Book of Sa'bara:
Relics of the Past

Michael Gene Thomas.

SPECIAL THANKS

Listed in no particular order are the various people I like to thank who helped either directly or indirectly make this book possible. My Aunt Ruth, who had her own real life adventure, which taught me that anyone can go on an adventure of a lifetime. My friends Seiyu and Craig, who helped me in this story in some way but could not be here to see it done within their lifetimes. Axel, Brian, Martha, Nicholas, Taelyn, Steve & Steve, who helped me with the story in innumerable ways and make it the best it can be. And always my family, for without them, I wouldn't be here today to make this book possible.

CONTENTS

Chapter 1 Chains of Freedom

The heavy chains attached to her metal collar rattled as Jesmine felt the cart sway side to side as it moved forward. Her wrists shackled and bound so closely together that there's not even an inch of clearance between them, forcing her to the bottom of her small cold wrought iron cage. A cloth cover kept her enclosure shrouded in darkness. Her pointed elven ears listened carefully to the neighing of horses and shouts of orcs, trying to discern what's happening outside.

A small town sat on the border between vast plains and seemingly endless forest. The town's buildings were barely passable; most were quickly put together and showed a distinct lack of knowledge on proper construction techniques.

The sleepy town awoke to the sudden arrival of the wagon train that rolled into the outskirts, pulling into a protective circle as a few muscular orcs close to seven feet in height dressed in leather armor approached them.

"What is it that you want?!" yelled the green skinned orc guard, his yellow eyes focused on the band leader, a tall, buff, red-skinned orc with a few battle scars on his face. His stern yellow eyes met the guard's, a practiced smile making his sharpened tusks become more pronounced. He leapt off one of the wagons, dressed in fine cotton clothes which looked out of place to all those around him.

"To give you a bit of entertainment as we are on our way to the great Sa'bara city of Rivera," he stated, slowly approaching them.

"Entertainment?" The guard looked past him at the wagons, his brow furrowing suspiciously. "What kind?"

"Shows to thrill, sights to please, and even rare curios not seen in this great land of Sa'bara," he explained.

"Curi-what?" the guard asked with an almost painfully confused expression.

"Don't deny a town of the rare chance of entertainment. I can see they are already curious," he stated, motioning to some town folk viewing from a distance. The orcs ranged in height of six to seven feet tall for the men, and about half a foot on average shorter for the women. Their green to dark brown colored skin was covered in minimal levels of animal hides.

He looked over his shoulder and then to his fellow guard before back to the orc caravan leader. "Fine," he grunted. "But remember to keep the peace or else."

"It won't be a problem." He looked to one of his armed companions, who was dressed in thick leather hide with well-kept heavy war axes and swords. "It's one of those towns."

The armed orc companion nodded, resting a heavy hand on the hilt of his weapon, responding, "As long as they have coin it won't be an issue."

"They'll have coin, the question is how much." he remarked before he yelled, "I want everyone to be at their best! Do not antagonize the locals! You all know what is at stake!"

He walked over to the wagon with Jesmine's cage and said in broken elven, "Do good, you eat."

Jesmine tensed, looking in the direction of the voice, responding in elven, "Yes."

"Good," he grunted, hitting the cage.

She felt it rattling through her. She tensed, slowly relaxing as she heard him walk away, letting out a soft sigh. "Out of the four, I had to be brought back to this one."

The town's guards watched the place with unease as they set up. Word quickly spread as people began to gather, half of whom were armed with spears or short curved jagged swords that looked well in need of a professional blacksmith.

As people gathered, the shows began. Orc dancers dressed in relatively fine clothing entertained and entranced the audience as one performer breathed fire to draw out an ever-larger crowd. The caravan's and town's guards faced off as they kept a distrustful eye on each other.

The audience cheered at the performers' theatrical display, a few of them showing their pleasure by tossing some coin their way, but as the performers pulled away, the leader of the band stepped up. He looked over the crowd that had gathered, gauging their relative mood and that of the guards that easily outnumbered his merry band, two to one.

"I told you, you wouldn't regret this show, but if you thought that is all we had. Ha! Only at Gorigon's show will you find two rare creatures that I bet that many of you have not seen in your life," he declared in a booming showman's voice.

The leader motioned his hand, one of the wagons was pushed forward by two stagehands. A tattered cloth hung over the top of the small cage no more than three feet in height or length on all sides. A mist billowed out from underneath the fabric as a layer of ice clung to it, despite it being a warm summer's afternoon. One of the stagehands took the blunt end of a sword and smacked the side of the cloth, bits of ice falling to the ground as the sound of rattling chains could be heard underneath.

"Your eyes do not deceive you. Ice in the middle of summer. This is no mere parlor trick. The creature held underneath this curtain comes from the far north, from the lands of Ashvala. A land crawling with an assortment of fearsome creatures! Some that may even rattle you to your very bones! Finding such a creature was no easy feat and capturing it alive to bring to you all here today before your very eyes is another thing entirely. Come closer if you dare, but I will warn you, it will require a fair bit of constitution and contribution." he said, rubbing his fingers together, "To keep such a thing alive is a costly venture."

The townsfolk muttered amongst themselves as one of the brutish orcs approached. "Yeah? Who says it's worth my coin?!"

The other orc continued to smile. "I assure you it is, but if you don't want to pay, you don't have to see it. However, if you think this is some kind of trick," he chuckled. "Come closer, feel the icy cold aura of death this creature emits."

"I will!" he grunted, walking past the orc leader and toward the covered wagon. He felt the air grow cold as he got closer until he stood within a foot of the cage, breath fogging. He grunted, about to take a step closer but two of the caravan guards crossed their heavy war axes in front of him. The town's guards responded, reaching for their weapons.

"No free looks. You could pay a simple sum and be the only one in your whole village to see this beast or... the whole town could contribute, and I will remove the veil and let you all get a closer look, and this is not even the best of what I have to offer." the orc leader chimed in, looking at the guards with a smug look.

The other orc glared at the leader with his yellow eyes, letting out a visible huff of air. He dug into his pouch, pulling out a few silver coins, tossing them to the ground in front of Gorigon.

"Here!" he grunted.

The orc leader nodded, one of his stagehands going to pick up the coins. "Does anyone else want to join in? Or shall we let this lone brave orc see the mysteries of the north?!"

Soon others joined in, tossing mostly copper pieces, a few stagehands collecting them, placing them in leather pouches. After several minutes the bags were brought to the caravan leader. He felt them up in his hulking green hands, hearing the jingling of coins within each one. "Yes, this will certainly do."

The orc leader motioned with his hand, stepping closer to the wagon. "Behold! A sight so rare that you will not believe your eyes!" he announced, grabbing the cloth, and with one firm pull, he ripped the cover right off. Ice cracked and broke, hitting the ground with a soft patter as the cage rattled. A white scaled lizard-like creature tugged at its chains, blue serpentine slit pupils narrowing as the light hit its face, which was covered by an ice-coated metal muzzle.

Shackles around its wrists and ankles forced it onto all fours. A pair of wings were heavily bound in chains, which added to the clanking of metal as it tugged at them. It snarled viciously at the crowd. A set of ebony horns jutted from the back of its head, the two largest having intricate carvings in them, but the left horn was cracked at the base that went halfway up the center. A heavy metal collar around the neck kept its head low.

"Behold! A baby white ice dragon! This fearsome beast was trapped in the ice and was left in deep hibernation, avoiding the death of the mighty northern dragons. So long has it been left in hibernation that it might be a child of the late Eisandra Everwinter, whose dragonflight used to rule the northern lands!" he shouted.

The orcs gave a mixed reaction of shock, awe, and confusion, the lizard being no longer than two and a half feet in length. One of the orcs yelled, "Eisandra is dead! Slain by the elves over sixty years ago!"

Another orc yelled, "It's so small!"

The orc leader chuckled. "Yes, which makes such a find so incredibly rare. Have any of you ever seen a baby dragon before? Let alone one of the great dragons?" he yelled.

The white lizard growled, a puff of icy mist flaring from its nostrils, causing a few of the orc children to pull back in surprise, while other children made fun of their cowardice.

A few more coins were tossed towards the orc leader as the townsfolk moved in. The lizard gave an icy glare at the orcs as they curiously approached. It growled and hissed, trying to flap its wings, but the chains held it in place.

"Fear not! We have securely restrained this beast and prevented it from using most of its defensive capabilities, but I warn you, do not touch the metal bars. Experienced hunters can tell you what cold steel can do against naked flesh."

The orcs stared and gawked, getting as close as they could to the dragon. After a good half an hour, the guards relaxed their stance as the orc leader continued his show. "We'll be keeping the white 'dragon' out for a while but believe it or not, it's not the main attraction to our show. We have something even rarer and more dangerous than this baby white dragon!"

The crowd turned to listen. "There is something not seen in these lands for over thirty years and thought to be extinct after the great green dragon Sa'bara put down their ilk after their insurrection." he said.

One of the orc townsfolk yelled. "What? Impossible! We killed every last one of those traitors!"

"Ah, so you say, but here…" Another wagon was pushed into view with a cage taller and wider than the first one with a black tattered cloth covering it.

The white lizard's hissing and growling slowed, eventually stopping as the attention was drawn away. It watched the show, claws tensing and raking across the cold metal base of the cage.

"Considering how much you have given already; it will only take just a little bit more to see what could very well be the last of its kind."

A collection was spread through the crowd and soon a sack of coins was presented to him. He reached out and fondled the bag, grinning and nodding to the stagehands. "This will do."

Jesmine winced as she was suddenly blinded by the removal of the cage's cover. She gently tugged at her constraints, her temporary blindness slowly fading as her soft, green eyes widened, looking at the crowd of orcs staring at her chained, bound, and naked form. Her snow-white skin was in desperate need of a bath, but despite that, it was easy to see from the neck down she was covered almost entirely in elegant, black tattoos. The only other exceptions were the soles of her feet and the palms of her hands. As she moved and squirmed in her bondage, the tattoos gave a soft, silver shine. Chest length black hair was tangled and frazzled, covering parts of her face, but her signature triangular elven ears poked though for all to see.

Some of the orcs gasped in surprise but a few of the older ones suddenly yelled in alarm. "It's not just an elf. It's an arcane user!" The town's guards moved to ready their weapons, glaring at the orc leader.

"Do not be alarmed. We have secured this elf to prevent any kind of arcane casting. She is harmless," he said.

The townsfolk muttered amongst themselves, the commotion bringing a smile to the orc leader's face as what little bit of coin the town had left to offer was pushed his way. The town guards uneasily returned to their positions as their leader motioned for them to relax. The show and the display of the two prize specimens kept the attraction going till late in the afternoon when the show finally ended, and the towns folk returned to their homes pleased with what they experienced.

The orc leader felt a single, heavy bag of coins in his hands, looking over to the 'dragon' and the elf, saying, "You two are a gold mine. I didn't think such a small town had so much money." He chuckled.

Jesmine said nothing, relaxing slightly, watching the orc leader walk over to the baby white 'dragon' he grunted, glowering. "I saw you relaxing on your act when you thought no one was looking. You can't let up on the act just because you THINK no one is watching. That's half rations for you for a week." He snorted, banging on the cage. The white lizard glared at him, giving a low growl. "That's it! Keep practicing," he said, chuckling, walking over to Jesmine.

"And you. I'm not going to bother speaking in that pathetic elven tongue. I bet you can understand me but pretend not to. You better put on a better show in the future. Struggle, squirm, show how much you don't want to be there, and how afraid you are. Till you do... half rations."

Jesmine said nothing, hands clenching into fists.

"I said fear!" he yelled, banging on the cage. "Don't worry.

You'll have plenty of time to learn your act," he said with a hearty laugh, walking away.

He looked over to the other orcs in his party, saying, "Come on. Let's get a move on. I don't want the town to get any fancy ideas of getting a refund!" They nodded, quickly packing everything up. The cloths were thrown back over the two cages once again delving Jesmine and the 'dragon' into darkness.

Soon enough the wagons were on the move. The chains rattled as they wobbled on the dirt road that followed along the forest. As the caravan got farther away from the town, the land became more rugged with tall grasses that swayed like the ocean under the near double new moons. Jesmine tried to rest as best she could given the circumstances, grateful for the cool air that flowed from the white lizard in the wagon ahead of her. Leaning against the bars, she attempted to get some sleep.

The head wagoner pushed through into the night, keeping a keen eye around him till he saw a figure in the darkness up in front. The orc squinted his eyes. "Who goes there!" he yelled, reaching for a set-up crossbow, nocking the bolt.

The shadowy figure did not respond as they got closer. "We aren't stopping! Move or be run over," the wagoner warned.

The figure remained still; the orc grunted pressing forward. The closer he got, the clearer it became. It looked more like a grass-stuffed scarecrow.

The orc chuckled. "Do they really think that was going to stop this wagon? Only a simpleton would stop for that." A bright flash moved across the night sky. It came out of the corner of the orc's eye, jerking his head to follow for a split second as a fiery arrow hit the scarecrow, which burst into flames.

"What th—" A sizeable explosion with shrapnel flew everywhere, instantly killing the orc and horse, the wagon rolling to a stop. The horses behind neighed and bucked loudly.

Orcs that had been sleeping leapt out of the wagons, yelling at the commotion. The grass rustled on either side of the caravan as orange-sized metal grenades rolled underneath the center wagons. Black smoke billowed out from the grenades, blinding and suffocating those within, causing some of the hacking and wheezing orcs to flee. Two were quickly felled by arrows, while the wagons in the smoke rushed off to the side into the grass to escape. The orcs within leapt out with axes and swords at the ready, looking around before the tall grass slightly shifted, one screaming out in pain, falling to the ground, silenced by an arrow to the neck.

Jesmine tried to sit up upon hearing the commotion, but the chains rattled as they instantly became taut, preventing her from getting up from a kneeling position, the cloth blinding her from the outside. "What's going on?" she muttered in elvish, looking in the direction of the sounds of combat, tugging hard at her restraints.

The white lizard opened its eyes, reaching to the edge of the cage to the very extent that its chained wrists would allow, slowly pulling at the cover till it fell off. The moonlight reflected off its eyes giving a faint eerie glow. Its nostrils flared, quickly sneezing as smoke was blown in their direction.

Gorigon, outside of his wagon, looked around while yelling. "Bandits! Take position, light the nearby grass on fire, and flush them out!" He rushed back to his wagon grabbing an oil lantern and with a few quick strikes of flint, managed to light it, illuminating the relatively nice interior. He rushed to the end of his wagon, not noticing the current state of the battle, pulling his arm back to throw the lantern when two bolts pierced his chest. He looked down as blood stained his otherwise clean clothes, grunting, stumbling forward, dropping the lantern and causing it to shatter on the floor. Within moments the wagon was set ablaze, and the orc leader fell to the ground with a heavy thud, the life draining from him.

After a few minutes the sound of battle faded, the nearby area lit brightly by the burning wagon. The horse attached to it bucked and tugged at the reins till they burned away, letting it run free out into the open field.

Jesmine's ears twitched, turning in the direction of the sound of rustling grass, *"I didn't think he'd come this fast for me,"* she thought, readying herself for her inevitable fate.

Off to the side, a scruffy-looking human dressed in black-studded leather stepped out of the brush. He had a bow and arrow drawn, his sheathed short sword around his waist slightly rattling as he moved in. He scanned the area, judging if it was safe enough to approach Jesmine's wagon. Sensing it was, he ran to it and with one quick motion he pulled off the cloth, which caused the elf to jump in surprise.

She stared at him, noting his brown eyes giving a look of concern and relief, "Jesmine Tanarelia?" he asked in human.

Jesmine's stern expression faded, letting out a sigh, as the human then added, "My companions and I are here to rescue you. Don't worry, we'll get you out of here in no time."

She tugged at her chains, speaking in a soft, soothing voice that hid the direness of her situation. "As much as I'm happy to be rescued, I really can't go anywhere. I'm a bit tied down and…" she looked over her shoulder down to the burning wagon, "If I am not mistaken, that wagon over there has the keys."

He looked at the blazing wagon with a little concern, "Right… that was Gnemi, and he can get a bit carried away at times, but don't worry, I can get you out of there without the use of keys." The human put his weapon down, digging into his pouch, pulling out a set of lock picks, quickly getting to work on the cage.

"Thank you, but tell me, what is the name of my rescuer?" she asked.

"Alderin," he replied, followed by a soft click as the lock unfastened. The cage squeaked open. He stepped inside, crouching down, while Jesmine looked to him with restrained eagerness.

"Alderin, is it her?" yelled a gruff-sounding voice. Stepping out of the brush was a stout, four-and-a-half-foot tall dwarf dressed in heavy leathers, his crimson blood-soaked dual-sided battle-axe was almost the size of his torso.

"Yeah, it is, Dran. Unfortunately, Gnemi and I accidentally set ablaze the wagon with the keys, so I have to do this the old-fashioned way."

A squeaky voice shouted from further ahead, "Sorry, I didn't know!"

"It's fine Gnemi," Alderin replied, working on Jesmine's wrist cuffs. "We'll get you out of here in no time. Orcs aren't known for their locksmithing skills."

Jesmine's chains rattled as she held her cuffs up to him, "Thank you, but I am afraid I have a request to make of you."

Alderin looked up at her, trying his best to avoid staring at her naked form. "What is it?"

"The kobold in the other cage. Can you release her too?"

Dran, who was washing off his blade with a damp cloth,

suddenly stopped and looked over to them, remarking, "Did she say a kobold? Why would we release a bloody kobold? They are servants to those damn, bloody dragons!"

The kobold silently watched the events unfold tilting her head to the side, looking at the elf with greater curiosity while tossing a glare at the dwarf.

"It's already giving me the death stare. You can't trust the thing," he grunted.

"Please, Alderin? No one deserves to be chained up and treated like an animal. And she doesn't deserve to starve to death."

Alderin looked at her and over at the kobold, which stared back at him, white scales shimmering in the light, sitting there with a faint mist surrounding her. "Are you sure?" he asked. "Something strange about that one. I never heard nor seen a kobold that fogged the air around them." A loud click followed as the cuffs were released from Jesmine's wrists.

She rubbed them, responding, "I do not know what causes it, perhaps a curse? Or she has strong draconic lineage in her veins."

Dran spoke up. "Both are excellent reasons to NOT release it from its bonds."

"I think that's all of them," yelled Gnemi, walking to the group. The three-foot-a-half-tall, slightly tanned skinned, green-eyed, brown-haired male gnome was putting away an apple-sized metal sphere into the side of his pouch. A pair of thick goggles around his neck suddenly fogged as he got close to the kobold's wagon. "So, what's this about a kobooohh—! Why is it so COLD here?!"

Gnemi took several steps away from the wagon, looking up to see the heavily chained up kobold. Jesmine answered, "That cold aura is from her. I've noticed it's something she can't help."

The kobold stared at the gnome with a piercing glare as he remarked, "Amazing, I'm sure I've never seen anything like that."

"That's what I said," Alderin remarked, as the elf's collar clicked open. It clattered to the ground with a heavy thud, Jesmine rubbing her neck.

"Thank you, but could you please do this? I couldn't live with myself if any more innocents died tonight."

"Innocents?" Alderin inquired, hopping out of the cage and holding a hand up to help her step out.

"Yes, most of those orcs were simple performers."

"They were keeping you prisoner!"

"They bought me off the slave market. They weren't the ones who captured me."

Dran rolled his brown eyes. "For the love of Basila, they were keeping you as a trophy on display."

"Yes, but that doesn't mean they had to die for it," Jesmine replied.

"And what did you expect us to do? Approach them and humbly request that they free you?"

"That's enough Dran," Alderin sighed. "Alright, we'll free the kobold, but I won't be held responsible if anything bad happens."

Jesmine bowed. "Thank you very much."

Alderin muttered to himself, "Saving a damn kobold, what is this world coming to?" He approached the cage, his breath fogging. "I better not regret this," he said, getting to work, looking at it, seeing the markings on its horns, making him tense.

The kobold let out a soft growl in response, staring at him. Alderin watched, feeling a cold shiver run down his spine. He shrugged, resuming his work, fighting off the numbness in his fingers, as he managed to get the lock undone with several minutes of effort. As the door clicked open, he jumped back, putting his lock picks away, rubbing his hands together. "Damn, that's cold," he looked to Jesmine. "Are you really sure about this? Something feels really off about it."

"Yes, I'm sure," Jesmine looked at the kobold, who eyed her.

Dran remarked, "This is a horrendous idea, I can feel it in my bones."

"It's going to take me a while to pick those locks, especially given the circumstances," Alderin said. "And I don't know about you, but I feel uncomfortable sitting near these woods, in the middle of a road, in orc country, next to a burning wagon with dead orcs. The scent of death is in the air and who knows what prowls in the night?"

Gnemi attempted to climb the back of the wagon, his feet dangling in the air, hands sliding across the wood before Dran gave him a leg up. "If that's the case we'll probably have to bring the wagon with us," he said, walking past the kobold, who watched him like a hawk. He took seat in the front, tugging on the reins, trying to ease and comfort the horse.

Dran groaned. "This is growing more problematic."

Jesmine softly interjected "You all shouldn't speak about her like that."

"Why? Not like it could speak human tongue. Kobolds speak only the tongue of the dragons. That is all they need to know to serve their dragon overlords."

"Rather she could understand you or not, you shouldn't."

Gnemi tugged on the reins, the horse hesitantly pulling the cart off the road. "Since they're a white kobold, that means they probably served Eisandra, right? That ancient dragon has been dead for over sixty-years. I saw her ice frozen preserved corpse in her lair outside of the capital city Drasin with my own eyes. They probably have no dragon overlord to serve. So, I say, I believe in giving them a chance."

Dran grunted, following a little ahead of the wagon. "Just because it has white scales doesn't mean it served a white dragon and there're other white dragons in the north."

"I believe there aren't any more," Gnemi replied, Jesmine tensing at the words.

"Regardless, we'll pick up our horses and find a safe place to camp for the night before it gets too late."

Jesmine walked beside Alderin as they kept a safe distance from the kobold's cold aura. "Not to be rude, but hopefully you'll have something for me to wear?"

Alderin blushed. "I think we have something that might fit you."

"I'd appreciate that," she replied with a smile.

After a fifteen or so minute trek, they reached the horses. Alderin walked over to his steed, opening a side pouch where he pulled out some worn leather clothes and handed them to her. "It's not much but it should do, I hope."

Jesmine smiled. "I appreciate it," slipping on the clothes. She gave a few minor tugs and adjustments, trying her best to get them to fit properly before finally giving up. She turned to Alderin and bowed. "Thank you very much."

He shook his head. "It's nothing. Sorry we don't have anything better. I'm the only one remotely close to your size," he stated, hopping onto his grey mount.

Gnemi said to Jesmine, "You may ride my horse, and I'll do my best to keep up with our extra passenger."

"Thank you," Jesmine replied.

Gnemi looking behind him to the caged kobold. "Are you doing okay back there?" he asked, hearing a soft chain rattle in response. "I guess that means 'yes'."

Jesmine took a moment to finally relax, "Hopefully we'll find a place soon to rest and we can get her out of there."

Alderin pulled his horse ahead of the group. "The last place we camped out was not too far, so we'll head there," he said, looking over to the caged kobold. "And once we are sure we are in the clear, we can solve our current problem."

Dran grunted. "Aye, hopefully one that shouldn't take us long to resolve," he said, as they headed out, deeper into the plains. Eventually they approached a few rolling hills and a small patch of forest. "There it is."

Gnemi commented, "For the great plains of Jerelsda, there are many times a distinct lack of plains."

Jesmine chuckled, replying, "It's mostly plains, but there are spots where it does not live up to its name, yes."

The kobold watched them as they set up camp, getting a fire going. Alderin returned to her open cage with a small flaming log, which he placed between the bars of the open cage door before crawling in. "Cold and cramped," he complained, his breath fogging over the kobold's face. She stared, tugging on the chains.

"Now imagine what it must be like to be her," Jesmine commented. "Cold and tightly bound in that small cage."

"You don't have to crouch next to it freezing your ass off in the middle of summer while doing a delicate job like this."

Jesmine replied, "I understand, and I am forever grateful for your effort."

"Please remember that."

"What?" she asked, stepping closer.

"Let me finish this then we'll talk, okay?" he asked with slight annoyance in his voice before Jesmine nodded.

Slowly, Alderin managed to pick the lock, taking breaks to warm his hands by the nearby fire. The kobold watched silently as he worked, her body twitching ever so often causing what chains remained on her to rattle. The very last lock, the one holding her muzzle in place, clicked open, the kobold quickly pulling it off of her face. Alderin crawled out of the cage, jumping off the wagon. "I thought I was going to freeze to death before I could finish," he complained, shivering.

"Thank you Alderin, I am in your debt," Jesmine replied as Gnemi tinkered with a strange mechanical crossbow in his hands, while Dran stood next to her. The kobold rubbed her wrists and then her snout, adjusting her jaw, gently feeling the locations where the shackles were. She attempted to unfurl her wings in the cage but only managed to get a third of the way through before she winced in pain, a soft growl escaping her lips. Dran tensed and held his axe up, walking over to the cage while Gnemi watched curiously.

Jesmine took a half step forward as the kobold shook off the pain and hobbled to her feet, her claws gripping the cage to give herself some support. Dran warned, "Don't let your guard down, it could be an act."

Jesmine shot Dran a curious look, "She's probably been caged for Gods know how long," she said. "Her muscles must be very atrophied."

Gnemi inquisitively asked, "How do you know she's a girl?"

"I've seen my fair share of kobolds," she responded.

The kobold stepped completely out of the cage, looking at the four before her, giving each one a long look before looking down to the ground. She released her hold on the cage, taking two tentative steps to the edge before suddenly stumbling forward, falling off the cart. She braced herself but was surprised to feel someone catch her. She looked from her upside-down position, seeing Jesmine.

Alderin rushed over. "Jesmine what you are doing?! We came all this way to rescue you and now you risk yourself trying to catch a kobold?" he exclaimed, unsure of what to do.

Jesmine's breath fogged up. "Could you be any more blind to her current state?" she groaned, gently placing the kobold onto her feet, who took a step back, while Jesmine instinctively rubbed her hands together.

"You should know what they are like," he warned.

"I'll be fine," she replied, waving him off, turning her attention to the kobold. "But you should be careful. It will take some time for your strength to return."

The kobold stood up once more, using the wagon as leverage, her body, wobbled, watching the party with her piercing, icy blue eyes, which slightly softened when she looked at Jesmine, "Thank you for saving me. It was unexpected but welcomed," she said in a strong feminine voice, a hint of a draconic accent underlining every word.

"You can speak my tongue?" Alderin asked in surprise.

"Yes, I can," she remarked.

"Perhaps you could thank me for freeing you. It wasn't easy you know."

The kobold's stern glare returned. "Why should I thank you? You wanted to leave me there to die. You were talked into it by Jesmine. I don't think thanks is warranted here," she growled, spreading her wings slightly before the pain forced them back closed.

"Why you…"

"Ungrateful beast!" Dran exclaimed.

"Relax," Jesmine replied, taking a few steps back. "If I was in her position, I'd feel a bit angry too. Though I'd have put it more eloquently."

The kobold took a deep breath and slowly sighed with a soft, icy fog coming from her nostrils. "I'm sure."

"What's your name?"

Her wings twitched, looking up at the elf. "You're asking me my name?"

"Yes."

She tilted her head. "Why?"

"We will be traveling together for a while. It would be nice to know my travel companion's name, would it not?"

Dran interjected. "Wait, wait, wait, what? We are not taking a kobold back with us to Tundaholm."

"I, too, would prefer not to go to a dwarven city," the kobold said, cracking her neck. "They'd kill me on the spot."

"See even it agrees with me!"

Jesmine sighed. "Look at her. She's weak and defenseless. I am not going to leave her here to die."

The kobold huffed at the remark, saying, "I can take care of myself." She let go of the wagon, taking one step forward before almost falling over again, catching herself on the wagon wheel in the nick of time.

"There is no shame in resting up and getting your strength back with the help of others."

The kobold gave a long, soft growl. "Fine, if you insist, I shall give you my company."

Jesmine smiled. "Thank you very much."

"The name's Histra Snow by the way."

"Histra, what a lovely name," she replied.

Alderin shook his head. "Great, we got a damn kobold now. This is just going to make this plan a thousand times more difficult!"

Gnemi walked over to him. "Yes, or you could have probably just have waited till after Histra left to mention there was even a plan."

Alderin groaned. "Damn it."

Jesmine turned to the two, "What plan?"

He looked over at Histra. "It's complicated. Best not to talk about it right now with our current company."

Histra waved a claw. "Go ahead and say whatever plan you want. I don't care what you tall folk want to do as long as it doesn't involve killing me... which I am sure is not out of the question," giving a glare to Dran and Alderin.

"I will have no more killing tonight!" Jesmine exclaimed, causing the group to look at her. She turned to face Alderin, continuing, "Sorry if I sound forceful, but it's been a long few months."

Alderin's shoulders drop. "Sorry, I was getting ahead of myself. But we are in need of your arcane capabilities. We can talk about it later, once we are in the safety of Tundaholm."

"I see..." she looked to the ground then back at him, "Yet whatever your plan is, there is one little problem."

"What?"

"Without my spellbook, I am nearly powerless."

"Oh... you wouldn't know where it is, would you?" he asked with a hopeful look in his eyes.

She sighed. "It was destroyed in the raid when I was captured."

He tensed before he collapsed to the ground.

Histra let out a weak laugh. "You saved her only to use her, didn't you?"

Alderin looked up. "What? No!"

Gnemi stepped in. "It's true we are in need of Jesmine's great arcane abilities but whether she agreed to help us or not, we still intended to rescue her."

Dran tightly gripped his axe. "Aye, only a creature like you would think of saving someone for their own ends."

Histra sighed. "Narrow-minded dwarves as always."

The dwarf took a step closer. "What was that?"

"You heard me. I do not need to repeat myself."

"Damn straight you don't, kobold…" he replied with fire in his eyes.

"Everyone please… just stop. Look, it's true I lost my spellbook and it's a loss that I don't think I could ever fully recover from, but…"

Alderin looked up. "But?"

"I do know the location of an older copy of my book. It doesn't contain all of my most advanced spells, but it will get me back on track. With it, I won't be mostly useless in a fight outside of a few select spells I know by heart."

"Great, where is it?" Alderin asked, standing up his demeanor doing a complete turnaround.

"In the ruins of my hometown, located in the center of Du'ralia Forest."

The human's shoulders slumped again. "That's the opposite direction of where we're supposed to take you."

Gnemi said, "Also, I believe I heard rumors that place is cursed? Even where I'm from, to hear of it would probably mean there could be a bit of truth behind it."

"I know, but it is also why I believe my book is still there."

Dran spoke up. "I say we head to Tundaholm. Where we can obtain the help, we need."

Gnemi answered, "Possibly, but that will most likely add a lot of time to go there and back, and I believe time is not our ally here."

"I'd vote Du'ralia Forest, but I don't think any of us have the right to decide except for Jesmine," Alderin said, looking to her. "What do you want to do?"

She took in everything, judging everyone's concerned

demeanor. Histra leaned against the wagon with slight amusement, the grass around her feet slowly freezing over. "We are already this far out, and the journey there and back is going to be dangerous. It would be best if we go there now rather than later."

Alderin cracked a smile. "That settles that then. We go to Du'ralia Forest, but for now everyone, get some rest. I'll take first watch."

Jesmine bowed. "Thank you all again." She looks over at Histra, saying, "You should get some rest too Histra."

"Eventually. I don't feel too safe falling asleep at the moment."

Dran grunted. "Funny, I had the same thought."

Histra glared at the dwarf, who walked over to Jesmine, saying, "You can take my tent for the night. It's made from Mixia fur, which will be far better than your previous accommodations."

Jesmine nodded, giving one last look to Histra, who remained near the cart before going to the surprisingly large tent by the small campfire. "And sorry for the trouble I've put you all through. I know this isn't what you were expecting."

"Life is full of unexpected events," Dran remarked, smiling. "Now get some rest. We have a long day ahead of us."

Jesmine slipped into the tent, Alderin and Histra squaring off at each other from a distance. The rest of the party moved to get some rest, none of them realizing that the real adventure, one with unforeseen consequences for them all and countless others, was just about to begin.

Chapter 2 An Uneasy Agreement

Jesmine awoke to the sound of chirping birds, stretching and peering out of the tent, seeing Dran standing a few feet away. The sun's rays revealing his fire red colored head of hair and well-kept, foot long, braided beard to match. His axe at the ready, keeping a watchful eye on Histra, who was about ten feet away.

Histra sat slumped against the wagon wheel. A layer of white frost had formed over the side with small icicles hanging from the spokes. She stared back at him, every so often her eyes beginning to close, head bobbing. Her head jerked back, wings twitching as she recommitted herself to stay awake.

"Morning," Jesmine greeted, slipping out of the tent.

"Good morning Miss," Dran said, waving. "Would you mind waking up the others? It is about time we should get going."

"Sure," she replied, walking over to Alderin's tent and tentatively opened it. "Excuse me," the elf said, seeing him sprawled across the floor, softly snoring. "Time to wake up." She gently shook his shoulder, the human jerking awake, pulling out a small dagger, and was halfway to bringing it to Jesmine when she quickly recoiled.

"Sorry," he said, fully sitting up, stretching with a long yawn before he rubbed the black scruff on his face.

"It's alright. I'm sorry if I startled you."

"It's fine. I apologize if I frightened you. When one travels alone you quickly learn how to be a light sleeper and to be ready at a moment's notice."

"I understand. I've traveled a fair bit myself, but I've never formed such a habit," she explained.

Alderin let out another long yawn, "Here, let me show you an easy way to wake one of us up," he said, crawling out of the tent, grabbing a nearby pebble. He walked over to Gnemi's tent. "Take a rock like so," he opened the flap to the tent. "And toss it in." He chucked the rock in, while standing off to the side.

A moment passed, a ruckus erupted from within, Gnemi yelling, "Alarm!" before catching his foot on the edge of the tent and tumbling out with a thud.

"Are you okay?" Jesmine asked, rushing over while Alderin let out a hearty chuckle.

"He's fine."

Gnemi looked around, dagger clenched in his hand, hair frazzled as the goggles around his neck were completely spun around. The gnome relaxed, noting everything was okay. He brought them back around, blowing some dirt off the lenses, looking up to Alderin.

"Morning Gnemi. Slept well?" he asked.

"I think I slept well, but I can't with certainty say the same for the morning," he replied. "I wished my watch was more fruitful though. I tried to talk to Histra, that is her name, right? I believe she didn't say a word to me. She only stared at me with those eerie reflective eyes of hers." He looked over to her, the kobold giving him a stare. "Just like that."

"I don't think you'd get much out of it, Gnemi," said Alderin, glancing over to Histra, then back at him. "Anyway, can you make us some breakfast? I'll check up on the horses," he said, walking over to the other side of the camp away from Histra.

Gnemi replied, "No problem." He pulled out some rations and cooking supplies from a bag from within his tent.

As Alderin checked over and fed one of the horses, he looked over to Dran. "Did anything happen on your watch?"

He shook his head. "Nay. Nothing suspicious, except it stayed up all night, watching me."

Jesmine looked over to Histra. "You didn't sleep?"

She held back a heavy yawn, dragging herself to her feet leaning heavily on the wagon wheel, breaking a few of the icicles.

"You should get some sleep Histra," said Jesmine, walking over to her. Histra watched her get closer, trying to stand tall. "You're not going to recover if you don't get some rest."

"Why do you care if this beast gets sleep or not?" Dran asked. "If it wants to stay awake, let it."

Jesmine shook her head. "Dran, you aren't helping." She stopped at the very edge of Histra's ice aura which was made clear by the white frost over the green grass, putting Jesmine about five feet away from her. "Histra, it's quite alright. You can get some sleep; no one here is going to hurt you."

She chuckled. "How are you so sure? You just met these people."

"Don't be so cynical, they just saved our lives no more than a few hours ago."

Histra's eyes narrowed, her wings spreading slightly before flinching in pain. "No, they saved your life, and not out of the goodness of their hearts, but for a reason. And whatever that reason is, it must be something big enough that they agreed to take you back to your hometown, even though it's infested with ghosts and monsters. In orc and avolariean infested lands, and under the control of the great dragon Sa'bara, who has his spies everywhere. I'm sure he knows about an elf in his lands, and it won't take him long to hear that she's suddenly gone missing. To go up against all that out of the kindness of their hearts," she said sarcastically. "Is outright laughable. So, it is not unreasonable to think that these untrusting bastards will kill me the moment I fall sleep."

Jesmine took a step closer, her breath starting to fog. "Histra, you need to be more trusting. They are good people risking their lives."

"For you, not for me. The only reason why they released me is because you pleaded." Histra looked off to the side, saying in draconic. "Surprised they'd even do it. They must really want you for something."

Dran gripped his axe tighter, taking several steps closer to Histra. "See, it speaks in the tongue of the dragons. Perhaps some of its ilk are nearby and it gave them a plan of attack," he cautioned, looking around.

Histra rolled her eyes. "Please, you'd think I'd have any of my kind here?"

"You can never be too careful."

Alderin spoke up. "I agree with the kobold, there is no chance it has any allies here. If it did, they'd have jumped us in our sleep."

Dran kept a tight grip on his axe. "Aye, you're right, or done something about her captivity with the orcs."

"It doesn't trust us, and we certainly don't trust it. We should just let it be on its way," suggested Alderin.

"No, she'll die, or be captured and enslaved in some kind side show again or something even worse," said Jesmine, looking to the others.

"We can leave it with the horse and wagon. Toss in a few rations and that should be enough to let it go wherever it wants.

That way we can be on our way, and it can be on its way, and we'll all be happier for it."

Histra let out a soft grunt, looking over to the wagon and back to the horse that was originally hitched to it, saying, "I don't get along with animals."

"Why am I not surprised?" Alderin said sarcastically.

"Alderin. You could be nicer about it, but even with a horse and wagon, I don't think she is in any state to go anywhere by herself," said Jesmine.

Gnemi spoke up, stirring the stew he was cooking. "I, for one, believe I wouldn't mind keeping Histra around. I've heard much about kobolds, but I think it's a rare treat to even talk to one." He turned his attention directly to Histra. "I think I would be very interested in learning more about you and your kind."

Histra turned her head to him, giving him a dismissive look, saying, "See, he wants me to stay only because he wants something from me."

Gnemi shook his head. "I didn't mean it like that. I thought I'd heard plenty about kobolds' reputation in relation to the dragons, and though that is interesting, there is so much more I'd like to know. What I do know, is that winged kobolds are rare. Isn't that true?"

Histra responded with a small wing flick which was quickly stopped by a shooting pain.

"If teaching me more about your kind so you can travel with us as you recover is the cost to pay, I think it's a logical choice to go along with it, don't you think?"

"Gnemi, does your curiosity ever override your so-called logic? Just because you haven't dealt with kobolds before doesn't mean you should go out of your way to do so," replied Alderin.

"One usually can't improve themselves simply from reading, and most likely the best knowledge comes from the source," Gnemi replied.

"But don't let your source end up getting us killed and ruin..." Dran said, head motioning towards Jesmine.

Jesmine sighed at their comments, moving closer to Histra. Her breath became even more visible, crouching down to get as low as she could, but unable to get low enough to be eye level. She took a deep breath, staring Histra right in the eyes. "Histra, I will admit that I have my own questions about you, but that isn't the reason I wanted to save you. If you must know, the reason I did was because it was the right thing to do. And if you or anyone else was in the same position, I'd happily do it again."

"Like that thing knows what the right thing to do even is," Dran said. "All their kind cares about is their own scaly hides and that of their dragon Masters."

Jesmine whipped her head around. "Dran, please just stop."

"It's the truth," said Dran, keeping a hand rested on the hilt of his axe. "I'm simply looking out for you and our well-being. Their whole ilk are nothing but dishonest. They are not to be trusted."

Histra stretched, cracking her neck in the process. "The dwarf speaks the truth. I do not care what you want out of me. I don't care about this little mission to retrieve your lost book. I only care that I live to see the next day and that I am better off than I was yesterday."

"See, I told you," Dran replied.

"I don't have to make it some kind of secret. Why should I concern myself with your problems? I have plenty enough of my own to deal with."

Jesmine sighed as Histra continued. "But I am not a fool. I do appreciate what *you* did for me. These others," she looked over at the rest of the party, "They could die today, and I wouldn't mind it one bit."

"Why you…" Dran walked into Histra's ice aura; his breath quickly became visible as he wiggled his nose, feeling the air growing cold around him.

"If I said it any other way, would you believe me? Would you trust me at all? No. As much as I hate to admit it, I am here because I have no choice. Ten years in those chains have withered my body. I am in no shape to go anywhere on my own. As sad as it is, you are all my best chance of making it out of here alive."

"It's upfront, I'll give it that," Alderin said, "But, that means you need us."

Histra glared at Alderin, but she soon softened, a draconic smirk crawling across her face. "Actually, you need me more than you realize."

His smile quickly turned into a frown. "That honesty didn't last long."

"Hah, we don't need you," Dran remarked.

"Would you two please just be quiet just for a moment? Let her speak before jumping to your own conclusions," Jesmine yelled before taking a long deep breath. "Histra, what do you mean?"

"When was the last time any of you were even near Du'ralia Forest?"

"Well over forty years. I left before the uprising occurred to study in the north," she took a deep breath, hands tensing, "And by the time word reached me of what happened, it was too late. It was all over."

Gnemi stirred the pot of food cooking away. "Never, I think this is the farthest I've been from my home."

Dran squeezed his axe tightly for a moment before relaxing ever so slightly. "This is the farthest east I've been," he remarked, taking a step back outside of the ice aura.

Alderin approached the edge of Histra's ice aura and looked her straight in the eyes. "I traveled into these lands several times… but I have never been to Du'ralia Forest. There was never a need to go there, but that doesn't mean we need you."

"Is that what you think? I wasn't hidden away behind a curtain for those ten years. They only took the time and effort to cover me up before a show or when they wanted to punish me for not putting on a good show. Often, they simply wanted ice to form on the cloth as part of the act. I'm sure they'd have done it longer and more often, but they learned that wasn't a good idea, as too much ice would form, and it was a chore to keep clean. Therefore, in the end I got a chance to see a lot, hear a lot. I understand the brutish thing the orcs call a language. It's almost as bad as human tongue."

Alderin scowled at her words, remarking, "Not nearly as bad as dragon tongue."

Histra ignored the comment, continuing, "You may be able to get there, but do you know the paths to take to avoid orc and avolariean patrols? How about getting through the great city of Rivera? Do you even know how to bypass security check points along the way? You see, their caravan didn't like to pay the local tolls, so they took other routes whenever possible. I know these routes, and if you want to get there quickly, with the least amount of trouble possible, and I know you do, you will need me to find those paths. By the time you get near that dreadful little forest, I'll be recovered enough to go my way where I won't need to deal with any of you ever again."

"What is to say that you don't try something to curry favor with the dragon of these lands once you're better?" asked Alderin, stepping closer. Jesmine looked over her shoulder at him then back to Histra.

Dran added, "Or lead us into a trap?"

"You think I trust the orcs to treat me any better than they already have? To them, I am merely a freak show commodity, and the avolarieans are no better. They'd rather hunt me down and string me up for being on their land. And seeing as I am not one of Sa'bara's kobolds, I have no protection from their wrath."

"I'd be happy to have your help Histra," said Jesmine.

She nodded. "I had a feeling you would."

Alderin interjected, "Do you think that is a wise idea? Granted some of the things it said is possibly true, but that doesn't mean we can trust it to keep its word."

Jesmine stood up. "Alderin, I am no fool, so trust me on this. I have a good feeling about her."

"A good feeling? About a kobold? Hah," remarked Dran. "Are you sure that isn't its cold aura? Though I am not sure how you could."

"I'll be responsible for her. I know the risks. This isn't the first time I've dealt with kobolds," said Jesmine staring off with Alderin for a moment. "If you are afraid of a severely atrophied kobold, then I doubt you'd be able to handle the way forward."

Alderin sighed, "You win."

"Breakfast should be ready, come and get it while it's still hot," Gnemi said. He poured most of the stew out into four bowls yelling to Histra. "We only have four bowls. I think we weren't expecting a fifth to be joining us."

"It's alright," said Jesmine, as Alderin and Dran headed over. Jesmine crouched down. "We have a deal then?"

Histra thought for a moment, then looked over to the trio, then to her. "You have my word I'll guide you to the forest, but after that you are on your own."

"I'm happy to have your help, Histra."

"You have no idea, but you will soon enough," she replied, leaning back against the wagon wheel, Jesmine heading to the campfire.

Histra remarked in draconic. "Not like I have any other choice..." closing her eyes for a moment before forcing them open, continuing. "I just have to be caref—" her words were cut off as suddenly in her field of vision was a steaming bowl of stew with a wooden spoon.

"Here you go. You need it more than I do," Jesmine said, Histra looking up at her and slowly reached out to grab it. "You better eat quick; it'll get cold fast."

She straightened herself up. "Funny," she replied, looking down. Her breath fogged over it as bits of ice formed over the top of the stew before it quickly melted.

Swiftly eating, she briefly revealed her hunger, forcing herself to slow down. Her tongue twitched, feeling the warmth of the stew run down her throat just before it was sucked from the food entirely.

She said in draconic, "Not bad."

As Jesmine returned to the campfire, Alderin held out his bowl, "Here, have it."

"Thank you but go ahead you can eat first."

"I can wait a few minutes, go ahead and take it. You're the one who needs to eat."

"Alright," Jesmine replied, grabbing the bowl. She looks over to Histra who is already half done with her food, calling out, "See, they are nice."

The kobold only glanced up at them, continuing to eat.

Dran positioned himself to keep a line of sight of Histra. "I sure hope you know what you are doing."

"It'll be fine, trust me," Jesmine replied.

"I trust you; I just don't trust it."

Jesmine sighed.

Gnemi spoke up. "Don't mind him, he probably has his reasons."

Dran gave Gnemi a look.

"Which are his own."

"I wasn't going to ask. It would be rude of me, and I do want to thank you all again for rescuing me and for putting you through all the trouble just to obtain my spellbook."

Dran rubbed his beard a few times. "I know a few things about magic. Especially the dangers of it. I've known people who died in their arcane studies, and though I am late to suggest this, but we do have arcane users back in Tundaholm. Couldn't we make you a new spellbook there? Or perhaps use one of theirs?"

"If it was only that simple," said Jesmine, with a soft sigh. "Anyone can cast magic but how our races have learned to cast it is different. I believe dwarven arcane users near you are specialized in earthen elemental magic?"

Dran nodded, "Aye, they are."

"I'm sure they know other kinds, but I've specialized in fire magic, and the way I tap into the fire element would be different than how dwarves by you do it. And that is to say if any even studied advanced fire magic techniques. Outside of that, the dwarven method of magical incantations, body movements, and hand gestures is something I would have to learn or translate to an elven style. Something that would take time for me to accomplish, and even then, I wouldn't be nearly as skilled in the arts as I would with my own book."

"Ah," Dran stroked his beard. "I thought as much."

"I'm sorry, but if there was another way, I'd happily do that. But I'm only a shadow of my capabilities without my spellbook."

Alderin nodded. "She's right. We need her to be at the very best she can be," he said.

Dran finished his food, refilling the bowl and handing it off to him, "Here."

"Thanks," replied Alderin, taking the bowl.

"There are other reasons why I'd prefer to get this book over going through the long process of making a new one," Jesmine said. "Even though it's a backup, it has spells that my mother helped me learn, and it would be nice to have a little something of her."

"That definitely settles that," replied Dran, as Alderin and Jesmine felt a sudden chill along their back sides. The small campfire flickered as Histra stood a few feet behind them. She tossed the empty bowl and spoon toward them.

Histra looked at them, all eyes turning to her. "We should be fine to travel along the road for the next two days," she said. "I recommend before nightfall we make camp away from the forest. It isn't safe at night, as it's best not to be a sitting meal for whatever is in there. It's not as bad as Du'ralia Forest, but one can never be too careful." Histra then added, "Also we should return to the caravan."

"Why?" Jesmine asked.

"To loot the money. They aren't going to need it, and we surely can use it."

"Unfortunately, it is right, we could use the money," Alderin said with an admitting sigh. "But we'll have to be careful, the smell of the dead could have attracted unwanted attention."

"Obviously," Histra remarked, slowly making her way back to the wagon.

"As obvious as you drawing attention to us?" sarcastically asked Dran, Histra brushing off the comment.

"What could be causing that ice aura?" Gnemi inquired, shivering at the lingering cold sensation in the air.

Dran shrugged, "I have my suspicions, but why don't you ask it?"

Gnemi turned and asked, "What causes your ice aura?"

Histra, who was in the process of trying to climb the wagon wheel. "My warm personality," she remarked, resuming her slow climbing attempt.

"It's her connection to the ice elemental magic," Jesmine explained, standing up, walking over to Histra, who had failed to pull herself up even over one spoke of the wagon wheel. "Here, let me help you."

"I got it," Histra growled. She didn't even look at Jesmine when she suddenly felt the elf's warm hands lift her up. Her wings twitched slightly, tensing as Jesmine effortlessly placed her into the back of the wagon. "I said I got it," she growled, turning to face her, but stumbled back, grabbing onto the cage to prevent herself from falling over.

Histra stared at her. "If you are trying to learn my secrets, forget about it. I am not going to tell you. I am going to do my part of the agreement and that's it, so why don't you go back to those others, and leave me be."

Jesmine gave fogged sigh, rubbing her hands together. "I'm sorry you feel that every good deed has an ulterior motive." Histra said nothing, staring at her, a moment of silence passing between them. "You'll see I speak the truth."

She simply shrugged, Jesmine walking away and back to the others.

As Jesmine approached Dran, he asked, "Are you telling me that kobold is an ice elemental specialized arcane user?"

She looked at Histra who peered over the side of the wagon back at the party. "No. She merely has a strong connection to ice magic. But if she doesn't know how to tap into those arcane capabilities, it's more of a curse than anything else. If she was trained, there would be no way she'd let herself be enslaved by the orcs for so long."

Alderin spoke up, grabbing the horses. "I've heard about that. The dragons are born with such a powerful connection to elemental magics that they can affect the land around them. But people and other monsters can have that, too."

Dran rubbed his beard. "Aye, everyone knows the dragons are magically attuned."

"I thought I read that, but it's curious to physically see anyone with such a connection," said Gnemi, looking back over to Histra. "I wonder if she feels cold."

Dran gave Gnemi a look. "Do you even need to ask that? Just take a look."

"Maybe…"

Jesmine continued, "One can also build a connection through study and training, but only the most talented and dedicated arcane users ever achieve such power, and in all my years, there have only been a few to reach that level of achievement. And I have only personally known one," Jesmine explained, moving over to mount Gnemi's horse.

"Your Mother, right?" asked Gnemi.

"Yes…" She trailed off, gently petting the horse. "I appreciate the use of your horse Gnemi, what's her name?"

"Gnaria. She and I have been through a lot. She's taken me all the way from Ashvala in the free North, through Dra'kesh, and to here in Sa'bara," he said, with a smile.

"Don't get him talking about his horse. He swears she's the luckiest horse there is," said Alderin, hitching a horse to the wagon. Gnemi climbed to the front and grabbed the reins.

"She is!" he exclaimed, Dran expertly pulling himself up onto a seemingly impossibly tall mare for his stature.

"See what I mean?"

Jesmine chuckled, "It's fine. I'm pleased to be on such a lucky horse, Gnemi. Gnaria is very pretty with her black mane," she said, looking to the others, "What are the names of your horses?"

Dran spoke up as he patted the side of his soft brown horse. "Her name is Dariel. I've had her for many years, and she's done me right."

Alderin gently stroked the black mane of his grey stallion. "I haven't had him long, but his name is Cetas."

"Cetas? Is that a southern name?" Jesmine asked.

"Don't know. It just came to me when naming him. I think it works," he replied as they set up and went back to the caravan.

A few moments passed before Gnemi looked over his shoulder to see Histra leaning her back against the side of the wagon. "Is it true that kobolds don't have parents?" Gnemi asked.

Histra gave him a look.

"I mean aren't they raised by the community in clutches? So, it's not that you don't have parents, it's just you don't know who they are. Is that true?"

"Don't talk to me," she replied, turning her head away from him.

"Another time then," said Gnemi, with a defeated sigh. "If you don't want to talk, perhaps you should get some sleep then. We have a long journey ahead of us."

Histra didn't reply, having already reluctantly closed her eyes and fallen asleep.

"Heh, couldn't stay awake forever," Gnemi mused, giving a tug on the reins to keep the horse in line with the rest of the group.

"We're going to be moving slower with the wagon," remarked Alderin, looking back at Gnemi.

"Aye, but I don't think the horses will take too kindly to have an ice monster on their back," Dran replied.

Jesmine interjected, "She's not a monster."

"You call it whatever you want, that still doesn't change the fact what it is."

"I've seen good and evil in all races I've come across, why is she any different?"

"It's a kobold, that's why."

"That doesn't explain anything."

"It explains *everything*," he said with a grunt.

Jesmine tensed slightly, squeezing the reins before she relaxed. "Talking to you on this will be a fruitless venture. How about we discuss something else then?"

Alderin replied, "That's a good idea. If we are shouting up a storm, it will possibly draw unwanted attention."

Dran nodded, "Agreed. We need to remain vigilant. Going back to the caravan is a risky venture."

"We shouldn't have much trouble with any orcs, our attack was far enough out of the way that any patrol will still be hours away."

"Aye, it was lucky we found Jesmine when we did, before they got too deep into Sa'bara's lands making a rescue attempt more difficult."

"How did you three find me?" Jesmine inquired.

"When all elves were supposed to have been killed or fled from Sa'bara's lands, word got around rather quickly when one showed up," Alderin explained. "The few human settlements here makes my movements easy."

Gnemi answered, "To my knowledge, orcs don't know much about us gnomes, so I pretended to be a child. For Dran, it is very probable that the dwarves in this land allowed him to get by unbothered by the more hospitable locals."

"Yes, but that doesn't explain how you knew where I was."

"When we were looking for you, we ran across people, who met survivors of the raid that led to your enslavement," Alderin said. "We followed those rumors and—,"

Jesmine's eyes lit up. "Do you know who the survivors were?"

Alderin shook his head. "I do not."

Jesmine's shoulders slumped, lowering her head slightly. "Oh."

"I heard it was a bunch of elven children," Dran said. "I wasn't too sure if what was said was trustworthy, but we had no other leads at the time."

"Really?" her eyes lit up once again.

"Aye."

Jesmine smiled, "That's good to know."

"Whatever the source, it led us to the Four Corner trade city where we heard an elf with long, elegant tattoos all over her body was sold to Sa'bara orcs. One thing led to another, and here we are."

"So, you're also from Dra'kesh lands then?"

"Dran and I are."

"I appreciate you've gone so far to find me. I honestly didn't think I was going to escape."

"We need to be thankful they didn't know who you truly were," Alderin said.

"I haven't done anything that was noteworthy. I just happen to be my mother's daughter."

Gnemi said, "But not everyone's mother is the one who killed one of the five ancient dragons. Not only that, I heard she single-handedly killed Eisandra, the White Terror of the North."

Jesmine clenched the reins of her horse. "My mother would be displeased to hear you speak of her such. She was one of many that fought and died to kill her. She'd weigh her sacrifice no more than anyone else's."

"I-I'm sorry, I didn't know. I remember growing up on stories about her exploits."

Jesmine took a deep breath. "It's okay," she replied, continuing to their destination.

"We're here," said Dran, approaching the remains of the caravan, birds and small beasts fleeing. Smoke fizzled up from the charred wagon.

"The burned wagon was the headmaster's. Most of the money should be there," Jesmine said.

Alderin dismounted, moving to it. He touched the remains, which instantly collapsed upon itself.

Dran chuckled. "Good thing money here doesn't burn."

"Let me find the coins; you can search for some food and feed in the other wagons," Gnemi suggested, hopping off. "You have the physique for it."

"Fair enough," Alderin replied, rummaging through them.

"I'll help," Jesmine said, dismounting, searching through the caravan, "I don't see any of the bodies... or horses."

"Thankfully, we aren't in the cursed lands, so they probably didn't walk off on their own," replied Gnemi, sifting through the charred wagon, tossing coins he found into a pouch.

"Whatever lies in the forest probably took them, all the more reason we have to be quick about this," said Alderin, taking some bags of horse feed, tossing them carelessly onto the back of their wagon, one of which partially landed onto Histra, suddenly waking her.

Histra growled, climbing to her feet with the help of the wagon's wall. Her blue eyes narrowed, seeing Alderin walking off. "Watch it, human."

"You're the one that suggested we come back here. Where did you expect us to put the horse feed?" he replied, back turned to her.

"You don't need to put it on top of me."

"Not my fault you decided to sleep while the rest of us worked."

Histra growled, her hands weakly gripping the wood, speaking in draconic. "Humans are so ignorant and disrespectful."

More bags were tossed in as Histra leaned on the side with a wide yawn, watching the others work. Out by the tree line movement caught her eye. Standing up she focused in that direction, noticing rustling of grass. "We need to get out of here."

Alderin, still not even looking in her direction replied, "We know, but you suggested we pick up the caravan's money and supplies."

"No, I mean we need to go right now," said Histra, pointing in the direction of the forest. "Something's coming!"

The others looked over there. "Damn it, it's right. We have to move now!" yelled Alderin as they rushed to their horses.

"Idiots," Histra remarked in draconic as Gnemi climbed his way to the top of the wagon. The horse nickered just as the others mounted up, four distinct trails of movement within the grasses quickly moved towards them.

"Does anyone know what they could be?" asked Jesmine, looking over in their direction.

"Don't know, don't want to find out if we don't have to," said Dran, as they got the horses under control and rode off.

"Easy girl, let's get out of here," Gnemi said, giving the reins a quick whip, the cart taking off with an unexpected acceleration.

Histra stumbled back, her foot catching one of the randomly thrown bags, falling backwards, hitting the back lip of the wagon; she tumbled over. The world spun for a few brief moments, before finding herself landing hard face first into the ground.

Histra gave a draconic growl, watching as the cart carried on without her. Her nostrils flared, smelling the pungent odor of the approaching beasts. "Idiots," she said in draconic, pushing herself back to her feet. "Of course, they'd continue to run," she remarked, turning in the direction of the nearest sound of one of the creatures approaching; a mixture of growling and snarling.

A large, feral beast about half the size of a horse came out of the bushes. Its grey, white, and black fur was a mangled mess, a mass of muscle snarling at her. Its yellow eyes focused on her, as the canid snout showed rows of pearly white teeth. Jutting from the back of its head were two long-curled horns over a foot and a half in length that ended in sharp points. The others were not far behind.

Histra attempted to spread her wings but a pain shot through her causing them to retract. Stepping closer, the beast's breath fogged the sudden cold causing it to take a moment's pause. "It's only going to get worse," said Histra, staring it down. Suddenly, an arrow whizzed over her head and lodged into the creature's shoulder, causing it to howl in pain.

The sound of hooves reached the kobold's ears, looking over her shoulder to see Jesmine riding back, hands moving in precise motions, muttering in arcane elvish, what little of her visible tattoos glowing a bright red. As she finished the incantation, a small ray of red energy left her fingertips at several times the speed of an arrow, hitting the creature in the face causing a small, lackluster burst of flames to pop in its face, singeing the hairs on its muzzle, the beast taken back by the sudden turn of events.

"That was… something," said Alderin, releasing another arrow at the creature, riding a few paces behind her.

"As I said I'm limited without my book," said Jesmine, pulling up beside Histra and dismounted. "Hop on," she said, crouching down to let her jump onto her back.

Histra looked away and groaned, climbing up. Jesmine winced at the cold sensation that suddenly gripped her. She climbed onto the horse just as another one of the creatures came out of the grasses. It was greeted with an arrow from Alderin before the three rode off.

"Humiliating," said Histra in draconic as the most injured of the beasts retreated while the one with the single arrow in it gave chase before being joined by the other two.

Alderin took aim, nocking back another arrow. "These wolkins are especially aggressive," he commented, firing, landing just short of the lead target. The beasts steadily gained ground, reaching their full stride.

"I have an idea that can help, just hold onto the horse," said Jesmine as they reached the wagon.

"What?!" exclaimed Alderin.

"Trust me on this, and whatever you do when I am done, don't look behind you," she said, holding out the reins.

"Alright," he replied, grabbing them.

Jesmine looked over her shoulder, "Hold on."

Histra looked off to the side as she leapt onto the wagon with a thud, Histra letting go just as they landed.

"Welcome aboard," said Gnemi, looking over to the kobold. "Sorry, this horse appears to be stronger than she looks. I didn't notice you fell off."

Histra didn't respond, as Jesmine stood up behind the small still open cage, its door squeakily swinging.

"Just buy me a few moments," said Jesmine, starting to wave her hands, her feet moving in small steps, taking slow, deep breaths in a steady rhythm, speaking in elvish-arcana.

"I'll do what I can," he replied, pulling out his mechanically enhanced crossbow. He fired a bolt which missed the leading wolkin. With a small click, the spring sprung into action, the rope automatically pulling back as another bolt was dropped from a small magazine into the chamber, ready to fire.

"I can't do anything like this!" yelled Alderin, pulling the horses ahead to Dran, who was keeping an eye to the front and sides. "Watch the horse," he said, tossing the reins over to him.

"Got it," he replied, catching them. Alderin slowed down, the lead wolkin leaping into the air, just missing the back of the wagon, causing it to fall behind the other two.

Gnemi took another shot, but it whizzed over their heads.

Jesmine kept a steady pace. A long string of words was spoken, special emphasis being put on specific syllables, the tattoos on her body glowing red once more, softly at first but brighter with each passing moment. The elf looked ahead of her, unflinching as Alderin fired off an arrow, which only grazed the back of one of the wolkin.

The wagon rattled and shook but Jesmine managed to keep not only her balance but her movements steady, fluid, the energy building in her fingertips, larger than the one from before.

Alderin notched and fired another, this time it hit the shoulder of the third wolkin, which caused it to lose several paces behind the fourth, the arrow's shaft snapping under the creature's muscular physique.

Gnemi tried to fire the fourth and last bolt within his mechanical crossbow but with a sudden jerk his arm went wide, and he tensed, seeing the bolt fly inches past the elf's head. She didn't even flinch.

Jesmine's words grew louder, her tattoos in full glow, speaking the last few words with powerful conviction. The new lead wolkin now in striking distance leapt into the air just as the energy left her fingers. A bright red-white glow shot forward, going off just in front of the beast with a brilliant, blinding flash and thunderous boom.

"My eyes!" yelled Gnemi, covering them with his arm. Alderin and Jesmine managed to look away in time. The lead wolkin hit the back of the cart, its claws scratching the wood, failing to find purchase, falling off and hitting the ground with a soft thud. The others let out a loud whine as they broke pursuit, shaking their heads and running around blindly.

Jesmine stumbled to the front, her god-like balance lost. Sitting down, she grabbed the reins from him. "Sorry, I forgot to warn you."

"It's okay... what was that?"

"A flash spell, one of the few slightly complex spells I know by heart," she explained.

"Are they still following us?"

"No, they broke off."

"Good... this isn't permanent is it?" asked Gnemi, blinking several dozen times while rubbing his eyes.

Jesmine shook her head. "No, it should go away in a few minutes."

"Thank the Gods," he replied as they continued at their current pace for a while before slowing down. Once the gnome's vision had returned, he was busily resetting his crossbow, pulling back and tuning each spring with a slow and steady turn of a knob.

"That's impressive, how did you obtain something like that?"

Gnemi smiled, "I made it myself."

"That's remarkable craftsmanship. Must be handy to have a self-reloading crossbow."

"It's helpful, but the issue I have is I have to make the bolts myself or they get stuck in the mechanism, and as you can tell," he said, grunting as he spun the knobs, "It's difficult to reload in combat," Gnemi lowered his head, turning to Jesmine, "Sorry about almost hitting you back there. The cart jerked and…"

"I wasn't hit, and you didn't mean to. I forgot to warn you about my flash spell, how about we call it even?"

"Yeah, but if I broke your concentration, I could have caused… what was it… a spell rebound? Not to mention a bolt to the head is something that probably no one would want."

Jesmine nodded. "Yes, it's a possibility, but with low level spells, it's easy enough to mitigate the elemental magic. It's only with the bigger spells that it becomes more dangerous."

Alderin, who was riding half a horse length ahead spoke up. "Thankfully, everyone is okay, despite certain things almost getting you killed."

"Histra saved us by warning about their approach. Can you at least give her a little credit? Don't you agree Histra?" Jesmine asked, looking behind her to see she was already asleep.

"It's still best not to lower your guard. It merely got lucky noticing the movement, and warned us because of its current state, not because of some desire, need, or want to be helpful."

"What gives you the right to speak about her like that?"

"What gives you such faith in it?" Alderin said with a groan.

"You tell me your story and I'll tell you mine?"

"Another time. It's best not to let our guard down. Those wolkin were oddly overly aggressive. I won't put it past them to continue the hunt."

Jesmine smirked. "Fine," she said, looking ahead to the split view of open plains and somewhat dense forest. "According to Histra, we should be fine for the next two days."

"Best we remain vigilant," Dran said. "But does anyone know what's up ahead?"

"There should be a few towns I think, but past that… no."

"We can ask our guide if you are really curious?" Gnemi

proposed.

"Why don't we let her sleep?" suggested Jesmine.

"I prefer we let it sleep," replied Dran as the group pressed on in their journey, having overcome their first bump on a long road ahead of them.

Chapter 3 Meeting in the Forest

Dark clouds hung in the sky as they traveled down the road. The wagon softly rattled and creaked. Histra walked back and forth in the back, holding a mostly empty bag of feed. Gnemi looked over his shoulder. "How goes your training?" he said. "You look like you can already walk without leaning onto something, that's a nice improvement, right?"

The kobold stopped, glaring at Gnemi, before turning her back to him and resumed what she was doing.

"Please don't be like that. I think you've been quiet for the past two days. If you want the other two to trust you, it might be good to talk to us."

Histra dropped the bag, turning to him. "There is nothing to be said. None of you are here to be my friend, and I am not here to be yours either. I only care that what I say is followed, for it is in my good interest to live to see tomorrow and that's it."

"Histra. I truthfully don't mean you any harm. I'm genuinely curious about you and your species. I don't blame your kind for serving the dragons; you are far from the only ones. As far as I know, almost everyone does."

Histra lifted an eye ridge. "Humph, I've been around too long to…" she said, trailing off, looking around. "Tell the others that we need to change our direction."

"Huh? What is it?"

"Just do as I say."

"Alright, alright," Gnemi replied, calling out to the others to stop. The horses let out a soft neigh, slowing down. Dran looked over to them and asked, "What is it?"

"Histra told me we need to change directions."

"Do we now?"

Histra walked to the side of the cart facing Dran. "Yes, we do. If we continue down this road, by the end of the day we'll reach the town of Agul. It's an orc farming town, but it's also a toll town, as it contains the only viable bridge to cross over the river for a three day's travel from here."

"I'd like to limit time spent with orcs. I've had nothing but bad experiences with them," Alderin commented.

"I like to avoid as many orcs myself," said Histra.

"Alright then, tell us, *guide*, what do you suggest we do?"

"We'll soon be upon a path that leads into the forest. It's a little hidden but I can point it out. If we follow through the path, we'll come across a fjord in the river. As long as it doesn't rain, it should be crossable with relative ease."

"You want us to go into the forest? The one you've been rather adamant about us avoiding this whole time? What do you make of this Dran?"

"I don't know…" he replied, rubbing his red beard, "I haven't had as much experience of the wilderness as you."

Histra let out a huff of air. "This forest is nothing compared to what you'll face in Du'ralia. If you are afraid now, you all better turn back and find a safe place to leave me," Histra explained.

"Unfortunately, I was never in this area, so I don't know much about this particular forest, but few are particularly dangerous, Du'ralia being an odd exception," Jesmine said.

Gnemi inquired, "Jesmine, if your home was so dangerous, why is it near Du'ralia Forest?"

"It's not near, it's deep within it. The forest was dangerous yes, but our home wasn't, and we had paths to lead us through it, usually without issue."

"Usually?"

"Yes, fascinating," Histra said, "But that isn't the forest we're going through right now is it? The path is mostly safe as long as you limit drawing any attention. Unfortunately, it will be slow going so we will not be able to reach the fjord before nightfall."

"What do you suggest we do then Histra?" Jesmine asked.

"Normally the caravan would wait and leave at daybreak, but we do not have this luxury, the sooner the better is what I am told?"

Alderin nodded, "You are correct. We can't just sit and wait."

Dran replied, "Aye, it's best."

"Luckily two to three hours before the fjord there is a clearing big enough to set up camp. If we are fortunate, we'll get there before nightfall. The last thing you'd want to do is travel the forest at night, especially when we have two new moons approaching. It'll be so dark even I won't be able to see the end of my snout," Histra continued to explain as Alderin approached her. She walked across the other side of the wagon to meet him. Cetas grew slightly uneasy, his breath appearing in the localized cold. "Is that enough from your guide or do you require more?"

"Perhaps you could tell us where this supposed path is?"

"I'll tell you when I see it. I can't give you all my secrets now." She partially unfurled her wings before stopping, feeling a twinge of pain.

Alderin looked down at her. "And I trust you could find it? What if you just so happen to miss it?"

"It probably would be for the best if we had more eyes to look for it," suggested Gnemi.

"Histra. Could you please tell us what the path's entrance looks like?" Jesmine asked.

She looked over her shoulder to Jesmine, her wings folding back. Her claws tensed slightly before they relaxed. "*Fine*. There is a blackened, fallen tree that marks the entrance."

Jesmine smiled. "Thank you."

Histra turned her attention back to Alderin. "There you go. Lead on," she said, waving him off.

Alderin humphed, "A guide who wants others to lead," he remarked, riding ahead of the group.

"Why do you do that?" asked Jesmine. Histra's wings twitched, folding her arms, saying nothing.

"It's in her nature," remarked Dran, riding off to Alderin, the wagon moving once more.

"Nature doesn't define someone," Jesmine replied.

"You should thank her," Gnemi suggested.

Histra turned to him. "Thank her? For what? I don't need to be defended. I don't need to be told what I am."

"I wasn't referring to that. She was the first to rush back to save you."

Histra tensed up, gritting her teeth and looked away.

"If you don't want to talk about it, can you perhaps at least tell me, is it true that kobold scales are like baby dragon scales?"

Histra responded with a grunt and rolled her eyes.

"I think I'll take that as a maybe," he replied. After a bit of time, they found the fallen tree, massive in length and girth, its charred bark seemingly out of place from everything around it. The branches were crooked, jagged, broken, far from a welcoming sign.

"Kobold, is this the path's entrance?" Alderin yelled.

"Yes, just go straight ahead… but one thing when we enter," she said, causing Alderin to stop his horse just short of the brush, the path becoming visible through the tall trees, light glittering through the canopy. The path was beaten from countless hooves, feet, and tracks, but there were signs the forest was trying to take it back, through the small sprigs and plants advancing on either side.

"What is it?"

"Whatever we find, whoever we run into, you must not be the first to strike or draw blood, especially your own."

"I do not plan to be cut in this forest," Alderin replied, turning his horse around.

"There are things in there that will come if the residence of the forest die, but blood of a sentient being will bring beasts far more terrible, which I wish to not run into. Do I make myself clear?"

"I will keep that in mind," he said, heading into the forest.

Histra sighed and remarked in draconic, "Humans, and they think dragons are the arrogant ones."

Entering the forest, the cart wobbled, cracking twigs and crunching leaves under its wheels. The horses moved slowly with slight agitation as birds fluttered through the upper canopy, keeping everyone on edge. Sounds of rustling brush and whistling winds echoed through the trees, making it almost impossible to discern its source. Deeper they traveled into the forest, the path winding and turning as marks in the tree trunks at set intervals helped them keep on track. Suddenly, a dark figure moved through the canopy, leaves and twigs falling to the ground, the top of the trees swaying under the creature's weight.

Gnemi and Alderin drew their ranged weapons while Dran pulled out his axe from his back, his thick fingers providing a tight grip on the hilt. "Don't fire," said Histra in a raised voice at an intensity that was below a yell.

"I didn't forget what you said, kobold but that does not mean I can't be ready," said Alderin, watching the creature.

"What is it?" Gnemi asked, his green eyes scouring the trees to locate it again, having lost it for a moment.

Histra looked up, the creature partially obscured by the foliage. "It's a kiapal. One would never attack a group, so we shouldn't be worried. It's only problematic if they form hunting parties."

"Hunting parties?" Gnemi asked curiously.

"It's moderately intelligent, if you can call them that. They're an aggressive bunch that pick on small animals. Me, you, and the dwarf are about the sizes they'd like to strike if given the chance."

"I've heard of those things, but no way I will allow it to carry me off," Dran said with a huff.

Histra replied in draconic, "You'd probably taste terrible anyway."

"What was that Histra?" Jesmine asked.

"Nothing. Let's keep moving," she said, the creature keeping a distance while they traversed the woods. The daylight steadily faded, the shadows growing larger, darker, and all encompassing. The sound of raindrops echoed through the forest as thunder rumbled out in the distance.

The rain slowly made it through the canopy, their clothes becoming soaked as time passed. The droplets that fell toward Histra froze and hit the wagon like little icicles. The kobold kept a watchful vigilance around her, muttering, "I hate the rain."

"It'll soon be too dark to see the path, we better find this campsite," Alderin said.

"I'm used to the dark, but it is best not to travel with a blind party," Histra said.

Dran's stern brown eyes peered into the forest, "You aren't the only one that can see in the dark, but aye it is right."

Jesmine softly sighed at Dran's remark. "Let me help. Dran, can you hold onto my reins?" she asked.

"Of course," he replied, grabbing them, Jesmine beginning to chant, moving her hands. Over the next thirty seconds, her tattoos glowed a soft blue before suddenly disappearing as three softball-sized glowing spheres emitted a light slightly greater than a lamp. She spaced them at ten-foot intervals as they floated ahead of her.

"Not that I am not appreciative, but we do have lanterns," said Dran, curiously looking at the spheres.

"Reins please," said Jesmine softly, Dran handing them back. "Thank you. This lets me be helpful. I can keep this up for a while without issue, but it will be up to you all to keep an eye out," she said, the light from the globes dimming slightly before she resumed her chant.

"Not a problem," he replied as their trek continued onward. The last rays of the day faded away and only the three floating orbs provided any light. The trees casted long shadows and the light drizzle remained constant. Water dripped from their bodies and weapons, and only Histra remained 'dry' as she moved in a quarter of an inch layer of snow-like icicles.

As the group turned a small bend, Dran held up a hand. "Jesmine, turn off the lights."

"What is it?" asked Alderin, Jesmine quickly waving her hands and with a short glow of her tattoos, the orbs instantly disappeared.

Jesmine blinked a few times, eyes adjusting to the darkness. "There's another light."

"Damn it," remarked Alderin.

"What shall we do? It's probably orcs," asked Gnemi.

Jesmine flipped a hood over her head. "I can feign being a human."

"You can't expect for us just to go up to an orc camp like it's nothing," Alderin replied.

"Elves should have been gone in this area for the past thirty years—it can work."

"That's not what I mean."

"We should approach with caution. If it's a small group we could get the jump on them," Dran suggested.

"You will do no such thing," said Histra, moving to the front of the wagon. "They are on the path; they should know the rules. Go there and stop for the night. Do any of you know orc tongue?"

"I know a little," Alderin replied.

Histra sighed. "That won't do. Humans and dwarves in this area are expected to know orc tongue. If you talk to them speaking broken orc they will be not only insulted; they'd suspect something."

"You could have warned us about such a possibility," said Dran, remaining vigilant.

"I didn't think I needed to explain it. It wasn't an exclusive path the caravan took. Others know of it, but it is still an overall secret."

"I'll go up ahead and see what's there. I'll come back, and we can figure out what to do next," Alderin said.

"You will not," replied Histra, who then leapt off the side of the wagon, her wings fluttering slightly, landing with a soft thud, stumbling almost following over. The wet foliage froze around her feet, slowly spreading outwards. She stood up, puffing out her chest, slowly walking to the front. "I'll talk to them, and the rest of you will follow right behind me. You may have your weapons out, but I strongly suggest you do not raise them."

Alderin looked down at the white kobold, trying to keep his horse calm, the water on Cetas' legs freezing. "Oh no, I am not going to let a kobold speak for me." He rode his horse in front of Histra.

"You aren't going to let me?" she said with some venom in her words, raising an eye ridge. "I am going do as I please. I can't trust a human to handle it without it involving bodily harm to my person, and I am very fond of that *not* happening to me," she said walking underneath his horse.

"Alderin, let her," Jesmine said.

"But it's a kobold. It'll sell us out."

"Aye, I agree," Dran replied, watching Histra stop ten feet ahead of the group.

"I can still hear you, follow me. If you are hiding it will not go well," she stated, turning to face them, arms crossed, wings slightly spread.

"If the other party knows what they can and can't do, they won't attack," Jesmine said.

"That's if what the kobold said is true," Dran replied.

"There is little chance we won't cross their path no matter what we do. Let Histra do her thing, if it goes wrong." Gnemi showed off his crossbow. "We'll be ready."

"I'm waiting," Histra called out.

"She has done nothing to break our trust in her. Give her this chance," Jesmine said.

"She hasn't had a chance to break it till now," scoffed Dran.

Alderin tensed and tugged on Cetas' reins, pressing his sides, breaking off small bits of melting ice, riding forward.

Dran sighed and followed, Histra giving a draconic smirk. "Say nothing, let me do all the talking and remember: Do NOT make the first strike," Histra said, heading down the path, keeping several paces ahead of the group as they soon heard with the sound of orcs chatting. As they approached their conversation stopped, leaving only the sound of the cackling of fire hissing under the slow and steady assault of the rain. A random lightning bolt illuminated the forest for a single moment showing the seeming endlessness of it.

Histra stopped just short of the opening in the clearing, yelling in orcish. The others stopped, Dran leaning over to Alderin, "What's it saying?"

"Hello, and what I think sums up one dwarf, three humans."

"That it?"

"I picked up orc tongue here and there, but I never had a real desire to learn it in depth."

"Perhaps it might be a good idea to start learning then?"

Histra motioned the group forward, continuing to speak in orcish. As she stepped completely into view of the orcs there was a sudden commotion amongst them. The party came into clearing where eight orcs, dressed in leather armor, had their weapons drawn. There were three females in the back with bows at the ready, two orc men with swords, and three others with axes.

A light-tanned skinned orc, wielding a massive axe that could fell a horse with a single blow, stood in front of the others. A large campfire burned in the center of the clearing which was big enough to fit a party six times their size. Felled trees were placed in a circle around the encampment up to three feet in height, with the only the one opening toward the path.

The orcs stared at them as they arrived, the archers keeping their arrows trained on the group, the large axe wielding orc yelling fiercely at Histra. His yellow teeth showed, tusks jutting from his lower jaw as his yellow eyes met hers.

"That's more than just a few orcs," Gnemi said, nervously adjusting his goggles, dumping the excess water that built up in them.

"Stay calm," Jesmine said.

"What are they saying?" Dran asked.

"It's going too fast… but it does not sound good," Alderin replied.

Histra spoke loudly, angrily, the orc leader shouting back even more, the talk between the other orcs dying down completely. The party watched as their two foot something kobold stood up to a seven-foot tower of muscle. Suddenly, in the strew of words between them, one word was spoken by the orc leader that everyone could understand.

"Sa'bara."

Histra growled speaking said name back, the conversation growing more heated.

"I'm not too sure, but maybe they think she's an agent of Sa'bara. Granted that could very well be true," Alderin suggested.

"What should we do?" asked Gnemi, fingers nervously drumming against his crossbow.

"Wait," said Jesmine, watching the 'debate' with great intensity.

The orc grabbed the hilt of his axe with both hands, approaching Histra. She walked towards him, spreading her wings. Their back and forth yelling reached a climax the orc swinging his axe down in her direction, her entire body disappearing behind it, mud flying up into the air.

Jesmine jumped at the sight, Dran remarking, "Well that's certainly one way to end an argument." Alderin notched an arrow, Gnemi slowly raised his crossbow.

Ice gradually formed around the axe and up along the orc's legs, his breath fogging as he spoke loudly in orcish. After a moment, the orc chuckled and lifted his axe, leaving a deep gash in the ground, showing the blade came within inches of hitting Histra. The leader said a few more words before turning to his group, everyone lowering their weapons, some of the tension melting away.

Histra lets out a huff of air, turning back to the group. "Horses are allowed near the center, but all of you are to set up camp near the entrance. In case something comes, they want you as bait. They don't trust you as far as I can throw you," Histra explained.

"The feeling is mutual," Alderin replied.

"Isn't the saying as far as they or I can throw you?" asked Gnemi, pulling the wagon into camp.

"Yes, but they can throw the lot of you pretty far."

"I believe that's fair enough."

Dran leaned over to Alderin whispering, "And they can throw her even farther," the two chuckling at that. "I suggest we double team our watch tonight," he said, dismounting, eyeing over the orcs, who watched them.

"Good idea, I'll take second watch. Jesmine, do you mind

helping me with that one?" asks Alderin.

"Huh? Sure, I can do that." she said, dismounting.

Gnemi hitched Gnaria to a large log. "Histra, why did you have such a heated discussion with the orc?"

She chuckled. "Heated? That? Hardly. Orcs are a hot-blooded bunch; they are aggressive and forth right. They don't like to talk using frilly words. They get to the point of the matter. Their leader was suggesting I was a spy for the great dragon Sa'bara. Part of a patrol to find those skipping the toll. I told him I was not, and neither were any of you, and then promptly tested my resolve."

"By throwing an axe at you?"

"I informed them an ice kobold would not be serving a poison-based dragon flight. Would be bad for my health, I proved my point and resolved in one quick go."

"How did you know he was not going to hit you?"

"Simple. To them it's dishonorable to strike an unarmed opponent, especially one of my stature, so I used that to my advantage." explained Histra, with a grin.

"Orcs have honor? I find that hard to believe," Alderin said.

"It's not far off from Dran's so-called hon—" suddenly the kobold found her mouth shut by Jesmine's hands. Histra glared at her fiercely.

"Sorry, but I am tired of hearing the three of you fight, and I think it's best for everyone if we do not show ourselves bickering amongst one another in front of foreign company."

Gnemi finished setting up his tent. "I believe that she makes a fine point."

Dran nodded. "Agreed."

Histra pushed Jesmine's hands from her muzzle, softly growling. "Don't ever clamp your hands over my snout again."

"Sorry, it was all I could think of."

Alderin thought with a smirk, *"And the smartest thing you've done so far."*

Histra sighed. "Get whatever rest you can. We'll be leaving first thing in the morning." She stated, heading over to the wagon, sitting underneath it in the soft muddy ground, which slowly began to freeze over and harden.

"Don't you want to sleep in a tent?" asked Jesmine, looking to her with concern.

"And be accused of freezing one of you to death as I slept? No thank you. This will do just fine."

"Okay…"

"I don't need your fancy equipment. Not like I need to worry about keeping warm."

"Actually…" Jesmine raised her hand.

Histra looked at her and after a short pause, "Yes?"

"Never mind."

Histra let out a little huff of air, the orcs tossing in a few more logs to the fire; it flickered and crackled. There were robust conversations amongst the orcs, taking shifts of two for their rotation. Jesmine and Alderin slowly made their way to their tents to rest while Gnemi and Dran set up a watch.

Night was no solace for those at the campsite, for the forest residents were out and about. Their calls echoed through the trees. The campfire light flickered illuminating small movements in the distance, and more concerning closer ones in the branches above. Despite this, both parties kept one person watching the other group, while the other kept a vigilance to what might be lurking in the woods.

The orcs changed lookouts twice before Alderin and Jesmine took the next watch. Jesmine slipped out from under the small tent, her hood thrown over her head, looking to see two male orcs near the slowly dying fire.

"It's still raining," said Jesmine.

"Aye, been raining all night. I'm soaked the bone," Dran remarked, he and Gnemi slipping into their tents while Histra was curled under the cart in a small nest of icy frozen mud. The wagon had small icicles hanging from either side that shrunk to nothing as they got farther away from her.

"Hopefully it will end soon. Otherwise the fjord could become difficult to cross," commented Alderin.

"Under this light rain?" Jesmine asked, holding out her hand to feel the gentle patter of water against her skin.

"Don't underestimate the power of what a steady rain can do."

The elf nodded, keeping a lookout, her attention shifting as the sound of branches bent and cracked up in the canopy that surrounded the clearing. The campfire provided enough light to illuminate the boundary between the top of the trees and the sky.

Alderin watched the orcs vigilantly, only giving glancing concerns to the forest that surrounded them. The orcs idly chit-chatted with each other before their watch eventually came to an end with two women orcs that took up the mantle.

Jesmine observed the opening to the campsite. "If you keep staring at them, it will only agitate the situation."

"They are staring at us just the same," he replied.

The two orcs bantered until a random noise in the forest drew their attention and their bows. After a few moments, they relaxed, the larger female orc, with soft green skin and black braided hair going halfway down her back, said something to her companion, taking a step toward Alderin and Jesmine. The other woman spoke a hair louder, reaching for her friend but was quickly shut down, continuing to walk towards them. The orc called out to them in orcish, as Alderin took a moment.

Jesmine kept one eye on the forest, the other on her, "What did she say?" she whispered.

"A simple greeting, so let me handle this," Alderin whispered back before speaking in orcish. "Hello. What is it that you want?"

The orc's soft, green eyes looked at him, then shifted her attention to Jesmine. "You are not able to speak any orc tongue, are you?" the orc asked in human.

Alderin quickly replied, "I speak orc tongue."

"Clearly you do… poorly. I meant you, human female."

Jesmine stammered for a moment before facing the orc who stood a few paces away. "How did you know?"

The orc let out a chuckle. "Way you act when little kobold confronted my husband. Obviously, you did not understand what was happening."

"I find it foolish to spend a night with strangers and not talk. Name is Durloch, she is Eghasha. Yours?"

"Jesmine."

Alderin kept a hand on the hilt of his blade, responding, "Alderin."

Durloch smirked, water dripping down her chin. "For one who doesn't know orc tongue, you are curious to head straight into orc lands."

"We're retrieving an item very special to me that was lost," Jesmine quickly said, Alderin tensing.

"Something a human has lost requires heading deeper into clan Ugosh lands?"

"Jesmine, I think you've said enough."

"It's not in these lands but elsewhere. It's a memento of my Mother. It was all I had of her."

Durloch looked at the two curiously. "How you lose it? Tidings to the dragon?"

"You can say Sa'bara is the reason it is lost, yes."

Alderin whispered, "Jesmine."

Durloch's eyes widened slightly. "You intend to take back what was taken by Sa'bara? You head to an early grave just to speak of such things. He has ears everywhere."

"Sa'bara didn't take it specifically, more like happenstance caused by his will."

"That's why you have kobold guide?" she asked, pointing over to Histra.

"Yes."

"You are desperate or stupid to trust kobold."

"I said the same thing," Alderin remarked.

"Alderin, not this again."

Durloch chuckled. "You two fight like a married couple, just like the kobold said."

"Well... I said my story, is it fair you share yours?" Jesmine asked.

"It is fair. We travel to borderlands. Get out of clan Ugosh lands."

"Why?"

Durloch tensed at the question, Eghasha quickly saying something in orcish before Durloch retorted back, causing Eghasha to tense up before Durloch regained her composure. "We're members of clan Tirghal. There is no future in Ugosh lands for any of clan Tirghal."

"Why is that?"

"When elves rebelled against Sa'bara, he learned that it was our clan that let the elves through to the north without hindrance to fight the dragon there."

"Orcs worked with elves?" asked Alderin in surprise.

Durloch nodded. "Once. Elves and Orc worked to feign hostilities to keep elven movement hidden from Sa'bara. In exchange, the elves would work to liberate our lands from him. But his spies are everywhere. They learned of the elf betrayal and were wiped out. Avolarieans and clan Ugosh quickly supported the extermination and were given elven lands."

"How did Sa'bara learn about your clan's aid to the elves?"

"I do not know. Homeland was given to the avolarieans. Our clan scattered. We want to return to our homeland but for now, need to find a place to settle within Sa'bara's lands. Rebuild and gain strength," she replied.

Jesmine looked away, hands clenching for a moment before looking back, asking, "That was thirty years ago. You are just now rebuilding?"

"Most of clan Tirghal was forbidden from travel."

"I see. We both have a long journey ahead of ourselves. I wish you luck."

"We do not need luck. We're strong. We will surv—," suddenly there was a loud snap in the trees above. Alderin and the two orcs drew their bows and aimed in the direction of the noise, as the soft clatter of falling sticks was heard. The firelight illuminated a set of glowing yellow eyes, followed by another, and soon over a dozen pairs could be seen watching all around the camp.

Chapter 4 Crossing the Fjord

Durloch whispered to the Eghasha in orcish, nocking an arrow. Eghasha nodded, slowly heading towards her encampment while keeping an eye on their unexpected visitors that hung above them. The campfire's fading light reflected off the kiapal's yellow eyes. They let out a series of low clicks, which was responded to by even more out in the distance. Flashes from distant lightning strikes reveal only for an instant at a time more movement in the trees. The roar of the thunder rolled in, causing a few of them to let out a sudden growl-chirp, briefly snapping at each other, their fangs visible in the low light. Parts of their bat-like wings showed through the foliage as they jump and flew to different tree branches.

"Wake the others, quietly," whispered Alderin.

Jesmine nodded, keeping an eye above, tapping the side of the tent. "Wake up we have company."

A groan emanated from within, Jesmine adding, "Be ready to fight."

The orc camp came to life, sounds of orcish being yelled along with metal clanking echoed out into the forest.

Alderin vaguely understood what Durloch mutter in annoyance. "Idiots don't know the meaning of quietly."

The creatures in the forest made out a series of calls to each other, one jumping from a crowded tree to an empty one, causing the branch to slightly crack and sway. Alderin drew his bow nocking an arrow.

"Do not shoot. Will cause frenzy," Durloch cautioned.

Alderin replied. "I know, I just wanted to be ready. I have been warned about spilling blood in this forest."

"Experienced guide. Your kobold."

Dran popped out of the tent with his axe in hand. "What is it?" he said, looking around over to the orc encampment until he saw Jesmine pointing up.

"Quiet," she said.

The dwarf looked up, his brown eyes giving off a soft eerie reflection in the fading light. His grip on the axe grew tighter. "Oh... that's a lot of them."

"Be ready for a fight but start taking down the tents, we'll throw them in the wagon."

"Aye, don't need to tell me twice," he replied.

Gnemi poked his head out of the tent with his crossbow in hand, quickly noticing the kiapals above. "I'm glad I probably didn't overact this time," he muttered, slipping his head back inside to get a few things before coming back out. "That appears to be a lot of them."

Jesmine crouched down by the cart, breaking off one of the longer icicles hanging from its underside and gently poked Histra's side. "Wake up, we have a problem."

Her wings twitched, letting out a soft growl, eyes slowly opening, narrow pupils quickly widening. She broke a super thin layer of ice from parts of her white scales.

"What is it? Did one of you piss off the orcs with your human tongue?"

Jesmine shook her head, motioning upwards. "It brought friends."

"Friends?" Histra slipped her head out from under the cart, wings twitching, claws tensing. "It wasn't a solo kiapal, it was part of a flock. Dammit," She spread her wings almost to their fullest before her body tensed with pain.

"Thankfully, they haven't attacked yet."

Histra stared up at them. "Of course not. They are waiting for a moment to strike. I'm glad none of you morons set them off."

"We're packing up and throwing everything onto the wagon right now."

She nodded in acknowledgement, keeping her gaze locked up to the trees as some of the raindrops turned into ice as they hit her. "I hate the rain."

Durloch warned Alderin. "Do not do anything stupid."

Histra headed to her encampment, while the orc archers were at the ready while the orc leader barked out commands to those loading up their equipment onto a large hand-pulled wooden cart. Their tents save for two were quickly taken down, and for the first time the party saw a half a dozen orc children ranging in age from a couple of years old to early teens being ushered into the larger huts.

The orc leader yelled at Alderin, approaching their horses,

which vocally expressed their unease with nickers and soft neighs. The human stared at the leader, motioning for Dran to come. "Get the horses ready."

"On it," he replied, the orc leader walking to Alderin, continuing to speak in orcish.

Alderin's gaze switched between the orcs and the increasing number of kiapals.

"Is it possibly close to sunrise? I don't like the idea of probably having to wait long to move," asked Gnemi, moving toward him, which caused the orc leader to yell in their direction.

Alderin stared at the orc, saying in poor orcish, "It's okay."

Gnemi looked confused at what is going on.

Histra growled, walking over to them. "Stupid, stupid, stupid. Gnemi stay there and don't do anything," she commanded.

"What is it?" he asked.

"They think you are a human child," she stated, approaching the orc, walking past Alderin in the process, talking to the leader in orcish.

A bright flash of lightning instantly followed by a thunderous boom, sending the kiapals into action like marathon runners sprinting at the sound of the starter gun. They let out an ear-piercing screech as they swarmed down onto the encampment.

The orc archers unleashed a hail of arrows, the kiapals' screeching and howling echoed throughout the forest. The orc leader struck down one in a single blow with his massive axe. The purple blood splattered across his chest and face as he let out a loud grunt, fending off the sharp, black talons of another attempting to rake along his back.

Gnemi fired off two bolts at one in quick succession, one lodging in its torso, causing it fall to the ground with a heavy thud, splattering mud in all directions, screeching in pain. It managed to force itself onto all fours, black fur wet from the rain, wings attached to its forearms by a thin-skinned membrane. It waddled across the ground with a hunched back, lips curling to reveal rows of tiny sharp teeth before lunging at Gnemi.

With a heavy thud, Dran's axe came down, slicing into the monster's back. Thick purple blood ran down its side, stumbling forward, dead. The dwarf and gnome prepared for another wave, when they noticed two kiapals grabbing the corpse, flying off with it.

"Are they are taking their dead?" asked Gnemi his gaze torn between that and the immediate threat.

"They'll eat their own," said Jesmine, staying near Alderin. She looked over to the horses who were bucking and tugging at the reins, but the heavy log they were tied to barely budged. "We have to guard the horses. Cover me!" she yelled to him, rushing over to them. He followed while Dran and Gnemi remained near the cart, fending off more attacks.

"Buy me some time!" Jesmine yelled, looking to him.

"I'll do what I can," he replied, firing an arrow at one kiapal.

Jesmine muttered in elvish-arcana, the tattoos glowing a soft, reddish hue.

Another kiapal swooped down, claws extended at Histra, who just managed to drop down in time to avoid the strike. Mud clung to her body, slowing freezing over as she growled, "Fowl beasts." She managed to roll away, dodging another strike.

Others swarmed, clawed, and bit the orcs. Their weapons flailed in an attempt to down them, only to be attacked along their backs, necks, and any exposed flesh. One orc was knocked over by the swarming kiapals, and though he swung his blade at them in vain as he was assaulted. They were soon feasting upon his brown-skinned flesh like a pack ravenous wolves.

One of his companions tried to rescue him, but he too, was swarmed. The orc struck out against them, trying to protect his face, stumbling back and falling onto one of the huts, which caused it to collapse. The orc children suddenly found themselves exposed and surrounded by the beasts. They screamed for aid, the eldest children armed with small daggers trying to stave off the attackers, but one young girl barely bigger than Gnemi rushed out into the middle of the chaos, frightened by one of the kiapals that got dangerously close to her.

Her long black hair was tied into a single braid that went halfway down her back. She bobbed and weaved between those fighting. The little orc stumbled, falling into the mud which sprayed into her face, shooting some of the mud out of her nose, curious to suddenly see her own breath. Two feet in front of her was Histra hugging the ground.

The kobold looked up and tensed, seeing the orc, their eyes

locking onto the other for a moment before two talons wrapped around the child, lifting her up into the air. The talons dug into her shoulders, drawing blood, and she screamed at the top of her lungs.

Histra simply watched her be carried off. Durloch noticed what was happening, yelling for help while taking a shot at the kidnapper. The arrow whizzed by grazing the creature's wings. The large orc leader struck down another, his eyes widening, trying to rush over but is blocked by more of the foul beasts. Dran and Gnemi were busy fighting off their own group, the gnome barely preventing one from dragging him into the air with the dwarf's aid.

Alderin tensed, the voice of the screaming child reached his ears. In an instant he pulled back the bowstring, aimed and fired. The arrow whistled through the air and the kiapal let out a screech as the arrow pierced its neck. Its limp body tumbled back down, letting go of the child, which landed on top of Histra with a squish. The weight of the landing forced the kobold's head into the mud. She lifted her head out of the muck, growing in annoyance, body twitches under the child as her arms shake, claws slipping across the mud, trying in vain to push the child off.

The girl's cries echoed in Alderin's ears, tightening the grip on his bow, his body shaking as heard voices spoken in human tongue of two young boys and a girl in his mind. They screamed out to him, "Father!"

Moments later, Jesmine raised her hand to the sky, finishing her incantation. The rest of the party realized at the last moment what was happening. Dran and Gnemi yelled, "Cover your eyes!" The elf let out a dazzling display of blinding light, and a loud cacophonic boom with little actual force behind it. Momentarily blinded and deafened, the kiapals which flew into each other, causing them to scatter back up into the trees. The few stragglers were quickly taken out.

"Get off of me," Histra growled in orcish, Durloch rushing to pick up the child, whisking her away to safety while the blinding light knocked Alderin out of his daze.

The orc leader bled from several small wounds, grunting heavily, looking over to Alderin and Jesmine once it became obvious the immediate danger has passed. He pointed his heavy, purple blood-soaked axe at them, speaking in orcish. Alderin nodded slowly, keeping his weapon lowered but at the ready.

Histra pushed herself back onto her feet, brushing off the slightly frozen mud. She spoke briefly to the orc leader; he responded loudly and verbosely which promptly quieted her. The kobold's eyes narrowed a little, turning to face Dran and Gnemi who had received only minor cuts and bruises. "Get the cart ready, double up the horses. We need to go now," she said.

"Aye, that much is obvious," Dran remarked, cracking his neck.

Gnemi panted heavily, "I thought I was probably going to die there," he remarked, checking over his quiver, "I'm down to ten bolts; it's most likely unwise for us to get into many more fights like that."

"All the more reason we need to go now before something far worst comes," said Histra, gazing over to the dead orc, which was being left behind, despite protests by some.

Dran rolled his shoulders. "Looks like they are going to need some help," he said heading over to Jesmine, who was having trouble calming the horses.

Meanwhile the orc leader stood in front of Alderin, the large muscle of a man towering over him. Their eyes met, the orc holstering his axe on his back, Alderin managed to understand one word clearly, a name.

"Krogg."

He failed to find the words to say "Welcome," before the orc leader Krogg turned, yelling at the rest of his party, who were quickly finishing preparations. The children were placed onto a cart with a tarp pulled over them and they departed, making their way up the trail.

"Human, do you even realize what you did?" Histra asked, Alderin giving her a cold stare.

"I saved one of their children," he remarked.

"I see," she replied with a smirk.

"What is it?"

"Nothing. Let's go before we have more company. Those kiapals might be back amongst other things," she said, struggling to climb back onto the wagon before Gnemi gave her a leg up.

"There you go," he said, rubbing his hands together, heading over to the front of the cart.

"I could have done it myself."

"We are most likely short on time, right?" Gnemi replied. She sighed in response.

Alderin eyed her for a moment before shrugging, hitching the horses to the cart, then mounting his. He turned to Jesmine who was climbing into the front. "It's still a little dark, do you think you can cast that light show again?"

"That will be easy enough," she replied, casting the spell as they left, the glowing orbs illuminating their way. They pushed ahead through the bending curves, searching for each marker to keep them on track.

"What resides within this forest that makes it so unhospitable?" Dran asked.

"A few types of massive beasts and possibly werewolves," Histra replied with a wing twitch, flicking ice from them.

Gnemi looked over his shoulder. "Werewolves? They even exist?"

"They do. There's a bounty put on them to be captured alive."

"Don't believe what the kobold says. Who would pay for a live werewolf?" asked Dran as a loud, deep, wailing howl echoed through the trees.

"What was that?" the gnome asked, looking around nervously.

"Nothing good, move faster!" yelled Histra. The horses clip-clopped through the forest, branches crunching under their weight, the cart shaking on the uneven trail.

Jesmine focused ahead of her, her hands shifting, guiding the orbs of light down the path. Echoes of snapped trees came from the direction of the camp. Gnemi asked, "Do you think it will follow us?"

"Maybe? I don't know, just keep going," Histra replied, keeping a vigilant watch. The treetops swayed, the calls of a couple kiapals could be heard above them.

"More of them? I haven't had time to reload my crossbow," remarked Gnemi, one of them bursting from the treetops, its black claws extended, diving at them.

Jesmine flicked her wrist, speaking her incantation, as one of the balls flew right into the creature's face, causing it to briefly pause and wince from the light. Its dive thrown off course caused it to crash into the cart with a thud, screeching out in pain. Gnemi pulled out his short sword driving the blade into the creature's gut.

It shrieked and clawed at the air, quickly bleeding out.

"That appears to be some quick thinking, Jesmine," Gnemi commented. She smiled while keeping to her spell.

Histra sighed, moving over, weakly pulling the still twitching creature to an empty section of the wagon. "Can't have the damn thing bleed all over the food," she remarked in draconic.

The other kiapal jumps from treetop to treetop, trying to keep up but steadily fell behind.

"I think we lost them," said Gnemi.

"Just keep going!" yelled Alderin, the last bits of night fading.

Jesmine ended her spell as the sun's morning rays began to illuminate the forest.

"Kobold, how much longer till we get to the fjord?" asked Alderin.

"We'll get there when we get there!" she yelled.

He sighed, shaking his head, "This is one hell of a way to start a morning."

"Aye, but I've seen worse," Dran remarked, his red beard dripping with water. An hour passed when a howl rang through the forest. "Are they following us?"

"That doesn't sound like what we heard earlier," remarked Alderin.

A wolkin busted from the bushes, leaping onto the path ahead. The horses kicked up, almost knocking Dran and Alderin from their backs, the cart veering slightly off to the side to avoid crashing into them. The sudden stop caused Histra to slide to the front of the wagon.

"Easy girl," said Dran, giving the wolkin a stern brown eyed stare. He drew out his axe, charging the black furred beast that bared its teeth with a snarl.

The wolkin pounced at him, who met it with a battle cry, swinging his axe, striking the creature with such force that he stopped it in its tracks. Bones snapped, blood spurting from the open chest wound, its teeth snapping out at Dran's arm, barely missing it. The beast yelped in pain, falling back. "They look tough, but they don't like to take an axe to the face."

"I believe there is more of them!" yelled Gnemi, as no fewer than five other wolkin approached from the sides and behind. Wasting no time, they took off. The wagon rattled, the wolkin striking at the side of it, their claws scratching the wood, just missing their opportunity to get to the horses.

"Histra, hold on!" shouted Jesmine, while the kobold was knocked near the back of the wagon. Her claws gripped the cage, ice steadily spreading outwards at the points of contact.

"Easier said than done," she replied, looking back, the pack that gave chase. The small horse-sized animals sprinted, their curled horns glistening in the light rain and matted fur showing the outline of their thick, muscular frames. They howled out, hungry for the kill.

A sharp bend in the trail caused the wagon wheels to skid, a rock caused the right back corner jump, making the items bounce within the cart. Up ahead the forest thins, revealing a murky brown river at least sixty feet wide.

"Is this the fjord?!" yelled Alderin, riding toward the riverbank.

Histra shook from her spot, her claws constantly breaking a layer of ice covering them. "Yes! Just keep going."

"The kobold better be right," Dran said.

Alderin looked to him, gripping Cetas' reins even tighter. "We don't have a choice!" The horses splashed into the water, going deeper and deeper as they pressed ahead, their hooves sliding across the smooth, rocky surface. The force of the current attempted to push them down stream as the water level reached the horses' upper thighs, just as the wagon reached the river.

Gnemi pushed the horses forward, the water slowing them down, the wagon wheels sliding sideways. They neighed as they fought against the river, trotting at an angle against the swift current.

The wolkin reached the riverbank moments later, barely pausing before leaping into the water, quickly gaining lost ground. Histra growled, seeing their advance. Gnemi focused on encouraging the horses, Jesmine occasionally looking behind them, updating him on the dire situation as Dran and Alderin were just about to reach the other side.

"Dammit," Histra muttered, releasing the cage, reaching for the edge of the wagon. Her claws dug into the wood with the nearest two wolkin only a few feet away and mere seconds from being able to claw their way onto the cart.

She stared at the yellow-eyed beasts. "How dare you lowly

creatures make me do this here," she remarked in draconic, spreading her wings, inhaling deeply, a blueish liquid drooled from the corners of her mouth, dripping down into the water, freezing anything upon contact. Releasing her breath at the peak of inhalation, an icy white-blue mist billowed out, instantly freezing the river in front of her, ensnaring four of the wolkin in a layer of ice about one to two inches thick. The last wolkin retreated with a fair bit of frost in its face.

A layer of ice clung to the back of the cart from the point of Histra's breath, wings folding back behind her. She panted heavily and the last remaining droplets of the freezing liquid escaped her lips before she licked up whatever remained, collapsing onto her back. "I was not ready for that," she said in draconic, looking ahead to see Jesmine watching her. She locked eyes with the elf, continuing to breath heavily, not fighting against the thin layer of frost forming along her body.

"Come on Gnaria, you can do this! I believe in you, you lucky girl! I'm sure you won't fail me now!" Gnemi yelled.

Jesmine looked at Histra for a moment longer before turning her attention to him. "You can do it; they are falling behind."

The gnome replied, "Good girl, I knew you could do it."

Histra raised an eye ridge, and several moments later Dran and Alderin were safe on the other side of the riverbank. Alderin readied his bow, taking aim but quickly lowered it. "They're falling back!" he yelled, seeing the last wolkin reaching the opposite side of the river and back into the forest.

"Seems those beasts don't like to swim for their meal," remarked Dran, keeping a look out while the wagon slowly crossed the fjord.

"Tell me this side of the forest is safer," said Gnemi, letting out a long sigh of relief.

"We will only be in it for a few hours, so we should be safe for now," Histra replied sitting back up, breaking the layer of ice that formed upon her. "I hate the rain."

"Everyone else okay?" Alderin asked.

"I'm good," Jesmine replied.

"A few scratches, but nothing serious," said Gnemi, handing Jesmine the reins, starting to reload his crossbow.

"I'm in one piece," said Dran, cautiously looking around.

"I'm fine, not that it concerns you," replied Histra, Alderin locking eyes with her.

"Now that we are not in mortal danger, there is something that has been bothering me," said Alderin, riding his horse beside her but kept it outside of the kobold's icy sphere of influence.

She chuckled, sitting in the center of the cart, her wings folded behind her. "This will be good, what is it human?"

"You told us that if we did not speak orc tongue that it would a problem, for it is *expected* that we know. Yet when Jesmine and I spoke to the female orc, she told to us that is not the case."

"Of course, not *every* human is going to know the orc tongue, but being this deep into orc lands and not knowing? That is a cause for suspicion."

Alderin glared at her, "And you not telling us your plans is a cause for suspicion."

"If I was going to lead you astray for my own benefit, I'd have done it already."

"You say that, but your secrets have caused us problems. When you spoke with that orc for one."

"And you attempting to engage in conversation with the orcs yet lack the ability to speak their actual tongue causes us problems," she remarked, jerking her head to the side.

"What? Forgive me for not knowing that Jesmine had to go deeper into orc lands to retrieve her book."

"You came into their lands and none of you had a firm grasp of the language? What kind of half-concocted plan did you come up with that you thought this would be a good idea?"

"And what was yours? To be all chained up?"

She glared at him as Jesmine interrupted, "Would you two please stop with this pointless bickering. Histra, if you feel it's a detriment for Alderin to have a poor grasp of the language, why don't you teach him the orc's tongue?"

"What?!" Histra and Alderin said in unison.

"Teach the human orc tongue," Histra said, cocking her head away from Alderin. "I don't think his limited intellect could have him learn it fast enough to make a difference. We're about three weeks till we reach the end of the orc lands at the city of Rivera."

"This human's 'limited intellect' was good enough to know how to pick your locks from your cage, kobold."

She tensed, "Why should I waste my efforts on—"

"Histra," Jesmine looked at her, their eyes meeting. "Please. It would be a nice gesture."

"Nice gesture? What, do you expect me to suddenly be..." she trailed off, letting out a deep sigh, her shoulders dropping. "Fine. I'll teach the human orc tongue."

"Learn from you? What guarantee do I have you will teach me correctly? What if I end up insulting the next orc we run into?" Alderin said.

Dran mused, "Then you'd know it taught you improperly!"

"Seeing that would be a detriment to my safety, it would not be a wise idea, now would it?" she asked, then muttered in draconic, "This is why humans are so stupid."

Alderin's grip on Cetas' reins tightens about to speak when Gnemi butts in, "It's probably not a bad idea Alderin. You don't trust Histra, it shouldn't hurt to have another know what is being said."

The human smirked, "Alright, alright. It'll be fun to prove how wrong it is about us."

Histra sighed. "Let's get started."

"Now?" he quirked his black-haired eyebrow.

"No, when we get done with this little trip, then we'll do it. Of course, now! Show me what I have to work with. Give me all the orc tongue that you know."

Alderin spent a moment speaking all that he knew, most of it being common phrases.

"Your pronunciation is terrible, the use of syntax and grammar deplorable, and your vocabulary is oh-so-limited."

"It's been a long time since I learned, and there aren't many orcs in Dra'kesh lands to practice with," Alderin remarked.

"Then why did you even bother to learn?"

"I'm from a border town, and we occasionally had run ins with orcs, so it's something I just picked up along the way."

"It could be worse," Histra said, "Now let's begin."

She conducted the lesson as they rode through the forest, while Dran and Gnemi were keeping a look out.

Jesmine asked, "Gnemi, do you have any other tricks?"

He kept attention outward, replying, "What do you mean tricks?"

"During my rescue, I saw a lot of smoke and explosions. Throughout my time in the north, I saw a fair amount of gnomish engineering. I can tell you studied the arts."

"Ah, yes, I do work with various substances that often create specific reactions, but I will be honest. The explosive power I used, I'm sure was invented by a human not gnomes. I believe their name was Parin Damelcia, and he died before I was born."

"I heard the name before. Do you have a lot of those items?"

He wiped his goggles. "Some. I used most of what I had in the ambush. I should have enough for one small bomb and probably enough material for a few smoke grenades, but that's it. In my experiences it's often not easy to obtain materials on the road, so I have to use them sparingly," he explained, gently tapping a bag on his side.

Jesmine nodded. "I do appreciate the efforts you are all going through for me."

"I wouldn't worry about it. What comes after is going to—," Gnemi's words were cut off when Alderin let out a throat-clearing grunt.

"Not in front of the kobold."

"Oh right, yeah."

Histra twitched her wings. "If you are done interrupting not only him, but your lesson, we can continue."

"I got this, continue," Alderin said motioning his hand to move her along.

"I'm sure you do," she replied.

"Sorry," Gnemi said.

"It's okay," comforted Jesmine, with a smile.

"You really appear to be understanding about this."

"The three of you risked your lives to save me, and now you are going out of your way to help me yet again. For better or for worse, I have faith in you three that whatever your intentions are, they are good."

Dran chuckled. "That's an understatement."

"Dran," Alderin said, giving him a look.

He shrugged, "I'm not dumb enough to speak about it in front of the kobold." A soft snap of a twig was heard, and all conversation stopped. Alderin, Dran, and Gnemi readied their weapons.

"What could it be now?" the gnome asked nervously.

"I don't know," Alderin replied.

"One thing is for sure, we didn't have this many problems with the local wildlife till we picked up the kobold," remarked Dran, as their horses moved forward, the cart softly rattling.

Histra tensed, hearing the comment, Jesmine saying, "By that logic, I'm causing the problem too."

"Hmm?" the dwarf replied.

"You can't blame her for something she has no control over. I'm the reason why we are going this way."

"Yeah but…"

"But what?"

Dran grunted, Alderin riding up to him. "This isn't the time for this." Another rustle came from up ahead, the party stopping as the human and gnome raised their ranged weapons when suddenly a large, antlered creature appeared from the brush. Its hooved feet stomped on the ground, looking at the party, its slender, soft brown body exposed to them. They lowered their weapons with a sigh of relief.

"It's a deer," Dran said as a few more crossed the path before the big one followed, allowing the group to resume. Eventually, they broke out of the forest and were greeted with hundreds of tree stumps. Out in the distance they saw movement, trees shuttering, falling to the ground with a thud and people shouting.

"Huh, the logging camp has been busy," Histra commented.

"You know of a logging camp?" Alderin asked.

"Yeah, they've been working in the area for the last five or so years. I wouldn't worry, they don't pay much mind to people coming in or out of the forest."

"I still say it'd be best we just keep going. But now that we are out, where to next kobold?" asked Dran from his lead position.

"That way back to the road, it will be less suspicious. There might be a few scattered orc patrols now but as long as you do what I say and nothing stupid we should be fine," Histra replied, pointing in their new direction, the light drizzle of rain finally stopping and sunlight occasionally breaking through the steadily thinning clouds. The land before them was more endless plains with faint rolling hills in the distance. The beaten path marked the road as they ventured forth with the occasional semi-dilapidated sign.

Alderin spoke to Histra in broken orcish. "How many villages along path?"

She winced, correcting with, "How many villages are along the road?"

"Yes."

"Dozens. Some like the ones you saw. Other's bigger. It should not be a problem if we simply pass through. Any that would have an issue; I'll warn you about."

Alderin looked at her, trying to translate all that she just said, and after a moment, Histra sighed and repeated it in human.

"Dozens of orc villages?" Dran exclaimed.

"Orcs are aggressive, powerful, and have a love of the hunt, but they aren't mindless bloodthirsty beasts. They won't attack you without cause. Whatever cause that is though, who's to say. It may be simple that they think you are outsiders and capturing you will make them look good in Sa'bara's eye. Speaking of which… you all know about Sa'bara's mark?"

Alderin eyed her. "Of course, we do."

"I had to be sure. I assume none of you have one?"

"Of course not. I'm not going to have a bloody mark scorched onto my right hand," Dran snorted.

"Same here," Gnemi replied.

"It would be more trouble than it's worth," Alderin said.

"Good to know, just wear gloves and you should be fine. They rarely ask for such things unless you raise suspicion, which *shouldn't* happen if you *listen to me*," Histra explained.

"Yeah, yeah," Dran said waving the kobold off.

"Let's continue the lessons," said Alderin.

Histra looking over to him, raising an eye ridge. "That eager to learn?"

"What can I say? I have a thirst for knowledge," he replied brushing his black hair off to the side with a smirk.

"Fine, we'll continue," she said as the party eventually found a pond not far from the road to camp for the night. Histra leapt off the back of the cart, ice clinging to parts of it. "Jesmine. I want to speak to you in private."

Jesmine, who was currently helping unhitch the horses looked over to her, saying, "Can you give me a moment, I want to get these horses to water."

"Fine, I'll be over here." She walked off to a set of nearby trees, leaning against one.

"What do you suppose she wants?" asked Gnemi, helping Jesmine.

"I don't know," she replied.

"Just be careful, you can't trust a kobold," Dran said.

"Yes, you made it very clear that you don't trust kobolds, but Histra has yet to do anything to break our trust. Show some faith in her."

"I am by letting her be our guide."

Alderin gently rubbed Cetas' sides as he drank. "How helpful her 'help' is, is yet to be seen. I do not trust it or anyone that serves the dragons."

"And how do you know she serves any of the dragons?" asked Jesmine.

"All kobolds serve the dragons. I have not once heard of a kobold not in league with them."

"If she is in league with the dragons, how did she become a traveling side show for ten years?"

"She says ten years, but we can't be sure."

"I traveled with her for months, and there is no question she was treated like a commodity."

Dran started to gather the equipment for the tents, breaking off the ice and pulling the frozen kiapal corpse out of the cart. "She may not be one of Sa'bara's minions but there are still three other dragons she could serve."

"She could have served Eisandra," Alderin said.

"Possible, but probably not though," Gnemi replied.

"Why is that?"

"Once Eisandra fell, I heard all those that served her were hunted down, so there shouldn't have been any left by the time I was born. I never saw a kobold till we found Histra," Gnemi explained.

Jesmine nodded with a subtle sadness in her voice, "It's highly unlikely, but when I was up north studying, I helped bring down the last two known white dragons. She doesn't even look old enough to have been around to have served Eisandra... I think." She glanced at Histra, who eyed her and the others.

"So, you really did kill a dragon?" asked Gnemi, eyes lighting up, "I thought I heard you did but I was never sure."

"They were relatively young, and I was with a small army. Though it's hard to say if they were the last or not. And it wasn't at the same time, they were years apart from one another."

"I've heard about your dragon killings, but that doesn't exclude the possibility she is serving one of them. Just because she's white, doesn't mean she served Eisandra. That dragon died what sixty years ago? How long do kobolds live anyway? Thirty years or something?" Alderin asked.

"Actually, there has been much debate about how long kobolds can live. I'll have to make a note to ask her that," Gnemi said.

"I should go over to her; she doesn't look happy waiting there," said Jesmine, looking over the horse to see her pacing.

She looked up, as Jesmine approached, folding her wings back, Jesmine beginning to say, "Okay Histra, what is it that you nee—"

"What is it that you want?" She said, cutting her off.

She pondered for a moment. "Want?"

"Me teaching the human orc tongue can't be what you are after. You saw what I did, and yet you said nothing to them."

"What you did was amazing, and you helped save our lives. I don't know why you don't want the others to know of what you did."

"They will only distrust me more."

"You can't know that."

"No, I do, and now you know, but yet you say nothing. Time and time again you 'defend' me, though I did not ask of you for it. I am fulfilling my part of the agreement. What more are you trying to get from me?"

Jesmine crouched down before her, getting close enough that her breath became visible. "I don't do things to get something out of it. I do it because I want to."

"Right, like they are on this little adventure to get your book because they want to? Out of the 'goodness of their own hearts' is it? They want something from you. It is painfully obvious. What I can't figure is what you want from me. So, let's be done with these games. Tell me what you are after. Is it about my ice aura?"

"No, it's nothing like that. Why do you assume because someone does something nice that they want something from you?"

"Because that is how the world works. I don't know what magical fantasy land you grew up in, but no one does anything nice just because they want to."

"My parents raised me to work toward a better future and life. And the place to start was with one's self."

Histra tensed slightly. "I will do what I can to get you to your damn forest, and I will teach the human as much, but I don't owe you or any of the others anything more than that."

"Tell me what you intend to do afterwards?"

"It is none of your business," she remarked.

"You could just come with us."

"With you? And the others? I'm lucky enough the human and the dwarf don't kill me in my sleep."

"Perhaps if you stopped insulting everyone, things could get better."

"I do not insult; I use appropriate descriptors."

Jesmine said, "Why don't you at least try to be a little nicer? At least call everyone by their names."

"Why? They don't use mine."

"Gnemi does."

"He just wants to get information out of me. Let's see how long his kindness will last once he gets what he desires."

"And what about me?"

Histra eyed her, "It will be made clear to me eventually."

Jesmine looked over her shoulder at the group, as Gnemi was busy preparing an evening meal. Dran kept a lookout while Alderin watched the pair. She let out a soft sigh and sat about a foot away from her. "You are all so stubborn."

"And you're too naïve," she replied, walking back to the group with a yell. "Alderin, if you want to stare at me all day, perhaps we can continue your lessons?"

Jesmine remained where she was, the chilly air quickly replaced by the warm, summer winds that blew across the plains, the sun disappearing over the horizon leaving a brilliant display of pink, orange, and red hues. The stars were already beginning to show on the other side of the horizon. She smiled and thought, *"She'll come around."*

Chapter 5 A Veil of Lies

Over the past few days, the endless grasslands were gradually broken up by farmsteads. Overcast clouds hung overhead as single orc-family sized farm homes could be seen in the distance with smoke coming from the chimneys as they cooked their mid-day meals. The buildings became steadily better built as they ventured deeper into Sa'bara's lands.

A few rolling hills, half of which were covered in ever thickening forests faded into the distance. Jesmine and Dran sat in the front of the cart as Gnemi took lead point. Histra sat in the far back of the wagon while Alderin rode nearby as they continued their orcish lessons.

"We are low on supplies. We should stop for provisions," said Alderin in orcish.

Histra leaned back against the wagon's side. "That was surprisingly fairly decent."

"No, I mean we are low on supplies. I'm looking at what we have, and we have two maybe three days left, five at best if we ration out," he explained in human.

Dran looked over his shoulder at the two. "We should have stopped at the last village a day ago. They didn't care that we passed through much like the others, of course we could hunt for food, but that may be a problem. I don't know how the locals would take us poaching on their lands."

"Probably not very well, much like the looks they gave me as we passed through," Histra replied.

"The hunting might have been a problem, but the looks? Not so much."

She sighed. "Town after next we'll stop for provisions, how about that?"

"Why the town after next?"

"The next one is fairly big, and they will take notice of us. I'd rather limit chances of complications."

Alderin gave her a long stare. "What was wrong with the last one then? We could have easily gotten supplies there."

"It wasn't a good town."

"Wasn't a good town? Which town is good? We're deep in

orc-controlled lands, none of these towns are good," Alderin said.

"The orcs aren't all bad," said Jesmine.

"You haven't seen them like I have," he replied, hands squeezing Cetas' reins.

"No…" Jesmine saw the stress in his face, her shoulders slumped slightly. "I guess not, then again I know many of these orcs are the descendants that helped kill off my people in the area, some of whom I've knew personally. I suppose something like that would paint my views differently than yours."

Alderin rolled his eyes. "How can you just be so…"

"Forgiving?" said Histra in orcish.

"Yes, that."

"What did she say?" Jesmine asked.

"Uh… nothing," he sighed. "Your experience is different than mine, that is for sure."

"I have to say your willingness to just let what happened go is really something else," Dran said.

Jesmine looked out into the fields. "It's not easy," she turned to Alderin, saying, "I didn't mean to come off as…"

"I know you didn't mean it that way," Alderin replied.

"Thanks, but I do feel the loss of my people… friends, family, but there is one thing I remind myself that helps me get through what happened, and forgive the orcs, the avolarieans, and the other races that helped in their slaughter," Jesmine said.

"What's that?"

"The dragons are the ones who are behind all of it. They manipulate everyone to fit their goals. Though we aren't in chains, we are slaves to their will. That is why my Mother went north to fight the rebellion against Eisandra. She worked with other races that have been traditionally our enemies, the orcs being one of them. She told me that one of the dragons' greatest strengths was their ability to manipulate and divide us. It's a lesson I have taken to heart."

Dran nodded, stroking his red beard with one hand while keeping the reins in the other. "Aye, I suppose I can understand that all too well. Dra'kesh split his lands into areas that must compete with each other to give the most tribute once every ten years."

"I've experienced that fighting firsthand. When I was traveling with the other elves, we were attacked only to be enslaved and sold off, so they could have money to give as tribute. It is strange to see how different Dra'kesh governs his lands compared to that of Sa'bara."

Histra eyed the conversation. "Right… anyway, I should let you know that we'll soon be going off road and heading through the forest over there. It will be a little rough, but those forests are far tamer than the one we were in ten days ago. Through there we can bypass the town, and in two days, we'll hit the next. But I will warn that when we at least get to Rivera tha—" she explained as a loud crack and thud occurred, throwing her from the cart, landing hard on the side of the road. The cartwheel, fractured and broken managed only a half more revolution before it split in half completely, bringing everything to a sudden stop.

"Histra, are you okay?!" exclaimed Jesmine, rushing over to her.

She rubbed her back and flicked her wings, standing up, refusing her hand offered in aid. "I'm fine," she grunted, flicking her wings again to get some of the dirt off them, patting herself down.

"But our cart sure isn't," commented Alderin, riding his horse to the other side. "It's completely busted," he said, dismounting and kicking the broken wheel, "I don't think we can get this fixed."

Dran hopped off the cart and walked over to the damaged section. "Aye, but no big loss though. We can just go by horseback the rest of the way."

"No, we can't," Histra stated. "Or did you forget that if I sit on the back of a horse for too long, I could freeze it to death?"

"We could alternate which horse you sat on," Jesmine suggested.

"Right… that won't be weird. Difficult, oh and wouldn't that be uncomfortable for who is with me."

"We could get winter clothing…"

"And that wouldn't be strange or difficult to obtain in the middle of summer and even if we could get that, it would be very suspicious. It is just far easier to get the damn wagon fixed."

Gnemi rode over and dismounted. "Let me have a look," he said, examining the wheel, the cart tilting toward the broken side, but not enough to hit the ground. "I am no expert on these things, but it does look like to me that the wheel itself is broken but the axel is still in good condition. If we can get the wheel replaced, it should be good as new."

"We could do that, but that would mean going into the town our guide doesn't want us to go into," remarked Alderin, looking over to her.

"The other option is we could have the damn kobold walk," said Dran, crossing his arms.

Histra's wings twitched, "That's the worst idea out of all of them."

"We are not going to have her walk while we ride," Jesmine replied.

"What? It's certainly an option to consider. If it doesn't want to try riding on a horse, why should we have to suffer for its stubbornness?"

Histra twitched, giving Dran a cold glare. She walked over to him as he stood his ground, breath fogging. "Stubborn like you? I don't care what you think of me. I don't care that you want nothing more than to take that axe against me." She gazed up at the dwarf, who had a clear two feet in height over her. "What I do care about is you do what I say when I need you to do it."

"Dran! Histra! Please. This is not a time to argue," yelled Jesmine, moving between the two. "She has only been helpful. She's kept her word, put some trust in her."

"Pah, trust a kobold? Only thing you can trust one to do is to stab you in the back when it becomes most convenient to them," he replied before looking down at Histra, "Better give me a damn good reason later on to keep 'doing as you say' aside from the arrogance dripping from that snout of yours." He replied curtly before pulling away, walking a short distance up the road.

Jesmine shook her head and looked at Histra. "Histra can you at least be a bit more sociable? We've talked on this," She looked up at Jesmine, who continued, "If there is anything you think I am trying to 'get out of you', it would be for you to work with me on this."

Histra rolled her eyes off to the side. "Fine. Only because all this fighting makes my job harder to do. A group of strangers fighting in the middle of the road just invites trouble."

Gnemi walked over to Dran, who asked him, "What is it?"

"I'm mostly certain that I know it's not easy for you, but Jesmine has a point, and Histra too, for that matter. If we are caught arguing, yelling, or fighting out here, it's probably going to draw attention to us. Right now, we probably have no one after us. Which should make it easy to get there and back without an issue."

"Through hostile orc and avolariean lands, controlled by a dragon that from what I hear is the most paranoid one of the four remaining ancients. Their spies are everywhere, and that kobold could be one of them."

"If she was a spy, why would she be that chained up and in such a terrible state when we found her?"

"I don't know. Those dragons care little about their kobold minions but they are too simple minded to not be loyal to them. I suppose no one would suspect the side show act to be a spy. It's a perfect cover," Dran explained.

"Now I think you are just trying to justify the idea in your head. But if true, why let us roam around freely for so long, at such a great risk to her?"

"I'm not sure. Perhaps we haven't run into its contact? Or perhaps it's trying to get what information it can before reporting us? Trying to be all sneaky and lay out traps for us like they always do."

"Wouldn't such an elaborate plan counter your other argument that the kobolds are too simple minded to do anything but be loyal to the dragons?"

Dran stood there for a moment, his hands gently stroking his beard, letting out a hmm. "Aye, I am man enough to admit you've talked me into a corner."

"Will you at least give Histra a break?"

"I do want to break something."

"I mean go easy on the conflict. Both you and Alderin have been relentless on her from the beginning. Right now, she's taking time to teach Alderin orc tongue. Now I know you can say it is to lure us into a false sense of security, but isn't that a silly way to do it? When us not knowing the language is to her advantage?"

"I suppose… I don't trust it, but I will cede to your point. If only to make things easier for us all."

"I believe it's the most sensible thing to do."

"You're right. Thanks, Gnemi, you know how to put things

into perspective," he stated, giving a hearty smack on his back, almost knocking him over. "When we get a chance, I owe you a drink."

"I really don't—"

"Nonsense! You help me, I help you," he chuckled.

"Someone is coming!" yelled Alderin, pointing further up the road, where orcs riding wolkin mounts rode towards them.

Histra climbed up the cart which wobbled and leaned down further. She stood, looking in their direction, her eyes widening slightly, wings spreading. "Damn, damn, damn those are military patrols. They definitely will stop and question us, checking if you have Sa'bara's ever watching eye on you."

"What do you suppose we do then?" Jesmine asked.

"I'm thinking," she said, looking over to the broken wagon wheel and then to Dran and Gnemi.

"Maybe we should just fight them?" asked Dran, resting a hand on the hilt of his axe.

"That would be unwise, there is no guarantee we could defeat them, without any of them escaping or us being killed in the process," Gnemi said.

"True," Dran grumped, hearing Histra yell.

"You two! Come back over here!"

"What does that bloody kobold want now?"

"We'll see," Gnemi said as they rushed back.

"What are you planning?" Alderin asked.

Histra glanced over to him. "I have an idea," she said, smirking. "Translate what I have to say to the others if you can."

"What are you going to do?"

"Just do as I say."

Alderin tugged at Cetas' reins, pulling him forward, "Fine."

"What is it?" Dran asked.

"Get under the axel wheel and try to hold the wagon up. Gnemi get in front to take the reins."

"What?" Dran exclaimed.

"Okay," said Gnemi, climbing onto the cart. The group of four orcs riding the large furry beasts grew ever closer.

"Why do I have to be under here?" Dran asked.

"Do what I say, and don't ask questions. This is all part of what I need you to do. Alderin, you have rope of some kind?"

"Yeah, what for?"

"I want you to try to use it to hoist the broken end of the wagon, and we are going to attempt to walk this cart to town."

"That's not going to help with what's coming."

"It will, trust me," she replied.

Jesmine said, "Histra. You can spend a moment telling us what you are planning."

She walked over to the edge of the cart, flexing her wings. "I'm going to get a promotion and you will all be my servants." She laughed.

"What?!" exclaimed Dran, getting out from under the cart.

Histra sighed. "This is why I didn't say it. Now do it. They are almost here!" Dran glared up at her before getting under the cart, his large hands pressing under the wood, creaking slightly, the cart leveling off.

"Jesmine, help out with the rope and wrap it around the axel," commanded Histra with a growingly aggressive tone.

She glanced at Histra before she nodded, getting to work.

The heavy rumbling of wolkin paws hitting along the dirt path, dusting rising up in the air being caught by the wind. The grey and black wolkin, with their long horns and snouts full of sharp teeth, come ever clearer. Their riders sat on brown leather saddles strapped to their backs. They were two male and two female orcs dressed in heavy leather armor; the latter had bows strapped to their backs while the former had black metal axes. On their heads were menacing animal skull helmets crafted with thin strips of metal casting over them for added protection. The wolkin snarled, as the orcs pulled back on their reins attached to their neck and head harnesses, slowing their approach.

Histra yelled out in human, "Move you lazy soft skinned bipeds! I will not allow any more delays!" Her wings outstretched, lifting her head and looked over to the four orcs.

"What do we have here?" asked the orc leader in orcish.

Histra walked to the other side of the cart, continuing to yell in human. "Get the cart moving, and I mean now!" The cart jerked forward slowly getting a few steps in, Histra saying in orcish to the leader, "What does it look like? I have a broken wheel."

The orc looked over the group as they continued to work on their task before returning his focus to her. "What's your business?"

"I'm trying to get to Rivera," she promptly replied.

"Rivera? Why?"

"It's important business and I don't need to tell the likes of you."

The orc let out a grunt, Alderin watching the scene unfold, but for the moment continued to help keep the cart balanced, moving forward.

The orc leader motioned his head as one of the archers rode in front of them, stopping the cart dead in its tracks, readying her bow, aiming it at Gnemi.

He raised his hands releasing the reins, dropping them to his feet. "Histra, I hope you know what you are doing," he responded nervously, eyes darting over to her.

"Shut up, child," growled Histra. The orc leader pulled out his axe and moved the sharp blade to within inches of her neck, who stared up into the orc's yellow eyes.

"You will tell us now. I have no problem knocking an unruly kobold down by the neck," he grunted.

Histra reached out and touched the axe with her hand, the moisture in the air condensing and freezing along the blade out where she touched. "Do that and you will piss off not one, but two great dragons, and someone even of your station would know what that would mean."

The orc twitched ever so slightly, eyeing the spreading ice over his blade, "Two?"

She let out a fogged sigh, pulling her hand back. "I was told that orcs were supportive and helpful to Sa'bara, and up till now that has been true. It would be wise to limit your questioning of me, orc."

The orc motioned with his free hand, the other archer readying her bow, the last orc moving to the other side of the wagon, the beast underneath him growling, the horses growing uneasy. Jesmine rushed to keep the two free horses from running off.

"Tell your purpose now or else. Sa'bara does not like outsiders traveling his lands. Where are you from and why you are here?"

"We're from the lands owned by the great dragon of Dra'kesh. Why am I here? To deliver a message to a contact I have been told to meet in Rivera. Why are these others here?" Histra looked over at the rest of the party "Well, to keep me company and ensure I make it to my destination."

The orc stared at her long and hard before replying, "What message?"

"You think I am going chance ruining my mission for you orc?"

He grunted, "Where is this message?"

She tapped her head with a claw, "Up here, where no one can get to it."

"Why go all the way to Rivera to deliver it?"

Histra shrugged "I don't know, and I don't question the will of the great dragons. I just do as I am told, just like you. You don't want to be poisoned to death, and I don't want my bones melted. It's a mutual beneficial thing, wouldn't you say?"

"I have heard Dra'kesh is a black dragon, so why did he send a white kobold?"

"Do you honestly think that every kobold of one color serves that dragon? That's like saying every kobold under Sa'bara is green. We come in different colors, and I just happen to be white."

"And what about this ice?"

"It keeps the bugs off me, and others away from me. Why do you think he picked me? Why don't you ask Dra'kesh yourself? I don't question my orders, but what I will do, is tell my superiors and my contact how my trip went and I'm sure they will find my tales of the orcs who made me *late* very fascinating."

The orc grunted, looking over to the archer in front of the cart, and she back at him, ready to draw and fire her bow at a moment's notice. He looked across to his other male companion who had his axe drawn, keeping his attention split between Alderin and him.

The human tensed, his hands ready to draw his weapon. Dran grunted, continuing to hold the cart level, while Jesmine kept her head low, her hood over her head, calming the horses.

The leader withdrew his axe from Histra's neck. "What's the cage for?"

She looked over her shoulder at the empty cage, "A contingency."

"What contingency?"

"You know humans and dwarves are stubborn morons who think just because they are out of their dragon's territory that perhaps they can get uppity. If that happens, I shove them in there and sit on the top of the cage. Let them freeze for a few days by my mere presence."

"Isn't that cage small for some of your traveling companions?"

Histra chuckled, "Do you think I care?"

The orc laughed, "Good point."

"You know, if you happen to help me get to town so I can get a new wheel on this thing and be on my way, I will be sure to mention the helpful orcs who have only proven their loyalty to their great dragon overlord. Isn't the time of Draksind near? Where your leaders vie for Sa'bara's favor so they can... better establish themselves within the dragon's hierarchy? I wonder how that could play out if I just so happened to mention how *helpful* you were to me, and to the one who could even directly report to Sa'bara *himself*. What was your name?"

The orc leader sheathed his weapon. "Urgon Da'gurl of clan Ugosh," he replied as the other three orcs relaxed. Gnemi finally lowered his hands, looking around confused.

Histra smiled. "Well Urgon, why don't you be so helpful and escort us to the town that's up ahead? Perhaps even find a way to help us get there faster? Every little bit can go a long way."

"Yes... there have been reports of bandits in the area, so it is good we found you. It would be dreadful news if ruffians managed to hinder your mission. We'll make sure you get to the town of Argesh and quickly arrange for the blacksmith to repair your cart."

"Really? Well that is most generous of you. I will be sure that my contact will hear of your understanding and helpful nature."

"Anything for the great dragons," Urgon replied, yelling at the other male orc to keep the wagon level using the set of ropes already in place with the help of his wolkin. Now with a point of comparison with the cart, it was shown that these wolkin to be about a fifth bigger than their wild counterparts.

The party remained deathly silent along the way as the town of Argesh came into view. A large wooden wall surrounded it as a layer of log-sized spikes jutted out towards the open fields with two-foot-deep four-foot-wide trenches dug in front of the spikes. Only the main road allowed easy access to the city. Two heavy, wooden doors with slightly rusted iron bands ran across the wood which could block the way in at a moment's notice. Animal hide armored orc archers walked along the top of the wall, watching the party enter only to be stopped by the guards.

"What is the meaning of this?" asked a red skinned orc with piercing yellow eyes, walking up to Urgon.

"We found a kobold on an emissary mission to the capital. She states she's from the lands of Dra'kesh."

The guard looked over to Histra, who stood on the cart triumphantly, still at a fraction of his height.

"What proof do you have of this?" he asked.

"We've checked it out. It doesn't appear to be anything suspicious, just three humans and a dwarf."

The guard looked over the party. "A child? That's unusually armed?"

Histra promptly stated, "It's a gnome."

"A gnome? I've never saw a gnome before," he continued, Alderin silently watching the events unfold, his body tensing upon mentioning of the gnome.

"I wouldn't think so. That one is *my* personal slave. He serves my will."

The orc chuckled. "Serves your will? How does something as small as you even manage to have a slave this small and puny."

Before Urgon could even speak Histra hopped off the cart and approached him. "Is that so?"

The orc eyed her, "I don't see many kobolds have a backbone like… why is it so cold suddenly?" he asked, Histra pointing to her horns.

"You think these are merely for show? You feel that sense of cold around you? Or would you like a demonstration as to how I broke my slave and kept these humans in line?"

The orc's smirk faded, holding his ground saying, "No need. I've seen enough." He waved at them.

"Good," Histra said with a grunt, returning to the cart. "Alderin. I am not going to climb up the cart myself."

"My apologies," he replied, dismounting, rushing to pick her up, placing her nicely onto the cart.

"Don't let it happen again," she remarked, eyeing Alderin, who returned to his horse.

"Right this way," said Urgon, leading the group towards the blacksmith. Histra stood tall and proud as orcs walking along the street stopped and looked at the strange display. They muttered and whispered to each other as they passed by. Eventually the sounds of metal against metal rang out and the pungent odor of burning coal hit their senses.

"We'll take your horses to the stables and make sure they are well taken care of," said one of the other guards, dismounting from his wolkin, tossing the reins to one of the women.

"Good, your help will be noted," stated Histra, hopping off the cart.

Urgon yelled, "Beslba! I have a job for you."

The sound of a banging hammer abruptly ended, and a deep voice came from the shop. "A job you say? What kind of job?" he asked as a stout, brown bearded dwarf stepped out.

"One of great importance. I need you to make a new wheel for this wagon," he said, pointing to it.

"You need me to repair a wagon wheel? I don't see why that is one of 'great importance' but it's a simple enough job to do. Will take me till near the end of tomorrow to do. Crafting a wagon wheel isn't easy."

"It's more of a matter of who the job is for." He pointed to Histra as the party gathered.

"I was not expecting to see another dwarf here," mumbled Dran, as the two caught each other's gaze before Beslba noticed Histra.

"Ah, I see."

"You will be compensated for your work," Urgon said.

"Good," he replied, cracking his neck.

"A day and a half?" grunted Histra in orcish, "I suppose that will do."

Alderin eyeballed her as Urgon asked, "Is there anything else?"

"Where's the inn? If I must be here for a night or two, I will need accommodations."

Urgon nodded, giving a quick set of directions to the town's only inn. "I will warn that it can be a very aggressive place to be at night."

Histra looked up at him. "I don't think that will be a problem. Simply inform them of my eventual arrival. It would be appreciated and noted to your list of contributions."

Urgon gave the kobold a long glare when she wasn't looking.

"Not a problem," he replied before heading off with the rest of his companions.

Histra turned to face the party who had a mixed set of reactions ranging from confusion, nervousness to extreme anger. "Alderin, Dran. I need you two stock up on supplies we'll need," Histra commanded.

"As you wish," Alderin replied.

Dran just glared at her, looking over to the other dwarf, who watched from a short distance away. "Yeah, sure," he said, the two departing.

Histra turned to Beslba. "There's not going to be any problems with our supplies being delivered here?" she asked in orcish.

He shook his head. "No problem, just don't expect me to load it."

"That will be fine," Histra replied, looking around. "Tell me dwarf, is there a weapon shop here?"

"That depends on what you are looking for."

"My servants have been rather on edge in this land. We've ran into less than welcoming wildlife and they've burned through much of their reserves of arrows and bolts."

"Ah, you're in luck, my shop has the finest of the sort in the area. There is a reason why the orc came to me for aid," he replied, motioning the three of them into the building. Histra walked to the very edge of the shop's entrance as Gnemi and Jesmine ventured in. There they saw axes, swords, and well-crafted metal shields in an orcish-style with jagged intimidating visage, but a few of them were finer balanced, broader in tune with a dwarven make.

Gnemi looked around curiously before turning to the dwarf, asking in human, "Excuse me but do you happen to speak human tongue?"

Beslba looked at the gnome, replying in orcish, "I speak only two languages, orc and dwarven."

Histra sighed, explaining the dwarf's reply to him. Gnemi said, "Oh. Um, Histra Miss?" Gnemi looked around, "Could you ask if he has unfinished bolts or arrows? I could use them for my crossbow."

She grumbled in draconic. "Now I am a translator… fine," she explained to the dwarf the situation. Jesmine looked over the items curiously before going over to Beslba and said softly in dwarven.

"I will admit I was not expecting to see a dwarf in this town. May I ask what you are doing here?"

He looked at her with a smile before glancing at Histra, who leaned against the door frame in disinterest. "I did not expect one of the kobold's servants to know dwarf tongue. A pleasant surprise, as it's been some time since I've heard it."

"How did you find yourself here?"

"That's simple. Business. There are a few dwarven settlements in these lands, but as you can tell, the orcs have a majority in this area. They are skilled in many things, but their weapons have little on dwarven steel. With that, I came here and set up shop. I occasionally send money back to my relatives at home. They appreciate it, especially during the Draksind."

"I heard it's tax season."

"You are knowledgeable then."

"I have to be for Histra. So, you are here freely then?"

"As free as the fact I need to eat and provide for my family. It is better to show cooperation than conflict, and what better way to do so by showing we have a value. With that being said though…" he glanced over to the kobold, "If she doesn't know, you best not speak in a tongue she can't understand. Kobolds that are drunk on the dragons' power have been known to be very egotistical and easy to set off."

Jesmine nodded. "I will keep that in mind."

"Hurry up, we have other places to go," grumbled Histra.

Meanwhile, Dran and Alderin walked down the main street, one of the few that's paved with cobblestones. The stench of waste of orc and beast alike lingered heavily in the air near the living quarters and steadily faded as they approached the town's market center, where orcs called out to potential customers, trying to draw them in with direct and to-the-point conversation. A few guards moved within the town. Occasionally an orc took note of the unusual sight of the two strolling down the street.

"I hope that kobold has taught you enough orc tongue to get by," Dran said.

"I believe so."

"Now that we're far enough away, what was the kobold blabbering about? I have an idea that it presented itself as someone of importance."

"Simple. A messenger of Dra'kesh to Sa'bara," he replied, the names causing a quick glance of a few orcs that were in ear shot.

"Best you say no more on that. Risky enough as it is that the kobold has had such a flamboyant display."

"It was surprising, and I am still very concerned."

"I don't blame you, but what choice do we have?" the dwarf asked.

"None."

"And I don't like it."

"Neither do I, but we do what we must. We have bigger things at stake."

"Don't have to remind me," he replied as they found a shop that fit their supply needs. The smell of cured meats overpowered the town's natural aroma as they entered. Large and small skinned animals hung from the walls and ceiling with a long, wooden table separating the area for the butcher and customers. A tall, light green skinned orc woman swung down a thick and heavy meat cleaver, blood splattering across the leather hide that covered her chest.

"Damn things are so stringy, hardly any meat on their bones," she grunted, raising her head as Dran and Alderin approached. She cracked her neck and swung the blade into the wood, leaving it sticking up as her bloodied self approached the counter.

"What's this? A human and a dwarf I have not seen before? Ah, you must be with that kobold. What do you want?" she asked, staring down the two.

Alderin took a deep breath returning the stern gaze with his brown eyes. "Food rations to make it to Rivera and back. Enough for seven people."

"Seven? To Rivera and back? That is a tall order. Do you have the coin?"

Alderin reached into a pouch and pulled out several silver and copper coins. The orc leaned in and held out her hand. "Show me."

"They are real," Alderin firmly stated, as Dran uneasily watched the back and forth banter between the two.

"So says a kobold's slave."

Alderin's eye twitched, Dran asking, "What's going on?"

"A friendly debate… Histra better have not led me astray with this," he replied in human.

"Bloody hell, this could end badly."

Alderin took a single silver coin from the pouch and tossed it to her.

She quickly caught it, running it through her fingers, giving it a close examination, "Local money. Acceptable. It will take me a day to prepare the supplies."

"Great. Do you know where to get feed for horses?"

The butcher gave Alderin a stare then held out her hand, "Pay first."

Alderin handed her more money and once the last coin was pocketed, she said, "The stables will have the feed. Talk to them. You come back tomorrow; I'll have it ready."

"Good," Alderin replied as they left.

"What happened?"

"It appears we're good. We'll have enough rations for us to get there and back here for at least seven."

"What? Seven?"

"It's good to have extra supplies."

"Right, smart move. I should have thought of that."

"But we're not done, we need to go back to the stables for feed for the horses."

"We're stuck in this town for a day and a half, there is not much we can do about it. Damn kobold sending me on this errand. I'd like to have talked to the dwarf."

"There's still time for it."

"Time, but if we are unfortunately supposed to appear to be on the kobold's leash, it looks rather suspicious, don't you think?"

Alderin nodded. "True. No matter how we look at it, we're unfortunately tied to the kobold."

"It's probably enjoying its power trip."

"Probably, which is concerning."

"Everything about that damn kobold is concerning. I feel better that there is another dwarf here, but this is still an orc town, we best be mindful of our surroundings."

"I know the feeling. Orcs are no better than the kobolds when it comes to bending a knee before the dragons." Alderin whispered, "But let's not talk about this in public, we don't know who could be listening."

"Right," Dran replied as they kept an eye around them, heading over to the stables.

Meanwhile in a clothing shop sat an older, green skinned, long black-haired orc in a creaking wooden chair, keeping an eye over the walls covered in clothes made of leathers, linen, fur, wool, and other materials. Light filled the shop through wooden slits, the door partially ajar so the sounds of the street echoed inside.

Dressed in cloth, he gave a far less domineering and intimidating look than those outside. He was picking one of his teeth with a sewing needle when the door swung fully open. Startled, he quickly pulled the needle back, watching as Histra stepped into the shop with Jesmine and Gnemi in toe.

"What are we doing here?" Jesmine asked, with curiosity.

"Don't speak back to me in public, it looks bad," remarked Histra, approaching the orc, who remained seated.

"A kobold? What brings you to my shop?" he asked in orcish.

"I'm looking for some clothes," she replied in the same language.

The orc chuckled, "Is that so? Did you want a custom job? I might have something that suits a child I could alter to cover you, though those wings will be a problem."

Histra's wings twitched and unfurled slightly, "Not for me. I don't need clothes!"

"If you say so. What are you looking for?"

"Something to cover my human servant behind me," she said, pointing to Jesmine. "The ones she's wearing don't fit and it's embarrassing."

The orc looked to Jesmine who stood there unsure of what to make of the situation with Gnemi beside her, who looked around curiously. The orc stood from his chair and straightened his back. "Did you want a custom job? That will require time and measurements."

"No, I want something you have readily made. That shouldn't be a problem, will it?"

The orc looked down to the kobold, and after a moment smirked. "It will be a pleasure to serve a servant of the dragons. I might have something that can work. Leather for protection? Cloth for something lighter and increased mobility? She looks rather frail and it's a debate if she can handle leather or it would even help."

"Cloth— and make it somewhat presentable with a hood to

keep the sun and rain off her head. The smell of wet human hair is dreadful."

"Is that so?" he replied, looking over Jesmine.

"Let him examine but keep that hood on," Histra said.

"Right," she replied, the orc grabbing her wrist, his big green four-fingered hands dwarfed her own soft, white, five-fingered one. He examined her for a minute or two as she watched the orc closely look over her body shape, his hands feeling through her clothes before pulling away. "I have something that could work. It was supposed to be for a younger orc woman, but she was killed before she could grab it. I kept it."

"Killed? By what?"

"Bandits."

"That's the second time I've heard about bandits. Do you know anything about them?"

"They don't approach the town. They attack those on the road, and from what I hear, often at night. I'd recommend not leaving town for a few days."

Histra lifted an eye ridge. "Why do you say that?"

"Tonight, is the start of the double new moons. With no light at night, the bandits can sneak up and take people by surprise. They don't care who you serve. I'm sure they would love to capture a kobold."

"I will keep that in mind."

The orc headed to the back of the shop, Jesmine asking, "Are you getting me clothes?"

"Your mismatched clothes given by Alderin doesn't do you much good."

"Thank you, Histra."

She flicked her tail. "Hmm?"

"For your help. You didn't have to do this."

"I did. It's best to keep a low profile and you wearing something local will draw less attention. If anyone discovered your species, we'd all be in trouble."

"That should be a good idea... but why don't you wear clothes?" Gnemi asked.

"What?" Histra said, glancing at him.

"Don't kobolds wear clothes? That's what I've heard."

Histra shrugged. "I do what I want. I don't need to. And they aren't all that helpful. Not like I need protection from the cold or heat."

"Right, but do kobolds wear clothes then? Or are you the norm?"

She rolled her eyes and looked ahead as the orc came out with a brown-hooded cloak with red trimmings. He held it up against Jesmine's form. "That's close. Will this do?"

"Yes, how much?"

"Five silver pieces."

"Five? Do you know who I serve?" she asked with a grunt. "Do you think that sudden chill you feel is for show?"

"This was a special custom order and won't part for less."

Histra walked up to him, the cold air eventually reaching up to the orc's face, breath fogging. "You sure you can't discount that even a bit?"

The orc's yellow eyes locked with the kobold's. "I do my part. I pay my taxes, but I need to make a living. I do not disrespect Sa'bara. My price stands."

"I am here in the name of Dra'kesh. What you do influences the opinion of not only Sa'bara but him. Do you really want to risk your current status of living over a coin or two?"

Silence filled the room for a few moments before Jesmine broke it, speaking in human. "Histra?"

"I'm handling this," she stated, not breaking her stare. "And what did I tell you about speaking to me in public without me initiating it?"

The orc looked up to see Jesmine's worried face before he let out a sigh, "I don't want to cause trouble to anyone. Four silver."

"That's acceptable," responded Histra, "Jesmine give him four silver pieces."

She nodded, digging through a pouch strapped to her side, pulling out four silver pieces and handed them to him.

The orc gave Jesmine the clothes, Histra saying, "Let's meet up with the others, we're done here." She turned, walking out.

"Sorry," Jesmine said, following.

"Kobolds are egotistical. I am too old to deal with it," he responded in human, returning to his chair.

The two groups eventually met up and headed to the inn. A large, two-story, wooden structure, the building towered in size over the nearby buildings. A few horses were hitched to the front with a cart visibly placed beside the building. Sounds of rabble-rousing, and music, came from the worn brown and black wooden door.

"We're going to bed here for the night?" Dran asked, cautiously looking toward the inn.

Histra let out a grunt. "You two don't talk unless I tell you to. Alderin, knock that door open with as much force as possible while I walk in," she commanded.

He looked down at her curiously. "What? Why?"

"I need to make an entrance, and we need to keep the orcs away from us. They know of our arrival, and we have to play the part," she explained.

Alderin reluctantly replied with a resigned sigh, "Fine."

"Aren't you being a bit too aggressive with this?" Jesmine asked.

"Do you know how to deal with orcs?" she responded.

She shook her head. "No. I never handled orc relations."

"Then leave this to me," she stated as they walked up to the front of the inn. Alderin forced the door open with a thud, the music continuing. Only a few orcs paid any heed as Histra walked in. Long, wooden tables and stools filled the expansive room. Several orcs had plates of food filled with cooked meats which they hungrily ate while enjoying heady mead foaming over the top after being poured by the nearby barmaid.

There was a small, raised platform in the corner where a band of three played, two with concussion and one woodwind instruments. A set of stairs led to the upper floors which were passed the bar, where several orcs sat enjoying their drinks, the rolling chatter amongst the orcs slowly starting to fade as more and more took notice of Histra.

She walked down the center of the room, the cold chill following her drawing the attention of a few that were still ignoring the intrusion. The rest of the party were a few feet behind, just outside of her ice aura where the lingering sensation of chilly air hit them. She kept her wings spread, walking tall and proud, ignoring the sudden stares and soft whispers between the orcs that watched her head straight for the bar.

"Who is the innkeeper?" Histra yelled in orcish.

A large, brown skinned orc on the other side of the bar responded with a grunt. "I am."

"Alderin," yelled Histra in human, snapping her claws and then pointed to the empty wooden bar stool beside her.

The human clenched his teeth, picking her up, gloves protecting him from the cold long enough to place her onto the stool without issue. Histra's gaze didn't pull away from the bartender, who still stood a few feet over her even when standing on the seat.

"Then you know why I am here. Two rooms. One for me, and one for them. Have them next to each other, I don't want my servants to be unable to hear me when I call them," she said.

"I've been informed of you," he grunted, reaching down to an iron-wrought key chain. He slid through a dozen keys before pulling out two. "The last two rooms on the top floor are yours. The fee has been covered," he replied, tossing the keys into an empty beer mug, sliding it in front of her.

"Excellent. If I need anything more, I'll be sure to have my servants contact you," she said, grabbing the keys before hopping off the stool.

"Of course," he replied, watching her and the rest of the group head upstairs, the sound of music and chatter between the orcs quickly returning to their normal levels. The upper floors were lit by enclosed lanterns that hung half a foot away from the walls. Wooden slit windows provided some extra light, which was beginning to fade with the setting sun. Reaching the last two rooms that sat across from each other, The kobold found the right key and unlocked the room with a click before tossing the party the other key. "Here. We'll talk in the morning," stated Histra, entering the mostly dark room.

A large, stray bed was pushed against the side of the room with a chamber pot near a bed post. Histra climbed up onto the bed using her claws to find purchase. She heard footsteps behind her. She turned, seeing Alderin lighting a small lantern on a small table.

"You aren't staying in my room," Histra said, catching Jesmine and Gnemi entering the other while Dran walked into her room. Jesmine looked over to them just before the door to Histra's room closed.

Alderin stared at her, sitting down at a chair next to the table.

"Are you insane? We are not to draw attention to us, and you go proclaiming you are a servant of Dra'kesh?"

"Quiet on what you say. Don't assume no one understands your tongue human," she replied.

"I have had experience on listening in on conversations, you need not worry about that."

Histra glared at him. "So, you say."

"I do say and do know. I've heard what you've been saying, I understand what you've been telling everyone. Something you could have easily pulled off sooner."

"It's a plan of last resort. Once we leave here, it's back to our normal plan, but I must say my lessons must have been going well if you've kept up. And you managed to do my chore without fail."

"Don't try to change the subject. I can understand the need to devise something, but you constantly try to keep us in the dark. Also, don't think I didn't see that threat you made to the orc guard with your horns."

"Aye, they've been bothering me since the very start," said Dran, approaching Histra.

"What about them?"

"They're wizard runes, aren't they? The equivalent of Jesmine's tattoos."

"They are merely for show. If I could utilize magic do you think I would have been a pet to those orcs for so long?"

"Tell me kobold, how did you become incarcerated? It looks like the orcs here have an annoyance but a fearful respect for your kind. That's quite a gamble for them to suddenly use you as a side show," Dran said.

Histra twitched. "That is something you don't need to know. I am keeping my end of the bargain, to get to where you need to go. Anything else is of no concern of yours."

"You're nothing but secrets and lies."

Histra smirked "Yes, but I keep to my word," she said, slightly outstretching her wings, "And my word is to get to where you need to go."

"A liar that keeps their word? You think we're dumb enough to fall for that?"

"Yes…" Histra answered seeing a stern look from Dran. "But my word is the only thing keeping me alive. You two aren't so different."

"What?" they said in unison, Alderin standing from the chair causing it to wobble.

"You are keeping secrets from Jesmine. You saved her for a reason. One of your own selfish accord. You may act like it's all righteous, but you have a purpose. And to continue this dangerous, but admittedly amusing quest of yours, entertains me. If for no other reason than I will enjoy seeing how Jesmine acts when she discovers the truth."

"We have agreed, Jesmine included, that we will tell her once we're safe. No different than you refusing to tell us what your plans are until the time suits you. And by then, you won't be needed, so you will not be there to see it," Alderin said.

"Are you two done? It's been a long day and I could get some rest. It will be nice to have a wall between us. Perhaps I'll get a real night's sleep tonight. Keeping an eye on you all is exhausting."

"Strange, I was about to say the same thing. Dran?" asked Alderin.

"I have nothing more to say or ask it," he shrugged, leaving with Alderin.

Histra let out a soft sigh, walking over to the lamp, blowing it out, locking the door before heading to bed.

"That kobold is so infuriating," grumbled Dran, entering the other room. Gnemi was currently setting up the floor with his sleeping mat. "Using us as slaves like that? I have never been so humiliated in my life."

Jesmine sat on the bed, replying, "She's keeping up appearances. How do you think they expect a kobold on a mission by the dragons to act? She's doing it for our sake."

"She just wants to be on a power trip is all," said Alderin.

"She's not that bad. Look what she got me," she said, holding up the cloak. "She wanted something that would fit and cover my head better."

"For orcish make, it looks well-made," commented Alderin, getting a closer look at it. "I was wondering where you got it."

"Histra is stubborn. She doesn't want to use niceties, but she's not as terrible as you two say."

"Wait till she no longer needs us, then we'll see her true

colors," Dran remarked.

"I bet she thinks the same about us."

"How could you be so supportive of the kobold? There is something about it that gives me chills, and I don't mean the whole ice thing," Dran said.

"She does give an odd feeling, but I think it's more of a personality quirk."

"I wish she'd tell me more about kobolds. She's so tight lipped it's driving me crazy," said Gnemi examining the bolt shafts with the aid of a nearby lantern. "But I agree with Jesmine. She doesn't appear show it, but she's not terrible compared to the kobolds I've heard about. She bought me ammunition. These bolts with a little bit of work can be used for my crossbow. We've been traveling for weeks without a break and despite the circumstances, we need it."

"We can't become complacent. We are in enemy territory," Alderin said.

"But if we act like they are the enemy, we won't get far. As far as they are concerned, we are a neutral group moving through under the yolk of a kobold who's under the command of one of the ancient dragons. We need to play it up," Jesmine said.

"No need to play it up. We're doing all we can to make this work. How can you just give the kobold a slide while…" Dran said, trailing off.

Jesmine tensed, "I'm sorry, I don't mean it that way."

"You sure could have fooled me." The dwarf thought silently to himself.

Alderin sighed. "Either way we should get some rest. We have to stay here for another day and there is nothing we can do about it," he replied as the party prepared for an evening of respite, not knowing the change in fortunes the following day will bring.

Chapter 6 A Veil Lifted

The next morning Jesmine woke to the scent of freshly cooked meats and ale. She sat up noticing the others sitting on the floor eating breakfast from wooden plates. Alderin looked over in her direction, smiling and waving. "Morning. We didn't want to wake you, so we let you sleep in."

"Not like there is a lot we can do yet. Nothing will be ready till the late afternoon which gives us some forced free time," explained Dran, finishing his meal, checking his red braided beard for any crumbs. He stood up with a soft grunt. "But that doesn't mean we should idly sit around in the room all day."

"Good morning to you all too," Jesmine replied, Alderin handing her a plate of food. "Thank you," she said, looking down at the slabs of bacon and other meats. "Orcs have a very heavy meat diet."

"At least their cuisine can leave me not for want," Dran said.

"I believe Dwarves are very hearty, and I heard your constitutions are legendary," Gnemi said.

Dran quirked an eyebrow, "What do you mean by that?"

"Well… uh, what I mean is that you have heavy meals and you can most likely drink me under the table several times over without even getting tipsy."

"Aye, this is true, when we first met you were so drunk after that I thought you were going to die."

"I thought I was going to, and then came the… well, best not to talk about that while others are eating."

The dwarf nodded. "Aye."

Jesmine ate some of the bacon, looking around and noticed a full plate of food on the floor. "Has Histra eaten yet?"

"The kobold hasn't left its room. I knocked on her door but no response," replied Alderin. "Honestly, if it wants to stay in the room today, that's fine by me. I could use a break from their arrogance."

"All kobolds have a superiority complex. Being the dragons' pets comes with the benefit of thinking they are better than us," Dran said.

"Histra is a bit rough around the edges but she's not as bad as you two constantly make her and other kobolds out to be."

"How can you be so protective over kobolds? Have you forgotten who they serve? And what those dragons have done? What they have—"

"Dran, it's probably best we don't go into that," said Gnemi, pointing to his ears and to the walls.

"Right, right," he coughed, turning his attention back to Jesmine. "You know what I mean."

"Yes... I do. But there is something I do know."

"Which is?"

"If you treat someone as if they are automatically the enemy and evil, you leave them little choice other than to fulfill it by being your enemy. For example, if you treat someone as only a common beggar who will steal and rob you blind, so you never give them the chance for decent work, guess what will happen? They will become that thief out of necessity rather than by choice. You need to give people a chance to better themselves."

Alderin quietly listens to Jesmine, poking at his food, rubbing his recently clean-shaven rugged face with his other hand before slowly taking a drink.

"And what do you do when you give them that chance, but they turn against you anyway and then it costs you dearly?" remarked Dran, walking over to the door.

"That depends what happens, if it happens at all," Jesmine replied.

"We can't afford a 'if it happens', Jesmine, and I would appreciate next time you not be so dismissive of my point, even if I acknowledged yours." The dwarf said with a heavy sigh before looking to Alderin, "Alderin?"

His head jerks slightly, lifting it up. "Yeah?"

"I want to scout the town and understand what's going on with these orcs. Mind coming with?"

"That's a good idea. Where do you intend to go? Downstairs and listen in on people?"

"Perhaps later, but first I want to talk to the other dwarf in town."

"Smart," he replied, standing up. "We'll be back. Is there anything you two need?"

Jesmine shook her head, "I'm fine. There isn't much I can do, and it's best I keep quiet."

"I should be working on these bolts, so I'm good," Gnemi replied, pointing to the stack next to him. In front of him was one of his completed bolts along with some tools laid out on the other side, currently midway in reshaping one of the shafts into an identical shape.

"I don't think we'll be out too long. But if we are, it will probably be because our supplies are ready."

"That or me and the blacksmith are having a long hearty conversation. I surmise he hasn't talked to one of his kin in some time," said Dran, opening the door.

"Do you mean with dwarves in Sa'bara or Dra'kesh? Be mindful that these dwarves may be much different than those back home. It could be like the Dra'kesh elves," Alderin remarked.

"Now why would you go say something like that?" grumped Dran as they left the door open giving clear view of Histra's room. The metal lock and knob are frosted over as a gentle fog bellowed out from the space underneath the door.

"Is Histra okay?" asked Jesmine.

Gnemi kept focusing on his work, replying, "We knocked, and I didn't hear her respond. I peeked through the eye hole and I believe I saw her sleeping. Alderin said don't bother her. We have food for her when she comes out."

"But her breakfast will get cold."

"I said that, and Alderin remarked, 'Like it matters with her.'"

"Alderin…"

"He has a point though."

"It's more of the thoughtfulness of asking. She expects that we are going to betray her when her usefulness is over. That is why she is so brash and secretive."

"Probably. She did state that when we first met," Gnemi replied, blowing some wood shavings from the shaft, checking it up against his base copy.

"Gnemi?"

"Yes?"

"You're from the, you know," she pointed up.

Gnemi looked at her for a moment as it dawned on him, "Oh, oh. Yeah, I am."

"So how did you meet Alderin and Dran?"

"Well…" he said, while still working, "If you want to know. I met Dran first and later Alderin found us. Then later as you know Histra recruited us for this mission," he replied, giving Jesmine a sly wink.

"So how did you meet Dran then?"

"Well, I don't want to go too much into his personal life, which I don't know much about to be honest, but when I came to a tavern in Tundaholm he was there. I was looking for a place to stay and he quite literally crashed into me. One thing led to another and most of the details are still rather hazy to me, but we got to talking."

"About?"

"You know, people, certain people," he continued, looking at her.

"Oh, I see."

"I wanted to find them."

"Why?"

"That, I think will be a better story to tell elsewhere."

Jesmine nodded, "So you left your home to find this person, but why would someone as clearly clever as you go on something so dangerous?"

"To be honest…" he stopped working, "I am not the best my family has to offer. Being the fifth child and though as good in mechanical wonders as I am, I'm completely unable to grasp magic and how to integrate it into my works. My other family members appear to have little trouble doing so. Many are responsible in keeping the Northern Frontier defenses secured against the cursed lands, but that is probably why I wandered into Dra'kesh lands. And when Histra found me, she was all too happy to make me do her bidding," he said, resuming his work to get a bolt tip attached to the finished shaft, "The northern wall always has a shortage of people, and my family seems to be very adept at mitigating the problem."

"Ah yes. I know of the issues they face. The cursed lands where the dead rise again to assault the living. Protecting the rest of the continent of Isharia from their attacks drains a lot of resources."

"Yeah but what can you do when that is the legacy of Eisandra that they've inherited."

"I'm to say at least I am fortunate that... perhaps it might be best to speak about this later. Sa'bara is known to be the most cautious of the great dragons, speaking about Eisandra could be taboo in these lands."

"You'd be the one who'd know."

"Yes. It was peaceful but an uneasy time growing up. Histra did inform us to never speak ill will towards him. For doing so would lead to a high chance of one going missing the next day or be put on display by one of his agents. It is true we don't know what the Great Sa'bara would think if we spoke about the others. Best not to chance it," replied Jesmine.

Gnemi looked up from his work, "What other things should we be cautious on?"

"Outside of not speaking ill about him, I'm afraid that I know nothing about that of which Histra hasn't already informed us. Things are much different compared to what I've heard."

"Is there anything in particular that stands out? Outside the obvious with... you know," he said, pointing to his right hand.

She nodded, "That's new. It must be something he put into place after he killed off all the elves for talk of the rebellion," she replied, poking at the food in front of her.

"It's not going to be easy is it?" Gnemi asked after a moment of silence.

Jesmine looked up, "This journey isn't easy."

"Yeah but I mean, well you know when we get to the end."

"Ah, yes. Honestly, I am trying not to think about it." She looked back at her half-eaten meal, "I fear I am may not have the strength needed when we get there. Histra would certainly not be pleased with me if I was, but till I do my part with her," she said with a moment of pause, "I'm more or less useless till I get what I lost. Anything I do is either small or carries great risk. I appreciate the help I am being given but this is all my fault. I was careless, and this is now my punishment with Histra dragging me along on this mission," she replied, wiping away a few tears, putting on a smile.

Peeking through a keyhole Histra watched and listened. She pulled back, adjusting her wings, letting out a wide yawn. The room frosted over as warm air from outside broke through the shuttered window, fogging as it enters.

"It seems they know how to have a conversation and not screw this up. And no talk of betrayal or plots against me while they think I am asleep. So far so good," she thought, quietly climbing back onto the bed. *"I'm still so tired. This is the first time I can sleep soundly in such a long time. Might as well get some more while I can."* She adjusted herself on the bed, curling up on herself, drifting back to sleep.

Meanwhile, Alderin and Dran headed downstairs. The wooden steps creaked under their weight as the once-bustling inn is now relatively quiet causing the few orcs there to take note of their arrival. The innkeeper-bartender eyed them for a moment before, saying, "Did the kobold like her breakfast?"

"She didn't say. She's being reclusive. We're out to continue what she desires," Alderin replied.

The orc nodded as the two departed. A few nearby orcs moved about their day. The dirt road was dried and caked as grey clouds overcast the hot summer's day. As they headed to the blacksmith's shop Dran remarked, "Your orc tongue has improved dramatically since we ran into the ones in the forest."

"Thanks. It's not as difficult as I thought, but hours of nothing but study does help."

"I'm just grateful that it taught you actual orc tongue."

"The kobold had to. If I said something that would enrage the locals, it would endanger it."

"Aye, makes sense," he replied, passing orcs, livestock, and carts loaded with items along the streets. Approaching the blacksmith shop, they found it to be strangely quiet.

"I wonder if he's working right now," remarked Alderin.

"He is. He's a dwarf after all. See look over there," replied Dran, pointing to their wagon propped up on the side of the shop by wooden planks. As they entered, the dwarf was busy at work shaving down the wood to be the right size for the wheel spokes.

"You were right," Alderin said.

"Aye, of course I am," he responded before whispering to him, "I hope you don't mind if I speak my native tongue for a bit?'

"Go right ahead."

"Thank ye," Dran replied, approaching Beslba, "Morning! Hope you don't mind us dropping by for a little while? The name is Dran," cheerfully greeting in dwarven.

Beslba stopped what he was doing and looked up.

"I know you're busy, but I thought we could chat a little?" he asked, Beslba saying nothing, causing an awkward moment of silence.

"Sorry, sorry. It took me a moment; I didn't recognize your dialect. You're the dwarf that is with the kobold, aren't you?" he asked in a different dialect of dwarven, one that took Dran a moment to unravel, "The human female, Jesmine was it? She surprised me speaking my version of our kin's tongue."

"Aye she is skilled," he replied, briefly looking around, "I hope we aren't interrupting too much?"

Beslba shook his head, "Not at all. I don't get to talk to many folks around here. But do you think it is a little rude to speak a tongue the human doesn't understand? Or does he?"

Dran glanced at Alderin, who was standing off to the side idly looking over the place as Beslba continued, "One might think you have something to hide from them. Unless you intend to hide something?"

Dran shook his head, "No, not at all."

"Will human tongue be alright then?" he asked in human.

"Yes, it will be fine."

"I appreciate the kind gesture. It is nice to hear someone speak my own tongue again, it's been a while," he replied, resuming his work, "From what I've heard, you're from the Dra'kesh lands?"

"Aye, I am."

"I've never met anyone let alone a dwarf from Dra'kesh lands, till yesterday."

"I could say the same about you for Sa'bara. I will admit I wasn't expecting the dialect to be so different."

"True enough," Beslba replied, glancing up at Dran then back at his work. "How are dwarves in your land?"

"We are broken into two kingdoms. I hail from the kingdom of Druhan. My hometown which is also our capital is Tundaholm. It lies at the base and within the Salvik mountain range."

"Kingdoms you say? Dra'kesh also allows kingdoms?"

"He does, but it is only to create conflict between us as we go about our once a decade tribute offering. Aren't there kingdoms here?"

"Only two groups under the great dragon Sa'bara are

privileged to have large kingdoms. Those are the orcs under clan Ugosh, and the avolarieans, which are more a loose confederation of tribes than any sort of kingdom. Us dwarves and humans are regulated to smaller settlements tied to orcs' hips."

"That's terrible, but why?"

"I don't know all of the great dragon Sa'bara's reasonings, but it might have had something to do with the elven uprising. The orcs and avolarieans were the first to throw their support behind their extermination. In turn, they got rewarded. They were given lands that were originally elven, human, dwarven and even some other orcish lands to those that helped him. My kin originally came from the other side of Rivera, as we mined the Sa'barian mountains for precious metals and resources. We shared the land uneasily with the avolarieans back then. After the war, many of us were shipped east and dispersed, myself included, though there are still many back home."

"That's horrendous!"

"It is, but…" Beslba stopped what he was doing and looked around briefly, "One may not like what Sa'bara did, but all we can do is work hard to regain his favor. Word of advice. While you are here, though you are only passing through under the indirect command of Dra'kesh, do not speak ill to Sa'bara, not even in jest."

"Our kobold has informed us of this several times," he replied.

"I'm confused on something, Beslba," Alderin said.

"Yes?"

"You say it's bad to speak against Sa'bara, but didn't you just do that?"

"Technically no. The great dragon Sa'bara is shrewd. If we were all to be killed for not liking an action of his, well there'd be a lot of dead folks around. The great Sa'bara only removes those that openly speak against or wish ill will towards him."

"Explain."

"Simple, if I said I wanted to do something negative to him for splitting up my homeland, then I might disappear before the end of the day. Depending on who heard me. But if I said, I dislike what he did, and I wish to find a way to regain his favor to restore my home? Then perhaps I might be given the opportunity to start doing so. And as an example of that, this is why I am here."

"You're blacksmithing in a middle of an orc town because you were asked to by Sa'bara?"

"Not directly, but I wanted to do better for my family and show that we dwarves can be trusted to return to our homeland. That it would be more beneficial for him if we did. A few weeks later I was offered a job here to shore up the growing lack of skilled orc labor in the countryside."

Dran quirked an eyebrow. "Do you happen to know why there's a skilled orc shortage?"

Alderin muttered, "Possible because orcs aren't skilled."

Beslba shook his head. "Not completely. I know many are heading to Rivera for whatever reason. There's always an influx of skilled labor and traders at the capital when the great dragon Sa'bara's tax is about to be collected. It's a time for those to garner greater favor from him for the coming year."

"I see."

"I've said much. How about you two? Tell me about this trip to the capital. As far as I know, it's a message to be sent for Sa'bara himself? From Dra'kesh? One great dragon talking to another, now that's something. I'd have thought there would be a larger group, better befitting the grandeur of such a mighty dragon," he said, blowing some wood shavings off the recently finished wheel spoke before starting the next.

"Unfortunately, or perhaps fortunately, we do not know anything about what the message entails. Only that the kobold's contact is in Rivera."

Beslba nodded, Alderin adding, "As to why not a big set of guards? I don't think either of us knows for sure. Perhaps he wanted a smaller group, or maybe it was left up to the kobold and it wanted to show off its prowess on how few guards it needed. If you haven't noticed, it's very arrogant."

"I noticed that myself during the brief time I've spoken to her."

"The kobold is high off the dragon's power. Marching in wherever it wants acting like it owns the place."

"Emissaries from the dragons should be respected but... I can agree that the kobolds I have seen tend to act superior to all of us. Just because they more directly serve the dragons than anyone else. And it's not because of skill, or strength. It's probably their lack of physical strength that the great dragons like to use them. Or perhaps it's something else entirely."

"Like what?" asked Alderin.

"Not sure but if I was a betting dwarf, I'd put my money on it having something to do with that ice aura she has."

"You think? Why?"

"It comes from a story my grandfather once told me that when he was a young one. The great dragon Sa'bara came to inspect the mines himself. A massive dragon; where he landed everything was poisoned and died. Sa'bara never weakened his poisonous aura he said. Nor did he change to a lesser shape, like his kin. Instead he had green scaled kobolds who were trained in the arcane magic to speak for him. They were immune to his passive aura. Perhaps that is why they are used, but that does make me wonder."

"Wonder what?" Dran asked.

"Dra'kesh, from what I've been told, is an acidic dragon. His breath melts bone and steel alike. To stand close to his presence would risk slowly being melted alive. If that's the case, why not send a black scaled kobold who might be naturally adapted to such magic? Instead of the relatively rare white? A kobold like that would have been more akin to Eisandra than Dra'kesh," he explained.

"I don't question the dragon's logic. He must have a reason for it. Just like there must be a reason why we're such a small group. But as long as completing this duty provides the benefit of gaining some favor with Dra'kesh, I don't have a problem with it," Dran answered.

Beslba nodded, "Forgive me, I am afraid I didn't catch your name human. What was it?"

"Alderin."

"Alderin. I've heard a bit from Dran here of the dwarves in Dra'kesh lands. What about you humans?"

"There are two notable human kingdoms, but I don't come from either. The area I'm from is more of a border region along Sa'bara's lands. It's thin, poor, gets raided by orcs with few organized military guards. Dra'kesh makes it difficult to move from one area to another, making one just live with the day to day problems."

"How terrible. You must really hate the ancient dragons then?"

Alderin took a deep breath, Dran giving him a cursory glance,

"There is one thing I learned about Dra'kesh; he is like a force of nature. And like nature, he can't be stopped, and you can't get angry over what happens. One must simply live with it."

"More truthful words have never been spoken," Beslba replied as the three continued to chatter for a while till the dwarf finished off the final spoke. "That's the last of them. And with that, I think I deserve a bit of a lunch. If you don't mind, I need to close shop and head upstairs. Your company was a nice change of pace," he said, placing the wheel spoke off to the side.

"We should be heading off. We have to check if the supplies for our trip are ready," replied Dran, offering Beslba a handshake.

He gave him a strong firm one. "Right. Remember you can leave your supplies just outside. Once the wheel is fixed you may load up."

"That goes without saying," Dran answered as he and Alderin departed. Beslba watched them leave, locking things up before going to a small rope that hung from the ceiling. He grabbed a stool to reach it, pulling it down to reveal a sliding ladder, which he climbed up, and pulled on the rope to withdraw it once at the top. The dwarf's living quarters were a little nicer than one would suspect, but there was one thing that stood out. Three small, winged wyvern-like lizards about the dimensions of a medium-sized bird, that hung perched from the ceiling. Their bellies ranging in color from a sky blue, to a pale grey while their backs went from a soft, earthy color to a vibrant green.

Beslba muttered something in draconic, an amulet shinning from underneath his beard. He peeked over the window, watching Dran and Alderin make their way down the street toward the butcher shop before pulling away as his incantation finished.

The blue-greenish colored energy flowed around him, form transforming, shrinking down in size. His hair withdrew into his body, stocky figure becoming slender, rough skin turning into purple scales, and flat face elongating into a kobold muzzle. Her black horns had carved runic markings with silver inlaid, red stripes marking along her body, while a golden amulet hung around her neck. A light cloak covered much of her small wingless form as the kobold's yellow eyes looked around, tail flicking.

"I know I shouldn't, but I just get so tired of that body," she remarked to herself, pulling out a small piece of parchment and an ink quill, squibbling a few words that appeared to be gibberish before rolling it up and placing it into a small tube. She whistled the dark bellied wyvern-bird over to her, the creature let out a soft chirp-like noise in the process. She petted it under its chin which caused it to chirp again, then tying the cylinder to its ankle.

"I couldn't get much out of them, but I think Sa'bara might be interested to know of someone coming to give him a message," she replied with a smirk. The creature spread its wings before it flew off. She stretched, heading to a private room to enjoy her planned lunch.

When Alderin and Dran reached the butcher, they found the supplies they'd ordered mostly done and ready to go. In total it was a few hundred pounds of food, which had to be carried by hand. The whole process took several trips to complete. When they came with the last of the supplies, sweat dripping down their brows, breath heavy, arms shaking, they noticed Beslba giving the new wheel on their cart a test spin.

"That's a lot of food you have there," Beslba said, eyeing the sacks.

"Aye, better to have too much food than not enough," said Dran wiping the sweat from his brow.

"True," he replied, lowering the wagon. "Good news. She's good as new."

"Great," said Alderin, looking over the wagon. "You have my thanks."

"No need. It's a job, but I appreciate it the thought."

"It's good *terrible* news," remarked Dran, Alderin and Beslba shooting him a curious look.

"Why?" Alderin asked.

"Now we have to put the supplies *in* the wagon."

Alderin slumped. "Oh…"

"Aye."

"I'd love to help a fellow dwarf, but I have orders I put on hold for this that desperately need my attention. Safe travels!" Beslba replied.

"Thank ye," said Dran. The stout dwarf grabbed the first sack, hauling it on board as Alderin struggled with his bag, panting loudly, but managed. By the time they finished their hearts pounded like beating drums, and the day's light was beginning to fade.

Alderin leans against the cart for support. "Damn, I thought this would never end."

"Aye, but that's the last of it," said Dran, cracking his neck and back.

"Thank the Gods for that. Let's head back before they start to worry. Hopefully we can get a good meal."

"Aye, that sounds like a brilliant plan," he replied, making their way back to the inn. Halfway there they heard a yell echoing out from behind them.

"Out of the way!" yelled an orc. A small caravan rapidly approached. They rushed off to the side as horse-drawn carts pulled past them with caged animals of all sorts. Wild wolkin were in two cages, while there were more exotic, clawed vicious beasts that rattled the cages that they were in. A brown skinned orc riding a horse alongside the caravan was draped in long orange and white fox skinned robes. His yellow eyes focused on one of the creatures that became more aggressive, tugging on its bonds within the cage.

The creature has thick black scales, its red reptilian eyes glaring, his long muzzle full of razor-sharp teeth ready to tear flesh from bone in a single bite. It growled out, the orc chanting in orcish-arcana.

His two-inch pair of tusks were engraved in arcane runes and inlaid with silver. They glowed a soft blue, the energy flowing down his arm to his fingers releasing a burst of electric energy. It shocked the beast which responded with a thunderous roar, shuddering.

Nearby orcs' attention was drawn to the noise. Sparks flew from the metal cage to the beast again, its body twitching before it collapsed with a heavy pant.

A well-built, muscular, dark green skinned orc rode up beside him. His body was draped in a mix of leather armor with metal plates adorned with intimidating spikes. Golden earrings dangled from his ears, with matching set of rings at the base of his tusks. He let out a grunt, saying, "Zed, be careful with the cargo. It's no use to us if it's damaged before we make it to Rivera."

Zed grinned, looking over to the other orc. "Fear not Garran. It can handle a few simple shocks."

"Yes, but you could use less harsh measures."

"It's not our big prize. Forgive me for being a little excited," he said, glancing at the cage in the middle of the caravan covered in a cloth.

He looked at the cage, grunting. "We lost a lot for that. I don't want to take any chances," he remarked.

"Orc hunters?" Dran wondered.

"Seems to be," replied Alderin, unintentionally following them. The caravan pulled itself up along the inn. The orcs in the caravan dismounted, securing the wagons while Garran stepped ahead of Zed to burst through the inn's doors.

"Irgha, get the ale flowing and food ready for we are going to celebrate!" he yelled interrupting the flow of the inn.

The bartender gave a tusk filled grin. "Garran, it's been a while! I was beginning to wonder if you died. Did you get a good haul?"

"You wouldn't believe it. With this haul I'm moving on up. Sa'bara is going to be so pleased with what I have for Draksind," he responded just as Alderin and Dran entered the inn, without anyone taking notice.

"You don't say? What did you get that lets you boast such a claim?"

Garran leaned against the table. "That my old friend, is a secret, but I'll let you know this," he said, moving in to whisper it.

Alderin and Dran headed up the stairs and back to their rooms. As the door creaked open, Jesmine and Gnemi instantly turned their attention to them. Jesmine greeted them with a smile, rushing to them. "You're back, thank the Gods," she said.

"What's wrong?" asked Alderin, growing anxious, looking around.

"Histra still hasn't left her room and the day is almost over."

Alderin's tenseness and apprehension instantly faded, replying, "So?"

"Look," said Jesmine, dragging them over. "There is a layer of ice hanging from the doorknob," she said, showing him the icicles. Cold foggy air continuing to flow through the cracks.

"I've knocked several times and haven't gotten a response. I'm just worried something has happened to her."

"So, the kobold is asleep? Big deal. The door is locked, what do you expect me to do about it?"

"You can pick it."

"You want me to pick the lock to its room? Just because it hasn't bothered us today?"

Gnemi spoke up. "It seems to have been an unusually long time. And if something happened, it could be very difficult to explain or possibly worse leave this fortified town without her."

"Fine, but if this causes something, this was your idea, not mine. How many times do I have to pick a frozen lock because of this kobold," remark Alderin, going to the door pecking away at the ice in the keyhole before beginning. "This is a simple lock, which normally wouldn't be bad, but the ice will make it tricky," he said, pulling out his lock pick.

"While he does that, what have you two been up to?" Dran asked.

"Nothing much. I finished shaping the bolts to fit my crossbow," Gnemi replied.

"I provided company. There isn't much we could do. We don't know orc tongue to learn anything from the locals."

"Aye true. But nothing more of interest has occurred?"

"Nope, unless you count Histra being stuck in her room all day?"

"I do not."

Seconds later a 'click' was heard from the door lock. "Easy," Alderin remarked, a layer of thin ice crunching as the door opened. A wave of cold air hit him in the face, causing water to condense on the metal on his person. Inside everything was covered in a thin layer of ice. The windows slats were completely frozen over. Histra was curled up on the bed. Small bits of broken ice laid around her.

"See, it's just sleeping. Nothing to be worried about," remarked Alderin, Jesmine running past him to the bed side.

"Histra? Are you okay?" she said, placing her hand on Histra's side. The warmth rapidly draining away like dipping her hand into ice water.

Histra's eyes shot open, dilating, letting out a draconic screech, leaping up like a surprised cat, unfurling her wings to their fullest extent. Her eyes darted around the room, she let out a soft groan, releasing the tension in her claws.

"Sorry, I didn't mean to startle you."

She gulped down what little freezing liquid she instinctively released, letting slid down her throat chilling her insides which she shrugged off. "What are you all doing in my room? How did you even get in here?!" she exclaimed.

"I asked Alderin to pick the lock."

"Alderin did… right, right I forgot he could do that. Glad I did, too, or I'd… never mind. What is it?"

"We were concerned that you haven't left your room all day."

She cocked an eye ridge. "I was sleeping. I needed my rest."

"I can see that now, but the sun has almost set, and you haven't come out once."

"What about getting sleep do you not understand? I haven't been able to sleep eas—did you say the sun has almost set?"

"Yeah."

"I'd say we have about another hour if that? Don't worry we got the supplies secured and ready for us to leave first thing in the morning," Alderin said.

"Aye, we got everything prepared. And look none of us got into trouble while you were sleeping the day away," Dran commented.

"Right… good. Glad to hear I don't have to babysit all of you for everything."

"Histra," said Jesmine with a stern look.

"What is it?"

"You don't have to be condescending. We came in worried about you. We have nothing but good news, and yet you speak down to everyone."

"Perhaps, but you shouldn't be talking to me that way. You are serving me when I am here, and while on this journey. I am charged with this mission, and I will let *him* know of your hard work, and concern for my wellbeing. I assure you it will go a long way," she stated, looking around the room.

Jesmine nodded. "Right, forgive me."

Histra hopped off the bed and stretched. "Let's get me some food. I haven't eaten all day and I'd like a nice *hot* meal," she said, glancing at Alderin. "Contrary to popular belief, I do enjoy them, sometimes."

"Right, could have fooled me. Shall we go downstairs then?" Alderin asked.

"Go get a table ready for me. I'll be down in a bit, I want to wake up more so I can make a proper entrance," she stated, stretching out her wings.

"We'll get a table then."

"You do that."

"I'm glad you are okay, if there is anything, we can do to make your night's rest better, let me know," Jesmine said.

"I'll inform you if anything crosses my mind," she replied as they left.

"Why do you care so much about that kobold? Especially after that display," Alderin asked.

"You know just as well as I. But if you want to talk about it, we'll do it later."

"Right. Remind me to take you up on that offer," he said as they walked downstairs. There, a few orcs took note of their arrival, but most were enjoying a meal. Two long, wooden tables were pushed together, and plates of food and drink were laid out for a dozen orcs. They sat at the table, verbosely chatting to each other, enjoying their food and drink while three spots on the table remained with a plate full of food and mugs filled to the brim with ale.

Garran curiously took note of the party but quickly returned to his festivities.

"Our great kobold will be down shortly and is wanting a hot meal, do you have a spot where we could all sit?" Alderin asked.

"We're busier than normal but I can make it happen," the bartender replied. A table halfway across the place was picked, cleared of the single orc sitting there, who grumbled at the treatment.

Garran eyed the events unfolding before him, but then Zed leaned up against him and bumped his drink to his, drawing his attention back to his group.

"I will be happy once we leave this town," Alderin commented, sitting down, resting a hand on the hilt of his short sword.

"Aye, the sooner we head out, the sooner we'll be done and, on our way, back home," Dran said.

"I still think we're two weeks from Rivera, and that's not the end of our travels," said Jesmine.

"We ordered enough food to last us," said Alderin.

"Aye, we have you to thank for that," replied Dran.

"One usually can't go wrong with more supplies," commented Gnemi, standing on the stool to keep his head over the table.

After a few minutes Histra made her way down the steps. Her wings unfurled slightly, making herself look larger. She stared down the orcs that took notice of her. She scanned the room, finding where everyone else was before making it all the way down the steps.

Whispers about the 'kobold messenger' filled the room but it was overshadowed by the uninterrupted celebration of the orc party, which she paid no mind as she walked by.

Garran felt the cold air brush against his back, causing him to turn his head, taking a swig of his drink, some of the beer running down his chin, wiping off with his sleeve. "Hey…. you look familiar."

Histra didn't flinch, turning her head in Garran's direction. "Of course, I do, I came here yesterday. It would be wise not to bother me during my meal."

Garran placed his mug down with a heavy thud, standing up. "I wasn't here yesterday. So that is not it," he replied, approaching her, who turned to face him.

Jesmine sat up as the events began to unfold. "Should we do something?" she asked.

Alderin shook his head. "We have to let it play out."

The orc towered over the small kobold, "No, no that can't be it either."

"I'm a messenger for the great dragon Dra'kesh. Perhaps you saw us passing on the road. We stopped here to get a wheel repaired. But I don't care where you think you've seen me. Stop interrupting me. I have a meal to eat," she growled.

The orc took a good long look over her, soon chuckling. "A messenger for the great dragon Dra'kesh, you say?"

"Yes. Are you deaf?"

"How long have you been this *messenger*?" he asked, standing almost toe to toe with her.

"I don't need to answer you. It would be wise of you to stop pestering me, unless you want Sa'bara to hear how you interfere with a messenger to him?"

Garran didn't flinch as others in his party curiously looked at the display, a few appeared worried, others more relaxed. Zed slowly drank from his mug, other patrons watching the display with increased concern.

"Well, it couldn't have been that long. I doubt any messenger from the great dragon Dra'kesh would allow him or herself to be put into a cage and carted around being declared to be 'a baby white dragon'."

Histra remained firm. "You must have gone mad if you think I'd have myself degraded in such a manner or be stupid enough to claim I am a dragon," she growled.

"I think *not*. I'd recognize that cracked, engraved horn and white scales of yours anywhere. You may fool others, but you won't fool me. And to pretend to be a messenger of the dragons? Abusing their power like that? Well that's a punishable offense," he stated, quickly dropping down to punch Histra hard in the face, causing her to spin and hit the ground with a heavy thud. Almost everyone in the bar stood up in shock. Histra's head throbbed with pain, feeling the point of impact lingering along her muzzle.

Dran thought the moment Histra hit the ground, *"I wish I could have done that, but this can't be good."*

Alderin intently watched, *"I've never felt so conflicted…"*

"Acting all high and mighty; abusing people because you think you can. This faux dragon messenger needs to be taught a lesson in mannerisms," Garran stated, glancing over at the rest of his party, "What do you all think?"

"Yeah. I thought I recognized that 'baby dragon' from somewhere. We saw that show about a half a year ago?" asked a red skinned orc to one of his companions.

Histra growled, unfurling her wings, her face throbbing, tasting iron on her tongue, she pushed herself back onto her feet. "You will pay for that," she said.

"For what? That or *this*?!" Garran stated, giving another heavy-handed punch to her face, blood flying from her mouth, which frosted over, changing from a deep crimson to a soft pink.

Jesmine took a step toward them, but she felt a hand on her shoulder pulling her back. Alderin shook his head, pulling her close.

"We need to help," said Jesmine, feeling Alderin's grip grow tighter.

Dran nonchalantly took a swig from his drink with a smirk, "Nah, the kobold's got this. If needed it'll call us."

Histra's claws raked across wood leaving light scratch marks. Another heavy blow struck her square in the back between her wings, causing them to flutter.

"I despise wretches like you, who have no respect for others. You don't realize how hard it is for us folk to work and make a living. Just because you are a kobold, you think you can make up whatever story you want to get what you want. I bet you think it's justification for what you have been put through. Well, *think again*!" he exclaimed, kicking her in the chest, sending Histra flying across the room almost hitting two bystanders who just managed to duck out of the way.

She landed hard against the wall; her head flung back into the wood so hard that her horns dug in with a crack. The force caused her fractured horn to widen a hair's breadth more which sent shock waves of pain through her head and in that moment, she saw a white starburst flash. Histra's eyes went wide, her pupils shrunk to tiny, vertical slits; a vision running past her, happening in an instant, but it all played out before her eyes like the day it happened.

Histra saw a massive, wide-open ice-covered cavern, the white floors stained with crimson blood, which froze all that it touched. Only her and the several white kobolds surrounding a mountain of a white-scaled dragon remained unaffected.

Labored breathing echoed in the room as they scrambled to each of the several gaping wounds that continued to bleed. Their horns glowed a bright white, putting their claws against the gashes, chanting in draconic-arcana, making arcane symbols in the dragon's scales using her own blood.

Histra was completely soaked in the dragon's blood, making her feel cold as she tried to tend the gaping wound that was several times her size. Between spell casts there was one sickening sentence being repeated over and over amongst the kobolds: "It's not working! The wounds aren't healing!"

Chapter 7 A Party Plus One

Histra landed face first onto the tavern floor, pain shooting through her body, as a mixture of confusion and excitement rung through the air. One of the orcs from Garran's party yelled out with a hearty laugh. "That kobold didn't even need to use its wings to fly!"

The bartender looked over to Garran, his yellow eyes showing concern, yelling, "Garran? Are you sure that kobold is lying? You know what will happen if you're wrong."

He looked over his shoulder. "I've spent my life trying to get ahead. I would not be so callous and risk it all if I wasn't dead certain. Not every kobold serves a dragon, and those who do not, need to learn it's disrespectful to *pretend* to," he replied, walking over to her. The orcs surrounding her moved out of his way. She looked, up pushing herself to her feet, stumbling for a moment, catching her balance. Her head throbbed, staring down Garran.

The bartender shook his head. "If it's true great, but if you're wrong, I had nothing to do with this," he said, raising his hands in gesture.

"I know what I am doing," Garran remarked, cracking his thick muscular neck. He pushed aside a table to get a clear view of his prey. The table shook and rattled, grinding against the wood floor with a moan, a few drinks being knocked over in the process.

One orc yelled out angrily at Garran. "That's my drink!"

"I'll buy you a new one," he scoffed at him, a few members of his party joining him. They spread out surrounding Histra as she tensed, flicking her wings.

Garran cracked his knuckles, Histra not breaking her gaze with him. She responded by spitting some blood off to the side. Which froze the ground, tensing her throat muscles, preparing her frothy mixture of liquid ice when suddenly Alderin yelled out in orcish, "Wait a moment!"

Garran stopped and looked at him. "What is it human?" he asked.

Alderin forcing his way through the crowd, "Out of the way!" he exclaimed, shoving one orc, who returned the favor forcing him up faster. "Are you telling me that this kobold here has been lying this whole time?!" he angrily exclaimed.

"Yes. I saw this kobold in a sideshow not too long ago, and previously a few years before that. I know for a fact that this kobold could not be a representative of any of the great dragons. And for her slights against them and me, she needs to be taught some respect," he remarked with a grunt.

"I will have y—" said Histra before the red skinned, medium built orc with dark leather armor gave a solid kick sending her back against the wall with a heavy thud. A few droplets escaped her throat, flying out of her mouth freezing bits of wood wherever they landed.

"We've had enough of your lies kobold," he stated, towering over her, his hand on the hilt of his blade.

"Let me deal with her!" Alderin demanded.

"What?" asked Garran, turning his attention to him, standing toe to toe, revealing the clear foot in height he had over the human.

"I want to deal with her," he stated.

"And why would I let you do that?" he asked, Histra slowly pulling herself back to her feet with the aid of the wall.

"Because this kobold here tricked me and my group. It told us that we were to be its guards through this land. See this," said Alderin, pulling off his gloves to show his hands. "We're from Dra'kesh lands. And if it wasn't for me being able to speak any orc tongue, we still wouldn't know what's going on."

"Alderin, what *is* going on?" yelled Dran in human from across the tavern.

"Now, we're trapped deep in Sa'bara lands, far away from home because we were tricked by it. If anyone has the *right* to show this kobold some *respect* it would be me and my friends," he said.

Garran took a moment to stare him down, looking over to Dran, then back at him. "Is that so?"

"Yes! Your minor slight is nothing compared to the weeks I had to travel with its never-ending demands and freezing body temperature. Do you know what's it is to feel like you are freezing in the middle of summer!"

Garran pulled out a dagger and up towards Alderin's face. "Are you saying that you, a human - an outsider human at that - have the right to teach *this* kobold a lesson?"

"I do! Do you have a problem with that?" asked Alderin, standing his ground, putting his hands on the hilt of his weapon, after putting his gloves back on.

Garran chuckled and withdrew his blade. "I like you. She's *all* yours."

The human smirked, walking to Histra who gave him a deathly glare. "You lowly human y-" she replied before Alderin kicked her right between the legs, lifting her up into the air, and with cat-like reflexes, grabbed her by the neck and pinned her against the wall. His fingers squeezed on her throat, the kobold gasping for air, claws grabbing onto the human's arm, digging into him, drawing blood. Her feet kicked in the air while her eyes stayed locked on his.

"I've had it with whatever you have to say, you got that *kobold*?!" he yelled, giving her a subtle wink before banging the back of her body up against the wall.

She growled in return, claws digging deeper into his arm. Alderin smacked her against the wall again. "You have no idea how much I've wanted to do this since the day we met!"

Alderin's tight grip blocked the flow of Histra's chilling breath fluid as some of it was squeezed up her throat, dribbling out of the corners of her mouth, hitting Alderin's glove, flash freezing wherever it touched.

The orcs cheered him on. "You have no idea how many hardships we've been through just because of you. Now we're stuck here, and do you realize how much trouble we are going to be in with the dragons because of you? *Do you*?!" yelled Alderin, smacking her against the wall again and again. Histra continued to gasp for breath as he pulled her away, carrying her to the entrance. She struggled and growled along the way, her wings weakly flapping.

"Needless to say, this is my resignation to your services and the money you gave me is mine!" he yelled, throwing her right out the front door. "You want to lord over something, lord over the dirt, but that might be too above you!" he said, the door closing behind her while she was still tumbling through the air.

Alderin turned around as he felt a heavy hand smack against his chest, which almost sent him toppling over. "Couldn't have said it better myself. I would have liked a few more hits in, but she's kept me from my group's celebration long enough as it is. Invite your dwarf friend," he said, calling over to the bartender. "Whatever bill that kobold racked up, it's on me. I like this guy! He has guts!" yelled Garran, dragging Alderin over.

Alderin called to Dran to join them, who looked at the turn of events with growing concern, "What happened?" he asked, eyeing the orcs, but with a pleasant smile tattooed onto his face.

"Your friend here got you invited to join our celebration that's what," said Garran in human tongue.

"Alderin?" he asked.

"Go with it," he replied as the two were about to take seats where there was untouched food and drink laid out, but as they were about to sit the nearby orcs pulled out their weapons and blocked their way.

"Some party," said Dran, resting his hand about to go for his weapon, giving Alderin a look of concern.

Garran cleared his throat, explaining in human tongue, "Forgive my friends. I did not realize you did not understand our traditions. Take a seat that doesn't already have food and drink," he explained, quickly informing his companions of the miscommunication.

"It's true, we don't know," replied Alderin in orc as he and Dran found a place down at the end of the table.

Alderin watched for a moment, taking note of three untouched meals. "What is this custom?" he asked.

Garran, who sat at the middle of the table, eyed the two, taking a long swig of his drink before replying, "This is a celebration of our group's very recent success, but it's also to respect and honor the three who could not be here to partake in it. We honor their sacrifice with one final shared meal with us," he explained as Alderin translated to Dran.

"A good tradition," Dran said, food and drink being laid out before him.

Before this conversation took place, another happened, when Histra was thrown out of the tavern. She instinctively spread her wings, attempting to flap them, but before she was even able to try, she hit the ground face first into the dusty grungy dirt. She rolled over three times before sliding to a stop on her back. Nearby horses bound to a post neighed and tugged at their reins. Her body twitched, slowly trying get back up, feeling a pressure building up within her.

Histra's claws dug into the ground as a cold rush ran up her throat, her body tensing as she threw up an icy blue liquid. The moment it hit the ground, ice formed and spread outwards, like a butterfly spreading its wings, with the ice half an inch at its thickest. She gasped for breath, coughing up a much smaller amount of freezing liquid which merely thickened the ice in front of her.

"I will kill that human for this," she growled in draconic, claws digging into the dirt. She spat of what remained off to the side, freezing the ground. Despite the unintentional release of her chilling breath, there was a clear border around her where the ice stopped.

"Histra are you okay?" said Jesmine, who was standing just off to the side next to the stabled horses. She rushed up to her, moving around the melting ice, reaching to touch her on the back when Histra spread her wings wide and yelled.

"Don't touch me!"

Jesmine recoiled. "I'm just…"

"Don't you dare touch me," she said, a growl rumbling from her throat.

Jesmine spoke a bit louder. "Histra, I think you've had too much to drink, come this way, off to the side." She motioned her towards the carts that were filled with wild animals.

The kobold let out a growled grunt, flicking her wings, looking up into her concerned face. She glanced around to see a few orc spectators watching at a distance, muttering to their neighbors but quickly stopping when she caught their gaze. She gritted her teeth. "Fine."

Histra took several deep breaths and pulled herself together, coughing. "We'll go over there," she said, heading to the carts. The animals became increasing agitated, starting to rattle the cages and pulled at their shackles. The wooden carts creaked under their shifting weight. "A little noisy, aren't they?" she complained.

"It will make it harder for people to hear us wouldn't it?"

"True… let's move under this one just in case the orcs come and check out what the noise is all about," she suggested, guiding Jesmine underneath the cart with the cloth over the cage.

"Why this one?" asked Jesmine, looking at the cloth-covered cage just a moment before ducking underneath with her.

"It's quieter."

She nodded, noticing that the chains ran through the wheels of all of the carts, which had thick metal locks in place, the chains growing taut as they shifted, except for the one they were under, and the beast that Zed slept.

"First we need to get out of here. My cover is blown, and we only have a small window to get everything and go. I didn't want to leave in the middle of the night with the bandit problem, but now we have no choice... just me and you and the gnome. As much as I'd love to repay Alderin for what he did, that's not an option," Histra said.

"You can't just abandon them."

"*Watch* me."

"What about your promise?"

"I promised to get *you* to where you need to go, not *them*."

"Histra... do you really want to prove to them the way they think about you?"

Histra cocked an eye ridge. "Do you honestly think I care?"

She sighed. "No."

She smirked, "You're not as naïve as I thought."

"I could say the same about you," Jesmine said.

She tensed, "What?"

"You are so focused on who is out to get you that you didn't even realize Alderin saved you from those orcs."

Histra twitched. "Sav—saved? Did you just infer he saved me?!" Her wings spreading out slightly.

She nodded again. "Yeah. He said he was going to give you a signal of some kind. I think he said a wink."

Histra stood there in silence for a moment. "A wink? What the heck does a wink mean?!"

"Honestly... I don't know either."

She let out a long, drawn out sigh, saying in draconic, "Stupid humans."

"Do you understand now? He did what he did for a show, so he could get you out of there and not have you be trampled by a bunch of orcs."

Histra turned her back to her. "Either way we need to—"

"If you are going to leave tonight, could you help me get out of here and take me along?" asked a soft, sweet, yet hoarse-sounding voice in human coming from above the cart.

Jesmine and Histra froze as they looked around. "Who said that?" Jesmine asked.

"I did. The one in the cage behind the curtain."

Jesmine moved from under the cart, grabbing the drape.

"What are you doing?" Histra asked, glaring at her.

"I'm going to see who it is."

"You don't know who or what it could be. I wouldn't recommend that. It could be one of those monsters that laying your eyes upon it could—" Histra stopped, seeing she had already picked up the corner of the curtain and was peaking underneath, remarking in draconic, "And she's a wizard?"

Despite the darkness, Jesmine's sharp elven eyes could make out the form of a female humanoid, seeing her naked form, causing a pit to form in her stomach. Her skin colored like a pale moon, her dark as night hair so long it almost came down to her butt. She stood on the balls of her feet, holding herself, arms chained across her chest. A heavy set of shackles were locked around her wrists and ankles with an equally heavy collar around her neck, which left little wiggle room.

She looked down at Jesmine, a glimpse of her midnight blue eyes reflected with what little light reached them. "If you would be so kind to get me out of here, I'll be forever grateful," she said in elvish.

Jesmine's eyes widened. "How did you… never mind. I have a friend, who can hopefully get you out. It might take a moment. If I may just have some of your patience," she responded in kind.

"Hurry. I don't know how long those orcs will be occupied with their celebration."

"Don't worry," she pulled her head from under the curtain and returned her focus to Histra.

"You know it could have been a trap. You have no idea what those orcs captured and why they had to have it covered."

"There are no such creatures in Sa'bara's lands."

"They could have traded for one."

"Do you have to be so untrustworthy of everything?"

"It keeps me alive. That's what matters."

"Not always... but I'm going to get Alderin."

"Are you seriously just going to release whoever or whatever is under there?"

"It's another elf from these lands. I recognized her accent when she spoke in human tongue."

"Sounded more guttural to me."

"Trust me I know. We need to save her."

"This is a bad idea."

Jesmine gave her a cold stare. "How could you even suggest that? With everything that has happened."

Histra's nostrils flared, raising a claw about to say something but stopped for just a moment before continuing. "You know... you're right. This will bring us trouble but that's already happened. My job is to get to where you need to go. Just remember you are making my job harder but go ahead. Save her. You have my support."

Jesmine smiled. "Thank you Histra. I knew you weren't as cold as you let on."

She sighed and rolled her eyes.

"I didn't mean it that way."

"I know. I'll be here. Go. If those orcs dragged him into their celebration, it might take some time to get him away from them without raising suspicion, and let me remind you, we only have so much time to leave before word spreads about what happened."

"I know. I'll be back soon."

Jesmine rushed off as Histra climbed up the wheel to reach the top of the wagon. There she slipped underneath the curtain, catching the predatory stare of the elven woman.

Histra shrugged off the look as she examined the cage and the woman inside. "I knew it. I don't have a sense of smell like you do, but at this distance even I can tell."

The elf didn't react to the cold around her, her breath fogging, though impossible to see in the darkness. "And you have the smell of death, it's been rather unpleasant."

She cocked an eye ridge. "Right. Another who doesn't like kobolds. This is going to be... interesting."

The woman growled and tugged on her chains.

"Don't worry. I'm not going to do anything to ruin your current plans. As long as it doesn't interfere with mine."

"If you don't intend to enslave me for your own needs. We will not have an issue."

Histra grinned. "Excellent. I have no intention of bothering myself with you."

"Good," she replied with another chain tug as Histra slipped out from under the curtain and back underneath the cart.

Jesmine entered the inn as the upbeat mood Garran's group brought with them spread throughout the place. The musicians in the corner picked up, a few coins tossed their way as the elf went over to Gnemi, who had been standing on a chair at the empty table, keeping an eye on everyone from a distance.

He looked up to her as she approached. "How did it go?" he asked.

"Well... but we have something new to deal with. How are the other two?"

"They are busy hanging with the orcs. It seems to be going amazingly well. Apparently, what Alderin did really helped hit it off with them."

"That's good, but do you think that we can get them away? We have to leave tonight."

"I think it's possible. But I am not sure how. I'm not too good with socializing and I don't even know the language."

"I think I have a plan, but first can you get everything from our room and get it outside? Especially the clothes I was wearing earlier? I want you to take them to our friend. She's outside by those carts."

Gnemi looked at her curiously. "Alright... there a reason for this?"

"It'll become clear soon enough."

"I'll get it done."

"Thank you Gnemi."

"Not a problem," he replied, hopping off the chair, rushing to their room. None of the orcs even noticing him as he moved about.

Jesmine quietly moved through the aisles between tables, the sounds of orcs clanking mugs together, laughter, and a few drunken arguments filled the room. She got within line of sight of Alderin who was busy telling a story of his own.

"And that is what it's like living in Dra'kesh lands," Alderin explained in human.

"I can confirm it's like this," Dran added, "We're from two different areas, so normally we'd be fighting each other. I find it enlightening to converse with someone outside of my area without the concern I am going to be killed or robbed."

Garran took a long swig of his drink before slamming it down on the table, motioning the nearby bar maiden to refill his mug. "Well that is something. It makes me feel better I am within Sa'bara's lands. Sure, we have to watch what we say but at least we can be our own people and not be arbitrary broken up on a dragon's whim."

"It's certainly strange to see how one dragon rules their land compared to the other," Alderin said.

Garran leaned back, finishing his drink. The barmaid came and topped everyone off. "You know, I am feeling generous. How about I talk to a few people to get you migrated over here? There are human settlements, and I'm sure you can find a good life."

Alderin looked at him curiously, the orc giving a toothy grin, his tusks jutting out. "Isn't something like that forbidden?"

"Yes, but as I said, I know a few people and I'm influential enough to get it done. I'm sure the great dragon Sa'bara and the other ancients are smart enough to have something in place just in case something like this were to occur. You were tricked to come over here. Instead of making a difficult and dangerous trek across the border, you might as well stay."

"I don't know... sounds risky," he said, his brown eyes focused on him.

"Hardly. If you remain honest, the worst that could happen is Sa'bara will deny the request and you'd be forced to go back. If it's an official crossing, less should happen to you."

"Should..."

"Garran why are you so helpful with this human and dwarf? Influential or not, it can be risky to meddle in these affairs," Zed said in orcish.

"He's a fighter, he doesn't let what life has dealt him stop him. I like that. Better than some of the squabbling humans we've run into."

One of the other orcs spoke up, "It's because he beat the shit out of his lying former boss isn't it?"

Garran replied in orcish with a chuckle. "It's a reason."

"It is a tempting offer bu—" Alderin said, catching Jesmine out of the corner of his eye. She not so inconspicuously winked at him several times, "But I'll be right back. My wife needs me."

Garran looked over to Jesmine, who stopped what she was doing, "That's your wife?"

"Yup."

"You humans should really get women with some meat on their bones. You need strong women to have strong children."

"That's my wife you're talking about."

Garran chuckled. "Relax. Bring her over. Let her join the party."

"She's shy and doesn't know any orc tongue and... she's had some trouble with orc raiders. I told you about them."

Garran gave a long, hard stare at her, who tensed before his attention turned to Alderin. "Shame."

"It is, but I'll be back soon. Thank you for all your kindness," Alderin replied in human.

Garran gave a nod, softly remarking to himself in orcish, "Such frilly words."

Alderin rushed over to Jesmine, whispering, "What is it? Why are you winking like that?"

"I wanted to get your attention without others knowing."

"That's... never mind," he said. "What is it?" he asked, catching out of the corner of his eye, Gnemi rushing through the room and out the door with Jesmine's old clothes and a few other items. "We're leaving tonight, aren't we?"

"Yes."

"I figured. Word of what happened to it will get around, which means we don't have much time, but Dran and I are stuck with some very joyful orcs. It will take us a while to get away."

"I need you right now," she said, reaching and gently grabbed his shirt, leaning in.

"Uh... well," he responded, looking at her curiously.

"Do you have your tools on you?"

"My tools?"

"For... you know," Jesmine leaned in close and whispered, "For locks."

Alderin's eyes widened, quirking an eyebrow, "Oh... OH! Yes, yes, I always keep those on me."

"I'm in need of your skills outside. The sooner the better."

He glanced at Garran and the other orcs, noticing they are lost once more in their celebration. "Alright, but make it look like you are leading me away."

"I am," Jesmine said, tugging at him.

"Why is your wife the one in charge?" yelled Garran, watching them walk away.

"She's stronger than she looks!" said Alderin in orcish, Garran letting out a laugh as Jesmine took him outside and over to the carts. There, Gnemi was standing near Histra underneath one.

"What... what's going on here?" Alderin asked, crouching down, looking around for anyone noticing them.

"I need you to please get someone out of a cage," Jesmine explained.

"What?!" he exclaimed.

"Shh, not so loud," she urged.

"You two are so inconspicuous," stated Histra with a sigh.

Alderin and Histra stared off at each other. "We need to get out of here, not break someone out of a cage. These are the orcs Dran and I are hanging out with. They appear to be professional hunters, and it would be dangerous to anger them. No one knows what we are up to, meaning no one is after us. This would chan—"

"She's an elf. She needs our help. This shouldn't be any different than before, right?" Jesmine asked.

Histra poked her head from under the cart and looked up at him with a smug grin. "Yeah, this shouldn't be any different. If I recall, you said you'd save Jesmine regardless if she'd help you or not."

Alderin raised an eyebrow. "You're agreeing with this?"

"Of course. After being trapped in a cage for a decade, I feel *sympathy* for others in the same position."

"Right...'sympathy' she says..."

"We'll probably be better off if we get this done quickly," Gnemi suggested.

Alderin looked around, Jesmine saying, "Is there a problem, Alderin?"

"No. None at all. I was just surprised," he replied.

She pointed to the cloth covered cage. "She's under there."

He climbed onto the cart, lifting the curtain up. "Keep a lookout," he said, giving one last look around. "I'm surprised there aren't any guards."

"They've locked the wheels tight. On top of that they are mourning their dead. They'd invite everyone who knew them, leaving anyone out would be an insult to their memory," Histra explained.

"How do you know that?" Gnemi asked.

"I've seen it."

"Right, right."

"Just keep a lookout," said Alderin, slipping under the covers to see the dark shadowy form of the elven woman who stared at him with predatory eyes. "Damn it's hard to see in here."

"I'll help with that," Jesmine replied, taking a moment to focus her magic, conjuring up a single ball of dim light, slipping it under the curtain. "Does this help?" she asked the woman's eyes giving an eerie reflection in the light.

"Yes, thanks."

"I will try to keep it steady, and bright enough to let you work, but not be seen through the curtain either. Since I can't see my spell it weakens my control over it."

"It's fine, thank you," he replied, pulling out his lock picks from a side pouch. "Don't worry we'll get you out soon."

"Thank you," she said in a soft but slightly gruff voice, her body twitching in anticipation, causing the chains to rattle.

Alderin adverted his eyes from looking at her bare form, "What is it with orcs and keeping you all naked? I'm noticing a disturbing trend here."

"Just hurry before they show," the woman remarked, watching him with an intent stare.

He tinkered with the first lock, replying, "Working on it. This lock is more difficult than I was expecting, but nothing I can't handle."

The elven woman took a deep breath, slowly releasing it, letting her body grow slightly limp. "Good… so the other one knows magic?"

Alderin nodded. "Yeah."

"Interesting. I wasn't expecting to see an elf here. Especially one that knows magic."

"It's a complicated story. I am sure yours is too."

"As true as we have one sun and two moons," she responded.

"Right," he replied, the lock clicking open. Alderin steadily opened the door, which made an uneasy squeaky noise, just enough to get better access to her shackles.

Jesmine crouched down, keeping a vague eye on the surroundings, softly muttering and moving her hands, looking in the direction of her spell every so often.

Histra walked to the other end of the cart, looking out from under it.

"Histra?" asked Gnemi, who was looking in the opposite direction.

She sighed. "Yes?"

"I know this might be a silly question. But when I saw you covered in that layer of ice in your room, I'd been meaning to ask. Do you get cold? Or are you just extremely warm in the summer heat?"

"Keep a look out. It's best not to be idly chatting, it might draw attention from people who have ears."

Gnemi slumped his shoulders, resuming his look out duties.

Alderin grinned, managing to undo the lock around the elf's wrists. The shackles swung free and hit the side of the cage, ringing out with a metallic clang.

Everyone froze in place, waiting for anything immediate to happen, the tension broke by Alderin. "What the…" he said as the elven woman was about to instinctively rub her wrists but only found that the shackles were part of a cover of another set of silver-blue metal bindings with stern lettering engraved along the sides. "Another set of shackles?"

"I was knocked out when they put me in here. I didn't even know these existed," she remarked.

Alderin examined them, running his fingers across the solid metal bands, finding not a single break in them. "I don't even see a way to remove these. But since they aren't attached to anything, we'll worry about them later."

"I'd like to get them removed but getting out of this cage is preferred," she said, running her hands over the cuffs for only a moment before pulling them away. "Perhaps these are magically locked onto me."

"You say magic?" Jesmine whispered.

"Worry about it later," Alderin replied.

She nodded, the human working his way down the shackles holding her in bondage, and as each piece were removed, it only revealed another pair of the same type underneath. When the last piece holding her place, her collar was removed, it too had another set, but before the chains even slid fully off her, she leapt out of the cage knocking him over.

"Hey, what the…" Alderin held back a louder exclamation as the elven woman landed between the cart and the inn. The cloth on the cage almost completely carried off with her. She breathed heavily through her nose, taking stock of her surroundings.

Jesmine released her spell, approaching her with a friendly smile. "Hello, here's some clothes," said Jesmine, holding them out to her.

The freed elf turned to Jesmine.

"Best you put these on to not draw notice."

She stared at the clothes for a moment. "Yes, right, good idea" she replied.

"Sorry I haven't asked this before, but what's your name?"

She slipped on her clothes, brushing her long hair out of the way the best she could, replying, "Ariana."

"Nice to meet you Ariana, my name is Jesmine. The one who freed you is Alderin, over there is Gnemi."

He waved. "Hello."

"And the one over there is Histra."

"We've exchanged names already," said Histra, still watching for any trouble. "It's best we get moving."

Alderin closed the cage pulling the cloth back over it. "Eager or not, you didn't have to jump out of the cage like that," he replied, slipping down. "I've never seen such strange looking cuffs before."

"It looks like mithril," said Jesmine, getting a closer look.

"Mithril?" he asked. "I've never seen it before." Histra casually walked over to the group taking note of the discovery.

Jesmine explained, "That doesn't surprise me. Mithril is extremely hard to mine and refine, and even outside its already legendary physical properties it's the best magically conductive metal, which makes it even more heavily sought after."

"If it's so valuable, why is it used as mere shackles?" asks Alderin.

"It's because they consider her valuable enough to use them," answered Histra.

"Why weren't they attached to the other shackles instead of underneath? Better yet, how do you get them off? I saw no lock or break in the metal."

"You need to know the command word to unlock them," Jesmine said.

"I'm sure that orc wizard knows it, but he'd be too smart to tell me."

"These things are troublesome," said Ariana grunting, constantly rubbing the shackles, adjusting her clothes in a vain attempt to get comfortable.

"There are other ways to break them, but for that… I'll need my book."

Ariana's eyes lit up. "Well go get your book. Get these off me."

"That's the tricky part…" Jesmine trailed off.

"I'll trust you in telling what she needs to know. I need to get back before the orcs get suspicious," said Alderin, heading off.

"Good idea. But do your best to get yourself and Dran away from them as soon as possible. Gnemi, do think you can get the rest of our personal effects from the room?"

"That should be easy enough. I believe due to their heavy drinking and my small stature that they won't even notice me."

"Excellent, once you get back, we'll head to our cart."

"So where is your book? Is it in the room?" Ariana asked, Gnemi heading off.

"No. That is why we're here. We're out to get my spellbook."

"Where is it?" she asked, constantly looking around, taking deep breaths through her nose.

"In the center of Du'ralia Forest."

Ariana's eyes grew cold and narrow, shoulders slumping, "What?"

"That's where it is."

"Why would it be there?" asked Ariana as Histra walked in between the two.

"Because that is where it is. Now are you going to try to head off on your own, or do you want to come with us? The city gates are locked at night and you are going to need us to open them,"

Histra explained.

"I don't have much of a choice," Ariana said.

"I'm sorry about this. I know you probably want to get those cuffs off and out of Sa'bara lands as fast as possible, but we need to head in deeper."

"Right. Yes. Exactly," said Ariana, looking down at Histra, who was already walking away from the two, resuming her look out position.

Alderin entered the tavern, the music having gotten even more joyful as the bar maidens rush to keep up with demand. When he reached the table with Dran, Garran, and the others, a buff but smaller-than-Garran red-skinned female orc with a single braided long black hair, was in the middle of telling a story. The left side of her face was scarred by a claw mark that went just below her yellow-green eye, and on the same side her tusk was permanently broken at the root which was only visible when she spoke while the other had a golden ring placed around the base. She stared at Dran. "Then I shot two arrows right between its eyes. The massive beast hit the ground so hard that the land shook. I saved Zed's life over there," she said, pointing to him.

"I had it under control," he replied with a soft grunt, banging his mug on the table after taking a hearty drink.

"Shana, do you not understand that the dwarf doesn't speak our tongue? He has no clue what you are saying," Garran remarked with a drunken orcish slur.

Dran kept a firm demeanor, only occasionally surveying those around him, noticing Alderin's returned, who spoke in orcish, "We had to talk about what has been going on. She's been concerned about will happen to us."

"I'm glad to have you back. I haven't understood hide nor hair of what any of these orcs have been saying outside of Garran, and that's only when he speaks human tongue to me, to which I much appreciate," said Dran, giving Garran a nod.

"I understand humans have weaker women. It would concern me too," Garran replied to Alderin as he sat down.

"She can handle herself but there is just a lot of uncertainty right now. Much of which, even with your offer, is very troubling."

"Of course."

Alderin cleared his throat and then spoke in orcish, "Can you tell me a bit about your fallen friends? This is a party for them, and it would only be fair to know something about them, since we are partaking in this celebration."

The orc paused for a moment, grinning. "A human with not only respect for himself but for others. I like that. Of course, we'll tell you about them but first," he said, commanding one of his men across the table, "Check our cargo."

Alderin muffled his reaction, inquiring, "I saw some of what you brought into town. Is selling beasts worth the risk?"

"Some are. Especially during Draksind when there are gladiatorial fights in honor of Sa'bara. None of us will be participating in the games, we are simply suppliers of entertainment."

Alderin nodded, ignoring the stumbling drunken orc heading outside, "That's interesting tell me more."

Meanwhile back outside Jesmine said, "It shouldn't be too much longer till Gnemi comes out and we can head to the wagon."

Ariana tensed, saying, "Sooner we move the better, I prefer not to be caught moments after being freed." She lifts her head looking toward the bar's entrance, grabbing Jesmine's hand with a surprisingly strong grip, pulling her underneath.

"What is it?" she asked.

"Quiet," said Ariana, crouching low to the ground, her body tensing, toes digging into the dirt, quietly staring out in the direction of the bar's entrance.

A moment later a stumbling, green skinned orc came into view. "Check the carts. He must be having one of his feelings," he slurred in orcish with mild annoyance, peeking through the bars of the cages.

He walked over towards them. Histra slowly backed away and toward the tavern, the orc stumbling, falling over but managed to catch himself on the very cart they are hiding under.

Jesmine covered her mouth, Ariana tensing, taking slow deep silent breaths, shifting her body weight uneasily on her bare callus feet.

The orc let out a belch, righting himself, spitting at the cloth-covered cage. "Infernal creature," he remarked, walking down the line before moving back toward the bar entrance where he almost stumbled over Gnemi in the process. "Watch it!" he grunted almost kicking the gnome, who dodged out of the way, arms full of items.

He turned the corner, running to them.

"We should go now," Histra said.

"That was close," Jesmine remarked.

"What happened?" asked Gnemi.

"Nothing to worry about. Did you see how Alderin and Dran are doing?"

"Having a few more drinks."

"Good, keeps the orcs busy," said Histra as the group rushed off towards the blacksmith. In the moonless night, the only light to be had was from the faint twinkling stars above and a few lit lanterns from a building here and there and along the city wall. They reached the blacksmith's shop to find the doors closed and shrouded in darkness.

"They've already loaded the cart for us? And they didn't even try to lock the wheels. Are they just asking for someone to come steal our wagon with all our food on it?" she grumbled.

Jesmine sighed. "Histra, can you be a bit more positive?"

"I'm sorry, were you the one that just got beaten against a wall today?" she grunted.

She let out another sigh. "Ariana, climb onto the wagon and please do your best to get comfortable and hide yourself. Histra and I will get the horses."

"What about me?" Gnemi asked.

"Keep Ariana company, we hopefully shouldn't be gone long."

"Then we are out of here before what influence I have is gone," said Histra as they headed to the stables.

"Shouldn't we find someone?" Jesmine asked, reaching her hand out in front of her, into the darkness.

"No, just grab our horses and let's get going. If they come to stop us, I'll know what to do."

"Histra…"

"What?"

"You could at least vocalize your plans more."

"What's there to say? I'll do what I've been doing so far. Now get the horses."

"You can say 'please'."

Histra glared at her as she mouthed the words. "You know why."

Jesmine sighed, cautiously heading into the stables, taking her time to get close enough to locate and identify the horses, "Easy, easy, I know it's difficult to move in the dark," she said, the horses neighing as she guided them out.

"Who goes there!" yelled an orc in orcish from on top of the wall. He lit a torch from a hanging lantern that was nearby, peering over the side. Jesmine stopped, looking up at him, while trying to keep the horses calm, tightly holding onto the reins. "What are you doing with those horses?" he yelled with a grunt as two more guards rushed along the top of the wall to their location.

"I told you not to mind the orcs. Now come, I want to leave now, not later," Histra yelled at Jesmine, two of the orcs notching arrows. She noticed the orcs, yelling to them, "I am getting my horses so I can be going. I'm already behind schedule, and I prefer not to keep the dragons waiting."

The orc with the torch, moves in her direction, letting out a grunt, "It's that kobold."

"Excuse me? What did you just say? Is there a problem with me getting *my* own horses? I was informed that everything was handled. So, what's the problem?" Histra yelled with a glare.

Another orc came from a small single room shack near the stables, letting out a big mouthed yawn, holding out a lantern in his hands. "What's going on here? Who's touching the horses?"

Jesmine brought the horses to Histra. "Go to the smith shop, I'll handle the rest," she stated.

"As you wish," she replied.

"Hey! You can't just take the horses!" yelled the orc, running over to them, but as Histra stepped in his way, the orc almost tripped over himself to stop.

"What did you just say? Did you say I could not get my own horses?!" she growled, spreading her wings out.

"Ah… oh. You're the one I've been told about."

"Yes. I am. Is there a problem? I'd like to leave now. And I don't need *your* permission to do so." The orc tensed slightly. "Perhaps Dra'kesh will like to hear about the disrespect and hindrance you've given me, or better yet, I could pass the message over to Sa'bara. Hmm?"

The orc shook his head. "No. No. I was surprised. I did not want some horse thief to take what is yours. Now that I see it's you, everything is good."

"That's what I thought. Now go back to whatever you were doing," she said, pivoting on her foot, walking away.

The orc's shoulders slumped slightly, giving her a mean glare, returning. The orcs on top of the wall dispersed, the one orc putting out the torch light, muttering, "Kobolds."

While that transpired, Ariana moved things around, making a hiding spot for herself. She nervously looked around, sniffing the air. Gnemi climbed to the front of the cart. "Things should get better," he said.

Ariana jerked her head over to him. "Things can never get better."

"That sounds a little pessimistic, doesn't it?"

She sniffed the air a few more times. "It's not safe here."

"We're in the middle of an orc village. I believe it's self-evident."

Ariana stared at him for a moment, Gnemi feeling a tingle down his spine as she hid behind the barrels.

Gnemi walked to the back of the cart, "Need any help?"

"No."

He stopped at the firm response and a few moments later he asked, "How did you end up getting captured by all those orcs?"

Ariana's head popped up over a barrel, giving him a long, hard, cold stare.

"Sorry, I understand that it's probably difficult to talk about," he replied, giving her some room. A little while later, Jesmine and Histra returned with the horses. Together they quickly hitched two to the wagon and temporarily tied the other two to the side of the cart.

"Wait here please. I'm going to get the others," Jesmine said.

"We'll be here," Gnemi said.

"Sorry for the wait. I'll be back as soon as I can," she replied, rushing off.

He slumped in the front seat of the cart, while Histra climbed into the back. "Sorry about Histra, she can't control her cold aura."

"Why are you apologizing?" Histra asked.

"I just want to be informative to our new guest. Is that wrong?"

"She can figure it out. She's smart enough."

"Ariana you're quiet. Are you doing okay?" Gnemi asked.

She peeked her head up, making a quieting hand motion. Histra eyed her for a moment, sniffing the air again. Her tail twitched, looking around. "Excellent idea. It's best not to wake the others," she remarked, finding a spot to sit and relax, feet kicked up onto a sack.

Gnemi sighed, thinking, *"Two people I would love to know more about, and neither appear to be talkative types. Wonderful."*

Jesmine entered the inn where the celebrations were going on as strong as ever, despite the crowd in the tavern having thinned out. She moved over to the same spot from before, looking at Alderin.

Alderin nursed his drink, speech slightly slurred, while Dran's words were showing some signs of being strung together, spots of his beard were damp from his multiple ales. Alderin immediately caught her standing there, giving him a wink. He sighed loudly. "Excuse me, Garran, but it seems my wife needs me again."

He glanced over at her, then back at him. "Go. She's important to you," he replied, his words slurring.

"Dran, why don't you come with me? Maybe you can help ease some of her concerns?" he suggested.

The dwarf chugged the rest of his drink, banging it onto the table with a thud, letting out a delighted sigh, "Alright," he replied, standing up with a slight wobble, his first steps a little unbalanced, before he recovered, speaking once they were out of ear shot, "What is it? I can tell you two have been up to something."

"We're going," said Jesmine just loud enough for the two of them to hear. Garran gave a cursory glance before returning to the party at hand.

"What about my things in the room?" he asked.

"Gnemi has already gotten everything," she explained, guiding them out of the inn.

"Things have gotten complicated Dran," said Alderin once they were far enough away.

His face grew stern, his brown eyes giving off the faintest reflection from a distant lit lantern, his slur in his speech slightly fading. "What happened?" he asked, Alderin explaining everything, finishing when they reached the others.

"Aye, you did good, but this will draw the ire of the orcs, which will be a problem."

"If they find out we are the ones that 'stole' from them after sharing all those drinks? Orcs are vengeful by nature. It won't be just a problem for us." Alderin said.

"They didn't give the feeling of bad folk, not that I could understand what most of them were bloody saying," he replied, mounting up on his horse, "But you are right. Let's hope they don't figure out it was us."

"I was surprised by how hospitable they were. That Garran fellow sounded like a nice guy. I never thought I'd say that about an orc. I don't know how to feel about this situation," Alderin said.

"Are you two done talking? We need to go to the other gate before what good will I have is gone," Histra grunted.

"Good will? I didn't think you had any to begin with," Dran replied, rolling his eyes.

Watching from the darkness in their room above the shop, Beslba stood in her kobold form, thinking, *"Well now. This certainly makes things more interesting…"*

Ariana remained low and hidden between the barrels, her nostrils flaring, staring in the direction of the kobold, unable to see anything. Her muscles remained tensed, ears open, while they made their way to a barred and locked gate on the other side of town.

"Who goes there?" asked an orc guard, stepping out from the shadows into the lantern light.

"Open the gate, we are leaving," stated Histra, walking to the side of the cart where the orc was standing.

"Leaving? During a no moons night?"

"Yes, I have already been delayed enough."

"But there are bandits that have been preying on travelers. It's not safe to go at night," he responded, the group recognizing him as one of the orcs they met yesterday.

"Did I ask you for your advice? I told you to open the gate and let us through. I'm already late and I need to make up for lost time. Those with me can handle a few simple bandits."

"Very well," the orc replied, removing the heavy wooden bar across the gate before pushing the doors open which creaked and groaned. The group pushed through seeing bonfires out in the fields surrounding the town, lighting the area. The gate closed and locked behind them. Ariana peeked over a barrel at the town unable to see the orc guards patrolling the top.

"Alderin…" growled Histra once they were far enough away that the town was now a faint glow in the distance.

"What is it?" he asked with a sigh, slowing Cetas just enough to bring himself in parallel to her, but outside her cold aura.

"I will warn you once. If you ever do something like that to me again, I'll make sure you'll find a cold, untimely death. Do I make myself clear?"

"Histra!" Jesmine exclaimed.

Ariana turned her head to the statement, watching silently. Dran brought his horse over to them. "After all that happened, that is what you have to say for yourself?!" he exclaimed, his hand resting on the hilt of his blade.

"Sorry, but I don't think you'd take too kindly to be suddenly bashed, beaten, kicked in the crotch, and then tossed out like a piece of trash, without ANY warning that this was part of some plan," Histra stated with a growl.

He looked at the kobold's vague darkened outline shape, "I saved your life from those orcs, and this is the thanks I get? A death threat?"

"A little warning would have been nice," she growled.

"Warning?!" he let out an exacerbated huff, "In a tavern full of rowdy orcs?! I had to act fast. You should be grateful for what I did! I even took the time to wink at you to let you know I had a plan."

"A wink? What does a wink mean? It could mean you have something in your eye."

"How can you not know of it?"

"Honestly… I didn't know about it either," Jesmine said.

"For the love of… does anyone else not know that winking could be used as a sign of 'trust me', 'I got this', 'follow my lead'."

"I didn't to be honest…" Gnemi said.

Alderin let out a defeated sigh. "Look, I did what I could. I saved your life. I didn't do it for your gratitude. I did it for Jesmine because you are our guide to get through this damn place. And you did well fooling those dumb orcs but next time, how about you tell *us* the plan and not leave it up to chance?"

Histra glared at him. "I tell you what you need to know to

increase our survival, that is all."

"Right, while you threaten *me* because *you* wanted a *warning* about a *plan*, you don't bother to do that with others! Damn, hypocritical kobolds," he grunted, pulling his horse ahead.

"It's okay Alderin. I knew what a wink meant," Dran said.

"Keep a lookout and don't make so much noise. I've been warned by several that there are bandits in the area. So, despite it being so dark, no light magic, Jesmine."

"I understand," she replied.

"I'll do my best so that we don't get lost but we should put some distance between us and the town. Those orcs aren't going to be too pleased once they discover that we took the elf."

"Right. Before we had the luxury of not being a target. I can only hope they don't realize it was us," Alderin said.

"What else could we have done? We couldn't have left Ariana there," said Jesmine.

"I know, it's just that... This is already not what I was expecting."

"I'm sorry you have to go far out of your way for me, but she's another survivor from Sa'bara's extermination. I couldn't just standby and do nothing."

Histra smiled, watching the conversation back and forth between Alderin and Jesmine with Dran adding a few supporting comments to Jesmine's case. Ariana held up her head sniffing the air. The wind suddenly shifted, and with it, she tensed, calling out, "Turn off the path. There are bandits up ahead."

The group's conversation ceased at Ariana's words. Alderin asked, "What? How could you know?"

"Even I'm having a difficult time seeing, how could you bloody know that?" asked Dran.

Ariana tensed. "It's hard to explain. Do it. Go that way." She pointed towards what looked like a half-grown farm field.

"Do it," Histra commanded.

"Why?" Alderin asked.

"You want to get there without an issue? Just do it, and without so much back talk. There are bandits out there and I prefer not to get ambushed due to your blabbering."

He grunted, muttering, "If it wasn't for Jesmine…" He tugged on the reins as they moved into field. Arianna kept a tense look out, constantly sniffing the air, keeping the party out of harm's way, as they pushed on through the night.

The following day, the orcs groaned, some grumbling about how bright it was, others complaining about headaches.

"You call yourselves orcs?!" exclaimed Garran, holding a piece of raw meat in his hand, approaching the cloth covered cart.

"It was a long night of drinking my friend," said Zed, before muttering in orcish-arcana, his rune engraved tusks glowing a soft green.

"Time for your breakfast. Don't want you starving to death before we get to Riv—" Garran pulled the cloth off the cart, his words stopping in mid-sentence seeing the empty cage. Zed slowed his incantation letting the glow from his tusks fade.

Garran's eyes grew cold and narrow, "Zed?" he grunted.

"Way ahead of you," he replied, pulling out a vellum bound book with silver inlaid markings, he flipped through the pages, while pulling out a small pouch of dust on his belt. He eyed the page, muttering an incantation, his tusks glowing a soft blue green. He blew dust over the cage, which clung in the air to two humanoid bodies, and one kobold in nature.

The blue-green glow formed a show of the movements from the previous night, hours condensed into a minute. Zed continued the spell with a lesser chant, his hands moving, reviewing the events that happened around the cage.

"Looks like the kobold that Alderin threw out was here, and…" said Zed in between chants, doing a few more hand motions the dust shifted and showed a clearer outline of Alderin, "He was also the one that let it out of its cage."

Garran gritted his teeth and clenched his fists. "They knew what we were carrying and its worth. They want to gain Sa'bara's favor with it," he said, his hand hitting the cage hard, ringing out with a metallic thud. "Shana?"

"Yes Garran?" she asked, standing behind him, a look of concern reflected in her eyes.

"Split the group. Leave just enough to guard our current cargo and bring it to Rivera. The rest will come with me. We are going to hunt them down and take back what is rightfully ours. We'll make them pay for their trickery," he spat on the ground, staring at Alderin's ghostly outlined mug.

Chapter 8 Decisions

Dirt flew up into the air as Garran, Zed, Shana, and two other orcs raced their horses down the road. "Keep an eye out! They couldn't have gone too far. The fools took their wagon," yelled Garran. There was nothing but a few scattered trees and tall grasses about two to three feet in height running a foot away on either side of the road.

"There is a chance they could have gone off road. If anyone notices anything no matter how small, let me know," said Shana, tightening her grip on the reins.

Garran added, "We will not let them escape. For the honor of our fallen comrades." The horses' hooves beat against the road till suddenly his eyes caught something up ahead. "Hold it!" he yelled, tugging back on the reins, the others quickly following suit. Zed pulled a red and black cotton scarf loosely around his face. As they slowed down, two orcs hidden in the brush pulled on a thick rope loosely wrapped around two nearby trees to raise it up to just over the height of the horses.

"Stop right there!" said a red skinned orc dressed in tan hide leather armor. He drew a battered short sword, staring up at him. "Hands in the air where I can see them, otherwise you'll get an arrow to the head," he commanded as four more orcs appeared out of the brush with bows drawn each aiming at a different person in Garran's group.

They raised their hands. "You are making a *big* mistake," Garran said, staring down at the bandit leader.

The red orc chuckled. "A mistake? I think not. I'm impressed you saw through our trap, but that only spares you a few unnecessary broken bones. Now give us all your weapons and valuables unless you want a few new holes in your body."

"You do not want to do this if you know what's good for you. I've had a shit day so far, and I am not in the mood for your antics."

The orc bandits pulled farther back on the bowstrings, the wood creaking under the strain. "You are in no position to threaten. Drop your weapons, get off those horses, and give us your valuables and then you're free to go. Refuse and we'll make it quick."

He looked over his shoulder a moment, seeing his group, hearing Zed crack his neck once. He returned his focus back to the bandit leader. "This is your final chance. Leave."

"It wasn't funny the first time, it's certainly not the second," the orc said, walking up beside Garran, moving his blade against his side, pressing it firmly against his armor. "For that I'll take that armor of yours too."

A sixth orc came out of the brush shortly followed by a seventh on the other side of the road. "You heard the boss, dismount!" yelled one, drawing her banged up short sword, cautiously approaching Zed. "What's with the scarf? Too ugly for anyone to look at?" she chuckled.

"I said *off!*" commanded the bandit leader.

"I can't get off without using my hands," Garran replied, gritting his teeth.

"Remove your weapons slowly, then dismount," said the bandit leader, pressing the blade against him a little harder. "*Slowly.*"

"Boss," said the female orc, looking at him, then back at Zed, holding the blade out in his direction.

"What is it?!" he said, keeping his attention focused on Garran.

"Something odd about this one," she replied. Her focus locked on Zed.

"Odd how?"

"He's wearing a scarf and not responding."

The bandit leader let out a grunt. "Remove the scarf... slowly!" he yelled, Zed remaining perfectly still.

The orc girl took a step closer. "He said take it off!"

"Do it or your boss will get it," the bandit warned, Garran looking over to him while very slowly and cautiously moving his hands down to his belt. Zed cracked his neck again, Garran looking to the others giving them a slight nod. Shana and the other orcs nodded in kind, slowly moving their hands to their weapons.

Zed cautiously lowered his hands and pulled back his scarf, revealing the green glow of his ornate carved tusks. The female orc's eyes widened, yelling, "He's an arcane user!" as she moved to attack.

Garran kicked the bandit leader's weapon away, grabbing his battle axe. Before he could even react, the orc slid off the side of his horse just as the arrow meant for him whizzed over his head. Shana and the other orc made similar moves just as Zed finished his incantation, his fingertips glowing an unearthly green.

The female bandit was about to strike at Zed just as green-brown fumes escaped from his digits. Zed's attacker leapt back covering her mouth with her arm, the gas moving in the direction of the four orc archers who panicked and fired without hitting their mark. They scrambled to nock another set of arrows just as the gas enveloped them. The female bandit regained her composure, charging forward coughing and hacking through her arm. Her weapon held high, she squinted, eyes burning and watering, desperately trying to find Zed.

Her eyes caught the green glow of his tusks, moving to strike. Suddenly an arrow pierced her neck; blood spurting from the wound as her going wide. She tried to hold her breath, using her free arm to pull at the arrow. She gasped for air, stumbling to the ground, coughing up blood, weapon slipping out of her hand.

Zed's tusks kept their soft, luminous state, focusing on the gas surrounding the archers. He remained unflinching, keeping his attention on the spell despite the battle now raging around him; the gas cloud remained stationary, easily overcoming a light breeze.

The orcs in the cloud made blind shots in his general direction. Two arrows hit different horses which darted into the fields. The third arrow hit Zed's horse who whined out in pain, but he used his legs to keep her steady.

One of the bandit archers stumbled out of the cloud. His eyes watering, lungs burning, coughing heavily, gasping for air. Drawing his bow, he took aim at the highest blur he could see when a six-inch dagger was thrust into his chest. He released the arrow, missing Zed by a wide margin, his crimson blood staining his battered leather armor. He looked at a red blur before him as the blade was pushed and twisted deeper. He grunted in pain; the warm trickle of blood flowed faster down his chest when the dagger was removed. He moved to put pressure on the wound before the red orc sliced his throat, and he soon fell to the ground dead.

The female orc grunted but her moment of victory didn't last long when another bandit rushed her. She moved to meet her attacker, but an arrow hit him in the head. He fell to the ground, revealing Shana standing behind him. Her and Shana's eyes meet for a split second before she grunted. "He was *mine*," she said, rushing back into the fight.

The fifth and last orc in the group let out a roar, charging with a heavy steel war hammer in hand. He rushed to the cloud of gas, speaking in orcish-arcana, silver runes inlaid into the sides of the hammer glowing a bright red, flames sprouting around the head. He swung into the cloud to no effect. With a scowl he yelled, "Isn't this flammable?!"

Zed shook his head. "No!" he yelled, and in that moment the cloud around the bandit archers shifted and began to dissipate in the wind. He resumed his chanting, bringing the cloud back to where it was. He watched as the war hammer wielding orc stepped into the cloud, and with a quick hand motion, parted it around his companion, revealing one archer who was on one knee with veiny watery eyes. The bandit gasped for air, rubbing his eyes, seeing a blur approaching.

"Gortha—," was all he managed to say before his skull was cracked open with the hammer. Blood splattered the ground, his body falling, legs twitching.

Meanwhile, Garran deflected a strike from the bandit leader. Without hesitation he saw an opening and grabbed his arm. In one quick motion, he broke it at the elbow. The bandit cried out in pain; Garran knocked him out with a head butt.

The leader found himself waking sometime later, his head throbbing, dried caked blood cracked over his left eyelid. A sharp pain ran through one arm, feeling the tight pull of ropes around his wrists holding his hands over his head, body tightly tied against a tree with several feet of rope. He grunted, struggling to break free but stopped the moment he felt the cold metal of Garran's heavy axe against his neck.

"I warned you," stated Garran, his vision clearing, revealing the bodies of his dead comrades lying nearby. What little value they had was stripped from their corpses. Zed stood beside Garran in support.

"If only you did wha—" he yelled, in pain Garran lowering the axe before punching him hard in the gut. Blood sprayed from the bandit leader's mouth. Among the dead was one of Garran's horses along with another panting heavily as it was being looked over by

Shana.

Coming in from the distance was the red skinned orc riding with the escaped horse in tow. She brought it over to the war hammer wielding orc, handing the reins over to him. "I managed to catch your horse Karrun. Try not to let her run off again."

He grunted, tightly gripping the reins while checking over his horse. "Not my fault I was given the cowardly horse, Orla."

She chuckled "A horse takes after their rider."

He gritted his teeth, glaring at her as she gave a big-toothed smile, showing off her silver ring pierced tusks.

The bandit leader wheezed heavily, glaring at Garran, who scowled back at him. "If you want to join your friends without a lot of pain and suffering along the way, you will answer my questions, got it?"

The captive spat directly at the domineering orc, who didn't flinch. "How's Greck, Shana?" Garran yelled.

"Not doing well, he lost a lot of blood. I'm trying to remove the arrows now, but one is lodged in the bone and it's difficult to remove."

His left eye twitched, before raising his axe and bringing the blade to the bandit leader's neck. "For your sake you better hope he survives, or this is going to get unpleasant. Now, you are going to tell me about the wagon that passed through here recently. Did you attack it? If so where is the cargo?"

"Why should I talk?" he grunted, tugging at his constraints which caused the tree to shake, a few leaves falling in the process.

"You have no idea what you have do you?"

The bandit looked away before he felt the hilt of the axe slammed into his gut. "You will not look away from me again. Answer the question. Where is it?"

"Garran!" Shana yelled.

"What is it?"

"I'm sorry but he's lost too much blood. There is nothing I can do."

He tensed, gripping the hilt of his blade, suddenly letting out a roar, swinging his axe. The bandit leader screamed, his left hand falling to the ground, blood spurting from the wound, the ropes so securely tied to his arms that he was unable to wiggle it free despite his best attempts.

"Karrun close the wound. I don't want this filth to die before I get answers," he commanded.

"As you wish," Karrun replied. He spoke in arcane orcish, the runes on his hammer glowing a bright orange, fire enveloping the head. He placed it onto the bandit's stub, the sound of flesh being seared, the smell of burning along with the orc's cries of agony going on for several seconds before the hammer was removed, revealing the blacked cauterized wound.

"You've cost me enough. Tell me where the wagon with its cargo is; the one with two humans, a dwarf, a gnome, a kobold, and one that looks like an elf."

The orc scoffed. "An elf? You're insane," he said before the process was repeated with his other hand. Garran watched in silence as Karrun cauterized the wound.

"You should watch that temper of yours my friend," Zed remarked.

"We are short on time. I must know if they have them. Rats like these always have a place to store what they have stolen."

The orc panted heavily, slumping against his restraints, his eyes locked with Garran's.

"There are more limbs to cut. We could just go down each arm or start with a foot or pull a tusk out from that mouth of yours. I will end this quickly if you tell me what I want to know."

The bandit leader looked over at his dead companions, then back at him before spitting in his face again.

Garran gritted his teeth. "Tell me if you've seen them. If you captured them was the elf alive?"

The bandit leader simply glared in defiance.

"You have no idea what she is, and there is not much time before she will be more than your ilk can contain. Tell me!"

The bandit chuckled. "No."

Garran looked at Zed. "What do you think?"

"It's hard to tell in his current state."

He nodded. "Prepare the spell."

"Understood," He replied, turning around, walking away just as Garran swung his axe and lopped off one of the bandit's ears.

"Stop wasting my time!" he yelled. The bandit screamed in pain while the interrogation continued.

Elsewhere as day turned into late afternoon, Garran's targets stopped to break for camp in the middle of a lightly forested area. As the group worked to unhitch the horses and give them some much needed rest, Histra leapt off the side of the cart and leaned up against a tree, watching everyone work.

Ariana looked around from her spot in the cart, her nostrils flaring, eyes darting around. "These woods are safe. There are no aggressive animals here," she stated, slipping off the cart, her arms brushing her black hair over the side, ensuring none of it snagged on the edge. Her toes gripped the dirt, remaining vigilant.

"I'm not surprised. The areas where most of us elves resided were long ago cleared of the most dangerous creatures. I don't know how much has changed in the thirty years since the orcs took residence, but I'd be surprised there'd be a resurgence given how much orcs are also not a fan of rabid beasts," Jesmine explained.

"Except for their mounts," Dran remarked, making a campfire, "I'll do the cooking today."

"You're cooking today?" Alderin asked.

"Aye? What's wrong with my cooking?"

"Nothing, but you make... um... rather flavorful meals."

"Unfortunately, we don't have many fine commodities out here to make such quality refreshments, so you'll have to make do."

"Such a shame," he replied, looking over his shoulder towards Histra. She noted his look, staring back while Jesmine approached Ariana.

"Do you mind if I look over your shackles, now that we have a moment?"

Ariana ran her fingers along the cloak, against their outline. "Sure. You think you might be able to remove them?"

"I won't know for certain till I get my book, but I believe I should be able to," she said, Ariana pulling back the sleeves, her white skin had a noticeable red rash along the point of contact. Jesmine ran her fingers across the engravings. "Whoever made these is extremely skillful and they appear not to be completely orcish made."

"What do you mean not completely orcish?" asked Gnemi, trying to get a look from his low vantage point.

"I don't know the orc tongue, but I've seen their writings, their forms of arcana. This has many orcish-arcana elements, but I see bits of draconic weaved into it."

Histra's wings twitched, listening to what she had to say before returning her attention back to Alderin.

Ariana recoiled to the news. "What do you mean by that?"

"It means that some level of draconic-arcana was used in their enchantment."

"And?" she asked ears twitching ever so slightly.

"It means I need to get my book. Draconic-arcana is the most primal and powerful of all the forms of magic. It will take some considerable skill to break the enchantment and get them off you."

Ariana slumped to the ground with a faint whining sigh. "That's what I was afraid of," she rubbed the shackles once more through the cloth.

"Don't let it get you down. We have a chance to get them off, till then you'll have to put up with them."

"So, it's possible that you can weave two arcana languages into one enchantment?" Gnemi asked.

"Yes, but it would take an understanding of both languages and arcana types to do so," Jesmine explained, "It's not done often though. It's rather strange to see it done like this."

"Will you stop staring at me like that, you... most aggravating human I have ever had the displeasure of meeting!" exclaimed Histra, spreading her wings.

"And why should I take my eyes off of you after your death threats!" Alderin yelled back.

"Those weren't threats, they were a promise and if you ever touch me like that again you will *pay* for it," she growled.

Alderin unsheathed his blade. "I knew you couldn't be trusted."

She tensed. "How dare you, after everything I've done!"

"Alderin! Histra! Stop this now!" commanded Jesmine, stepping between the two breaking their line of sight. "You two need to stop fighting like this."

"Are you defending it again? After it threatened me? You heard what it said."

"He's right. It did threaten to kill him," Dran added, staying by the campfire to prepare the night's meal.

"I am not an *it*!" Histra growled in draconic.

Jesmine took a deep breath. "Look. Put your weapon away."

"Why are you still defending it?" asked Alderin. He tensed for a moment, before reluctantly sheathing his blade.

"Despite what Histra has said, all she's done has been helpful. Her ways are rough, but she hasn't led us into any traps."

"And I wasn't the one who had to be convinced to free Ariana," Histra remarked.

"Histra, you aren't helping. You shouldn't have threatened him. He saved your life; a little more gratitude would go a long way," she replied, looking over her shoulder.

Histra looked up at her and let out a soft grunt while her wings unfurled slightly. "Saved my life? I was moments from having it handled."

Alderin stepped past Jesmine. "Excuse me? Being beaten and kicked around was having it handled? Don't make me laugh. I didn't have to save you, but I *did*."

"You only *did* it because I know the way. I speak orc tongue which *I* have taught you. I have done my best to keep you all out of trouble and out of the eyes of any possible agents of Sa'bara. You only *saved* me because you *needed* me. The moment that's gone, I know what will happen."

"I, I, I! Me, me, ME! Listen to your little snout yapping away! Everything is about *you*! Every selfish action you've taken is ultimately for you and no one else! And don't presume to *know* why I *did* anything and the *reasons* behind my actions, so get off your high horse, *kobold*! …*We* should have left you in *that,* where you can't harm anyone," said Alderin, pointing to the metal cage still bolted to the wagon.

Histra's wings twitched, claws tensing, her deep blue eyes glaring at him. Ariana looked over to the cage, then back to them.

"I said that's enough! Alderin, you will not harm Histra, and Histra, you will not make any threats or actions against Alderin or anyone else here, do you understand?!" Jesmine yelled staring down Alderin. He tensed before lowering his gaze.

Jesmine turned her full attention to Histra, walking to the kobold, who stood her ground. The elf's breath fogged while she crouched down before her to get as close to eye level as possible. "Look, you might think something bad will happen to you when your task is done, but it's not, I won't allow it."

"You won't allow it? What could you possibly do—"

"Alderin?" Jesmine said, keeping eye contact with Histra.

"Yeah?"

"I know you are doing this to get my aid in something. I know whatever it is, it's big enough that you don't want Histra to know. I am going to tell you this once and only once. If you or Dran do anything that purposely leads to any harm befalling her, no matter what you do, I won't help. Do I make myself clear?"

"What..." Alderin tensed for a moment, gritting his teeth, before taking a deep breath, "Alright, but the kobold better not do anything in return."

"I'll get to that point, but first. Dran?" Jesmine asked.

Dran got the fire going before responding, "Aye, I agree to it. It's a small price to pay. I accept your terms," he answered.

Jesmine reached up and gently rested her hands on Histra's shoulders.

"What are you doing? Don't you tou—"

"What have I done for you not to trust me?" she interrupted, holding her firmly, the warmth from her hands steadily draining away.

Histra's tail twitched, feeling the warmth against her scales before it faded back to nothing. "What?"

"What have I done for you not to trust me? I don't know what others have done to you, but I am not them. I've asked nothing from you when I got you out of the cage. You offered the deal, so you had time to recover."

"I thanked you for saving me, what more do you want?"

"To *trust* me. Trust me that I will not allow any harm to fall upon you. That whatever plan you have once we're there, you are free to pursue it. Haven't I earned the chance to earn your trust?"

Histra tensed more as the two stared off for a moment longer. Her gaze broke from hers for a split second, seeing Jesmine's hand's turning beet red from the cold. She sighed, looking back into Jesmine's eyes. "Fine, and to be fair, I promise not to do anything that will lead to any harm befalling upon you or anyone else here while we are travelling together."

Jesmine smiled. "Thank you." She pulled her shaking hands away, rubbing them together while blowing on them.

"Are you going to be—" Alderin remarked but quickly grew quiet when Jesmine gave him a fierce glare. "Never mind. I'll keep it to myself."

"Please do."

"Well... that was something," Gnemi said.

"How did you all survive this far?" asked Ariana after a moment of silence.

"It wasn't easy with these three always going at it," Jesmine replied with a sigh.

"I've never seen such disorganization and lack of cohesion in a group in my life."

Alderin gave one last look at Histra, who kept an eye on him before turning his attention to her. "We're somehow managing but tell us, how did you get captured? Were you outside of Sa'bara's lands like Jesmine? I noticed I didn't see the mark of Sa'bara on you."

Ariana looked at her hands. "No, I was never forced to be marked and those orcs you saw were the ones that captured me. They had gotten wind of where I was, and after several attempts, they eventually succeeded. Those orcs are tenacious, I give them that."

As Dran poked the fire, cooking the evening meal he asked, "Is there anything you can tell us about their methods?"

"They're a tight knit group. They trust one another and understand each other's strengths and weaknesses. One of them is a magic user specialized in poison-based arcana. They have at least one who wields a fire enchanted war hammer, but after that, things are hazy..." she said, trailing off.

"In other words, we should try to avoid them as best we can. This is far worse than I thought," Alderin remarked.

"If what we saw at the celebration is all of them, I believe with enough preparation, we can handle them," Dran said, being mindful to keep his beard away from the heat of the flames. "Once food is served, I'll douse the campfire. With a double new moon tonight, it's unlikely they will travel far enough to catch us, but I'll take first watch. My vision is better suited for the darkness than most of yours."

"I'll take the second," Jesmine said.

"I'd like to take the third. You all rescued me, and I need to do my part to help," said Ariana, sitting up.

"Thank you, Miss," replied Alderin, Gnemi walking over to Histra.

She eyed him for a moment, his hands rubbing nervously together. "What is it?" she asked in a stern voice.

"I presume with everything that just happened, it's a little forward of me, but I have been curious— your cold aura fascinates me. Would it be too much to ask if I could just touch your scales?"

"What?" she cocked an eye ridge as she stared at him.

"Sorry, sorry, I simply want to know more."

"It's cold, what is there to know?"

"I want to know what's it like for myself."

"You have to be one of the weirdest and most curious gnomes I have ever seen… not that I've met many," she commented.

"Well I haven't met any kobolds before."

"I wonder *why* that is," she said, giving a soft growl.

"That was before my time… does that mean you're from th—"

"I prefer you not speculate where I am from," she stated with a cold glare.

"Sorry," he trailed off for a moment. "Um, so how did you do that whole ice thing out in front of the bar? I hypothesize that it was you that made it, right?"

Histra took a deep breath, sighing, walking off.

"Oh… okay. Well, if you change your mind I'd love to know!"

"Don't mind it, Gnemi. It won't tell you anything, and if it did, it wouldn't be too truthful about it," Alderin remarked.

Jesmine softly sighed.

Alderin took a moment to look over his bow, "Gnemi was clearly bothering it. I'm trying to be helpful."

"I didn't say anything," Jesmine replied.

Gnemi sighed in defeat, returning to the group.

"You're a curious gnome, aren't you?" Ariana asked.

"I think we're all curious to some degree. There're probably other races that are just as curious, if not more so. I think humans can be more tenacious in their curiosity, but what about you? I have little doubt that you have many stories to tell."

She eyed him for a moment before looking off into the woods. "It's a long story and we've been traveling all day. Perhaps another time?"

"Yes, but of course. I didn't mean to make you uncomfortable."

Ariana smiled at him. "That's alright. It's nice to have people to talk to. I've been on my own for a long time…"

Jesmine sat beside her. "You don't have to be alone now. You'd be pleased to know that Sa'bara's extermination isn't as complete as people say. A lot of small groups managed to sneak into Dra'kesh lands to the east and some to the free lands in the north. I don't know if any made it to Darikaan lands in the south."

Ariana smiled. "It's good to hear that," she replied, looking at the kobold, who was leaning up against a tree some distance away. Histra eyed everyone while getting into a relaxed position. "There is something that doesn't feel right about her."

"I'd say the ice aura makes her a little cold but—" Gnemi said, his words were cut off by Histra yelling.

"I heard that gnome!"

"I didn't mean it that way."

"Are you talking about Histra?" Jesmine asked.

"Who else would she be talking about?" Alderin commented.

Ariana glanced at him. "Yes."

Jesmine made herself comfortable on the ground, saying, "We've all heard the stories and seen many kobolds who are closely aligned to the dragons, but she's been nothing but helpful. If she is aligned to any, it's not Sa'bara, or Dra'kesh for that matter. She's rough around the edges but she's rather nice."

"Nice? How do you… never mind," Dran said. "Food will be ready soon."

Ariana shook her head. "No, no it's not that. Just something else, it puts me at… unease. After helping me, I felt that you should know."

"Was it something she said when you two were alone?" asked Jesmine.

She tensed up. "No, no. Nothing like that."

"Then what is it?"

"You know, it's nothing. Forget I said anything about it."

"Okay… but really Histra isn't as bad as she seems," she said, leaning in. "She's just been through a lot. I don't know how true it is, but she was shackled worse than you were."

"That one?" Ariana asked with a slight head motion towards the cage.

Jesmine nodded. "Best not to talk too much about it. I think it's a sour topic and she still might hear us. I find it rude to talk about something like this especially in their presence."

"Eat up. We've had a long day and there are many more in front of us," said Dran, offering them warmed up meat pies. The pie crust was particularly hard and crunchy, but once the exterior was broken, it revealed soft tender meat, gravy, and vegetables inside.

Ariana bit through the crust with surprising force, chewing through it to get to the supple, juicy insides.

"If I realized you were this hungry, I would have made more. I can make some if you'd like?" said Dran.

"I'm good," Ariana quickly replied, continuing to gnaw ravenously.

Histra, with her open meat pie watched with slight amusement. Jesmine curiously biting into the hard crust with some difficulty, remarking, "I think Ariana is making a point in that we shouldn't waste any of this."

"Waste? I was thinking of giving it to the horses once we soak it in some water," Dran said.

"Water should make this more edible," Gnemi commented, trying to chew the hard bread in vain.

"Do whatever you want. Soak them in water, feed them to the horses, but don't waste it and get some rest," said Dran, dousing the campfire with some dirt and a little bit of water. "We have a slight lead over our pursuers but that won't last long. The wagon will slow us down, but we don't have much of a choice."

Histra gave him a glare, while Jesmine said, "It will, but we don't have any other options to carry all the supplies we need to get there and back without it."

The kobold relaxed slightly, the dwarf nodding. "Aye. And till we are sure we aren't being followed by them and have assuredly lost them; we'll be at a disadvantage."

"Dran's right. Get some rest and we'll leave at first light," said Alderin, walking over and slipped into his tent.

"I wish I had thought of obtaining more tents. I'm sorry for this inconvenience." said Jesmine.

Dran stretched. "I can sleep with Alderin, and you and Ariana can share mine. Gnemi's tent is too small to be much use."

"I offered Histra to rest with me, but she refused," said Gnemi with a soft chuckle, checking the integrity of his tent.

"You'd die if I did that," she remarked, getting comfortable underneath the wagon.

"You say that, but I don't believe you."

"Gnomes," she grumbled in draconic.

Ariana looked out into the forest, her toes clenching the grass underneath her feet. "I'll be fine. I'm used to sleeping outside."

"It's fine. I won't bite," Jesmine chuckled, going over to Dran's tent.

Ariana smirked. "I'm not worried about that," she remarked, walking over to her, looking inside the tent. "For a dwarf, this is a rather nice and big."

"I like to be over-prepared than under. Good thing too with how big our group has become," Dran replied.

"Jesmine, remember to wake me when it is my turn to go on watch."

"I will," said Jesmine, entering the tent, shortly followed by Ariana.

As the night progressed Dran remained vigilant, hearing the noise of small bugs and nocturnal animals scurry about the forest. Without incident he switched with Jesmine.

"Rest well Dran," she said with a soft whisper, exiting the tent.

"I'll do my best. It's unlikely they will find us here, but you never know what else might," he replied.

"I will keep that in mind," she said, Dran retiring to his tent. She walked out and looked up to the night sky, thinking. *"One can see so many stars during a no moons cycle. I left during one…"* She turned her focus to the dark forest around her, "I need to keep focus.". The hours passed without incident and when Jesmine popped her head into the tent, she moved over to tap Ariana on the shoulder.

"I'm awake," she said, opening her eyes.

"It's your turn."

She sat up. "I figured, thank you," she said, stretching, sliding out of the tent. "Rest well."

"Thanks. And good luck to your watch, it's been quiet."

"Good to know, rest well," she replied then closed the tent behind her. She looked over the camp while making a few rounds, her nostrils flaring, sniffing the air, her pupils going wide as she watched. She moved silently, cautiously, around the campsite waiting, listening till she suddenly stopped. *"They should be asleep by now,"* she thought, rubbing her shackles. *"It's nice they want to help, but that won't last."* She turned to the forest and silently walked off. The elf walked several yards away, stopping to look over her shoulder in the direction of the camp. "Bye. Thanks for everything," she said softly, continuing to walk away.

"Leaving so soon?" asked Histra as she jumped and spun around to see her standing there.

Ariana let out a soft growl, staring down at the kobold, who was smirking, the starlight barely providing anything more than the vague outline of her form. Ariana tensed, her nostrils flaring.

"Did I surprise you? I should be pleased that I managed to do that, but then it was a simple task so long as I remained downwind from you."

"How did you know what direction I was going to take?"

"Simple, you'd want to make sure we weren't going to follow you, and if we were, keeping track of us and our scent makes it a trivial task for you to avoid us."

She glared at her, her hands tensing. "What is it that you want? If you think you can stop me..." she managed a semi-feral growl, "...you are sadly mistaken. I won't be taken like the others."

Histra chuckled. "Despite how I look, I am still fairly atrophied from my *decade* of captivity. I have no intention of going along with whatever plan those orcs had for you. I'm here to tell you that you should strongly reconsider your decision given your current situation."

Ariana eyed her, standing tall, crossing her arms before walking around Histra, who followed her movement but didn't budge.

"Those shackles aren't going to come off on their own, and the only person who would be willing to help you despite what you are is that elf in that camp over there."

"And what makes you so sure she'd help me?"

"She defended me. All she knew was I am a kobold and that I should be freed from my enslavement. And then she stopped the two idiots back there from killing me. If she is that concerned about my well-being, she'd be more than sympathetic about yours. And she will keep the others in check without issue."

"What makes you so sure?" she asked, stopping her pacing

right in front of her.

"Because whatever those guys want her for, she has them by the balls."

"I noticed that… what's in it for you? Why are you so concerned about *my* freedom? So, concerned about helping me? On trying to stop me from leaving?"

"I promised Jesmine that I'd get her to her location safely. If you run off, we'd have to spend time looking for you, and the odds that those orcs would find us would be increased dramatically. Speaking of which… they captured you once but now you are weak and shackled, do you think you could so easily avoid them again? Your only chance of survival is with that dysfunctional group back there."

"They are disorganized, bickering people who have little chance of making it through Rivera by themselves let alone with me. I'd be heading straight to where they were taking me."

"It's going to happen either way. You could either do it with them, and the one person who could help you, or could just wait for the inevitable with the orcs to bring you there in chains. One provides you a chance of real freedom, the other does not."

Ariana tensed, resuming her pacing. "I don't like this. You… you have some other motive behind this. I just don't know what it is, and it's driving me crazy."

"Is it because of that bad feeling you get from me?" she asked with sarcasm.

"No. That is something completely different... tell me Histra, do you have a problem with animals? I noticed those others in the cages were none too happy about your presence and I don't think it's your ice aura."

Histra flicked her wings and eyed her. "I've been in a cage for a decade. You think I'd know," she said, staring at her for a moment before she continued. "What's it going to be? Are you going to take the risk and leave? Or take the risk and stay? If you stay, I recommend you tell them today, for they will find out by next nightfall."

"There's something about this that doesn't feel right," she growled.

"Take it or leave it. But do you see any other way to get those off you?" she pointed to her wrists.

Ariana ran her hands against her cuffs. "I will find out what's in it for you, and when I do… if it is close to what I am suspecting," she said, towering over Histra who stood her ground, the cold air surrounding them, "I will not hesitate to tear you limb from limb."

"You are certainly free to try. Now don't you have a watch to finish? We've been gone a long time, what if we get ambushed?"

"Don't flaunt yourself to me, kobold. Even with these shackles… I won't need to *try*. But with that said, they aren't anywhere nearby. If they were, I'd know," she replied, pointing to her nose. "I suspected they'd possibly reach us tonight but maybe we lost them before this chase even began."

Histra shrugged. "I've seen too much to be hopeful on that. Come, we should head back," she said as Ariana eyed her for a moment before sighing, following. Histra slipped under the wagon and tentatively kept an eye on her as she finished her rounds. Half an hour before dawn the others awoke and began preparations for their morning meal.

Ariana watched everyone as they went about their routine. She tensed, glancing at Histra who had a sly grin on her face, standing beside the cart.

"Ariana are you okay?" asked Jesmine with a concerned look. "Did you get enough sleep? You can rest in the wagon if you like once we get going."

"Aye, you had a long day yesterday. If you need rest, get it," said Dran, checking over the food.

"Thanks, but it's not that," she said, pacing a bit more, rubbing the shackles on her wrists. "Something I've put a lot of thought into, and I think it's something you should all know," she said, taking a few steps back from everyone.

"What is it?" asked Alderin, giving her a curious look.

"What's got you spooked?" asked Gnemi, with a concerned look in his eyes.

"You can trust us. Though I had no part in it, the rest did free you from the cage," Dran said.

"They're right. Whatever it is you can tell us," said Jesmine, taking a step closer as she took a step back.

Histra said from off to the side. "Yeah. Whatever could be troubling you Ariana? I prefer not to have unknown trouble. It'll make my job harder."

"Don't mind it," Alderin said, while Ariana shot the kobold a look. "We're here to help."

Jesmine stayed where she was. "I do apologize for the inconvenience. I know where we're going isn't easy, and if you have concerns, we'll do our best to ease them."

"Getting to your spellbook, though troubling isn't the problem," she replied.

"Then what is it Ariana?" she asked.

The cool breeze of the early morning blew through the trees, birds singing their morning song, the party looking at her with a mix of curiosity and concern. Dran stroked his red braided beard, Gnemi idly cleaning his goggles, while Alderin's black haired stubbled face expressed worry but also frustration at the words of yet another problem.

Ariana took a deep breath, giving one last look over everyone. Her muscles tensed, rubbing the cuffs once more, her toes digging into the soft earth. Her heart pounded, saying without hesitation, "I'm a Lycan."

Chapter 9 The True Weight of the Situation

Ariana stood tall, legs tensing, toes digging into the soft earth, ready to sprint the moment the words left her lips. A soft wind caused the leaves in the trees to rustle, while birds chirped in the distance. Silence has befallen the group over the next few tenuous seconds. Ariana studied each person's reaction. Gnemi's green eyes were wide with excitement, while others had a mix of skepticism and a hint of fear. Histra leaned against the wagon behind the group with a smug grin. She looked to Jesmine who raised an eyebrow as there was a hint of something else going through her mind.

"What did you just say?" asked Alderin, keeping his distance, hands near but not on his weapon.

"I'm a Lycan, and at the start of the new moon phase from Amaya, I will quickly regain my lupus characteristics."

"Really? I thought that werewolves couldn't talk. But is it true that only silver can hurt you?" asked Gnemi, approaching curiously.

Ariana tilted her head to the side; a small smirk crossed her lips. "A werecreature is a simple term referring to anyone who turns into another animal from one trigger or another. A werewolf like myself or say a for example a werebat."

"Isn't a werebat a vampire?"

"I don't know anything about vampires really, but no. Those are completely different."

"Hold it one bloody moment. You said you are a Lycan?" Dran asked, giving Ariana a stern stare.

"Yes, I did. I knew this was a bad idea…" She took a step back. "You did save me from the orcs bu—"

"Relax. No one here is going to hurt you," said Jesmine, approaching her.

She took another step back, muscles tensing, looking at Alderin, who grew agitated when their eyes met.

Dran approached and rested his hand on Gnemi's shoulders whose excitement continued to grow. "Relax Gnemi. It's best to not make her feel cornered."

"But she's a werewolf… a once in a lifetime opportunity," he responded.

Ariana remained on edge, looking to Histra, who kept her smug composure. *"Was this what you had planned?"* she thought as Jesmine moved in front of her.

"Careful," cautioned Alderin, Jesmine taking another step closer.

She sighed and turned her head to them. "If she was going to do something, she'd have done it when we were asleep. Why don't you two relax," she said, returning her attention back to Ariana. "I know coming out like that wasn't easy," she smiled and held her hand out.

The other elf instinctively pulled back.

"I'm not going to hurt you, and neither is anyone else here. I appreciate you telling us. I'll do my best to get those shackles off you. The mithril must be extremely uncomfortable."

"Jesmine. She's fine now but when the moon comes up, she'll become a vicious monster. She'll attack us all on sight, care not of friend nor foe, and her bite will turn you into one of them!" yelled Alderin, moving his hand to the hilt of his blade, Ariana looking around for the best route of escape.

"Alderin. Not another word. It is clear you only have minimal knowledge of lycanthropy."

Ariana's eyes met Jesmine's, her muscles relaxing slightly.

Alderin didn't move an inch, asking, "And you do Jesmine? I've heard plenty of tales about them. None of them are good. Viscous creatures with the power of ten men. They can't be reasoned with. She'll turn and attack us."

"Yes, I do. In my hometown of Ami'ralia, there were two renown alchemists who had a fascination with all forms of lycanthropy. I happened to learn a few things from them when my Mother brought me there from time to time during her research visits."

Ariana swallowed a lump in her throat. "Those stories aren't untrue though. Many of us Lycans are very vicious and do not take well of strangers walking into our territory. We tend to live in packs of just a few to even a few dozen. We can be hard to approach," she said, relaxing slightly. "Instincts can be hard to control during a single full moon, and far worse yet during the rare double," she turned her gaze back to Jesmine. "Those orcs won't give me up easily. They were mourning the death of the comrades that I killed. They were celebrating my capture."

"I appreciate she is telling us this, but she admits how dangerous she is. Perhaps it is best we simply part ways," Dran suggested, his axe pulled out but not at the ready.

"Dran. Not another word from you either. Let her speak. After that, we can figure things out. How does that sound?"

He let out a long, drawn out sigh. "She still has her wits about her, for now, so it's fine by me."

"I'd love to hear more myself honestly. I'm curious to know more about her pack," Gnemi said.

Ariana tensed at Gnemi's words.

"I'm glad someone does," Jesmine said, taking a step back. "Can you tell us more about your condition? I know some things, but I am no expert like the Teramori family was." Ariana gritted her teeth at the name before she took a deep breath, closing her eyes. Jesmine gave her a little more space.

"I wouldn't call it a condition. Not by any means, but the orcs are after me because I am a Lycan."

"Why?" Gnemi asked.

"I don't know why, but Sa'bara has been hunting Lycans for decades now. There were others of my pack but over the years, we were hunted, killed or captured, till only I remained. You all know little about my kind. Half-truths, things about us only told from one perspective. Though Jesmine, I suspect you might be the only exception besides me..." Ariana trailed off for a moment, focusing on Jesmine, "Afterall, you knew my parents."

"Wait, what?" Jesmine said, staring at Ariana for a moment, before her eyes widened. "You're *Ariana Teramori*?"

"Yes. I don't have many memories of my extreme youth. That was over sixty years ago, and I believe I was no more than ten at the time."

"I remember when I was there, they had a daughter, though you look nothing like her, but then again you were only a child. When I heard your name, it sounded familiar, but I had no idea you were her. I would have never suspected anyone from our hometown to still be alive."

"We never really talked. I became a Lycan about fifteen years before Sa'bara exterminated the elves."

"So, you're a daughter of werewolf experts, and now you are one. So, what? You just know better how you will lose control and attack us?" asked Alderin, keeping his hand on the hilt of his blade.

"Alderin, be quiet. How often does anyone even get a chance to talk to one stricken with lycanthropy? Never," said Jesmine.

"That's what bothers me," he replied.

Ariana continued. "As I said. We're very protective of our homes and those who have poor control over their instincts rarely are able to distinguish between the random passing traveler who won't mean us any harm or someone who is there to hunt us."

"And how well can you control your instincts?" Jesmine asked.

"Better than most. It wasn't easy. I spent time with my pack. I learned a lot from them, but I was naturally better able control my gift than the others."

"Gift? Did you just call it a gift?" Dran asked.

"Call it what you will. The only problem with this gift is of course the overwhelming instincts that can take over my higher faculties. It took years to tame it. I even manage to remain in complete control of myself under a full moon. I helped others in my pack, and some were close to achieving a level of control such as myself. We are not vicious monsters. Our instincts are simple. Eat, sleep, mate, survive, and defend our home from invaders."

"Are you saying you are a 'nice' werewolf who won't attack us once you turn?" Alderin asked.

"Basically yes. Once the moon shines, I will become more anthropomorphic, and near full moons, I will become more feral in my physique to the point that vocal communication for the duration will be impossible. But I will not maul you without justified provocation."

"I appreciate you coming forth in telling us, but I know you are doing this with a reason. Are you planning to continue to travel with us?" Jesmine asked.

Ariana took a deep breath, "Yes."

"We are already in a difficult situation. We are in a foreign land, having enough trouble as it is with one elf. Two elves does make it more complicated, but fine. But now we have someone actively trying to find us, on top of that… We have to hide a werewolf? I think that might be a bit much," Alderin explained.

"I don't want to sound like I don't care, but Alderin has a

point. It'll be hard to hide a Lycan through the city of Rivera," Dran said.

"Don't worry on that. I have a way to sneak us through," said Histra as everyone turned toward her.

"*You?*" asked Dran quirking an eyebrow.

"I've had a plan for a while now."

"Let's hear it then."

"I think it's best you all finish your little chat here first. We'll worry about the future when it comes."

Dran and Alderin gave Histra a long, hard look before turning back to Ariana who shifted on her feet.

"I know it's a difficult thing to ask, but I am in desperate need of your help. Everyone I know, for the second time in my life, is gone. With these shackles on me, I am a fraction of my current strength and," she shakes her wrists, "...even when I transform these will remain on me and irritate my skin."

"Mithril? I heard silver was the only metal that could harm a Lycan," Alderin said.

"If you lop off my head, I'll die just as readily as anyone else. We are resilient and have relatively strong self-regeneration capabilities. A broken bone won't keep us down for more than a few days, but the magic conductive metals, such as silver, gold, platinum, and mithril, to name a few, slow the regenerative process to a near standstill. When in shackles like these, it's physically draining."

Jesmine nodded. "That explains the use of mithril."

"I'm still concerned about the whole possibility of being mauled and turned into a werewolf," Alderin said.

Ariana sighed. "I am not going to maul you. I've trained myself over the years to remain in control. Even in my most primal form, I am not stupid. I wouldn't attack without reason. I know the situation, and I wouldn't harm those who've helped me."

"What about after? If we manage to get there, and Jesmine gets them off, what then?"

"I'll leave. No 'civilized' town will accept me. Also..." she trailed off for a moment but before anyone could respond she continued. "It would be nice to say goodbye to my family one last time. There are things I've always wanted to say, but never got the chance to." Ariana looked up into the trees.

"What happens when you transform?" asked Dran, returning his axe to his back, taking a moment to adjust his brown tan hide leather armor that's placed over his earthen colored clothes. Histra eyed the dwarf curiously but didn't move.

Ariana looked at him, responding. "Lycans have four forms. The one you see me in now, then there is the one you'll see next when I bask in the moonlight. It is not my most commonly used form, even when given the choice, but it will best suit our needs as it will be the easiest for me to hide in."

"Which is?" Dran asked.

"An anthropomorphic wolf. The next is my preferred form as it is stronger, faster, has deadlier claws, a stronger bite, but is much harder to communicate in. The last is my four-legged feral form and I have found speaking in that state is quite impossible. It took me over a decade to learn how to speak in my different forms. Which is something few take the time to do, and fewer still even want to do, given that our reputation often precedes us. There is not much purpose in communicating with those not like ourselves. Also, our primal language communicates our day to day needs just fine."

"So why did you?" Dran asked.

"It's my family's work. Becoming the very subject of my study has honestly been amazing."

Jesmine took a step forward. "I never asked but what was the purpose of your family's research?"

"They were trying to find a cure."

"And you've continued that research?"

"To a degree. My motivations have shifted a little given my new insight, but it's difficult given no alchemic lab or even a place to put it. I've kept some studies, but it's all been minor… and speaking of studies, I will let you all know a Lycan's bite is the source of the spread of lycanthropy but only during at least one of the full moons."

"That's good to hear, that means we have thirty-seven days till a Drakvin becomes a full."

"And ninety-three days till Amaya is. I find what you've said fascinating, but you've gotten me curious," said Gnemi, shifting his weight on his worn leather shoes, "I thought I heard you kept saying you were able to and allowed to when it came to your forms, what does that mean?"

"I'll explain that later. But for now, I need to know. Am I able to stay? Or shall I take my leave?"

"She did come out and tell us. I think she should stay," Gnemi replied.

"I am uneasy about this, but we already have a kobold, can't be worse than that," said Dran. "You've been upfront, honest. Just don't take offense if we keep an eye on you for now."

"I'd be surprised if you didn't," Ariana replied with a faint smirk.

Alderin sighed. "True. You're a step up from the kobold. You told us what's going on. Let me guess then. It was your sense of smell that told you about the orcs up ahead the other night?"

"Yes, which will be even better once the moon comes out. I also know orc tongue, and some of these surrounding lands, since this is the general area I lived in once I became a Lycan."

"That's a good thing. Perhaps you could continue to teach me orc tongue," suggested Alderin, Histra pushing off the cart, watching the events unfold with a raised eye ridge and a twitch of her wings, head tilting slightly to one side.

"I can do that. Though forgive if I am a bit more guttural in the language after tonight."

"I won't mind as long as you don't mind that I will also try to keep an eye on you. Your story is hard to believe but then again, I never talked to nor heard of a talking werewolf before."

"Lycan," Ariana corrected.

Alderin adjusted his belt that held his sheathed weapons. "Lycan... Got it."

"That went better than I thought. So, we're good to continue?" asked Jesmine, everyone voicing their agreement. "Histra?"

Histra twitched, focus shifting to her, shoulders slumping, noticing Ariana giving her a cold long stare while all eyes were on her. "I have no problems. I recommended we free her. I promised to get you safely to your destination. That's what I'll do."

She smiled. "Good. Let's head off then. We've spent enough time in one spot and if Sa'bara is that keen on having you for Draksind, the orcs will be very keen on trying to recapture you."

"Thanks. I appreciate the vote of confidence," she replied, helping pack up the camp while Histra climbed up onto the wagon.

Halfway through the process Dran motioned Ariana to the side, "What is it?" she asked.

"You haven't voiced any strong opinions about the kobold. It might not be as suspicious of you. Perhaps you can keep an eye on it?"

"I already am, but why do you ask?"

"Something doesn't smell right about this whole wanting to free you scenario. Not to mean any offense to you, but it's been adamant about keeping a low profile, yet was okay with freeing you and risk being chased by orcs?"

"She's never smelled right by me. I thank you for your trust in letting me know how you feel. But remember for now we all need to work together and force aside our distrusts. If we fight amongst each other, it's not going to go well."

"I'll be honest," Dran said. "We've been digging ourselves into a deeper hole than we'd ever expected to find ourselves in. We've been lucky we've gotten this far."

"That's been my only explanation from what I've seen," she replied with a smirk.

"Right… I'll say this once. I've heard many tales about Lycans, back home we had one of the bat variety take up residence near us and it wasn't pretty, but what you've said did ring true. They rarely attacked outside of their hunting grounds, and it wasn't till an incident where a child had gone missing that things got heated."

"Is there a point to this? Are you telling me if I make a mistake I'm gone?"

Dran shook his head. "No. I'm saying even though I don't trust you that much right now, I trust you far more than our current guide," his head pointed over toward Histra sitting in the corner of the cart watching over everyone else.

"I understand," she replied with a nod, helping to load everything up.

"We are a bit off from the path, but if we continue in this direction, we should find a side road that will avoid some of the next few towns. At our current pace we're about a week from Rivera," Histra said.

"And are you going to tell us your plan of how to get through the city with a werew—Lycan?" asked Alderin, mounting Cetas.

"I have to see the situation myself before I can say. Anything before that will be pointless," she explained, waving him off, looking to the side.

Alderin shook his head, "And our point is made," he said, while he and the others kept a vigilant look out.

After a while Gnemi looked over his shoulder to Ariana and asked, "You said something about your various forms? And you were going to talk about them once we got going?"

Ariana's eyes shifted and focused on him, "I did, didn't I?"

"If it's not too much to ask. It's a long trip."

"I am also curious about that. I haven't heard of anything about multiple Lycan forms before," Jesmine said.

"To be fair, not many stay around to find out, and those who get too close are often perceived as a threat..." she cleared her throat, taking notice that Alderin and Dran slowed down their horses to get closer while Histra paid no heed.

"During the rare double new moon, we revert back to our original born selves and are stuck like that, but once a sliver of a moonlight is present I will no longer be able to retain this shape as I shift into my most anthropomorphic form, which will be the one I will keep for you all as it will be the easiest to control, communicate, and best of all, hide in."

"You can shift between your Lycan forms?" asked Jesmine, the cart rattling and squeaking as it made its way through the brush, running over small twigs which snapped under its weight.

"Yes, I tend to, like most other Lycans, prefer the one between our most bestial and the one you will see."

"Why?" Gnemi asked.

"As I explained already. it's stronger, quicker, and I honestly feel safer in it. If both moons are near full, I won't have a choice in the matter, but I don't see that being an issue before we get where we are going."

"I certainly hope not. And that whatever Histra has planned, I hope it goes better than her last one," Alderin remarked with a wink.

Histra tensed her claws, giving Alderin a quick glare as he smirked in response.

"I, for one, am very glad to hear you talk so candidly about this. Anytime I ask Histra a question she just... well look. Hey

Histra. With those wings of yours, are you able to fly or just glide? I've heard conflicting accounts on it, and it would be great to know!" Gnemi yelled.

Histra looked over her shoulder at Gnemi, staring at him, letting out a huff of icy air, before turning away, adjusting her wings to block his view of her.

He hand gestures to her. "See?"

"Some don't like to talk about themselves. I have to for a matter of necessity." Ariana replied.

"You're damn right. If you turned tonight without letting us know, things could have gotten very complicated," Dran said.

"It's a risk on my part, but thus far it has been paying off," she replied, giving a cursory glance at Histra, who kept looking out of the back of the cart. A thin layer of frost gathered on the cage as water slowly condensed and froze over, competing with the warmth of the summer's day.

About midday, they broke out of the forest and into a large clearing of farmlands. The area before them laid fallow as out in the distance they could see the waving of crops in the wind, the smell of livestock rolling over them as they pressed on, the cart shaking side to side as it rode on uneven ground.

"I don't like the idea of just riding through farmland. It's just asking for trouble," said Dran.

Alderin replied, "If I were them, I would be angry. Though we've seen some decent orcs, I doubt it will go well for us if we are caught here."

"See, you can't judge people for how they look," Jesmine said.

"I appreciate the sentiment, but I have often found that one can make some good judgements about someone based on how they look. A hunter will dress like a hunter. A farmer will dress like a farmer. Only those trying to hide their true nature will use their appearance to hide the fact," remarked Ariana, her head suddenly shooting up, turning in the direction of the blowing wind. "Four are coming."

"Four are coming?" Jesmine asked.

"Four orcs, on horses." Ariana sniffed the air a bit more. "Yes, just four."

"Are they the ones after us?" Alderin asked.

"No. They smell of livestock. They're probably farmers."

"That was damn fast," Dran said.

"We are out in the open on their land. It's not surprising," she replied.

Histra grunted. "I'll handle this," she stretched and flexed her wings. "News of what happened at the other town wouldn't have reached here so we should be good. Just do what I say. All of you."

"I have an idea, Histra" Ariana said.

She eyed her curiously, "You do?"

"Let me do the talking. Pretend you don't know any orc tongue. The rest of you will move into a defensive position around her. As a messenger for a dragon, you'd want to defend her. I'll play as your humble translator and explain the situation to the orcs of how we had a run in with bandits and we are looking for an alternate, less used route to get to Rivera. That way we can perhaps get a different path."

"I know the way," stated Histra, turning to face her.

"You know of one, but what if there are more? If we are being chased, wouldn't it be good to know of others?"

"I think she's right, it's probably a good idea," Gnemi said. "It's worth a shot."

"She does make a good point," Jesmine said, pulling her hood over her head. "And it will allow you to continue playing the one in charge without speaking with the locals directly. That does sound like something a kobold who has some ranking would do."

Histra huffed, flicking her wings. "I suppose it can work," she said, looking over at the others, "Do it. I'll speak only in dragon tongue to give context. Do you understand dragon tongue?"

Ariana shook her head, placing the hood of her cloak over her head, "No."

"Won't matter but good to know," she replied, the orcs approaching on horseback. They slowed their cart to a stop. Alderin and Dran took a defensive position between the cart and them, weapons at the ready but not raised.

Two of the orcs, a few years shy of adulthood have dark green skin, their bows pulled at the ready. One young adult red skinned orc was armed with a long hunting knife and the oldest one with leathery sunbaked skin, weathered leather armor hastily adorning his body, has the only war forged weapon amongst them, a heavy battle axe. The two older orcs rode up to just a few feet away from the group as the eldest one yelled out in orcish.

"Who are you and why are you trespassing on our lands?!"

Ariana raised her hands and yelled out. "We did not mean to trespass!" She slid out of the cart and walked over to them, hands still up and head low. "We are a special envoy from Dra'kesh, and we were attacked by bandits that forced us to take refuge in the forest."

The eldest orc grunted. "An envoy from Dra'kesh? You?"

"I'm not. I am just the translator. These are the guards. The envoy is the kobold over there," she said, pointing to Histra.

"What did I tell you about pointing to me? Have you resolved the situation yet? Why do I even have a translator if she does not translate what they say!" she growled, huffing and spreading her wings, speaking draconic.

The two younger orcs tensed and raised their bows, Alderin responding in kind, but then the elder raised his hand. "Who told you to raise your weapons?" He gave the two younger orcs a glare.

"No one, Father." They lowered them, Alderin doing the same.

"Forgive me. I was simply explaining our situation to them," Ariana explained in human.

"I didn't tell you to explain that to me, did I? You tell me what they say first then I tell you what to say!" Histra yelled.

The eldest orc eyed the kobold before turning his gaze back to Ariana. "She speaks orc?" he asked.

Ariana shook her head and said in human, "He says he was surprised by our arrival. He asks how he can help our situation."

Histra let out a huff. "Ask for an alternative route to get to Rivera, preferably one not covered in bandits. I'd like to get there and back home quickly without a chance of death by the locals," Histra said with a growl.

"As you wish," she responded in human before saying in orcish, "I told her you are asking how you could help. I know I should not lie about my translation, but I must placate the kobold. She has a nasty temper. We do not wish to cause you trouble, we just want to find an alternative route to get to Rivera. Any help will be appreciated and rewarded as our mission does involve contacting Sa'bara himself."

"Father, you can't seriously believe this. It is true there have been bandits a day's travel away, but an envoy from Dra'kesh?"

asked the eldest son near his father.

"Quiet! I will decide," he said to him, then speaking Ariana, "Have everyone show the back of their right hand. Kobold excluded."

"I will let them know," she said, turning to Histra, "He wishes to help but asks to have everyone show the back of their right hand. Except you of course great one," she explained with a slight bow.

"What? Wh… Sa'bara's mark. Do it!" Histra commanded.

"Show the back of your right hands," she translated in human, and the party did so, giving the orc father a clear view.

"Hmm, I've seen enough. I believe you."

The son's jaw dropped. "Father, but why?"

"What have I told you about speaking out of turn?" he grunted.

"Yes father," the eldest son huffed.

"Only those who live outside of this land would not have Sa'bara's mark. And to show it without hesitation means they aren't afraid to let him know they are without it. Only a fool would do so otherwise," he explained to his son.

"We appreciate your assistance," Ariana replied in orcish, turning to Histra speaking in human, "They are giving us direction to routes that we can use."

"Good," she replied.

"Do you happen to know of any other way to the city?"

"There is only one trail that you could use with a cart like that. It's used by a few people who want to avoid being seen. Despite the chance of running into less law-abiding folks, they won't cause you trouble as long as you leave them alone," he explained, giving the directions which Ariana conveyed in human.

"This is the same route I know," Histra thought. *"Wait… did she plan this so the others would know it too? If so, I will need to be extra cautious. I've foolishly underestimated her,"* she continued to think, then yelled, "Good. Now we've wasted enough time here. Go!"

"I'll be sure to make sure your help is not forgotten," Ariana said as the farmers gave their names and parted ways. She turned to the others, saying, "That went well, don't you think?"

"You did a great job. Is this path different from the one you know of Histra?" Jesmine asked.

172

"A little. Perhaps we'll take that one, since everyone knows of it. It's in the same general direction," she replied, sitting back down in her corner.

"That was good, you have a knack for that," said Alderin, riding up alongside the cart.

"Thanks. I've learned I have to be sneaky in more than one way when my other strengths don't pan out," she explained with a smirk.

"Speaking of which, when does that happen?"

"Within an hour after sunset."

"Is it painful? The transformation?" Gnemi asked.

"It can be uncomfortable but it's more of a rush than anything. It's rather thrilling actually," she responded, with a hint of longing.

"It's going to be strange camping with a werewolf... Lycan, but you've done right by me so far. I'm thankful for your help," Alderin said.

"Aye. I am still uneasy about this, but you've been upfront and communicative thus far. I, for one, appreciate that," Dran said.

"I won't play down the fact that we Lycans haven't earned our reputation, but you have nothing to fear from me as long as neither of us mean to do the other harm."

"That's good to hear," Jesmine said. "See Histra. Perhaps if you take after Ariana's example, it will ease tensions here."

Histra took a deep breath and replied, "If it were that easy for my well-being, I'd have done so. I have a knack to be able to read the malice the others have for me. Though you and Gnemi have been surprisingly lacking. the others will not trust me. I do not trust them. It is a mutual understanding. I have my word to keep with you. You saved my life after all, and my word is the only word I can truly trust, and I will uphold my end of our agreement."

Jesmine softly sighed as they continued their travel. Moving through the farmland, they eventually made it back to the forests and to the trail that was described to them. When the sun was getting close to setting, they took a small detour from the path and setup camp.

As darkness overtook the land, and the only light was from the flickering campfire and a sliver of moonlight from above, all eyes were upon Ariana, who placed Alderin's cloak off to the side.

"Do you have to be naked for it?" inquired Dran, who had

finished cooking meat pies, while Alderin watched her back side, keeping his gaze slightly averted.

"I prefer not to accidentally ruin the only piece of clothing I've had in decades," she replied with a smirk, brushing her long black hair away from her, grabbing her meat pie, tearing into it.

"Good point."

Her ivory skin began to darken as short black fur sprouted up all over. She voraciously ate her meal as fingernails darkened and curved, thickening into sharp claws. Ariana's nostrils flared, smelling the uneasiness coming from Dran and Alderin. Her body tensed as she ate.

"Do you have to eat during it?" Alderin asked.

"It helps," she said with a soft gurgling growl, fangs growing and protruded from her steadily elongating muzzle. A thick black tail sprung from behind as her lithe form thickened, muscles rippled and grew, legs and arms bulging. Her elven ears widened and became softer triangular shaped as they twitched and moved.

"I wish I had some parchment and a quill to record this," Gnemi said, intensely studying the transformation, heart racing.

"I'm sure you would," Ariana replied, body cracking and popping, the fur thickening as her long black hair faded into a moonlight white. Her underside grew a grey-white colored fur which contrasted with the rest of her black, and over a period of a few minutes the transformation was complete.

Sitting before them with a strong, yellow-eyed gaze was an anthropomorphized version of a wolf. Her clawed hands and muzzle were dirtied with what was left of the meat pie. Her long canine tongue licked her lips and hands, cracking her neck. She looked over the rest of the party, studying their reactions. Her ears turned to Histra, focusing her gaze on her. "Histra? You don't seem to be surprised by this."

She continued to tear into her meat pie before the last bit of warmth was sucked from it as parts of the bread already had frosted over. She stopped and looked up. "What? Do you want me to congratulate you on your lycanthropy? We knew it was coming. So, what's the issue?"

"We just saw a real Lycan transformation. You know how many people have seen that? And probably not be Lycans themselves? This is absolutely amazing!" exclaimed Gnemi.

"I'm pleased that you are so happy about it," she answered with a hint of sarcasm.

"You've seen it before, haven't you?" Ariana asked. Histra stared at her for a moment before going back to what remains of her meal without saying a word. She stood up and walked over to Histra, staring down at her.

"Ariana what's wrong?" Jesmine asked.

"I was uneased by the fact you knew I was a Lycan from the very beginning."

Alderin stood up. "It knew?!"

Histra looks over to him, "Yes, I knew."

"And you didn't tell us?!"

"It wasn't mine to tell," she replied with a smirk. She looked up at Ariana who crouched down and moved onto all fours in a primal stance, bringing her head down to be level with hers. "It would have really ruined any chance of freeing you, now wouldn't it, Ariana?" she asked with a continued smile. Ariana's breath fogged in front of her, bringing her head closer.

"I didn't survive this long by ignoring what troubles me. You know more about my kind than the average kobold."

"And how would you know what the average kobold knows?"

"Being hunted by greedy hunters looking to benefit from my capture, included many uninformed kobolds."

"I've been around. I didn't spend my entire life bound in a cage by a bunch of covetous orcs who paraded me around as a sideshow. I had a life before that, and that life included seeing a Lycan transformation or two."

"Where are you from? Everyone here has been upfront about themselves, except you," Ariana said with a growl.

"Where I am from does not matter. Where we are going, does."

Jesmine spoke up, "Ariana. I just went through this with Alderin and Dran. Do I have to do this with you? Histra insisted on saving your life. Give her some trust in the matter," said Jesmine.

Ariana's ears turned in her direction, followed by her head, "I am taking necessary precautions. I want to make sure my rescue isn't in reality a theft of opportunity. The temptation to impress one of the ancients is hard for many to ignore."

"I will say this. I have never been under the service of Sa'bara or Dra'kesh nor do I intend to serve them. I don't like their style of ruling."

"Whose rulership did you enjoy?" Gnemi asked. "Were you one of Eisandra's kobolds? I mean you are cold in a literal sense. I could theorize that, but that would make you old. How old do kobolds get?"

She completely ignored him and continued to stare at Ariana. "If you must know, one of my motivations is that despite the difficulties of getting you passed Rivera, is that your skills will be most useful getting through the lands controlled by the avolarieans. Getting past those birds will be tricky and they aren't going to be as negotiable as the orcs have been so far. Your sense of smell to help us avoid them will compensate for the trouble of freeing you and getting you across the Great River."

"You wanted me as your bloodhound. To sniff out threats before they arrive."

"Is that a *terrible* thing to ask for *freedom*?"

"Histra! You didn't have to be so secretive about this," Jesmine said "Why can't you just talk it out and tell us? We work better as a group."

Ariana cleared her throat, standing tall once again. "I can agree to that. Those after us will work as a tight unit. We need to do the same or we won't even make it to Rivera."

"You're both right," Dran said, standing up. "The kobold needs to tell us its plans. It's our guide, not our leader. It can't be making such decisions that affect the whole group without us, and rarely does a leader make such decisions without informing those around them. But it's late. We can continue this conversation in the morning. I'll take the first watch. Ariana, if you wish you may rest in my tent."

"Appreciated, but I prefer to remain outside," Ariana said, shaking her head. "It makes it easier to sense trouble when it's coming. I know the scent of those orcs, and after what they've done, their scent will wake me in a heartbeat. They shouldn't be able to get within a mile of us without me knowing."

"Shouldn't?" asked Dran, pulling out his axe.

"If they approach from downwind, it will limit my capabilities, also weather can be a major factor."

He nodded. "Best to put out the fire," he said, kicking dirt over the flames snuffing them out as the others headed off to sleep.

Elsewhere though, their pursuers were not done for the night.

The nearby table rattled as Garran finished his drink. "I need another," he grunted, leaning back in the chair taking a moment to relax in his room at a local inn. "After all that searching it turns out they weren't even at the bandit camp!"

Magical lights filled the room providing ample light for the whole party as Karrun checked over his war hammer. "We at least collected on the reward for ending the bandit threat."

"So?! I lost Greck and the window of opportunity to capture our cargo while she was in her weakest state is now gone!"

"I should have been more vigilant. It was fool's luck they happened to be in the same direction as the bandit camp," said Zed, laying a map of the area out on a nearby table, which included the city of Rivera that sat on top of a massive river.

"It was my fault. I didn't see where they left the path," replied Shana.

Garran said with a deep grunt, "It's now going to be difficult to catch her. More so if they fail to keep her under lock and key."

"The other villagers did say they had a cage bound to their cart. If anything, they shoved her in there," said Shana.

"Well get her Garran and those who stole her," said Orla, leaning against a wall cleaning her fingernails with one of her daggers. "We all have fault in this."

"With the new horses we purchased from the reward we can renew our chase at full speed," Karrun said.

"It won't be that easy," Orla said. "We all know how difficult it was to catch her the first place."

"She was but she's now weakened by the mithril shackles I placed on her, and if she's still caged, all we have to do is get the thieves and she'll be as good as ours," explained Zed, pulling out a light blue, cone-shaped crystal tied to a leather strap. He held the crystal over the town on the map. "Make sure the map is perfectly aligned to the cardinal directions."

"I got it," said Shana, pulling out her compass, making minor adjustments to the map as Zed continued to mutter in orcish-arcana. His tusks began to glow a light green, and after a minute, so did the crystal. At that point, he released the leather strap holding it, but it remained taut, held by some invisible force while continuing his mantra, hands making specific gestures.

Garran got up and walked over to the other table, watching silently as the crystal pendulum suddenly tugged in one direction, the leather strap keeping it from flying off. Zed continued for another half a minute as Shana marked the map with a coin. He finished his chant and grabbed the crystal just as the tension of the leather strap gave way.

"It looks like they aren't taking the main roads," stated Shana, looking over the results.

"Catching them out in the middle of nowhere away from patrols will be to our benefit. No one will be there to question us as we have no proof of ownership over the Lycan," said Zed, placing the crystal securely into his pouch.

"That is an option. Does anyone know of the paths in this area?" asked Garran as they shook their heads.

"We must not underestimate them. Not only did they manage to trick me about their relationship, they have the kobold, who was with that traveling circus. I believe they were from one of the lesser clans, and there is a chance they know paths to avoid the authorities."

"Their cart will slow them down. We can catch up to them with no problem," Karrun said.

"Assuming we are chasing after them and not the Lycan."

"And if the Lycan escapes?" Orla asked.

"We'll check every night. If the direction suddenly changes, then we'll know. Till then we'll assume they have her under lock and key."

"What do you suggest we do then Garran?"

"We know they are heading to Rivera. Draksind is upon us and they will want to collect their reward. These side paths will not be faster than a direct route. I suggest we take a moment and set an ambush ahead of them."

"Most of the land is flat and open space between here and there. Even if we set an ambush, they'd most likely be out of the forest," said Shana, pointing to the small nearby woodland where she placed the coin.

Garran studied the map, thick fingers running across the parchment, muttering incomprehensible words to himself, focusing on one marked forested area on the map before Rivera, "What do you think the odds are their path leads them here?"

"It's four days before Rivera. You sure you want to give them that much time?" Shana asked.

"Make them complacent. Have them feel they've escaped. We'll get there a day ahead of them. More than enough time to learn of any paths they could take. We'll ambush them, take back our treasure, and meet up with the others in Rivera. The sooner we get her there, the sooner we can cash in."

Shana nodded. "It can work."

"If that's what you want, I will do all I can to make it succeed," Zed said.

"You're the boss," said Karrun, laying his hammer down with a heavy thud.

Orla cleaned her daggers before she sheathed them. "You've done us well thus far. I feel trying to catch them there is an all or nothing gamble, but I trust your judgement."

Garran nodded. "We're in agreement then. Get some rest, we'll set out at first light."

Chapter 10 Ambush and Surprise

Histra stirred from underneath the carriage. The soft ground had become hard and frozen, the metal bits of the wagon wheel white with frost and bits of ice. She felt a hand wrap around her muzzle; her eyes shot open as she instinctively reached forward. Her claws wrapped around a wrist, as her vision came into focus. Alderin was on top of her, his hand tightly clamping her snout shut.

"About time you fell asleep. I've been waiting for a while to do this," he said, thrusting his dagger into Histra's gut, his breath fogging over her face. Pain shot through her body as red crimson blood flowed down her belly. Her eyes widened, claws digging into Alderin's wrists, barely able to break through the cloth, blood slowly soaking through.

"Shh, I don't want you to wake Jesmine," he continued, driving the dagger deeper into her. Histra's wings twitched, feet sliding against the hard ground, trying to open her mouth. She stared into Alderin's eyes, trying to work up the liquid for her ice breath.

Dran spoke up, standing off to the side with his battle-axe in hand, "Ariana told us all about your manipulation, and with her ability to continue to educate Alderin orc tongue along with her survival instincts, we won't be needing your kind anymore."

Alderin forced the kobold's head off to the side and pinned it to the ground. Gnemi stood on the other side of her. "I wanted to get more information out of you before this, but perhaps dissecting your cadaver will have to do," the gnome said cheerfully with a wide grin, Alderin dragging her body along the ground till her head was out from underneath the wagon, neck exposed to Dran.

Histra's eyes gave a soft glow in the moonlight as the blade reflected in them which swung down with a sickening crack. Her body jerked, eyes opening to find herself leaning against the back corner of the cart.

"Finally, you're awake. You know if you slept when everyone else did you could stay up and help keep watch," said Alderin in orcish, riding beside the cart.

She cleared her throat and stretched, giving him a long stare. "A momentary slip of consciousness," she replied in orcish.

"You're doing a great job Alderin. And you said you have only been learning this for a little while?" Ariana asked in orcish.

"Some before reaching town with Histra. It's an attempt to smooth things over or something."

Histra let out a huff of air through her nostrils. "Try to be nice…" she grumbled in draconic.

"What was that?" Alderin asked in orcish but she said nothing.

"Don't mind her. Keep focusing on your lesson. The more you know the language, the better off we'll be," said Ariana in human tongue, sitting near the front of the cart.

"Learning the eloquence of the tongues of other races was never my forte. It's why I only know gnome and human. Humans are most likely everywhere, so it was a safe bet language to learn," said Gnemi. "Histra, what languages do you know? You seem to be well versed in a few. I believe I heard that kobolds know a what others might call a 'bastardized variant' of dragon tongue, is that true?"

She looked over at him for only a brief moment before rolling her shoulders, looking out into the surrounding forest.

He gave a sigh of defeat, resuming his watch over the horses.

Jesmine smiled. "Don't worry Gnemi. She'll open up to you soon."

"You think? I'm not sure I know anything about kobolds except a few scant lessons and written works of second-hand accounts of those who fought them, which is not always the most reliable information, I tell you."

"Histra is a little rough but she does things the way she wants at her own pace. Once she's ready, she'll tell you what you want to know."

"I can hear you two talk about me you know," Histra said, not turning to face them.

"I know," Jesmine replied.

"I'd prefer if you did not presume things. You know nothing about me," she said.

"You've made that abundantly clear," replied Gnemi, looking over to her.

"I do not presume. I say it how I've seen it," Jesmine replied.

Histra looked over her shoulder, asking, "Why do you want to know about my kind so much?"

"Huh, uh, oh me? Sorry I wasn't expecting you to ask me a

question," stammered Gnemi, looking over his shoulder again while trying to keep the horses on track. Dran was up ahead by two horse lengths.

"Who else would I ask?"

"Truth be told. I am curious. I probably won't get another chance like this ever again. I want good honest information about your kind."

She nodded and looked back over the cart, while he looked at her for a few moments before sighing softly to look ahead.

"I feel cold."

"Huh?"

"I feel cold, but it doesn't bother me. It's comforting. You asked me that once, didn't you?"

"Uh, yes… yes I did."

"There's your answer."

Gnemi's eyes lit up. "Thanks. I will try to remember that. I appreciate it."

She shrugged. "Keep a look out. I prefer not to get jumped. It's been quiet and we're at the last forest before it's all plains from here on out. Seeing that it's tax season we might want to shift to a main road at this point."

"The main road? That will put us at a huge risk!" Alderin exclaimed.

"Actually, it might be a good idea if the orcs are after us. Moving to the main road within a day's ride to Rivera would be a good move. If we can keep Ariana hidden, we'll be safer mixing in with others," Jesmine explained.

"Others?"

"It's Draksind. The road to Rivera will be full of people heading there to pay their taxes."

"You mean tribute."

"Sa'bara wishes it to be called a tax."

"Dra'kesh calls it tribute."

"It's tax here. People from around the land will collect what they can offer, and send representatives of the villages, towns, cities and come to Rivera. There you'd pay your Draksind and depending on how much you pay, it is possible to increase the influence you'd wield within his land."

"And what happens if you can't pay the minimum?" Alderin

asked.

"Depending how short one is, you could be imprisoned to work off your debt or simply disappear. But there are many ways that Sa'bara allows Draksind to be paid. It could be through goods or services, the value of which can change year to year."

"Really? I've heard that Dra'kesh probably just wants precious items, gold, gemstones, and the like. How does your system work?" asked Gnemi, looking to Jesmine with curiosity.

"Halfway between each Draksind we are informed of what Sa'bara will prefer in tax, and those items and services will have an extra weight. Like when Eisandra fell, there was an increased tax value on stone, artisans, and military service to build and defend a series of forts along the northern border."

"You haven't been here in decades how do you know Rivera is still the central tax location?"

"It still is. My previous captors always went there, as it was a good place to not only pay their Draksind but drum up some money due to the influx of people and large crowds that needed their twisted entertainment," Histra explained.

"And the kobolds there to watch over the tax didn't help you? You'd think a baby ice dragon would have brought some attention," Jesmine asked.

She looked over her shoulder. "They didn't care. You assume every kobold is allied and friends with one another. We're not. We're just as grouped and divided as humans, orcs, and the other races."

"If you all don't mind, I'd like Alderin up here with me. While we are in the forest, it would be wise to keep watch," remarked Dran, motioning Alderin forward.

"He makes a good point," Ariana said, "I have been paying attention, but extra eyes can't hurt."

"Easy enough. Thank you, Ariana, for the lessons," Alderin replied, squeezing the sides of Cetas, tugging on the reins, riding ahead and up alongside Dran.

"Enjoying your lessons?" asked Dran, giving him a quick glance before returning to his survey of the forest. The leaves in the trees rustle as small woodland creatures jump between branches in the ample sunlight making it through the forest canopy.

"Yes. I've also learned a lot," Alderin replied, keeping watch on his side, moving through a beaten path, with signs of overgrowth already trying to reclaim it. Shrubs and twigs were crushed and broken under the weight of the horses and cart.

"Aye. I don't mind it. I prefer it. I think you have a talent for learning other tongues, but the current situation doesn't sit well with me, and I'm not referring to those behind us. Those orcs were able to capture a damn Lycan. That's no easy feat. They have at least one good tracker. One who uses magic, and even if they keep some members of their party back to watch over their other beasts, they will not let Ariana go without a fight."

Alderin's hands tensed on Cetas' reins. "It hasn't left my thoughts. Perhaps they are waiting at Rivera?"

"Hmm, that is a possibility... Jesmine! Question about this city."

She raised her head, "Yes?"

"When we get there, what's the chances we'll get attacked? If the orcs figure we are heading through the city, will they try to get back what is so called theirs? I don't think we can take on an entire city of orcs."

Jesmine shook her head. "No, I don't think so. Order and control are paramount during Draksind. Punishment for even minor disruptions are usually heavy handed."

Histra turned around. "They have no proof of ownership. Robbery of tax goods before getting to Rivera is common. Why do you think there were reports of those bandits? If I were them I—"

Ariana's ears perked, lifting her head and holding her hands up. "Stop. Stop!" she yelled as Histra held onto the side of the wagon, the cart stopping, horses neighing softly.

"What is it?" Gnemi asked.

"I smell them, five. Just up ahead, the leader, the wizard, the one good with a war hammer..." she lifted her head higher, sniffing the air, her body tensed as her tail wagged quickly. "The female who managed to track me down and another."

Alderin pulled out his bow while Dran his axe. "How close?"

"I can't tell, the air here is strange," said Ariana as suddenly a large, brown colored fog appeared twenty feet ahead of them, but quickly it lit up into a brilliant display of fire, rushing towards them.

"Run!" yelled Ariana as Jesmine sat up and began to mutter an incantation. Cetas and Dariel bucked up in fear, the heat of the flames blowing across their faces, singeing their hair. The horses hitched to the cart became increasingly agitated with each passing moment. The ball of fire roared towards them.

Those on the wagon felt a quick chill, Histra sprinting past them, leaping off the cart, and with a few hard wing flaps propelled herself over the hitched horses and landed between Alderin and Dran. Her right horn had a faint bluish glow tracing along the engravings. With a deep breath, she spat up the ice-cold liquid, unleashing a white frozen mist which smashed into the wall of flames, snuffing them out moments before the fires reached them.

In front of them, what was green, and lush forest was now covered in a thin, white layer of frost that went out a few feet before fading into charred brush. The bucked-up horses landed with a thud as Histra panted and coughed. A combination of white mist and grey smoke mixed and twirled like miniature tornados on the path but were no fiercer than a gentle breeze.

"Push ahead!" yelled Dran, tugging on the Dariel's reins.

Alderin following suit, yelling, "We'll keep the path clear!"

Gnemi, with his crossbow in one hand, tugged on the reins with the other commanding the horses forward. The horses sprinted, the cart jerking forward, causing some of the supplies to slide towards the back.

"Histra get on!" yelled Jesmine, the kobold panting and looking over her shoulder, the cart rushing to her. With no time to spare, she jumped and gave her wings a single hard flap, which boosted her just high enough to let her legs and tail get caught by the wagon. She spun and tumbled past everyone, landing with her back and head into the cage with a loud ding. Her horns poked through the metal bars, having just missed them. Histra groaned, a white flash passing before her vision.

The cart sped forward, rocking and bouncing, while in this same instant, coming out of the smoke was Karrun wielding his war hammer, its runes blazing a fiery red. He swung at Dariel. The dwarf's axe clashed with Karrun's hammer, deflecting the blow, flames "sparking" as the weapons met. The heat of the hammer further singeing the hair on Dran's face and the side of his horse.

An arrow whizzed past Dran and landed right into Karrun's

arm, the orc yelling in pain, blood flowing from the wound while Alderin and Dran rode past him, the human nocking another arrow. He tightly gripped his hammer, turning his attention to the cart, raising it up into the air. A scream of pain echoed through the forest.

An arrow lodged into the back of Alderin's shoulder, blood staining his clothes, unleashing his shot, the arrow sliding across Karrun's armor to no effect, while they continued to ride ahead. Karrun's swing was delayed by the arrow striking him, the cart rushing by his eyes wide in shock, seeing Ariana free. A whistle echoed through the forest as he fell back into the brush, while Orla pulled out from behind on horseback, giving chase.

The cart ran into smoke, blinding the group for only a moment. As they burst through, they noticed that Dran and Alderin were riding about five horse lengths in front of them.

Standing just ahead of all of them off to the side, partially covered in the brush, was Zed speaking loud and clear in orcish-arcana, his hands moving in calculated motions. Alderin attempted to bring his bow to bear at him. His muscles tensed, pain shooting through his arm, unable to even partially draw his bow as he clenched his teeth, feeling the warm trickle of blood down his back.

Gnemi fired a shot from his crossbow, the bolt whizzing inches past the unflinching orc arcanist. Zed continued his chant, focusing on the cart riding past him. His tusks glowed purple along the arcane markings.

Gnemi wrapped the reins around his arm, turning to fire another shot just as Zed finished his spell, with a plume of purple colored haze appearing in the space between the horses and the cart. They ran right through it just as his bolt hit Zed's lower torso.

The orc grunted, hands dropping, chant stopping, the purple haze instantly beginning to dissipate but managed to linger over the cart for a few seconds.

Orla rode past him, the purple cloud gone by the time she gets to the same location.

Garran rode through the forest with a second unmounted horse in tow. "Are you okay?"

Zed grunted. "Just a flesh wound, but I believe I got those on the cart, including the Lycan," he replied, mounting the horse, with a loud groan, not bothering to touch the bolt as its end bobbed up and down.

"Are you able to continue?"

"Of course," he replied, Karrun and Shana riding past them as they got going.

When the purple haze cleared around the cart, Jesmine released her held breath. "That was close. Is everyone else okay?" she asked. Gnemi was hunched over the back of the seat unconscious, barely holding onto his crossbow.

"I knew it was sleeping gas," she said, grabbing the reins from him, gently pushing him into the cart.

Ariana lets out a huff of air from her nostrils. "I fell for that once, not again."

Jesmine gained control over the horses, Alderin and Dran pulling farther ahead. She turned her attention to Histra. "Are you okay?"

She gave a big, open mouth yawn, rubbing the back of her head. "All things considering…" she said, Jesmine observing Orla catching up.

"Histra, do you know how long till we're out of this forest?"

She raised an eye ridge, giving a quick look around. "I can't be sure. It will be a little while still if nothing else stops us."

Jesmine nodded. "Ariana can you take the reins?" she asked, holding them out to her.

Her ears twitched, tilting her head to the side, before grabbing them with her clawed hands. "It's been decades, but I can."

"Please do it, I have a plan."

"Got it," she replied, switching places with Jesmine, who climbed into the back of the cart, pushing items off to the back, clearing a space around her.

"What are you doing?" asked Histra.

"I need space for my spell. Can you use Gnemi's crossbow?"

She pulled herself up, watching the orc that was only moments away from catching up to them with Shana and Karrun not much farther behind. She rushed over to the crossbow and picked it up. She looked over the mechanical contraption curiously before taking aim. The small bits of metal that composed parts of the crossbow frosted over, pulling the trigger. Nothing. "It's not working," she grunted.

Alderin groaned, looking over his injured shoulder. "Dran, you can handle anything that happens here right?"

"Aye. It looks clear," he replied.

"Good, I am going to try to slow our pursuers," he said, slowing down.

"Don't get yourself killed!" Dran yelled, Alderin now riding beside the cart, watching Histra fumble with the crossbow.

"Histra, give that to me!" he shouted. The width between him and the cart ever shifting, his injured arm holding onto the reins, working to keep Cetas on the path.

Without a word, Histra tossed it and Alderin managed to catch it by the wooden stock. He turned and aimed at Orla who was about to reach them. Her body was low to her horse, bouncing against it. She yelled in orcish, pushing her steed to its limits, weapons jingling on her side.

Alderin steadied himself the best he could and fired. The bolt pierced her armor and into her leg. She grunted, feeling the warm crimson blood trickling down her thigh. Orla looked to the human with a crossbow in hand still aimed at her before glancing behind to see the others. She slowed down, pulling farther away from the cart till she was now riding alongside her companions.

"This is not going as planned," she said, eyeing the bolt in her leg, "Jumping onto a moving cart with a free Lycan onboard is suicide."

"I've disabled their archer," Shana stated.

"What do you call this then?!" said Orla, motioning to her leg.

"I saw the crossbow fire, and it hasn't reloaded," she explained, drawing her bow while another crossbow bolt whizzed by her head.

Orla counters, the arrow piercing into Alderin's arm, a few inches away from the first injury.

His body jerked, hand twitching, gritting his teeth, staring down the orc, taking aim.

"Alderin!" yelled Jesmine, finishing sliding enough provisions out of the way to provide a sizable area in the cart.

"I'm fine," he replied, blood dripping down his fingertips.

Orla said, "Looks loaded to me."

"There is something strange about that crossbow, fall back. I'll keep them in sight. Confirm with Garran what to do next," she commanded, the others retreating till only Shana was left in view of the cart.

"They aren't giving up that easily. They must be planning something," Alderin said.

"Stay ahead of us, we need to keep going and make it out of the forest; I'll handle the rest," said Jesmine, turning to Histra. "Histra, climb onto my back."

She tilted her head to the side. "What?"

"Climb onto my back and hold on tight, and whatever you do, don't let go."

"Do you want to be frozen?"

"I won't, but I need your ice aura, or this won't end well," she said, looking her straight in the eye, swallowing a lump in her throat. "Please."

She sighed. "Fine." Jesmine lowering herself allowing her to climb onto her back. Histra's arms braced around Jesmine's shoulders and neck, legs around her sides with her tail wrapped around her waist. "Like this?"

"Perfect, I need to keep my hands and arms free."

"You better know what you are doing," she remarked, Jesmine standing up, adjusting herself to her new center of gravity.

"What are you doing?" asked Ariana, keeping her attention focused on the horses.

"Empowering a lesser spell, the hard way," she explained, taking a deep breath and slowly releasing it, her breath fogging.

"Be careful," cautioned Alderin, moving only slightly ahead of them.

"This is humiliating," Histra remarked in draconic as Jesmine began to speak in elvish-arcana, her hands and body moving fluidly around the open space on the cart. Her focus locked on the horse far behind them, her tattoos within seconds giving off a soft, red-orange glow.

Shana grunted at what she saw, nocking another arrow. "No, you don't!" she said, firing, the arrow whizzing right past her head.

Jesmine didn't flinch, continuing her arcane dance ritual, her tattoos glowing steadily brighter.

Histra silently watched her, keeping a tight but not constricting grip.

"Damn. Sir! The human is a spell caster!" Shana yelled behind her, a moment later hearing a long whistle. Shana tensed, grumbling as she fell back, nocking another arrow.

Garran, who was not far behind her, motioned her over "Do you think you know what kind of spell it is?"

"Don't know. I don't recognize it. I saw some orange glow appearing on her body."

"It's probably fire magic. At this point, don't break it. If it backfires it could catch our prize, and a dead Lycan won't do us any good. Zed went that way to circle them from the side. Catch up and tell him of the situation."

"What about you?"

"I'll follow out of sight. She can't hold the spell for long and will have to dissipate it. Zed is preparing a major fog of sleep to envelope all of them. After that you'll know what to do."

"Yes sir," she replied, riding off.

Meanwhile, the party rode as fast as the horse drawn cart would allow. Gnemi was still fast asleep, his body propped up in the front corner as Jesmine's arcane dance continued. She repeated the whole incantation and movements over and over, her tattoos glowing ever brighter, to the point that the radiance was noticeable in Dran's peripheral vision.

"Jesmine what are you doing? I don't see any of them," he asked with concern.

Alderin kept a vigilant look out, ready for the next blow to come from anywhere.

Jesmine didn't respond, continuing the spell cast. Her body grew warmer, the fogging of her breath fading to nothing. The cart shook as the sound of the wheels breaking over small brush echoed through the forest. The horses panted heavily, their hooves clopping across the ground. Jesmine focused in front of her, hands glowing alight, flames appearing on her fingertips.

Ariana looked over her shoulder, her eyes widening with concern, ears flattening as the cart hit a dip in the path. The cart bounced, the items in the cart jostling around. Gnemi slid from his spot and towards them.

Histra eyed his limp body about to collide into Jesmine.

Her foot bumped into him, the fire on her fingertips spreading along her fingers and around her hands growing stronger and brighter.

Ariana grabbed Gnemi, pulling him away.

The wood darkened and smoked underneath Jesmine's feet while Histra no longer felt her cold aura. She tensed, claws and wings twitching as parts of her body felt as if heat was being applied to recent burn wounds, yet she remained completely silent.

Jesmine quickly regained her composure as the wild flicker of the flames stopped, but they remained just as large, sweat pouring down her brow. The scent of burnt hair filled the air, her tattoos now a bright, burning red, flames dancing around her palms.

Ariana slid to a corner, feeling the heat blowing onto her back, the forest before her thinning out toward open fields. "We're almost out of here!" she yelled.

Jesmine continued her arcane mantra, her eyes burning with energy.

The orcs emerged from the forest in a big U-shaped formation. Zed's tusks glowed a bright purple, his orcish-arcana spell near its completion. He looked to the group, taking one last deep breath, pointing in their direction, holding in the other hand a leather-bound tome with silver runic markings along the back and sides, which glowed a matching purple.

Jesmine pointed her hands at the far end of the forest and as she spoke the final phrase of the spell, two giant pillars of fire burst forth from the ground far away from each other. The two fires, about ten feet tall, spread quickly in a line towards the other, following Jesmine's hand movements as she brought them together in a loud explosive clap.

A massive wall of fire burned brightly, and roared with vigor, as a few trees caught within the wall instantly burst into flames and billowed up black smoke. The orcs yelled in surprise, tugging on the reins of their horses, slowing them down to avoid the wall of fire, the animals kicking up uneasily.

Garran turned his gaze away from the brightly burning fire wall just as a puff of purple smoky haze suddenly appeared to his far left. "No!" he yelled, riding toward the smoke.

The convection of air from the heat of the flames pulled the haze away so quickly that by the time he got there, the purple fog was gone. Laying on the ground dangerously close to the flames were the unconscious bodies of Zed, Shana, and their horses.

Garran gripped his reins tightly, calling for the others who rushed to his aid, pulling them away from the unmoving flames which charred the nearby land, with only a few disconnected fires spontaneously combusting.

Sweat continued to pour down Jesmine's brow as she now stood still, her gaze focused on the fire, her hands making slight motions, continuing to chant under her breath.

Everyone couldn't help but look at the wall of fire, riding blindly ahead. Histra tensed, gritting her teeth, feeling the constant heat pounding against her form while raising an eye ridge of surprise.

"I have never... useless without your spellbook she says..." Dran muttered.

"That's certainly one way to get rid of them," remarked Alderin, moving beside the cart. "Do you really need your spellbook?"

Ariana growled. "Quiet. She's still focusing on the spell." The Lycan's ears folded back, looking behind her one last time at the display of Jesmine's prowess.

"Sorry," he replied, looking at the two arrows sticking out of his body. "We should find a place to hide."

"There is a pond in that direction, and it can be a good place to rest but it's an hour away," Histra said, using her tail for a moment to point in the direction before wrapping it back around Jesmine's waist.

"Will you be okay with that Alderin?" asked Ariana, looking at his wounds from a distance.

"I'll be fine for a while. I think the bleeding has stopped. I'll let Dran know of the direction," he said, catching up and explaining it to him.

Dran looked over at Alderin's injury, watching the arrows wiggle slightly with each trot. "Do you think you can make it?"

Alderin looked at his wound. "Yeah."

"Good," he replied, changing direction and the others followed suit. The flames still visible even at a distance. "That is going to draw a lot of attention."

Alderin said, "Hopefully we'll be long gone before anyone comes to investigate"

"How are the others?" he asked.

"Gnemi is unconscious, but he looked alive. Everyone else

appears to be in one piece."

"That's good. The blessed Earth Mother must have been watching over us to get away so unscathed."

"Speak for yourself," he groaned.

"Considering they jumped us, we got lucky."

"They underestimated us. It won't happen a second time."

"Aye they did, not that there will be a second time," Dran replied, giving one last look at the wall of flames. "Even from here she keeps them up. That is something."

Jesmine remained focused on the fire wall, her tattoos glowing while she made slow and calculated hand motions in conjunction to her chant. Sweat dripped from her nose, and only where Histra was holding onto her remained drenched.

Just as the fire began to fade out of view, Jesmine took a single, deep breath, her hands slowly rising, and deliberately exhaled while pulling her hands down, the wall of fire shrank and shortened until it suddenly puffed out of existence. The glow from her tattoos faded completely. The wall of fire left charred earth and a few natural born fires in the forest.

Jesmine though, only saw the billowing smoke rise into the sky. She collapsed to her knees almost falling over before she caught herself with one hand. Short of breath, she barely managed to say to Histra, "Are you okay?"

"Don't do that again," she replied as the sweat on Jesmine's body froze and melted in pulsating waves. She let go and took a few steps back as the rate of freeze slowed but the heat emanating from her body remained.

"I don't think I will," she replied before collapsing. Histra sighed, grabbing an empty, folded provision sack before placing it under Jesmine's head.

"Jesmine!" shouted Alderin, riding over, "What happened? Is she okay? How about Gnemi?"

Ariana nodded. "Gnemi was knocked out with sleeping gas from the orc wizard. I don't know how long he'll be out. Jesmine is exhausted. Anything else I don't know."

Dran made his way back to the cart, saying, "I've seen this. She's suffering from magic feedback."

"Will she be okay?" Alderin asked.

"I don't know. Casting a spell of that magnitude is no simple feat. Most wouldn't have been able to survive the casting…" he said trailing off for a moment, his hands tightly gripping the reins. "This is why I chose not to learn the arcane arts. The risks are too great. I prefer enchanted weapons. They are far safer to deal with."

"She should be okay," Histra stated.

"How can you be so sure?" Alderin asked, giving her an inquisitive look.

"She used my ice aura to help nullify the effects of the heat caused by focusing the spell. She planned this out," she said, looking to Jesmine. "I'll keep an eye on her and keep her cool. The rest of you keep watch. We can't assume we are safe yet," she said with a wing flick. "There is nothing any of you can do right now. Get to the pond and from there we can figure out what to do next." Her attention turned to Alderin, "Such as getting those arrows out of you. I'm sure you'd love that."

The two stared at each other for a moment but Alderin's gaze was broken when Ariana called his name.

"Yes?"

"What kind of medical kit did you bring with you on this journey?"

"A basic one. A surgical knife, some herbs, bandages and a sewing kit."

"Good. I'll get those arrows out of you when we stop. For now, don't touch them. It's better for you to leave them in there than for you to try to remove them."

"Easy for you to say. I can feel them move with each step," he grunted. "But this isn't the first arrow wound I've seen. I know the basics."

"Excellent," she replied as their pace slowed, and with it, the anxiety of the fight. Ariana kept a nose out, trying her best to overcome the smell of charred wood and dried blood, while Dran and Alderin kept watch.

Histra stood over Jesmine watching the freeze and melt cycle slow with longer and longer periods of freezing before the melt. Eventually there was no melting period, Jesmine beginning to shiver. Histra walked over to the far end of the cart, sitting on a pile of supplies, looking out over the plains. The grasses swayed and moved like an ocean. She gazed over the horizon, unable to see the black smoke anymore, her wings slightly unfurled, shoulders dropping.

Ariana every so often looked over to Jesmine and Gnemi, who was still fast asleep. When she noted Jesmine's improved state, her tail wagged a little faster. She listened to Dran and Alderin chatting it up, while taking a moment to attempt in vain to adjust her mithril cuffs.

A long drawn out yawn broke the overall tranquility of the moment, followed by the sound of something hitting wood. "We're under attack! Where is my crossbow?" yelled Gnemi, looking around frantically.

"It's over," Histra stated. "We escaped."

"Huh? What? But... what happened? I fired a shot at the orc with the glowing tusks and then... I don't know."

Ariana spoke up. "You hit him and broke his concentration of the sleep gas spell. You probably saved us during that part of the ambush."

"I did? Well, hmm probably," he replied, brushing himself off, adjusting the goggles around his neck.

Ariana smirked. "You just were the only one not to notice the sleep spell and fell victim to it."

"Ah, that explains that, is eve... Jesmine! Are you okay?" he yelled, stumbling over to her.

"Quiet. Jesmine is resting. She cast a large firewall spell that covered half the forest and is understandably very exhausted from it. I believe she's recovering from the spell's aftereffects. Isn't that right Histra?" Ariana asked.

Histra replied, "More or less."

"She cast a huge spell?" asked Gnemi with a hint of excitement.

"Biggest I've seen in my life," Ariana replied.

"Damn it. I would have loved to see it at work... but there is still one important question to ask."

"Hmm?" she inquired, ears turning in his direction, her tail giving an inquisitive wag, brushing some hair away from her eyes to keep a visual on him.

"Where is my crossbow?"

"Here," said Alderin, holding out the crossbow. "Sorry, but I had to use it as my bow arm is out of action, till we get the arrows out."

"Careful!" Gnemi yelled, fumbling with the crossbow before he wrapped his arms completely around it.

"Sorry. But it was better than the kobold fumbling with it and breaking it while trying to figure it out."

Gnemi examined the weapon, running his fingers over the wood and bowstrings. "I understand. Not that I was much help, seeing that I slept through the whole thing."

"It's fine. We made it and that is what matters. We're hopefully near the oasis where we can rest and get these damn things out of me." Alderin head motioned to the arrows.

Gnemi winced. "Oh, my Gods… Those look painful just looking at them."

"You have no idea," he replied.

"Also, not to sound rude, but it wouldn't be called an oasis."

"Huh?"

"You said we are going to an oasis, but we aren't in a desert, so it wouldn't be an oasis."

"You know what I mean Gnemi."

"I do."

"Then don't worry about it," he replied with a soft chuckle as he climbed into the front seat of the cart.

"I didn't know you could drive."

Ariana tilted her head just enough to have one eye trained onto him, responding. "You never asked."

"Touché."

"I learned before I became a Lycan."

Gnemi nodded. "Ah," he replied, looking around. "Anyone seen my bolts? I had them in the back of the cart."

Histra let out a soft sigh, wandering to the other side of the cart and pulled a few sacks out of the way to retrieve a completely enclosed partially frozen over quiver case, walking it over to him. "Jesmine moved things around to make space to perform her spell," she explained, motioning to the charred wood markings under Jesmine which had a runic shape.

"Thanks. I appreciate it Histra."

Without saying a word, she returned to her corner of the cart as he unlatched the top, pulling out a single bolt to check it over and started the process of loading the crossbow.

"Is it a wise idea to have it loaded like that all the time?"

Ariana asked.

"I built in a safety feature. If this isn't pushed in this way and made flush with the wood, the trigger shouldn't work," Gnemi explained, showing a small level rod on the right side of the crossbow. "I've found having it always at the ready far outweighs any other risks."

"How clever."

"Thanks," he said with a smile. "Besides, these things usually take a while to load, a luxury not often given in combat."

Ariana replied, "True."

Eventually they found the pond with a few sparse trees. Willow wisps lined the edges as a little bit of green algae sat on the surface, which they cleared as they brought their horses to drink. A few birds chirped in the lush green trees as small woodland critters dispersed when Dran and Gnemi began to set up camp. Alderin laid on his belly with Ariana kneeling beside him with his leather armor already removed and the arrows' shafts broken halfway down. Dried blood was caked onto his tanned skin. A small fire was lit near them, Ariana examining the wounds, sniffing them, getting close before wiggling the arrow in his arm.

"Do you have to do that!" yelled Alderin, tensing in pain, gritting his teeth.

"I am seeing how deep it went. The leather armor provided a fair bit of protection, and it looks like the arrow didn't get too far here. I'll start by removing this one."

"Just make it quick."

"I'm going to do it right," she said, putting the tip of the small surgical blade into the fire for a few moments before dipping it into a small cup of water, which hissed and steamed upon contact. Despite her large seemingly unwieldly pawed hands, she handled the blade with surprising precision. She offered a stick to him. "Bite on this."

Alderin steeled himself while she cut into the wound slightly widening it. Alderin muffled his own screams the best he could, hands digging into the ground. Dran and Gnemi continued to keep themselves busy as Histra watched from on top of the cart, her attention split between them and Jesmine.

"There we go," Ariana said, finding the arrow's head, easily pulling it out and tossing it to the side. "Now to stop this bleeding and help the healing," she said, reaching for the grey stone mortar with the matching color pestle still inside. She dips her finger in to pull out a green-yellow paste.

"Wait, what? You are going to use that on me?"

"Yes, why do you think I spent five minutes on it as you got your armor off."

"Use what we have. Not some... whatever that is."

"I don't trust what you have. I'm a trained alchemist. Did you think I collected plants during our stops for fun? Now deal with it. This will sting but it should triple the normal rate of healing and prevent infection."

"Dran, you can't let her do this..."

"Be a man, and take it," Ariana said, rubbing the paste into his open wound. Alderin grunted and groaned as she rubbed it, then sewed the wound closed, before taking some of the cotton roll and wrapping it around his arm. "That's one."

Alderin panted heavily as he said, "If I told anyone I would receive medical aid from a Lycan, they'd call me insane."

"Yes, they would, now accept it, this next one might hurt more," she responded, gripping the shaft of the second and attempted to twirl it.

"What are you doing!" Alderin screamed.

"Testing if it's stuck in your bone... and," she sighed then continued, "It is. This one is going to be difficult." Ariana got onto Alderin's back. "Don't move, this is going to hurt a lot," she warned, beginning to make the incisions into his back-shoulder blade. The human muffled his pain once again. Ariana cut down till the arrowhead was revealed. Crimson blood flowed from the wound, giving the arrow a firm tug. He grunted again as she tugged harder, but it didn't come out.

Jesmine suddenly sat up looking around. "What's wrong? What's happening?!" she asked as she attempted to stand but stumbled back down.

"Relax," Histra said, glancing at her. "Alderin is getting an arrow removed from his shoulder by Ariana. She has it all under control." she explained as he yelled even louder, Ariana placing her knee on Alderin's shoulder blade. She grabbed as much of the broken arrow shaft as she could, pulling hard.

"There anything we can do?" asked Gnemi, wincing.

"This your first time seeing an arrow being removed?" Dran asked.

"From someone living."

"Aye," Dran said. "Alas there is not much you can do. If those buggers get stuck in bone, they can be very difficult to remove. We can only hope the shaft doesn't come free of the arrowhead. You don't want to leave one of those in you. But we should continue. He will need time to recuperate."

Gnemi nodded. "Okay," he said just as the arrow came free, and the sudden release of tension sent Ariana flying backwards, landing on her back with a hard thud.

"These cuffs are making me so weak," she growled, seeing the arrowhead still attached to the shaft. "Small miracles." She grinned, getting back to her feet, patching up the second wound the same way as the first. Alderin remained still, panting heavily, dirt mixing in with his ever-thickening black facial hair, hands full of torn grass.

"Please don't do that again," Alderin muttered.

"Don't get hit with an arrow and I'll be glad to grant your request," Ariana answered with a smirk, tossing the arrow shaft into the fire.

He watched from his face-down position. "We could use those arrowheads."

"We can retrieve them once the fire goes out." Ariana answered. "For now, you worry about healing so lay there and don't move." She helped Dran and Gnemi set up camp.

Jesmine jumped off the cart stumbling and almost falling over as she landed.

"I don't know the effects of the overuse of magic, but I give you the same advice," said Ariana.

"I'll be fine," she said, walking over to Alderin. "I'm so sorry I put you through this."

Alderin coughed, brushing some dirt away from his face. "It's fine. I'll recover in no time, but what you did back there was nothing short of amazing. Those orcs had to be fried in such a large fire."

"I can agree to that. We may not have to worry about them specifically, but there were more to their group, and they will be none too happy," Dran said.

Jesmine looked away, gently rubbing her hands together. "About that...,"

"She didn't hit or get a single one of them," Ariana said with a soft growl, looking to her.

Dran turned to Ariana, "What?"

"I know the smell of burning flesh, I didn't catch a single whiff. That big display was just to stop them from chasing us, wasn't it Jesmine?"

She looked down before answering. "Yes."

Histra softly sighed, thinking, *"I knew it."*

"What? Why?" Alderin asked.

She closed her eyes and took a deep breath. "I couldn't without real justification."

"Real justification? They shot at us. With intent to kill!" Alderin exclaimed. "How is that not justification?" He winced, sitting up.

Jesmine took a deep breath and looked at Alderin. "Yes, and if it got any worse, I'd done so to defend us, and I was ready to do so but when I saw a chance to escape without having to, I took it."

"But why!"

"They were doing what they thought was right. We stole from them and they wanted it back."

Ariana gave a long low growl. "They hunted me! Them and countless other people wanting my hide for some benefit. If I had any idea of how strong you were, when we broke their trap, we should have turned on them and got rid of them for good."

"It's not completely their fault. They are doing what they think is best."

Ariana walked to Jesmine who pushed herself up onto her feet. "Not their fault?" she growled, the two facing off, Ariana with a clear foot in height over Jesmine." They deserve to die for what they did to me."

"Calm down Ariana. We're in this together," Dran said, moving closer with one hand on the hilt of his axe.

"Are we?" She turned and glared at him, her body tensing, tail wagging furiously.

"I'd say so. Jesmine risked her life to save us. I've seen spells a fraction of that size kill the caster when done improperly. I don't agree with her decision, but I have to give it to her that she has some conviction."

"Jesmine. What you did, did not only endanger yourself but all of us. They will still be after us"

"You don't know that," she replied.

"I *know* their type. They won't stop," she growled, her lip curling. "Don't be so damn naïve."

"We have to give them the chance. Alderin, you talked to them, did they seem like an evil bunch?"

Alderin sighed. "No. They were helpful in getting us migrated over here, believing we were trapped here. Their leader Garran talked about having connections to make it possible. They are not only angry for their so-called theft, but for breaking their trust. If I was in their position, I hate to admit it, but I'd probably do the same."

Ariana tensed, "I can't believe I am hearing this."

"That is not to say I agree with Jesmine for not killing them. With that kind of power, you could have made it smaller, more concentrated and burned them. Instead, you risked yourself to make a giant wall of fire. I'm with Ariana, you should have killed them."

Jesmine tensed, "I'm not going to kill just because you say so. Only when there are no other options. It is not their fault that they are in their current position."

Ariana took a step closer. "And whose fault is it Jesmine? Hmm? They aren't some puppets. They have a choice of what they do."

"Do they? Or are you forgetting one important fact? That they, you, me, all of us are under the influence of the dragons. You know just as well as I, Ariana, of how Sa'bara's tax system works. It's a form of control. Do you honestly think they just up and wanted you? No. They want what you represent, a chance to gain his favor. Do I agree with their actions? No. Not one bit, but I do sympathize with them."

Ariana let out a huff of air from her nostrils. "Fine. But remember anything that happens next because you let them go, will be on your head," she said pointing at Jesmine.

Her shoulders slumped, nodding. "I know that."

"No, I don't think you know, and I believe once again your naivety is showing through. They were caught off guard. They didn't know I wasn't some caged beast being transported to Rivera, nor did they know of your skills. Now they do. They won't make that mistake again. We had our one chance, and *you* blew it," she growled. "I'm going to take a walk; I'll be back before nightfall." She walked past the cart, snatching an empty bag before continuing on her way.

"Shouldn't we do something?" asked Gnemi.

"Do you want to go after an angry Lycan?" Dran asked, Gnemi winced, looking at her.

"I'm sure she'll be fine," Alderin said.

Histra sat on the edge of the cart her feet dangling off, looking up at Jesmine. "That's some resolve you have there, Jesmine. I can respect someone who can stand up for their morals, as wrong as they are. The orcs attacked us. They deserve death."

"Says the one who keeps secrets from all of us," remarked Alderin, "I shouldn't have been surprised, but you have an ice breath?"

"Yeah, what of it?"

"It could have been a good thing to know."

"Like I'd tell my possible future murders what I can or can't do? Yes, now you know I can ice breath, but any limitations of it, I will not say."

Alderin grunted, pushing up to his feet and walked towards her, keeping his injured arm relaxed to his side, "Why you."

"Alderin," Dran said, "She saved our lives. If she didn't put out that fireball, we'd have been toast."

"I know that," he said, staring into Histra's eyes. "And for that, thank you, Histra. I won't forget what you did."

"And neither will I," said Dran, "You have my thanks for what you did. But that won't excuse your attitude." He sat by the fire taking a moment to look out toward the seemingly endless plains, a few random birds fluttering out in the distance.

"I couldn't let you two die. And it wasn't a fireball spell."

Dran turned his attention back to her. "It wasn't? What was it then? A ball of fire coming to us looked like a fireball to me."

"It looked to me like a gaseous based spell that was set aflame," Jesmine said. "I suspect from the few spells I've seen that their orc wizard is specialized in natural gas spells."

"The orc with the fire enchantment war hammer. He could

have lit the gas and the wizard simply pushed it towards you two," Histra said.

"That would have given them extreme control over the fire as he controlled the source of its fuel. Their intent was probably to burn you two alive," Jesmine suggested.

"Ariana said there were only five?" Gnemi asked.

"She said she smelled five," Jesmine answered.

"So, we're equal in number. Do you think it's wise we stay here? We haven't travelled that far."

"After what they saw, we probably bought ourselves some time," Dran said.

"We easily bought ourselves a day," Jesmine said, slowly walking over to the campfire, sitting back down, slowly stretching.

Histra raised an eye ridge. "You seem to be confident on that assumption."

"The orc wizard's spell backfired when I made the fire wall. I saw the purple haze as we rode off. Gnemi was knocked out for over an hour with just a few breaths. I'm sure he's gotten a larger dose and will be out for a while. They won't make a move till he recovers."

"A fair observation."

"And Histra?"

"Yes?"

"Thank you again for your help. Channeling a small fire wall spell meant to be a fraction of that size was only doable thanks to you."

"You used my natural born ice aura to negate the feedback of the fire spell to keep yourself and the cart from bursting into flames. I'll say it's the first time I've seen or heard anything like it, and to feel warmth like that was… an experience. But don't do it again. If you get yourself killed, I won't be able to keep my end of the agreement."

Jesmine smiled. "So, concerned about our agreement, are you?"

"Of course. I keep my word, but I suppose that makes us even on the saving each other's lives."

"Except for when the wolkin attacked, or the time the kiapal attacked in the forest. And there was the time I saved you from the orcs. You're still in debt there," Alderin explained.

Histra turned her gaze to glare at him, who smirked in response. "I had the orcs handled in the inn, you simply interrupted my plan," Histra said.

"If you say so…"

"Jesmine, something has been bothering me," Gnemi said, approaching her. "I will admit I never got my head around spells and spellcraft. But from what I've heard you did something amazing. What will your spellbook do that you can't already?"

"I admit I was wondering the same thing," Alderin said, sitting back down by the campfire with a soft grunt as Dran started cooking.

"First, I will have access to spells I know how to cast, but don't know how to cast from memory. Some spells have specialized movements and incantations that must be heeded to or risk spell rebound. The second, is I could cast spells like the ones you saw, safer and a little faster."

"How does that work?" Gnemi asked.

Jesmine paused for a moment, considering her answer. "How to put it. Ah, you know how to do math?"

"Of course."

"It is sort of like math. Where if you had two and two you get four. And if you keep adding two to the number gets bigger, but it takes more effort, and the chance of a mistake increases as you spend time calculating the spell and holding it there before release. Now if you do the same with multiplication, you will get to the same answer sooner. They are the same in power, but one is achieved faster than the other. What I did was simply empowering a spell by repeating my draw of magical energy and holding it as I continued to do so. The longer I held it, the larger amount of energy, the bigger the risk as it wanted to burst free as it does not like to be controlled."

"Any method has risks," Dran added as he stoked the campfire's flames. "The bigger spells are more complex, easier to screw up, and blow up in your face. Empowering smaller spells to be larger risks you not being able to hold the energy long enough or making an error in repeating the spell so many times. Either way it's a danger that one must understand before casting any spell."

"I believe you said you knew a bit about the arcane but here you sound very knowledgeable on the subject, Dran," said Gnemi.

He nodded. "Aye. I've had basic education on it before I decided it wasn't for me. The risks versus rewards were just too great..." he said, turning his attention to his cooking.

"I didn't have much of a choice. You don't say 'no' to my mother," Jesmine said.

"What was she like?" asked Gnemi, walking over to her. "I've heard so many stories, but you knew her. That had to be amazing."

"She was a strong and forceful woman but loving. She never took no for an answer... or that I'm tired... But then she stood face to face to Eisandra and played a major part in taking her down. Despite the difficulties, I appreciate what she's taught me."

"Tell me, Jesmine," Histra spoke up, sliding off the cart, "You talk about giving people chances and not wanting to kill them unless you have to."

"Yes. I believe everyone deserves a chance. No one is pure evil."

"Except the dragons," said Alderin and Dran at the same time.

While Histra asked, "Even the dragons?" Alderin and Dran stared at her.

"Of course, you'd ask that. You're a kobold," remarked Alderin.

"I think it's a fair question," she replied with a smirk.

"To someone like Sa'bara. Who ruthlessly killed everyone I knew and loved? Who had every elf in their lands hunted down no matter who or how old they were? Who laid siege to our biggest city Rivera and slowly starved and poisoned the people till they was nothing but corpses littering the streets? I'd be a fool to say that someone like that could be redeemed," she replied, her hand shaking, closing her eyes, taking a deep breath. Histra continued to smile.

"But... that is not to say every dragon is born that way. I personally don't think it is impossible for a dragon to be good. Perhaps there are a lot out there but with how the world is right now they remain silent. Perhaps powerless to do anything."

Histra's smile instantly faded as Dran laughed. "Good dragons? They are all a greedy and controlling sort," he said almost falling over before regaining his composure. "How they manage to work with each other is beyond me."

"I agree. The dragons are cruel and sadistic creatures. They think of us as nothing more than mere pawns or playthings," said Alderin.

"I don't know myself. I've never had to deal with living under a dragon's reign till I left my country in the free lands. I will say I have noticed their presence, though I have never seen one," Gnemi said.

"I still don't understand why you left in the first place, but it doesn't matter now," Dran said, poking at the stew he was making out of some of the meat pies.

"Histra, what do you think?" asked Alderin.

She raised an eye ridge. "Of?"

"The dragons. Despite being their favored race in every land, you were held in bondage for, what was it again? Ten years? And yet nothing was done."

"I don't expect them to handle trivial matters of the everyday person. My predicament was caused by myself. I should have handled it myself. And speaking about my thoughts on the dragons. That's the way they will remain. As mine."

"I'm glad you two are getting along a little better," remarked Jesmine.

"What?" Alderin asked.

"You're calling Histra by name," she said with a friendly smile.

Alderin broke his gaze with Histra, turning to her, "Well after all that has happened, and what you've said. As much as I still don't like her kind, her personality, and the way she treats us, actions speak louder than her words. I'd be no better if I didn't."

"Hopefully this will lead to better cooperation. The orcs worked with each other. They constantly communicated and changed their plan on the go. Much like you three when you rescued me."

"Aye. We executed that rescue without a hitch. It was almost too good to be true," Dran said.

"We need to come up with a plan to get to and through Rivera without an issue. Now that we have an orc band after us and a Lycan, it will be that much more difficult," said Jesmine, looking out toward the plains. "But we should wait till Ariana returns."

"Why?" Alderin asked.

"She's part of the group. She needs to be part of the process, and whatever we decide involves her just as much as anyone else."

Histra spoke up from her off the corner spot. "I've already stated that I have a plan to get through the city once we're there. You all need not worry about it."

"And what's the plan?" Dran asked, eyeing her.

"When we get there, you will know."

Jesmine softly sighed, getting up, walking over to her. "Histra, you can't keep on keeping secrets like this."

"Why don't we use a boat?" asked Gnemi, everyone turning to him, "You said the city was nestled on a massive river and that the city is the only place where one can cross on foot right? Why don't we get a boat and cross?"

"That would be a good idea except it's not feasible," replied Jesmine, "Sa'bara has banned the use of boats to cross the river unless under strict controls and all of those crossings have to occur near the city, which by the way is the only safe area on the entire river. The rest are either full of uncrossable rapids or creatures that we'd have no hope against if we were to draw their attention," Jesmine explained.

"I couldn't have said it better myself," Histra said, then explaining, walking along the top of the cart. "It's far easier to cross through the city than any other means. Which is why I have thought out what to do when we get there."

"So, you say," Dran said dismissively.

"It's best not to argue about it right now. We'll work on a plan when Ariana gets back," Jesmine said as Dran finished cooking.

The group ate, chatted and waited for Ariana to return. Histra sat off to the side as usual, and just when the sun was about to set, the light of the day dimming and the campfire becoming more prominent, she returned with a half full bag in her hands.

Jesmine stood to greet her. "Welcome back."

Ariana let out a huff of air, her ears folded back. "Thanks," she said, tossing the sack onto the cart. "Hardly anything useful around here."

She walked up to Alderin, getting close, examining his shoulder. "Good, you kept the bandages on."

"I'm not crazy enough to just up and remove them because I think whatever you put on them is not to my liking. I don't know anything about medicine, but what I do know is to trust my gut, and my gut tells me that you know your stuff."

Ariana's ears raised slightly. "Good."

"Now that you are here Ariana, we can start on coming up with a plan to get to Rivera without issue," Jesmine said.

"You waited for me?" she asked, walking closer to the group, crouching down, yet remaining on her feet, slightly hunched over.

"Yeah, we didn't want to make a decision without your input," she said, stretching a bit, her hands gently running across her black tattooed arms, which faintly reflected in the campfire light.

"I've kept what's left of the stew warm," said Dran, pouring the last bit of it from the pot to a bowl.

"I did eat earlier but the rabbits weren't much of a meal," Ariana remarked, grabbing the bowl, "Thank you."

"You caught and cooked some rabbits?" asked Gnemi.

Ariana stared at Gnemi for a moment. "Yes, I caught some rabbits. I had some frustrations to get out, and a little hunt was rather nice. It was also good to confirm my suspicions that these cuffs and collar don't hinder me becoming any of my other forms. Though, the fact I had trouble catching the rabbits was troubling," she remarked, looking off to the side.

Histra paced as she spoke. "It may sound weird but as I mentioned earlier today, getting to a main road and continuing to Rivera will be the safest way there. We'll be one of many travelers to the city. There are checkpoints to enter it proper. But there's a town that grew on the riverbanks where we can stay and continue on with the next part of the journey."

"There is just one problem with that, Histra. I'd stand out. I could hide for a while but eventually, I will be seen and called out, by those that Jesmine refused to kill..." Ariana glared at her, "Or someone else. This form, though friendlier than the others will likely be a dead giveaway of my Lycan nature."

"Despite few, if any having seen this form of yours, it is a risk..." Histra responded, crossing her arms.

"Why don't you go full feral then?" asked Gnemi.

"What?" everyone asked, turning to him.

"I was thinking about it ever since you mentioned you could shift forms unhindered. You could pretend to be some kind of wolf or wolkin-like protector and then you'd be able to hang out in the open without issue."

"What?!" Ariana growled. "I am no one's pet!" She rushed over to him; her fists clenched.

He stuttered slightly, continuing, "H-hear me out. Does anyone here even know what a full feral Lycan looks like? Outside of you?"

"I don't," said Alderin.

Dran shook his head. "Neither do I."

"I do, but I'd count myself as a special case. It is not common knowledge," Histra replied.

"I do from sketches that your parents made," Jesmine answered.

"See? I doubt many orcs or whatever is at the town will know what a feral Lycan will look like. You could transform into it, pretend to be under, say Histra's control."

Ariana growled at the comment, staring Gnemi down who winces.

"It's not a bad idea," Histra added in.

"Or perhaps someone else here if you don't like it? But then we don't have to hide you. You'd stand out but not in a bad way. After the initial looks no one will mind us… I think. But certainly, few would try to bother us with someone as powerful looking as you. Not that I have seen your form, but I bet it's rather fierce looking."

"It is more powerful to be sure, and though my instincts will be stronger; they don't dictate my actions. Though I won't be able to talk in my feral state," Ariana explained, looking at everyone. "Alderin, you will be my handler. I will pretend to listen to you, and only you. When we get near the main road, I'll shift and walk beside your horse. Keep him under control."

"You want me to pretend I trained you?" he asked, giving a curious look.

"Yes. I want to stick close to you, seeing you are the most injured one amongst us. You'll need the extra protection. After all you did pick my locks. I owe you that much."

"I will do my best, and don't worry about Cetas. He's a smart and well-behaved horse."

"Good," she responded as the party started to hammer out details of the plan. Histra was the least responsive of them all while she watched and monitored everyone else.

Elsewhere as Garran's group recovered, they were making

some plans of their own.

Zed opened his eyes, grunting before jerking to full reality, checking over his person, the bolt in his gut gone, but the pain lingered, letting out a groan. "I'm alive," he sighed in relief.

"You're awake already? That's good. We'd thought you'd be out cold for a full day," Orla said, standing over him.

Zed slowly sat back up, looking around, discovering they set up camp in the woods, their horses hitched to some trees including the still two unconscious ones which were off in their own spots. He saw Shana beside him still fast asleep, armor removed and made more comfortable.

"I'll have something ready for you in a few minutes," Karrun said, poking the campfire which provided most of the surrounding light, the glow from the two waxing moons shining above them. Garran sat across from them, legs and arms crossed, silently staring endlessly into the fire.

Zed cracked his neck. "Damn that wizard. When that wall of flames appeared, it broke my line of sight and concentration. I had no time to react before the spell went off."

"When we noticed your spell rebounding, we rushed to your aid," Orla explained.

"I am amazed you pulled not only us but the horses out of harm's way," he added.

"The fire wall remained where it spawned and barely caused any nearby brush to catch ablaze."

Zed's eyes went wide. "I see… continue. I should be able to heal this wound and that of the others." He dug into his shirt, feeling through a set of chains, pulling out a golden amulet of a dragon's claw gripping a green gemstone with runes engraved on them. He gripped the amulet, pressing it near his body, beginning to chant in a guttural, draconic-arcana language.

"The fires stretched across the entire forest and blocked our path to give chase. The heat was unbearable, it was like nothing I've seen before. Yet it remained steady and burning bright, catching flame of anything that touched it. When we were dragging the horses away, after we got you and the others to a safe distance, it disappeared, leaving a long-blackened scorch mark on the ground."

Karrun sat down with them, carrying some cooked meat. "They

had a powerful arcane user with them. It was the human female. I saw markings of red along parts of her body. The kobold for some reason was riding her back."

"I found that to be odd myself," remarked Orla.

Zed continued to chant as a white glow appeared on the runic markings of the amulet. A minute passed before the light faded, his chant stopping. He sighed in relief, pressing his hands against his injury. "Mostly healed. I'm glad to have learned the basics of healing magic. It makes recovering minor wounds like this easy. I'll get to the others next, but one thing. Did anyone see a book? Magic of that level almost always requires a book."

"I didn't see one," Karrun replied, passing him the food.

"Neither did I," said Orla.

"Zed, what type of magic do you think it was?" Garran asked.

"Fire."

"No. Not the element. The type. You've been around for a while. You've seen many other races cast their magic. Do you know what race of magic it was? From what little I saw; it didn't look human to me. Unless human magic in Dra'kesh's lands are far different than here."

"Hmm. I couldn't say. But her skill in the elemental arts of fire are something not to be trifled with."

"We've been tricked more than we thought," Garran said. "I don't know what they said to the Lycan, but she is traveling with them uncaged. They have a wizard that has magic beyond anything we possess. With enchanted auto-firing crossbows. We ambushed them, and we came out more injured. What does that say about us?"

"We had no way of knowing," said Karrun.

"We underestimated them! We cannot be so foolhardy again! We all should be ashamed at this failure."

Zed sighed. "I have equal part to blame. I did not anticipate the kobold would have an ice breath and one strong enough to snuff out the flame attack."

"We did not plan thoroughly. We had no back up. We did not block the escape routes. If we put a single log out in the path, we could have easily prevented their escape. We can't let this failure happen again!" Garran yelled.

"Yes, but what are we supposed we do? They'll be at Rivera

before the rest of our party gets there. We don't have the strength to go after them with just the five of us," Orla said.

"Once they are in the city, there is nothing we can do. If they tricked the Lycan in some way. They will get the glory of turning it in for Draksind."

"That is if they were going to stop at the city. I don't think that is their end goal," said Zed.

"What?" Garran asked.

"Right before they caught onto us because the Lycan warned them, I overheard what they were talking about. They mentioned going through the city. Perhaps they don't intend to deliver the tax there?"

"I see. The kobold has proven herself one of lies and deceit. It could be part of her plan to keep the Lycan complacent."

"Also, with such a valuable tax, they may not trust anyone to handle it properly. Perhaps they know of an alternative spot?" suggested Orla as she passed some food off the fire to her companion.

"It is a possibility. The land past the city is far wilder now that our clans have been pushed out of them. Perhaps they know of a drop off point? I can't be sure," replied Zed, tearing into the meal that was handed to him.

"If that's the case, we have a chance to slow them down in the city. If not, we can wait for the others, provide our initial tax offering and then go to retrieve our bonus. I don't have to remind you of the importance of this Draksind. Sa'bara's tax priority is hinting to something big. And that means there is plenty of new opportunity for growth and positions of power. We can uplift ourselves and clan Or'gla at the same time. We won't have a better opportunity like this again in our lifetimes, perhaps a dozen lifetimes." Garran paused and looked over the group.

"Shana, our tracker, will be out for about half a day still. So, will two of our horses. We're stuck here till then. I'm not afraid of losing them, but the issue is, what do we do if we find them before the others arrive? I want to hear from all of you." Garran stared at them, the fires reflecting in his eyes as their discussion about what to do next was kicked off.

Chapter 11 A Few Revealed Secrets

A warm wind blew across the open fields as their group cut through the waist-high long grass. The sun hung overhead, clouds dotting the blue sky. Histra sat on top of the metal cage, her ice aura condensing and freezing the water in the air. Icicles hanging from the top that thawed when the warm summer breeze blew by. A bucket at the base of the cage caught the dripping water as the fight between Histra's localized winter and summer rages on.

"Judging by how long we've been travelling, we'll be reaching the main road soon," Histra said.

"I agree. I can smell the road from here," Ariana said, slipping out of her full-bodied length cloak, revealing her black and grey fur. Her ears twitched in the wind, her long silver hair flowing behind her as she leapt off the side of the cart. "A reminder, I won't be able to speak while in this form."

"Will you be fine walking the rest of the way?" asked Jesmine.

"This will be nothing. I'm more curious how well this plan will pan out."

"You did appear to look like one of their bestial mounts when you showed us the other day. I have faith in this plan," Gnemi said.

"We shall see," she replied with a smirk. "And I'll keep my instincts in check. Walking with non-Lycans, let alone in a major crowd will be interesting." Ariana's body rippled, fur growing fuller, muzzle extending as muscles thickened throughout her body. The sound of bones cracking and shifting caused Jesmine and Gnemi to tense while Alderin and Dran watched with a defensive posture. Histra watched with partial disinterest, keeping one eye on their surroundings.

Ariana's teeth grew sharper and longer. Her claws dug into the ground, taking a feral four-legged stance. Her body grew in mass till she was one and a half times bigger than before. Her anthropomorphic feminine features faded away. The transformation taking place in under a minute. Ariana shook her body, the mithril cuffs and collar magically adjusting to her size, remaining flush. Her long silver hair became a long silver stripe along her back; her predatory yellow eyes looked around, ears surveying the area, sniffing the air.

"Don't tell us there is someone nearby we have to worry about," remarked Alderin.

She looked up at him, shaking her head, taking a position near Cetas, who whined softly as she drew near.

"Easy, everything is fine," Alderin said, calming his mount, the group continuing on their way.

"We are about three days away from Rivera, so let me remind all of you that it's the time Sa'bara collects his tax. Everyone from his land is coming to pay their yearly dues. Which means there is going to be a lot of traffic on the roads now that we are this close, and the area around the city will be packed with all the races in his land. Don't draw attention to ourselves. Even I won't be able to save you like previous mishaps," Histra stated, flicking her wings.

Ariana let out a soft growl, glancing over at her.

"What? There is only so much that even *I* can do."

"You act as if you are the only reason why we managed to get so far," Dran complained.

"I'm your guide. It is my job. I am giving you a fair warning. You should be more *grateful* for my help."

"Grateful? Maybe if you didn't talk down to us, we might be," said Alderin.

Histra focused on them, her eyes narrowing as Jesmine jumped in, "Histra has been very helpful. Yes, her ways are, for lack of a better word, cold, but we asked her to let us in on her plans. Though she could say it better, warning us that we'll be in the very heart of Sa'bara's land, during a time that will be crawling with guards, and his representatives, we will need to be even more cautious than ever."

"Always ready to defend her no matter what. If only we could be so lucky to get that same consideration now and then…" Alderin thought to himself.

"You mean kobolds?" asked Dran.

"Yes. They collect the taxes. It's one of the few times you'll see so many out in the open in one place," Jesmine explained as Dran's and Alderin's gaze shifted from her to Histra.

"I know what you are thinking, and no. They are not my kin." Histra said. "They let me sit in the cage being a fake white dragon for a decade. I have no love or care about them."

Dran shook his head. "I don't like your kind, but it didn't cross my mind."

"I never noticed," she responded with an icy sarcasm.

"If you wanted something like that, you'd have been better off not saving our lives, but you did. Whatever the reason, the fact is, you did. I would be not who I am if I didn't show gratitude and thanks for that. We need to work together to get out of this alive," Dran said, cracking his thick muscular neck. "This doesn't mean you can act like you are better than any of us. You don't know us."

"Dran, I couldn't have said it better myself," Alderin added.

"And none of you know me," Histra replied.

"I've been trying to know you better, but you seem not to have been the most forthcoming," said Gnemi.

Histra's eyes narrowed, letting out a soft huff of fogged air. "See?"

"We are all hiding something from one another. I don't feel an obligation to tell you anything," she explained.

"Fair enough, but I am willing to tell you more about myself to hear more about you," he replied.

"I have no desire to know more about you."

"That's so cold." Gnemi said, freezing the moment the words escaped his lips.

Dran chuckled, "Nicely done."

"I didn't mean it that way."

"It was still a good one."

Histra let out a soft sigh.

Gnemi took a moment to adjust the goggles around his neck, picking out a random lose brown hair from them. "Actually... I do have some questions I've been meaning to ask."

"What is it this time?" she asked, staring down at him.

Gnemi shook his head. "Not you, but Jesmine... and well Ariana, but I kind of forgot to ask this before she lost the ability to speak."

Ariana let out a soft growl.

He swallowed a small lump in his throat, "I'm sorry. I've been meaning to ask but with everything that happened, I forgot. However, now that Histra has mentioned Rivera, I want to inquire you, Jesmine, and now that I am thinking about it even more, perhaps you too, Histra. What's the city like?"

Histra crossed her arms. "I only saw bits of the city from my cage. I've never been there myself."

Jesmine leaned back. "Rivera was the heart of the elven kingdom for centuries. Truth be told even though everyone calls the city Rivera, the real name is Sa'el'taria."

"Rivera is much easier to remember," remarked Alderin.

"Why does everyone call it Rivera rather than Sa'el'taria?" Gnemi asked.

"Sa'el'taria is elven tongue for 'Sa'bara's Great City'. And why Rivera? It's always been an apt name. It's a great city built on a series of islands within the Great Sa'bara River, which splits his land in half."

Gnemi blew away some of the brown hair growing down over his eyes. "Tell me more."

"I haven't seen it in perhaps forty years, so I am not sure what's changed, or how much is left. The extermination of one's people tends not to leave a lot of cities intact."

"Oh…" Gnemi looked away. "Sorry, I didn't mean to cause you any problems."

Jesmine placed a hand on his shoulder, smiling. "It's alright. It happened thirty years ago. I've made peace with what happened… and in a way, it's nice to talk about it. It keeps it alive. Sa'bara destroyed my people, and now only a handful of his elves even remain, scattered to the other lands."

"I've met a few," Gnemi said. "None wanted to speak about what happened."

"It's understandable," Jesmine replied, looking at the surrounding fields. "Much of where we are traveling through used to be part of elven lands. We used to control vast portions of his land and till the extermination, we were Sa'bara's favored race. Over a century ago there was an avolariean uprising and once we put it down, the avolarieans were stripped of their winged companions. In return we received even more land, much of which is near Du'ralia Forest."

Alderin looked over his shoulder to her. "Wait, wait. Are you saying that the elves put down a rebellion against Sa'bara? And all that happened to these avolariea people, was that they were stripped of some mounts and some land? But when your people rebelled, they were completely wiped out?"

Dran commented, "Aye, I was wondering the same thing."

"This was before Eisandra was slain. My relatives, who were there at the time told me much about the war while growing up. My mother always voiced her negative opinions about it to us in private, even though she fought in it."

"Your mother was either brave, stupid, or very sure of herself to voice opinions against Sa'bara," remarked Histra.

"She always worded herself to not directly mention anything against Sa'bara. My mother was one of the most talented and strongest people I've ever known. I'd appreciate if you didn't insult her," Jesmine said, shooting her a look.

Histra let out a little humph.

"Histra, the least you can do is apologize to Jesmine," suggested Gnemi.

"Apologize? For what? I didn't call her mother stupid, I merely suggested given the dangers caused by the paranoid Sa'bara that speaking out was a dangerous gambit. That is all."

"It's best not to fight about it," said Jesmine, turning her attention back to Gnemi, "But you wanted to know more about the city, Gnemi?" she asked just as the dirt road came into view, halting the conversation.

Grooves from countless wagons crisscrossed each other down the dried earthen path, which was about three times wider than the roads they were on previously. Brown dust was kicked up by seven different caravans that were visible along the road, the heavy wagons pulled by the orcs' beasts of burden.

"Should we worry about others seeing us coming out of nowhere?" asked Gnemi.

Jesmine shook her head, "No, it's nothing new."

"Exactly. There is nothing to worry about," Histra replied.

Gnemi nodded as Alderin and Dran moved closer to the cart, Ariana walking just beside Alderin, keeping her ears up, body alert, nose sniffing the air constantly, tail quickly wagging.

"You sense anything?" Alderin asked her.

She let out a huff of air and shook her head.

Gnemi watched the other caravans. "Will it be fine to still talk about Rivera?"

Jesmine chuckled. "Of course. We're just talking about a city. There's nothing wrong with that."

"I wish I had a way to take notes, but you said the city is on a major river?"

"No. It's not simply a major river, it's *the* biggest river in all of Isharia. It's so wide at this point that you can't even see the other side. The city is like a giant bridge from one end to the other, built upon several islands, but truth be told I have no idea how many."

"Strange, why is that?" Gnemi asked.

"Because it's been so built over that it's all connected. Water flows underneath the city, and there're giant wheels that catch the flow of moving water, which powered the city's economy in the past. We had the best forges in all of Sa'bara. We were able to smelt and forge metals in large quantities of such fine quality that it makes gnomes and dwarves, who pride themselves on such matters jealous."

"This I would have to see to believe," Dran remarked letting out a huff.

"The river powered the forges and smelters. Along with other engineering marvels like the rotating bridges."

"Rotating bridges?" Gnemi asked, his eyes lighting up with curiosity.

"There are twelve massive stone bridges that connect the city to the riverbanks, six on each side. During times of war, or by command of Sa'bara, they'd rotate out into the river, making the city almost impossible to breach. With a fresh supply of water, and food from the fisheries that simply dip their nets into the river, the city could hold out against any siege for years."

"Impressive… but has the city ever been sieged? If it's Sa'bara's main city, it seems foolish to attack it."

"To my knowledge only twice. The first time was centuries ago, when the orcs tried to take the city and claim it as their own. The second time was also done by the orcs but at Sa'bara's behest, when the extermination order was given… I don't know what's really left of the city. I heard rumors that it was completely destroyed after a several month-long siege, but word between lands doesn't spread quickly."

"The death of Eisandra sure did," Dran chuckled.

"It's hard to stop that news," she replied as their cart steadily caught up to one of the slower moving caravans. They quietly pulled up beside them, staying out of their way as an orc armed with a short bow sat in the front beside the driver. The cart's wheels creaked and moaned as they churned; a grey tarp over the cargo hid it from view. The background noise caused by their travel drowned out the party's conversation. A green orc tapped the shoulder of the red driver who stared blankly at the wagon ahead of him.

They watched the orcs from their peripherals, carrying on with idle chat. The orcs pointed at Ariana and then at Histra, who simply stared at the orcs that glared back at her. The green orc turned his attention to Alderin and yelled in orcish over the noise, "Where did you get that beast?"

Their eyes meet as Alderin stared into the orc's yellow eyes. "She's not a beast, but my companion. She protects me and those I am traveling with."

Ariana let out a growl just loud enough for the orc to hear, which drew his attention.

"She doesn't like strangers," he explained.

The orc chuckled. "A strong fighting beast. I like that."

He continued his stern stare. "Not a beast."

"A little much for such a small traveling party."

"It suffices, for what we need to protect."

"What are you protecting?" the orc inquired, eyes darting over to Histra, who silently glared at them with her arms crossed, wings furled.

"You first. What are you protecting?" Alderin responded, subtly nudging in Histra's direction.

The orc smirked, lips curling over his tusks, showing his yellow stained teeth. "Our humble offerings to Sa'bara. It is exactly what he desires, and which we are happy to give."

"I couldn't have said it better myself, and we need the protection. The raiders have always been bad this time of year."

"True," the orc said, leaning back, resuming his talks with his companion as the party pulled up ahead.

"I always get nervous when that happens. I have no idea what's going on," remarked Gnemi.

"It is times like this, I wish I learned the orcs' tongue, but then when given the chance, I had other priorities," Jesmine said.

"Aye, one can't predict the future. All we can do is do our best to overcome the challenges that are thrown our way," Dran said.

As the group moved away from the nearby caravans, well

outside of earshot, Jesmine looked over her shoulder to Histra. "Histra?"

She looked down at her, "Yes?"

"Don't you think you may want to compliment Alderin? He did do a good job with the orc there."

"He's a grown human. He doesn't need me to compliment him on every good job. He should have a general idea how orcs work. What he did sufficed."

She sighed. "It might help group unity if you recognized it. After all the trouble you've given him these past weeks with the orcs."

Histra raised an eye ridge, "Trouble?"

"You know from earlier? In the forest? Not the recent one but the one with the monster attack."

"It's hard to forget."

"Don't you think, then, you should be more appreciative?"

"I appreciate that he doesn't get us killed nor try to kill me, despite his feelings towards me and my kind. Isn't that enough?"

"Histra, shouldn't you be a bit more considerate?"

"Jesmine, don't strain yourself with it," Alderin said. "I don't need her to give me any compliments. I can live my life perfectly fine not being acknowledged by a kobold."

Histra smirked. "See, he doesn't need me to say it. He knows it already."

"I didn't... never mind, forget it," he replied, waving her off.

Jesmine softly sighed as she adjusted her hood.

"It's okay Jesmine, you tried," Gnemi comforted her, his small gnomish hand gently patting her on the lower back.

"I just want us to get along. It will make the journey that much nicer."

"There's nothing nice about this," Histra said.

"How about getting freed from that cage?"

Histra opened her mouth but quickly closed it. A few moments passed before she replied. "My cage has merely gotten bigger, but... it has been nice to be able to move and stretch my wings," she said, unfurling them for a moment. "I'm still not back to where I was, but it's getting there." She furled them back.

"There you go. Something nice."

She sighed, "You make me more and more curious just to what

they want from you, to go to these lengths."

"I'll find out soon enough."

"And we'll still be sure not to let you know," Dran remarked.

Histra smirked, "I knew as much," she replied as they continued to travel down the road. A few more caravans joined in from smaller roads that spanned out into the countryside. Endless fields of farms filled the view with the occasional town built to support the travelers on their way.

Unlike the previous towns these had a different feel to them. Many of the buildings were constructed of wood, with sharp ends, and a fearsome visage, common to orcish architecture, but there were a few buildings made of soft grey, or a pale white stone. Crystals built into the stone gave them a shimmering look when the sunlight hit their surface. They were sleek, curved, and elegant in their creation, like a beautiful woman.

"After all these years, a few elven structures still stand," remarked Jesmine, gripping the reins a little harder.

"They are beautiful," said Gnemi.

"Unfortunately, there's a lot of dirt and grime on them, dulling their beauty. Elves here liked to build homes out of a mixture of wood and stone. It took a lot of work, but the results were worth it."

"My home was nothing more than wood, dirt and hay for the roofing. We couldn't afford anything else," said Alderin.

"Ours are made out of stone or built into the mountain itself. The finest dwarven craftmanship," said Dran.

"Wood, stone, or clay. We made our homes out of anything that worked," said Gnemi, looking over to Histra.

"Don't even ask," Histra remarked.

"Please?"

Dran answered, "Kobolds tend to live in mountains, and caves. They dig out their homes, much like we dwarves do. It makes them ideal in improving and expanding dragon lairs."

"You never told me you knew about how kobolds lived."

"I know a few things. No expert, but we had to know the very basics of our enemy. The kobolds near us are from a different zone, and are always problematic for us," he explained.

"Look, you don't need to bug me with these questions. He can answer them for you," Histra said.

"But you're the expert. As knowledgeable as others may be, I still believe you are the most likely the accurate source."

Histra let out a soft humph, looking up ahead, "Well… that's something I wasn't expecting," Her eyes narrowed, standing up on the cage, her body wobbling, trying to keep balance.

Alderin looked ahead, "What is it? I see nothing but a heavily trafficked road ahead of us."

"It's nothing to be concerned about. Just follow those ahead of you and we'll be fine," she replied, sitting back down.

"What is it?"

"Nothing to worry about."

"Which is?"

"Histra… there is no reason to not say," said Jesmine.

She sighed, "It's road construction."

Alderin, Dran and Gnemi all replied in near unison, "Road construction?"

"Yes, road construction. I told you there was nothing to worry about."

"They're finally building out this way. This must mean they finished the roads to the north," remarked Jesmine.

"Orcs build roads?" asked Alderin in surprise.

"Orcs help build roads, but many races take part in it. It's one of the taxable jobs one can do for Sa'bara. He determines just where and when the roads are to be built."

Dran looked over to Jesmine with a curious gaze. "The ancient dragon bothers himself with road construction?"

"Sa'bara commands a lot of things to be built. Roads, mines, even some towns are built by his will. A lot of road construction happened to the north and to the mountains on the other side of the river," she explained.

"Why?" asked Gnemi.

"The mountains had riches, and traffic to the north was heaviest when Eisandra demanded people from the other lands."

"I remember hearing stories about that from my Grandparents. Eisandra took people from the other lands to continue her undead experiments or something like that," said Alderin as Histra tensed ever so slightly, her wings pulling tighter against her body.

"It would be best if we did not talk about such things near the road construction. There are bound to be a few overseers, ones who will have ears open for any voice of discontent or odd conversation," Histra warned.

Alderin looked at her and nodded. "Right," he replied, quietly moving forward. Three heavily armed orcs with axes stood a hundred yards ahead of the start of the road assembly, yelling and motioning for everyone to move around, splitting the traffic in two, taking a wide berth around the construction area. The grass flattened and crushed under countless hooves and wheels, the ground was even more irregular causing the wagons to shake and wobble from side to side.

A large ditch was being dug which was wider than the original road itself. Humans, orcs, and dwarves with metal shovels scooped dirt into wheelbarrows which were carted off to the side and dumped. The several stages of road construction steadily came together as sand and gravel were poured into an already dug out section. Past that, the partially filled ditch was compacted tightly together with heavy logs, while even further down a group of dwarves slid precut stones into place. The whole process utilized a few hundred people, taking an hour to ride by all of it. A bunch of brown leather skinned huts were nearby, smoke rising from campfires while the smell of cooked meats reached them.

Near the end of the construction, where the controlled chaos became more organized and less chaotic, a black scaled kobold spoke with one dwarf, an orc, and a human. The three workers towered over the small, scaled lizard, speaking to them in draconic. His claws pointed to a map in his hands, the others listening intently.

A little while later they merged back onto the completed section of road, the cart bouncing as the path was raised above the ground. The sound of hooves on dirt and plants being crushed were replaced by wheels running across smoothed rock. The flow of traffic increased, the wagon becoming far more stable on the newly finished road.

"I've never seen anything like that before," remarked Alderin once they were far enough away.

"I've seen it. Roads are common where I am from," replied Gnemi.

"Aye, we have a few roads like that, mostly by our capital. But many of those are centuries old and require only occasional upkeep," remarked Dran.

"They do last a long time. The roads by my home were already two centuries old when I was born," Jesmine said.

"Hopefully, this means we can get to Rivera soon and be done with this step in our journey," said Alderin.

"A little, but not much unfortunately," replied Jesmine.

"They are smartening up a little bit. At least I don't have to stop them from asking why Sa'bara was doing this," Histra thought as the party continued until near dusk. They made camp off the side of the road, one of many. So many campfires were beside it that it was illuminated enough for the occasional person to continue to travel at night.

Without incident the party continued for the next two days, the patrols of orcs on wolkin mounts steadily increasing, but so did the amount of traffic on the road, which slowed their pace to half of what it was before.

Ariana never shifted out of her feral form the entire time, staying near the group. Her ears twisted and turned, nose flaring. When they were about a quarter of a day's travel from the outskirts of the city her ears perked, head rose, letting out a growl, lips curling.

Alderin looked down at her, then quickly in all directions. "What is it?" he asked as the party's idle banter ceased. They scanned the area, but the countless wagons around them made it difficult to notice anything out of the ordinary.

"Stay calm. If you look like a bunch of frightened children, they'll know something is wrong," Histra muttered, scanning from her vantage point, but to her dismay, with the roads so packed with carts with their goods covered in tarps that everything blended together.

"Ariana, do you know which direction?" asked Alderin in a soft whisper.

Ariana sniffed the air, taking deep breaths, processing the hundreds of smells. She thought, *"I can smell one of them...damn it! I can't find them. Too many!"* She shook her head.

A loud screech sounded up and overhead. A large winged bird with golden-brown feathers, wings spanning twice the width of the road, soared just a foot over the wagons. It sped down the road, its mighty wings flapping as it passed over head, causing a woosh of wind to blow across them with enough force that Histra grabbed onto the cage to prevent herself from being knocked over.

Her eyes went wide, Jesmine's hood blown clear off her head, revealing pointed elven ears poking through her black hair. She scrambled to pull her hood back on, looking around nervously, but everyone's attention was up on the bird. Horses neighed, and beasts of burden groaned. The large fowl flew up into the air, turning to make another pass over the road.

"What is that?" exclaimed Alderin.

"That was an avrius. A giant bird used by the avolarieans as mounts. Most likely one is riding it right now," Jesmine explained.

"I thought they were stripped of their privilege to ride them?" asked Alderin.

"They were, which means the avolariean riding the avrius has earned the right to do so and is patrolling to keep the peace."

"It's nothing new. To prevent bias protection, the avolarieans oversee the security of the orcs, while the orcs oversee security of the avolarieans," explained Histra, continuing to look around, noticing no unusual reactions by any of the nearby orcs.

"None for the humans and dwarves?" asked Gnemi.

"Orcs manage them because they make up a much smaller portion of the population. Few see them as guard material… perhaps it's best not to talk about this in public," said Jesmine.

Gnemi nodded. "Probably a good idea," he replied, the avrius flying high up overhead. The giant bird swooped down and landed a few yards up ahead and off to the side of the road, its brown leather harness straps shifting slightly. Its eyes kept a constant vigil as a black scaled kobold slipped out from behind the bird.

The two-and-a-half-foot scaled lizard with swept back horns and yellow eyes was dressed in a green cloth clothing with a yellow eye of Sa'bara's mark sewn into the back. The kobold stretched, remarking in draconic. "That was certainly exhilarating."

An anthropomorphic avian stepped out from behind the bird, standing behind the kobold. The seven-foot-tall avolariea sported a breathtaking display of colorful feathers of blues, soft shades of purples, reds, and blacks. Sharp talons poked out of the leather-bound shoes wrapped around its feet. Clad in black tanned leather armor, the bird had a long spear strapped to its back. It let out a few chirps and trills from its sleek curved black beak, petting its mount, the ebony scaled claw hands visible as the rest of the arm was covered in feathers about a foot in length. The avolariea pulled out a piece of cured meat, which it tossed into the bird's hungry mouth before giving the kobold its full attention.

Gnemi quietly remarked, "Wow, she is a pretty avolariean."

"He's a male actually," Jesmine replied as Gnemi tensed at his correction. "The males are often more colorful than the females," Jesmine explained.

"I don't care how pretty they look. I only care why they stopped," Dran remarked.

"It's best not to worry about it, just continue forward, unless they do something."

"That's what I'm worried about," he responded, giving a quick glance to Histra.

"We shall see," replied Jesmine. As their cart drove by.

The kobold reached out and yelled to Histra in draconic. "Hey! You, come here!"

The avolariean's yellow, piercing eyes looked over the parading caravans in silence.

"He wants to talk to us. Pull off to the side of the road and dismount," Histra stated in the human.

"As you wish," said Alderin, the group pulling a few yards away from the traffic-filled road, dismounting.

Histra jumped off the top of the cage, her wings unfurled, catching the air, barely managing to slow her descent and land on the ground with a soft thud, stumbling forward, just catching herself. She turned to face the black kobold, approaching and responding in draconic. "Is there something wrong?"

"I was taken by surprise to see one of us among these orcs," he said, stopping just as his breath became visible. "I was not expecting that," he remarked, placing his hand into the cold air, "You should suppress that when I approach," he remarked with a glare.

Histra's eyes locked onto his. "I would if I could." she replied.

"Shame. You should really do something about that. I hear uncontrolled magic like that eventually leads to death."

"I will keep that in mind, but sadly I am magically attuned, not inclined."

"Interesting, a rarity then," he looked over at the others.

"Unusual group you are traveling with."

"My protection from bandits. They suffice."

"Orcs would be stronger."

"So would the smell."

The black kobold laughed. "I'll have to remember that one."

"Feel free to do so," she replied, keeping her gaze locked with his.

"I shall," said the kobold, and after a moment of silence, broke his gaze with her. "It is unusual but not unheard of to see one of us traveling with these masses, but I have to ask something. What happened to your clothes?"

"Clothes don't last long with me. Water gets into them, it freezes and tears them to shreds in short order, and with these wings," she spreads them, "It's expensive to get something tailored that fits me well."

"Hmm, I did not know that."

"Not many white ice kobolds around here?"

"You're the first I've seen."

"That doesn't surprise me. I haven't seen any besides myself."

"That's a shame really," he looks over Histra for a moment, "What happened to your horn?" he asked, pointing to his own horn, which mirrored hers that was cracked at the base.

"Bandits. Those behind me are not only my escorts but saviors. They nursed me back to health and killed my attackers. I'm here to vouch for their efforts and apply it to their tax."

"That would explain why you are traveling with them."

"Is there anything else you would like to know or need help with? We are not far from the city, and I would love to be able to finish this trip as soon as possible."

"If you want, I could take you to the city. There's enough room on the bird's back," he replied, pointing to the avrius. "You would not believe how wonderful it is to fly."

She looked over to the bird mount as it preened its feathers, idly waiting. "I could imagine, and I appreciate the gesture, but if I part from the humans, the odds of me finding them in the surrounding area again is more trouble than it's worth. And my presence this close to the city has kept the orcs in line."

The black kobold nodded. "Good point. Once you are done with that, if you want to talk more, you can find me in the main city in the kobold district. My name's Argyl. As an overseer, I'll be easy enough to find."

"I'll certainly keep you in mind," she replied with a smirk.

"May the last leg of your trip be uneventful."

"It should be," she replied as Argyl walked back to the avolariean.

"We're done here. Let's go," he commanded.

The avolariean let out a chirp in acknowledgment as the two mounted the bird. The mighty avian's wings spread out as it let out a screech, beating them several times. Loose grass and dust kicked up as it took to the sky. Meanwhile, Histra climbed back onto the cart.

"What was that about?" asked Gnemi, watching the bird fly off.

"Nothing important."

"You could at least tell us what it wanted," said Alderin, remounting his horse.

"It was about nothing," she said, climbing onto the top of the cage.

Dran mounted his horse. "If it was nothing then you could tell us what it was."

"After all this time, you could at least trust me that when I say it's nothing, it is nothing."

Alderin and Dran stared at her, Ariana letting out a soft growl.

"Not you, too."

"Everyone, it's alright. If Histra says it was nothing, then it was nothing," said Jesmine.

Alderin slumped, muttering, "Not again."

Dran let out a sigh. "I have a bad feeling about this, but there is no point in arguing about it."

"It is best not to make a scene. I have no obligation to tell you what I say to another kobold. Doing so raises suspicion," Histra explained as they merged back into traffic. A few more hours passed, the horses neighed, moving up a modest hill that blocked the view toward the city.

"We're almost there," said Jesmine, hands tensing, heartbeat quickening.

"Finally," remarked Alderin.

"I'm a bit excited if I am to be honest," commented Gnemi,

sounds of hooves to stone, orcs yelling, beasts groaning. They crested the hill; the massive white stone city of Rivera came into view. An impressive castle sat at the center of the city, its large towers reaching up to the sky, the stones sparkling like diamonds. The clear blue waters shimmered in the sunlight, providing a grander display than the city itself, even though the opposite side of the river could not be seen.

The stone road led straight toward the city bridges where four large dragon statues made from jade were at the entrance, the green contrasting with the surrounding area. The road itself split in two, while a dark and dreary shanty town hugged along the riverbanks, though none of the buildings were within a hundred yards of the road.

Smoke billowed out from parts of the city and the smaller town, its wooden structures with their thatched roofs were a pale comparison to the soft grey and red clay roofs of the city. The surrounding area was filled with people arriving from all over Sa'bara. All the camps and temporary shelters made the city itself look as if it was under siege by a mighty orcish army.

Jesmine's grip on the reins loosened, almost to the point of slipping out of her shaking hands as she stared at the capital with a gaze of awe. Her eyes glistened with tears softly muttering, "I don't believe it."

"The city looks that different from before?" asked Gnemi.

"No… it looks just as I remembered it. It's as if it was never touched."

"How is that possible? Wasn't it besieged?"

"It was. Or so I heard…"

"It is best not to talk about it right now," said Histra, pointing to one of the worst-looking corners of the town along the riverbank. "In Little Rivera, we are to head there, to a tavern called the 'The Battle Hardened Lady.' Alderin, you are to meet with the tavern owner once we arrive. His name is Garmesh."

"Me?" Alderin asked.

"Yes, you. Now, come here," she stated, slipping off the cage and moved to the edge of the cart. Alderin pulled up beside the wagon while other caravans on the road pulled away, heading toward their final destinations.

"What is it?" asked Alderin.

"You are to say to him first that you have a message from Krogg. When he asks about the message, you respond, in orc tongue, 'We are one. Never to be divided no matter how far apart we may be,' then you will say 'Greshek'akis' to finish it off."

"What does that mean?"

"It's gibberish, but it will gain you the trust of the orc there. Then, you tell him you want to get through to the other side of the city."

He gives her a long inquisitive look.

"What?" she asked.

"How do you know all of this?"

"The tavern owner is from the Tirghal clan. You gained the trust of their chief after you saved his daughter back in the woods."

"I did what? Wait, is that why you yelled at me?"

"No. I yelled at you for the sheer dumb luck you possess, and how it was wasted on someone who at the time couldn't speak proper orc tongue."

"Is that why you were so keen on teaching me?"

"It was a factor, yes."

"And you couldn't tell us this earlier, because?"

"It wasn't important to know till now."

"And what if I hadn't saved the chief's daughter?"

"I had other plans, but none as great as this one."

Alderin squeezed Cetas' reins. "You are infuriating to work with. You make things needlessly complicated."

"To you, maybe, but not to me," she replied.

"You mean, except you," he remarked.

"Let's just get into Little Rivera and the tavern. The sooner we secure transportation through the city, the better off we'll be," reasoned Jesmine.

"Yeah, yeah. I know," replied Alderin, preparing to ride back to his place up in front.

Histra raised her claw to stop him, "One more thing."

"Yes?"

"Make it painfully clear that you have a kobold in your party, and that he will know me."

"What? He knows you? Why couldn't you do it then, if you like to do everything yourself?"

"He knows me, but we've never spoken to each other."

Alderin eyed her for a moment before softly sighing. "Alright," he replied, moving back to where he was. Ariana remained by his side the entire time.

As they approached the town, they saw six mounted avrius flying overhead and heavily armored orcs mounted on wolkin patrolling the grounds. Several avolarieans were posted at key points. In the distance dozens of kobolds with orcs and avolariean guards checked over goods to be taxed. One kobold with runic engravings in his horns spoke in draconic-arcana, horns glowing along with the paper in his clawed hands before handing it to the orc in charge of the group he represented. It was one of countless identical events happening around them.

Entering the town, the streets were nothing more than dried dirt paths worn flat by the constant travel. Orcs busily moved through the streets as merchants shouted out to all those who came near to see their wares.

A group of performers performed their trade in a small confined area, the streets so crowded that it put the group's progress to a crawl. Most orcs pretended not to notice them as they went about their day, but others gave stern looks at Histra, curious glances at Ariana, or at the rest of the group's unusual makeup.

Ariana, with her fur on end fluffed out, keeping a vigil, growling at anyone who got too close. The scent of cooked meats mixed with the pungent smell of so many orcs in tight quarters, along with the unhealthy droppings of the beasts of burden that moved through the streets, gave the town a unique aroma.

Eventually they reached the tavern, a two-story tall wooden structure with thin shutters for windows. The building was worn and in dire need of improvements, with a few broken shutters and the front door no longer level on its hinges. The sign heavily worn by the elements showed a female orc in full battle armor and an axe. The hitching posts were packed to the brim as they pulled up behind the building, one of the few areas that still had room.

"Good luck, Alderin," said Jesmine as he dismounted.

"Thanks," he replied, turning to Histra. "Do you mind telling me what this Garmesh looks like?"

"Red skinned orc, missing a right tusk, and right eye. Last I saw him, he had a patch over said eye, so he's hard to miss," she replied, leaning back in the corner of the cart. She looked behind her, seeing down the alley to the busy street in front of the tavern.

"We'll be right here, so holler if you need us. If Ariana runs off after you, we'll be not far behind," Dran assured him, grabbing Cetas' reins.

"Thanks. Hopefully it won't come to that," replied Alderin, walking off.

"Remember to mention you have a kobold," added Histra.

"I won't. You are hard to forget," he muttered, walking onto the main street. When he entered the tavern, the door creaked and scraped across the ground. The place was packed with orcs, feasting and drinking with a festive energy.

A female bard sang as two others in her troop played musical instruments. The tune was drowned out by the cheers and chatter of the local patrons, barely catching a few lines of the song. "Her bloody axe in one hand and her banner held in the other, she rallied…"

He weaved through the crowd, standing on his toes, trying to get his head over the massive orcs. *This is like looking for a needle in a haystack,"* he thought, bumping by one orc, who grunted.

"Watch it!" A moment later, he heard the same orc say, "Look, a human. You don't see that every day." The orc chuckled and took a swig of his drink.

"Where is he? He better be here," Alderin thought as the orc in question caught his attention. Garmesh, the six-and-a-half foot tall fire-red skin, a battle-scarred face with one tusk and one eye, his black hair tied back behind his head, manned the bar with two others, struggling to keep up with the constant stream of orders. The muscular orc looked more in place on the battlefield than standing behind a bar serving drinks.

He squeezed between a few orcs to a corner of the bar as his presence went completely ignored for a few minutes. He waved and yelled for him by name. A few moments later, Garmesh, after serving another mug of ale, turned to him from halfway across the bar, his yellow eye focused on him, before tilting his head to the side, approaching him.

"A human? How do you know my name?" he asked, grunting, staring him down.

"I come with a message from Krogg," he responded.

Garmesh's eye widened ever so slightly, leaning in. "You? What could you possibly have to tell me from him?" he grunted. "If you want a drink, you better have the money, because it's going to cost you."

Alderin said the phrase along with the words of gibberish.

Garmesh kept himself composed, turning to the other two at the bar, "I'll be gone for a bit," he turned his attention back to Alderin, "Follow me," he stated, walking out from behind the bar and motioned him deeper into the tavern.

He followed without hesitation as Garmesh made a path through the patrons into the back where an orc man and woman, were busy preparing two kinds of meals: a type of thick soup and slabs of fried meat. The scent of smoke was heavy in the air, the chimney struggling to funnel everything out of the room. The two of them were too busy to acknowledge their entry as they approached another door which Garmesh opened and stepped to the side.

"Inside," he commanded.

Alderin entered the room, a simple furnished living quarters and the only room with glass windows. Hunting trophies adorned one side of the wall, a massive bed taking up a third of the space. Garmesh closed the door behind him, locking it by sliding a latch over the end and grabbed a heavy war axe that leaned against the wall by the door.

He spoke a single word of orcish-arcana, as a bluish crystalline sphere hung from an iron wrought chain glowed and filled the room with a blue light. Alderin turned to see Garmesh, taking a step back, reaching for his sword.

"That won't be necessary," Garmesh said, putting his axe down, "I had to be sure before we spoke."

Alderin eased slightly, but his hands still trembled, "Sure of what?"

"That you were not a kobold."

He looked up at the light hanging overhead, "I assume that has something to do with it?"

"A true light sphere. It reveals the true form of a person. Now tell me, how did you come by this phrase?"

"I ran into Krogg in the woods with my traveling companions. We spent the night camped together, and the following morning we were attacked by kiapals. I saved their daughter from being carried off by one of them. He gave me the phrase as gratitude."

"You saved the chief's daughter... well isn't that something," the orc cracked a smile, "But how did you know to come to me?"

"Someone in my party knows you and told me to talk to you about making arrangements to get to the other side of the city."

The orc's smile faded, "Across the city? Why do you want to do that?"

"It's in the direction where we are traveling. Through the city is the only way to get there. That is unless you know another way?"

"I do not," Garmesh took a step closer to him but he did not budge, "Who exactly told you about me?"

"One of those I am traveling with. A kobold. She says she knows you."

His eyes narrowed, staring him down, "Did you say a kobold?"

"Yes."

"I don't know of any kobolds personally."

"She says she knows you, even though you have never spoken."

Garmesh quietly muttered a few words to himself, eye widening, "Where is this kobold?"

"She is behind your tavern with the others of my party, composed of a dwarf, a gnome, and a female human."

"Show me, then we'll talk more," he stated, grabbing his axe.

"Of course," Alderin replied as Garmesh unlocked the door and stepped out.

"There's an exit in the back over there," he said, pointing with his axe. He unlocked the back door as the two orcs took notice of him.

"What's wrong? What's with the human?" one asked.

"Nothing yet, I'll let you know," he replied as they stepped outside. Haze from within rushed out through the door, and only a few feet away was the rest of the party, who looked at the two in surprise upon their sudden arrival. Ariana let out a low growl, focusing on Garmesh.

"Easy, everything is fine," Alderin responded in human. "He wants to see Histra. As I did mention her," he explained, then repeating in orcish.

"I understand human tongue," he replied, looking over the group as Histra stood up and walked over to the edge of the cart.

"Hello Garmesh, it's been a while," she said to him in orcish with a grin.

He rushed over to her, "You're my younger brother's baby white dragon... where is he? He was supposed to be here over a week ago," he stated in orcish. Alderin's eyes went wide, but he remained silent.

"Dead," Histra answered, as Garmesh brought a blade to her throat.

"How did he die?!" he yelled, as his breath fogged before him.

"Wait, wait, what's going on? Let's be calm about this," said Jesmine, jumping, raising her hands up.

"Killed by bandits. Him and his entire troupe. I was left in this here cage behind me to starve once the bandits saw I was nothing but a kobold."

He stared into her blue eyes before looking at the wagon, "It is one of his wagons... How did you escape?" he grunted, while keeping the blade to Histra's neck.

"We can talk about this," said Jesmine.

"We are," stated Garmesh to her in human as Alderin walked over to her and whispered.

"Let this play out."

"That human there freed me at the behest of the female beside him. In exchange for letting me recover, I am to guide them to where they need to go, which just so happens to be on the other side of the city."

Garmesh tightly gripped the hilt of his axe, taking a deep breath, pulling his blade back.

"I did not want to go to you. The brother of the one who tossed me into a cage for a decade, but you are the only one I know who has connections."

"Tell me. Did Gorigon die fighting?"

"I was in a cage, I couldn't see much... but from what I heard, yes."

"Where did it happen?"

"A few weeks to the west. If you travel to where you head to Four-Scaled City, you'll be sure to find the location where it happened."

"He did mention he was going there to buy something good for his show, to draw even bigger crowds."

"And he was ambushed and killed for it."

Garmesh took another deep breath and turned to Alderin, "All of you need to get across the city?"

He nodded, "Yes. Including, if possible, our supplies, horses, wagon and my protector here," he motioned toward Ariana.

Garmesh looked over everything, "How quickly do you want this done?"

"As soon as possible."

"How much do you have on you?"

"Give him all the money. You don't want to skimp on this," stated Histra in human tongue.

"All the money?" asked Dran.

"If you want to get through the city without catching anyone's attention, it would be a wise move. The bridges are heavily guarded, and everything is checked, coming and going," said Garmesh in human.

"That is fair," he replied as they quickly pooled their money together into one hefty bag. Copper, silver, and a few gold coins jingled as they handed it over to him.

Garmesh's thick, red orcish fingers felt the bag for weight before peering inside. "This will be more than enough," he said in orcish, putting the bag away, looking to Alderin, "I will have everything set up by tomorrow."

"Tomorrow? Really?" he asked.

"Yes. As the kobold stated, I have connections," he looked over to Histra.

"I have no interest in your connections. This isn't my home, I don't care what you do," she replied.

"It's true. She's been rather *cold* to everyone..." said Alderin in orcish.

Histra glared at him.

Garmesh chuckled and spoke in human, "Come. I'll give you a place to rest and hide till tomorrow." He went to a locked latch, and pulling out a key, he opened it with a click. The metal chains slid away, opening the doors to a set of stairs that went straight into the cellar underneath the tavern, "I have no rooms, but seeing you want to get through the city discreetly, it would be best if none of you were to be seen," he explained, walking down into the dank and dreary cellar.

Wood creaked above as the noise of the tavern could faintly be heard. In one area, there were cured slabs of meat hanging from hooks, and on the other half, kegs of alcohol.

"I've slept in worse places," remarked Alderin as he was right behind Garmesh, the others were not far behind.

"I hope you aren't afraid of the dark. You'll be in it for a while," chuckled Garmesh.

"We'll survive. Thank you for your help. We really appreciate it," said Jesmine.

"I appreciate the coin," he replied, heading back to the door, "Just keep the kobold away from the meat. I prefer it not to freeze. It never tastes the same once it's frozen."

"Shouldn't we get our gear?" asked Gnemi.

Garmesh stopped and looked at him, "Don't worry about that. Your transportation is going to be tight with such a large party. I can get the cart and horses to the other side without much of an issue," he explained, climbing up the stairs, which creaked under his weight, the doors closing behind him with a thud, leaving the party in near pitched darkness with only a few faint streams of light coming through the cracks in the door.

"Why do I get the feeling that this was a bad idea," remarked Dran as Jesmine quickly cast her light spell, forming two small orbs, causing a few rats to scurry away.

"It is the best I could do given the circumstances. Rivera is Sa'bara's pride and joy, and everyone and anyone gets checked before going in. And they will check to see if you have Sa'bara's mark," explained Histra.

Alderin looked over to her who stood off in a corner, the wet walls freezing over with a thin layer of white ice, "How trustworthy is he?"

"I've never seen him break an agreement and I've seen him do a few. You'd be surprised what people talk about near you when you're chained up, unable to speak. Speaking of speaking, we should be safe to talk. The tavern overhead will cover up any noise we make."

Jesmine nodded, sitting on a barrel, "That's good," she said, looking to Ariana who was sniffing along the room, "Ariana, are you going to change back for a while?"

She shook her head.

"So, what was with the axe being pulled back there? How do you know that orc?" asked Dran.

"He's seen me a few times as the traveling side show as this was the troupe's common end of the year stop. Garmesh was surprised to see me out of my cage, and being a kobold, I tend not to get a warm welcome when one can get away with it."

"Alderin. You understood what was said, what happened?"

"It is like what she said," he replied as Ariana let out a huff of air from her nostrils.

Dran nodded, "Now we wait. I can only pray to the Earth Mother that this is not a trap."

"I don't think so," said Alderin.

"Oh? What makes you so sure?"

"I've dealt with my fair share of shady folks in my past and those you can trust are the ones that ask the fewest questions or don't question the answers you give them. For the most part, he did both."

"Hmm. It would be wise that we don't let our guard down. This is the most dangerous step on our journey yet... but since we can talk about it, what is up with the orcs here? It appears like they are having a celebration rather than paying 'taxes' to Sa'bara."

"It is a celebration. After one pays their tax to him, they then praise him with festivity that lasts for about two weeks, or until all the tax is collected. Most celebrate a day at most before they must head back to work though," Histra explained.

Dran stroked his dirtied red braided beard, looking to Alderin, "Much different than back home. The year before and the year of tribute are stressful times for all. Banditry, kidnapping, and wars between kingdoms increased, as everyone vied to not only meet Dra'kesh's requirements, but also to not be the poorest tributary."

"I honestly find this all to be fascinating. I have never seen so many kobolds before," said Gnemi, as he sat on a small wooden stool.

"The only ones you'll see are those in a position of power, as they oversee tax collection," said Jesmine as the lights dimmed slightly, "There's a small district in the city designed for kobold occupation."

"You'll have to tell me more in detail once I have a place to take notes," he said as the group broke into idle chatter. Ariana laid down and rested her head on her paws, her ears still up and alert.

Histra stayed in her claimed corner, watching the others talk, when suddenly she caught Gnemi looking in her direction every so often. After a few minutes, she stood up and annoyingly asked, "What is it?"

"Ah... um... well I was thinking maybe you could answer a question or two of mine? I know you aren't one to answer, but they'd only take a moment," he replied, hands rubbing against each other anxiously, looking down and then back up at her, "If you answer them, I'll try to make you one of my automatic crossbows."

"I don't think we'll be together long enough for that to happen," Histra replied.

"Histra, why don't you answer at least one question of his? Outside of me, he's been nothing but helpful and nice to you. You can at least give him something," said Jesmine, the lights slowly dimming.

She gritted her teeth and let out a long, drawn-out sigh.

"It's a strange one, but one that I heard about since I was young. And when I saw all the other kobolds around, I was reminded of it." She stared at him as he got closer. He looked her in the eyes before looking off to the side, "It's a silly question but I want to know if it's true."

Histra's claws twitched a little, slowly asking, "What is it?"

"Histra... is it true that if a clan of kobolds have too many of one gender that some can switch? Like if there are too many males, they can become female to help the clan?"

Dran let out a soft chuckle, "What? That is—" his words were cut off by Histra yelling, her wings spreading out to their fullest extent.

"What kind of idiotic question is that!" She glared at him, body shaking, "You want to know more about kobolds? Don't ask me! I don't know! I haven't been around others of my kind in decades! Want to know why? It's right here!" she pointed to the cracked part of her horn. "All I know about kobolds is from broken confusing memories since before I got this injury. I don't even know how old I am," she took a deep breath and continued.

"The only things I do know is that I've been hunted, used, and abused for being what I am, and that every single waking moment I am in excruciating pain. I feel as if I am being stabbed in several parts of my body and no amount of magic or herbal medicines can cure me! But you know what I do know?! That we don't change genders! Whoever came up with that is worse than an imbecile, and… and…" Histra's eyes darted around the group, their eyes locked upon her, taking a slow deep breath, and her outstretched wings slowly pulled back in, "And I've said too much," she remarked in draconic. Ariana softly growled already back on her feet.

"Histra… I don't know what to say but," he stepped up to her, "I'm sorry. I didn't know," Gnemi recoiled a bit, "When I was young everything dragon in nature was killed, including kobolds. I knew they were servants of Eisandra, but to hunt them down for decades after was something that if I was aware at the time I would have been against," he said, slowly approaching her. She stared at him intently as he placed a hand on her shoulder, "I didn't mean to offend you," he replied, as she let out an icy misty huff, looking up at him.

"You're from the north, aren't you Histra?" said Jesmine.

Histra tensed, staring at her, "What of it?"

"I took part in some of those exterminations. I was called upon to help hunt down and kill the few remaining younger white dragons after Eisandra was slain."

"I wouldn't call it exterminations. Many of those bastards were far from innocent," stated Dran as Histra gave him an icy glare.

"My father was ambushed and killed by kobolds. His head was put on a pike along with several others, many of whom I knew. Don't act as if none deserved it."

Histra turned her attention to Jesmine, "How many dragons did you kill?"

"I took part in four. All of which were young. None were no bigger than this tavern we're under," Jesmine replied.

"They had to be less than three hundred years old if they were only that big," remarked Histra.

"I never did agree with the policy of killing every dragon and kobold to ensure the safety of the people, but I had limited options… and I was a bit caught up in it all. Being the daughter of my mother, people had certain expectations of me, and then when my home was destroyed…" she trailed off before resuming her focus on the spell.

"So, you killed four others," stated Histra.

"I thought you said you only killed the last white dragon," said Gnemi.

Jesmine shook her head, "I said I killed the last known white dragon, not that it was my only one," she explained, taking a deep breath, bringing the light of her spell back to full strength before continuing. "When I heard rumors that there were survivors of Sa'bara's extermination in Dra'kesh, I began to make trips there to rescue and bring them to the north. Dra'kesh isn't as alienating as Sa'bara but being a small group of outsiders in a foreign land, with the punitive tribute system, I had to help."

"It's okay Jesmine. You can't beat yourself over a bunch of kobolds or a few isolated dragons who cared nothing but for themselves," said Alderin.

Histra replied with a soft growl, "You know nothing of the dragons."

"And neither do you!" exclaimed Alderin, "You don't remember anything but yet you still hold some grand idea about them, but I've seen them. I've seen Dra'kesh. Watched him as he…" Alderin swallowed a lump in his throat, hands shaking, heart pounding heavily.

"Asked for those to be sacrificed as payment for our poor tribute. Years of training, thieving, blackmail, all so my area would not be the poorest tributary, things I did not want to do, but had to do, all for nothing. In the end he selected my village to be punished," Alderin said, walking up to Histra, looking down at her as she stared up at him.

"I sacrificed everything for my family. I volunteered to be killed by him. And when it came to the moment, he picked those we wished to be spared. He said something about only those willing to sacrifice get to live, then he melted my family before my very eyes. He MELTED them with his acid breath! And who was there making sure we could do nothing but watch? Who made sure we WATCHED!? Who enjoyed their time like it was some kind of party? Kobolds! Black… scaled… kobolds! Do you have any idea what kind of screams people make as they melt!?"

Histra remained silent, looking up into his water filled eyes as a single tear ran down his cheek.

"Alderin. I am so sorry," said Jesmine, walking over to him, the strength of her light spell fading in and out.

Alderin's hands continued to shake, taking a deep breath and slowly let it out. He swallowed down another lump in his throat. "Don't think you've had it the worst. You haven't. I haven't. I lived. I was spared. I was spared because I wanted my family to live instead of me. Maybe you should think about how you aren't the only one making concessions here." He turned and returned to the keg he was sitting on, walking past Jesmine, who softly sighed, and went back to her seat.

"I don't know what to say here. I've had nothing as terrible as that happen to me…" said Gnemi.

"Be grateful for that," said Jesmine, turning to Alderin. "I was not there when my mother was killed. I was not there when my father, my family, and most of my race was killed by Sa'bara. It is shocking to see the city I knew when I was a child to be exactly as I remembered it."

"Sa'bara is purposely preserving the city," said Histra.

"What?" asked Jesmine, giving a curious look of disbelief.

"Orcs live there now, but based on what I've heard, Sa'bara makes them live like the elves once did when they ruled. From the use of metalworking, the clothes, down to the meals and music that is played in the city… everything."

"Why would the dragon do something as crazy as that?" asked Dran.

"To show power and control. To remind everyone who visits the city who was there, and they are gone because he willed it," said Alderin in an exhausted, beaten tone of voice. He looked down at Histra from his seat. "You said you are in pain in every waking moment that cannot be cured?"

"Every moment. It makes sleep difficult, though I have noticed over the past two decades it's been slowly getting better, it's still painful."

"You aren't the only one, and no matter how much time passes, it does not fade. Every time I close my eyes, I see them, as they were, and what happened. Maybe now you'll take into consideration the constraint I have when dealing with your secretive nature."

"I will keep it in mind. But maybe perhaps you understand why."

"Today… I do, but maybe not tomorrow. Keep *that* in mind."

Jesmine took a deep breath and softly sighed, "Gnemi. That was some question you asked."

"I got a lot more than I intended," he replied, slowly backing away.

"Despite the ruckus above us, we were rather loud. I hope no one heard us," she commented, looking at the wood ceiling.

"If someone did, we'd hear about it eventually. Perhaps it would be best if we cut the lights and get some rest? Tomorrow is going to be a trying day," suggested Histra.

"Aye, I can agree to that," said Dran, as Jesmine nodded and dimmed the lights, and once everyone was ready, Gnemi set up to keep first watch near the stairs. After that, she ended the spell.

While they got rest, Garran was about to get a piece of news that would change everything. At their camp far off the road, one of hundreds of others with campfires burning, and food cooking, Shana was by the flames simmering several salted meats. Garran looked at Zed as he finished casting his tracking spell. "There is a strong chance they are in the town, maybe the city itself."

Garran squeezed his fists, "Hmmm…"

"What is it?"

"There's something about this that has been bothering me."

"How so?"

"I'm not sure. It's been a feeling ever since they said they want to go through the city. There is something else to this, and I need to know."

"Garran, they're here," said Karrun from just outside of the tent.

"Finally," he replied, stepping out to see the rest of his hunting band, carts and cages empty.

"We paid ourselves several times over with our catch," said a dark brown skinned orc with a pair of axes attached to his belt, and a bow with a quiver full of arrows strapped to his back.

"Good to hear Kra'mek," said Garran.

"And I have some other news for you, that you might like," he replied, leaping off the cart.

"About?"

"Those that took our prize. I saw them on the main road."

"Yes. We figured they took the road to hide and claim as the innocent party if we attacked them."

"But you won't believe what I saw," he replied, looking around.

Garran raised a curious brow, motioning him closer. "In the tent."

"Yes sir."

"Zed make sure no one can hear us outside of this hut," said Garran, stepping inside with Kra'mek right behind.

"Give me a moment," Zed replied, pulling out a leather-bound tome with silver runic markings from under his robes. "I haven't done this one in a while," he explained, flipping through the pages of orcish-arcana, with pictures depicting hand motions, body movements, and notes explaining each step of the different spells. "Here we are."

He read over the page before beginning his cast, and a minute later a flow of blue-green light flowed outward around the hut. "You have ten minutes before I have to upkeep the spell."

"They had the werewolf walk out in the open in full feral form! And that's not even the most surprising thing!" exclaimed Kra'mek.

"Bold. Very bold. They know few have seen a werewolf, and who would think a fully feral werewolf was walking beside them. She looked like a breed of wolkin when in that form… but you say that isn't the most surprising thing?"

Kra'mek shook his head, "No. I wasn't sure at first, as it happened so fast, but when an avrius came swooping over the wagons, it blew the female human's hood back."

"And?"

"She is no human, but an elf. They are traveling with a damn elf!"

Garran nodded, looking over to Zed, "What do you make of this?"

"It could explain the Lycan's passive nature. She was an elf, and seeing another elf, might make her more complacent."

Garran stroked his chin, "I see. So, the human wizard is in reality is an elven wizard. Zed, do you happen to know of any towns past Rivera that housed powerful elven wizards before

Sa'bara wiped them out?"

"Yes. There is a town deep in the forest of Du'ralia. It is where the slayer of Eisandra lived, and where Sa'bara made his first stop when he began his elven extermination. The place was covered in deadly poisonous gas for years, and rumor has it now that it's haunted by the ghosts who were killed there."

"If you were an elven wizard with immense power and you wanted more, where do you think you'd go?"

"I'd go there."

"Tomorrow, I think we will visit the local avolariean representative in Rivera and get a rite of passage through their land."

"Don't you think we should enlist more help?" asked Zed.

"Now that we're back together, I believe we have all the help we need. Speaking of which, do you have the writ?"

"Right here. We already took our payment from it," Kra'mek said, pulling out a rolled-up piece of parchment.

"Next time wait for all of us," grunted Garran, unfurling the paper which had the eye of Sa'bara on it with runic markings around it.

"What's the word?"

"Ekum."

Garran placed his marked hand over the paper, saying the word, the paper glowing with a golden light, and a moment later so did the mark on his hand. As the light faded, the runes on the paper looked more non-descript than before. Garran gave the parchment over to Zed, who did the same as Garran, the runes fading even more.

"Make sure the others get counted as having paid the tax. If we are late returning or the Gods forbid, we fail, we'll at least have paid our dues and then some."

"Yes sir," Kra'mek replied, taking the paper and headed out of the tent.

"With your current payment, there's a good chance you could get a commanding position in the army," said Zed.

"Of a small group of warriors at best, but I have bigger plans. Sa'bara is planning something with this Draksind. I must exemplify to everyone that our clan is to be trusted with carrying out his goals. We will not stop here. We must press on. But for now, get something to eat, and some rest. We have a big day tomorrow."

"I trust your decision on this," Zed replied, leaving the tent.

Garran took a deep breath and closed his eyes, his hands running across his blade, "We won't fail. We have too much to lose and everything to gain from this."

Chapter 12 Passing Through, Nothing to See Here

Jesmine sat on a small barrel of mead, a softly glowing orb remaining near her to illuminate the dark cellar. She listened to her companions get what sleep they could, the rumble of activity up above and outside steadily increasing as the night faded into day. She turned her attention to the only other person awake, Histra, who leaned against the wall. Her eyes gave a bluish glow as the light caught them. Her wings furled tightly up against her, spending a moment to adjust position.

"Do you not sleep because the pain you say you are in or another reason?"

"It doesn't make it easy, but this is not a place to rest," she replied.

Jesmine nodded as Dran stirred awake. "Argh, is it daylight already?" he asked, stretching out with a soft groan his brown eyes reflecting like Histra's in the light.

"Not yet. I wish I knew when they'd come to pick us up," Jesmine said, looking up to the cellar doors.

"They said in the morning but not when," he replied, standing up, checking over his gear.

"Do you need a little more light?" she asked.

"This is plenty," he replied, the jingling of his equipment stirring Alderin awake.

"We're still in the cellar, not sure if that is a good thing or a bad thing," he remarked, rubbing his back. "I'm going to be feeling this later," he stretched, "Is it morning yet?"

"Close but not yet," Jesmine replied.

"Can I get a little more light?" Alderin asked, pulling out some dried meat from a pouch.

"Sure," she replied, chanting, three more spheres appearing, glowing brighter, filling the room with light which woke Ariana and Gnemi.

"Thanks," he turned and nudged Gnemi. "Looks like we won't be cooking today."

"I've been the one doing most of the cooking the last few days," remarked Dran as Ariana let out a soft whining yawn, stretching, tail wagging, sniffing the air.

"Everything okay?" Alderin asked.

She gave a simple nod, walking towards the entrance, her ears held high, twisting and turning slightly.

"I'll take that as a yes, but guarded."

"Given the situation, that is the best answer we can hope for. I for one don't like this one bit," Dran remarked, taking a bite of his dried jerky. "We don't know where our supplies are, and though these orcs have been hospitable, we can never be too careful."

"We have to do what we must to get through without getting noticed," Jesmine replied. "Hopefully once we are past the city the other orcs will have lost our trail."

"I hope so. I don't think I could take another arrow," said Alderin, rubbing his shoulder. "Thank you, Ariana, for the medicine, I'm healing much faster than I thought I would."

She kept her attention towards the door, her ears turning to him as he spoke with a quickened tail wag.

"But that is why I am so concerned about this plan. We are taking so many risks, and judging from what I saw, these orcs are equally not a trusting bunch. Garmesh, the orc we dealt with, had a magic crystal to check if I was really human and not a kobold in disguise."

"Of course. You'd expect me to take you to some upstanding citizens, who are happy with the current social order?" Histra asked, standing taller, "You can't tell me you aren't fond of working with those who work below what is considered lawful? Considering your skill set and what was said last night, you shouldn't be a stranger to such things."

Alderin glared at her. "I'm not. But that does not mean I am put at ease."

"There is something I'd like to say, that I should have said yesterday," said Jesmine, standing up, the lights dimming for a moment as she closed her eyes, focusing.

"There was a fair bit said, things that shouldn't have been said," Histra remarked, eyeing everyone.

"I wasn't expecting to talk about my past, but now you know where I and Dran are coming from," Alderin explained.

"Alderin, you asked me many times why I give Histra so much trust despite being a kobold," Jesmine said.

"I have."

"I've wondered about it, but it was not my place to inquire," Dran said.

"Do you remember when I asked you about how you learned where I was?" Jesmine asked.

"I remember," Alderin replied.

"Those kids only managed to escape my fate because of a kobold."

Alderin and Dran's gaze grew more focused on her as Histra watched with a curious look, while Ariana's ear turned in her direction, Gnemi remaining as curious as ever.

"A kobold from Dra'kesh, helped you?" asked Dran in disbelief.

"Why would one of those things help you?" asked Alderin.

"I was escorting several elves that survived Sa'bara's extermination. They had set up a home near the Murical Swamps, where the shek live, but it was recently attacked. I was escorting the survivors north to our settlements there. At one of the stops for supplies, a group of local human children were brutalizing this one defenseless kobold."

"Kobolds are never defenseless," remarked Dran, making hand claw motions.

"Will you let me finish?"

"Apologies," he replied, lowering his head slightly, Histra giving a sly smirk.

"I helped her. Checked to see how injured she was, giving her a little bit of food, and sent her on her way. She was very thankful for what I did. A week later when the caravan was attacked and I fell back to defend a group of children, it was to my surprise when I met the same kobold again."

"And this explains your trust in kobolds how? You saved one and, in the end, they attack you with the rest of their kind," Alderin remarked.

"Let. Me. *Finish*," Jesmine stated firmly.

Histra let out a soft chuckle.

"Histra, don't try to undermine what I am trying to say. Please, be quiet and listen," Jesmine stated as the lights around her grew dimmer, looking at her for a moment before turning her attention back to the others.

"Entering the hut, she was just as surprised to see me as I was to see her, and after one quick look at what I was doing, without me saying a single word she waved off the other kobolds from coming in. After that, we had a brief exchange where she'd guarantee the safety of the kids if I wouldn't cause them any problems. She was aware of my arcane ability, but she didn't know I lost my spellbook during the mass panic that happened when the fighting broke out. And after what Alderin told me how you knew where I was, I knew she kept her end of the deal."

"Because a kobold who helped put you into slavery, but didn't enslave some children, you were willing from the very beginning to give Histra a chance?" Alderin asked.

"Kobolds aren't inherently bad but if you treat them as nothing more than dragon serving monsters, what else do they have going for them?"

"But why did you help the kobold in the first place?"

"My mother, outside of her dedication to bringing the death of the ancient dragons with every fiber of her being, did feel that those under them deserve a chance. It is how she and others managed to broker an agreement with the Tirghal orc tribe to safely travel to the north. It's why I don't feel we should condemn Histra for being a kobold but judge her by her actions. As questionable some of those may be," she looked over to Histra, who had her arms crossed. Jesmine continued, "Or I should say as secretive as they may be. She's been immensely helpful. And though we all have our own history with kobolds, orcs, and even the ancient dragons themselves, we all share a similar goal right now. So, it's best we work together."

"I understand, but then there is one problem that's bothering me," Alderin said, looking to Histra.

"And what might that be?" Histra asked.

"What do you intend to do once you lead us to the forest."

"Does it matter? Once there, I should be well enough to head off on my own. I've spent decades by myself. I can get to where I want to go easy enough from there."

"It might. You keep a lot of secrets from us."

"And you do the same. One where me leaving would be a good thing for you."

"There's a lot not said between all of us. But that doesn't matter. If it's not important to the here and now. There's no need to ask. In the meantime, we must be ready for what's to come," Jesmine said as Ariana let out a soft growl.

"What is it?" Alderin asked, standing up, rushing over to her, his hands on the hilt of his blade as the sound of a metal latch slid across the cellar doors. Jesmine dropped the spell moments before the doors opened.

"Wake up, it's time to go," stated Garmesh in orcish, only a small amount of light entering through the opening, revealing that it was still about an hour till dawn. "Ah, I see you are already awake. Good, let's make this quick."

As they stepped outside into the back alley, they saw a horse drawn canvas-covered wagon with two muscular orcs of towering physique, one a deep dark green, the other a dark red, standing beside it with the back latch already open revealing an empty but dirty wood floor.

"You'll be hiding in here," Garmesh said, the two orcs pressing a finger into the side of the wagon, pushing a small block of wood and lifting a false bottom. "It won't be till late afternoon that you'll get to the other side of the city. Your wagon, horses, and supplies will be there waiting for you."

"Does it take that long to ride through the city?" Alderin asked.

"No, but these two fine men are going to risk their lives to get you through. In order to remain outside of suspicion, they will need to perform their daily routine without alteration, which means you will have to wait til they are done. Hopefully, you can remain in one place for hours without a problem, not that you have much of a choice."

"H—" Alderin started before Histra quickly cut him off.

"He said we have to get into the wagon. We'll be there all day til late afternoon. The question is, what order do we want to go in there?" she asked.

"Why don't you go in first and my companion here can go in right after. That would be the best way to make sure there is enough room as it already looks like a tight fit. At least Ariana's fur can handle your cold without an issue, and hopefully, isolate it from the rest of us," Alderin suggested.

"I can't fault that logic," she replied with a soft grumble afterwards, jumping to grab onto the back of the lowered wagon door, clawing her way up and inside. She wiggled towards the back, which felt rather spacious to her. *"This is going to be tight with the others,"* she thought.

The ox in the front of the wagon mooed and tugged at its harness slightly. "What's got into him?" the red orc remarked, working to calm him.

"You're next girl, inside," Alderin said with a soft whistle, Ariana letting out a soft growl before leaping up and climbing inside. Her fur fluffed and fully filled the empty space. Histra pressed herself up horizontally against the front of the compartment, feeling Ariana's fur brush up against her. The fur blocked the cold air from spreading but a thin layer of frost had already begun to form.

"I'll go next," said Jesmine, stepping up.

"I should have mentioned two things. Don't scratch the runes on the sides. They will keep you from being sensed by the low-level detection magic that they use at the gates. Second, there are a few wood knots you can pull to peek outside and provide a little more air. Best not to use them unless you have to," Garmesh explained as Alderin translated.

"Why are the extra holes there?" Jesmine asked, about to step inside.

"How in the nine hells should I know? If you meet the one who made it, you can ask them, and remember to push those two first blocks in once inside," Garmesh replied.

Alderin was next to go in, followed by Gnemi and Dran who were small enough to line up facing away from each other, leaving barely any wiggle room. The orcs placed the wooden plank over the opening while they shoved the blocks back into place. Delving them in near complete darkness, the two orcs slipped onto the wagon, starting their day.

They tried their best to get relaxed in the cramped and cold conditions. Ariana felt the constant chill of Histra's ice aura along her side, her breath visible, cramped but not too uncomfortable in her four-legged form.

The wagon rumbled, moving through the streets, the sound of the town fading as Jesmine and Alderin found a knot hole close to their position. She pulled it out, revealing some of the countryside with pitched tents as far as the eye could see.

"I don't like the looks of this," remarked Alderin, plugging up the hole.

"We can't make any quick judgements yet…" she replied.

"All I could see was the river," Gnemi said.

"Shh, we shouldn't be talking," warned Dran as everyone's chatter ceased. Several minutes passed as they moved farther away from the city, until suddenly the cart pulled off the road, causing it to wobble and creak under the uneven surface. Sunlight began to peek through the small cracks in the wood along with an ever-increasing stench of animal droppings. The wagon stopped as the red orc grumbled, "This is the worst part of the day."

"It is what the plants need to grow. And with the arrival of one of Sa'bara's representative in two weeks, we have to make it look as good as possible," remarked the green orc, getting to work shoveling a cartful of fertilizer onto the back of the wagon which rocked slightly with each shovel load. Small amounts of it filtered through the cracks, landing on those below.

"Disgusting…" muttered Gnemi, pulling a cloth from his side pouch, using it to cover his face, pulling his goggles from around his neck to cover his eyes. The wagon creaked as more manure was shoveled into it. When the two orcs finished, they closed the back, locking it securely before turning back toward the city. The shakes and bumps of the road shifted small bits of manure down onto the group.

The grotesque smell was overpowering Ariana's nose, but behind it was something more sinister, the aroma of burning flesh. Her ears turned toward the sound of an orc screaming in pain as the red orc driver remarked, "Sounds like a weak one is getting their mark today."

"My eldest didn't even flinch when he got his," replied the green.

"How long till your daughter gets hers?"

"Next Draksind," he explained.

"She takes after you. Strong and fierce. I'll bet she won't even flinch."

"She takes after her Mother."

"If that's the case she'll make the damn kobold flinch when they mark her," he chuckled. Sounds of orcs with their beasts of burden bled through the thin wooden walls. A sudden jerk and wobble of the wagon, sound shifting to that of hooves and feet onto stone. The wagon pulled onto the main road made of well-crafted interlocking sections of stone, its breadth wide enough to encompass the entire width of the two bridges and everything in between.

The party was unable to see the two sets of massive jade carved dragon statues that stood at the entrance of the bridges. The statues' wings spread wide, sitting on their haunches, posing like mighty lions, their heads held high but also looking down at those that entered the city. The bases were made of obsidian and carved into them with white marble inlaid, were words of greetings to Sa'bara's great city in Elvish, Orcish, Avolariean, Dwarven, and Human in that exact order.

Past the statues was the guard station where dozens of orcs dressed in shimmering elvish armor, who checked in everyone who entered the city. The wagon slowed at the behest of one of the guards. "Working with the plants again?" one of the orc guards asked.

"Always," replied the red orc.

"You know the drill. What do you have in your wagon this time?" he asked, walking to the back.

"Shit for the plants," replied the green orc, the guard investigating the back of the wagon. He let out a huff of air, seeing the pile of fertilizer along with several gardening tools.

"Go," the guard commanded, walking away, the wagon continuing. The party heard the shifting sound of stone as they moved from pavement to the bridge, the sound of rushing water following soon after. They reached a small island that split the bridges, water wheels creaking as they turned, ready to power the bridges' engineering marvel at a moment's notice. The unique sound between the stone bridges and the islands shifted a few times before reaching the city proper.

White stone composed the defensive walls that faced the bridge side of the city. Orc guards in well-kept but seemingly mismatched elvish style metal plate armor adorned their massive muscular bodies.

As they moved deeper into the city, the sounds and even a few smells that managed to sneak through the stench of the fertilizer brought back memories to Jesmine, causing her hands to shake. Her thoughts rushed to when she was a child visiting with her mother, and she reached for the knot hole. Alderin looked to her with concern, whispering, "What are you doing?"

"I have to see. Just something about this…" she trailed off, pulling the knot out, peering through, seeing one orc guard in the elven armor, a flash memory of the exact same armor adorning the elves of the city. A bakery with elvish style breads, and meals prepared were bought by well-to-do orcs dressed in light clothing composed of whites, blues, and greens, distinct colors of the elvish nobility.

Jesmine tensed, seeing a living twisted memory of her people. Everything felt familiar but also clearly different. The guards, the workers, even the few children at play dressed in elegant elvish clothing, speaking a rough accented version of elvish. Her native tongue twisted by the orcs who occasionally interjected a word of their own that had no good translation.

A set of street performers played wooden and string instruments that were played by her people. Elvish music she had heard many times in years past reached her ears as the wagon rode by. Her heart quickened, a weight pressing down upon her.

The height and size of the buildings shifted depending on where they were in the city. Those built over the water were smaller, and lighter. Forges and smithing were done with the aid of the water wheels to power the furnaces and provide a constant supply of cool clean water. The clang of metal rang out, drowning out other sounds nearby; the distinct ringing of mithril being forged. It was an unforgettable noise as the material was often described as a metal that "sings" when it is worked. A heavenly sound that she first heard when she came to the city.

Jesmine swallowed a lump in her throat and plugged the hole, her breathing heavy and labored, placing her hands over her mouth, breathing into them. Tears filled her eyes which soon rolled down her cheeks. Alderin with a look of concern leaned in. "Are you okay?"

"I'll be fine," she muttered, taking slow deep breaths, closing her eyes, forcing more tears to flow down her cheeks.

"We'll talk about it once we are out of the city," Alderin whispered, feeling a slight nudge from Dran who looked over to him with an inquisitive look.

Alderin mouthed the words, "I will tell you later."

Dran nodded while Ariana shifted slightly, her tail wagging side to side, gently brushing up against the wood behind her. Her yellow eyes looked at Jesmine's reactions before checking up on Histra, who had fallen asleep.

Deeper into the city they went, the busy streets slowly growing lighter as the wagon suddenly stopped once again as an orc yelled in roguish elvish, "Halt! Who goes there!"

The red orc stared at the yellow-green skinned orc in fanciful heavy armor, "You know who it is. We're here to do our royal duty, and you know full well we don't speak elf tongue."

"You two? Come to make the plants all pretty?" he asked in orcish with heavy sarcasm, chuckling to the other guard with him at the gate of an inner-city wall.

"You know of the importance of our work. Sa'bara wants the gardens in pristine condition."

"Ah yes. They are important. And a mighty task that only the weak inferior Tirghal clan can only hope to manage with two of their best 'warriors'," he laughed.

"It's only a couple of weeks till one of Sa'bara's kin comes to see the end of Draksind. We have a lot of work ahead of us," said the green orc.

"Right, right. Hard work that only the bravest of Tirghal, who can't even make a bird tremble at the sight of them, can manage. But before I let you in, you know the rules." He whistled to another orc dressed in light airy clothes. Around her neck is a silver symbol of Sa'bara's eye with a green gem in the center. She held up the symbol and chanted in orcish-arcana. The gem glowed for a moment, soon followed by her eyes. The symbols within the wagon began to glow a dull greenish.

Quietly those inside pulled away while Jesmine looked at the runes with curiosity, but after a few moments the orc stopped her chant and the glow within the wagon faded away just as quickly.

"Nothing unusual in the wagon, except the shit in the back," she stated.

"You, stab your spear into it just to be safe," commanded one guard as the other gave his companion a glare. He nevertheless moved to the back and stabbed the spear into the black mucky steamy fertilizer. He pulled it out and rubbed the spear tip against the wagon's canvas cover.

"Nothing," he remarked.

"Get inside and get this rotten aroma away from me, and whatever smell that so-called plant food is making," stated the commanding guard as the metal gate leading inside the castle was raised.

The outer defenses of Rivera castle were made with forty-foot-high stone walls, and it was constituted with battlements, towers, murder holes, and other defenses that would protect it from any possible attacker. A second such wall separated the outer castle from the inner, which housed the massive towers, and finally, the magnificent palace itself.

The party remained still, unable to lay eyes upon the bailey's grand gardens before the stronghold. which had a smooth stone walkway that weaved through them. In the center of the grounds was a fountain made of marble with noble elves standing tall and proud. Looming over them in jade coloring was a massive, grand depiction of the great dragon Sa'bara.

Hundreds-of-years-old trees with long branches covered in hanging green vines and white flowers grew nearby, providing shade and symmetry. Flowers of reds, pinks, and purples bloomed on shaped bushes and trees with dark blue leaves and blood red flowers abounded in the early morning sunlight. Dew dripped from the leaves, evaporating as the day progressed. Guards walked the premises but paid no mind to the two orcs and their wagon as they worked to pull in at the edge of the open field.

Alderin peaked through the knot hole to see a fraction of the garden's beauty before plugging it up. He motioned for Dran to look through the wooden block, but he shook his head. Gnemi, though, did not hesitate, looking through to see the slender blue leafed, red flowered trees that seemed to shift color in the wind.

An hour passed, perhaps more, as the orcs worked. Ariana shook and rolled herself onto her back, brushing up her partially frozen fur along her mid-section.

Jesmine looked at the ice and whispered, "Let me help you with that." She breathed slowly and deeply, pressing her hands against the ice, tattoos beginning to glow faintly red, whispering a chant of elven-arcana.

"What are you doing?" whispered Alderin as Jesmine continued and after some time her hands burned with an unnatural but comfortable warmth. With slow strokes, she melted and then dried Ariana's fur. The Lycan squirmed at first, but soon relaxed, feeling her fur shift from cold to wet to pleasantly warm and dry.

Her paws twitched as she relaxed. Once her side was dry, she shifted and turned back to her original position, revealing her only slightly cold backside. After a few pets Jesmine stopped. Several more hours passed as the orcs continued to do their work, shoveling more and more of the fertilizer out of the wagon and into wheelbarrows. During one of these trips Ariana's ears suddenly rose, becoming more alert, tensing. Her lips curled, growling softly. The sudden movement and noise jolted Histra awake, who let out a yawn before Ariana's demeanor put her on alert.

"What is it?" Jesmine whispered.

She tensed, her tail wagging faster as the elf heard a low blowing horn. The kobold stretched a little more before catching the sound. Another deep burling horn blew, the sound almost as faint and distant, but then another louder one.

"What's that noise?" asked Alderin as massive bells from across the city rang out.

"What's going on?" asked Gnemi.

Histra tensed, thinking, *"It's too soon for one to arrive."*

"Dragon," whispered Jesmine.

"Dragon? What do you mean?" asked Alderin, looking to her with fearful concern.

"No one say anything. They have excellent hearing," Jesmine warned.

"I know," Alderin replied, clenching his fists. The ringing of the bells steadily faded and gave rise to a new sound. The flapping of wings which grew louder and louder as a massive green dragon flew above the river. The smooth surface of the water rippled under the wind generated by its massive appendages.

The dragon quickly approached and flew over the city, darkening an entire block as it made its way to the heart of the capital, the palace. It slowed and turned itself upright as the mighty dragon hovered over the very gardens the group was in. Its massive wings flapped several times, causing a gale-wind like force to blow down upon them.

The wagon rattled violently, and the ox sounded in distress as the two orcs tried their best to keep the carriage from tipping over and the steer from running off. The trees rattled as a few weak branches broke, a mighty roar rippling out over the area. Everything in the city stopped dead in its tracks, all eyes looking in its direction.

The green dragon's yellow slit pupils looked around only for a moment, speaking in a booming voice, its tongue fierce, feral, and powerful in ancient draconic. Its mighty back-swooping horns were carved with draconic runes, filled out with mithril and dozens of jewels attached to golden chains that wrapped around the horns with purpose and elegance.

One of these gems suddenly glowed a blue green as the dragon lowered itself, continuing its incantation. As it descended, it shrunk down to a fraction of its original size, becoming an anthropomorphized version of itself. Its wings spread at least ten feet in either direction as it slowed its descent even more, approaching the gardens below.

No longer having to worry about the wagon being knocked over, the two orcs fell to all fours and lowered themselves in submission as they kept their gaze averted from the dragon, which landed not far from them.

As it got closer to the ground, the grass underneath its shadow browned and died within seconds. The dying grass spread in a circle centered by the dragon itself, making its gentle two-point landing, wings folding back as the rolling death surrounding the dragon quickly approached the two bowing orcs. They watched in surprise as they saw the advance of the withering grass.

They covered their mouths as their lungs and eyes burned. The dragon issued a single ancient draconic command, another jewel glowing green as an unseen force withdrew back to them. Only the shifting of the grass towards them gave any indication of what transpired.

The two orcs continued to gasp for air, their bodies shaking, and a blue tint began to show in their lips as the dragon spoke in ancient draconic-arcana. The mithril in its horns glowed a dark green as it held out one of its claws to the suffocating orcs.

Histra's ears perked at what she heard, claws tensing and eyes going wide as the familiarity of these words thrust her back into a similar moment…

She fell to all fours, gasping for air, along with four other white kobolds nearby. Her eyes burned, lungs feeling as if they were being torn from the inside out, blood dripping from her nose, as a large feral green dragon landed in the entrance of a snow-covered cave. Her horns glowed, pointing her massive claws at them, and like with the orcs the pain and suffering subsided, the poison coursing through her veins disappearing as her lungs filled with cool crisp air. A rush of cold ran past them, which slammed into the dragon's green scales, a layer of ice forming over them.

"It is impolite for a guest to poison my servants in my home," growled a fierce female-draconic voice, speaking ancient draconic.

Histra snapped back to reality as this same dragon spoke in its ancient draconic tongue. "Be grateful I took the time to spare your lives. Remember to not be so foolish and be near where I land," she stated as rows of sharp white teeth could be seen when she spoke. Standing at an imposing twelve feet tall, she towered over the groveling orcs.

The jewelry woven around her two sets of back swept horns shrunk down to match her new size. One of the jewels glowed a bright green, but the other gems of a multitude of colors and runic markings on them remained dim.

"Razashra," Histra thought as she tensed even more, holding herself still.

Razashra adjusted her massive wings as they furled back behind her, hanging over a foot over her head. Her obsidian claws, sharp and deadly pointed to the orcs who kept their heads low to the ground.

"I just spoke to you. Respond," she growled as they remained still, swallowing their fear, not daring to move a muscle.

"Unintelligent and brutish creatures," she stated, once again speaking in her arcana tongue, the mithril markings on her horns glowing green-blue for a few seconds and then faded down to only a very soft glow. The two orcs felt their heads pound. "Do you understand me now?" she asked with annoyance.

"Y-yes great one," said the green orc.

"Yes, we do, mighty dragon," answered the red one.

"Good. I am not going to resort to speaking that primitive language of yours. May this experience be a reminder that you should keep a respectful distance from me. Next time I won't be so generous to such a folly," she stated.

"Yes of course. We appreciate you for sparing us," said the red orc.

"It was our mistake, for not knowing," the other replied.

"Quiet," she responded, looking around. As she walked, her feet sunk into the ground, crushing the dead grass beneath her, approaching one of the trees near the fountain. She reached out to one of the branches with dozens of flowers on them, leaning in close, nostrils flaring. Her wings relaxed ever so slightly, looking over the garden. The guards stood at their posts, unsure what to do as she turned her attention back to the still groveling orcs

"Judging by your looks you two work in these gardens?"

"Yes, we do great one," said the red orc.

"It's been a few decades since I've been here. It looks as good as I remember it. My father will be pleased with your work."

"You honor us great one."

"Very much so, great one. Kinder words have never been spoken to us," answered the green orc.

Razashra smirked. "I assume not. Tell me, have you two paid your taxes yet?"

They shook their heads as the red one spoke. "No great one. We've been busy preparing the gardens for the arrival of one of your status. We only take the time to do our tax on the day before your planned arrival."

"Yes. I am unfortunately here, and early," she remarked, looking over to see a rush of four green scaled kobolds dressed in elegant elvish clothing with guards and a dark green muscular orc and his wife dressed in soft silks, with jewelry adorning their bodies including elegant elvish designed crowns upon their heads.

Razashra looked back at the orcs. "For your work I will grant each of you the value of ten taxes collected for the effort you've made to keep these gardens the way they were, but in return I have two tasks for you."

"What is it, great one?"

"We are your humble servants."

"You two will learn draconic and replace the grass of this garden with Elven Blue Grass. It's more resistant to my landings and I like the color."

"Yes, great one, it will be done."

"Good," she replied as one of the kobolds yelled in a softer draconic.

"Endless apologies oh great kin of the great Sa'bara. We were not expecting your arrival on this day. Please forgive our tardiness and inappropriate welcoming," the male kobold proclaimed, kneeling before her, soon joined by the other three kobolds, the orc royalty, their retinue, and local guards.

The sheer weight of her presence was felt upon everyone there, including those in the wagon. They held still as possible, their breaths slow and heavy, hands covering their mouths. Ariana struggled with her animal instincts to either run or to fight, using her feet to stifle her tail wagging.

Alderin's heart pounded in his chest, memories of the last time he saw a dragon causing a cold shiver to run down his back. He closed his eyes, steeling himself as best as he could. Jesmine closed her eyes and simply listened intently, holding back the fear that weighed upon her. Dran held firm and did not move a muscle.

Gnemi tightly closed his eyes, thinking, *"You can do this. Just think of something else. Think of the stories you probably can tell when you get back."*

"Yes. I know. Father in his infinite wisdom decided to send me here, as something important has caught his attention," she responded, with the slightest hint of annoyance in her voice.

"What has happened?" the orc king asked, while keeping his head low and remaining on one knee.

"We'll get to that. First, you." She pointed to the closest kobold to her.

"Yes, great one?" he looked; his shaking hands pressed close to him.

"Provide those two orcs over there a tax payment of ten persons each and unhindered access to enter the avolariean territory, *immediately*. I want them to harvest and bring back Elven Blue Grass for cultivation and upon their immediate return I want them to be given a dragon tongue tutor."

The small two-foot tall kobold stood straight, swallowed a lump in his throat, bowing graciously. "Yes, great one. Right away!" he replied, running off.

"Now that is resolved." Razashra stated, turning her attention to the kneeling orc royalty. "It has been brought to my attention that there's a message from Dra'kesh coming here, via a white ice kobold and a small set of guards, numbering two humans, their child, which is perhaps a gnome, and a dwarf."

One of the remaining kobolds looked up curiously at the other two. "A message from Dra'kesh with such a strange party? Why would the mighty Dra'kesh send a kobold to the even more powerful Sa'bara?" she asked.

"That is what my father would like to know. Therefore, I am here to greet this messenger, who should be here any day now if they aren't already. You," she pointed to one of the kobolds. "Inform the local kobolds, and you," she pointed to one of the orc guards, "The orc guards, spread the word. I best not be kept waiting."

"Yes, great one," said the kobold, rushing off.

"As you command," the orc responded, keeping himself low, backing away until he's sufficiently far enough to run off.

"Do you think this might have anything to do wi—," began the orc king, his words cut off by her raising her claws.

"First," she said, turning and walking over to the orc gardeners, who remained in a submissive bow. "Resume what you were doing. Pay no heed to what you hear."

"Yes, great one," said the green orc.

"As you command," replied the red.

With a soft utterance in draconic-arcana and a motion of her claw, the soft green glow on her horns faded and the mithril returned to its original color. The pounding headache the two orcs were suffering faded away as they rose. Razashra took a step toward the king but stopped. She took a deep breath through her nostrils, turning her attention toward the cart.

"That is our fertilizer. It smells terrible but it's the best for the plants," explained the red orc. She walked over to the cart, her heavy footsteps growing louder as she got close. Alderin's heart raced, an overpowering sense of death and dread filled him. Her nostrils flared, taking another whiff.

"I can have it removed if it displeases you, great one," said the red orc.

"No need," she remarked, waving her claw at them, walking back towards the king.

The two orcs glanced at each other, letting out a soft sigh of relief as they moved to grab their dropped tools, getting back to work.

"No. I don't think so. After all, Father is not increasing his territory. You're simply expanding into unclaimed lands left by the fallen Eisandra. As long as you pay the toll for the use of his border, there won't be a problem."

"Of course, great one. The aid and freedom Sa'bara has given us will not be forgotten. We will repay his generosity several fold."

Razashra grinned. "Good. You've taken after your Father," she stated.

"Shall we talk inside? I will have my servants prepare a banquet for you."

She looked down at the orcs as they slowly stood back up, waiting patiently for her to respond. She looked over to the nearby white flowered trees. "I am famished from my flight," she said, walking past them, towards the castle. "Come," she commanded, the orcs and kobolds following in her footsteps, leading them inside.

With each step, the weight of her presence faded. A soft sigh of relief escaped from everyone. Histra's wings twitched and brushed up against Ariana, who shifted at the touch. Jesmine kept her breathing slow, deep, and steady, slowly opening her eyes. She looked over to Alderin, whose hands were shaking, sweat dripping from his brow. She reached over and gently held his hand. She mouthed the words "It's okay," cracking a smile.

Alderin smiled in return, swallowing a lump in his throat, mouthing the word "Thanks."

A few more hours passed as the orcs came and went, unloading more of the wagon, when suddenly they heard soft footsteps and someone yell in orcish, "Come. Your payment is here. From the great kin of our mighty lord Sa'bara himself," It was the same kobold from before, with three rolled up scrolls in his green claws.

The two orcs, dirtied from their constant yard work, rubbed their hands on a soiled cloth, reaching down for the scrolls. "We greatly appreciate it," said the red orc, grabbing the first two scrolls while the green one took the third. They unfurled the paper to look over the arcane markings on the page, a light reflecting the silver in the ink.

"The command word for your paper is Turkek. And for yours it's Thurgar," the kobold explained. "The other is orders of protection and passage through the avolariean lands, granting protection by them against any bandits or monsters as you go to retrieve the Elven Blue Grass."

The red orc read over this paper. "Great. We just finished our work for the day. We'll get right on this."

"Good. And be quick about it. This is a wish from one of Sa'bara's closest kin!" he yelled.

"Understood," replied the red orc as the kobold ran off. The two orcs sighed, the red orc remarking, "Power tripping little lizards."

"But the dragon on the other hand…" the green orc trailed off.

"We lived. We were rewarded. And given a more convenient excuse to head to the other side of the city."

"But now we have to go to the other side and travel. Elven Blue Grass grows in the northern plains by the Iron Forest. That will take us weeks to get there."

"Weeks we don't have to garden but have a real danger to deal with," replied the red orc.

"I didn't think of it like that. We'll have to make real preparations for such a trip, but for now let's go. This cart is really starting to stink," he grunted as they loaded up the wagon with their tools and headed out.

Through the city they went, the party feeling their sore and numb limbs absorb every bump along the way. The stench of the fertilizer filled their every breath. Ariana flipped over, Jesmine using her magic to warm her half-frozen body.

Slowly the sounds of orcs faded and were replaced by something new. At first it sounded like simple birds chirping but as it got louder, it became clear that it was more complex with different tones, pitches, and distinct syllables. The curious nature of the avolariean tongue, soft, elegant, and beautiful, but at times harsh and ear popping when an argument broke out.

The avolariean females stood almost as tall as most orcs while the males on average had a foot in height over their counterparts. The males had colorful feathers, of blues, greens, reds, occasionally shades of blacks and purples, with a chance of some orange. The females were stockier, with their feather scheme oft lacking the beautiful display of the males with blacks, browns, and light blue with the occasional white. Avolariean parents have children in clutches, meaning that they have on average two to five children in each clutch. The avolarieans sang to each other, visiting the few local shops that are run by their kind in this half of the city.

One orc shopkeeper sighed as an avolariean tried to speak to him in broken and battered orcish, the words coming out closer to a compilation of poorly mimicked words strung together to form sentences.

The wagon continued toward the bridges that mirrored in design of those on the opposite banks but were all together about a third shorter in total length. Orcs guarded the entrance, but avolarieans helped man the first and last checkpoints into the city. Unhindered as they left, they pulled onto the large paved road that headed further west.

Hundreds of circular leather tents with smoke billowing out of the top marked the places where the avolarieans have come to rest and pay their Draksind. Dried smoked meats hung in some of the huts as leathers, finely crafted bows, and countless arrows are presented before orcs and kobolds who mark and judge the payment, they brought this year.

The party heard screeching squawks, the red orc remarking, "They could never handle their marks like us."

"They are a stealthy bunch, but when it comes to a real fight, they don't stand a chance," commented the green.

"If anything happens when we venture out, they will fall back and let us handle any real fighting. Which will be fine by me. These birds don't know what it really means to be a warrior," the red orc scoffed as they travelled for another half hour away from the city. The wagon suddenly bounced harder as they turned and stopped at the edge of a small forest. The orcs went around and pulled down the back of the wagon, knocking on the sides.

"It's time," stated the red orc.

With a sharp pain in Gnemi's and Dran's bodies they lifted the wooden bottom, bits of fertilizer trickling down as they squinted from the late afternoon sun. The stench of the fertilizer seeped through their bodies as they tumbled out.

"I do not wish to do that again," remarked Gnemi, wincing, slowly stretching out his limbs.

"We probably will have to in order to get back," commented Dran, cracking his neck as one by one each of the members slipped out of the back. They looked out from the edge of the forest; the white stone city sparkled in the background while countless leather huts with smoke rising from them covered the landscape. Their arrangement far less chaotic than the orc encampments on the other side with no avolariean shanty town equivalent hugging the riverbanks.

"One of the longest days of my life," commented Alderin, stretching, his back, joints popping as Jesmine climbed out in short order. She stretched and looked out at the city before turning away to see the two orcs waiting impatiently as their own wagon and horses were brought out from deeper within the forest by a brown skinned female orc.

"You're here earlier than expected," she remarked.

"We were a bit hurried with the dragon nearby," said the red orc.

"The dragon? I saw it. How close were you?"

"Closer than I'd like. I'll tell you on the way back, but our Draksind has been paid for us and the children with some left over," he explained.

Her eyes lit up. "Really?"

"Yes, but I will be on a mission to collect some damn grass the dragon wants," he explained, showing her the scrolls.

"If this pleases the dragon, that is the best we can hope for. It could possibly raise our standing."

"Yes, but first," he turned to the others as Ariana shook her body, flecks of ice and water spraying off her along with some fertilizer. Histra half tumbled out, catching herself before flicking her wings with a grunt.

"I hate this feeling," she remarked in draconic.

"We have done our part. Now go," said the red orc.

"Tell them thank you," said Jesmine.

"I don't know how to say thank you in their tongue," Alderin replied.

"Histra? Can you thank them for their help?"

She looked over her shoulder at the orcs who barely paid any attention to her and shrugged. "They don't care," she said as the two climbed onto the wagon with the green one getting into the back with a reluctant sigh.

"I know you don't understand me, but thank you," Jesmine

replied.

The female orc looks over the side, saying in human, "It was a paid job. Now go before anyone sees," she stated firmly as they pulled on the reins, riding off.

"I told you. They aren't a soft-spoken language people. Actions, admittance, and promises speak volumes. Not soft, kind words such as thanks and welcome," Histra explained.

"I'm going to smell like shit for a month, but it kept us from being detected by the dragon. I'm okay with that," stated Dran, taking inventory of what's in the wagon.

"That was really a dragon wasn't it? I'm not too sure but we were close, weren't we? I didn't even get to see it and it pales in comparison to what I've read!" Gnemi exclaimed.

"I have, and I can tell you that Dra'kesh is worse," stated Alderin, hands clenching into fists looking out toward the city.

"Worse? How much worse?" asked Gnemi, swallowing a lump in his throat.

"Far worse. Sa'bara like Dra'kesh is an ancient. What we just experienced was one of their kids. It's probably not as big and powerful as them," Alderin explained.

Histra climbed into the cart. "She's close. That was Razashra. Sa'bara's eldest living daughter."

Everyone turned to look at her as she raised an eye and flicked her wings. "What?" she said, her body ever so slightly tensing. *"I said too much,"* she thought.

Jesmine replied, "How do you know that?"

"It's not like you can recognize the voice, or do you?" said Alderin with a look of concern.

"I speak the tongue of the dragons. I understood what was being said. Her name was mentioned, and it's not the first time I've heard it. She's the most well-known of Sa'bara's children. Simple as that."

Jesmine looked at her curiously. "Do you know what was said then? It's not every day you get to eavesdrop on a dragon and live to tell about it."

"It was about their tax collection. She was there as Sa'bara's dragon representative."

"It sounded like her arrival was a surprise to them. You would think the eldest daughter of an ancient dragon would get a better reception."

"She came early. Sounded very annoyed she had to do the job. Perhaps she came early just to get it done? I don't know. I don't care," Histra remarked with a grunt.

"Either way, it is good she didn't notice us," said Dran before adding, "It looks like everything is here. Let's take their advice and put some distance between us and the city."

"I wholeheartedly agree," said Alderin, walking over to Cetas, who bucked and nickered softly as he came close. "Sorry Cetas, but you are going to have to put up with a smelly rider for a little while," he said, gently patting the horse's back before getting on. Ariana sniffed the air, looking around, her ears pointing in several directions, looking at the party.

"Are you going to change back yet?" asked Alderin.

She shook her head.

"Is everything okay?" asked Jesmine.

She nodded, looking into the direction of the forest. "Are you suggesting we go this way first? It will take us a little away from the direction we need to go."

"It's not a bad idea. We can avoid being noticed by those approaching the city," said Dran.

"Good idea. Thanks Ariana," said Alderin as they set up to head deeper into the woods. About ten minutes into the trip, though, Jesmine turned to Gnemi. "Mind handling the reins? I want to talk to Histra for a moment."

He looked at her curiously but nodded. "Sure," he replied, taking them from her. Alderin eyed her crawling into the back of the wagon while Histra sat in the back corner. She stared at Jesmine as she came close enough for her breath to be visible in the air.

Histra tilted her head slightly, sitting straight up. "What is it?" she looked over to Gnemi, who curiously watched out of the corner of his eye, noticing that Alderin and Dran were making idle conversation up ahead.

Jesmine leaned in and whispered, "It would be a good idea if you told them what really happened."

She gave her an inquisitive look, wings twitching. "What?"

"With the dragon. It would be good if you opened up and told them," she said, staring her square in the eyes.

Histra tensed. "Whatever could you mea—"

Jesmine interrupted her, speaking in draconic. Her voice producing feral vowels that felt out of place for her voice. "You aren't the only one who knows the tongue of the dragons."

Her eyes widened ever so slightly as her claws clenched, responding in draconic, "You never mentioned this."

"Do you think that I am that naïve?"

She stared into her eyes for a moment before looking away, responding in human, "No. I'll tell them once we make camp. How about that? But they aren't going to respond well to it."

Jesmine rested a hand on her shoulder. "Don't worry. I'll give you support, and I won't mention that they did not say her name."

Histra tensed slightly, sighing. "Alright."

"It'll be fine," she said with a smile before heading back to the front of the wagon.

She slumped back into the corner, defeated, *"How could I have been that foolish? I never once considered she knew dragon tongue."*

"What was that about?" asks Gnemi.

"Just clarifying something that was bothering me."

"Okay."

They traveled for two and a half hours the afternoon turning to night. The stars visible up above through the tree canopy, the moons providing some light as they set up camp. The mouthwatering scent of cooked meat filled the area as Gnemi prepared dinner. Everyone but Histra gathered around, stomachs growling.

"I can't wait to eat. I'm starving," said Alderin as Ariana stretched, shifting back into her anthropomorphic form.

"Shifting takes a lot of effort and makes me famished..." she said, eyeing the food with a little bit of drool coming off the side of her muzzle.

"Do you feel better in that form?" asked Alderin, eyeing the drool.

"No. I feel weaker, and more vulnerable, but... I can converse easier with you all, speaking of which," she turned to Jesmine, "Thank you for warming my fur."

"You are most welcome," she replied with a smile, glancing over at Histra who stood by the cart leaning against the wagon wheel. Their eyes met, giving a subtle nod to her.

Histra tensed and flicked her wings, sighing, walking up to the campfire. "Everyone... there is something important I want to tell you now that we are this far out away from the city," she said. The other idle conversations stopped dead in their tracks, all eyes upon her.

"This can't be good," remarked Dran, stroking his red beard.

"Are you leaving us? You feel you've done enough, and you can go?" asked Alderin with a hint of optimism in his voice.

"No. My promise is to take Jesmine to Du'ralia Forest, and I aim to keep that promise. It's something else," Histra looked over everyone, taking a deep breath. "Razashra has a big reason why she came so early. To put it simply, it is because of us."

The sounds of crickets and crackling of firewood filled the silence that followed, eventually broken by Dran, "What do you *mean* because of *us*?"

"She stated she was looking for us."

"Why would she be looking for us?" Alderin asked, glaring down at her.

"Because she heard that a white kobold has a message from Dra'kesh, and she is there to receive it."

"What?!" he exclaimed, standing up.

Dran took a deep breath, turning to face Histra. "Repeat that one more time. For I thought I heard you say that big dragon that we heard today... *is looking for us*?!"

Histra sighed, and muttered in draconic, "I knew this was a bad idea," before saying in human, "The story I composed to get us through the town when our wheel broke. It seems one of Sa'bara's agents caught wind of it and sent it ahead. I did hope I was low key enough that it wouldn't spread bu—"

"Low key? Low KEY?! You paraded around the town like you owned the place. How do you call that low key?! And now thanks to you we have caught the eyes of the damn dragons!" yelled Alderin.

"I had to keep appearances. I did only what had to be done," she remarked, staring up at him.

"Do you realize how terrible this is? We've been trying to avoid getting their attention," he said, pacing. "If he finds us and sent forces against us, that's it. We're done."

"Do you not think I realize that? But think for a moment. Does anyone know where we are going? No. Does anyone know where we are? Those few orcs do, but if they were going to speak out against us, they'd have done it when one of Sa'bara's CHILDREN was right in FRONT of them. If we keep moving, we'll be fine."

"What about the orcs that are after us? They might get suspicious. They could be talking to their fellow orcs about us as we speak," Dran said.

"They still don't know where we are going," Histra replied.

"We could have avoided all of this though, if you didn't make all the plans on your own. You decide something without talking to us and you expect us to blindly follow. And then you keep secrets from us. So many damn secrets," said Alderin.

"I'm your guide. I guided you through this. We all have our secrets, that's nothing new."

Jesmine spoke up, "There is nothing wrong with not telling us everything. And I've already said Histra should talk to us more. Isn't that what she's doing now? Despite this one mistake, she's been doing a great job."

Alderin turned to her and said. "A mistake? Getting the attention of the dragons is no mistake, it's… it's…"

"But she got us through the city."

Ariana spoke up, her tail quickly wagging, "She did. She even got me, a Lycan, through," turning her attention to Histra, "It was lucky though that the brother of the one who imprisoned you had underground connections. He was even willing to help you despite the death of his brother by some bandits. If I was him, I'd have been far more suspicious," she said as Histra and Alderin froze.

"Wait, what was that?" asked Jesmine, standing up. Her eyes went wide, looking at Histra and Alderin. "You both knew, didn't you?"

"Knew what?" Ariana asked with a head tilt.

"The bandits you just mentioned are these three," Jesmine said motioning toward Alderin, Dran, and Gnemi, "When they rescued me."

Dran gave a stern look at Histra. "Did you have us pay our way through the city with the very coin we took from the brother we killed?"

"Yes," Histra replied. "Not like he needed to know that."

Alderin let out a soft sigh. "Yes, I knew. But I figured it out as the deal was being struck, not before."

"And neither of you two were going to tell us?" Jesmine asked.

"I honestly don't know what to say. First we have dragons then this?" Gnemi remarked.

"Alderin. You could have at least told me. I'd have expected Histra to hide this from us, but you?"

"I couldn't think of a good time to bring it up. Hey, you know that orc that helped us? We killed his brother. I couldn't do it while we were there. And after the dragon, I had other more important things on my mind," he replied.

"I knew it was going to cause a problem; it was better that the rest of you did not know. Otherwise, you could have done something accidentally suspicious and made matters worse. It was safer not to tell you," Histra said.

Jesmine took a deep breath. "I know all of you have been risking your lives for my sake. Afterall, it is my backup spellbook we are getting, which we would not have to go get if I wasn't so foolish with my original. It is a burden of a journey that I am ever so grateful for all of you to share with me. But..." and she gave a stern look at Alderin and Histra, "I think keeping secrets that affect the group as a whole has been causing us nothing but trouble. Histra?"

She looked up at her, her arms crossed, as Jesmine continued, "You've done a lot. And I thank you so much for it. But from now on don't hide anything like this from us. You aren't used to working with others. Especially after so many have treated you poorly. I understand that, but you are with us, and you will need to work with us. I've supported you this far, and I will support you to the end. I will try to help you in any way I can. I won't force, nor even ask about your past, but secrets that affect us? That needs to stop."

Histra took a deep breath and sighed, an icy fog escaping her muzzle. "Hopefully there won't be a need to, but fine."

"That goes for everyone."

"Aye, I have no problems with this," Dran said.

"I never had anything to hide. I've been upfront," Ariana stated.

"Same goes for me," Gnemi said, stirring the pot of stew.

"We've had a lot of friction, haven't we?"

"I've seen worse actually," Jesmine said, sitting down.

"You have?" Gnemi asked.

"Somehow I don't believe this," Histra said.

"You've seen worse fighting than our small ragtag group in the middle of enemy territory?" Dran asked.

"Yup. But after a long day like today, I think a nice hot meal and a good rest is in order."

"Aye, I couldn't agree with you more," Dran replied, looking at Gnemi.

"I pray to the three sovereigns that this doesn't come and bite us in the rear," Alderin said.

"It wouldn't do me any good either," said Histra, sitting several feet from the rest, who eagerly awaited a hot meal. She took a deep breath and closed her eyes, thinking back over the day. *"How did I know her name?"* something she'd wonder over the next several days of their journey.

Meanwhile, Garran, stripped of his weapons, stood waiting impatiently in front of one of the large avolariean huts. Two colorful, feathered guards in blues, greens, and reds stood at the entrance way. Long spears were held in their black-scaled claws, their yellow eyes staring down at him and Zed who stood at his side. In the background, mounted orcs patrolled the area.

Zed leaned in, whispering, "I beg you to reconsider this course of action. If you simply tell the others about what you know they can dispatch forces to quickly end this."

Garran grunted, giving Zed a firm stare, his teeth grinding, fists clenching. "And be nothing more than a messenger? That would spit on the names of our friends who died to get this far. I can't fail them or my clan's name."

"We're already several days behind due to the strict monitoring of who goes in and out of the city looking for that very same white kobold and her friends."

"I know. And without some help, it would be foolish to continue. It is why we are here."

"Yes, and I support you. I will do all that I can to see you succeed, but could you at least consider the alternative?"

"I've weighed all options. This is the only way to glory. To regain our honor. If we take the easy path it will simply show how weak we are. We are not weak. We are strong. Resourceful, but not foolish. We will seek aid when we need it. Your advice is good and that is why I have you by my side."

Zed nodded, replying, "As you wish." There was a soft chirp followed by a much louder call by one of the guards, "They're calling us in."

Garran marched in to see a large, semi-circle of avolarieans surrounding a low burning fire that lit up the interior. Leather rugs covered the ground where they sat on their legs in a perch-like fashion. Alternating between male and female, they watched, the two orcs stepping inside, sitting at two empty rugs placed several feet away from any of the avians. A half dozen armed male guards lined along the walls.

The leader, a male avolariean with red plumage and dark shimmering purple chest with blue and black feathers filling the rest wore a headdress made of brown and white feathers from an avrius. His hawk-like eyes stared at the two, speaking in his native tongue.

Once finished Zed replied, "He said that we've come here talking about needing aid and a big reward, but he wonders, what aid would we need, and that you will need to clarify the reward you speak of."

"Chief Tarnaka. Do you understand my tongue?" Garran asked.

He let out a quick trill.

"No," Zed translated.

"This is going to make it more difficult," Garran said.

"Mind if I ask if he understands another tongue?" he asked.

"You know other languages?"

"I do," he replied, looking at the chief and spoke in draconic. "Great chief Tarnaka, do you speak the dragon's tongue?"

He responded with a quicker higher pitched trill.

"He understands draconic," Zed said.

"Good. It would have been problematic to get a translator now. We're already short on time. Go ahead. You know what we need."

Zed said in draconic, "Great chief Tarnaka, leader of the largest tribe to the southern regions of the great land Sa'bara. We are in need of some of your finest warriors to track down and capture a ferocious beast, as well as grant us safe passage through your lands while we hunt the beast down."

Tarnaka responded which Zed quickly translated to Garran, "Why would orcs want to hunt in our lands? And how do you know of a beast that is there even though you've never been?"

Zed translated for Garran, "It is a crafty beast that managed to get through this great city undetected."

"How did such a beast make it through the great city of Rivera?"

"It is clever, and has the aid of allies, each who need to be captured alive."

"Why?"

"Their value to Sa'bara alive is greater than dead. Each is a dangerous foe that must not be underestimated."

"How many are there?"

"Six if you include the beast."

"How many are you?"

"Twelve."

"And you still need our aid?" he asked raising his plumage slightly.

"We've fought the beast when it was alone. It's extremely dangerous. Now it has powerful friends. We are not foolish to go at it alone and in your lands without permission."

"We could hunt this beast well enough on our own."

"We have a way to track it."

"We have good trackers."

"We've come respectfully. Would it be rude to take another's hunt after they've tracked it for so long?" Zed asked.

Tarnaka talked to the brown feathered female to his left and the black one to his right, they whispered back and forth for a moment before he responded, "You do not come with ignorance. We won't interfere with your hunt, but what could you offer to have us give you our aid?'

Garran told Zed, "Tell him great rewards. Our influence will be greatly increased, and we'd be sure that their help will be equally rewarded for the assistance they give."

Zed said in draconic, "Aiding us will yield the reward of at least one of you to receive the gift of flight from the great dragon Sa'bara."

A silence in the room, which was broken moments later by chirps and trills, the avolarieans speaking amongst each other.

Tarnaka's plumage raised high. "How could you be assured of such a great reward?" Zed translated without alteration.

Garran didn't flinch when he responded. "The value of our targets to Sa'bara is that great."

Tarnaka's feathers lowered, leaning back and talking to those beside him. A few minutes passed, the two orcs patiently waiting when Tarnaka suddenly let out a loud bird call. Garran sat firm staring at the chief with his gaze slightly lowered when a few moments later a seven-foot-tall avolariean stepped into the hut.

He was dressed in fine leather armor, a bow strapped to his back, a long spear with a hook at the tip. Blood red feathers made up much of his plumage with a mix of purple along the chest. Black feathers ran across his cheeks, with some of the purple ones fading into a sky blue around his waist and tail. He lowered himself. "You called father?"

"Tetsunage. You will gather six of your best hunters and assist these orcs in their hunt of a great beast. They tell us that by giving our aid that one of us will be given the gift of flight."

Tetsunage's black claws tightened around his spear, feathers rising slightly. "Could this really be true father? They are orcs."

"Such an offer cannot be taken lightly. Go. Pick those you wish to hunt with you. Make me proud and I will make sure you will be the one rewarded with the gift of flight."

Tetsunage lowered his head more. "Yes, Father. I will not fail you," he replied, standing up, walking out.

"What was that about?" Garran asked.

"We are going to be given the chief's son and six of his best warriors to aid us," Zed said.

Garran gave a toothy tusk grin. "Perfect."

Chapter 13 Bestial Wrath

Tall wild grass swayed in the hot dry summer wind that blew across the plains. The sea of green with some hints of brown covered much of what the party could see with only a few random individual trees standing out. Some of the grass broke under the horses' hooves, others bending underneath the cart, springing up behind them with a quick whip action. Histra sat on top of the cage, looking out into the distance. The bits of ice that had formed on the it was broken off by Ariana who handed it off to Gnemi.

"Thanks," he said, placing it into his mouth.

"It's been three days since we've seen any source of water, Histra. Are we getting close to a river? A lake? A pond of some sort?" asked Alderin, looking over his shoulder at her.

"We have to be careful not to draw the attention of any of the avolariean tribes, so we have to avoid common sources where they'd gather, but we are close to one."

"How close?"

"Not that much farther, I'm sure."

"Jesmine?" Dran asked.

Jesmine, who was mindlessly watching the horses in front of her, looked up, "Yes?"

"I know it's been decades since you've been here. But you wouldn't happen to know of any places to get some water? Our horses can't go on much longer."

Histra tensed, "We are close. Why don't you believe me?"

"Does it hurt to get a second opinion from a local? Jesmine might know something that you don't." Dran said.

Histra crossed her arms, remaining silent.

"It has been many years but…" she trailed off and looked off to the east, "If we head in that direction, we'll hit the main road that leads to my hometown. There were several villages along the way where one could rest and trade."

Dran looked out in the direction, noting nothing but more endless plains. "That sounds like a good plan."

"And risk drawing the attention of the avolarieans by being on the road?" asked Histra.

Jesmine replied, "Avolarieans prefer cross country over roads as they often follow game that they hunt. It is a risk, but the Great Sa'barian Plains can be unforgiving if you don't know where to go."

"What's the name in elvish? I prefer not to call this place after one of the dragons," Alderin said.

"Sa'el'pa'ria, which means the same thing."

"It sounds far nicer than saying Sa'bara everywhere you go," Dran remarked.

"The only good thing about Dra'kesh, if you can even say there is anything good about him, is that he doesn't force his name into everything around us," Alderin said before continuing, "But back to what's important. We need water. This sounds like a good plan, don't you think, Histra?"

"Fine," Histra said with a sigh. "I suppose we try the route. As long as we keep a lookout for any avolariean encampments we should hopefully be fine."

"About which direction is it?"

"I believe about that direction," Jesmine pointed. "I've tried to keep track about where we are since we passed Rivera, but I am not exactly certain."

"Works for me," Dran said, turning Dariel toward the new direction the rest following.

They drove through the grasses for another two hours before jutting out over the plains in the distance were wooden and stone structures.

"That town should have a well," Jesmine said.

"Excellent. Hopefully we can get ourselves cleaned up while there. I don't know how much longer I can stand to be this grungy," remarked Dran.

"That would be good. The smell has been making it harder to notice other sce—" Ariana stopped midway through her sentence, ears perking up, head turning out toward the plains.

"What is it?" asked Alderin.

"Don't tell me those orcs followed us this far?" Gnemi said.

"I doubt they could have tracked us after this long without knowing where we are going," said Alderin.

"It is unlikely, but I am not letting my guard down…" Ariana said, relaxing. "It's nothing."

"Nothing?"

"I thought I maybe smelled a wolkin."

"A wolkin?"

"They do travel the plains but... hmm."

"What is it?" asked Gnemi.

Ariana looked over to Histra then back to the group. "It's nothing. We should be fine, I'll let you know if anything changes."

"Wolkin don't tend to get near towns which would mean..." Jesmine trailed off.

"That there shouldn't be anyone in the town," Alderin said, riding a bit faster. "Come, we should see what's there. Hopefully their wells are intact."

Dran picked up speed and Gnemi whipped the reins following suit. Jesmine kept her head low while Ariana kept hers raised and alert. Histra watched Jesmine from her perched spot when Gnemi asked, "Are you okay?"

"Yeah. I'm fine," Jesmine answered with a nod.

"You've been quiet since we got through the city."

"I've just been thinking that's all." She lifted her head and smiled. "Nothing to trouble yourself with."

"Okay," he replied as they broke through the thick grass to reach the main road that parted the plains straight towards the town. The road was wide enough to easily fit four of their carts. The heavy interlocking pieces of stones were slightly worn, and green shrub grass poking through the cracks.

The blowing wind whistled through the long-abandoned buildings, many of which were collapsed into themselves with tall grass growing in and between them. Many of the wood structures were blackened and charred and mostly destroyed with white and yellow flowers growing out of some of the wood, while those made of stone remained standing. Roofs were caved in, doors torn clean off their hinges on some buildings while others were swung open with vines wrapped around them.

Jesmine tensed, looking through the town, swallowing a lump in her throat, feeling each heavy steady beat of her heart. The air was heavy, each breath filled her lungs like a lead weight, feeling a pressure upon her like she was trapped under rubble that surrounded them.

The grass swayed in the wind, a random bug jumped from one blade of grass to another, the only places not overgrown were the main stone road and the few cobblestone side streets.

The horses clip-clopped their way through the town. They looked for any sign of life but more importantly a source of water. One stone building had a black charred sign that was too damaged and worn by the elements to read what it once said, hanging from a single rusted chain that squeaked in the wind.

"That was the blacksmith's shop," remarked Jesmine as they came to a stop.

"How do you know?" asked Gnemi.

"I remember," she softly replied.

Dran and Alderin dismounted from their horses, taking the reins and hitched them to the cart. "We'll look around to see if we can find a well or something. There has to be something here," said Alderin.

"I'll help," said Ariana jumping off the cart, her tail slowly wagging. "I think I might remember where a well is."

Jesmine looked over to her, who began to walk away. "I forgot you've travelled too."

Ariana stopped but doesn't look at Jesmine, "Yeah. I remember too what it was like," she responded, disappearing into the tall grass.

"This was an elven town wasn't it?" asked Gnemi.

"From Rivera to my home was all elven lands. Four or five-day's journey from here there's even a castle that belonged to the noble family of Ashrania."

"Did you ever go to it?"

"I've seen it many times, but only been in it once. It was one of many stops I made heading north. Since I was the daughter of the great dragon slayer, they wanted me out of dragon-held lands in case they ever discovered where my mother came from."

"It must have been a hard time for you."

"At the time it was exciting. Despite it being over a decade since Eisandra fell, word that my mother was killed in the fighting had not reached us."

Gnemi's eyes went wide. "You didn't hear from your mother for ten years and you didn't suspect anything?"

"It was fifteen years by then. Once Eisandra fell, the borders became even harder to cross, and with it news of what happened. It was only once I arrived that I learned the truth."

"I couldn't imagine what that was like. I'm sorry."

"It's alright. It happened years ago, and I think the truth of her death was purposely kept a secret."

"Why do you say that?" asked Gnemi.

"We got a memento from my mother's achievements. Father and I both thought she was still alive but unable to say anything... I don't even know if he knew."

"I'm sorry to hear that. I didn't realize that things were so... complicated after Eisandra was slain."

"It was. The hunts after her death lasted for decades," remarked Histra.

"Yes, the hunts... Once I got there, I discovered the real reason why they wanted me was to use my magic abilities to help hunt down and kill the remaining white dragons," Jesmine said.

"I remember you mentioned that."

"Younger dragons, though powerful in their own right, are only a fraction of the older ones, but all of the eldest dragons died during the war against Eisandra."

"What was it like? Hunting down a dragon?" Gnemi asked.

Ariana popped out of the grass, howling.

"What's wrong?!" Gnemi asked, grabbing his crossbow.

"I found a well."

"Why did you howl?" asked Histra.

"It's the fastest way to get the other two to come," she replied as Alderin and Dran came running back.

"What's wrong?!" asked Alderin, his bow drawn.

"I found a well."

"What? You let out a howl just to tell us that?" asked Dran, giving Ariana a curious look.

Her tail wagged quickly, grinning. "It worked, didn't it?"

Jesmine let out a soft chuckle. "Unorthodox, but effective."

"Come," Ariana said, motioning everyone to follow.

Carefully she guided them through the brush to the stone well tucked away in the back of several destroyed homes, the roof over it was wrecked as the grass has grown so tall around it that it was impossible to see till they were almost on top of it.

"That's definitely a well, but how do we get the water?" asked Alderin.

"We have a rope and bucket, we can easily use that," Gnemi

said, hopping into the back of the cart to look for it. Histra pointed it out by the gnome's foot, "Thanks."

"I can't believe I forgot we had that," Alderin said, rubbing his grizzled facial hair.

"It's fine, it happens to the best of us," Dran remarked.

Gnemi tied a rope to the end of the bucket, handing it to Alderin who lowered it down.

The wooden bucket echoed, bumping against the side of the walls, disappearing into the darkness as it descended. A few moments later the distinct sound of a splash of water echoed up. With some effort Alderin pulled the soaking wet water-filled bucket back up.

"Looks clean," he said. "Ariana, would you like first drink?"

Ariana tilted her head ever so slightly to the side. "You're going to let me have the first drink?"

"Yeah. You found the well. It's only fair," he replied, holding it out to her.

"You aren't concerned about contracting anything if I drink from it first?" she asked curiously, taking it within her wolf pawed hands.

"I never heard of anyone contracting lycanthropy from drinking water."

"Neither have I," said Dran.

Ariana's tail subtly swayed faster. "Thanks," she said, holding the bucket towards her lips and poured the water slowly out, lapping it, attempting to funnel it down her throat. She panted, licking her lips, her muzzle fur wet and matted against her face, handing the half full bucket back to Alderin, "I needed that," she sighed in relief.

One by one each quenched their thirst, letting their parched horses have a drink. Once the horses had their fill, Alderin pulled out another bucket full of water and dumped it over his head.

"It will be great to get this damn smell off of me," he said, rubbing his six-day old unshaven face. "I might even be able to get rid of this. I've never enjoyed having a beard."

"You just want to keep that youthful baby-face appearance," Dran replied with a chuckle.

"It will be better for my nose too," Ariana said with a huff through her nostrils.

"It shall be nice to wash up a bit," Jesmine said, taking off her cloak and shaking the dust off of it. "If you don't mind, I'd like to go next. In exchange I'll make the water a bit warmer."

"Wouldn't that take a lot of effort or cause that whole overheating thing?" asked Alderin.

"Warming up a simple bucket of water is not too difficult and it's one I can do verbally as I transfer the warmth of the fire magic from me to the water," she explained.

"A hot shower? I'll take that. Go right ahead," Dran said.

"Was that the spell you used in the cart to warm me up?" asked Ariana.

Jesmine nodded, "It was. Not every spell requires a somatic component. Extremely skillful wizards can cast some moderate level spells only through incantation and the use of a focus. My mother was one such wizard, and she took time teaching me how to accomplish such feats. This was one of my training spells. So even without my book, I can do it with ease," she explained, grabbing the bucket of water.

She focused on it, beginning her incantation. Her intricate tattoos glowed a slight reddish-orange and after thirty seconds, the glow flowed down to her hands, glowing brighter until it too faded. The bucket's exterior steamed and dried at points of contact with her hands, till the water within the bucket heated. Jesmine dipped a fingertip into the bucket, quickly pulling it out. "A little too much. I'll let it cool for a minute."

"You could have Histra cool it off," Gnemi suggested, suddenly feeling a shiver run down his spine. He looked up, seeing Histra standing on the edge of the cart behind him.

"I'm not a tool to be used to cool things off," she said, claws gripping the side of the cart.

"I didn't mean it like that."

"Histra, he meant no harm by it," Jesmine said.

She looked up at her. "I'm going to look around a bit as you all bathe," she said, walking over to the other side of the cart and climbed down the wheel.

"What are you hoping to find?" Alderin asked, walking over to her.

"I will know when I see it."

"We'll let you know when it's your turn," Jesmine said.

"I'm not much for water. It doesn't agree with me," she remarked.

"I'll make sure its extra warm to compensate then."

Histra was already several steps away, pushing through the grass simply responding, "I'm good."

Alderin looked at the others. "I'll keep an eye on her."

"She can take care of herself," Jesmine replied.

"Just for a little while," he answered, walking in her direction.

Jesmine let out a little sigh, muttering, "That's not going to build trust."

"Let him. There is no harm in it," Dran said.

"I am not too sure about that," she replied, looking over to Alderin as he disappeared between two buildings. She then dumped the hot water over herself, washing away a thin noticeable layer of dirt and grime.

"I'm next," Dran said with excitement.

Meanwhile, Histra looked around, pushing through the grasses. She stopped near the outer edge of town, where parts of a broken stone wall stood tall enough to jut out over the grass.

"Perfect," she said in draconic, pushing her way through the grass, using a caved in section of the wall as a stepping stool to climb to the top. She stood there, feeling the wind blowing across her, taking a deep breath through her nostrils. The kobold stopped and looked around, listening for a few moments to the sound of swaying grass.

She relaxed and closed her eyes. Slowly she spread out her wings, her body jerking slightly, catching the wind, feeling it flow over her extended wings, feet clenching the quickly cooling stone underneath her.

"You've done this before, haven't you? You can do it," she thought, flapping her wings and jumped, the sensation of flying over the ground flashing in her mind for an instant... until she landed face first, the grass breaking under her, scratching along her wings.

Histra let out a grunt, claws digging into the ground, tearing at the base of some grass, before standing up and looking around, her vision completely obscured by the plants. Climbing back up to the stone wall, she gave another cautious look around before positioning herself against the wind. She unfurled her wings, flapping them, leaping into the air with the same disastrous results. Undeterred she tried again, failing.

"Damn it. You have done this. You need to remember how. My wings can't still be that weak," she growled in draconic, trying again.

Alderin watched through the cracks of a burned wood and stone building. After several more failed attempts he thought, *"Amusing, but worthy of privacy,"* slinking away.

Histra tensed, looking in his general direction. Her blue eyes scoured for any sign of movement, but after a short while she relaxed, resuming her flight attempts. *"I'm not weak. I can do this,"* she thought.

When Alderin returned to the others, Gnemi was having hot water poured onto him.

"This feels amazing. I don't believe I ever had a hot shower before."

"Really?" Jesmine asked.

"No. Back in my home, such things are reserved for the rich or those who have accomplished something…" he trailed off, looking away.

"I wouldn't worry about it, Gnemi. When we get back to my home, you'll be treated to one," Dran said, squeezing out some water from his beard.

Gnemi's eyes lit up. "Really?"

He nodded.

"That will leave just you, Ariana, and Histra when she gets back," Jesmine said, lowering the bucket back into the well.

"Histra will be busy for a while," Alderin answered.

"What is she up to?" Dran inquired.

"Nothing special or worth worrying about. I think she wanted to just have an excuse to get away from us for a bit," he replied.

"Did she catch you spying on her, and bite your head off?" Jesmine joked.

Alderin smirked. "I'm quieter than I look."

Jesmine nodded, pulling the bucket up, beginning her incantation.

"How was the hot water?" Alderin asked curiously.

"Amazing," Gnemi replied, "I recommend you try it."

"I'm good for now," he answered, watching Jesmine heat the

water, looking at the glowing tattoos. Alderin questioned, "I've been meaning to ask, why do you have those magic runes tattooed onto you?"

Jesmine finished her chant, steam emanating from the bucket, turning her attention to him. "Runes help focus magic. The closer you are to the runes used for your spells, the greater and more refined the control you possess over them. But this greatly increases the risk of injury or death if a mistake should occur, especially if you don't know how to deal with it."

"And the effects of it can be rather…" Dran remarked, trailing off, looking away, hands clenching.

"When my mother felt that I was skilled enough, she tattooed the runes onto my person as the next step in my training. She used a special mithril-based ink, making the runes on my body even more effective in the art of spell casting."

"Mithril? In a tattoo?" Alderin questioned.

"Aye, I've only seen two dwarves back home with such markings, our Grand Arcane Master and his current apprentice. Even then, theirs aren't as intricate as yours."

"My mother insisted I had the very best," she trailed off, seeing her reflection in the water. "You can see the metallic sheen of the tattoo in certain angles of light. See?" she said, holding the bucket with one hand, moving the other to get the right angle to show the tattoo's faint reflective nature.

"I see that. It is very pretty if I must say so," Alderin complimented.

Jesmine turned back to him and smiled. "Thanks." she dipped a finger into the water, "I think it's about the right temperature, you ready Ariana?"

She nodded, her tail quickly wagging. "Not that I need one, but I would be lying if I didn't say that I—" Ariana abruptly stopped, ears perking up. She lifted her snout in the air, taking several deep whiffs. "Where is Histra?"

"Ariana, what's wrong?" Jesmine asked.

"Opposite side of town in that direction." Alderin pointed in her general direction with an inquisitive look.

"Wolkin are close," she stated, sprinting off at breakneck speed, leaving swaying grass in her wake.

"I'll follow. The rest of you protect the horses till we get back,"

Alderin said, running off after her. Gnemi rushed to climb up the cart, grabbing his crossbow, Dran pulling out his axe.

"Why did the damn kobold wander off that far on her own?" remarked Dran.

Jesmine took a deep breath, running after them. "I'm going after them. Stay here." She then began to chant, moving her hands in elegant motions.

Dran took half a step before stopping. "Why by the Gods would you…" he let out a soft sigh. "We'll just stay here and guard the horses then Gnemi."

Gnemi kept a vigilant look out, his crossbow primed and ready. "Already on it."

Meanwhile, Histra climbed back onto the top of the stone fence. She grumbled brushing away some of the grass stuck to her scales, which quickly grew hard, and frosted over, much like the grasses where she's landed several times before.

She softly growled and flicked her wings, spreading them, glaring at them, running her claws along the 'fingers' of her wings. "Work! I know you can work… I can—" she cut herself off, looking out to the plains before her. Her nostrils flared, taking a slow, deep breath.

A big, black furred wolkin leapt out of the grass. Histra jumped back as it came barreling at her. Her already spread wings flapped once, trying to push herself farther away, but the beast with teeth bared moved too quickly. The wolkin swiped at her, its claws scratching along the insides of her wings, red blood oozing from the wounds. Her body was flung several feet away, smacking against a wood frame of a mostly collapsed home with a thud.

Histra fell face first to the ground, the grass bending and breaking around her. She dug her claws into the ground, pushing herself back to her feet. The wolkin growled, rushing towards her. The kobold took a deep breath the icy freezing fluid leaking out of the corners of her mouth.

The wolkin pounced, jaws open, sharp teeth ready to rip into her, but a spray of white mist bellowed out from Histra's mouth, covering the wolkin's face. It let out a short, whining yelp, head flash freezing, ice forming around it, slamming hard into Histra, pinning her against the building, knocking out what little liquid she had left adding to the ice on the wolkin's head, freezing parts of the ground.

Histra gasped for air, ice pressing up against her neck and face which covered all of the wolkin's head, up around parts of its horns and down its neck. The wolkin pulled away as it thrashed about, attempting to bite through the ice, it laid on the ground hind legs trying to claw and push it off its head.

She let out a huff of air. "Serves you right for attacking me," she remarked, walking away, leaving it to suffocate, pushing through the grass, blood dripping from her wounds, which clung to the grass, slowly freezing over at the points of contact. *"Damn beast thought it could—"* Histra's train of thought was lost upon hearing multiple wolkin approach her from different directions.

"I'm not going to let some meager creatures get me," Histra thought, running headfirst into another one, but before she could even react, its fangs bit into her shoulder, blood flowing down her side. She let out a growl, while being hoisted into the air, a piercing pain rushing through her. It jerked its head side to side, digging its jaw deeper into her, tearing at her flesh.

Blood dripped onto the wolkin's tongue, freezing it. Shocked, it loosened its bite. In that moment she clawed its eye, digging into the soft tissue, ripping it out. Blood oozed from the wound, the wolkin flinging Histra onto her back.

She panted heavily, the creature howling out in pain, blood oozing from her wounds, trickling down her arm and claw tips. A memory flashed into her mind, her unfractured horn glowing a soft white, but it stopped the moment she caught a third wolkin sprinting towards her. It leaped toward her; jaws open wide, sharp teeth ready to clamp down on her neck.

She tried to back away, feet sliding across the grass, her good arm held up in a vain attempt to block the blow. Suddenly the wolkin was hit hard on the side and flung off into a nearby building with a heavy thud and a canine-like whine.

A deep guttural growl drew Histra's attention. Standing over her was an eight-foot-tall mountain of a beast with a midnight black body with silver-white fur along its underside and back. Its piercing yellow eyes were as bestial as the wolkin that were attacking her. Barely noticeable humanoid female features were visible underneath the thick fur, her one claw bloodied from the strike as rows of sharp teeth were shown under her curled lips. Her posture was slightly hunchbacked, the mithril cuffs and collar poking through the fur.

Ariana did not even look at her, growling out in barely intelligible words, "Run!" striking at the one-eyed wolkin that was baring its teeth with a low, guttural growl.

Four unseen wolkins joined into the fray, dog piling onto Ariana. They clawed and bit at her thick hide. She grabbed one, biting it on the neck, blood gushing from the wound. Clenching her jaws hard the wolkin whined till there was a sickening snap, its body becoming limp. Two more wolkin rushed in to strike when an arrow whistled past Ariana, piercing the side of one of them, causing it to trip and run into the other.

"I was not expecting this…" Alderin remarked, Histra pushing herself up to her feet. He took aim and fired on the wolkin clawing at Ariana's backside who then grabbed and threw it at the two that had failed at their recent attack. The wolkin pack fell back to regroup, the scent of blood heavy in the air. She stood before them; teeth bared, ears folded back, and claws out, letting out a deep spine-tingling growl. The wolkin growled back, standing their ground, moving to encircle her, but another arrow from Alderin ended their flanking attempt.

Histra remained hidden in the brush, holding a claw to her wounded shoulder. She muttered in draconic-arcana, eyeing Alderin and Ariana, who were distracted by the fight. Her undamaged horn glowed a soft white, moving deeper into the tall grass.

Alderin nocked another arrow, taking aim before hearing elvish-arcana from behind, which caused him to look over his shoulder. Jesmine's tattoos glowed a bright red as she spoke even louder and clearer, and with greater focus. With a wave of her hands, a wall of fire erupted between them and the wolkin in a semi-circle, the ends of the fire wall starting and ending at two different nearby buildings. The fire roared and nipped at the wolkins' noses. They yelped at the heat, quickly retreating into the plains.

Ariana panted heavily, blood staining her black and silver colored fur. She let out a deep, tense growl. Blood dripped and stained her teeth, sniffing the hot air, the scent of burning grass overpowering most other smells.

"Ariana?" he called out, but she didn't respond. Her ears went flat, sniffing the air again, turning in the direction of Histra, rushing to her. Ariana, with a laser focus, readied to strike. She looked up in surprise, the glow of her horn gone, a small burst of flame appearing between them. Histra jumped back, Ariana stopping and paused.

"Ariana, what are you doing?" he questioned, keeping a lowered arrow nocked. Jesmine was unable to say anything, focused on chanting to maintain the spell.

Ariana licked at the blood on her teeth, taking another step back from the flames. She looked to Alderin and Jesmine, slowing her breathing. Her muscles relaxed, shrinking down in size. Her long, silver flowing hair sprouted from the back of her head, absorbing the silver color of her back, making it black once more, taking her more anthropomorphic Lycan form, though the injuries she took in the fight remained. She kept an eye on Alderin and Jesmine, licking a wound on her left hand. "I told her to run," she growled.

"Because I didn't run, you decide to snap at me?! You didn't think I may not been able to?" Histra questioned, walking to her.

"You have no idea how difficult it is to control..." she trailed off, sniffing the air. "I believe they are retreating." Ariana looked at two of the dead wolkin nearby. "They've lost at least two packmates and suffered other injuries. Even with the drive to attack they aren't dumb enough to try it again."

Jesmine took a slow, deep breath, lowering her hands as the wall of fire faded away at the same rate of her tattoos. "I've never seen so many aggressive wolkin in my years living here. Occasionally they'll attack someone, but normally that is desperation during a famine. They'd much prefer to go after livestock rather than anyone who could fight back."

"Perhaps they saw Histra as an easy target?" remarked Alderin as Histra let out a huff, pushing through the grass to reach them.

"I heard that remark," she grunted.

"Histra you're hurt, here let me help you." Jesmine offered, moving to pick her up, but stopped when she raised her uninjured claw.

"I can walk. The bleeding has already stopped," she said, taking a few steps away, but she stopped again, looking over to them. "Thanks for the help," she said, resuming her walk.

"Did she just thank us?" Alderin asked in surprise.

Jesmine cracked a little smile. "Yes, she did," she responded, following.

"I can tell you why they are so aggressive, but I'll wait till we're back with the others," Ariana stated.

"You do?" Jesmine asked, raising an eyebrow.

Ariana nodded, checking over her injuries.

"Ariana?" Alderin asked.

She raised her head and looked at him, "Yes?"

"What form was that?"

"The one I told you about. It's between this and my four-legged one. It's the one most people see... before they die."

"It was impressive."

"Still not as impressive as I should be," she remarked, motioning to her cuffs.

"We'll get them off of you," Jesmine assured her.

"That would be nice," she replied, moving through the town, reaching the others without incident. Gnemi tensed and took aim at their approach but soon relaxed. "You're okay. We heard some of the fighting from here and we were worried."

"Nothing happened here," said Dran.

"Histra and Ariana were injured," Jesmine said.

"Once we get cleaned, I can attend to the wounds," Ariana told them.

"I'm fine," Histra remarked.

"You are not fine, Histra. Look at your shoulder," Jesmine said, pointing to the gashes in her white scales where some pink flesh could be seen. "That is not fine."

"I can handle it myself. The bleeding stopped. That's good enough for me," she replied.

Jesmine turned to Ariana, walking to the well, "Ariana. You said you knew why the wolkin were so aggressive. Mind telling us?"

"It's Histra," she responded.

Histra looked at her. "You can't blame this on me."

"I never heard wolkin going out of their way to attack kobolds," Jesmine said as Ariana turned to the group.

"This is the third time we've seen wolkin unusually aggressive to us," Dran said.

"Histra, perhaps you can explain why you have that scent about you that makes horses uneasy? That it nags at predators like me to hunt you down like a weakened animal ripe for the kill?" Ariana asked.

Histra gave her an inquisitive look. "What are you talking about? Horses and other animals don't like the cold that surrounds me. Nothing more than that."

"I contributed Cetas' reaction to that," Alderin said, petting the side of his horse.

"What do you mean Ariana?" Jesmine asked, picking up the water filled bucket, warming it up.

"Histra has a smell about her... more than that. It's a sense that makes me feel uneasy yet... aggressive. Like she's a dying animal. This uneasiness puts me and animals like wolkin on edge, more aggressive. The sense of an easy meal draws them in."

"That would explain why we keep getting attacked by the local wildlife, but the question remains is why?" Alderin asked, looking at Histra.

"What are you looking at me for?" she asked.

"Histra, do you happen to know why this would be?" asked Jesmine.

"No, I do not. I always thought they were this aggressive. The caravan I was enslaved to always had a few beast attacks here and there. I had to deal with them before that with... it was always a problem. And if I did happen to know why, I certainly don't know anymore," she pointed to her cracked horn. "Or did you all forget?"

Alderin stared down at her for a moment before he sighed. "It doesn't matter why. We know it happens at least. If it was something you could control, you'd not be the type to let it happen."

"Of course. You think I'd want lowly beasts attacking me?"

"We'll just have to do our best to help mitigate it. Which means, we need to get you cleaned," said Jesmine, approaching her with the hot bucket of water.

Histra took half a step back. "I said, I'm fine. I do not need that. Me and water don't get along. It freezes fast if you haven't noticed."

"I made it hot enough to compensate," she replied, getting closer.

"I think not," she responded, stepping back only to bump into Gnemi, who blocked her escape.

"It's just a bath. I'm sure you'll like it," said Gnemi.

"Don't assume what I will or won't like," she snapped, turning her attention to him. In that moment, a rush of hot water ran across her scales, washing away dried blood, dirt and grime from her body. Histra tensed as her feet dug deep into the ground, gritting her teeth. The soothing hot water felt good on some parts of her scales but paled in comparison to the pain from her wounds. Her wings shuttered, twitching, water dripping off her, a heavy fog rising. She held back a groan, feeling the warm water on her scales fading. After less than a minute some droplets started to freeze.

Jesmine took a rag and knelt before her, chanting, her tattoos softly glowing as she funneled warmth into the rag to wipe more dirt from Histra's scales, melting any frozen water, drying the rest. "This isn't so bad is it?" she asked.

She flicked her wings before flinching, reminding her of her wing injury. "You have no idea," she grunted, reluctantly standing there. "Hopefully this will help with some of the 'smell problem' as you so elegantly put it?"

"It certainly can't hurt," chuckled Dran.

"Once I get cleaned off, I'll attend to your wounds. It's best to prevent infection," Ariana said.

"Save it. My injuries look worse than they are," she replied as Jesmine finished.

"They look rather bad from here, and I could see the pain you are in," Jesmine said, looking over the wounds before Histra pulled away.

"I'm not weak. I'll be fine."

"No one said you were weak, Histra."

"If she feels she doesn't need our help, let her be. We don't have a large supply of medicine. Save it for when someone wants it," Dran said.

"It works rather well. I don't think I could have fired my bow so soon without it," said Alderin.

Histra glared. "I'm good, okay? You gave me a shower. Isn't that enough?".

Ariana lowered her ears. "If you don't want it, I won't make you. I can use some of it myself. Even with the cuffs I heal faster than all of you, but that doesn't mean I can't help it along."

"Are you able while on the move? I prefer to get going before anything decides we're an easy meal," Alderin said.

Jesmine looked over the destroyed town. "I'd prefer to leave this place sooner rather than later."

"I can do it in the cart without a problem," Ariana replied.

Histra struggled to climb up onto the wagon, refusing to use her injured arm. She gritted her teeth, fighting against the pain when suddenly she felt a pair of warm hands lifting her up, placing her into the cart. She tensed at the touch, noticing Jesmine standing there, "I can do it myself."

"But it doesn't hurt to get some help from your friends," Jesmine said as Histra raised an eye ridge ever so slightly before getting settled in a corner of the cart.

"Let's just get out of here," she remarked, trying to get comfortable as they set out once again.

Three days after their departure from the elven-town ruins, the sun was close to setting, Garran and his band of orcs on horseback with seven avolarieans following alongside, Tetsunage beside Garran with Zed on the other. His fists clenched the reins of his horse, looking over to Zed, "What do you think?"

"We are still a few days behind, but the horses need rest. This would be a good place to do so. Towns like this should have a well where we could get some water."

"We'd have caught up to them already if these birds didn't insist on walking," Garran said.

Tetsunage looked up at the orc, speaking as Zed translated. "We are a people of one animal. Not many like you. We have kept up with your pace, but it is best not to reach your prey tired."

Garran grumbled. "We have to hurry."

Tetsunage tilted his head, "And why do we need to hurry?"

"It will be more difficult to hunt her if she's not in the open," Garran remarked, looking over the ruins. "But seeing as we do need to rest; we'll make use of what these town ruins has to offer."

"We will not be staying there."

Garran looked at the avian curiously. "Why?"

"It is a place where the dragons have defiled. We do not go

there."

Garran laughed. "A place where the dragons have defiled? Do you think one of them would have gone to the trouble of destroying this small village? No. You see the burned-out buildings? That's something that we orcs have done on the behest of them. Avoid it if you wish but it is where we will make camp," Garran said, informing the rest of his troop.

Tetsunage looked to Zed, who simply followed him as the orcs rode ahead. A black feathered female avolariean with white tipped feathers stood nearby, her body adorned with golden rings with chains that went from the rings to three pairs of bracelets that went up her arms. Woven between golden chains were a few precious stones with runic markings on them. "What do you make of this Penisiya?"

"The village does appear to be what he described. But I feel an uneasiness in the air. There are details the orcs are not telling us," Penisiya responded, staring toward the town.

"We've known that from the beginning. Based on what they offer in exchange for our help."

"I suggest we camp just outside but take a look around the town. Maybe there is something that may give us clues on what we are facing."

He nodded, looking over the others dressed in light leather armor, bows strapped to their backs with backpacks full of supplies necessary for this trip. "I want one of you who understands orc tongue to stay with the orcs tonight. I want three others to search the town for any clues about our prey. As for the rest, I want you to look around the village with me. If you find anything inform me immediately," he commands.

"I'll stay with the orcs," said one green and purple avolariean with accenting red colored feathers before they split up.

The orcs explored the remains of the town, setting up a camp in the center, making campfires using some unburnt wood from the collapsed buildings. Shana looked over to the lone avolariean, walking over to Garran, "They were here."

Garran's eyes lit up, walking over to her, "Show me." As they walked off, the avolariean followed not far behind, remaining in earshot as he was led to the well.

"They spent time here. See? Tracks from their wagon. Judging by these tracks here, they not only got their cart but their horses across the city."

"I assumed they probably had horses; the cart is a bit of good news. It means they aren't traveling as fast as we initially thought."

"Three maybe four days and we'll be able to catch up to them. That's what? You think a week or so before they reach the forest?"

"I think, but I'm not sure. It won't matter if we catch them before then. No need to ask the birds about it."

Shana leaned in. "We might have to mention it, they have one watching us."

Garran looked over his shoulder at the avolariean, who was trying his best to appear inconspicuous. He shrugged. "If they ask, they ask. We haven't lied to them about anything. What we are hunting is dangerous and the rewards are immense."

Shana whispered even quieter into his ear, "Do you think we can trust them? They did bring an arcane user."

"I saw. Zed informs me she appears to be one trained in the wind elements, but without seeing her cast he can't be sure. For now, remain cautious. Don't do anything that will betray their trust unless they do it first."

"Understood," she said, leaning back, speaking normally. "We should head back to camp and talk to Zed. He can provide a better estimate on how far away they are."

"Agreed," he replied.

Elsewhere, another one of Tetsunage's warriors informed him and Penisiya of something he had found. They approached the outskirts of the village, where the fight with the wolkin took place. The dead wolkin partially eaten by scavengers, the stench of death hanging in the air, the sun's rays fading over the horizon.

"What do you make of this Penisiya?" asked Tetsunage, looking over at the dead beast.

"I'm not sure yet," she replied, waving her hands in the air, speaking in avolariean-arcana. One of her white gemstones began to glow and after twenty or so seconds four bright glowing orbs appeared in front of her and with a flick of her wrists, they were scattered to light up the battle.

Tetsunage studied his surroundings. "There is a lot of strange things here. I see a struggle between multiple wolkin against a powerful beast, one that has jaws powerful enough to break this one's neck. The other appears to have died by other means, but I am not sure how," he commented, studying the area more, reaching down to the spot where Histra was landing repeatedly from the wall.

"Can you bring me some light here?" he asked. Penisiya nodded and does so with a flick of her wrist. The light hovered over his head as he reached down to feel the blades of grass. "Some of the grass here is dying like it has suffered extreme cold, but it is the middle of summer."

"Do you think the creature we are hunting has innate cold magic capabilities?" asked one of his fellow avolarieans.

"I don't think so. Whatever made this was small," he replied.

Another avolariean chirped out, "I see use of fire magic here."

Tetsunage raised his head and tilted it to the side. He rushed over to the long streak of burnt grass four or so inches wide, claws running across it with concern. "Penisiya, what about this?"

She slowly walked over to the area and brought one of the orbs illuminating the spot. She followed along the entire burnt path. The glow of her lights dimmed to the point they appear no brighter than a star in the night sky while focusing on what she saw.

"A very skillful fire wizard," Penisiya told him. "Fire likes to spread and feed on all around it. To contain that hunger takes a level of skill that perhaps not even my teacher possesses. We need to learn more. Everyone, stand back and give me room," she commanded, reaching into her backpack and pulled out a vellum book, its brown colored exterior marked with runic markings with silver inlaid.

Tetsunage motioned the others back as Penisiya ran her black scaled claw along the exterior of the book speaking a few arcane words. One of her blue gemstones on the same hand glowed, resonating with the markings on the book as it suddenly opened. She flipped through the pages, filled with symbols and other runes. She scanned through them in the fading light as she stopped two thirds through the book. Her claws ran across the pages, reading through it and spoke another word of avolariean-arcana. The page glowed, as did the avian's soft emerald color eyes in a soft blue-green light.

She elegantly danced around the edges of the battle that took place. Other more mundane looking gemstones glowed brighter and brighter in the same soft blue green that matched her eyes. Over the next four minutes she completed two circles around the area before making her way to the center and when she did a glow of blue light filled the outer edges of where she had just danced.

The area was lit up by the magic, moving her hands, as ghostly versions of the blades of grass shuddered, slow at first but then faster and faster. Ethereal versions of the dead wolkin were pulled from their current locations back to where they originally died, showing for brief moments the random scavengers that picked at the carcasses reversing the damage done to them.

The farther back she went, the heavier Penisiya panted. Her hands shook, movements slowed as if she was moving through some viscous liquid. Tetsunage took half a step towards her but one of his fellow avolarieans stopped him, shaking his head.

"You mustn't interrupt her," he whispered.

Penisiya arrived at her intended goal, the time where the fight had occurred. There they watched Histra attempting to fly before being attacked by the wolkin, only saved just in time by Ariana in her Lycan glory with Alderin assisting with his bow. Jesmine approached from behind, casting her spell.

She continued to play the battle in real time till it was over, the wall of fire fading away and the Lycan shifting back to her more anthropomorphic form before she paused the play of events.

She looked over to the others, chanting, head motioning them to approach and inspect the scene.

"Go back to that creature's larger form," Tetsunage ordered a hint of concern in his voice.

She moved and danced till the spell was at the earlier moment.

He walked near the spectral being, feathers rising. After a few more minutes, the ghost figures faded away, and the glowing runic markings on her jewelry and spellbook faded in kind.

Penisiya took a moment to catch her breath, Tetsunage rushing to give her support.

Garran clapped. "That was quite a show you did there. I'm impressed you managed to go back so far. Zed can only go back a day at most and that's with the aid of a spell component."

Zed grunted, "It's not an area of my expertise. I am more adept at combat magic."

Garran chuckled and slapped him on the back. "Yes, I know.

Your magic has saved us many times."

"You have some explaining to do," Tetsunage said, his eyes narrowed. "We were told we are hunting a great beast not this strange party which includes not only an elf but a kobold. What is it that we are truly hunting?"

The avians approached him but stopped when he raised his hand.

"You already know the answer," he said, walking over to Tetsunage. "The creature in the center, that is the great beast. How she managed to get through the city was because of them. I don't know much on the elf. The kobold is a liar, and one of those lies has reached the ears of the dragons, who are currently looking for her. It is a big hunt, with big risks but the rewards are even greater. Wouldn't you agree?"

Tetsunage watched Garran with reservation, "That does explain a lot."

"I came to your tribe, because you are the ones, who could get it done. The ones, who deserve the glory of this capture. I suggest you rest up. We have a long day of travel ahead of us tomorrow."

"Yes. Yes, we do," he chirped.

Chapter 14 Storm Clouds Gather

A light drizzle fell upon the group, water soaking through their clothes and fur, while Histra flicked her wings and shook her body every so often to break the thin layer of ice that formed on her. Thick grey clouds hung over head, while darker clouds with signs of distant flashes of lightning followed by the low rumble of thunder were pushing in their direction by an ever-quickening wind.

"I hate the rain," Histra grumbled, sitting in the back corner of the cart.

"I find it funny that a few days ago we were sorely in need of water, and now it's falling all over us," remarked Gnemi.

"The weather here in Sa'el'pa'ria, can be unpredictable at times," said Jesmine, looking over towards the darker rain clouds. "We should find shelter."

"I would appreciate anything to get me out of this rain," remarked Histra.

Alderin called out, "I don't see any place where we could shelter from the storm. Where was that castle and town that Jesmine talked about? Do you two know?" he asked, riding beside them.

"I believe we are close?" Histra answered.

"I think we are about an hour away," Jesmine said. "If the weather was nicer, we'd be able to see the outskirts of the town from here."

"See? Close."

"We better hurry then," Alderin replied.

"Aye. That would be good. I never experienced weather like this," Dran said.

"It's rather normal for here, but…" Ariana trailed off, looking at the flashing clouds, the wind blowing across her damp fur. "I'm more concerned if we get tornados. If that happens, we'll definitely need shelter."

Gnemi looked behind to her. "Tornado? What's that?"

"It's a swirl of powerful, magic-like windstorm that tears through buildings like they aren't even there. Seen it once. It's not something you want to be close to," she explained.

"Yeah… that does sound rather dangerous. Jesmine, you said it's about an hour till we get to the town?" Gnemi asked with a hint of urgency in his voice.

"I believe so."

"Let's not waste any time then."

"Yes, let's not," Histra stated with a slight groan, flicking her wings, breaking the newest layer of ice. The cart bounced and swayed as the winds rocked it side-to-side. Water flowed toward the back of the cart, rushing through small drainage holes as Ariana tugged a tarp that was over the supplies, water rushing across it like a river down a mountain.

Lightning flashed across the sky and struck the ground, the roar of thunder reaching them in under a second. The lukewarm rain turned into a total downpour, pools of water grew in the back of the cart, it gushing out of the drainage holes.

Slowly the outskirts of the town appeared out of the rainy haze. Steadily, the outline of a castle on top of a hill towering over the town came into view, though the weather made seeing the embattlements a challenge. The tall grasses became shorter and shorter as they reached the town's edge till only a few sprigs and short sprouts grew here and there. Water flowed off the roofs of the intact stone and wood buildings with some of their windows cracked or shattered, while others were shuttered up. The wind whistled through the town as the horses' hooves splashed on cobblestone streets, a thin layer of water rolling across the surface.

"There has to be a place to stable the horses," states Alderin.

"Over there!" yelled Dran, pointing to a set of horse stalls big enough to fit them and the cart. Across the stalls in a small open yard with a well in the middle was a small servant building that looked to be in good condition near the castle.

"You can get the horses," remarked Histra, leaping off the side of the cart with a splash, rushing over to the closed door. She reached for the handle and pushed, but the swollen waterlogged door wouldn't budge as her feet slid against the slick stone.

Ariana approached, the muscular feminine outline of her body showing through her wet fur. "I got it," she stated, pushing the door, which groaned and creaked against the stone, the door popping out of its frame. The only light illuminating the inside was from a cracked glass window facing toward the horse stalls and the recently open door.

Laying on the floor was a humanoid skeleton, the bones a faded brown as a layer of dust and mold clung to fragments of clothing. The blowing wind caused the fragments to flutter and shake, the skeleton shifting slightly.

Histra only gave the skeleton a passing glance, rushing around it before getting to the far end of the room, flicking her wings, breaking off the forming ice. "I hate the rain."

Ariana walked into the room and past the skeleton. "That explains the smell." She moved to an opposite corner and shook her body, flinging water in all directions, some of which landed on Histra, instantly freezing.

"Watch it," she remarked, flicking her wings.

"It's only water. You'll live."

She let out a huff of cold foggy air just as Gnemi walked in.

"They almost have everything secured. They'll be bringing th—by the Gods!" he exclaimed, stopping in the door frame.

"It's nothing. You've killed before. A long dead skeleton shouldn't bother you," remarked Histra.

"I was just surprised is all." He walked around the corpse. "We should do something about him? Her? I'm not sure. But it feels wrong to just leave them there," said Gnemi, taking a moment before getting closer to examine it.

"What can you do? They've been dead for decades, and the weather outside is atrocious. What do you want to do? Bury them here?" asked Histra.

Ariana looked over to her and then back to Gnemi. "It would be best not to touch it. That fungus is poisonous."

He slowly stepped back. "Good to know. Would it be safe to stay here?"

"As long as you don't eat them, yes."

"Duly noted," he replied, moving away from the corpse.

Dran walked into the room with the canvas filled with supplies that hung over his shoulder and on his back. "We'll have to go through our supplies and see what we can salvage," he remarked, taking a few steps before noticing the corpse. "Forgive us for using your place of rest." He bowed his head, walking toward a small fireplace on the opposite side of the room. A pot sat over black ashes which shifted a little from the wind blowing from the chimney. He put the sack down onto the table near the fireplace kicking up dust before pulling up one of two chairs that were nearby, the wood creaking as he sat down.

"The horses are secure…" Jesmine said, entering the room. Her voice trailed off, attention shifting straight to the corpse. She stared at it, the rain hitting her backside, hands tensing as Alderin bumped into her, almost knocking the elf over.

"Sorry, sorry," Alderin said as Jesmine stumbled forward, barely able to prevent herself from disturbing the corpse. He grabbed the door, forcing it closed with a moaning creak and the sound of wood grinding against the frame.

"The horses should be fine in the stables. For being abandoned for thirty years, the condition is not that bad," Alderin continued, turning around, seeing Jesmine silently staring down at the corpse. "You okay?" he asked, walking over to her.

She took a deep breath, softly replying, "Yeah."

He looked down at the skeleton. "Did you know them?"

"No. And even if I did, there is no way for me to tell who they were. I can't even tell if they were a male or female elf."

"How could you be certain they were an elf?" asked Alderin.

"This was an elven town, so it's probably safe to assume they were an elf," Gnemi said as he stood beside Jesmine.

"It's a male elf," Histra said.

"How can you tell?" Gnemi asked, taking a moment to dry off his goggles.

"The shape of the skull tells me it's an elf. They are shaped slightly different than say a human's skull and their bones are slender too, a dead giveaway."

"And him being a male?"

"The hips."

"How do you know that?" Alderin asked.

"I know a bit about elven biology."

"Tell me, how do *you* know elven biology? That is a peculiar bit of knowledge for a kobold to know," Ariana said.

"I don't remember," Histra said, pointing to her damaged horn. "There are things I know, but I don't know how I know them. Or did you forget that?"

"I didn't forget it. But *you* should remember I don't know what you do or don't remember," Ariana replied with a smirk.

The kobold responded with a light huff.

Jesmine pulled away from Alderin, who was gently touching her back. "No fighting. Especially here," there is a momentary pause before she continued, "And we should do something for him. He shouldn't just be left there like that."

"What do you intend to do? Go outside in this weather and bury him? After that, are you going to go around this entire town which is filled with countless others and bury them, too?" asked Histra.

A loud metallic clatter interrupted as the pot in the fireplace fell over, the lid wobbling on the hard-cold floor, the pot rolling away. Dran jumped to his feet in surprise. "That was… unexpected. It suddenly just jumped out," he replied, looking inside the pot, "Smells terrible."

"Probably filled with a poisonous fungus from the food that was left there," Ariana said.

"Aye, looks like it."

"It is not right to speak ill of the dead," said Jesmine.

Histra raise an eye ridge as her wings twitched. "Really? I heard plenty of—never mind…" she trailed off.

"What is it?" asked Jesmine, walking closer to her.

She took a deep breath and closed her eyes a moment before opening them and looking up at Jesmine. "You're right. One shouldn't speak ill of the dead, especially in their presence. Sorry."

Dran's jaw dropped. "Do my ears deceive me, or did Histra just *apologize*?"

She tossed him a stern glare.

Alderin stuck a finger in his ear and wiggled it. "So, it wasn't just me who heard that."

Histra's attention turned to Alderin before turning back up to Jesmine. "What do you intend to do then?"

"It would be best to give him and the town their final respect. Gods know they deserve that much."

"That sounds like a great idea, but what would be um… good to say? I have never done anything like that before," said Gnemi.

"I know how I'd do it, but I think it would be improper for me to give final dwarven rights to elves," remarked Dran.

"Don't worry. I know what to do. My father was educated in spiritualism and was a doctor," Jesmine said.

"I remember. He helped diagnose me a few times when I was sick. My parents made the medicine." Ariana said.

"Your Father. I believe I have never heard anything about him. Only your Mother," said Gnemi.

"He was a kind and generous man," Jesmine said, taking a deep breath, turning to the corpse. "Mother was the stern one.... which isn't a bad thing. She taught me much which has gotten me through many difficult times, but I feel I wouldn't be who I am today if it wasn't for him."

She took a few slow, deep breaths, beginning to sing. The beating of the rain and the howling of the wind muffled the singing at first but steadily her voice grew louder, singing the elven final resting rights, calling for the earth and nature to guide them to life thereafter. After a minute her song faded into the backdrop of the storm raging outside. "Forgive us that we don't know your name. Forgive me for this tragedy to have befallen you and the town," Jesmine said in honor of the dead elf, lowering her head, hands held together, doing her best to steady their shaking, a moment of silence befalling the group.

Jesmine continued, "I know it might be awkward, but does anyone else want to say anything?"

Ariana's ears perked, remarking "As the only other sort of elf here, I might as well." She looked down at the corpse. Her ears folded back; her tail slowly swayed. "You didn't deserve what happened to you. No person does. You lived a hard life. May your life in the next be far kinder to you."

"I'll give it a go," Alderin said. A moment passed, thinking over what to say. "Death is a certainty in life. It is the end result. Don't be sorry that death has happened, even though your journey was cut short. Think of it as a head start on your next life. One perhaps that doesn't have dragons to end your life on a whim."

Histra's wings twitched, silently watching the ceremony.

Dran rubbed the back of his head, walking over to the corpse. "I was never good at these things. But next time I have a drink, I will be sure it is in memory of you and all the elves of the town who suffered from Sa'bara's extermination. You may be gone but your people aren't forgotten."

Gnemi paced. "Sorry. I don't know what to say."

"It's alright. You don't have to say anything," Jesmine replied, giving Gnemi a smile before looking over to Histra. "Did you want to say anything?"

From her corner, she looked up at her then back down at the corpse, "I don't know what you want me to say. You have all talked about dragons, kobolds and those who support them as evil and anyone else as merely a victim of it. I've seen elves, humans, dwarves, gnomes lie and be just as cruel as any other race," she said. Everyone in the group gave her a stern stare.

She notes hints of sorrow in Jesmine's face, her hands tensing as she spoke. Histra closed her eyes for a moment and took a step towards the corpse. "But... I understand what it is like to be treated a certain way because of your species. To be judged because of it. In that way, we are no different. Death might have been the kinder fate. Regardless, of that, your fate was not deserved. May you forever rest in peace," she said, looking up to see everyone still staring at her. "What?"

"That was rather nice, Histra," Jesmine said with a smile.

"I'm a bit surprised myself," remarked Alderin.

"Same after your earlier remarks," Ariana said.

"You weren't all that fazed by it either," Histra said.

"No, I wasn't. I've seen plenty of death, killed much myself, especially in my earlier years as a Lycan."

"We've all killed before and haven't given much of a passing thought on those that fell," Jesmine said, stepping away from the corpse. "I have a strong idea of how much you've been through. I appreciate the fact that despite your experiences you said something."

The window facing the horses cracked slightly as wind smacked hard against the building. The roof overhead creaked, water dripping from the ceiling.

"We should dry ourselves and see what we can salvage of our supplies. I'm fearful a lot has become waterlogged," said Dran.

"I'll start a fire," Jesmine said. She took a few steps away from the corpse, her hands moving in slow elegant motions, performing a small dance. She muttered in arcana for about ten seconds, her tattoos only giving a soft glow when a small magical fire appeared in the fireplace. "Should that work for some warmth?" she asked, the fire flickering in strength.

"Aye, that will do. Thanks," Dran said, taking out a pot and tossed some of the most waterlogged food into it, "Might as well eat these."

"The storm is really getting rough. We're lucky the town was so intact, or we'd be in some trouble," Alderin said.

Jesmine sat on the other chair by the table, staying near the fireplace, her attention focused on it. "This is probably where one of the dragons personally attacked. The northern white dragons' ice breath is terrible, but I can only imagine how horrible a black dragon's acidic breath is."

Alderin cringed "You don't want to know."

"Nothing compares though to that of the green dragons' poisonous breath. It spreads through every crack, finding every hole. If you can't run fast enough, there is nowhere to hide. That is what probably happened to him over there," Jesmine said.

"Although Lycans were my parents' primary focus, to the point at times that is all they seemed to care about, they were always curious about the dragons' poison breath. But samples were always hard to come by. The only ones my parents ever managed to get were soil samples from a few of the younger dragons, obtained after the avolariean rebellion," said Ariana, thinking for a moment longer. "They were always focused on their work..."

"I couldn't imagine anything being worse than being melted alive, but it is eerie to see this town so intact after the others we saw," Alderin said.

"Aye, but it's not surprising after we went through Rivera," replied Dran, stirring the pot.

"What gets me is how empty these plains are. We've barely seen any sign of avolarieans outside of some smoke from a few encampments. We've traveled down the road and seen nothing nearby. It makes me wonder why Sa'bara is encouraging the orcs to attack the north when there is so much unused land here," Alderin said.

"Wait what? The orcs are doing what?" Gnemi asked, rushing over to him.

"The orcs mentioned it when talking to the dragon, though I only caught half the conversation."

"Razashra said that this isn't supported by Sa'bara to expand his territory. He is only giving the orcs free reign to take new lands in exchange for paying higher taxes," said Histra.

"How is that not expanding his territory?" Alderin asked.

"I never figured out why the dragons never did attack the north once Eisandra was killed. But it sounds like Sa'bara is trying to do it without angering the other dragons," suggested Dran.

"Probably. She did say that Sa'bara was officially not supporting the attack, therefore none of his children will take part in it," Histra said.

"What should we do? We need to warn the free north about this attack," Gnemi said with concern in his voice.

"What could we do? The trip there is longer than where we need to go, and it is probably more dangerous, as they are preparing for war," Alderin added.

"Aye, and I think the free north are well aware of any activity along their border. I'm sure they can handle whatever is tossed their way," Dran said.

"Not necessarily," Jesmine chimed in.

"Why is that?"

"The cursed lands are in the far North. One reason the free nations took so long to clear their lands of the remainder of Eisandra's followers was because a great deal of their military might was tied up defending the northern border from the undead."

"Yes! Exactly that. My family oversaw research and development to improve the undead defenses. To enhance them to require fewer people to man the Great Wall of Eskal Mountain Pass," Gnemi said.

Histra quirked an eye ridge. "Weren't they called Everwinter Mountains?"

"They were."

She let out a soft sigh, "Depending on how long this storm lasts. I say we continue on our way once it's over?"

"Maybe, but the horses are exhausted. We need to think of them," Dran said.

"I agree. The town is deserted. It's a safe place to spend a day to rest," Alderin said, crouching over by the fire, rubbing his hands together.

"I should have done something to dry us," Jesmine said.

"This is fine. It is best not to abuse your magic for everything," Dran said, checking the pot.

The gnome climbed up onto the other chair and started to go

through some of the supplies.

"A little water shouldn't hurt us, and the supplies aren't as bad as I feared," remarked Gnemi, sifting through them.

The aroma of Dran's cooking filled the room, overpowering some of the musty smell. Water dripped through the crack in the window, flowing down the side like a constant stream, blurring the view of the stables.

"This is more than just a little water," remarked Histra.

"Storms like this can get worse, but they tend to not last long," Ariana said.

"We can hope," Dran said, stirring the pot.

"It's going to be weird eating with a corpse nearby," Gnemi remarked.

"Wouldn't be the first time I've done it," Ariana said.

"Neither have I," remarked Histra.

"Unfortunately, it's not the first time for me," said Jesmine, keeping her attention on her spell.

Dran got up from the fireplace and walked over to Gnemi. "Don't worry," he said, giving him a hearty pat on the back which caused the chair to wobble, "You get used to it."

"I'd rather not," he sighed.

The party spent the next three hours weathering the storm, eating, and talking. Histra spent most of the time in the corner, with a clear shot of the door.

"You shouldn't be doing that the whole time," Alderin said to Jesmine, grabbing the now empty second chair and breaking it apart.

"What are you doing?" asked Dran.

"Oh, I know," said Gnemi as Alderin tossed the pieces of wood into the fireplace. The dried wood quickly caught light, releasing black smoke up the chimney.

"Now you can relax a bit," Alderin said.

Jesmine smiled, "Thanks. I was okay, but I appreciate it nonetheless," she replied, ending her spell and took a rest in the chair.

Eventually, the drumbeat of rain waned. The rattling of windows, the whistling of wind through the cracks in the building faded. Alderin stood by the window, peering outside. The rain had slowed to a drizzle, the ground muddied, puddles of water everywhere as the stables were now clearly visible as well as the castle that towered over the town. The whitewash on the stone walls faded from the elements as dirt clung to them, while on other sections the paint and stone had crumbled.

"Jesmine, you were in that castle over there?" he asked.

She walked over, peering through the window. "Yeah. That was the noble Ashrania family's home."

"That's their home?" exclaimed Alderin, looking at it again.

"Yeah. That is what a castle is. A home. Otherwise, it'd be a fortress."

"I didn't know that."

"Really? You robbed people and didn't know that?" asked Histra.

"What do you expect? For me to rush into some well-defended place and rob it blind? What am I? Stupid?"

"No. I was judging from your lock picking skills that you might have risked it."

"It is something I picked up over time. It is useful, but not to rob a fortress."

"Castle," Gnemi corrected.

Alderin sighed, "Gnemi, really?"

"Sorry," he replied.

"Those skills have come in handy," said Jesmine.

"Anyway. I shall check up on the horses. They probably need a drink," Alderin chuckled, pulling the creaking door.

"I'll help," she said, following him out of the room.

"Think we should help?" asked Gnemi.

"I'm happy enough to sit down for a bit longer. But perhaps once they get back, we could find a place to rest with less of those resting in peace," Dran said.

"That's a good idea," he replied.

Alderin and Jesmine walked through the open field, their feet squishing in the mud as the short, slow-growing grasses were completely drowned by the rain. "I could do it myself," Alderin said.

"I needed a little fresh air," she replied.

"I understand. It's not easy going through places you remember before they were destroyed. I never returned to my home after Dra'kesh took everything I knew...." Alderin stopped for a moment. "Sorry. I shouldn't have brought it up."

"No. No. It's fine," she replied as they continued until they entered the stables. Water leaked down some of the roofs. "As much as it pains me to see it, it's good to be home after all these years."

Alderin nodded, checking the horses and cart. "One day I might go back. To visit their graves, but right now I don't think I could face them."

She reached into the cart, pulling out the bucket and rope, "Why is that?"

"Well…" he trailed off, looking to the ground, "We really need to find you some shoes."

She looked down at her muddied feet, wiggling her toes. "It would be nice, but it doesn't bother me all that much."

"There is bound to be something in this town that could help."

"Histra will definitely not like that," she chuckled as they headed out.

"She doesn't like a lot of things. I can't figure her out. At times she's a complete pain, being secretive, acting as if she's better than everyone else, then at other times she is helpful, does what she says, and… let's say I am surprised at what she said earlier," he explained, tying the rope to the bucket before tossing it down the well. The bucket bounced against the stone walls, lowering it till an echoed splash of water was heard.

"I understand her feelings. What happened in the north is not much different than what Sa'bara did here."

"I don't know much about what happened there. But I can tell you no matter what happened up north, the extermination of your people like this, is inexcusable."

"So was what happened in the north. What I helped in. Two of those dragons weren't much of a threat at all. They were hiding, trying to survive and we hunted them down."

"They were at the time, but if they were to get older, they'd try to take up Eisandra's place," he replied, bringing up the water, which swirled in the bucket, "But to be honest, I don't care about the free land's politics. It's a land I'll never see," he said, lifting the bucket up to his lips. "I will be glad once we get back home and—"

A voice yelled. "Drop it or you will die!" Alderin looked

around and saw a middle-aged man with brown hair steadily greying on the sides, with wrinkles on his face becoming ever more prominent. Dressed in simple clothing, a walking stick in hand, he sternly stared at him.

"What? Who are you?" he yelled, quickly looking around, stepping in front of Jesmine, seeing two younger men with their bows notched but not drawn standing off on two opposite sides using the buildings as cover.

Alderin dropped the bucket as it splashed to the ground, he held up his hands. "Look, I don't know who you are. But we are just passing through. We didn't know you had claim on the water. There is no need to get violent," he said, looking over to the building with the others. Ariana peeked through the glass, making a few hand motions.

The man slowly approached, continuing, "You don't understand it's…" he trailed off, looking past Alderin to Jesmine. "By the great God Toval, it's an elf."

Alderin muttered under his breath, "Damn." He looked around, catching two more people out of the corner of his eye behind him. Jesmine followed his gaze taking note of them.

She stepped past Alderin, replying, "Yes, I am."

"Jesmine," Alderin muttered.

"They can tell I am. There is no point in hiding it," she said to him before turning back to the man. "We are just passing through. We mean you no harm."

"We don't mean to cause a problem either," replied the man.

"Yelling that I will die if I don't do what you say is a strange way of going about it," Alderin said.

"If you drank that water, you'd be dead in a day. The poison of the dragon's breath still lingers in the soil and groundwater. If it's not properly treated, it is rather deadly," he responded, getting closer.

His beard was short and scruffy with white and grey hairs mingled in with the brown. His brown eyes looked over them and after a pause, the misty rain caused water to drip from his nose. "The words you are looking for is thank you for saving my life."

"How do I know it would have killed me?" asked Alderin, shifting his focus to the other four who watch them from afar.

"You must not be from around here," the man said as Alderin

tenses. "The elf I figured, but a human traveling through here? Unaware of the lasting effect of the dragons' poisons? How did you two and the others get so far without getting caught by Sa'bara's spies?"

"How do you know there are others?" asked Jesmine.

"We checked your wagon. We thought we saw someone approach the town when the storm was getting worse, and then when we saw smoke coming from the stable hand's house, we had to investigate," he explained, halting his approach, stopping about six feet away from them.

"Damn, I didn't think about the smoke," Alderin remarked.

"Neither did I," Jesmine said, taking a step closer. "We appreciate the warning and saving my friend's life here. Would you mind telling us why you are here then? Last I heard this is avolariean lands."

"You tell us first why you are here. No elf in their right mind would come here after what happened."

Jesmine looked over to Alderin, who whispered, "They know you are an elf… it's up to you."

She nodded, turning to the man. "I want to visit my home. I know of the risks. But after being away for over thirty years, I want to say goodbye to my family one last time. Risks be damned."

The man straightened his back slightly. "Hmm, is that so? And who is everyone else?" he asked, glancing over towards the building.

"Friends of mine who are willing to risk their lives to help me see my goal. We are a mixed bunch, that includes us two, a gnome, a dwarf, a rare race of wolfkin found in the far reaches of Dra'kesh, and a very respectable guide who has proven their trustworthiness many times over and is the reason we made it this far without incident."

The man raised a brow. "A wolfkin? I never heard of that."

"Not many have. I never did till I escaped to Dra'kesh."

"Hmm, well then. Let's see this group of yours."

"Not till you tell us why you are here," she responded.

The man thought for a moment, a smile creeping across his face. "Very well," he said, looking over his shoulder to a glaring look of one of the archers. "But first, show me the top of your hands. And then I will. If you aren't from here, you wouldn't have Sa'bara's mark."

"I hope you know what you are doing Jesmine," remarked Alderin.

"What choice do we have?" she replied, showing their hands to them. "See?"

"You satisfied?" Alderin yelled.

The man nodded, "Yes. We're on our trip to deliver our taxes. We took refuge here, as the avolariea avoid the settlements that the dragon struck during elven extermination like the plague. It makes traversing the plains far less confrontational. Now if you please, let's see who's with you."

"Okay. Come out of the building. I told them of you. They aren't here for a fight," yelled Jesmine.

Dran was the first to step out. "This is a big risk, but I trust you have an idea what you're doing," he said, holding his axe in his hand. "Forgive me for not disarming myself. As I can see," he motioned over to two of the archers, "Your friends have not done the same."

"I understand. We weren't intending to talk but I couldn't watch as this young man was about to unwittingly kill himself."

"I heard," Dran replied as Gnemi was the next to come out, his repeating crossbow in hand, looking around nervously.

"Ariana you can come out, too. I explained to them that you're the rare wolfkin race."

Ariana let out a huff. "You didn't have to say my name, we haven't been properly introduced," she remarked, holding back a growl, her ears twitching, tail wagging quickly, stepping out. Two of the archers tensed up but the older man held up his hand.

"Apologies. A little introduction should be in order, yes. My name is Amir."

"Amir? Sounds almost elvish."

"I live close enough to where many elves lived…" he responded with a shrug.

Ariana sniffed the air. "There are four more I don't see. Since we showed ourselves, it would be polite if you did the same," she said, sternly looking at Amir.

"Right, right, of course," he replied. He motioned his hand and two male, and two female humans dressed in light leather armor, armed with sheathed short swords came out from behind some buildings. "That is quite a nose you have there. I'm surprised we surprised your friends with an ability like that."

"The dead elf in the building, the storm and a few other factors blocked your approach till it was too late."

"Hmmm," Amir said.

One of the recently revealed men approached, his hand on the hilt of his weapon, looking over the group. "Amir, they said they had a guide. I don't see them."

"Sorry, we didn't have a moment to bring her out," Jesmine said, turning to the door, "You can come out."

Histra yelled, "I prefer not to be shot!"

"No one is going to shoot you."

The guy next to Amir whispered to him as he waved him off. "No one is going to shoot you for stepping out. I prefer we have this meeting without any bloodshed."

"I'm sure you will find a need!" Histra yelled, remaining out of sight.

"Do you mind if I go in and get her? She's untrusting of people. It was only special circumstances that we got her as our guide," Jesmine explained.

"I see no harm in it, but please hurry. I prefer to get back to some place a bit drier."

"Thank you," Jesmine replied, walking to the building. Amir watched curiously, noticing her distinct lack of shoes.

Jesmine entered the house searching for Histra, not seeing her initially till she felt her cold aura coming from behind the door. "Histra?" asked Jesmine as she stepped into view.

She looked at her with a stern glare, "Yes?"

"You can come out now."

"So, they then can overreact and shoot me?" she responded.

"They won't shoot you."

"I have heard that before."

"Why don't you come out right behind me, how about that?"

Histra clenched her claws. "And hide like… hmmm," she grunted. "I'll go ahead. This is a *terrible* idea."

"It wasn't one of choice."

"Story of my life," Histra remarked. She flicked her wings, walking around Jesmine and muttered in draconic, "Damn rain."

"It's a kobold!" yelled one of the archers, lifting his bow but not drawing it.

She let out a foggy sigh, some of the mist crystalizing and falling to the ground like a light snow before it melted immediately upon hitting the ground. "As I was saying," she remarked, walking into view of the others, putting all the humans on edge.

Amir gripped his walking stick tighter, staring her down. "Unexpected," he remarked.

Jesmine followed behind her, "She has proven herself very trustworthy," she said. There was a laugh or a scoff from the others in Amir's party, but he remained silent.

"I was just as hesitant at first, but she knows the language, the lay of the land, and managed to get us through Rivera undetected," explained Alderin.

"Hmm. Let's get to the castle. I'd feel better if we continue this conversation there. Get your horses and cart. It would be wise to keep everything together," said Amir.

"Is this a good idea? This could be some test from Sa'bara," said one of the archers as he approached him.

"Don't be so paranoid. This is far too messy to be a test."

"Are you sure?"

"One thing I know is how Sa'bara tests people," he said before muttering softly into his ear, "But keep an eye on the kobold."

Ariana's ears twitched, looking at him and then down to Histra as they uneasily walked to the stables. They hitched their horses to the cart, Histra climbing inside, keeping an eye on the humans, who kept an eye on her, while the party gathered their things.

"You've been traveling for some time, haven't you?" asked Amir, walking ahead of the group, while the three archers followed them, the remainders keeping to their flanks.

"We have been," Alderin replied.

"I'm not a fan of being surrounded," stated Dran as they took a closer look at the imposing castle with battlements. A section of wall near the drawbridge was smashed in, not only making the drawbridge impossible to raise but also revealed a second taller stone rampart behind the first.

"If we wanted to do you harm, we'd have done it by now. There is no point in putting up a charade like this," said Amir, looking up at Dran as they stepped onto the wooden bridge which creaked under their weight.

"Forgive me for being cautious. Sa'bara's lands have shown to be filled with paranoia and thanks to my home, it is hard to trust anyone outside of your area," explained Alderin. "But you said you intended not to contact us?"

"Yes, but I could not let you drink poisoned water."

"I understand that, but why this? Moving into the castle?"

"It's safer, and even less likely for the avolarieans to come and notice our presence."

"Are the bird people that bad?"

"I heard they weren't terrible before the rebellion from my grandfather. But personal experience has taught me otherwise. They've become extremely defensive over their new lands; they like to keep control and attack anyone caught trespassing."

"They've always been protective of their lands, but I've never heard of them being that aggressive," remarked Jesmine.

"Not sure what to tell you. A lot has changed over the years," Amir replied. Ariana's ears perked, her attention constantly jumping from one to the next, tail wag quickening.

"We appreciate running into some friendly faces. The orcs as you'd expect are less than welcoming," Jesmine said as they passed through the gate. Water dripped down from the murder holes, the cold-water hitting Gnemi on the head, causing him to flinch and look up. The horse steps echoed as they passed through the second similar gate, the slot for the castle's portcullis were empty.

"That's one benefit of living where we are. We don't have to deal with orcs. They never travel through avolariean areas," Amir explained as they entered the courtyard. Stone barracks stood near one side of one wall, stables larger than the other sat across from them on the opposite side. Across from the gate was the keep, a large stone building, the whitewash was almost completely gone, showing the grey stonework underneath. The three intact floors had narrow windows and arrow slits while what would have been a fourth was completely collapsed, the roof nearly demolished, but one section of it somehow stood defiantly. Thick slabs of stone, part of the keep's upper most floor, laid scattered across the courtyard, most of it near the base. The ground was brown and muddy with only a few hearty shrubs growing.

Jesmine tensed, seeing blossom trees barren, their bark blackened and slowly rotting away, memories rushing back to her when they were full of life.

The cart slowed, wheels grinding through the mud as they were guided toward the stables. "Orcs don't come through here often then?" asked Alderin.

"Often? More like never," Amir replied as Alderin nodded, glancing at Histra, whose attention was still drawn by the other humans. Once the cart stopped the kobold jumped off, her feet squishing in the mud, flicking her wings again to remove the thin layer of ice.

"I hate rain," Histra grumbled in draconic.

"Watch it, kobold," stated one of the humans who stood a few feet away, his hand on the hilt of his weapon.

She grunted, glaring up at him. "Or what? I've done nothing. Amir! Where do you want us to go, so we can keep this gathering amicable?"

He replied, using his staff to point, "The barracks over there are empty. We've been staying at the keep."

"Fine with me," she grumbled, walking off in that direction, one of the humans following a few feet behind her.

"I'll go too," said Ariana, leaping off the cart, chasing after her.

"The wolfkin has peculiar items adorning her body," commented Amir, watching her walk off before turning his attention back to Alderin and Jesmine as they dismounted from the horse and cart.

"It's not a choice, nor something we want to talk about," remarked Alderin.

"I'm sure you understand," said Jesmine.

"That's perfectly fine," he replied, watching Ariana for another moment longer.

"It's not difficult for me to see that your people are not too pleased with your decision," said Dran, looking at the others.

"They are on edge, but I have done this for many years. They respect my decisions, even if they don't understand," he said as a few of the others look over to him.

"I'm going to check on Erkin," said one of the female archers, going off to the barracks.

"I'll go too," said Gnemi, walking off.

"I apologize for the inconvenience," said Jesmine, looking at the others around her.

Amir smiled. "No need to apologize. Toval wouldn't forgive me if I willingly let someone die, without just cause."

"Thanks, on that. So, do you know where we could get some more water?"

"The next town with a reliable well is about a day away. But we can still get water here if its properly treated," he said, looking over to one of the men and motioned for him. The man walked into the now gentle misting rain toward the well, drawing water.

"Is the water here not poisonous?"

"It's the same water. It's gotten better but it will be perhaps another decade before it is drinkable without treatment," Amir explained.

"You're a priest," said Jesmine.

He nodded. "A priest with some study in water magic. It has proven to be important to have clean water for my patients. But, forgive me, what is your name, sir?" he asked.

"Alderin."

"Alderin, I noticed you had some difficulty mounting your horse. Are you injured?"

"Ah… I took an arrow to the shoulder over a week ago. It's been healing."

"Would you mind if I take a look at it?"

"Uh… sure," he replied, removing his armor to reveal the injury.

Amir leaned in and examined the wound. "Whoever removed your arrow knows what they are doing, and you said this happened a week ago? It's healing amazingly fast."

"Ariana, the wolfkin, has strong alchemic healing skills."

"I would love to know what she did then. Call it payment for what I am about to do, if you don't mind me taking some time to heal this."

"You can cast healing magic?" asked Alderin with some surprise.

He nodded. "That I can."

"Go right ahead."

"Amir, do you think this is wise?" asked one of his companions.

"It is always wise to help those in need. This is not going against anything Sa'bara has stated. We paid our Draksind. We are causing no trouble or harming any dragon. The years of elven extermination are long past. If one lone elf visiting the graves of her family posed such a threat, the dragons would not be in the position they are today."

"If you say so."

"Now, please, let me focus," he stated, beginning to chant, his voice soft, silver engraved runes on his staff beginning to glow a soft blueish-white. The light travelled halfway down the staff, moving it with one hand, while pressing his other on Alderin's wound who felt a soft throbbing pain from the touch.

A minute passed while one of his men brought the bucket of water. He stood there silently as Amir placed the staff against the wound. A warmth filled the point of contact. Alderin tensed from a sharp but quickly fading pain that caused his entire arm to twitch. When the pain surge disappeared so did his initial ache.

"How's that?"

He rotated his shoulder. "Much better, thank you."

"Perhaps that will build a little trust between us," he said, going to the bucket of water, beginning to chant, making new unique hand motions. He moved around the water, the staff glowing that same color as before, but then another set of runes on the second half of the staff radiated a dark blue. The water lifted from the bucket, flowed through the air like a floating river into a trough which the horses happily began to drink. What remained in the bucket was a very thin, faintly green-tinted slime which was only visible when viewing it at the right angle.

The glow from his staff faded, taking a deep breath, peering into the bucket. "If you'd be so kind, can you get another."

"Of course," he replied, walking off to the well.

"That's... that's something," remarked Dran.

"I'm unfortunately not skilled enough to neutralize the poison even when it's this diluted, but I am skilled at detecting and separating it from the water."

"How did you know it was for the horses?" asked Alderin.

"I overheard you talking about it. Once I am done here, would you mind coming to the keep with me? There are a few things I'd like to discuss."

"I don't see why not," he replied.

"Neither do I," replied Jesmine.

"I hope you don't mind if I come along as well? I'm curious what you have to say," said Dran.

"Not at all," he replied, turning to the others. "Return to your posts. Remember to light the lanterns when it becomes dark and take four-hour shifts."

They responded with a nod before half split off to the walls, patrolling up on the battlements.

Dran rubbed his beard curiously, asking, "Lanterns? Wouldn't that draw attention here?"

"It would, yes, but there are a few reasons why," he replied as the water is brought to him. "One is that the avolarieans are notably superstitious and take it that the place is haunted by the ghosts of those who were slaughtered here. The second, amusingly enough, is to keep watch of the ghosts which do haunt this place."

"Ghosts here?" asked Alderin, shooting Amir an inquisitive look.

"Yes. Do you think such horrendous death would not mark the land? Though the ones seen here over the years are harmless, echoes of the past events," he said, turning his attention to the bucket. "Excuse me, I'll need a moment," he said, repeating the magical chants and motions from before, the clean water flowing out of the bucket and into the trough.

"I have heard of such things. I have been fortunate enough to not experience any of it myself," said Jesmine.

"Aye, neither have I," replied Dran.

"I knew it was a possibility though. Thankfully, ghosts are not the undead, where the physical form is brought back to an unnatural life. Undead tend to be the body while ghosts are lingering souls. Ghosts, if I recall, can persist for decades or even centuries where the event occurred before truly passing on," explained Jesmine.

Amir's eyes widened ever so slightly. "I'm impressed. I didn't expect you to be knowledgeable on such matters. Benefits of elven longevity."

"My father was the town's spiritualist. I picked up a lot from him."

"I see. Well, let's get inside, where we can properly discuss matters at hand," he said, leading them over to the keep with two of his people following in tow. Jesmine looked at the keep, grey clouds overhead keeping the light of the sun at a perpetual dusk-like level. Memories of a brighter time flashed for a moment in Jesmine's mind. Like a flickering flame blown out by the wind, there for only an instant, images of the period when she was here. The whitewashed walls, the well-kept field, the blooming trees, the guards stationed at the ramparts. As she looked up to the torn top floor, a guard stood there looking down at them as they entered.

Earlier, Histra walked into the barracks, the door swinging open with little effort, which pushed a thin layer of dust, scraping some mud that was along the door entrance. Long tables and stools sat silent, barren. Half-open wooden shutters allowed light through with puddles of water in front of them. A musty aroma lingered in the air, albeit not as bad or filled with the sense of death like the stables. She flicked her wings to break the new layer of ice, looking over her shoulder to see the guard walking in right behind.

"Last I checked, I, nor anyone else, was your prisoner. So why don't you just go?" she remarked, waving off the human, looking around.

Erkin took another step into the barracks, leaning by the door, his hand never leaving the hilt of his weapon, eyeing her moving about.

She lifted her head, jumping onto a stool noticing the second archer entering. "Two of you? Do you honestly think I could do anything? Better yet would even do anything? That fearful of someone less than half your height?"

Ariana entered, shaking the water from her fur, sending it flying everywhere, causing Erkin to flinch, feeling the spray of water on his face.

"A little warning, will you? We are giving you hospitality here," said the archer.

She looked over to her. "This isn't your home. You aren't giving us anything. We are merely co-existing by each other till we part ways. Now, get out of here. I don't like being watched," she stated with a faint growl.

"We aren't here to watch you," she remarked, motioning to Histra.

"I didn't ask you who you were meant to be watching."

"I don't want any trouble with you."

"Then leave."

She looked over to Erkin who nodded to her. "Go. I'll stay."

"I'll be in earshot if you need me," she replied, stepping out of the barracks.

"You too," Ariana stated, eyes narrowing.

"If it makes you feel any better, I'll keep my hand off my weapon. Amir is in charge. I will do what he says, but I won't stop you from doing whatever you want to do. Try to start something and I will finish it, but I would rather not cause trouble here."

Ariana let out a huff of air as Gnemi entered. "It's good to be inside again…" he said, looking around, "It looks bigger on the inside. And it appears to be incredibly well preserved. Ariana, do you think you could tell if there is anyone here making their final rest?"

Ariana slowly turned her attention to him, sniffing the air. "Not that I can tell."

He let out a soft sigh. "Good. The body of that elf was giving me the chills."

Ariana looked over to Erkin, then back to Gnemi. "Really? One dead body gave you the chills?"

"No. That one corpse did. And then when that pot moved all by itself."

"That was the wind from the storm," she remarked as Histra continued to make her way through the rooms, checking out the living and sleeping quarters. The straw bed stuffing and the cloth sheets are partially rotted away, giving off a moldy smell.

Inside were open chests, fragments of some of them laying by the ends of the beds. A smashed in window faced out towards the courtyard. Histra noticed and grabbed a small fungus covered wooden stool, using it to peek outside, her feet squishing the small brown mushrooms as they began to freeze over. She watched Amir using his magic to purify and move the water into the horses' trough.

"I knew he had skill," she muttered to herself, the same archer from before, walking toward the window, causing her to duck.

"How could they have a damn kobold guide? Are they insane or just stupid? Maybe Amir will talk some sense into the elf… an elf. I never thought I would see one. They don't look that much different from us," she muttered before she stopped in front of the window, peering inside. Histra kept low by the wall, looking up. She saw her breath just start to form as she pulled away, walking off.

"This is where it starts, isn't it?" Histra thought, climbing back onto the stool and looked out of the window, *"I need to know."* She sighed and muttered, "Back into the rain again," jumping off the stool, which broke under her feet but not before she managed to hoist herself up and through the window, landing with a soft thud, her feet squelching in the mud. Looking around she found a large round piece of stone. She sprinted toward it, constantly looking around, hugging the stone, placing herself between it and any of those patrolling the wall, catching the conversation coming through the door.

"What did you want to discuss?" Jesmine asked standing by the keep's entrance, the broken hinges making it impossible to properly close the door.

Amir took a deep breath. "The kobold. What do you know about her?"

Histra thought, *"I knew it."*

"Histra? She was enslaved by orcs for a decade. She's not from this land, and has little love for the dragons here," explained Jesmine.

"She has little love for anyone for that matter," remarked Alderin.

"Alderin!" exclaimed Jesmine.

"What? It's true."

"Aye, that it is. She is a pain. Acts as if she's better than everyone else, and that you don't deserve to know what is going on unless it is absolutely necessary. She likes to power play."

Histra listened and tensed up, Amir replying, "That doesn't sound like someone you want as a guide."

"But she has been invaluable and once you get past her rough edges, she's not a bad person. I am happy to have her with us. She's a good friend, who has saved all of our lives," said Jesmine, motioning to her companions.

"That's also true," Alderin replied.

"Aye," said Dran, rubbing his beard, the braids fraying, starting to come undone.

Amir nodded. "Kobolds are a… peculiar bunch. They have often proven to be spineless, sneaky, and underhanded."

Histra growled, flicking her wings to break the ice that accumulated on her backside.

"Don't talk about Histra like that. I know kobolds can be any of those things, but they can also be good, kind, trustworthy, and courageous. And she has proven to be so."

Alderin shoots Jesmine a surprised look, thinking, *"I wouldn't put kind in there."*

"Perhaps, but I will warn you, even for a kobold she is not normal," said Amir.

"We know. The ice aura gives it away," said Alderin.

"That is odd, but that is not what I am talking about."

Dran moved over to a nearby chair, sitting down the chair creaking under his weight. "What else is there?"

"Is it the fact she has probably never been here before?" asked Alderin.

Jesmine turned to Alderin. "What?"

"She said she has been to where we need to go. Amir said that the orcs never travel this way. I find it hard to imagine that an orc traveling side show came this far. A lot of risk for little reward," explained Alderin, going to a nearby wall and leaned against it. "There are a couple other little things that she's said that have bothering me, but let's face it, Histra lied to others in front of us. Why would you be surprised if she lied to us?"

"Damn, this isn't good," thought Histra, looking around, peering over the rock to the guards who walked the walls. *"If I just sneak through there, they will shoot at me. And I am in the middle of nowhere! What to do…"*

"No. But when we met, she had just as much reason not to trust us as you two had not to trust her. Wouldn't you have done the same?" asked Jesmine.

Alderin sighed. "Slow down with being so quick to turn what I say back on me, Jesmine, please. I'm not saying she is horrible. She saved my life. She's a pain, though, and I am really tired of her looking down on us."

"Her superiority complex is her worst trait," Dran added in, "She has her problems, but I cannot deny that she's done good by us and stuck by her word."

"I am not sure if I am relieved or concerned you think of your kobold 'guide' this way but none of that is what I am referring to," Amir explained, positioning himself so he could see everyone in the group. "Even if it's somehow true that she's not a kobold that serves Sa'bara, she is no run of the mill kobold. A kobold doesn't get intricate runic magic engraved in their horns for no reason. Has she even told you she's an arcane user?"

"Damn that human," Histra thought, tensing.

"I suspected, but it was never mentioned," remarked Dran.

"I asked, but Jesmine waved off the notion," said Alderin.

"I knew she was versed in magic but given at the time half the party was more likely to kill her than work with her, I didn't want to make her appear any more threatening than she really was."

Histra relaxes slightly. *"I was wondering."*

"I appreciate your words of caution, but we aren't naïve travelers," said Jesmine.

"Apologies, but I would not feel right if I didn't say something," he replied.

"We appreciate it. Your thoughtfulness means a lot."

"Doing what I can."

Alderin stood tall again. "Let me ask. If we stay here a day or two, to let our horses get much-needed rest, would that be a problem?"

"No problem at all. We plan to leave tomorrow in the morning."

"Is there anything else we should know? Are there any major avolariean clans nearby? I noticed how heavily armed you keep the guard here, despite the fact the avolarieans avoid the former elven settlements, you even have a guard on the fourth floor of this keep," said Jesmine as Amir and the guards nearby who were silent up to this point muttered amongst themselves.

"Did you say you saw someone on the fourth floor of this keep?"

"I did," she looked at the others, reading the concern on their faces. "There is no one on the fourth floor is there?"

"The stairwell to the fourth floor is collapsed. There is no way to get up there."

"You saw the watchman," said one of the archers.

"The watchman?" asked Jesmine.

"It's what we call the ghost of the castle. They're only on the fourth floor. People who are on the third say they hear footsteps and creaking wood above them, but you said you saw them?"

"Yes."

Amir took a deep breath, closing his eyes for a moment before he focuses on her. "That's not good."

"Why?"

"Anyone who has seen the watchman had something bad happen to them not long after."

Alderin spoke up, "How bad?"

"It depends. Sometimes, it's a broken ankle or arm from a simple accident, robbed by a local orc when visiting the city of Rivera, but… over the years of doing this trip, two people on two different occasions who have seen them have died."

"Blessed be the Gods, but there is no way I'd let that happen," said Dran.

"Just because someone has died, doesn't mean you will, just be careful about the next several days."

Histra thought, *"Mental note. Don't look up. I can't risk…"*

"Hey! What are you doing there!" yelled the archer from earlier.

She looked over her shoulder, seeing her approach. "I was relieving myself."

"In the middle of the field?"

"Does it matter?" Histra remarked, walking toward the keep.

"Don't walk away from me."

"I don't care," she said, waving a claw. She squeezed through the ajar door, then she smirked at the group, wiggling off any last bit of ice around her. "So, this is where you all have been hiding. Having a fun conversation? We've been wondering where you all have been and as much as I love to be reminded of the time when we first met, where half of you would rather have killed me than work with me. But now I feel more comfortable being around you than the random humans, who have been following me," she said as the human archer pulled the door open.

"Sorry Amir, she's snuck past me."

He waves it off. "It's fine. I don't think she is going to pose a major threat to us."

"Shall we make our way back to the barracks? There still some daylight left but the day has been long. Some rest would be nice," said Histra, looking to her group.

Jesmine smiled. "That's a great idea," she said, turning back to Amir. "Thank you for the help."

"Toval would expect nothing less from me."

"Thank you. Our travel has been long, and a bit of relaxation will be nice," said Jesmine.

"That is an understatement," commented Alderin as they headed out of the keep back to the barracks with Histra taking point. The party enjoyed some much-needed rest and relaxation, without realizing that tomorrow they would need that rest as Garran and his party were almost upon them.

Chapter 15 Clash

The storm passed, the clearing night's sky showing the fading twinkle of stars. The two moons in different stages of waning crescent shone while dawn approached. Garran looked over the town before turning his attention to Zed, who had just finished casting his spell, the glow from his tusks fading. "There?" asked Garran.

The other orc looked in the direction of the castle. "Yes."

Tetsunage let out a long yawn, saying while Zed translated, "We should wait till they leave the town."

"No. We move in and use the town to our advantage. We can box them in and cut off avenues of escape," stated Garran.

"The elven ruins are cursed. You can see the ghost lights from here."

Garran let out a groaning sigh. "You fool. That's them."

Shana rides up beside him, saying, "I do not think it is wise to attack the castle. There is only six in the party, yet I see two with torches there. Something about it does not feel right. Perhaps it is best to wait till they leave and then ambush them?"

"They are on edge because of what happened. They took refuge in the castle as a defensive measure, but in doing so they have trapped themselves. Tetsunage, I want half of your forces to guard the rear of the castle, make sure they don't try to escape. The rest will assist us in taking them out."

Tetsunage looked up at Garran and then to Penisiya. "What do you think?"

"This is one of the towns the dragons attacked. Nothing feels right."

"Do you want to take the warriors around the back? To counter their arcane user?"

"No. I think it's wise to stick together with the orc's arcane caster. The elf is powerful, and it will be advantageous to work with him."

Tetsunage let out a soft chirp of agreement, as Zed then translated, "We don't like the idea of going into the town. The ground is cursed."

"Cursed? It's not cursed, it's merely abandoned. If you birds took over the settlements, you'd be far better off."

"We learned that it is best to keep moving."

Garran glanced down. "Humor me. Why?"

"Makes it harder to be hunted if you aren't penned up," he remarked before adding, "We'll support your plan. Penisiya, half my hunters, and I will support your attack. We aren't good in melee, but our archery is superb."

He sighed. "Your kind is weak-boned, but it's better than nothing." He looked to Shana. "I'll leave you and one other to support the rear guard. I don't want them to escape."

"Yes, sir."

"Remember, the elf, the beast with the cuffs on it, and the kobold must be taken alive, and if possible, capture the human alive. I want to *personally* repay him for the trouble he has caused," he ordered as the orcs and the avolarieans split up accordingly.

Back at the castle, an archer stopped and looked out over the town. "Hey, do you see that?" she asked another archer with a torch held in his hand, looking at her and following to where she was pointing.

"Huh? Hmm…"

"I think I see movement."

"That can't be good, get the others," he remarked as she rushed down the stairs from the wall to the keep.

Dran watched her running from within the barracks "That appears troublesome," he said, waking everyone up. The grogginess from Alderin and Gnemi's faces faded in an instant at the sense of Dran's urgency. Jesmine stretched and stood up while Ariana leapt to her feet.

"What's going on?" asked Ariana, sniffing the air, her ears twitching, looking around.

Histra peeked her head out from underneath one of the tables. "What happened?" she asked, letting out a long-drawn yawn.

"One of their guards just rushed down the wall and into the keep," Dran explained.

Jesmine's grogginess quickly drained from her, walking over to him. "Do you think it's them?" she asked, hands tensing.

"No, how could it be? They have no idea where are going, or even if we got through the city," said Alderin.

"It is possible the other orcs told them after the fact," remarked Histra.

"They managed to capture me once. I wouldn't underestimate them," Ariana said, rubbing her cuffs.

"Either way, we need to find out what's going on," said Jesmine, rushing outside just as Amir and others of his entourage were coming out of the keep.

"What do you see?!" he yelled to the guard still on top of the inner wall.

"A group on horseback, and people running beside them. They've split into multiple groups. The largest will enter the town in a few minutes while the others are moving to surround the castle. They know we are here."

He looked up with concern. "The avolariea don't ride horseback. Those are probably orcs with avolarieans beside them. The question would be, why are orcs and avolarieans working with each other?"

Jesmine walked up to them. "I believe I can explain the orcs."

Amir and the others turned to her. "Tell."

"On the way to Rivera, Ariana, the wolfkin, was captured to be sold off as part of their Draksind. We freed her and they aren't too fond of what happened."

"Do they happen to know you're an elf?" he asked with concern in his voice.

"I believe not. But we couldn't abandon our friend."

"Orcs are hard to reason with when they have their minds set. I can't let them take your friend. Set up a defensive line. Hopefully, we can discourage them," he said.

Erkin stepped up. "Wait. Are you asking us to risk our lives for these strangers? One of which is a kobold?! Have you lost your mind Amir?"

"I am of sound mind and body. I am in charge. Do you think if we just let them do what they want that we won't be harmed?"

"If you hadn't taken them in this wouldn't be an issue."

"I am doing what Toval would want."

"What Toval would want? Or what your father would have wanted?"

Amir's eyes narrowed slightly, gripping the staff a bit tighter. "This isn't the time to talk about this. We need to prepare."

"I have an idea to scare the orcs off," said Jesmine.

"What idea?"

"I could not live with myself if I put you all in danger. I could create a wall of fire between the two walls. This will deter them from attacking and maybe, perhaps, retreat."

Ariana spoke up. "I do not think some fire will stop them, but it could delay them."

Amir nodded. "A wall of fire between the walls? That requires some advanced magic. You didn't tell me you practiced the arts."

"Sorry, but that isn't what is important right now. What is, is that I can do it. But if I am to do so, I need to place the anchoring sigils in the ground immediately."

Amir looked at Jesmine and the rest of his own group. "What do you need from us?"

"Just delay them. They aren't going to be expecting you here. That will give them pause. I would prefer if we can avoid a fight."

"And what if they do? And won't leave?" asked Erkin.

"There is an escape tunnel behind the keep," said Jesmine.

"How do you know of it?"

"It was used once when I was here. A stone slab covers it, it will take some effort to open," she explained.

"Do what you need to do. Everyone else, man the inner wall and guard the main entrance. We'll try to stall, delay, and convince them that they aren't here. Try to avoid a fight, and let them make the first aggressive move," commanded Amir as they took to their positions, with a few softly spoken remarks.

"Thank you, Amir. You have done much, without needing to."

"It is the least I can do," he replied, looking at the rest of Jesmine's group, his gaze catching Histra's, who watched from the doorframe of the barracks. "Be ready to do your part but remain out of sight until necessary."

Alderin rushed to Jesmine. "I'll stay with you."

"As will I," said Dran.

"Amir, will it be alright if I use the third floor? It will help me keep line of sight once I complete the glyphs. Is it also possible to have someone ready to provide rope to lift me out of the back? I don't want to risk coming through the front."

"No need. The second wall behind the keep is smashed. The first wall is thankfully intact and should hopefully provide a deterrent long enough for you to get the spell working."

"Histra?" Jesmine asked, turning to her.

"Yes?"

"Could you wait at the third floor? You know. Just in case?"

Histra sighed. "I prefer that not to happen again, but I'd rather you not fry yourself."

She smiled. "Thanks."

Amir raised an eyebrow. "I hope you know what you are doing. I didn't see a spellbook on you."

"This is something my mother instilled in me as a defensive measure. I will be fine."

Dran spoke up. "Why not have Histra near the front?"

Histra remarked, "What?"

"You have your ice breath. That could be useful if they storm through the front door."

"I'd rather you not speak of what I can do in front of others," she remarked before clearing her throat. "But now that you pushed me into a corner, I must admit something. I can't. My breath is unfortunately a once a week ability. My glands aren't as productive as say, an actual dragon. And seeing as I used it a few days ago. I can't right now."

Dran sighed. "And here I was hopeful."

"Do you mind, Histra, staying up there and waiting?" asked Jesmine.

"No, not at all," she replied, walking towards the keep.

"The secret escape route is behind the keep? Inside or outside?" asked Ariana.

"Outside."

"I'll try to look for it," she said, running off.

"Time is of the essence. Get going, we'll do what we can," said Amir.

"Where do you want me?" asked Gnemi.

"Try the second floor of the keep. That crossbow should be useful there if things turn sour," Amir suggested.

Gnemi looked to the keep, pulling out his weapon. "Got it."

As everyone moved into position, Jesmine said to Alderin and Dran, "When I start, it will be very important that I focus. If you need my attention, do it gently."

"How risky is this?" asked Alderin.

"Magic always comes with risks," remarked Dran.

"I'll be fine," said Jesmine.

"If you can create giant walls of fire, why do you need, *you know what?*" Alderin asked, looking around, seeing the other humans watching them as they headed to the gate.

"Firewall is the most advanced spell I know without aid," she explained, going to a patch of muddy ground about two feet away from the gate.

"And these anchor sigils you spoke about?"

"A sigil, or glyph, as some call it, can provide an attachment for my spell. I transfer the elemental energy from me to the glyphs which will allow me to create the wall without having to see the entire location."

"Don't you need valuable metal to bind the transfer?"

"For advance spells and enchantments, it's very helpful but not necessary for something like this. It won't last long. Now, let me focus," said Jesmine, beginning to chant. Her hands moved in slow, elegant motions, her steps calculated, walking in a circle, once, then twice. Her tattoos glowed a soft red, drawing runic symbols into the mud with her hands, her chant growing slightly louder. The elf danced around the glyph again, which gained the same soft red glow, the water around it evaporating, the mud drying into hard earth. Jesmine rushed to the next location, keeping her chanting going, repeating the process all over again.

Gnemi looked over his crossbow as he and Histra walked up the stairs. "What do you make of everything?" he asked.

Histra raised an eye ridge. "Everything of what? The fact that a bunch of random humans are helping all of you? Or that the orcs managed to find us?"

"They are helping us, and both I guess?"

Histra laughed. "Us? No, there aren't helping *us*. They are begrudgingly helping, and their human healer gives me the same untrusting look the others do."

"They are risking their lives to help. Don't be so... healer? Which is a healer?" Gnemi asked curiously, looking around to find a chair, which he dragged over to the window.

"Amir."

"How do you know he is a healer?"

"I can tell from the spell he casted."

"When did he cast a spell for healing?"

"For one who is so curious, you don't pay attention to what is around you. I'm going upstairs," Histra remarked, walking over to the next staircase on the opposite side of the room.

"Alright... thought we could probably talk a little bit."

"No time to talk," she said, climbing the stairs, reaching the next floor. Dust covered the floor, rubble and pieces of broken staircase popped into view, stone from the upper floor blocked off the pathway completely. She grabbed a chair and dragged it over near the window, which was the main source of light into the room, peering over the edge.

Histra looked down at the humans who were on the wall, bows nocked and at the ready. She looked past the wall to see the town and the quickly approaching orcs and avolarieans. *This plan better work,"* she thought, hearing heavy footsteps overhead. She curiously looked up to see dust fall from the cracks of the wood planks. The kobold took a deep breath, slowly releasing it. "Restless spirits become more unrested when death is in the air..." she trailed off and flicked her tail. "Wait, how do I know that?"

Ariana searched behind the keep, behind the broken section of the second wall, caused by parts of the keep having fallen onto it. Her tail lowered and wagging hard, seeing the muddied ground, remarking. "Wish she had a moment to point out where it was." She looked around along the stone wall of the keep, digging her paws into the mud.

Garran and his party rode through the town, quickly at first but slowed as they drew closer to the castle, noticing the multiple humans on the wall. Amir stood at the entrance to the castle, holding his staff, looking down the path past the drawbridge watching them ride into view. "I don't recognize these humans. Careful. They might be in the town proper. Zed?"

"I'll need a moment. Find out who these people are," he replied.

"There shouldn't be any humans here. They are trespassing on our lands," Tetsunage said with annoyance.

"That would explain their defensive nature," remarked Garran after Zed translated.

"Just say the word and we'll rush them," said Karrun.

"Stay on guard, but I prefer not to make more enemies than we need to. Our current targets are dangerous enough," he said, riding up with Karrun, Tetsunage and Penisiya. They stopped several feet before the drawbridge, the archers standing on the wall at ready but showed no initial hostile intent.

Tetsunage chirped to Penisiya, "Can you prepare a wind wall? Just in case? You know how these humans can be."

"I'm already on it," she whispered, her fingers running through the pages of her book, hiding behind the horses, finding the right pages, she began to softly mutter her chant.

Amir called out, "Who goes there?!"

"That should be my question to you. I am Garran from clan Or'gla, and we are hunting a group of bandits that have stolen property of mine. We believe they are in this town. It is in your best interest to tell us if you have seen any of them. I will warn you that they are deceitful and very dangerous," he replied in human.

"We are just a small band of travelers, moving through to pay our dues to Sa'bara. We are not here to hunt or cause problems to the avolarieans. Be sure to tell them that," Amir said, motioning over to Tetsunage.

Garran looked to him and said in orcish, "Do you understand human tongue?"

Tetsunage shook his head, saying in poor avian style orcish, "No."

"Karrun you translate," he ordered.

"Yes sir."

"They understand orc tongue. He will translate," he said and motioned to Karrun. "Now answer the question. Have you seen them?"

"No, unfortunately we have not. We've made camp here to shelter us from the storm. We planned to move on today."

Garran's eyes narrowed on the human, riding his horse a few steps closer to the edge of the drawbridge. The archers drew back on their bowstrings but not taking aim. "These are dangerous people. There is a wolf creature with them that's especially dangerous. They have killed and won't hesitate to kill again. If you value your lives, you will tell me."

"I have been truthful. What makes you think otherwise?" Amir asked.

Garran looked over to the archers. "For humans who have

nothing to hide, you are very protective."

"We don't like to be surrounded. We are from a simple village. We are only here to pay our Draksind to the great Sa'bara. And many times, we have suffered attacks from bandits trying to claim that payment for themselves."

Jesmine and the others listened to the conversation as she approached from the other side of the gate. Dran and Alderin tensed slightly while Jesmine continued her chant, dancing around the newest glyph as it glowed, drying the ground around it. Jesmine's tattoos glowed an orange red, approaching a spot several feet away from the gate's entrance.

"Is it possible to do it quieter?" Alderin whispered as Jesmine moved to the next spot without response.

Amir glanced in Jesmine's direction for a moment, Garran gripping his reins a bit tighter. "Then you will let us look around. These bandits are sly and dangerous, and they could be hiding here without you knowing."

"Unfortunately, I must decline. We've kept watch on the gate. The defenses of this castle have been more than adequate to keep out any random beast or roaming bandits of which you speak of."

"It's for your safety. Let us in," he said as his horse took another step closer, the archers taking aim. He stopped, eyeing them.

"I disagree. It's best if you leave. Once we are on our way you can look around all you want. We do not want to cause trouble."

Garran glared at Amir who stared back at him. "It will mean your death if you let them roam free," he said, turning around, the archers becoming more at ease. He approached Zed, asking in orcish, "And?"

"It's in there. Perhaps they have more connections than we thought, or they tricked them into defending them, but either way they are in there."

"Do you think you can take out the archers? The old man isn't going to be much of an obstacle into the castle."

"Smoke or poison?"

"Smoke. It's a faster cast."

"Penisiya has a wind wall ready to deflect the archers," Tetsunage said.

"Do you think the others are in position?" Garran asked.

"They should be by now."

While they talked, Amir watched them farther down the path with uneasiness. "Please leave!" he yelled.

"Don't tell us what to do," Garran grunted, keeping one eye on them, whispering in orcish to Zed, "How long till you are ready?"

Zed blinked twice to him, continuing his chant, his tusks glowing a light green.

"Charge when the smoke comes up," Garran said.

Karrun nodded and said, "With pleasure."

Amir took a few steps back. "We do not wish to fight!" he yelled.

"Neither do we," Garran said, Dran taking position closer to the gate, Jesmine finishing the final glyph, walking toward the back. She chanted, the runes glowing just as bright as her tattoos as the mud on her feet dried, cracked, and peeled off, while she kept focusing.

"Amir," whispered Erkin from on top of the wall.

"What is it?" he asked, not looking away from the orcs.

"I see a glow from one of the orcs."

"One of them is a caster," Dran said.

"Damn it. Fire!" Amir yelled, the archers unleashing a volley. The arrows whizzed through the air, Penisiya loudly speaking a command word, which sounded like an avian trill, her hand raising up, wind rushing upwards, the force of which caused even Amir's hair to be blown about. The wind howled, the wave of arrows deflecting upwards. The archers took aim and fired at Penisiya. Her claws moved and adjusted the wall, deflecting the second wave of arrows, the wall ending moments later just as Zed finished his cast.

He moved his hands before him, as thick, black, blinding smoke puffed into existence along the top of the first wall blocking the view of the archers just as they released a third volley. The arrows whizzed by as Karrun charged ahead with a loud battle cry.

Garran's horse led out a neigh of pain, an arrow piercing its eye, blood flowing from the wound. It kicked up, bucking him right from his horse, landing hard on the edge of the raised path that led to the drawbridge. He reached out only to grab mud, feet sliding across the slippery surface, tumbling down the side.

One of the other orcs rushed down to help while a second

charged in right behind Karrun. Amir was already sprinting away from the gate as the orc rushed in. He spoke out in orcish-arcana as the runes on his war hammer turned bright red, flames bursting around the head. He raised his weapon, readying to slam it into the back of Amir's skull when Dran swung his battle axe into the leg of Karrun's horse.

The horse's whine echoed between the two castle walls, tumbling to the ground almost taking Dran with it as Karrun was flung forward, barely missing Amir.

The dwarf yelled, charging the orc. Alderin stepped out from between the walls with his bow at the ready, firing his arrow at those charging in before falling back.

The arrow hit but was deflected off the horse's leather armor. Gnemi fired his first crossbow bolt at Karrun as he hit the ground, piercing his side.

Karrun's muscles tensed, grabbing his war hammer and pulled it up just in time to deflect Dran's attack. Fire burst from the hammer upon impact.

Dran winced at the heat of the flames licking at his face before Karrun jumped to his feet.

Jesmine moved past the fight, her arcane chanting steady like a swinging pendulum, rushing inside and up the stairs. Gnemi took aim at Karrun not even noticing Jesmine scurrying past behind him just as the mounted orc and two avolarieans crashed through the gate.

Alderin barely dodged out of the way of the orc's axe. Gnemi switched attention to the other orc, firing. The arrow whizzed past him, piercing into the horse's backside, neighing out in pain.

One of the avolarieans noticed Gnemi, notching their arrow, taking aim. Gnemi ducked down just in the nick of time as the arrow whizzed over his head, lodging itself in the wooden ceiling.

Histra watched the fight unfold. The second avolariean looked up, their eyes meeting. With her arrow nocked she fired at one of the guards on the wall. The arrow pierced his chest, gasping for air he dropped his bow, collapsing to the ground. A volley of arrows hailed from the back side of the castle, landing all around, a few just missing Ariana, who had no time to take cover, growling angrily.

"They're in the castle!" Amir yelled as Erkin and the other

archer turned and fired at the orc on horseback. The orc swung his heavy battleax at Alderin, the blade whistling through the air. The arrows struck the orc's back, his attack cutting a few hairs from the top of Alderin's head. He fell from his horse, hitting the ground with a thud, splashing mud everywhere.

"Got you!" yelled Alderin, brandishing his short sword, moving to finish him off but the heavily injured orc parried the blow. He glared at Alderin with weighty labored breaths.

Karrun yelled as he and Dran faced off, blades clashing, fire sparking from each hit.

Tetsunage with his bow notched and ready yelled to Zed, "Lower the smoke!" and without saying a word he lowered his hand, the thick black smoke flowing down the side of the wall. Tetsunage and the other avolarieans unleashed a volley of arrows, two of which hit the back of one guard at the gate. Coughing up blood, he stumbled off the wall and landed with a squelch face first into the mud.

Erkin cried out in pain as an arrow hit him in the back. He pulled himself up against the wall providing cover from those outside. With the archers at the front gate cleared, Orla and her fellow orcs, along with two more avolarieans, rushed in.

Histra watched the approaching second wave of orcs, hearing Jesmine's footsteps behind her. She pulled away from the window. "I am not a fan of being your cooler, but this is an exception."

Jesmine continued to chant, looking out to the gate, her tattoos glowing a bright orange-red, a faint smell of burnt wood emanating from where she stood. Her eyes focused, her chant growing louder, pulling hands behind her, the glyphs glowing brightly. Pillars of fire, ten feet taller than the wall shot up into the sky.

Histra stood her ground, feeling the hot air blow across her face like a soft desert wind, her wings twitching with a dull throb of pain. Jesmine's hands moves from behind to the front in a big circle. Following the movement of her hands, a giant wall of fire spread from the back glyph and out in both directions. With each new glyph the firewall hit, her hands jerked slightly as if hitting resistance. Within seconds, the massive wall of fire surrounded the castle, snug between the walls. Those on the battlements were taken back, ready to leap to safety but they were shocked to find no heat despite how close they were. One curiously reached out but recoiled when his hand got too close.

"Stop!" Orla yelled, halting her horse, which slid to a stop a few feet before the roaring flames. For those outside the wall, the battle ground to a halt. Garran looked up at the fire with a grunt, climbing back up. "Who's on the inside?"

"Karrun and Urka," remarked Zed, dropping his smoke spell.

Tetsunage looked to Penisiya. "Do you think you can break through it? We can't leave Shika and Amakasha by themselves," he said with concern.

"Working on it," she replied, flipping through the pages of her spellbook. Her black claws stopped at the desired spot, and she began to chant, eyes lighting up, along with the runic symbols on the page, followed by her jewelry.

Zed reached into a bag and pulled out his worn silver inlaid spellbook. He muttered a few words, the lock glowing and clicked open. "This is going to take some time," he muttered to himself, thumbing through the pages of his tome.

"Hurry," Garran stated, tightly holding the hilt of his sword, while those near the wall fell back.

"This should work," Zed replied, chanting, the runic symbols on the page glowing, eyes focused on the burning wall of fire, tusks glowing a brighter blue green with each word he uttered.

Dran and Karrun faced off, dodging and parrying each other's blows. The avolarieans moved to flank him and Alderin, forcing them to fall back closer to the keep out of line of sight of the those on the wall.

Erkin attempted to draw his bow but pain shot through his arm, blood trickling down his back, "Damn."

Urka relentlessly attacked Alderin, the avolariean Shika moving in from behind. With a loud trill she struck with a short sword. The blade slashed against his back; his leather armor took most of the blow but the avian's blade still tasted blood. He felt the force of the strike, causing him to fall back.

Gnemi fired off a third bolt which struck right through her neck at a steep angle. Shika let out a shrill of pain as blood stained her brown feathers. She gasped for air but found none, stumbling to the ground.

Urka continued his attack forcing Alderin to retreat, their blades clashing with a metallic clang. He stepped back, dodging another blow, tripping over the dying avolariean, landing hard on his back. Urka chuckled, raising his blade, their eyes meeting as a pit forms in Alderin's stomach, trying to raise his sword. His heart leaped out of his chest as he realized it was too late. There was nothing to stop the axe from cleaving into his skull.

Alderin saw his family, his wife, her long brunette hair, slightly weathered tanned skin, three children two boys, one daughter, ten, eight and seven respectively. They stood there holding each other, fearful. A loud metallic clang drew him back to reality. The axe deflected, a deep growl coming from the side.

Ariana stood over him, minor cuts on her arm and hand, the mithril cuffs not even scratched from the force of Urka's blow. Her lips curl, sharp teeth baring. He grits his teeth, staring into her feral eyes. She grabbed his wrist, claws digging into his skin, causing blood to drip down his arms. Ariana let out a long, drawn-out growl as the orc struggled against her.

"You bitch! You aren't escaping here!" Urka yelled, swinging with his free arm. Ariana countered, grasping it. His muscles tensed, fighting against her strength. Her muscles shifted underneath her fur.

"I could say the same to you… *weakling.*" she responded in orcish, rearing her head up and then clamped down onto his neck. Urka's scream of pain was muffled, struggling against her in vain. Blood poured down his neck. She clamped down harder and with a sickening crunch, snapped it in half, watching his body go limp. Ariana dropped the lifeless form to her feet as blood dripped from her still bared fangs.

Karrun's eyes burned with anger, tightening his grip on his war hammer. The flames licked around the weapon's head. With Ariana's back turned to him, he charged her. He made it no more than two steps before he felt the piercing pain of Dran's axe deeply lodged into his lower back. Pushing through the pain he lunged, swinging his hammer at the Lycan.

The heat of it singed some of her fur as she dodged. Dran sliced into Karrun's back once more, breaking through his leather armor with the second strike. Blood splattered across the axe while orc coughed up more before seeing Ariana lick crimson red fluids from her lips. His body burned with anger as he raised his hammer, before falling to the ground with a heavy thud, his strength all but gone. Mud splattered in all directions, the hammer sizzling as the fire snuffed out, the glow of the runes fading.

Amakasha's eyes darted around, taking stock of his current position. His brilliant feathers dirtied, ruffled, enemies moving in all around him. Fire roared, blocking his only escape. He looked to Shika's lifeless body, hands shaking, tightly gripping his bow, shoulders dropping along with his weapons. He held his hands in the air. "I surrender!" Amakasha chirped in his tongue.

Dran charged him, yelling at the top of his lungs before slowing to a stop.

"Capture him!" yelled Amir, checking on his fallen comrade. His head held low, muttering a few words, closing his companion's eyes.

Erkin grunted, climbing down the stairs. "Fine damn mess you got us into Amir," he said, glaring at the avian.

Outside the blazing firewall, Zed finished casting his spell, tusks glowing a bright blue green, the air in front of them shifting and changing. Zed formed a vacuum which was barely visible by the shimmer of arcane energy forming around its edges. With one hand motion he thrust it towards the roaring flames which only fluttered and weakened slightly.

Jesmine countered, hands gracefully moving, the glow of her tattoos brightening slightly before diming. The glyphs glowed brighter as the flickering of the flames became a roar, pushing back Zed's spell. Sweat poured down her body from the exertion to maintain concentration over her cast.

Histra moved closer, the heat brushing up against her scales. She gritted her teeth, wings twitching. "Thank me for this when you can."

Zed fought back against her, loudly chanting, keeping his focus, exerting himself into the spell. His tusks glowed, hands shaking, sweat dripping down his brow. He ended the invocation, heart pounding, heavy of breath. He looked to Garran, who stared at the wall of flames before looking away in shame.

Penisiya continued to prepare her spell for another half a minute, unleashing a gale force wind, which she elegantly guided towards the gate. The stone shifted and cracked, focusing all the energy of the spell toward the opening.

Garran stepped back, flames flickering, beginning to part. Dran and Alderin were thrust up against the keep, the heat of the wind curling some of their hair, Shika's lifeless body tossed like a rag doll. Ariana leapt back, fur blowing wildly.

The orc grinned, about to speak as Jesmine fought back, cutting through Penisiya's spell, forcing it to end prematurely. The wind flew back into her face, feathers blowing wildly, flying off her feet. Tetsunage rushed to catch her, knocking him off his feet, landing hard on his back, the air knocked from his lungs.

Garran braced himself against the wind, sliding back half a foot, eyes locked at the path closing before him. His hands clenched into fists. "What do you suggest now, Zed?"

"For her to be this responsive and powerful, she must be watching the spell. If we can break her line of sight or her concentration we can break through," he explained.

Tetsunage gasped for air, helping Penisiya back to her feet, just managing to say, "Are you okay?"

"I'll be fine. I was caught off guard but, how are you?" she asked.

"Yeah. No broken bones," he replied, brushing the mud from his feathers.

Penisiya looked to the fire, "Whoever she is, she is even more powerful than I thought."

"Where do you think she could be?"

"She has to keep a view on the spell's location. Most likely someplace elevated, like the keep."

Tetsunage nodded, backing away.

Garran raised an eye ridge, yelling, "What are you doing?"

"Getting a shot!" he yelled. He backed far enough away, looking over the flames, locating Jesmine, her tattoos lighting her up against the grey stone backdrop. His hawkish vision focused on her as he nocked an arrow, gauging the distance as he began lining it up. "Penisiya, I need you," he chirped. She rushed over to him, and he pointed out where Jesmine stood, taking aim. "You know what to do."

"Of course, thirty seconds, count it down," she replied, beginning her chant. The sound of songbirds escaped her beak while Tetsunage counted down. He looked down the shaft of the arrow, carefully adjusting his aim.

Garran watched curiously, splitting his attention between Zed, the wall, and them.

Penisiya's jewelry glowed a brighter and brighter blue, casting her spell as Tetsunage said, "Zero." He released the arrow. She finished her spell, jewelry giving out one last burst of light, wind swirling around the arrow, tripling its speed, over the flames, threading the needle of the window.

Jesmine's body jerked, eyes going wide as a burning pain seared into her chest. Her hands quickly made a single motion. The glow of the tattoos faded completely, fire jutting out straight from the wound in her chest with such force, the blast destroyed a section of the window.

Stones flew out over the field as the wall of fire burned even hotter. The clothes of those still on the wall burst into flames. They screamed, jumping off the wall, dropping and rolling in the mud. One landed hard on their leg, breaking it. The whitewash on the stone walls blackened and peeled away.

Histra was forced back, raising her claws to shield her face, eyes squinting, cold aura non-existent. The heat faded a moment later as she approached Jesmine, who was on the ground, blood staining her clothes, the shaft of the arrow burned and blackened, the arrow's feathers completely disintegrated. Blood escaped the elf's lips, gasping for air.

Amir looked up at the display in astonishment. "A spell rebound," he muttered, rushing into the keep.

"Jesmine!" Alderin yelled, rushing in behind him.

"This can't be good," Dran remarked, following.

Ariana flinched for a moment ready to follow but stopped, looking over to the tied and bound avolariean, arms wrapped around a horse stall.

On the other side of the wall, Zed took several steps back as the fire burned out of control, the heat beating against his face. Garran yelled, "What happened?!"

"Spell rebound," he answered.

"If it's a spell rebound, why is the firewall going crazy?!" he asked, backing up.

"She must have somehow transferred the energy of the spell rebound into the spell itself. I'm not even sure how that's possible."

Tetsunage looked over to Penisiya, slack jawed. "Spell

rebound?"

"I don't know… If it is, we have to wait till the spell expends its energy."

"How long will that take?"

"I wish I knew," she replied.

Jesmine with labored wheezing breaths, barely moved as blood oozed out of her wound. Despite the burns on her clothes, her skin was untouched. Histra stood over her, staring down. The elf's skin grew paler, feeling her ice aura wash over her. *"Something about this… feels familiar,"* Histra thought.

Amir almost tripped over the last step, rushing into the room. "No, no, no," he said, moving over to Jesmine. He reached down to look at the wound, arm bumping into the arrow shaft which disintegrated into ash.

"Jesmine!" yelled Alderin, reaching the room, stopping, hands shaking. "Amir, you can heal her, right?" he asked, swallowing a lump in his throat. Dran and Gnemi come up seconds later, Gnemi gasping.

"What happened?" he noticed her lying on the floor, eyes going wide, "Jesmine?!" he yelled.

Dran remained silent, lowering his axe.

Jesmine's body twitched, feeling the blood pounding through her. Desperate eyes moved to those that had gathered. "I—I," she tried to speak.

Alderin moved beside her and held her hand. "Don't say anything. Amir, you can heal her, right?" he asked, looking at him with pleading eyes.

"I can try, but I never healed an elf before, nor have I healed a wound this serious. I should remove the arrowhead but there's no time," he said, examining the wound once more. "Stay back," he pleaded as everyone, but Histra took a few steps back. He began chanting as the faintest glow started on the head of his staff. Histra grabbed it, stopping the spell in its infancy.

"No," Histra stated with a glare.

He gave her a dagger-eyed stare. "How da—"

The others moved in to stop Histra when she interrupted. "If you do it. She'll die," she said, forcing his staff away. "I'll do it."

"You?" everyone in the room exclaimed as she moved over Jesmine.

"Amir was right, these aren't for show." She pointed to her horns.

"You're a kobold. You don't have any blessing of the Gods to perform healing magic."

"One doesn't need the Gods to heal," she remarked, beginning to chant in draconic-arcana, her one intact horn glowing with a soft white, running her claws over Jesmine's wound, which she pried open wider with her claw tips. Jesmine weakly moaned, feeling her flesh spread and torn, Histra's cold aura slowing the flow of blood. She chanted over the elf's weakening groans, opening the wound even wider, claws digging into her. Gnemi looked away, covering his mouth, while everyone else silently watched.

"She can't be a healer, can she?" muttered Dran.

"I-I don't know," Alderin replied, clenching his fists.

Histra's claws slid into Jesmine's pinkish flesh. The elf gritted her teeth, tensing, heart pounding harder. Dran and Amir prayed to their respective Gods. Histra dug for the arrowhead, finally grasping it within the first minute.

Jesmine's toes curled, hands tightly gripping her cloak which steadily weakened as it became harder for her to discern if the cold, she felt was from Histra or death knocking. With a soft squelch Histra pulled out the arrowhead, tossing it to the side with her elegant hand motions.

"Thank Toval," said Amir.

"Blessed be the Earth Mother," said Dran, shoulders dropping.

Alderin remained tensed.

Now both of Histra's hands danced over the wound. Her claws clearing the frozen blood away, before cutting into Jesmine's skin, crafting sigils around the wound, which glowed upon the moment of their completion. Her wings fluttered and shifted in calculated motions, undamaged horn glowing brighter, the pink from Jesmine's face fading.

Jesmine's eyelids grew heavy, her vision blurry. Body grew cold and numb. The world around her slowed to a near standstill.

Histra placed her claws on the open wound as Jesmine's breath slowed, becoming nearly nonexistent, runic tattoos glowing white. The kobold's incantation grew louder and more complex the wound sealing up as if time itself was reversing to undo the damage.

Suddenly, Jesmine took a deep breath, eyes opening wide while a numbing pain shot through her chest. Histra stumbled back, panting heavily, claws twitching as the glow of her horn faded and Alderin rushed over to Jesmine.

Amir stood there in disbelief for a moment.

Gnemi's peered over his shoulder, eyes lightning up.

Dran held his head low, hand to his chest, "I would have never thought in a dragon's lifetime…"

"Jesmine! Are you okay?" Amir asked, crouching beside her, moving to lift her head but stopped just before touching her.

Jesmine coughed, pushing herself off to the side, spitting up some blood before another deep aching breath. "Yes. I think," she said, Alderin gently helping her sit up.

Amir looked to Histra. "How?"

"I felt that I've worked on elves before," she replied, shooting him a glare. "And, though similar, they are different from humans. I couldn't risk you trying."

"I have no experience with elves. I haven't seen one in almost thirty years."

"That is how I knew you'd do it wrong," she replied.

"Histra?" Jesmine said softly, slowly pushing up to her feet, her body shaking stumbling back into Alderin's supportive arms.

"Yes?" she asked.

She attempted again to push herself to her feet. "Thank you."

"You saved my life. We're even," she huffed, looking at the others. The sound of the roaring flames mixed with that of breaking stone. A small section of the outer wall collapsed, falling down the hill.

"We need to get that fire back under control," said Amir, glancing out the window, the raging flames blocking the view of the town. Smoke billowed up; the drawbridge burst into flames.

"I don't have the strength to do it. We need to get out of here," Jesmine replied in a soft wispy voice, her breaths short, leaning on Alderin.

"We better hurry then," said Dran, heading downstairs.

"Right," Gnemi replied, following.

Alderin and Amir helped ease Jesmine downstairs.

Histra stood off to the side, letting them take lead. Once they were out of the room, she approached the stairwell hearing footsteps overhead. "It'll be good to leave this place," she remarked.

In front of the keep everyone gathered. Erkin, the arrow still in his shoulder approached Amir. "What do we do now?"

"She can no longer control the spell. We must escape through the secret passage," he explained.

Jesmine held her head low, "I'm sorry everyone."

"Don't talk," urged Alderin.

Erkin sighed, tensing trying to keep his one shoulder still. "Do we even know where the passage is?"

Jesmine softly replied. "It's in the back of the keep."

"Which none of us have found in all our time staying here," he replied.

"I already found it," said Ariana, dragging Amakasha toward the others, his wrists and ankles bound together and also now gagged and blindfolded. "I don't know what languages he speaks but I told him it would be best not to follow us."

"Not that it would do us any good," said Erkin, glaring at Amir. "We would have been fine, and our friends would still be alive, had he not felt an obligation to help the elves like your father did."

Amir tensed. "That's enough. We'll escape through the hidden exit. I'll take full responsibility for what happened, but now is not the time to discuss it."

Jesmine looked at the bodies of the fallen in front of the keep and the two slightly burned humans, one leaning on a friend as he held one leg off the ground.

The mud along the walls had already dried and cracked, nearby brush catching fire, releasing black smoke into the sky. Jesmine lowered her head. "I am sorry for the trouble I have caused all of you. If I was only fast enough, I could have stopped the attack and prevented their deaths."

"You did all you could. No one is blaming you," assured Amir.

"Come, I'll show you," said Ariana, guiding them to behind the keep.

Before Dran followed, he looked over to Karrun, his war hammer still clenched in his hand. With a little bit of effort, he liberated it from his grip. "You fought well but you won't be needing this anymore," he remarked, giving the hammer a few test swings before holstering it.

"Where is it?" asked Erkin, looking at the empty muddied ground.

Ariana stared at him, digging her claws into the mud. "Right here," she said, pulling out thick rusted chains. "I'll need help," she stated.

Amir looked at his burned comrade. "Are you able to hold Jesmine yourself? They need my help." asked Amir.

"Go right ahead," Alderin replied, adjusting his grip.

Amir began casting a healing spell on his companion while everyone else who is able bodied grabbed the thick muddied chains, rising it up out of the muck.

Jesmine weakly said. "Pull toward the wall."

"What if its arcane sealed?" asked Erkin.

"It's not. The family was noble but not that wealthy and powerful to afford an arcane sealed escape route."

"And how do you know of this again?" he asked with a distrustful look.

"I used it once many years ago," she explained as the chains were pulled taut.

Dran cleared his throat. "On three. One... two... three!" he yelled, the sound of stone grinding on stone rang out. Their feet sunk into the muck as inch by inch, the mud-covered stone door slid back into a secret compartment in the ground. Mire slid off the top of the stone onto the grimy fungus covered steps. Insects scurry away as light shone on them.

"And here we have our escape," said Dran, cracking his neck, flicking the mud off his hands.

"What about the horses?" asked Alderin.

Jesmine looked to him. "It's big enough to guide them through in a line."

"No more cart then, but at least we won't leave Gnaria behind." said Gnemi.

"I was about to say the same for Cetas," said Alderin. He looked to one in Amir's group, "Mind holding her for a moment?"

With the briefest hint of hesitation, he relented, "Sure," moving to take her.

"Sorry," she replied.

"It's alright. You did save us," he replied as Dran, Alderin and

Gnemi rushed over to the stables, which began to smoke, the wood darkening. The horses neighed and nickered, tugging against their reins. Others in Amir's group rushed to help as sections of the stalls burst into flames, grabbing supplies from their cart in the process.

"Easy Cetas, we'll get you out of here," Alderin said, rubbing his side, calming him.

"Come Dariel, a little fire never hurt you before," said Dran.

"Careful with Gnaria," said Gnemi, trying to help in vain.

"I'll lead," said Ariana, stepping down the stairs as Amir finished casting his spell.

"That should help, I'll do more later," he said.

"Thank you," she replied, heading down the steps, followed by the other injured.

Amir turned to Jesmine. "You should get going too."

"I will once everyone else gets in," she replied.

"You can barely stand. I recommend you go now," Amir insisted as the horses were brought to the hole.

Gnaria bucked back a little, reaching the edge. Gnemi stepped in front of her, grabbing the reins, reaching up to rub her head, which she lowered. "Don't worry Gnaria. Just follow me. One step at a time," he said, slowly easing her down, the other horses following. Amir and the rest of the party stood by the escape route. Alderin returning to support Jesmine.

Dran looked at her. "The horses are in, hopefully they won't be too spooked. I know Dariel will be fine, but the others may not be used to being underground."

"We have torches," Amir assured him.

Alderin, looked to the flames and then the dark dank hole. "Let's get going."

"Wait," said Jesmine.

They look at her curiously. "What are you waiting for?" asked Dran.

She motioned with her head toward Histra who stood halfway between them and the stables, her back turned to them, staring at the wagon with the bolted cage. "Histra? We are going," she called out.

"Damn kobold! Get your scaly hide over here. Unless you want to stay here as a last-ditch defense. But I don't think that's your style," Dran called out.

Histra looked over her shoulder. "Do me a favor," she said sternly, eyes revealing a hint of turmoil.

"A favor? What favor could that be at a time like this? Cook a hot meal?" he laughed heartily.

Histra tensed. "Please," she said, Dran's laugh abruptly ending.

Alderin furls his brow, adjusting his hold on Jesmine. "What could you want now? Can it wait till we aren't in mortal danger?"

"Push the cart into the fire. I want it to burn," she stated firmly, looking back at it.

"Burn the cart? What for?" he asked.

Jesmine spoke up. "That's the cage she was locked in for the last decade."

Dran turned to her. "Of course. We had to bring it along with us because... oh," he said, sighing, walking to the wagon. "Alderin?"

"Of course," he looked to Amri, "Amir?" asked Alderin.

"I got her," he replied as Dran and Alderin ran past Histra.

She folded her wings behind her, silently watching the muddy wheels turn, the wagon wobbling the several feet needed to be pushed into the burning stalls. Within moments the wood blackened, bursting into flames. Fire engulfed it, the repaired wheel breaking first. As the metal cage collapsed into the back, a smile crept onto the kobold's face.

"Histra, we need to go," said Jesmine as loud as she could.

She let out a huff, her wings fluttering slightly, walking over to the hole and down the steps along with the others. As they headed down Jesmine slipped on one of the wet stones but Amir and Alderin quickly saved her.

"Careful," Alderin cautioned.

"Sorry, I know I have been a burden," Jesmine replied, keeping her head low.

"I don't think anyone here considers you that," he replied, reaching the bottom, greeted by a long dark tunnel. Water dripped through the stonework. A glimmer of light visible up ahead, voices echoing down the tunnel.

"I apologize for the anger of those in my care," said Amir passing through an unlocked rusted metal gate, the moss forming a small bridge from the gate to the stone wall.

"You don't need to apologize. It's because of us you were dragged into this and lost two of your people."

"It's a decision that I must live with."

"The only one you should be apologizing to, is me," remarked Histra, following behind them.

"I see you were not exaggerating on her personality," he remarked.

"I heard what you all said about me."

"When you barged in last night, I figured you did," remarked Alderin.

Amir looked toward the kobold, the light of the torches in the distance reflecting in her blue eyes to give an otherworldly glow similar to Dran's and to a lesser degree Jesmine's. "Your kind has not been on the best of terms with my village, especially me."

"I get that excuse a lot," she remarked as they continued to walk. Their footsteps splashed as a small stream of water flowed down the tunnel.

"It's well earned," said Amir.

"Not by me," she remarked.

"If you cooperated more, it could help," Alderin suggested.

"I have been," she replied.

"Cooperative, perhaps, but your attitude shows anything but that." Dran replied.

"Amir. Thank you again for your help," said Jesmine.

"It's nothing…" he trailed off for a moment, looking away before continuing. "Erkin, though his words were harsh, they were also true. When I saw an elf after thirty long years, I couldn't help but feel the need to help. Perhaps it's to cover my past mistakes."

"Mistakes?" she asked.

"When Sa'bara began his extermination, elves sought refuge in our village. My father, along with several other skillful mages, helped ferry elves across the grand river, avoiding Rivera, which was under siege at the time. Despite my ability to help, I was fearful of what Sa'bara would do if he found out what was happening. Which turned out to be one of the worst decisions of my life."

"And where does hating me come into play in your 'I am sorry I did nothing' story?" asked Histra.

"Histra!" remarked Jesmine, coughing and wincing in pain.

"What? There has to be a connection."

"Oh, I am getting to it right now, don't you worry. One of the elves that took refuge in my father's home was actually a *kobold* in disguise. I should have known when they tried to ask me questions, but I shooed him away, telling him that I had no part in this. When I awoke the next day, I saw my father, mother and four others I knew with their heads on pikes along with the bodies of a dozen elves laid across the ground. If I had not been so concerned about myself, I could have noticed what was wrong and saved them."

"I'm so sorry Amir," said Jesmine.

"It's not your fault. But that was the last time I saw any elves until yesterday, and when Alderin here was about to accidentally poison himself, I felt as if Toval was giving me a second chance to redeem myself. Then, when you said you were going home to pay final respects to your family, I was sure of it."

Jesmine nodded. "Either way, I thank you."

The tunnel continued, the incline slightly lessened, the water becoming a few inches deep. They passed another two gates before Alderin spoke up. "Amir. Do you think this water is also poisoned?"

"Possibly. It is best not to try, though," he replied as almost an hour passed before everyone came to a stop, the others catching up. Ariana calls out. "I need some strong able-bodied people up here. This cover is heavy."

"I'll go, I can see better than you in these dim conditions," Dran replied, wiggling past the horses. Moving through others, "Pardon. Pardon," he said, the water here a foot deep before a set of steps led up toward the stone covered exit.

"This better not be a dead end," said Erkin, holding a lit torch up for light.

"Jesmine said she came through here, so there has to be an exit," said Dran.

"I can smell the outside on the other side. Now help me push!" Ariana yelled.

"Don't need to yell. I am right here," he remarked as they push against the cold stone wall. One attempt, two, three, nothing. "Perhaps it's locked?" Dran asked.

"I checked. There doesn't appear any locking mechanism."

"Did you not notice how many gates there were?"

"Yes, and they were all unlocked."

"That doesn't mean this one was left unlocked. Everyone look around. Perhaps there is something keeping the door in place," Dran called out. The horses in the middle of the group whined uneasily in the confined space and after five minutes of searching one person yelled.

"I found something." She brushed past some moss as a built-in optical illusion into the wall revealed a small alcove big enough for someone to put their arm in, and when she did, she found a heavy chain.

"Good, check to see if there is any more," said Dran, smirking at Ariana, who let out a huff.

"I'll help unlock it," said Ariana, slipping over, helping pull the chain. Metal grinded against stone as a low vibration coursed through the tunnel. The chain slowly pulled back a full foot before stopping with a thud. The process was repeated a second time when a second alcove was found on the opposite side of the wall. Once pulled, the wall shifted, dust and pebbles fell to the ground, bouncing down the steps, splashing into the water with a soft echo. She moved back to the front.

Dran rubbed his beard triumphantly. "Told you."

"Don't rub it in," she replied, pushing against the door. Roots were torn up as the door moved. Tree branches broke, lumps of dirt falling into the tunnel, fresh air rushing in. They pushed the door down, landing with a heavy thud, crushing the brush on the other side. They winced at the sunlight, sighing in relief, everyone exiting.

"Good girl," said Gnemi to Gnaria, rubbing her sides, taking her off to the side to eat some nearby grass.

"Is the fire still burning?" Amir asked, trying to peer over the small mound of earth that hid the door.

"I highly doubt that," Erkin remarked. "A spell burning off that much energy wouldn't last long. I'm relieved we didn't hear orcs marching down the tunnel after us."

Dran looked out in the direction of the castle. "Aye. I think so too. It's best to keep going."

"I would love to take a moment to heal those who need it, but Dran is right. We should move on," said Amir.

"If you need to heal, we have a moment," said Jesmine gently letting go of Alderin, taking a few steps on her own. Alderin moved to help but she held her hand up. "I'm okay. I've had some time to recover."

"How much of a moment?" asked Amir.

"A spell of that power, with the level of energy I was expending, in that small of an area, along with the energy of the rebound I managed to transfer into the glyphs preventing myself from bursting into flames? I think it should last about three to six more hours," Jesmine explained.

"Did you say three to six hours?!" asked Alderin in shock.

"Yeah."

"There is no way. How?" asked Dran, eyes wide in disbelief.

"I exerted a lot of force to keep a tight control on the fire. Therefore, there was more energy behind the spell than normal."

"She's probably lying," remarked Erkin, climbing on top of the small mound of earth, pushing through fallen branches, looking in the general direction of the castle, but was unable to see anything.

"I have no reason to lie."

"It would be best if we took a moment to rest. Histra?" asked Amir, looking over to her.

"Yes?"

"Are you adept in human healing?"

She thought a moment, looking at him with apprehension before answering. "Why?"

"Would you be able to heal his leg? While I attend to some other wounds?"

"I don't know…" she remarked, looking at them all. "But I will look. It will be amusing to have one of them owe me a favor," she chuckled, stepping over to the burned human, who's currently leaning against a tree for support. Half the hair on his right side is burned away down to his skin, with second degree burns visible along his arm.

He eyed her approach. "A kobold to heal me?" he questioned.

"Remove his pants so I can take a look," she stated, looking at the person sitting beside him.

"What? You aren't going to remove my pants!" he remarked, staring down at her.

"I'm not. She is," she motioned to the woman.

Amir spoke up, going over to check on Erkin's wound. "The

kobold knows how to heal. Surprising, yes, but she healed Jesmine from a mortal arrow wound to the chest. If she can do that, she could heal your leg better than I can."

He stared at the kobold, who stared back with a sly grin. "Time is of the essence if we want to get out of here before the orcs show up."

The injured man sighed. "Fine, but don't try anything funny. I don't want to see my leg covered in kobold scales or something," he answered.

"It doesn't work that way," Histra replied.

He grunted, wincing in pain, while his companion slowly removed his pants. Histra ran her claws along his leg, feeling the bone. The human tensed and twitched. "Your claws are cold."

"Of course, they are." She shook her head, mumbling to herself, finding the broken bone. She closed her eyes for a moment in thought. "We first need to pop it back into place. Push hard here and quick," she said to the woman.

"Wait, what?" asked the injured human.

"You may want to bite onto something," Histra remarked as the woman looked over to Amir, who was busily working to cut out the arrowhead from Erkin's back who silently took the treatment.

"You better know what you are doing," she said, pushing hard on the bone, and with soft crunch the injured man cried out in pain, gaining the attention of everyone nearby.

"Damn, that hurt!" he yelled as Histra began to cast a spell, her intact horn glowing once again. Over the next four minutes, she cut into the human's skin crafting her sigils. The human gritted his teeth watching with concern.

Her horn's glow faded, taking a few steps back, looking over her work. "Feel better?" she asked.

He slowly moved his leg, wincing, expecting to feel a shooting pain yet was only greeted by a mild, but manageable throbbing ache. "Yeah, much better," he said. He stood up, leg collapsing underneath him, falling to the ground.

"It will be weak for a few hours, so you should stay off of it, and you won't be able to run for a few days. I think," replied Histra, with a smirk.

"You could have started off with that," he remarked.

"You could have thanked me," she replied, walking off.

Jesmine watched her, saying, "You don't make friends treating people like that."

"I'm not here to make friends with people, who I will hopefully never see again," she replied.

"Not doing a great job with those whom you will be seeing in the upcoming days and weeks either," Both Alderin and Dran unknowingly thought together.

"About that," Amir said, approaching Jesmine. "We'll all be heading out soon. Perhaps it will be wise to split up, so we'll be harder to follow. But once you visit your home, if you need a shortcut through the great Sa'bara river, come to our town of Sabra. It's to the south of Du'ralia Forest. But I must warn you to be careful. Du'ralia Forest is dangerous and filled with massive beasts. If you take the path that's to the eastern side of the forest, you will pass by most of the dangers without an issue."

Jesmine nodded. "Thank you, and we will take that into consideration. Du'ralia Forest is actually our destination."

Dran and Alderin looked at her and she returned the gaze. "After all that has happened, I think they are trustworthy enough to mention where we are going."

Amir gripped his staff. "Did you say that Du'ralia is your destination?"

"Yes, because my home was there."

"There were three elven villages in that forest. Which one do you come from?"

"Ami'ralia."

Amir's shoulders dropped. "You shouldn't go there."

"I'm afraid I must."

"Ami'ralia is no place for the living."

"I know of the stories."

He shook his head. "Stories? No. The land around the town refuses to grow, since that tragic day. People have tried to raid the town, but few have returned, and those who have, spoke of vengeful spirits."

"I know a bit about spirits. My father was a spiritualist."

"Then you know of the possible dangers you will face."

She weakly clenched her hands, swallowing a lump in her throat. "Yes, but I must go."

Amir took a deep breath. "If you must, don't stay long, say your final goodbyes, and go. I'd hate to see you fall to the same fate as others."

"I would prefer not to, but it's my home."

He nodded, putting a hand on her shoulder. "I can't stop you. But be careful."

Ariana ears folded back, her tail quickly wagging, taking slow, deep breaths. *"Soon. They'll know how I feel, after all these years, I will be able to tell them,"* she thought.

Jesmine smiled. "I will, and I thank you. I have friends who will give me support and the last thing I want to do is to put them in danger."

Alderin cleared his throat. "We've heard about it but here we are. We will do our best to make sure we get in and out of the town. We don't intend on dying there."

"People rarely intend to die anywhere except in their beds, but often that doesn't happen," said Amir.

"Aye, that's the Gods' spoken truth," remarked Dran.

"Thank you again, Amir, for your help. Thank you everyone for your sacrifice. I won't forget this as long as I live," she said, lowering her head. "Thank you so much," she continued as those with Amir gave mixed reactions. As they mounted up on horseback, Alderin helped her on.

Gnemi rubbed the side of Gnaria's mane. "No more cart pulling for you, girl. I bet you are glad to know that," he chuckled, Gnaria letting out a soft huff of air.

"Histra, will you ride with me?" asked Jesmine, pulling the horse beside her.

She looked up at her. "For a while, but you know what will happen."

"I know, but let's get some distance before worrying about switching," she said looking to Alderin. "Mind helping her up too?"

Alderin replied, "Sure," he reaches down.

Histra furled her wings, remarking. "Tell no one of this."

"I won't," he replied, hoisting her up onto the horse, which nickered when she was placed on its back.

"You won't mind if I ride with you, Gnemi? You're the lightest and put the least strain on the horse," said Ariana, leaning against

Gnaria, causing her to softly whine.

"Sure. Gnaria can handle it, isn't that right girl" Gnemi replied, patting her on the side. Ariana mounted in one quick motion as the horse shifted with slight unease. "See, no problem."

They gave one final farewell, riding off through the forest. Amir's group left a little while later taking a different direction.

Meanwhile, hours passed while Garran angrily paced, fists clenched, grumbling to himself. They waited impatiently, some staring at the castle others lying low, ready to rise up at a moment's notice. Sections of the wall cracked and crumbled, the bridge leading to the castle burnt to a crisp, a section of the first gate tower collapsed in upon itself. Each passing moment Garran's anger grew, raging like the fires before him.

He cursed and screamed as Zed and Penisiya tried again and again to break through the firewall. Suddenly the fire receded, retreating towards each glyph. The pillars of flame poofed out of existence as if someone was blowing out candles on a birthday cake, leaving the blackened and burned area in its wake. Everyone jumped into action, a pair of orcs pulling out a hastily made temporary bridge to cross the gap to the gate.

Zed casted a spell, black smoke covering the front of the castle, blocking the view from either side, Penisiya continuing her chant, keeping a spell at the ready. Garran yelled in orcish, "Charge the front gate. Tetsunage remind your people not to touch the stone, it'll be hot."

Tetsunage remarked "We know." They rushed into the castle under the cover of the smoke, Zed guiding the smoke screen along. They charged in ready for battle only to be greeted by bodies of those who had fallen, and one bounded but alive avolariea laying against the keep.

Garran, ready for action, tensed, laying eyes upon his friends. He grits his teeth, hands tightly clenched on his weapon, approaching them, alert for any movement. "Your deaths won't be in vain," he grunted as Tetsunage unbound his friend. Zed cleared the smoke as it became obvious the castle had been abandoned.

"The bird says they left hours ago," Zed translated.

Orla yelled "Garran! There is a tunnel back here!"

"They escaped…." Garran remarked, taking a deep breath, releasing a massive roar of anger looking up into the midday sky.

Shana approached him. "They fought well. There is no way we could have known she'd create a firewall around the entire castle like that." she replied. Garran continued to yell, suddenly stopping. He blinked, looking up to see movement on the very top of the keep.

"There is one still here," he grunted, charging in.

Shana looked at him perplexed. She looked up, seeing the rubble on top before rushing in after him. Garran licked his lips in anticipation, his footsteps heavy on the stairwell, getting to the third floor before stopping.

"No… no!" he yelled in frustration, causing Shana to run up after him.

"Garran what is it?" she asked, reaching him.

"I saw someone. Up on the top floor… but the stairwell is broken." he grunted.

"I didn't see anyone, but if whoever is up there, they aren't getting down. Let them starve. Right now, we have to bury the dead and continue the hunt."

Garran took a long, slow deep breath, closing his eyes, letting out a guttural grunt, "Yes… Yes, we do."

Chapter 16 Almost There

Only a few hours passed since the firewall spell ended. Garran and his fellow orcs stood just outside of the town, the two fallen orcs still in their armor, weapons to their sides. They laid upon a pillar of wood made up of mostly broken furniture from the town.

Garran's thick fingers tightly gripped a lit torch, the fire flickering in the wind as he stood by Karrun's pyre, "You have fought bravely in many battles. May your ashes reach Garthund and that he finds you worthy," he said, putting flame to the pyre, setting it ablaze before turning to Urka and repeating the process. The fires engulfed the two, smoke billowing up, the smell of burning flesh filling the air. Garran took a moment standing there, watching his friends burn before turning, walking over to the others. "Those birds better be done with their ritual. We've given them too much of a head start already."

Shana let out a grunt. "We traveled all night to get here. We attacked while exhausted. We should have waited."

Garran growled, "There was no way to know they had reinforcements. I did what I thought was best. Their deaths are on me, but we can't stop and let all be for nothing," he stated.

Shana glared at Garran. "We will not. We will rest and then come back twice as strong, kill those who get in the way, and capture those we need so we can get Sa'bara's favor for our clan."

"We will, but we must press on. We'll rest come nightfall but not before," he stated, looking at the others. "Do I make myself clear?"

"Yes sir," they replied.

"Remember this is not for ourselves but for them. They who made the ultimate sacrifice so that we may benefit from their efforts," he stated, pointing to the burning fires. "Let's check on those overgrown chickens," he grunted, heading to the avolarieans, who are over a mile away from the town and the smoking castle.

The avolarieans gathered around their fallen comrade, the grass around him cut and laid underneath like a bed, stones of random sizes and shapes circling the body. Underneath the stones were Shika's feathers. From the neck down she was completely defeathered, revealing her soft pinkish skin.

They sung like the birds in the trees. A sweet song about life, and death, Penisiya led the chorus, her runic jewelry glowing, blocking the wind around them, providing a perfect stillness in the air. Tetsunage knelt beside the body, a curved bird of prey claw shaped weapon in his hand. The steel weapon had silver runes inlaid into the blade. With his free hand, he ran his claws along the body.

"May the birds return you to the sky, to which you belong, Shika my friend," he said, tightly gripping the hilt of the blade, softly muttering in arcana, the runes glowing a soft white blue. He swung the blade with a high-pitched whistle, wind engulfing it, slicing through her body with unnatural ease.

The blood already drained, and none touched the knife-edge. He symmetrically carved up Shika into small pieces while the rest continue to sing through the process until only the head remained, which was placed at the base of the biggest rock of the circle, head facing out to the carved body. Tetsunage ran his hands over the head, opening the eyes as his chanting ended. The blade's spell ended, saying, "May you watch over us from above and grant us strength to carry on."

Penisiya ended her chant, slightly out of breath. Garran and his orcs approached. He yelled, "Are you done?"

Tetsunage stood up, shooting him a fierce look. "Almost."

Garran heard Zed's translation. "What could take you so long? We suffered more than you," he stated, glaring at Amakasha, who's claws twitched in anger, feathers fluffing out.

"Time and effort are given equally to each fallen," stated Tetsunage.

"Time? How much time is needed to…what in Garthund's broken tusk…" he trailed off, looking at the carved up avolariean corpse.

"What is what?" he asked.

"That!" Garran exclaimed, pointing to the body.

"What of it?" Tetsunage asked, tilting his head to the side.

"That's just despicable," he remarked.

"We are giving ourselves back to the sky," he replied.

Zed further explained. "They carve up the dead so it may be easier for the birds to consume."

Garran let out a grunt, "If they are so eager to return to the sky, maybe they shouldn't surrender so easily," he snorted.

Tetsunage let out a sharp trill. "We are here to help you. You asked for our help. We are risking our lives."

Zed translated, "They don't like what you said."

"I bet they don't. We are risking our lives, and I need to know we can count on you when the fighting happens. You will be compensated for your losses."

"Compensation or not, you had better watch your tongue next time when insulting our traditions for honoring the dead..." the avolariean said, a sharp shrill sound escaping his beak as his eyes narrowed threateningly. "I for one find the burning of the bodies of your comrades to be a dreadful wasteful act and reflects on the brutish, thick-headed nature of your kind. To me, there is no admiration in a pointless display such as that, but you do not see me coming over and mocking you for it, now do you?"

Zed hesitated for a moment upon hearing that before slowly repeating it in full, and he was not surprised at all to see Garran's eyes go wide, gripping his axe and pounding over to the bird.

"What?! How dare you THINK that you can even begin-"

"Perhaps it is YOU who should be thinking, orc! You are angry because of the loss of your friends, and so are we, but that does not give you the right to mock us, the ones who agreed to help you on this hunt."

Tetsunage stepped up to him, the avolariean having a good foot in height over the orc but had nowhere near the muscle and body mass. Garran let out a grunt, staring up at him, hands gripping the axe so tightly his knuckles started to drain of blood. "We are brave but not stupid. We will fight, but I will tell you now. If given the choice between bringing honor to myself or saving the lives of my people, their lives will come first. There is no honor in sacrificing others for personal gain," he chirped.

Zed translated, "He will fight. But not to what he would consider a pointless death."

"This is more valuable than you can imagine. And Sa'bara will reward all of us greatly. Prepare to move; we've lost much time. We'll rest when the sun sets. We have to get to them before they reach their destination."

Tetsunage's eyes narrowed, "And where is that?"

"Du'ralia Forest."

His eyes widened slightly, feathers rising, holding his tongue.

"Now you know why we must hurry. I prefer not to fight them there, and if you find that ruin a cursed place, perhaps knowing where they are going will motivate you to go faster," he stated, leaning in closer. "Do what you need to do, then we leave. You do not want your friend's death to be in vain any more than our own."

"I understand," he chirped in poor orcish.

"Good," Garran said, turning to the other orcs, "We won't be taken by surprise again. Prepare the horses."

Tetsunage turned to his people, "We shall carry on. Our enemy is strong, but not heartless. We shall treat them with the same respect as they have given us." Their faces were as stern and expressionless as wild birds of prey, yet their subtle body movements, told him everything he needed to know. They silently lowered their heads, turning back to their fallen friend, giving one last farewell.

A few hours earlier, Jesmine and the others stopped, Histra dismounting, spreading her wings to softly land in the grass. A layer of frost clung to the horse's fur, moving up along the back of Jesmine's cloak. Histra asked, "How are you holding up?"

Jesmine slid off the horse, casting a spell to warm her up. "I'm fine. The horse on the other hand is not going to like me."

Dran pulled up beside her. "Aye, the frost has gone all the way down to her tail."

"I told you that it wasn't going to work the first time," Histra said.

"And we listened to you, but now we have no cart for you to ride in," answered Alderin, dismounting his horse, letting it graze on the nearby grasses. "Perhaps you could try to suppress your ice aura? I saw Dra'kesh use magic to control his."

She stared at him. "If I could, I'd have done it by now."

"You mean like healing me when you clearly have the ability to do so?" he asked.

She tensed and flicked her wing. "Look. That was completely different."

"Different how?" he asked, walking up to her.

She stared up at him, eyes narrowing, Jesmine stopping her soft chanting, saying, "Histra, no one here is going to harm you. You've proven yourself to everyone here several times over. You saved my life only a mere few hours ago."

"Speaking of which you shouldn't be using magic yet. Your body is still recovering," Histra said.

"I believe Jesmine's right. Some of us may have gotten off on the wrong foot, but despite your seemingly standoff attitude, I consider you a friend," said Gnemi.

Histra twitched at the word, Dran saying, "Aye. Believe it or not Histra, as much as I think you are a pain in my arse, you have proven to be very trustworthy and faithful to your word."

"It's not so much you trust me," she said.

"Histra, I heard what you said to Amir. I have seen some healing magic over the years, and like my skills, that requires studying and a spellbook. What you did is no small feat."

"This is true. It is very regulated back at home. It takes years of study before even being allowed to start the arcane training," Dran said.

"Of course, it does. If one doesn't know the biology of the person you are working with, you can't effectively heal them. You could even inadvertently kill them, or worse," Histra explained.

"We've been traveling together for a long time. Survived several life-threatening experiences together, some of which you have brought down upon us," Alderin said.

"Not purposely," she responded.

"It's true. Histra can't help that animals don't like her," Jesmine defended.

"That is not the point I am trying to make. We know she has never been this far. You and Ariana know this area far better than she does. Ever since we crossed through Rivera you have had no value to us, worse yet a burden," Alderin explained.

Histra took a step back. "I knew it," she remarked, eyes darting around.

"Alderin!" Jesmine yelled.

He held up his hand. "Let *me* finish," he said, keeping his gaze on Histra. "My point is if we wanted to kill you or toss you to the side because you have outlived your usefulness, we'd have done it by now." The tension in Histra eased up slightly. "And I won't lie. I tolerated you back then only because of Jesmine."

"Aye me too," Dran said.

"I know," The kobold replied.

Alderin continued, "But that was then, this is now. We are in this together. And as someone who is part of this group, I want to know who you really are."

Dran spoke up. "Effective healers are few and far between, fewer still who could heal more than one race. You've shown you could heal two races that aren't even your own. It is not a stretch to think you know how to heal your kind best of all."

Histra sighed. "Yes. I at least know how to heal them... as far as I can tell."

"As far as you can tell?" Alderin asked.

"I told you, I can't remember much," she said, pointing to her horn. "There are things I can do, but I don't know I can till I try, or something else triggers the memory. Healing magic is not something to just test out. I believe I know how to heal a few races, but I can't be sure. All my memories are snippets. A piece here, a piece there with nothing connecting them. No context. No way to know if what I am recalling is real or some delusion. But when I saw Jesmine injured there," she hesitated and thought, looking to Jesmine who was watching and warming the back of the horse without magic.

She continued. "You saved my life. I made a promise to you. To get you to Du'ralia. I recalled a moment. It was brief. There was a battle. People crying out in pain, metal clashing. There was an elf. I don't remember many details, but people had arrows in their chests. They were bleeding out. We were being overrun, there was nowhere to go, so I kept healing. I felt as if I was going to die there... but then we were saved..." she trailed off before looking back at Alderin. "The point is. I keep my promises. My word is all I have left."

"Is it?" Alderin asked, a smile coming across his face.

"Yes, it is," she said with a hint of annoyance.

"I recall you asking for a favor earlier today. I want to call it in."

"What?" she asked sharply.

"Alderin?" Jesmine asked.

"Please let the man finish Jesmine," Dran said.

"At this point you are going to either trust us or never will. Tell me who you really are to the best of your knowledge, and what do you intend to do once you fulfilled your promise with Jesmine."

Histra's claws tensed. "You know… I could just say whatever I want, and you'd never know the difference."

"True. But if your word means that much to you, I don't think you would."

"How could you be so sure?"

"Call it a hunch."

"A hunch?"

"Yes."

Histra let out a soft chuckle. "I don't think you'd believe me even if I told you."

"Try us."

She eyed him for a moment before looking to everyone else, watching the back and forth between her and Alderin. "Jesmine?"

"Yes?"

"Do me a favor."

"What is it?" she asked with a hint of concern.

Histra turned her head in her direction. "If they kill me for what I am about to say. Whatever thing they are trying to get from you. Whatever they want you to do. Don't do it."

"What?!" Dran exclaimed, "You think we'd just kill you for—"

Jesmine said, "If it puts you at ease. Yes. I promise."

Histra turned her attention back to Alderin. "Good."

"What was that? How do you just trust her and ask her to do that when—" Alderin said, Histra interrupting him.

"I served directly under Eisandra Everwinter."

Alderin stopped dead in his tracks. Everyone but Jesmine stared at her with complete disbelief, Gnemi almost falling off his horse. "Huh?"

"I thought I made myself clear. I believe, based on what fractured memories are in my head, that I served directly under Eisandra Everwinter which is the dragon Jesmine's mother murdered. And before you ask, the reason I believe this is I have one clear memory: of her dying. My magic and the others trying to heal her, but it was not working," she looked up at Alderin and continued, "That is why I know so much healing magic. And what I want to do when we get to the forest is to head to Tria'Cil, known to you as Four Corner City or perhaps known as the Four Scaled City. This is where the last servants of Eisandra Everwinter live."

"You want to go to the four-dragon trading city? Where Jesmine was taken and sold? That slave hub?" Dran asked.

"Eisandra was the only one not to have her land directly connected to the city, and because of this, she was the one in charge of the city's care. To my knowledge it still is with those last few alive that served her."

Jesmine answered, "It is. I remember noticing a few white kobolds running the city. But after being enslaved for so long, do you really want to go there?"

"What else do I have? Everyone I have known is dead, and no other dragon land will have me," she explained, looking back to Alderin. "Satisfied?"

"You served Eisandra?" Gnemi asked, eyes glowing with curious excitement.

"I believe I did, of course if I could get all my memories back, I'd be completely certain."

"Really? You? Serve Eisandra? You couldn't come up with something more believable?" Dran quipped.

"I believe her," Jesmine said.

"What?"

Alderin balled his hands into fists before relaxing them slowly. "I do too."

"Why?" Dran asked.

"All this time she's been concerned for her own safety. Her survival, but while sticking to her word. She knows what happened to me. What happened to my family? To just state… that she served directly under one of the dragons that ruled the land. Like the kobolds that held my…" Alderin swallowed a lump in his throat before finishing, "If she were to lie that would be the worst lie, she could have ever made. She'd be better off not making one up that would make me want to kill her where she stands," Alderin said.

"Alderin! After all that Histra has done," Jesmine yelled.

He turns to her, "Give me a moment before jumping to conclusions. After all that Histra has done…" he stated, taking a deep breath, calming his nerves, "That is why I won't. You served the most hated dragon of them all." Jesmine lowered her head.

"That's a matter of opinion," Histra said.

Alderin tensed. "True. I hate Dra'kesh more than anything else in the world. And those slimy, snaky kobolds that serve directly under him. But you are not one of them."

"I am not. It would be like me wanting to kill Jesmine for her Mother murdering Eisandra, but Jesmine is not her. I don't think Eisandra would have been that vindictive," Histra replied.

"I wouldn't be too sure about that," Dran said.

Ariana spoke up. "Perhaps, it's your relation to Eisandra is why I feel so on edge around you. From what I heard; she did practice necromancy."

"I wouldn't know," remarked Histra.

"I had a suspicion you had a history like that, Histra," Jesmine said.

Alderin asked, "What? How?"

"I have heard of white scaled kobolds with advanced runic markings on their horns that were amongst Eisandra's most elite kobold arcane users. But I wasn't sure since any such kobolds I saw with such markings had mithril inlaid in their runes."

Histra turned her attention to Jesmine. "What now?"

"I saw a kobold like you about fifteen years ago, when I was hunting the last white dragon."

"And what happened to them?" Histra said.

"I was told they, along with the other kobolds under the white dragon, were killed as they fled. I only saw them once. They stood out to me due to the shine on their horns, but then I had a white dragon trying to kill me, so my attention was elsewhere."

Histra said, "I don't recall anything like that myself."

Jesmine continued, "It was said that most of Eisandra's clerical kobolds were killed not long after she was slain. They were a top priority to be hunted down, but I thought they were all dead by the time I arrived, till I saw that one... I was... Too taken up at the time and even after what happened to my people... Mistakes were made."

Histra said, "After Sa'bara killed your people, I can see why. You know how I feel."

Jesmine shook her head, "Honestly, I don't think I do."

Histra raised an eye ridge.

"I have memories. Although they are bittersweet, I couldn't imagine not having anything."

"Honestly. How could anyone want memories of serving under

the wickedest of the ancient dragons," Dran said.

Histra's wings twitched. "If I had enough, I'd tell…" she looked off to the side. "I knew I shouldn't have said anything."

Alderin shook his head. "No. You did." He crouched down to get to eye level with her, placing his hand on her shoulder. Histra eyed it and then looked back at him.

"I told you no—"

"Thank you for telling me. As much as I hate dragons and the kobolds that serve them, this is the first time I heard you say something I felt like I could trust completely," he said, pulling his hand away from her and rubbing them together.

"Coming from you, I am not sure if I should take that as a compliment or an insult."

"Why don't you try taking it as a compliment for once?" said Alderin, standing up. "We should get going."

"Wait," Histra said.

"What?"

"It's your turn."

"My turn?"

"I told you my secret. Why don't you tell me… and more importantly Jesmine, the reason why you have been so willing to go this far for her sake. What do you want her to do that is worth all this trouble? To the point where any of you would never whisper more than a half-hearted complaint about anything you'd disagree with."

"Histra, I agreed to wait till we got out to hear what they wanted."

"They only said that so I wouldn't hear. Which means it's something important, because they don't want a KOBOLD to spoil their plans."

"Histra!" Jesmine said, giving her a little look.

"I'll talk it over with the others. I'll let you know when we make camp tonight," Alderin said, looking to Histra, "Perhaps showing our trust in you is necessary at this point."

Dran and Gnemi looked at Alderin curiously. "Alderin, are you really considering this?" Dran said.

"I'm not against it, but…" Gnemi trailed off, getting closer to Histra. "You have to tell me then. How old are you? You must be at least sixty years old! I didn't know kobolds lived that long."

"I must be older than that. A healer takes years of training. I had to get that before Eisandra was murdered. But my exact age? I don't know. I certainly don't feel aches and pains of old age. Maybe I am unnaturally young for my kind, having used healing magic, but I'm not sure."

Gnemi's shoulders slumped. "A shame. I would have loved to learn more."

"I've noticed that you have mostly stopped asking questions I can't or won't answer."

"I probably won't know which ones they are till I ask. And maybe it will help jog your memory?"

Histra shrugged. "Wish it worked that way."

"Have you tried?"

She sighed. "Honestly, I never talked about this before."

"How does it feel?" Jesmine asked with a smile as Histra looked over to her.

"Well, I'm not dead yet, so that's something."

"As much as we can talk about Histra's opening up, we have a few problems, one of which I can help with, the other is more problematic," Ariana stated.

"What problems?" Alderin asked.

"I'll start with the one I have a solution for. Switching between horses and warming them up is a slow process. We are being followed. It's best we don't slow down needlessly."

"Yes, we know that. It is why we used the cart the first time," Histra said.

"Solution, one I do begrudgingly but will benefit us the best. I'll shift into my feral form and Histra can ride my back."

Histra lifted an eye ridge. "Ride you?"

"You were freezing just as much in the cart as when we went through Rivera as the horses now," said Jesmine, giving the horse's cold back a gentle rub.

"While in a small, tight compartment, unable to move to help warm me up. I didn't feel *that* cold. I've survived harsher, colder winters than the cold air around Histra."

Jesmine said, "If you feel like you can do it, I won't stop you, but if you need to stop, don't hesitate to tell us. Hopefully, I will be able to perform some of my magic by then."

"I recommend not using magic today. Your body is strained

enough as it is, and I worked to heal any damage to your tattoos. I'd like a closer look tomorrow just to be safe. Last thing I need, is you to accidentally blow yourself up due to a damaged rune."

"Mother stated that there was a redundancy built into them, but I'd appreciate the look."

Alderin walked over to Ariana. "Let me guess. The other problem is how they found us?"

"It's been nagging me. The more I thought about it the less right I've felt."

Alderin rubbed his thick unshaven chin. "Same. I've tracked targets before. And I am perhaps no expert like these orcs, but there are limits. We passed through an entire city, took off into the woods, before going by road. On top of all of this they didn't know where we were going. There were other carts leaving the city. They had aid from those birds, but we avoided any of those encampments. I don't think they noticed us."

"No avolariean got close enough to bother me," Ariana responded, pointing to her black wolf nose.

"You better not be suggesting that I am leading them to you," Histra said.

Jesmine answered, "No, Histra. I don't think anyone was thinking that."

Dran said, "It crossed my mind."

"Dran? Why?" she asked with a sigh.

"It's the Gods given truth. But it was too unrealistic. If you wanted us to be captured, Histra, you'd have done it at the city. Not out here."

"This is true. At least you dwarves at times use your heads," she said.

Dran walked over to Histra. "I'll let that one slide, but perhaps you best lay off the insults. We're trying to foster better relations in our group now that more things are out in the open, or did you forget that already?"

She glanced in his direction, Dran reciprocating with a stern look. "You did help a lot... I will work on it."

He turned his attention to the others. "Now then, what do you think they are doing? A lucky guess? Their tracker was that good that they could follow us all the way out here? Perhaps they followed your scent?"

"Orc's sense of smell isn't that good. It's worse even than that of a human," Histra said.

"That would explain their smell," the dwarf remarked.

Gnemi turned to Jesmine. "Jesmine, what do you think, seeing you are the expert on arcane? Are there spells to track someone?"

"I wouldn't consider myself an expert. There is still much I could learn. And I have never heard of any spell that could just tell you the location of a person or any way to spy on them from a distance to determine where they are…" Jesmine trailed off, thinking, "Unless they are tracking an object they have marked. It's basic wizard training to mark your book so you can find it in case it was lost or stolen." She turned to Ariana, her gaze moving down to the shackles, eyes widening, "The cuffs! They must have a similar mark on them!"

"That would explain a lot," Alderin said.

"Why didn't I even think of this possibility before!" exclaimed Jesmine. "I put everyone in greater danger because I didn't even think of the basics of arcana! It's obvious that their wizard would know how to do it. It's stupid not to have thought they'd not put it on the mithril cuffs. They are made of MITHRIL!"

Alderin gently placed his hand on Jesmine's back. "It's okay. Don't blame yourself. We've had an exhausting couple of weeks. No one is blaming you."

Histra let out a sigh. "I didn't think of it either. I should have."

"This is all the more reason why we should move now," stated Ariana, immediately transforming. Sounds of cracking bones and shifting flesh caused Gnemi to look away but occasionally he took a peek.

"I couldn't agree more," said Dran, returning to Dariel and mounting up while Alderin helped Jesmine back onto her steed.

"Thank you."

"I'm just trying to help," he said as Ariana, her change complete, walked over to Histra.

"I hope this works," Histra remarked, climbing onto her back. She situated herself and gripped the back scruff of her fur, causing Ariana to let out a long, rolling growl.

"I need to hold onto something."

She let out a huff of air as Alderin said, "Dran and I need to have a conversation. Keep Histra out of earshot." Ariana nodded.

He looked to Histra and continued, "You know why."

She gave a soft glare. "I do. Have your little conversation. I eagerly await to see how this will turn out."

As Alderin and Dran rode several paces ahead, Jesmine said to Histra, "Why did you do that? There is no difference in me knowing now or later."

"You can't tell me you aren't curious."

She let out a soft sigh. "I'd be foolish to say I am not. I am not naïve either. Whatever it is, it's important. It's worth risking their lives, isn't that right Gnemi?"

He nodded, gripping the reins tightly. "That it is… but I will let them decide on what they want to say and when."

"And to whom," Histra said.

"Histra, why do you have to be like this?" Jesmine asked.

"Curiosity, but not on what it is. I don't care what they want. I want to see if they will tell me."

"You don't hold a lot of trust in people, do you?"

"No. Experience has taught me to be skeptical. Others are only helpful on what you can do for them. On what power you have over them."

Jesmine quirked an eyebrow. "Power over others? I don't know about that."

"That sounds a bit draconic to me," Gnemi said.

Histra explained, "Really? Why did you need us to go get your book? Because you don't have the power to do it yourself. Why did you need me? Because I had the power to help get you there. Why did I need you? Because I didn't have the power to get out of the cage or be on my own because how weak I was. Why is Ariana with us? She doesn't have the power to get these cuffs off her." Ariana let out a growl, shaking her body, almost causing Histra to slide off.

"It's true. And they," she pointed over to them, "Are helping you because of the power you can provide them with whatever it is they lack to accomplish what they need. Life is based on what power one has, and what one wants or needs."

"If that's true, would that possibly mean kobolds provide a kind of service or power to the dragons?" Gnemi asked.

"Yes actually," Histra turned her attention to him. "Not that I remember much of anything, but it is easy to see. The dragons provide a source of power, protection, place for my kind. They give purpose to our overall frail species."

"I wouldn't call you frail," he replied.

"Compared to you, but say an orc? Then it becomes painfully clear. Outside of our clearly draconic features we provide numbers. We can go and exert the will of the dragons and keep them out of harm's way. Why go yourself when you can send someone else in your stead?" Histra explained.

"That sounds closer to being used," Jesmine said.

"And didn't your royalty do the same? Why go themselves when they could handle other more important matters?"

"I suppose, but I will say that your thinking of the world is… rather sad."

Histra jerked her head to Jesmine. "Sad? It's the way the world works."

"What about family?"

"The power to continue your line after you have died. Only dragons are ageless."

"Friends?"

"Mutual sharing of power that they have to benefit each other as a whole rather than separately."

"How do you explain my insistence to get you out of that cage? You had nothing I knew that could benefit me at the time. I even suspected, as slim as the possibility was, that you were a cleric to the very dragon, who killed my mother."

"You aren't a vengeful type," Histra replied.

"That doesn't answer my question. How does it explain what I did? How do you explain charity work? Helping those in need for no benefit to yourself, in fact it often costs you. Time, effort, resources to help."

A moment of silence passes as she looks ahead. "Let me think on that."

"Please do, and let me know what conclusion you come to."

Up ahead, Alderin said, "I wonder what they are talking about."

"I don't know, but don't assume because you can't hear them that they may not be able to hear you," Dran replied.

"I know," he said, looking to him. "What do you make of her request?"

"What I make of it? It's a test. If we say nothing, it shows that we still can't trust the damn kobold. And make us look bad before Jesmine, who has a soft spot for her."

"And if we tell her, she'll have information she could use to get herself out of trouble, or worse yet, propel her to a new place within one of the other dragon lands."

"Aye. Either option is not good for us."

"This is too important for not only us, but for countless others. We could just not say anything and be done with it. Screw her trust issue. She still expects us to kill her in her sleep," Alderin said.

"If she makes herself to be a danger to the mission... Of course, any of our lives is worth getting her back into Dra'kesh lands with book in hand. If she's not at her full strength, this has all been for naught. We wouldn't have the time for her to get a new book. And the Dra'kesh elves are more problematic than the orcs here."

"They're exempt from the tributary. They wouldn't care."

"Aye, true enough. If we do tell, it could build trust with Jesmine and any reservations she has we could work it out along the way," Dran said.

"I have been concerned about her passiveness," Alderin remarked, glancing back to her for just a moment.

"Hmm, perhaps..." Dran remarked, rubbing his beard. "If we do tell her, we can always remove Histra if it turns out to be the wrong decision."

Alderin gave him a long look. "And risk the anger of one of the most powerful mages in the world?"

"Not if it happens after we part ways."

Alderin raised an eyebrow. "Go on."

"We are going to a village attacked by Sa'bara himself. If the other elven city's water was poisoned, sure enough, the water there will be too. Fill a water pouch with water. Give it to Histra as a parting gift as we will remain a fair distance away from the Four Corner City. We leave, she'll surely get thirsty on the way there, and before her ice aura freezes the water, she'll drink some, die, and Jesmine will be none the wiser."

Alderin looked away for a moment, thinking. Slowly he nodded, looking back to Dran. "I've had to do a lot of underhanded things in my time to save my family. Many things I am not proud of…"

"I don't like the idea any more than you, but what else can we do? If it's either our chance of our plan succeeding or her living, we'll choose the plan," Dran said.

"I know. And worst yet, I agree."

"We'll see. Maybe it won't be needed."

"Maybe," Alderin replied, returning his focus to the plains ahead of them. They continued to travel, breaking camp only about an hour before sundown.

"I suggest we don't set up a fire tonight, to keep attention being drawn to us," suggested Alderin once they started to set up camp.

"I haven't caught a whiff of them since we parted ways with the other humans," Ariana remarked, shifting back into her anthropomorphic form.

"Good to hear," Alderin replied, sitting down by his tent. "But seeing now that there is a good chance, they are tracking us with Ariana's bondage, Dran and I have come to one big conclusion."

Ariana let out a soft growl. "If this is going where I think it is," she said, staring down Alderin.

"If you mean doing anything to you, no. Definitely not."

Ariana's ears relaxed. "Good."

"We need to stop these orcs and birds from chasing us," Dran said. "It is too risky to just keep running when we know they can find us no matter what we do."

"What are you suggesting then?" Ariana asked, walking over to them.

"We know they are coming our way. We keep going till we find an optimal spot for an ambush and then attack them," Alderin said, Ariana smirking.

"I do like the idea of taking them out. Their numbers were reduced slightly by the attack on the castle."

"Are you serious? They outnumber us three to one? Perhaps more? And need I remind you that they have two arcane users. That arrow that hit me wasn't done by skill alone," Jesmine said.

"We are outnumbered, but so were we when we ambushed the caravan that held you prisoner," Gnemi chimed in. "If we do this right, we might have a chance. And after all this time running, they'll probably never expect us to stand and fight."

Ariana flicked her tail and continued to smile. "Yes, but we need to find a place. One of the villages could work, but it could also mean we are surrounded. I suggest we try to press on as hard as we can until we get to the forest. There we could set up traps and still provide ourselves with an escape route if things go wrong."

"No. It is too much of a risk. It would be better if we pushed to our home. There we can get my spellbook and find the spell that can break the magic lock on your cuffs. After that we can dump them off somewhere and lose them without the need of a risky fight," Jesmine suggested.

"But you are assuming we can outrun them. Stopping now is already a risk," replied Alderin.

"Aye, the man's right. We had possibly several days ahead of them last time and they caught up," said Dran, sitting down, pulling out his war hammer. "There is no guarantee we'll make it before they run into us again, and next time we won't be so lucky to have a bunch of humans helping us in a defensible position."

"But we were moving slower due to the cart and took refuge because of the storm. We're travelling much faster now. They need to sleep just as much as we do. We got a head start. We can do this," Jesmine retorted, looking at everyone with growing concern.

"We bought ourselves a few hours at best. There is a chance they could reach us tonight. If it wasn't so open, I'd suggest we try to set up some traps here and now," Gnemi said.

"It's too dangerous... Histra, you've been strangely quiet on all this. What do you think?" Jesmine asked

The kobold standing off to the side, wings furled, thought for a moment, replying, "Killing them would make our lives easier but there are risks. Considering that yes, they do out number us. They have two arcane users, even though I believe they are no match for Jesmine's prowess. And we do have the benefit that they only want to kill a few of us. Probably just you three, Alderin, Dran, and Gnemi."

"Hey, why do you say that?" asked Gnemi, shooting Histra a concerned look.

"One of the avolarieans looked at me with a clear shot and instead of attacking me, they turned their attention to someone else. I suspect they wanted to take me alive."

"Because you got the attention of the dragons with your lies," remarked Dran.

"It was a calculated risk, and that is probably why they want to take me alive," she said with a scowl before she suddenly relaxed, grinning. "Much like how you brought up this heated discussion instead of telling me if you are going to tell us your secret."

Jesmine let out a soft sigh, "Was that why you brought this up, Alderin?"

"No. We needed to discuss this."

Histra inquired, "Then why don't you tell me the secret? The one you've kept hidden from me, Jesmine and Ariana?"

"Ironic that you are so eager to get us to tell you when you want to know everything when back when we did the very same thing asking your plans you kept your mouth shut and refused," The human replied with a sigh and roll of his eyes. "Again, when it's *you* wanting to know other peoples' business you are all over it, but when others ask for the same consideration, you think you are the superior one."

As he was speaking, Ariana looked over to Histra, then to Alderin and Dran, "To answer Histra, it wasn't my place to ask. I am happy enough to get these things off me and be on my way."

"You didn't want to stay with us?" asked Jesmine.

Ariana tilted her head to the side. "Stay? I'm a Lycan. What makes you think I'd stay?"

"What were your plans once they are off then?"

"I... hmm," she crossed her arms and looked off to the side as she thought. "I never got that far. If those orcs are still hunting me, I'd get rid of them. After that, maybe stay in Du'ralia Forest. Few go there, it will be out of the way. My family's alchemy items are nearby. I could continue my research. After that, try to find out what happened to the others of my kind. Sa'bara is collecting us for a reason."

"That could be easier to achieve working with us," replied Jesmine.

"Yes, hopefully we kill the bastards before we part ways. That would be nice."

"That's not what I meant," Jesmine said sternly, Ariana letting out a huff.

"Now that has been said. Alderin? Dran? What say you? You going to trust me and tell, or keep it to yourselves?" Histra asked with a smirk.

Alderin looked over to Dran as he nodded, "To note we have been trusting you, so we'll tell you, even though I agree with Alderin as far as you not giving us the same consideration in the past," the dwarf said, her smirk lessening slightly.

"I will say there are too many variables to explain it all here," Alderin said.

"Then you are going to wait till we get there then," Histra remarked.

"It's fine, it wasn't going to affect me," Ariana commented, sitting down.

"I'm still willing to wait," replied Jesmine.

"That's not it. What I am trying to explain is, I will simply tell you our end goal. The only goal that matters," Alderin said, taking a deep breath. "We intend to have you help us kill Dra'kesh."

There is a moment of silence. Ariana's smile widened and perked up, while Jesmine tensed, "Dra'kesh. *The* Dra'kesh," Ariana said, breaking the silence.

"Aye," replied Dran, Histra bursting out in uncontrolled laughter causing all attention to swing over to her. Histra held her sides as her wings twitched, tail stiffening.

Alderin's eyes grew cold. "It's not funny."

"Not the reaction I was expecting," Dran remarked.

"Histra…" Jesmine replied, trailing off.

"My sides… they hurt… oh… ow, ow," muttered Histra, trying her best to keep from falling over, her laughter slowly dying down. "I thought it had to be something big. Help fight some war or something like that. But to kill Dra'kesh? With her? After all her passiveness and refusal to hurt others, despite the fact they have no problems trying to kill her? That's just…" she continued to laugh.

"Histra!" Jesmine yelled, walking over, crouching in front of her, placing her hand on her shoulder. "Show a little respect for once, please. They risked their lives to save me and to get us this far. You shouldn't laugh at their motivations."

She stopped, their eyes meeting. "Tell me this. Would you help them?" Jesmine's grip on her shoulder tightened. The kobold continued, "Could you? You think others haven't tried once Eisandra was killed? It's been sixty years since she was murdered by your Mother, and I've heard of only whispers of one planned attempt, and you know what happened to them."

Jesmine took a deep breath and slowly released it, fogging before her. "I don't know..."

Alderin stood up, walking over to them. His hand touched her back. "We know it's a big decision, and the risks. Take your time and think on it. Right now, what is important is getting your spellbook and returning to Tundaholm in one piece," he said.

Jesmine loosened her grip on Histra's shoulder. "Yeah... I'll need to think on it."

"We appreciate it."

"Jesmine. I know you've had a lot thrown at you at once. But, could you assist me with this hammer?" Dran asked.

Jesmine pulled away from Histra, standing up. "Sure. What do you need?"

"This hammer has arcane runes inscribed into it. I know it's fire, as I've seen it in action, but I don't know the command words to activate it. You, being an expert in fire magic, do you think you could figure it out?"

She sat down in front of him, running her fingers over the runes of the hammer. "These are orcish-arcana. You said it's fire?"

"Aye. I saw the flames and the heat singed my beard," he said, showing the burnt ends of his hair. "I assumed it was orcish made."

"Most likely. I don't recognize these particular runic structures. Each language carries meaning, and that meaning with the correlating runic symbols, by force of will and language in itself is simply a means to an—."

"Jesmine?" Dran gently interrupted.

"Yes?"

"I know the basics of magic. Do you think you could figure out the command word for these runes? A fire hammer could be very useful."

"Unfortunately, I can't read orc or their version of arcana. Much like I can't with dwarven. The only two I know are elven and draconic."

"Draconic?" asked Histra.

"My mother was driven in my education," she replied, turning her focus back to the hammer. "My best suggestion is to say different phrases in orc tongue that could unleash the stored magic. Remember, you can't just speak the words but must express the meaning."

"Aye. That is what I was afraid of," his shoulders slumped.

"There are ways to learn it, but I am not trained in those arts."

Alderin spoke up. "It's bound to be a simple phrase. We can work through some and hopefully we can stumble upon it."

"There is also the possibility that the word is in pure orcish-arcana," said Jesmine.

Dran sighed. "Great."

"Sorry, I didn't mean it like that."

"It's fine," he replied, lifting the hammer. "Regardless, I'm impressed with the craftsmanship. It put a few dings into my axe. I'll need a smith to fix it," he said, pulling out his axe, showing the blunted edges.

"Good idea on taking the hammer, then," said Alderin.

"I'm sorry I couldn't be more help," said Jesmine, standing. "I think I'll head in early. I'm still exhausted from earlier."

Histra stretched. "I agree. Healing magic is exhaustive to the caster and the recipient. I'll let you all figure your watch cycle," she remarked, pushing a bunch of grass down and simply collapsed onto it.

"I'll take second watch. I need a little rest. After all, I did walk, unlike the rest of you," said Ariana, pushing down some grass to turn it into a bed, curling in on herself.

"Don't you want to come inside a tent?" asked Jesmine.

"I don't want anything to limit my sense of smell," she replied, pointing to her nose.

"Got it," Jesmine said, ducking into the tent.

"Oh, and Alderin? Dran?" asked Ariana, staring at them with her yellow eyes.

"Yes?"

"Say hypothetically, if you managed to kill Dra'kesh, then what?"

"Well… I'm not sure to be honest," replied Alderin.

"I'd be hopeful that it would start a wave of new rebellions against the remaining three. Killing one might have been a fluke. Two? There is no denying that they can be killed. Their days of oppression and manipulation of our races will be numbered," said Dran.

"Do you think Sa'bara would be next?"

"I couldn't tell you, but it is a possibility."

"Hmm," she mumbled as the group got some much-needed rest. The night passed without incident. For the next week and a half, they pressed on. Each night brought a sense of uneasiness that it would be the night that the orcs caught up.

As the sun reached its zenith, a cool breeze blew across the plains, a shimmer of color appearing in the distance. With eagerness, they pushed ahead, Jesmine and Ariana feeling a tenseness within them as their exhausted horses approached.

Massive trees reached up into the sky, their trunks wider than a person was tall, towering over the view. As the wind blew, the color of the leaves of about half the trees shifted from green to blue, red, and orange. They reflected the light like the ocean. It continued to change as they came closer, but other trees of blue or green leaves remained stagnant like islands in a sea of color.

Vines with blue flowers hung from some of them with green and blue leaved shrubs covering the forest floor. Small patches of blue grass clung around some that stood alone outside of the forest proper. Their pace slowed, reaching the outskirts of the forest. Birds sang and chirped in the treetops, one flying from one to another, revealing a dazzling soft white glow, which ended the moment the bird landed and stopped moving.

"Du'ralia Forest. It's as gorgeous as I remember it," muttered Jesmine, riding up beside Dran and Alderin.

"How far until we reach your home?" asked Alderin.

"Two days travel by horseback," she answered.

Ariana kept her ears perked, scanning the nearby area, remaining ever vigilant. *"Home,"* she thought.

"We'll travel until we are less than a day away from your home. Then we'll set up the ambush," said Alderin.

Jesmine looked over to him, "We've gone over th—"

"Look. We were lucky to make it this far without them catching up. Would you rather we deal with them before we get to your home? Or chance it there? And deal with that and whatever crazed hauntings there?"

"He's right Jesmine. Given the chance, I prefer we not fight them there. Not only because of the ghosts, but I wouldn't want to see your home further damaged by violence," Dran added.

"I would add that ghosts react negatively to violence, becoming more active," remarked Histra.

Jesmine tensed before dropping her shoulders and head.

"Do you want them to risk destroying any more of your home? We've tried to avoid them. Outrun them. But they have been relentless. If we do enough damage maybe they'll realize what a mistake it is and back off," said Alderin.

Jesmine swallowed a lump in her throat, gripping the reins of her horse ever tighter. The horse neighed softly.

"We are only defending ourselves," said Dran.

"From something we caused," Jesmine muttered.

"We freed one of your people from slavery. A slavery you know all too well. No one is going to think badly of you. We have a mission, which is bigger than all of this. We are out to free people from the dragons' control. Something your mother knew well."

Jesmine squeezed the reins even tighter. "I know. I'll do what I can."

Dran nodded. "Thank you, Jesmine. We did all we could, but there comes a time where we must fight, and fight we will. Come, let's get going." He squeezed the sides of his steed with his legs, pushing into the forest.

Ariana let out a soft growl as they stepped in.

"What's wrong?" asked Jesmine.

Ariana relaxed after a moment before shaking her head, which almost knocked Histra off her back.

"Careful!" she yelled.

"Hopefully it's nothing, but let's keep going," said Alderin.

Less than six hours after they entered, Garran and his people reached the outskirts of the forest.

Garran grunted. "I knew we should have pushed harder!"

Zed, who rode beside him spoke. "They've been pushing themselves just as hard as us, now that they know we are coming."

"It is my fault, Garran. If I didn't think they were slowed down by the other humans on the first day, we'd have ridden longer," said Shana.

"Yes, it was. But what is done is done. We didn't want a repeat of what happened at the castle," grunted Garran, looking over to Tetsunage. "If we were faster, we'd have reached them before they got to the forest. You better not chicken out now."

Tetsunage gave him a long cold look. "We'll press on," he said, Penisiya leaning in close while Zed translated.

"There is something wrong with the forest. It's a darker sense than I got back at the elven castle," she whispered to him.

"We'll be careful," Tetsunage replied.

"Good. You've been more of a hindrance," stated Garran.

"Lest I remind you that you are here because we gave permission."

"And your lack of permission was a huge problem for them to move right through your lands," he retorted.

Tetsunage let out a soft annoyed chirp. "We'll continue forward. But remember, the lives of my people outweigh this reward."

He looks down at him, "The lives lost weigh heavily on my decisions," he said, looking to the forest. "We're moving until the sun sets."

As they stepped into the forest, Penisiya's feathers slightly ruffled. "I have a real bad feeling about this," she whispered.

"We can do it," Tetsunage replied, pressing onward.

Chapter 17 Battle in Du'ralia Forest

Sunlight pierced through the tree canopy, speckling the ground with its warm glow. The shimmering leaves caught and refracted a fraction of the sun's rays, which peppered the forest with faint rainbow colors. A dazzling display caused by a white bird fluttering through the changing leaves, caught Jesmine's attention as it hid behind some branches nearby.

A large bird of prey, its multi-colored feathers mimicking that of the shimmering trees, screeching out to snatch the light bird in mid-air. As it dove, the smaller one created a small burst of magical energy, which increased the intensity of the dazzling light show, causing the bird of prey to just miss its target which escaped into the treetops.

Jesmine slowly and quietly chanted, her tattoos glowing faintly, resisting the urge to adjust the rope tied around her waist. She took slow deep breaths, keeping her focus out ahead of her. Her glyphs on the ground were covered by random leaves and brush, hiding their faint orange glow.

Underneath Jesmine at the base of the tree trunk was Ariana in her normal anthropomorphic wolf form. She kept her ears pointed out in the expected direction of their pursuers. Alderin and Dran took wide positions along the right flank, while Histra and Gnemi took the left, hiding within the forest's brush.

They waited patiently for what felt like an eternity. The quiet before the storm. Ariana's nostrils flared, ears perking as she let out a soft surprising bird-like call. Everyone tensed as Alderin nocked an arrow. Dran stayed low with the war hammer in hand, pressing up behind a tree while Gnemi pulled up his goggles, his crossbow at the ready, but also three metal spheres around his waist, two the size of oranges and the third slightly smaller. On his right hand were two bands with flint built into them. Histra waited farther back than everyone else, her ice aura slowly frosting the nearby plants.

Tetsunage walked beside Garran, eyes peeled, ears open. The sound of twigs and underbrush snapping under the weight of the horse's footsteps made his feathers rise ever so slightly.

"Your horses make too much noise," he remarked, Zed

translating.

"It won't matter, our primary target can smell us before we could even be heard."

"I sti—" Tetsunage lifted his head, letting out a soft chirp while raising his right hand. He motioned with his hand twice to the right and twice to the left, the other avolarieans except for Penisiya fanning out to the flanks.

Garran looked at him with concern. "What is it?"

"I heard an unnatural bird call."

"What?" he looked at him skeptically.

"Are you doubting my avian ears?" he asked with a soft inquisitive trill.

Garran nodded, pointing to two of his men. "Support them on the flanks."

They peeled off. Garran whispered to Zed. "Check about how far we are from our goal."

"As you wish," he responded, Zed riding a few steps behind Garran, casting his spell.

Penisiya walked up behind Tetsunage. "We should spread out more. There is a chance the wizard survived the attack. If they get a jump on us, it's not going to be pretty."

"I agree, the odds she lived are slim but still, it is best to be safe. Prepare a wind wall and I'll advise Garran," he replied, noting Zed's spell casting, his tusks beginning to glow. He cleared his throat and spoke in broken orcish. "We spread. Bad magic. Chance. We close."

Garran looked down at him and chuckled. "You can't speak a real language, eh? Their arcane caster is unfortunately dead. We talked about this. If we spread out too much, they will pick us off," he explained. Penisiya's jewelry faintly glowed.

Slowly the orcs and avolarieans came into Jesmine's view. She moved her hands in elegant and well-planned motions, her chanting growing a little louder. The others felt the tension in the air, their hearts racing, sweat running down Alderin's brow, noting their spread-out formation.

Jesmine's tattoos glowed brightly, unleashing her magic. Six hidden arcane runes positioned in a shape of a diamond, shot jets of fire six feet high. The horses reared up in surprise. Within seconds, a wall of fire connected, locking all but six within the flames.

Alderin and Gnemi jumped out from under the brush, firing at Garran, who was in clear view on top of his horse. The arrow and bolt whizzed over the fire. He yelled, feeling the piercing pain of Alderin's arrow in his arm.

Penisiya raised her hand, creating a wall of wind, catching and deflecting Gnemi's bolt. The spell ended moments later. Gnemi fired again, hitting an orc in the chest. He looked at the bolt jutting out of him. Eyes wide, blood trickling down. The grip on his horse's reins loosened. He fell hitting the ground with a thud.

"Dismount!" yelled Garran, slipping off his horse, Alderin's arrow whistled over his head.

"Now!" yelled Alderin, pulling out a metal sphere with a fuse at the end. With similar finger flints, he lit the fuse, tossing it over the fire wall. A trail of smoke bellowed out from the bomb, following its trajectory while Gnemi in quick succession threw the smaller grenade. It landed behind Penisiya, fuse sparkling with a hiss.

Tetsunage grabbed Penisiya, placing himself between him and the bomb as it exploded, unleashing a hail of shrapnel. Piercing pain ripped across his back and legs as blood stained his feathers.

"You okay?" he asked, wincing in agony.

Penisiya looked at him with complete wide-eyed shock. "I'm fine, but..."

"I'm good," he responded, seeing Zed dropping to his knees. The orc grunted, blood oozing out from several small wounds in his legs. A nearby orc lied motionless in a pool of his lifeforce that spilled out from his ravaged body.

Garran yelled in frustration as a second smoke grenade landed amongst them, smoke hissing out of the top. The grey-white haze filled the air, blinding them. Their lungs and eyes burned, coughing loudly.

A brown skinned orc outside of the wall of fire drew his axe, charging Alderin. He let out a loud battle cry, the two avolariean nocking their bows and taking aim.

"Remember, Tetsunage wants them taken alive," said one of the avolarieans.

"I know," replied the other as they released their arrows, which whizzed by the unflinching orc. The first arrow raced across

Alderin's back, bouncing off his leather armor, the second pierced his lower torso.

Alderin winced in pain as the orc lunged at him. Dran popped from behind the tree, swinging the war hammer, hitting the orc in the knees. Bones cracked loudly and the orc tumbled to the ground with an angry yell. Dran followed through his attack, hitting the orc along the head with a sickening crunch, knocking him down.

The two avolarieans took aim at Dran. Jesmine with a quick hand motion, spoke an arcane phrase, causing another hidden glyph off to the side to light up. A pillar of fire rose before lashing out and connecting to the diamond, which caused the overall height of the flames to drop by a foot. She took a deep breath, continuing her chant, the flames slowly rising back up to their original height, tattoos glowing even brighter.

On the other side, moments after Gnemi tossed the grenade an orc and two avolarieans appear from the brush several yards away. "That's probably not good!" he yelled. He panic fired his shot, missing Amakasha.

Amakasha took aim and fired as Gnemi loosed another bolt, the arrow and bolt passing each other in mid-air. He let out a shrilled chirp, the bolt hitting his abdomen while the arrow lodging right into the gnome's crossbow, making him jump in surprise.

He yelled, pain shooting up his leg as the other avolariean's arrow pierced it, warm blood trickling down his thigh. His heart raced as he looked down to see the wound, eyes going wide, and falling to one knee.

A green orc with a scarred face and a broken tusk raised his massive great sword, lunging towards him. He barely rolled out of the way, crying out in pain, the arrow shaft in his leg snapping in half, pushing deeper into him, muscles tensing and tearing.

"You won't get away from me!" the orc grunted assaulting Gnemi, the heavy blade crashing down on him.

The gnome held up his crossbow in a vain shielding attempt, heart racing once more, as his eyes locked on the blade before he winces, closing them. Metal clanged against metal. A feral wolf growl knocked him back to reality.

Ariana stood between him and the orc. She used her mithril cuffs to deflect another blow, her claws slashing across his leather armor, revealing the padding underneath, missing his flesh. Ariana howled in agony as an arrow pierced her tough Lycan hide. Muscles tensed; pain shot through her before she shrugged it off and grabbed the orc by the wrist. In one quick motion she grabbed his other arm and flung him into Amakasha.

Bones snapped as the orc slammed into the bird, sending both to the ground. He trilled in pain as the other avolariean connected with an arrow in Ariana's upper thigh.

She tensed and growled, lips curling, fangs bared. Her claws twitched, taking a single step towards them, nostrils flared, salvia dripping from her maw.

Gnemi tossed his last grenade, landing between Ariana and the avolariean, smoke billowed out obscuring him from view.

"I had him," Ariana growled.

"You're hurt, you need to fall back," Gnemi said, pushing to his feet, wincing in pain, trying to not look at his injury.

"You're worse than me," she remarked.

The smoke within the firewall rushed up hanging ten feet in the air like a fog, blocking Jesmine's view of the battle. Desperately she looked for an opening to aid her, while upkeeping her spell.

Zed continued his incantation as more smoke from the bombs was funneled up into the sky. Garran coughed, clearing his throat. "Good work." The flames surrounding them grew weaker, losing height.

Tetsunage looked to Penisiya. "Do you think you can get us out?"

"Yes, but you need to be careful," she said, pulling out her spellbook, flipping through the pages.

"I'm okay," he coughed, body tensing, feeling countless injuries burning in his back. Penisiya found her spell, beginning to cast.

Tetsunage turned to Garran, pointing to the fire wall. "Push out," he chirped.

"You were right, Zed. She is in the trees. The spell's weakening," Garran remarked, looking at the barely flickering flames. "Not as much as I would like."

As the smoke hung over their heads, Dran struck down at the fallen orc. He dodged out of the way, the hammer hitting the ground with a heavy thud. He evaded the follow up, rolling back onto his feet. Blood dripped from his wound; head throbbed like it was in a vice. He gritted his teeth, fighting the pain.

"Wish this had a spike on the end," Dran remarked, pulling back countering the orc's attack. The sound of clanging metal sang out as the weapons clashed.

Alderin landed another arrow in the orc's side, causing him to stumble. Dran ducked under his failed attack, swinging the hammer and nailing the arrow further into the orc's side.

Blood spurted out of the orc's mouth, falling to one knee. He swung wildly against the dwarf, who easily defected the blows. Dran bashed the hammer into the orc's sternum, knocking the air out of him, bones cracking as he was slammed to the ground. The two avolarieans made it around the edge of the fire wall.

"Look out!" Alderin yelled, firing one arrow off in the birds' direction, making them duck behind some cover. The dwarf fell back behind a tree, panting heavily.

"These are times I wish I had a ranged weapon," Dran remarked, peering over the side, an arrow piercing the tree, barely missing.

"If we get out of this alive, in the future, we'll make sure you have one!" yelled Alderin, taking cover.

Meanwhile, Ariana jumped back, dodging the orc's renewed assault.

Gnemi limped away, thinking, *"What to do? What to do?!"*

The uninjured avolariean used the smoke cover to drag Amakasha out of harm's way.

"You've killed my friends, you bitch!" the orc yelled in a furious rage.

The blade cut an inch and a half gash in her side, blood slowly oozing out of the wound. Ariana growled, baring her teeth, feeling the burning throb of each injury, making her heart pound. "And I will kill you too," she replied, clawing him.

Inside the firewall, Penisiya's jewelry glowed brighter, dancing toward the edge of the flames. The heat caused her feathers to ruffle, a few singeing as her arcane song grew louder. She reached out toward the wall, a burst of wind flowing from her claw tips. The firewall flickered, the wind piercing through it, the flames fighting back, but were no match for her, as she created a clear route of escape.

"You are doing it, Penisiya!" Tetsunage yelled, following

behind her with a limp.

Garran commanded, "Stick together, protect Zed, he's blinding the wizard."

Shana pulled out her thick wooden bow. "Understood," she replied, moving behind Zed, who kept a steady chant, while splitting his attention between his spell and Penisiya.

Kra'mek readied his bow. Orla had her daggers in hand. Penisiya pushed through the wall, the heat of the flames shriveling and darkening some of her feathers. She turned toward the firewall, keeping the path open as Tetsunage followed.

He suddenly trilled, "Look out!" Dran striking at Penisiya from behind, pain slowing his reaction. The avolariean drew his short sword, trying to intercept.

Dran's hammer whistled through the air, barreling down upon her.

Penisiya leapt back, the hammer knocking her chest. She let out a trill of pain, bones snapping, her jewelry glowing bright as gale force winds blew out, pushing Tetsunage off to the side while also pushing Garran and the other orcs back away from the hole almost into the opposite side of the firewall. Garran screamed in frustration, the horses neighing in panic.

The wind thrust Dran a half a foot back. His red beard and hair blowing wildly. "I thought he was the arcane caster," Dran remarked in dwarven. Tetsunage rushed to get between Penisiya and him.

Garran turned to Zed. "Can you break out of it?"

Zed shook his head, quickly saying, "Not possible," the haze of smoke over their heads weakening slightly.

Jesmine's eyes darted across the fog, her sharp elven ears focused on the sound of combat. She felt as if her heart was about to jump out of her chest. Movement to the right suddenly caught her attention. A shiver ran down her spine, heart beating even faster. She made a few quick hand motions, uttering elvish-arcana ending her spell, the glow of her tattoos snuffing out, yelling, "Run!" She worked to untie herself from the tree.

Alderin barely managed to hear her words, but before he could react the firewall blinked out of existence, leaving black charred ground in its wake. "Jesmine!" he called out.

Tetsunage dodged Dran's attacks, who did his best to keep him on the defensive. Penisiya stood a few feet behind him, holding her side with heavy labored breathing.

The hammer battered orc pushed himself to his feet once more. Blood rolled down his body, adrenaline snuffing out the pain, rage filling his eyes. He charged Dran, axe held high ready to cleave his head in two.

The dwarf caught the movement. Distracted, Tetsunage drove his blade into his shoulder, only piercing a half an inch thanks to his armor. He groaned in pain, finding himself stuck between a rock and a hard place.

The orc swung down when a massive head of a snake burst through the smoke cover with lightning quick reflexes snatching up the orc within its massive jaws. The force of the blade felt through Dran's hair as it now clearly missed its intended target.

The orc called out for help, the massive scaled serpent, with brown and greenish coloration along the top of its head and back with brilliant rainbow-colored scales underneath, bit into the orc, its curved fangs piercing through his leather armor like it was not even there. Three feet from the base of the head were long leathery scaled wings that spread out from its back. The underside showed a ghostly view of what was behind it, constantly shifting as if looking through a slightly imperfect glass window, showing an ingenuine view.

Garran and the other trapped orcs were about to charge into battle when the massive snake attacked. His eyes burn with a hatred, his attention shifting from Dran to the colossal serpent.

Zed dropped his spell as the twelve-foot-long wings flapped, blowing away the smoke revealing the hundred-foot-long behemoth. The serpent pulled its head back, the orc in its mouth screaming out, his legs flailing as with one quick head motion forced the orc completely into its mouth, swallowing him whole. Its massive black forked tongue flicked, the horses' panic growing. Its gigantic wings flapped, and in quick succession the snake was propelled forward, striking one of the horses, fangs piercing its side. The horse whined out in pain, blood dripping down its sides. It wrapped its tree trunk sized coils around the horse, squeezing the life out of it until a sickening crack, sent the other mounts fleeing.

All eyes locked on the creature as the will to fight ceased. Their blood ran cold as a second heavy loud hiss echoed out through the forest. The last of the smoke dispersed revealing another equally massive snake, slithering from one tree to the next causing the trees to rattle down to the trunk. Leaves and broken branches tumbled to the ground. The serpent moved and coiled around the tree Jesmine was on, which shook violently. The branches under the elf's feet swayed and wobbled, her feet slipping. The rope only allowing her to fall a few feet before going taut while she hung on tightly to it.

The snake's yellow slit eyes surveyed the area for only a moment, as its fellow serpent devoured its prey. It followed one of the fleeing horses and struck out at it just as the horse ran past Gnemi. Unable to react he watched as the creature's fanged mouth opened wide, barreling at him as the gnome's heart stopped, feeling the cold grip of death forming over his body.

A blast of ice slammed against the creature's face forming more along the side of its head, which caused it to recoil and veer off just enough to miss Gnemi by half a foot. The snake slammed its head and body into the ground, trying to knock off the ice, the force of which caused Jesmine's tree to rattle even harder.

Her fingers slipped from the rope, falling to a lower branch, which cracked under its weight, but held, wrapping her hands around it, helplessly dangling from the branch.

Gnemi blinked several times, staring at the massive snake moving less than a foot away from him. His heart was ready to jump out of his chest, taking a few steps, almost tripping over himself, "What is that...WHAT IS THAT!?"

The serpent shook its head, knocking off the remaining ice from its scales. Its tongue flicked, looking in Histra's direction, who spat off to the side what little of her frost breath remained, the ground freezing where it landed.

Ariana grabbed Gnemi from behind, running off. "No time to waste," she stated, giving a momentary glance at the creature, running past and picking up Histra, wrapping an arm around her.

"Watch it!" the kobold yelled.

She glanced down at her. "We need to get out of here, or do you prefer I leave you with the acon'nada?" she asked with a sly, toothy smirk.

Histra let out a defeated huff, looking back at the serpent.

Jesmine's branch broke, smaller ones scratching her body, as she tried in vain to catch one. The last ten feet were a complete free fall, and the elf braced for the inevitable impact.

Alderin caught her with a loud groan, feeling a piercing pain in his gut.

"Thank you," she replied as Alderin put her down.

"We need to go," he said.

Dran held his hammer up, eyes darting between the orcs, the avolarieans and the acon'nadas.

Alderin yelled, "Run!"

Dran not looking to him, "Aye, that sounds like a good idea!" he remarked, running away.

Tetsunage kept a defensive position, his attention split between Dran and the snake, his feathers fluffing out.

Garran surveyed the situation, watching the utter chaos enveloping him. The avolarieans already turned their attention to the direr threat, firing a volley of arrows against the acon'nada, which barely penetrated its thick scaly hide. "How much time do you need to take it out?" He asked Zed, pointing to the serpent.

"A couple of minutes," he replied, pulling out his spellbook, flipping through the pages.

"I was afraid of that," he said. "Distract the beast! We need to buy Zed time!"

Tetsunage continuously shifted his focus, stopping on the nearby serpent, eyes narrowing. "You think you could help me pierce its hide?" he said to Penisiya.

She winched, standing up. "Of course. I can't let anything bad happen to you. You're all he has left," she replied, Tetsunage's feathers rising.

The acon'nada thrashed about, its massive body slamming into one of the avolarieans, flinging him several feet away. The creature spread and quickly flapped its wings, propelling itself, avoiding a volley of arrows.

Shana and Kra'mek fired their heavy bows with arrows twice the thickness of the avolarieans', which pierced into the creature's hide. It twitched and hissed, turning its attention toward them. They ran in different directions away from Garran and Orla who kept a defensive position in front of Zed, tusk runes glowing green.

It snapped at Shana, a lightning fast arrow piercing its right eye, causing it to barely miss her. Its body slammed into a tree snapping it at the base. The tree groaned, branches breaking, falling over with a heavy thud, causing birds nearby to scatter.

Red blood oozed from the snake's tightly closed eye; the very end of the arrow's shaft visible between the eyelids.

Penisiya prepared another spell cast.

Tetsunage notched another arrow, yelling, "Run!" His two nearby companions barely dodging the snake's strike. It slithered after them, breaking a small tree in the process, before coiling up a thicker one, gaining height over everyone, its body appearing translucent against the forest canopy.

The forest rocked, it seeming to fly from one set of trees to the next, coiling around several of them. Its black tongue flicked back and forth, eyeing what to attack next, glancing briefly in the direction of the other acon'nada.

Zed spoke loudly in orcish-arcana, hands and body moving in calculated motions, spellbook glowing in one hand. He looked up to the serpent, pointing to it. A cloud of blackish green smoke formed over the snake's head. He continued his chant and with a few quick hand motions he forced the gas into the snake's nostrils and mouth.

The acon'nada's head jerked; its body convulsed. Its thick muscular coils squeezed and snapped the top of a tree, tumbling a few feet before being caught in the branches of the surrounding trees. Over the next minute it jerked its head side to side, breaking free from the cloud for only a moment before it enveloped its head once more.

It tried to flee, its body convulsing, crashing into the ground with a heavy thud, unmoving. Zed finished the spell and the smoke dissipated. Parts of the serpent's body were still entangled in the trees; its full impressive length on display like a fisherman dangling its biggest catch by the tail.

Garran patted Zed hard on the back. "Good work," he said, assessing the damages.

Zed panted heavily, putting away his spellbook. "I know it was."

Meanwhile, Ariana weaved through the trees holding Gnemi and Histra under each arm with the other acon'nada was not far behind. It elegantly slithered through the forest, flapping its leather wings propelling it faster along the ground. Gnemi yelled, "It's catching up!"

"You don't have to tell me that," Ariana growled as Jesmine, Alderin, and Dran ran parallel to the group several yards away, behind the chasing snake.

Jesmine sprinted ahead leaving Alderin and Dran in the dust but still trailed behind the snake. Her heart raced, beginning an incantation. Bushes broke and trees rattled as it moved. Small, hidden woodland creatures fled the area in all directions. Ariana's ears twitched, focusing on her pursuer.

"Ariana!" Gnemi yelled. She leapt to the side, the acon'nada's strike just missing.

"Quiet!" she said, glancing at the snake. Mixing into the surrounding noise were fearful neighs of horses. Gnaria tugged at the reins tied to the tree trunk.

"There is no way we can mount up!" said Gnemi, Ariana simply running past her.

It struck towards them again, Gnemi stiffening up as he could only watch the next events unfold. With supernatural reflexes, it snatched and coiled around Gnaria which neighed out a death cry, the signal of her life being snuffed out.

"Gnaria!" yelled Gnemi, feeling a pit form in his stomach.

Just as the acon'nada swallowed the horse whole, two glyphs on either side of the creature lit up and burst into flames. Jesmine ran closer to the snake and, bringing her hands together, a wall of fire formed right on top of it. Her tattoos glowed brighter, speaking with greater force, the fires burning hotter, parts of the snake's head catching on fire.

The serpent writhed in pain, hissing as it darted away, rolling and rubbing its hide against the foliage, catching some of the nearby brush on fire. Jesmine took a deep breath, ending her spell, snuffing out the flames of the fire wall and the smaller nearby fires before relaxing, the glow of her tattoos fading. With a heavy pant she walked over toward them.

Ariana ran till she heard the snake hissing in pain, fleeing the area. Gnemi squirmed in her grasp, crying, "Gnaria!" She placed him and Histra on the ground, the gnome looking off in the direction of the burned snake.

Ariana looked down at him letting out a huff of air. "Get on my back, we aren't safe yet." She shifted into her feral form, one of the arrow shafts lodged in her broke.

Histra let out a grunt. "That could have gone better," she said to Gnemi and Ariana, noticing their wounds, looking to the broken arrow, "That is going to make it harder to get out."

"Are you three alright?" Jesmine asked with a heavy pant.

"We're fine... more or less. We did what we could in the ambush, and now they have a giant snake to deal with. We need to run while we still can," Histra said.

"I could be better," said Gnemi, looking down to the arrow stuck in his leg. He reached for it, Histra smacking his hand away. "No, leave it in till we can handle it. When we aren't in mortal danger."

Ariana let out a low growl, positioning herself for them to get on.

"Get to your horses, we'll be fine," said Histra.

Gnemi climbed on, wincing in pain. "Right... horses," he sighed, tears still in his eyes as he held onto Ariana's fur.

Jesmine ran off to the other horses tied to a tree several yards away, reaching them just as Alderin and Dran did.

Alderin commented between heavy breaths. "I didn't know... elves could run... so fast."

"I've had practice," Jesmine replied with a faint smile, mounting up.

"Aye, something we're becoming good at," replied Dran, turning to Alderin. "Need a hand up?"

Alderin waved his hand. "I'm fine. Let's get out of here before they manage to handle the other snake," he said, mounting up with a held back groan.

While they got farther and farther away from their pursuers, the orcs and avolarieans took note of their losses. Garran clenched his fists tightly, looking over the body of his fallen comrade. He lifted his head, turning it to Zed, who limped his way over.

Zed lowered his head, saying, "We're down two. Most of the avolarieans are injured." He let out a long drawn out sigh and continued, "The same could be said about us."

Garran grumbled, "How did that wizard survive? Even you said it was impossible for her to have lived. The birds said the arrow hit her in the chest."

Tetsunage chirped in the best of his broken orcish, "Did. Saw, arrow hit."

"Once again. Unforeseen circumstances have robbed us of victory," Garran said.

"The winds of fate at times determine our paths. It is best not to go against the winds," Tetsunage said in avolariean.

Garran walked up Tetsunage as Zed gave a loose translation, his hands clenched into fists. "What does that mean?"

"I've already lost one of my people, and three are badly injured, including myself."

"You lost one. I've lost five. FIVE stout warriors. FIVE of my best companions. You birds can't stomach more than a single loss and a few scratches?!"

Tetsunage's eyes narrowed, his neck feathers ruffling, calmly but sternly replying, "I told you how far I am willing to go. We've done our share. We didn't succeed. We will return home empty handed."

"They were also injured. They don't have the ability to set up another trap. We out number them and have fewer injured. If we strike now, we can win."

Penisiya chirped in, holding her side. "I've been sensing a great dark sadness ahead of us. It's gotten stronger with each step we've taken. We're already too close."

Garran's eye twitched, Tetsunage adding, "We're heading back," and in that moment Garran reached up and squeezed his throat.

"How dare you say that to me!" he said, noticing three avolarieans quickly drawing their bows, aiming at him. Tetsunage held his claws up, keeping a firm stance against the orc.

"Release me… now." he managed to say in orcish, eyes unflinching.

Garran grunted, the other orcs weapons drawn, Zed keeping an eye on Penisiya. The orc gritted his teeth, hand shaking before releasing him.

"We're leaving. We'll take your dead and injured out. We'll wait for you at the forest's edge for ten days. After that you will be on your own to get back."

"Tetsunage, you don't have to give him that. He just attacked you!" squawked one of the avolarieans.

"Part of our agreement is to guide them through our lands and back. We failed them in their hunt, but we won't fail in escorting them back," he replied, clearing his throat. "Am I understood on that?" he asked, feathers raising, staring at his companion.

"Yes. Completely," he responded, giving Garran a glare, feathers rising.

"You can come with us now, or we will wait. That choice is up to you if you want to pursue this insanity."

Zed limped over to Garran. "I suggest we turn back," he said, the orc giving him a stare most foul. "But I will support whatever decision you make."

He took a deep breath, staring at Tetsunage for a moment longer. "Zed, how much can you heal?"

"Minor injuries only. I can't do broken bones."

He nodded. "Start with yourself."

Zed found a place to sit, pulling out his runic symbol, beginning his draconic chant.

As night began to fall over the forest of Du'ralia, Gnemi let out a cry of pain as Dran held his leg down. Histra slowly cut into his flesh with her claw, digging down to the arrowhead.

"Stop your whining and fidgeting. Do you see Alderin complaining as Ariana works on him? No. And she has arrows still stuck in her!" she said, continuing to work. "You also don't want this to freeze, so I have to work fast."

"This is the first time I've been shot before, okay?" he yelled.

"Hope this teaches you not to get shot in the future," she replied.

"Easy for you to say! Are you going to do healing magic on me afterwards?"

Histra cut into the flesh a little more before gripping the base of the arrow shaft and pulled the arrow out with relative ease. "Didn't hit any bone. That's good," she replied, tossing it off to the side. "The most I can do is to stop the bleeding and close the wound." She pinched the bleeding wound.

Gnemi moaned in pain. "Why not heal it fully?"

"Because I am not sure if I know your biology. Now, no more questions," she responded, beginning to chant, horn glowing as Gnemi gritted his teeth.

"She's right, Gnemi. Healing magic can be very powerful but it's also very dangerous. That's why only skilled priests, who have spent years honing their skills as doctors are allowed perform it. Without the proper knowledge she could just as easily kill you as heal you," Dran explained.

"This is why she is not going to try to heal me either. I may have been an elf, but I am no longer," Ariana said, pulling the last arrow out of Alderin.

"Thanks," he replied, looking over the injuries.

"You were lucky. It appears the avolarieans weren't trying to kill you with these shots," she remarked.

"It sure doesn't feel like it."

"I'd bandage you, but Histra should be able to handle these injuries once she's done with the whining gnome."

Gnemi tensed and muttered under his breath. "That's cold. That's cold." He looked over to Ariana. "Ariana, there's something I have been wanting to ask you."

She looked over her shoulder, her tail idly wagged. "You're in pain, but yet you want to ask me a question?"

"I believe it distracts me," Gnemi replied, wincing.

"Sure, go ahead what is it?"

"Did you… use Gnaria as bait?"

"Yes."

Gnemi balled his hands into fists. "How could you do that!?"

"Simple. The acon'nada would go after something easier to catch than us. Even though it was angry at Histra for injuring it, the horse would have been too good to pass up."

"But Gnaria…"

"Would you rather us be dead or your horse?"

He took a deep breath just as Histra pulled her claws away from his leg. "I know… but just me and Gnaria went through so much together. She's been with me since I left home."

"It was just a horse. It did you well," Histra remarked.

"Histra, Ariana. You should be a bit more tactful about what happened. She and the other horses have saved our lives and gotten us through this far," Jesmine said, sitting beside the fire poking at the pot that hung over it.

"Forgive me for never having a fondness for horses. They've never done anything for me," Histra replied, going over to Alderin.

"Except drag the cart you were on for weeks, and then some," replied Gnemi with a sour look on his face, staring daggers at the kobold.

"A cart that... never mind. I have work to do," she remarked, working to heal Alderin's wounds.

"Gnaria was a member of the team, and she won't be forgotten," Dran said, patting Gnemi on the back, "But that's not the only thing you've lost, is it?"

He nodded. "My crossbow took an arrow, may have saved my life, but it damaged some components. I can still load and launch a single bolt, but I won't be able to fix it for multi-firing till we get back to Tundaholm. That and I'm also out of all my bombs."

"They were very useful once again, Gnemi."

"Thanks. We took out a few of them, and we were lucky that none of us were too seriously injured."

"Speak for yourself. I took a few hits that normally I'd never have taken if I wasn't..." Ariana trailed off. "I'm not used to fighting with such frail people."

"You saved my life there. Thank you, Ariana," Gnemi said.

"I wasn't going to leave you and Histra there. When the acon'nada showed up, my instincts said to run. And so, I did."

"I'm not sure if it was good or bad that they showed up, but the bigger question is... why?"

Jesmine spoke up, "I was wondering that myself. They aren't normally that aggressive. We could have disturbed their nest from all the fighting. Or it could have been..."

"Histra drawing the ire of the animals upon us," said Ariana.

Histra didn't flinch, focusing on sealing the wounds, her horn glowing white.

"Whatever the reason, their horses were sent off running. That will slow them down if they weren't killed off by the giant snake," Alderin said. He winced, feeling Histra's cold claws on his bare skin.

"From here, we're only four hours from our home... I wonder how much of it is going to be left," Jesmine said, staring into the fire, gently poking the flames with a nearby stick.

Ariana looked up toward the moons. "I never gave much consideration of returning home. There were things I'd like to have done if I got here. Now to be so close, I feel... off," she said, looking out in the direction of their home. Her ears folded back, tail wagging quicker.

"Off? How?" asked Gnemi.

"A sensation, of something is… wrong. I've felt it ever since we entered the forest. But it's been faint, like a smell of a flower in the background. Just one flower out of many, it's noticeable but not fully known. But as we've gotten closer, it's gotten stronger and it's made me feel uneasy."

"I've heard about the stories of our home being haunted. Part of me had wished it was just that, stories," Jesmine said.

"I'd prefer there be no ghosts but given the circumstances. If we say, run into ghosts, what will we do?" asked Gnemi. "I know a few things about fighting the undead. But ghosts and spirits are different than the bodies of the dead coming up to rise against the living."

"My Father was a spiritualist. He has mentioned that magic could disrupt and block harmful spirits. I'm hoping that is enough to stop anything from happening to us."

Histra pulled away from Alderin as he thanked her. "Magic can… I think. The cursed lands have their fair share of ghosts and ghouls… but," she growled, "I feel as if I know something but it's like holding onto air."

"It's alright Histra. I don't plan to take long. We go in, get to my home get the book… and perhaps some real clothes for me and get out."

"I'll be visiting my home if it's still there," Ariana added.

"I see nothing wrong with that."

"Same, you deserve to see your home as much as anyone," Gnemi said.

"We should get some rest then. Today was a long day and we don't know if they are still following us," Alderin said, looking over everyone. "Who wants to take the first watch?"

"I will," Histra replied as everyone stopped and turned to her. Her wings twitched as she flicked her tail. "What? I barely sleep anyway. Most of you have sustained injuries and need rest. I'll wake you if something happens. And if you don't trust me to take watch at this point, you never will," she growled.

"We didn't say you couldn't, Histra," Jesmine said.

"It's more we never expected you to offer," Dran remarked.

Histra let out a long-drawn-out sigh, "Get some rest. I'll wake one of you when it's time," she replied.

"I'll go next. I got lucky and came out with only a few scratches," Dran said.

Histra looking over to Ariana. "Did you want help getting that last arrowhead out of you?"

"No. It will come out on its own. And I prefer not to get my blood on any of you. My parents theorized that one way to contract lycanthropy is through the blood. And I never heard of a kobold Lycan. Perhaps you aren't compatible, and you'll die, and if you are? I prefer not to give you this gift."

She chuckled. "I prefer not to have it myself."

"But there is something I would like to give you. If it works."

She raised an eye ridge. "And what could you have that I could possibly want?"

"My parents were extremely talented alchemists. They had cures for all sorts of ailments, some were purely physical, while others used the magical essence of ingredients to craft potent potions. I believe there is something in my family's archives that could assist you."

"I doubt it."

"Histra, why do you have to be so negative?" Jesmine asked.

"I tried. I looked around. I used my own magic, nothing worked. Occasionally I get glimpses of my past, but if it was so easy to just drink a potion, I'd have done it by now."

"You never know, Histra."

Histra slumped her shoulders. "If there is? Great. But I am not placing any hope on it." She turned and walked off to the edge of the camp, climbing up a tree, perching on a branch like an owl. She looked down at the group as they got ready to get some rest.

Alderin looked up at her, seeing the firelight reflecting off her blue eyes like a cat in the darkness. Histra turned her gaze out in the other direction, thinking, *What is she trying to do? Lure me into a false sense of security? She has nothing to gain from it except my complacency. I will do what I want because I want to do it. Not because of another empty promise.*

The night passed without issue and after a few hours of travel, Jesmine stopped her horse. The others quickly took notice and stopped, Alderin asking, "What's wrong?"

"There," she said, pointing and riding off to the side.

The others followed, Dran yelling, "What's there?!" They only rode a short distance when Jesmine stopped her horse which neighed uneasily, entering a small section of the forest that was completely devoid of life. The trees stood tall with ghostly black and dead branches reaching out in all directions.

"What in the Gods is this?" asked Dran, looking around. The section of dead trees was only six feet in width but slowly grew wider in the direction toward the village.

"One of the dragons," remarked Jesmine, turning the horse in the direction of the expanding dead forest. Her hands tightly clenched the reins, pushing the slightly reluctant stallion forward.

"But the other town the dragons attacked; things were growing. Slow, but still growing," Alderin said. Ariana let out a low growl, ears perking as they walked. Gnemi held tighter onto her back.

"What's wrong?" Gnemi asked.

"She doesn't like the feel of this," Histra replied. "Neither do I," she added. Wind blew through the dead trees, causing them to creak and moan, the backdrop of birds chirping in the trees growing quieter and quieter til there was nothing but the creaking of dead wood.

Thump, thump, thump; the sound of heavy wings beating echoed through the forest, the horses neighing as they tried to regain control over them. The sound grew louder, seeming to come from everywhere as a deep, vindictive ethereal echoing voice spoke.

"We need to move!" Jesmine yelled, riding off in the direction of the village, the others quickly following suit as the heavy beating sound of wings and voice grew louder and louder. Wherever they looked, there was nothing but lifeless trees.

Unnoticed dead animals littered the forest floor; birds and larger creatures, their bodies in different states of decay which grew less as they drew closer to the town. They raced ahead, the sound of the beating of wings and the feral voice resounding out all around them, growing ever deafening until they burst from the dead forest into a completely barren field followed by a deathly silence.

"What was that!?" Gnemi yelled, looking around to see nothing but clear blue skies and signs of death all around him.

Dran looked around, pulling his war hammer out, tense and ready for a fight. "I don't see anything."

Bow drawn Alderin looked up. "Me either."

Jesmine turned to the group. "You heard it, right?" she asked.

"Aye, of course we heard it. It was thunderous, but what made it?" Dran asked.

Alderin swallowed a lump in his throat, heart pounding. "That sounded like a dragon to me," he remarked.

Jesmine answered. "It was speaking draconic. It said 'Die. You will all die.'"

"I don't see anything," he said.

"Neither do I," remarked Dran.

"It might have been an echo," remarked Jesmine, the tension slowly easing out of her.

"An echo? From what?" he asked.

"From the time it happened. Father told me that sometimes an event is so powerful that echoes of it can be heard in the land decades or even centuries after they occurred. I never experienced one before till now," she explained.

Ariana shook Gnemi and Histra off her, shifting back into her humanoid form.

"I think I know where the dragon landed then," Alderin said, pointing to the barren field, huge mounds of earth pushed up, two or three feet high and several feet across.

Ariana stared in the direction of the town, "It's almost like I remember it," she stated, brushing off some dirt from her hands. Her ears folded back, tail wag quickening.

The massive town in the forest clearing became everyone's focus. Everything appeared to be perfectly preserved, except for the destroyed stone building at the very top of a hill which rose in the center.

For Jesmine and Ariana, everything else was unchanged, save for the empty barren fields, filled with dead dried out livestock, surrounding the town, and the skeletal dead forest bordering it. Despite the open area, there was no wind. No singing birds. Nothing but a ghostly silence.

The elegant elven structures with their winding and curved forms was a stark contrast to the surrounding area, along with the bodies of a few dead visible from their vantage point. Jesmine tensed more, seeing her home, a two storied building, built into the hill side. It appeared untouched, as if time had no meaning since that one fateful day the dragon came to pay it a visit. After weeks of travel, fraught with danger, they were finally here, and as everyone wondered what this town of death had in store for them, Histra had one thought, giving a curious look at Jesmine.

"How does she know ancient dragon tongue?"

Chapter 18 Ghosts of Ami'ralia

Dran looked to the town and the dead barren fields in between. "Not to speak ill of your home, but we should get in, get your book and get the hell out. This is very unsettling."

Jesmine squeezed the reins of her horse, heart pounding ever quicker, hands subtly shaking, the air feeling heavy. A few moments passed until Gnemi broke the surreal silence. "Do you think we could head over there?" he asked, pointing over to the mounds of raised earth.

"Why?" asked Alderin, looking down at him.

"If our goal is to fight 'you know what', then perhaps getting a closer look at what one left behind would be beneficial? And as far as I know, unlike half of you, I've never seen a living one. I believe it won't take much out of our way, and when will we get a chance like this?"

"I don't know…" Alderin said, looking over to the mound of earth.

"It's fine. It shouldn't take too long and besides, I would like to get an idea which dragon came to my home," said Jesmine, riding over there and with each step, she felt the weight growing heavier upon her.

Dran gave another look around him. "We saw what happened at the other villages. It was nothing like this," he commented, keeping a hand on the hilt of his war hammer. "After thirty years there was growth and life, but here… there's nothing."

"I watched Dra'kesh's acid aura melt the world around him. Trees slowly died as their bark turned to slime, dripping down their sides. Some of those in the village were killed simply by being chained to the ground, letting his aura eat away at them. While others were…" Alderin trailed off, swallowing a lump in his throat, a tingle running down his spine.

"I don't recall the breath or power of Eisandra's ice aura, but I did get a taste of the poison once from one of Sa'bara's children. It wasn't pleasant," Histra remarked as they reached the point of landing. Each footprint was big enough to easily fit several horses with plenty of room to spare.

Gnemi approached the edge of one of the dragon's footprints, which was well over a foot in depth. The claw indentations were even deeper though somewhat weathered. "Just how often do dragons get this big?" Gnemi said, looking around, wide-eyed.

"I don't know. The dragons I fought were much younger, and were a fraction of this size," said Jesmine, looking down at the impressions.

"There is only one dragon that can be this big in Sa'bara's lands, and that is Sa'bara himself," remarked Histra, climbing up the mound of dirt to get a better view.

Jesmine's attention focused on her like a laser. "How can you be so sure?" she asked with tenseness in her voice.

Histra turned. "Razashra. She is his eldest living daughter, which makes her the eldest living dragon in his land after himself. She is almost but not quite this big. Who else could it be then but Sa'bara?" she asked, looking to Alderin. "You've seen an ancient dragon. Wouldn't Dra'kesh be about this size?"

Alderin took a deep breath and nodded. "Yes. He is like a flying mountain made of scales, claws and teeth. I have never seen any other dragon, but he caused similar destruction simply by landing near my village."

Ariana spoke up, "We should be careful not to disturb anything except what we must. Much of what we see here is probably still poisonous," pointing down the field, "Look over there. That acon'nada ate something that didn't agree with it," she adds as they looked in that direction, seeing the massive skeletal remains of the snake.

Its bones a pale disgusting yellow, parts of its body curled up on itself, its head upside down, the curved teeth jutting up into the sky, and trapped within those bones was a partially digested bovine. The undigested parts of its flesh were dried to its bones in an undecaying mummified state. Littered around the corpse and other animals were skeletal remains of scavengers that were unlucky enough to stumble upon their final free meal.

Dran gave an affirmative nod. "Aye. Its best we don't linger," he remarked, turning toward the town.

Jesmine took a deep slow breath looking toward the place she once called home. "Yes… but try to be careful. Those who have not fully departed this world may not take kindly to our presence.

Be respectful. Take nothing, disturb nothing that did not belong to myself or Ariana," she stated, pressing the sides of her horse, riding off in the direction of the town.

"That sounds about right," remarked Histra, jumping down from the mound of dirt.

Gnemi turned to her with a curious look. "What do you mean that sounds about right?"

"I lived in the north. I…" she closed her eyes for a moment, trying to think. "Believe I recall a battle with the undead. Though the undead and the ghosts who refuse to leave due to whatever reason are… different in an aspect. What she said sounds appropriate. In other words, don't step on any bodies, don't go into anyone's home, and be apologetic," she looked to Jesmine, speaking louder. "But I surmise Jesmine knows what to say to help put the dead at ease!"

Jesmine tensed, slowing her horse. "I will…" she trailed off.

Ariana looked down at Histra. "Did you have to do that?"

She looked up at her. "What? She's the best chance… outside of you to not incur the wrath of the undead."

Alderin remarked, "Unless they are vengeful for you two escaping their fate. Which would mean it would just anger them."

"It could be a possibility maybe? If I knew, I'd say, and I am saying what I know."

Ariana asked, "And what do *you* think you know?"

Histra sighed, "I'm trying to help."

"You are trying to appear to be useful," she stated, walking ahead enough to catch up with Jesmine, who was several paces ahead of the rest of the group. "Will you be okay?"

She nodded "Yeah. I knew this would have been difficult from the start…"

"You were expecting it to be different?"

She let out a long drawn-out sigh. "Yes. Almost everything is as it was. Except for the temple on the top of the hill."

"A place where some of them might have ran. Or just the best place to unleash his breath upon the town, but you fought dragons, what do you think?" she asked.

"I prefer not to talk about what possibly happened. What's dead is dead and there is nothing we could do about it," she looked to her. "You seem rather calm about coming home."

"You're right, I seem calm, by instincts are telling me that I should run. That there is something wrong about this place. It's a feeling even greater than what Histra gives me. My skin crawls, my fur is on edge, and I feel as if I am being watched."

"I feel the same way," she replied, reaching the outskirts of town. The bodies of dried out elven corpses littered the streets, running in a direction away from where Sa'bara had landed. Their mummified bodies were twisted and contorted as they gave a silent, deathly scream of agony. Some were reaching out for help that would never come, one was holding a child against them, only a few steps outside of the open front door to their home.

Jesmine stared at the bodies. "I don't know if I should be grateful or sad that I can't recognize anyone yet..." she muttered to herself, slipping off the horse. "I think we should tie off our horses here. It will be easier to avoid disturbing anyone's place of rest," she suggested, tugging on the reins, the horse slowly and reluctantly moving over to a nearby post.

"Aye, I believe that would be a good idea. Dariel doesn't like this place any more than I do," commented Dran, riding up to Jesmine, dismounting and hitching his horse, soon followed by Alderin.

"Do you think they will be okay here?" asked Alderin, patting the side of Cetas, calming him.

"I hope so," Jesmine replied, a shiver running down her spine, "I know a few things from my father. Restless spirits were his area of expertise, but if you are asking me, will they be fine without a doubt? I don't know. They should be okay being this far out of town given how long we plan to spend here. ...Yeah, I think so. If he was still alive, he'd have had a field day doing his best to learn about these restless spirits, the root causes, and most importantly bringing them to their final rest," Jesmine explained, looking in the direction of her home, stomach clenching. "To say I am afraid of what I am going to find there, is..." she trailed off.

Alderin gently rested his hand on her back. "It's alright. I know this can't be easy for you. I'd hate to think if my family..." he looked at the dead bodies, "You know."

She closed her eyes, taking a deep breath, "I know what you are thinking. I don't know what I'd do if I just saw him trapped in this world as a ghost or something worse, like a ghoul."

Gnemi inquired with a mix of curiosity and fearful concern in his voice. "What's the difference between a ghost and a ghoul?"

Jesmine looked down at him, thinking for a moment. "How to best explain it..."

Histra suddenly answered "Ghosts are an undead spirit that won't leave this plane of existence. A ghoul is that but will cause harm to the living, and perhaps even other ghosts."

"That would be correct," Jesmine added.

Gnemi nodded "I see," looking at the random corpses down the street, placing a hand on his loaded crossbow.

Ariana walked past him, shaking her head. "I don't think that is going to stop an undead spirit," she remarked.

"It never hurts to be prepared," he replied, making their way into town.

They ventured down the cobblestone road, walking past several dead elves of all ages. Each in the same state of dried out but not decayed flesh, bodies twisted and contorted, some reaching out, as if they were dragging themselves against the ground. Some homes had their doors wide open; others were partially ajar. One curved door frame with an elegant floral pattern around it had a body collapsed in the frame, desperate to get back into their home.

Gnemi weaved through the bodies, giving as much berth as possible around them. Jesmine carefully walked through the streets, hands held together, giving a few elven words of farewell. Ariana followed right behind her, eyeing the corpses, her tail barely wagging. Alderin moved right behind Dran, walking through carefully while keeping vigilance as Histra followed behind the group, looking with an almost child-like curiosity.

The deeper they ventured into the town, the greater the silence became, with only the sound of their footsteps echoing out. There were other dead animals, pets and horses tied to stalls, their bodies as withered and mummified as the elves.

"Look, one of the bodies has decayed," said Gnemi, pointing over to an oil lamp post where there was a skeleton of a human male. His body lay crumpled against the white and golden curled metal leaf pattern at the base, his head a few feet away. Dangling near the end of the lamp post arm was a thick rope tied into a noose.

Jesmine stared for a moment, forcing herself to look away.

"Why would someone… I am so sorry," she muttered.

Ariana let out a soft huff. "It's not your fault. The better question is did he do it, or someone else?" she asked, looking around.

"Why is this body rotted away, unlike the others," Gnemi said, keeping his distance, "It's as if… Jesmine were there many humans visiting your town? This is a human skeleton, right?"

"It is," Histra confirmed.

Jesmine shook her head. "Not often. We kept to ourselves," she responded, looking to Gnemi then back to the body. "Why do you ask?"

"It's just a hypothesis, but I think those who died when it happened aren't rotting away, but those who have come here and died afterwards decompose naturally. The question is why?"

"The bodies are poisonous. So much so that they don't even rot away," remarked Ariana.

Alderin commented, "All the more reason not to touch them."

Gnemi nodded and swallowed a lump in his throat, feeling the pace of his heart quicken, "Good idea," he replied, the sound of softly creaking wood filling the air. He jumped, looking in the direction of the noise, a door slowly opening. He took a single step toward the home, Dran placing a hand on his shoulder causing the gnome to jump, dry firing his crossbow.

"Relax. Remember, the only place we are going is Jesmine's home," he said.

"Right, right," he replied, taking a deep breath.

"I will be going to my home when we get close. And I prefer to go alone," stated Ariana.

"What? Are you mad?!" exclaimed Dran.

"No. It's my home. I want to be alone and it will be quicker that way," she remarked.

Gnemi looked up to her. "But what if a ghost or ghoul comes?"

Ariana gave him a stern look. "If we are to compare supernatural occurrences. I am one. I'm not going to be held up by something as simple as that."

Dran raised an eyebrow. "I don't think supernatural forces cancel each other out like that," he replied.

"This is my decision, and you're not going to stop me."

"I won't stop you, but do be careful. We don't know the extent of what can happen here."

"Nothing goooooooooood!" exclaimed Histra, feeling something wrap around her ankle. She looked down to an elf corpse with its cold gangling boney fingers wrapping around her. The kobold growled and kicked at the hand, snapping it off from the body and sending it flying a few feet away.

"Histra, what's wrong?" asked Jesmine, rushing over as the others turned to her.

"The corpse grabbed me," she remarked, pointing over to the body that's now two feet away.

Jesmine's hands shook, crouching down, looking at it. She said an extra prayer in elven before saying to Histra, "Perhaps it's best if we stay closer together."

"Maybe," she remarked, looking back at the body, which was undamaged and unmoved, causing her to twitch. "Or the ghosts are playing tricks on me... and I don't like tricks." She let out a huff of cold foggy air.

"What do you mean?"

"It's nothing... nothing dangerous," Histra remarked, moving up to next to Gnemi.

"It grabbed you?" Gnemi asked, looking over to the next closest body.

"No. I thought it did, that's all."

"How?"

"Spirits occasionally try to scare the living away as a warning not to stay," Jesmine explained.

"That doesn't make me feel better."

"It's not supposed to. It's to keep you vigilant and mindful of where we are," she added as sourceless screams filled the air. Ariana's ears perked, looking around as they bunched up. The voices of countless people cried out.

Jesmine tensed as Ariana remarked, "They are speaking elf tongue," Just then, a deep draconic growl rolled over the area, the screams growing louder, and louder. The sounds of people running down the streets as another draconic roar bellowed out. An echoing rumble of a crushed building comes from the direction of the hill as he door from the house that was opened moments ago slams shut and in that instant the silence returns.

"Uh... we should probably move," remarked Gnemi.

"You don't need to tell me twice," said Dran, quickening his pace.

"This place is more than a little haunted," remarked Histra, following the dwarf, flicking her wings.

"All the more reason we do not linger," he remarked, walking deeper into the deathly silence, a sensation of being watched coming over them. A shiver ran down Alderin's spine, looking up at a two-story building with dirty glass windows, seeing nothing. They approached a large open area near the base of the hill that commanded the view of the town.

"This was the town square where smaller shops would open up and local festivities were held," commented Jesmine, walking into the clearing.

Destroyed and mangled shops line along the sides of the square, the dead seen through the rubble, while others were huddled up against the side of buildings. In the very center of the square was a well. There laid six skeletons, five humans, their clothes weathered down as it clung to their frames, the sixth a kobold. The small skeletal frame sat awkwardly in a human sized armor, it's dragon-like shaped skull with a set of jutted horns coming from the back of the head fallen off, lying beside the body.

They slowly approached the well on their way toward the hill. Gnemi looked at the deceased with an apprehensive curiosity. "It appears that someone drank the well water."

"Aye," Dran replied, looking at the kobold skeleton before pushing on.

"I'll be heading over to my home. It's on the other side of the hill," said Ariana.

"What? After all that you've seen? You still want to go alone?" asked Alderin.

"Yes. Strange voices aren't going to harm me," she remarked.

"I don't like the idea of splitting up but at least one of us should go with you, just to be safe."

"No," she let out a soft growl. "This is my home, I will go, and none of you will follow. I can handle this on my own."

Alderin took a step back. "Alright. No need to get so aggressive. I'm only concerned," he replied.

Ariana let out a soft huff, her tail's wag slowing, ears folding back slightly. "It is simply something I need to do alone. I've handled myself in far more dangerous situations than this," she stared at him with her amber colored eyes, "Jesmine is the one who needs the protection, not I."

"Ariana, I don't think you need to be that way," replied Jesmine.

"I agree, Jesmine is important but--" Alderin trailed off, looking around, "Do you hear that?" he asked.

Ariana's ears perked up, turning her attention to the well. "I heard it. It's a cry for help in elven tongue," she stated, "It's coming from the well."

Histra remarked, "All the more reason to avoid the well."

"It sounds like a child," said Alderin, stepping toward it.

"Help me. I'm cold and it's dark down here," said the female voice in elven.

"And there is no reason a child would be alive here. Just keep walking," urged Histra.

"Yes, but what if it's not?" Alderin asked, the tremble in his hands growing with each step he took.

"Alderin, I agree with Histra, this is a bad idea," said Dran, rushing up to him. "We need to keep going."

"Help, please. I'm cold," she echoed from the well.

The voice was incomprehensible to the human, but the meaning was clear. A young child in distress. He closed his eyes, a vision of his family before him, his children yelling for him not to sacrifice himself to Dra'kesh. "But what if it's not?" he asked, looking to the well. "The well's cover and what was used to pull the bucket up looks to be in working order. We can wheel it up, if no one is really down there, nothing will happen, if there is, we saved a life. How can you not try?" he reasoned.

Histra shook her head. "It is best to leave it alone and continue. Isn't that right Jesmine?" she asked, looking over to her.

"It's impossible for it to be anyone from here," Jesmine said as the voice of the child caused her to close her eyes but not to turn away.

"See?"

"But, if it happened to be someone trapped down there, it is best to check."

Histra sighed, "Why? Really? Why?" she let out a groan, her wings twitching.

Alderin grabbed the handle. "If you can understand me, grab onto the bucket, we'll pull you up," he said, glancing down the well, unable to see the bottom in the darkness.

Jesmine took a step closer, repeating the phrase in elvish. Alderin turned the handle, but after one and a half revolutions the rope grew taut, becoming difficult to turn. "It feels heavy," he remarked, slowly making a single revolution.

Ariana groaned. "Let me help," she said, walking over to the well and grabbing the handle. Her feet dug into the earth that gathered around the base. She turned the crank with surprising difficulty, her body sliding against the stone, bumping into one of the skeletons.

Jesmine gave an apologetic prayer, while Histra and Gnemi stood off to the side. The kobold, with her arms crossed, sighed in annoyance, the gnome keeping vigilance for any movement as the pulley creaked. The rope slowly raveled around the wood cylinder, the two struggling to pull the bucket up.

"I told you it's heavy," said Alderin, looking at Ariana, who huffed.

"Not that heavy," she remarked, the sound of wood against stone echoing up from the well. All their effort brought up a bucket mostly filled with water, droplets dripping down the side as Ariana's ears flattened. There was no one there.

"See? Nothing," Histra remarked. Suddenly, the bucket kicked away from the two, the swift movement causing them to release the handle in surprise. The bucket flew over the stone side, hanging over the edge.

A ghostly elven voice whispered out into Alderin and Ariana's ears. *"Thank you."* A small child sized footprint appeared on top of the stone, causing the human to jump back, feeling a shiver running down his spine, hair standing up on end. He breathed heavily, looking in the direction of the footprint.

Ariana huffed; her fur puffing out, as Histra said, "Told you."

"She said, 'thank you,'" replied Ariana before she turned to the kobold with an exasperated look, "'Told you?'"

Alderin replied with a shaky voice. "Ah, uh, welcome."

"Not what I was expecting," said Dran, stepping away from the well. "Best we continue."

"Yes, yes. Let's…"

Jesmine softly sighed. "At least nothing bad happened. Maybe it was a good thing, as you might have freed their spirit from being trapped in the well."

"Right. Either way we should continue to move. How much further is your home?" asked Alderin.

"Not much, about two thirds of the way up the hill," she said pointing it out.

"You already know where my home is. If you happen to need me, I'll be there, but I'll be done before you all are," said Ariana, running off.

"It's not a good idea to split up like that," remarked Histra.

Jesmine nodded. "I know, she knows, we all know. All the more reason we should hurry," she said as they headed their separate ways, walking up the winding road that snaked its way up the hill. Dead trees and bushes filled the spaces between the road, which split off into smaller streets that led to homes.

"This place must have really been something," said Gnemi, looking up at the dead trees.

"It was. You could see the forest from the top balcony of my home, which was a beautiful sight, especially when the wind blew just right and you could see the shifting color of the leaves," she replied, looking through the desolate woods. Her home was now only a few minutes away. A weight pressed down onto her chest "It's been so long since I've been here. I never thought I'd return after what happened. Now a part of me wishes I hadn't."

Alderin walked up beside her. "I'm sorry that we had to put you through this again, but you see why we need you? You are the daughter of the great Ameria, the slayer of the evil…" he said, Histra interrupting him with a cough. Alderin looked over his shoulder down at her. "Outside of you, no one else thinks otherwise. Look at what Sa'bara has done. Do you think this level of destruction is justifiable?"

Histra sighed. "No, but he wasn't the first to do it, was he, Jesmine?" she asked.

She shook her head. "No, unfortunately not." She took a deep breath. "But that doesn't justify it. Let's keep going," she said, speeding up her pace.

Gnemi walked beside Histra, giving her a look. "Did you have to go there?"

"Excuse me for pointing out that she wasn't the only victim of an extermination of one's people. When my kind and those I served were killed off, it was justified, but when they do it because of a perceived threat of the exact same thing, it's horrible. Neither is acceptable to me, but I won't accept any hypocrisy over it."

"You are certainly eager to accept your own acts of hypocrisy, so long as they are justified in your head..." Alderin thought quietly to himself with a sigh.

Gnemi lowered his head in thought for a moment, and then back up to her. "I'm the youngest one here out of the group. I'm only twenty-seven."

"Why tell me this?" asked Histra.

"I was raised in the free north. Without the threat of dragons, I grew up hearing the great exploits of Ameria and the sacrifices she and others made. The work Jesmine and others did hunting down dragons that threatened the freedom that so many sacrificed to achieve. To me, Jesmine is a hero, and I am honored to be in her presence."

"I am not a hero. I did what I thought was best with my abilities," Jesmine replied.

"And comparing what happened in the north to your kind to what Sa'bara did here is not fair either. You could fight back, but this was a total slaughter," said Alderin.

Histra looked up at him with a glare. "We were powerless just the same to avoid the fate." She turned her attention back to Gnemi. "If I ever get my memory back, remind me to give you a real history lesson," she replied, walking ahead of everyone.

"You think you'll even be able to remember asking me to do that for you, Histra? Or if that precious memory of yours is even accurate?" Alderin called out after the kobold before rolling his eyes in disgust.

Dran shook his head. "It would be best if we keep the talk of dragons out of the conversation. We are not going to see eye to eye on the matter, but Alderin is right, this shows just how punishing it is to be under the dragons' rule. This, here? This is what happens to half a village every ten years where Alderin and I are from."

"I know. I heard about it when I slipped into Dra'kesh lands to find other Sa'bara elves to bring them to the north," she replied, turning down the street where three large homes built into the hill stood.

She looked at them, crossing the path of the first home. "That home there belonged to a relative of what you'd call a mayor of Ami'ralia. He was of a strange sort. Stayed at home fiddling over books of all sorts. He was very standoffish."

Histra turned to her. "And why tell us this? Does it really matter?"

"He was my neighbor. Though, someone else could have moved in since I was gone..." she trailed off.

"Who cares about that?"

"It's just, they were people who lived here. People I knew."

"People who you barely talked to. They just happened to live next to you. Yes, they are dead. Yes, it was horrible that they died, but why mention this now?" she asked.

"It's my home," she replied, looking down to her. "Wouldn't you talk about it if we were back at yours?"

Histra took a deep breath, sighing, fogging the air in front of her. "Perhaps..." her words were cut off as in the cold fog a long boney spectral hand was briefly visible. It grasped around her neck, lifting the kobold up into the air.

"Histra!" yelled Jesmine as the others were taken back. Histra's legs twitched, gasping for air, her claws holding around whatever was squeezing her throat. She tried and failed to formulate any words. "Let her go!" The elf yelled, reaching for Histra before the kobold was tossed like a rag doll through one of the second story windows. Glass shards flew out everywhere, cutting her along the shoulders, legs, and wings. She crashed into an empty bookcase which wobbled upon impact.

Histra fell on top of several books which were thrown all over the floor. She panted heavily, giving a long draconic growl. "How dare you touch me; you foul undead thing." Her body throbbed with pain of the impact, blood slowly spilling out from her cuts along her form. Her wings twitched, feeling pain spike along the wounds. The others were yelling as they rushed to the house. She pushed herself back to her feet as the bookcase creaked and wobbled. She leapt out of the way as it fell. Like dominos, it knocked over all the others.

She rushed to the door across the room, jumping over fallen bookcases, a vellum-bound book smashing into the back of her skull. Her head ached with throbbing pain; cracked horn added to the sensation like someone was drilling into her brain. She jumped to the door handle, hanging from it as it clicked open. The door swung itself wide, throwing her onto the balcony that overlooked the main entrance hall of the house. The sound of pounding against the front door echoed from downstairs.

Outside, Dran pulled out his war hammer. "Stand aside and let me," he stated, swinging hard, smashing through the lock as the twin doors opened.

Histra was shoved through the guard railings, which snapped and broke. As she tumbled down, she managed to spread her wings just enough to slow her descent so just the wind was knocked out of her.

Jesmine rushed to her and picked her up. "We need to run" she stated, feeling the kobold's cold scales against her. Droplets of her blood stung with a burning freezing sensation as she ran her out of the house. The sound of heavy footsteps was heard from the floor above, followed by a several thuds as pieces of the railing that fell to the ground broke under some unseen weight.

"You don't have to tell us twice," remarked Dran, rushing from the house and down to Jesmine's home. They looked behind them, seeing nothing. Their hearts raced, reaching the front of the house.

Histra groaned and twitched within Jesmine's arms. "Are you okay?" she asked as the others stood in a semi-circle behind her.

"I'll be fine. Put me down," she stated with a cough, her body twitching, pain shooting through her.

"But…"

"Do it, please."

Jesmine relented, doing so, looking over to the others who were apprehensive. "Anything?"

"No, it's calm again," said Alderin, looking over to the other house, thinking, *"Perhaps Histra shouldn't have insulted him like that."*

"He might be bound to the house," said Jesmine, looking over to the home. "He always spent all his time there."

"It is best we play it safe. Gnemi, do you mind staying out here with me?" asked Dran.

"I…I was hoping to enter, if that is okay with you, Jesmine?"

"It's fine by me."

"I'll stay outside too," said Alderin, Dran looking over to him. "Yell if you need us, okay?"

"I'm coming too," stated Histra, holding her claws to her side, her wings twitching slightly.

Jesmine looked down at her. "Do you really think that is a good idea? Wouldn't it be safer out here?"

"We've gotten this far. This is the home of the one who murdered the one I served. Call me curious, but I want to see what's inside. And don't worry. I don't intend to do anything. I'll spend most of my time healing what wounds I can."

Jesmine nodded, placing her hands on the front of the door, the handles shaped like elegant curved leaves. She took a deep breath, pushing the door handle with a soft click. It opened freely with a soft, echoing creak. The elf stepped inside, her bare calloused feet tapping against the hardwood floors, kicking up a thin layer of dust that covered everything.

Gnemi and Histra followed behind, the first thing greeting them was a large painting of a family portrait of Jesmine as a child with her parents standing behind her, each with a hand on her shoulders, dressed in their finest attire. Her father had a soft warm smile on his face, kind and gentle green eyes. His black hair was swept back, with two golden studded earrings in the bases of his pointed ears. Her mother, Ameria, stood out with her piercing fiery red eyes, her hair a blazing red. The fierceness was balanced by a small but sincere smile and her ears had three separate sets of earrings with different colored precious gems, while parts of her tattoos were shown curling out from underneath her white dress.

The weight grew on her, eyes quivered, staring at the painting. She walked closer to it. "It's still here, after all these years," she muttered to herself, Gnemi looking up in awe.

"That's Ameria? She really did have red hair."

Jesmine nodded. "Yeah. A rare trait amongst us elves."

"I thought all this time that was to describe her magical ability."

"Her skills were formidable."

Histra stared at the painting, drawn to the image of Ameria. Her heart raced, her claws tensing, wings twitching, pain shooting through her. She felt a burning ache in her chest and wings, tearing herself away from it. "She is something alright," she remarked, closing her eyes and began to mutter her incantation, her horn beginning to glow white.

"Where's the book?" asked Gnemi, admiring the room.

"It should be in my room," she said, heading up the stairs, which creaked under her weight. The sensation of soft red carpeting against her feet was as she remembered it. She felt the elegant curves of the railing, making her way up. The memories of a time long past rushed through her. Gnemi and Histra followed behind. She ran her claws along the cuts of her body, slowly sealing each one up.

Jesmine stopped at the door, slowly pushing it open. "Do you mind if I go in alone? I want to put on some clothes."

Gnemi stopped dead in his tracks. "Yes, yes, of course, go right ahead."

"Thank you," Jesmine smiled stepping inside, closing the door behind and leaving her alone in the room that was exactly like she left it. A dresser with a half-length mirror, a sturdy work desk with an empty inkwell and quill at the top, a wall full of books, and a canopy bed with soft silken white sheets with a fine layer of dust over it.

Images of her youth played out in her mind. Brief moments of happiness were instantly crushed by the reminder that it was all gone, yet everything was as she recalled. The view from the window, one that was of color and life, where she could see the town center and the forest out in the distance, a reminder just how dead the place had become.

After what felt like an eternity, she slipped on some clothes. Though dusty and old, they were the best she had ever felt. The elf rubbed the dirt and grime off her feet before slipping on some stockings and a pair of leather-bound shoes. She turned to see herself in the mirror, her hair a frazzled mess. She grabbed an ivory comb and brushed out some of the snags and random debris caught within.

"I still look horrible," she remarked, pocketing the comb. She looked around the room, pulling out drawers, shuffling through papers and clothes before stopping for a moment when she found a claw broken at the base with a thin layer of frost around it. She picked it up and it felt icy to the touch as she rested it in the palm of her hand and ran her thumb across it, feeling the warmth sucked out before pocketing it. "I might be able to do something with that later," she muttered, resuming her search.

In front of the house, Dran looked to Alderin. "Now is as good a time as any."

"What? Now? After what we saw?"

"Aye. I don't want to take more time here than needed and there was water in that bucket."

"I don't want to leave Jesmine alone with just Gnemi."

"You won't. I'll just go."

"What if what happened to Histra, happens again?"

"I'll be quick. There won't be another opportune time as this. Or do you want to risk it?"

Alderin looked back to the house, then over to the town square. "Be quick about it. I don't want to explain to Jesmine why you aren't here. It's bad enough that we let Ariana go alone."

"Aye, I know," Dran said, rushing off.

Alderin watched him leave, giving a wide berth away from the neighboring home before disappearing out of view. "If Jesmine finds out about this, we're done, but if we don't plan for it, we're also done," he muttered, resuming his watch.

There was a sudden knock as Gnemi called out through the door of Jesmine's room. "Everything okay in there?"

"Yes, yes," she responded, opening the door. "My book isn't in here."

"It's not? Where could it be then?"

"It has to be in the house somewhere. My father would never let anything bad happen to it. Let's check the study downstairs," she suggested, looking over to Histra, who was still chanting. Most of her minor cuts had been healed, breathing with less pain. "How are you doing, Histra?"

She continued to chant for another fifteen seconds before stopping, the glow of her horn fading with shortness of breath. "Tired. I stopped any bleeding, but my ribs are still bruised, possibly with a few fractures. It will take time to heal, and to heal correctly. It's far harder to heal myself than others."

"Is that why you were Eisandra's healer?" asked Gnemi.

"One of many, but yes," she replied as they headed downstairs into the study in the back of the house. It was full of books and everything was in order not a single one seemed out of place.

"That's a lot of books," remarked Gnemi.

"Mother and Father studied a lot. More so Mother as she was very obsessed with the arcane, which means I've read almost every book in here, some more than once," she explained, running her fingers across the spines of some of them, glancing at the various titles.

"If this library doesn't throw its books at me, I'll be happy," Histra remarked before adding, "What does your spellbook look like?"

"Leather bound with runic markings engraved with silver and gold. It has a latch on it that is protected by a runic lock."

"That would make it easier to find. None of these that I see have any precious metals engraved into them."

"Don't worry, Jesmine, we'll find it," said Gnemi, looking up, most of the books out of reach. "Perhaps we should get Alderin to come and help? He is taller than me," he remarked.

Jesmine chuckled. "Maybe, but for once it feels rather peaceful. We can take a moment to look, and if we need their help we can ask," she said as they searched. Several minutes passed with no luck, no book left unturned.

Eventually Jesmine approached a back wall of the library. She stood there looking at a set of books before reaching up to run her finger across the wood space where two bookcases met. She muttered words in elven-arcane and a set of hidden glyphs glowed bright for a moment before the door swung open with barely a sound.

"I'm going to check my mother's personal private study!" she yelled, Gnemi turning to peer past one bookcase to see the secret door.

"I'll come with you," he said, taking a few steps.

Histra smirked, adding in. "Me too."

"Keep looking up here," Jesmine stated, standing in the door frame. "This is one place I prefer no one outside of my family sees."

"Why?" asked Gnemi, Histra giving a long cold stare.

"We arcane users like to keep our secrets and it's not that I don't trust you. It is just that if there is one place I preferred not to disturb, it's here. I hope you understand, but if I really need your help I'll call."

Histra relaxed her shoulders. "We all have our secrets. You respected mine, so I'll respect yours. Come, Gnemi, maybe we missed something over here."

"Okay," he said, watching the kobold walk off. He looks back to Jesmine. "Be careful, okay?"

She smiled. "I will, don't worry," she said, heading downstairs. Gnemi resumed looking over by her. Jesmine took a moment to create the glowing light spheres, heading down a large set of steps that went into the hill. The stone walls showed minor structural fractures.

Gnemi watched Histra sit down, leaning against a bookshelf. "We'll just wait here until she comes back," she remarked.

"Aren't we going to continue to look around?"

"It's not going to be up here."

"Are you sure? If so, despite the secrets, perhaps it would be better to go down and help?" he asked.

"It's a hidden passageway. It's not meant for you, me, or anyone. As much as I'd like to know what's down there, it's not something to inquire about."

"But what makes you sure it's down there and not up here?" asked Gnemi.

"It's a spellbook, so it's bound to be down there, and I need you to keep an eye out for any more possible ghosts wanting to give me a bad day," she stated, gently rubbing her side and winced. "Damn, it still hurts."

"After you healed Jesmine, what happened to you shouldn't be too hard. Right?"

She chuckled and winced. "If it was another kobold? Sure. I could do more. But it's several times harder to heal myself."

"Why?"

"Outside of not being able to reach all of my injuries, the difficulty of being able to remain focused as pain shoots through my body exists. Losing half of my runes also limits my power," she stated, pointing to her cracked horn. "There are a lot of reasons."

"Why don't you try to heal your horn?"

"It's not that simple. And I know that as a hollow version of my old self. There are complications, and without knowing them all, I won't risk it. Last thing I want to do is accidentally damage my brain."

Gnemi winced at the comment. "Yeah. I can probably see that."

She nodded, tilting her head to the side. "Speaking of seeing something," she pointed as he tensed. A shiver ran down his spine, turning around slowly, just in time to catch the secret door closing.

"No, no!" he yelled, running to the door just as it closed. He banged on the bookcase. "Jesmine? Can you hear us?"

Histra sighed. "We'll have to wait. It's magically sealed," she remarked, closing her eyes. "I'm so tired."

Jesmine reached the base of the stairs, looking around. She waved her hands and with a forward walking like dance she stated a few arcane command words, a series of torches magically igniting. She stood on a balcony that was attached to another set of stairs that led straight down the center of the library. The elf took a deep breath, catching the musty smell of old books that lingered in the air when her chanting abruptly stopped. Her lights flickered out of existence, the magical torches now providing the only light in the room, but they provided more than enough for her to see sitting off to the side, legs crossed, with an opened book in his lap, the dried-out corpse of her father.

Jesmine gasped, covering her mouth. Her heart sunk to her feet, going over to him. His golden earrings reflected the ambient glow of the room. His hair was pulled back and his face was strangely serene despite his dried out mummified state.

Tears flooded her eyes, putting her hands together, lowering her head to sing him his final rights. Tears fell to the floor, hands shaking, voice cracking, spending several minutes performing the full vocal ceremony. When done, she looked up at him, saying in elven, "I am so sorry father." she looked away, "This… is all my fault," she said, then looking back at him, "I can only hope that I can one day earn your forgiveness." With one last wave goodbye, she turned toward the stairwell, taking one step down when she felt a hand on her shoulder pulling her back and a gentle voice speaking in elven.

"Don't go down there Jesmine, it's still filled with Sa'bara's breath."

Jesmine stumbled back and would have fallen over if it wasn't for a set of ethereal arms catching her. Her heart skipped a beat, scrambling back to her feet, jumping away from the stairs. Standing there with a ghostly but gentle smile, dressed in the same clothes as his corpse, stood her father. "Welcome home, my precious songbird. I've missed you so much."

As this all transpired, Ariana moved through the streets with quickness and agility, passing the fallen without disturbing them. She leapt and landed on all fours, sliding on the stone, stopping inches away from another dead elf. Slowly she stood tall, brushing any dirt off her hands, looking at the single-story home. The door was ajar as the smell of alchemical ingredients tingled her nose. Her ears folded back, tail wag slowing as she sniffed the air again before stepping inside.

"I'm home," she said, her voice softly echoing, and in return she got nothing but silence. "Not that you cared if I returned home," she muttered to herself, venturing forth. Her dulled claw tips tapped against the wooden floors, moving through the main greeting room, where withered herbs and other plants sat on stands near the windows.

"Not much has changed, what a surprise," she sarcastically remarked, entering the next room, the long, wooden dining table chairs knocked over as the body of an elven woman laid on the ground underneath two of them.

Ariana's ears folded back even more, crouching down beside the body. "Hello Mom. Been a long time," she said, taking the chairs off of her. "Part of me is so angry, angry at what happened, but…" She took a deep breath and let out a long, drawn out sigh. "It is good to see you, even like this. But I've been dead to you and father for a long time, haven't I? I'm not regretting what I did. I encouraged you to leave, I just wish," she trailed off, looking away, "It was always harder to speak to you than it was to Dad. I wonder if he's in the lab? I bet he is," she said, standing up and walked off in the direction of the lab. "May you rest in peace, Mom."

The smell of alchemical ingredients grew stronger and stronger, overpowering the smell of death that lingered throughout the town. She let out a soft huff of air, remarking, "And I thought it smelled bad when I was an elf."

She stepped into the lab with its large, long tables with all kinds of beakers, vials, some still filled with liquids, others with the dried stains of what was there before. Locked glass cabinets showed hundreds of different ingredients, many of which had withered away. Light came through thick glass windows providing a moderate amount of illumination. Across the room at a desk below one of these windows sat the corpse of her father hunched over the desk, with yellowed notes laid on the floor.

Ariana walked through the lab, memories of times long past echoing in her mind. She said to him, "Sorry I didn't come back to visit, but things have been difficult for me. I'm sure you don't mind if I take some of your equipment. You would want it to be put to good use." She grabbed a large backpack designed to carry lab equipment and ingredients. She unhooked the buttons that fastened it closed, tugging on strings that strengthened the enclosure to open it up revealing pockets, hoops, loops, and still soft cushioning.

Ariana grabbed any clean alchemic equipment, test tube holders, portable focused flame burners, and other items that she could. She filled a second bag with some of her parents' research books before checking the cabinets, which rattled when she tugged on them. "Still locked," she said, turning to her father.

"You always had the key on you," she thought, walking over to him. "Sorry father, but I need this more than you, to continue the research that was so precious to you and Mom, to me really. But I now have no choice in the matter, don't I?" she said out loud, examining him. She noticed a vial that was tightly grasped in his hand with a black rubber stopper firmly pressed into the top, thumb still folded over it.

"What do we have here?" she said, ears perking up, gently unraveling his fingers, peeling the thumb back and bones creaking and suddenly snapping, dried brittle skin breaking apart.

"I don't mean to disrespect you, but you always knew how curious I was," she said, pulling the vial out of his hands. Inside was light green gas which swirled around when she moved it. On the very bottom was a thick, viscous, dark green liquid only an eighth of an inch deep.

Ariana's ears perked, her eyes going wide, jaw dropping. "Did you..." she said to him, "You did, didn't you? Even when death approached, you couldn't help but think of your work." She gingerly placed the vial in a layer of cloth, then placed it into a larger vial, which she sealed with a rubber stopper. She did this one more time, placing it into the largest vial she had before wrapping that in another cloth and putting it securely in her vial bag.

She returned to her father, obtaining his small simple key that was in a pouch strapped to his side, unlocking the cabinets with a soft click, going through various ingredients, most of which were unusable.

"You two must be sad to see so many of your hard-searched components went to waste. It took you years to get some of these, and thinking back, it was fun coming along to get some of them. For me it made it worth the effort, but I know the goal was the most important thing, wasn't it?"

"I told Mom, that if given the choice, I'd do it all over again. I love what happened to me. I'm stronger, faster, and less prone to injury. I even have a few arrow heads stuck in me, and I'm doing fine. They hurt, but I will survive," she said, going to another cabinet, sifting through the bottles of various ingredients. "I control my instincts; they don't control me. I wish you could have seen me. But once I was blessed with this power, you…" her ears flattened, "I had to do it all on my own, but that's fine. As I said, it's made me stronger." There was a loud thud across the room, ears turning in the direction of the noise.

Ariana went silent, walking in the direction of the disturbance. She looked around, initially seeing nothing, and was about to walk away when her foot bumped into something. The elf looked down to see a book lying on its spine open to her. Her ears perked and tail slowly swayed from side to side, picking it up, skimming through the first page. Her ears flattened, and her tail became idle as she squeezed the book. She looked over to her father, then back to the book, reading the page again.

"It's been years since Ariana sacrificed herself for our safety. No child should ever die for their parents. If only we knew sooner that she wasn't killed, but became infected with lycanthropy herself, we could have cured the early stages of her curse.

But all is not lost. Through our knowledge of it, we managed to give her potions to help her regain her faculties through feeding local wildlife the treatments which she fed upon.   A'shiria and I are hopeful. Our last trip to her pack showed promise, but that was

432

unfortunately years ago.

Sa'bara's interest in our research has been helpful in furthering it, but we are concerned with why he is so interested. We do not want anything to happen to our dear Ariana. We have been giving Sa'bara outdated information on the Lycan pack's location. We hope that will help keep her safe. Though A'shiria calls me foolish for writing this down, it helps put my mind at ease.

But I have other concerns. Our trip to study the Lycan pack has been delayed, and according to our contact, by none other than Sa'bara himself. He wants to conduct a census of every race in the land. A'shiria says it's nothing. She says he has conducted censuses in the past, but I worry. We are told that once it's complete, we will be able to go. We are hopeful that we can try to make first contact with her this trip. Time will tell.

Sema'ariak

She closed the book, her ears folded. "This can't be true. I would have noticed if you were watching. It was my focus, my control that helped me tame the beast within me," she said with a growl, gripping the book ever tighter. "You," she trailed off, looking away. "All this time, I..." her ears folded, her tail subtly slipping between her legs. "Thank you," she said, putting the diary into the bag and resumed collecting materials.

"Oh, you know Jesmine? Ameria's daughter? She's still alive. A dwarf, a gnome, and a human escorted her here to get her spellbook. She lost her original. They rescued me from captivity from orcs and..." she said, recapping the whole series of events while cleaning out the lab. "To top it all off, there is a kobold in the party. She was the one that insisted I be freed. And get this, she says she's a cleric of Eisandra Everwinter, the dragon Ameria slew. How weird is that?" she asked, finishing packing all she could.

"Not sure what else I can say. I'm glad to have had this talk..." she swung the bags around her back with a soft grunt. "This is goodbye. May the knowledge that you did help comfort your rest in peace," she said, walking to the door, giving one last look over to her father before leaving. She stopped at her mother's body, crouching down. "Goodbye Mom. I'm sorry about the things I said... I didn't know what you both did for me. Thank you. May you rest in peace," she said, suddenly her ears perked, hearing a creak coming from the door.

Her nostrils flared, getting a strong whiff of the alchemic ingredients in her bags. Cautiously she headed toward the door, feeling herself grow tired. Her eyes grew heavy, limbs sluggish; she sprinted out of the house as a net was thrown over her. She thrashed about as Orla and Shana pulled the net completely around, taking her right off her feet. She growled, feeling the sting of small, silver hooks built into the net digging into her skin, further sapping her strength. Zed stood across the way, his tusks glowing a soft purple, a similar colored haze forming around her head.

Garran chuckled. "Finally, we got you back. You've cost us a lot of trouble," he said, crouching down to her. Her struggling grew weaker and weaker. "No matter. The others will be paying for it several times over," he said, everything for Ariana went dark.

Chapter 19 Resolution

Dran's footsteps echoed on the town square's stonework, approaching the well with a soft pant. His eyes locked onto his goal, the bucket, laid on top of a worn human skeleton at the base of the stone well wall. He crouched by it and peered inside. Deceptively clear water showed his reflection.

"Good, some is still in there," he muttered to himself in dwarven, pulling out an empty water sack, looking at the body. "I didn't mean to disturb, apologies," he said, gingerly pouring water into the flask, careful not to get any of it onto him. He closed the cover, putting it in a different pouch before standing up. He took a single step away, looking at the bucket then back to the well.

He grabbed the rope. "In case there are others trapped down there," he muttered, throwing the bucket. It flew into the well, suddenly stopping, levitating in the air in the center of the well, causing Dran to jump back. A sharp whistle followed by a massive orcish arrow pierced the bucket, puncturing the first wall and lodging itself into the second. The bucket fell quite unnaturally into the well after that, clattering all the way down, ending in a splash. He ducked down and up against the well beside a dead leather armored covered skeleton.

"They caught up to us," he remarked in dwarven. He looked in the direction of Jesmine's home. "I can't lead them back there. They won't know where they are because Ariana's... Ariana! She needs to know." He pulled out the war hammer, getting back to his feet but remained crouched. "I can't sit here," he said, looking over to the dead body.

"Forgive me but you might save a life today," he muttered, grabbing the corpse's leather armor, chucking it in the opposite direction of where he intended to go. An arrow pierced the body, bones shattering, and before the body hit the ground Dran sprinted toward Ariana's home.

Kra'mek gritted his teeth, notching another arrow from his hidden position amongst the torn stands on the other side of the town square. He drew his thick longbow, taking aim, but quickly relaxed as the well blocked his view.

"Damn," he muttered, sprinting after the dwarf. His heavy

orcish boots crushed an elf skeleton, upon reaching the well he took another shot. The arrow slammed into Dran's back, shattering on the blade of his war axe, the impact making him feel as if someone punched his back. Fragments of the arrow shaft cut along the nape of his neck and ears, drawing a little blood before he disappeared down the street.

Alderin stood by Jesmine's door, looking over to the neighbor's home. He felt a shiver down his spine, looking away. "We need to get out of here so—," his words were cut short, eyes widening, seeing Dran being chased by an orc. Without a second of hesitation he burst into Jesmine's home. The doors swung open with a heavy thud, yelling, "Jesmine! Gnemi! We have a problem!" His voice echoed in the living room, looking around. "The orcs! They are here!"

Gnemi rushed from the library, his crossbow drawn. "They're here? Where?"

"Town square! One is chasing Dran! We need to go now! Where is Jesmine?"

"She went into a secret library and hasn't come out yet."

"Get her, we need to go."

Histra spoke up, leaning on the door frame, "It's magically sealed. We can't get in."

"What? Open it then."

She shook her head. "I can't open it. I didn't watch her do it. That is even assuming I know how to do that particular kind of magic. You two go and help Dran. I'll wait here and tell Jesmine what's happening when she gets out."

Alderin stared at her, his body tensing as the kobold stared back at him.

"You're not coming to help?" Gnemi asked.

"I'm in no position to," she answered, looking to the secret passage. "And someone needs to tell Jesmine what's going on. You two need to inform Ariana what's happening."

Alderin nodded, looking to Gnemi, "She's right. We need to go. I saw Dran running to her and he needs our help."

"Got it," Gnemi responded as they rushed out.

Histra let out a drawn-out tired sigh, walking back into the library, to the front of the secret door leaning against the side of a bookshelf. She closed her eyes, muttering in draconic, "Don't take too long."

Alderin and Gnemi raced down the street which curved around the hill in the shape of a giant oval. "Do you see him?!" asked Gnemi, looking in vain.

"Not yet, but we'll need to get down there. Ariana said her home was on the other side of the hill. We'll run down through the back to avoid detection," he explained. The homes were separated by dead bushes and trees, which were easy enough to slip through.

Dran looked over his shoulder, unable to see anyone chasing him. He sidestepped and avoided the elven bodies on the street, hearing an echo of one being crushed under orcish footsteps. He turned a corner, almost tripping over himself at the sight that befell him. Hanging in front of Ariana's home from a lamp post was an unconscious Ariana, her body tightly held within the net that clawed at her hide. The alchemist's bag pressed against her back while Zed stood nearby with his hands up and focused on her, muttering words in orcish-arcana. Garran looked up at Ariana with a smirk, turning to Dran just as he appeared.

Orla stepped out of Ariana's home. "No one else is here, only dead elves and a--" She stopped midsentence, throwing a dagger at Dran with lightning quick reflexes. The blade sunk into his shoulder. He groaned from the stabbing pain, blood soaking into his armor, the discomfort growing as he tightly gripped the hammer.

Shana, who was standing off to the side drew her bow, taking aim when Garran yelled in orcish, "Take him alive!" Dran took a step back, "Run and she dies," he warned in human, pulling out his battle axe, pointing it over to Ariana.

Dran's eyes darted from orc to orc and up to Ariana, the axe moving closer to her. "Drop the hammer," Garran commanded. In this moment of hesitation, he heard the heavy footsteps of Kra'mek from behind. He looked just as the orc cracked his fist on the back of his head, knocking him to the ground, forcing the dagger deeper into his shoulder. He yelled from the tormenting pain, Kra'mek putting a foot on his back.

He reached down, ripping the hammer from Dran's tight grip. "This was Karrun's. You have no right to wield it, rock digger," he said in orcish.

Dran tensed, looking up at the orc, only to hear him saying a word in orcish-arcana, the symbols on the hammer glowing bright red, bursting into an aura of fire. "Perhaps I should show you why," he grunted, bringing it down, the heat licking at his face.

"Kra'mek! Don't waste the magic like that. Tie him up and bring him here," Garran commanded.

Kra'mek eyed him and let out a grunt, speaking the word again, the flames sputtering out. "Yes Garran," he replied, quickly tying him up, dragging him over and leaving a small trail of blood in his wake. Orla walked over to Dran, who looked up at her with a stern gaze before she pulled the dagger out. He gritted his teeth, muffling his groan, his shoulder throbbing.

"Cauterize the wound. We can't have our second bargaining chip bleed out," stated Garran, looking to Kra'mek, who nodded.

He spoke the words, the hammer bursting into fire once more, the heat of the flames licking at Dran's face, a few of his hairs curling and singeing as the corner of the hammer was put to the wound. He cried out in agony as it was cauterized, the smell of burning flesh permeated through the air as Garran spoke to Zed.

"Prepare for the others. The werewolf should remain unconscious."

He nodded and relaxed, the glow of his tusks fading. "Hopefully. These werewolves are hardier than we expected," he remarked.

"I know," he responded.

"Now that we have the werewolf and one of them, we should leave. They are now too disadvantaged to follow us, and it would be advantageous for us to get back to the others."

Garran grunted, "They've cost us too much. I won't stop till we have each and every last one of them," he stated, walking over to Dran, holding a blade to his throat, "Where are the others?" he asked in human.

"What do you mean? They aren't here?" snarkily replied Dran.

"Don't try my patience," he brought the blade closer.

"Maybe the ghosts got them. We've had problems," he remarked.

Garran pulled the blade away from his face, nodding to Kra'mek, who gave him another heavy-handed punch, knocking him onto his side, saying, "When I saw this rock digger, he came from the direction of the hill, but when I chased him he ran here."

"I see. They must be somewhere over there," he motioned with his head, "Be on guard. Shana take a position on a nearby roof and provide us with some cover. They probably know we're here by now."

"As you command," Shana said, walking up to him, whispering, "As much as I want to avenge them, there are times we need to fall back. I don't want to lose anyone else, including you."

"We won't lose this time," he grunted as she nodded, climbing the side of a nearby building. "Zed, take a hidden position; prepare more sleep gas for our guests for when they arrive."

"Of course," he responded, moving into a nearby building that faced toward the hill. He caught the musty smell of the place, kicking up dust as he moved, giving a look to the dead bodies huddled in the corner before he began to slowly mutter an incantation, tusks glowing a soft purple.

"You two keep an eye on the dwarf and the wolf," he said to Orla and Kra'mek. Garran walked to a less exposed spot. He took a deep breath, yelling in human, "I know you can hear me! We have two of your friends. If you want them and yourselves to survive, surrender now. If you do not. I will not hesitate to remove the dwarf's head from his shoulders!"

Dran, already sitting back up, yelled in dwarven, "Don't worry about me! The plan is more important!"

"Who said you could talk!" yelled Kra'mek, punching him to the ground with a thud. He spat up some blood, sternly glaring at the orc, tensing at the bindings that held his wrists behind his back and ankles together.

Alderin and Gnemi moved toward the commotion, taking positions just out of line of sight. Gnemi looked to Alderin, whispering, "What do we do? He said to leave him."

He nodded, pulling out his bow. "I'd say the same."

"What shall we do then?"

"The same thing he would. Rescue him without dying."

Gnemi tightened the grip on his crossbow. "We need a plan. There are only two of us and probably ten or so of them, and they could have two mages."

"Dran mentioned he injured the avian mage, but it's not safe to assume he is out of the action."

"What do you suggest we do then?"

"You think they've heard the same ghostly things we have?"

"Probably, why?" he asked curiously, looking down at the little gnome.

"We can't win head on, but if we buy time for Jesmine, we could put them on edge by making a few random ghostly distractions."

The human looked at him curiously. "How?"

"Shatter one of the nearby windows with an arrow; it will draw them away, while we move around. We'll keep them on their toes. Who knows maybe we'll get some ghostly help?"

"I don't think we should rely on the dead for help, but splitting them up and causing unease sounds like a good idea to me," he responded, taking aim at a two-story tall home from the alley. "We don't mean to disrespect your graves, but it is to save one of your last people," he whispered to himself, unleashing the arrow, shattering the window followed by a loud crash. Alderin and Gnemi ran away when the orcs turned their attention to the noise.

Garran yelled in orcish, "Do you see anything, Shana?"

"Nothing."

He yelled, "If we suspect you are doing anything but surrendering, say goodbye to Dran. If you try to attack us, it's over for your friends," he looked to Orla, "Think you can check it out?"

She nodded. "They have no real fighters left," she said, walking off in the direction of the noise.

Dran muttered in dwarven, "What are those fools doing?" He looked up at Kra'mek, who kept an eye on him and the surrounding area.

"*Push him into the house… when you are free,*" whispered a female voice that left a cold shiver down Dran's spine. He held himself back from looking around frantically, feeling a hand caressing his back, ropes slowly beginning to loosen. He tensed, swallowing a lump in his throat, feeling the same around his ankles.

"What in the name of Basila was that?" he muttered in dwarven, heart beating quick and heavy.

Kra'mek grunted, "Quiet," hitting him in the back of the skull. His head throbbed from the blow, remaining calm, his binds further loosening. All the while no one noticed that the knot that held Ariana's net up was slowly unraveling.

Ariana slowly cracked open an eye, feeling the stings of at least a dozen small hooks digging into her hide. She winced, heart pounding, vision blurring as she spied Orla running in a random direction. Her nostrils flared, catching the scent of the other orcs. She took another whiff and subtly turned her attention toward Dran.

"He's here," she thought as she sniffs again. *"Alderin, Gnemi. Did they come for me?"* she wondered, vision slowly coming into focus.

Garran gave a passing glance at her. "Hmm?" he took a step closer, her eyes shutting before he saw anything. "She can't be awake yet. Zed was sure to give her a form a sleeping gas that she was not resistant to," he muttered before resuming his watch. "Anything Shana?"

"I'll let you know if I see anything," she stated, keeping vigilance while using a chimney for cover.

Gnemi peered around a house noticing her before ducking back behind, leaning over to Alderin and whispering, "One of them is on a roof."

Alderin quickly peeked and ducked back. "No clear shot. Keep moving," he whispered, moving to next building, Shana just missing them.

Orla entered the home with the shattered window. Her daggers at the ready, making slow, calculated, stealthy steps, looking around.

Gnemi and Alderin quietly moved, trying to find a vantage point, mindful of their prey. The gnome took a moment to carefully and steadily reload his crossbow. "I don't see any of the birds," he whispered.

"Don't count them out yet," Alderin replied.

Ariana twitched, cracking her eyes open again just as Garran yelled, "My patience is running dry. Come out now or Dran dies!"

Kra'mek put his foot on the dwarf's back, pushing him into a kneeling position, holding the war hammer over his head.

A moment later, Orla came out of the home. "The window was shattered by an arrow!" she yelled.

Garran yelled, "You have till the count of five. "One. Two. Three."

Alderin drew his bow, keeping his back tight against a stone wall. He looked over to Gnemi, holding his crossbow at the ready, giving each other a nod. Kra'mek raised the hammer high into the sky.

"Four!" yelled Garran, and at that moment Ariana's rope unraveled. Her eyes widened, falling back first, hitting the ground hard, rolling just enough to land on her shoulder, protecting her bags from impact.

A cold whisper in Dran's ear said, "*Now.*" He became free of his bindings and with a mighty shove he pushed to his feet, throwing Kra'mek back into Ariana's home, along with himself. Shana took aim and fired, but the door closed the moment they were through, hitting it.

The orc looked surprised but noticed Alderin and Gnemi, "Garran watch out!" she yelled. Garran ducked as an arrow whizzed overhead. Shana counter fired, barely missing them. Gnemi sat down behind cover, using his feet to reset his crossbow while Alderin fired a shot at Shana, which bounced off the stonework of the chimney.

"Come on!" Alderin said, motioning Gnemi to follow, just as he got another bolt ready. Garran squeezed the hilt of his battle axe, moving to get better cover while Orla moved silently around. The sound of breaking wood echoed out within Ariana's home. She twitched, trying to move, finding the net's silver hooks digging deeper into her skin, further sapping her strength. As the party fought headlong into a life or death struggle, Jesmine was face to face with death itself.

The elf stood before the ghostly apparition of her father. His smile felt cold and empty, despite the compassion behind it. His ethereal form, translucent and surreal, yet full of detail. A near perfect representation of how he was when she last saw him, except for a few more wrinkles.

"I apologize for startling you. I wanted to simply watch, but no parent could let their child walk to their own death unwittingly."

She covered her face, holding back the swelling of tears. Her breath was heavy, her legs feeling weak unable to stop herself from switching her gaze from her father's ghost to his corpse only a few feet away.

He let out a breathless sigh "It is so very good to see you," he said, looking over her, before looking away. "I know how hard this must be to see me like this."

Moments of deathly silence passed. Jesmine swallowed a lump in her throat, hands shaking, voice cracking. "Father?"

He nodded. "I know it's hard to believe but—," he responded, his words cut off.

"I am so very sorry," she replied, tears streaming down her face.

"There is no need for you to be sorry, there's nothing to forgive. I decided when Sa'bara's breath was seeping into the house that I'd stay."

"It's my fault. It's entirely my fault," she stated, tears hitting the floor.

"Jesmine, you are too hard on yourself and I'm pretty sure don't have a poison breath," he said, moving closer. "I made the decision to stay."

"No… it's not that…" she trailed off for a moment, throat aching. "What happened to our home. Our people. It's my fault."

"Jesmine. What are you talking about?"

"I am the reason that Sa'bara caught wind of talk about rebellion. The free North told me if I could get a rebellion going in Sa'bara's land that they'd assist. I sent letters enlisting the aid of those I knew…" she looked up, tears continuing to stream down her face, "Months later. MONTHS. Sa'bara killed you, exterminated our people… countless had to die because of my hubris and naivety. I helped exterminate the remaining dragons in the North and my reward was the death of everything I knew and loved. If only… if only I wasn't—," Jesmine words were cut off by the cold sensation of his ethereal hand on her shoulder.

"You cannot blame yourself for the decisions others have made."

She looked up at his smile, a smile devoid of warmth but full of love. "But you died because of me. You are dead because of me."

"Jesmine… were you holding this in all this time?"

"Could you please forgive me? I was so stupid. If I only didn't send those letters, you and everyone else would still be alive."

He let out another airless sigh. "Jesmine. You did not kill us. The avolarieans revolted in the past, and did they get wiped out? No. Sa'bara wanted to do this."

"But I gave him the reason to do so!"

"Jesmine… when does a dragon ever need a reason to do something they wanted?"

Jesmine took a deep breath and slowly sighed, replying, "Never."

"Don't take the actions of others as sins upon yourself. It does neither you nor those who died any good."

"I should have done something. If I didn't leave home—," Jesmine said, her father interrupting her.

"You left home to pursue what you thought was right. No one could fault you for living for what you believe in, and I couldn't be happier, and I know your Mother would be too."

"But if I was here I—."

"You'd be dead as well. There was no warning, no time to react. Sa'bara came with such swift brutality that many have been unable to move on. Some trapped in loops of the time of their death; others protect what they had in life from the rare plunderer, while others have become so embittered by their deaths that they've become vengeful spirits, borderline ghouls. Like our neighbor."

Jesmine nodded. "We noticed. We saved one spirit trapped in a well that was crying for help, and then we were attacked by said neighbor."

"Are you okay?" he asked with deep concern in his ghostly voice.

"I'm fine. I wasn't the one attacked, but Histra."

"Is she the kobold?" he asked.

"Y-yes. How did you know?"

"I've been watching since you walked in. Histra's presence has not gone unnoticed."

"I know. She's a kobold, and they are the most loyal followers of the dragons, and she's rather harsh and rough around the edges, but she's been nothing but helpful. If it wasn't for her, I'd have not made it here. Please don't judge her for what she is father."

"You misunderstand. It's not that she's a kobold. It's something else."

Jesmine looked at him with a curious look, wiping some tears from her face. "What do you mean?" she thinks, wondering, *"Just how far does this aura she gives off go?"*

"She has an aura of death around her. I've never seen nor read

444

anything like this before, but she gives off a sense that she should be dead, but clearly, she's not. To those who wish to remain amongst the living, such a thing can easily incite anger in them."

"Is that why she was attacked?"

"That, or the fact she is a kobold."

"Don't tell me you think she's evil? She even saved my life from an arrow to the chest which caused a powerful spell rebound," she said, pointing to the hole in the cloak. "See? She's a powerful healer."

Her father leaned in and inspected the cloak. "She did? That would mean she knows elven anatomy, but I didn't see a spellbook on her, does that mean she knew the incantations from memory?"

"Yes."

"Hmm, interesting, it is rare to see healers that can heal other races, moreover, to cast without a spellbook."

"Father, can you promise me something?" she asked, looking at him before averting her gaze, the weight of seeing him pressing down on her.

"Of course, my precious songbird, what is it?"

"Don't do anything to Histra. She saved my life, and those in the party, and she knows who mother is."

"I promise."

"Histra said she's a cleric of Eisandra. Do you think her relation to Eisandra has something to do with it? She suffers from amnesia and only remembers bits and pieces of her past. She doesn't even know how old she is, but she's mentioned how she doesn't feel old."

He nodded, "Hmm. Eisandra was known for necromancy. I don't know how long kobolds live, but to be that knowledgeable she must be old. It's possible that Eisandra did something to Histra to give her an unnatural long life."

"Which would mean she should have died due to old age, but is alive and well?"

"I honestly don't know," he replied, "But you aren't here for that, are you?"

Jesmine swallowed a lump in her throat. "No. I'm here for my back up spellbook. My original one was destroyed when...," she trailed off, averting her gaze. "I know how important it is, but there was little I could do."

"Things happen that one can't control. Your Mother would not be pleased but I won't tell her if you don't," he let out a ghostly chuckle.

She took a deep breath and sighed, "Father…"

"I'm only trying to lighten the mood. I know this can't be easy for you."

"That's an understatement. Going through our former lands, to see the destruction of places I visited. The city Rivera was just as I remembered it, but now there are orcs there living like our people did. Wearing our armor, making our weapons, speaking our language… Sa'bara is mocking our ancestors!" she yelled, looking at him. Her hands tensed. "It constantly reminded me just what was lost. What I helped cause."

"I bet they don't look as good as we do, but Jesmine you can't—."

"Who's to say that Sa'bara did it as reprisal for the extermination we did in the north? An extermination that I helped make a reality."

He let out another long, ghostly sigh, rubbing his temples, "You've inherited my sense of compassion, but your mother's stubbornness."

Jesmine looked down. "I wish I could have done something. If I only knew. If I didn't go off to follow in mom's footsteps, this could have been avoided," she muttered, more teardrops added to the puddle on the floor.

"Tell me. Do you think you'd have been happy staying here?"

She looked up, "Huh?"

"Why did you leave in the first place?"

"To make the world a better place. To free our people from Sa'bara's control so we could live how we want, and not how the dragons believe we should. To make you and mom proud… and not let her sacrifice be in vain."

"Your mother was the same. When I met her, she was already obsessed with finding a way to take down the ancient dragons. Like you, she wanted to free us from Sa'bara's control, and so, she wanted him to be the first to die."

"Then why didn't she?"

"Sa'bara is clever. He's never seen. Always using his children to exercise his will. He also coerces other races to follow him. She realized this when we elves fought the avolariea rebellion where they were stripped of their winged mounts. Eisandra on the other hand was well known, seen often, and feared by all. None wanted to be shipped to the north to be under her cold reign. Out of the five lands, hers was the harshest. Which is why she went there. To free those who were in greater need. You could say her decision to kill Eisandra led to the deaths of our people here. If she focused on Sa'bara and killed him, we'd still be alive."

"How could you talk about mom like that! She sacrificed herself to make the dreams of countless people to become a reality!"

"How could *you* talk about yourself the same way when you were only doing the same?"

His words echoed out into the silence, the weight in her chest growing even heavier.

"You and your mother made sacrifices to do what you believed in. Decisions come with consequences, and we all must live with those consequences, but don't blame yourself for the decisions of others that you had no control over. Your mother wouldn't blame herself for the death of our people, and neither should you."

A moment of silence passed, taking a deep breath. "Those I came with want me to help kill Dra'kesh."

Another moment of silence passed. "And how do you feel about that?"

"I... I don't know. Alderin the human wants him dead for the death of his family. Dra'kesh made him watch as he melted them with his acidic breath. Dran, the dwarf, wants him dead because the fighting caused by his decadal tribute makes countless people suffer. And Gnemi? He seems to want to make a name for himself. Oh! Ariana, the alchemists' daughter, she's here, alive and well."

"It is good to know your friends' motivations, but their reasons are their own. I asked you how you feel about it?"

"I wish I knew. I don't want to let them down, but I feel like this is a repeat of history. If we succeed it will surely lead to the deaths of countless people, even kobolds. Many think kobolds are evil, who are nothing but the dragons' pets, but I've seen them do good things. They aren't as bad as people think they are. I'd hate to see them killed just because they had no other choice but to follow the dragons."

"And if you fail, you fear a reprisal and the deaths of countless more."

"But if I do nothing, people are going to suffer and die due to Dra'kesh's tributary system. No matter what I decide, people are going to die. They are going to die because of me! Because I happen to be my mother's daughter, the slayer of an ancient dragon!" she yelled, body tensing up, tears resuming to flow down her cheeks.

Suddenly, she felt a ghostly hand on her chin gently easing her head up to look into her father's cold, yet loving smile once again. "No one said you had to be a dragon slayer like your mother."

Jesmine let out a soft huff. "Mom sure made it feel that way."

"She wanted you to be prepared for whatever life was going to throw at you. She knew the storm that was to come if she managed to kill Eisandra."

"But there was no storm. The other dragons didn't invade Eisandra's land once she fell. They only made life more difficult for those in their lands. Sa'bara now marks everyone with his all-seeing eye and imbues it with magic as part of his tax collection."

"I am not going to pretend I understand what the dragons are thinking, but I will ask you again. What will you do?"

Jesmine swallowed a lump in her throat.

"The only one who can decide this is you. I can only support you in what way I can."

"I want to help them…" she looked at her father. Her body shook, feeling the urge to look away. "You know how hard it is for me," her voice cracked, "To just talk to you? To see you like this."

He closed his eyes, "I know. And I am sorry that I'm causing you such pain."

"Don't blame yourself. You aren't the one who did this."

"But it was my decision, my dedication to this world the desire to see you again that has kept me here all this time."

Jesmine blinked, a few more tears rolling down her cheeks, following the tracks of the ones that came before. "I'm so sorry. You could have been waiting here forever for me to come. The only reason I am here today is due to chance."

"I knew one day you'd come. I had faith in you."

"But to be here alone, all this time."

"Time has little meaning when nothing changes. And I've had

my and your mother's books to keep me company. Which I kept perfectly in the order she has left them. She'd kill me if I didn't."

Jesmine's eyes narrowed, "Father... Your sense of humor hasn't improved at all."

"It hasn't gotten any worse either," he responded with a ghostly chuckle.

She let out a long, drawn-out sigh, wiping her face clean.

"It is fascinating. I remember what I've read. I'm not just living in the moment, my existence is continuing and, in a way, growing. My spirit is remembering what I have experienced. I would have never guessed anything like this when I was..." he trailed off, "If you meet anyone else in my field, let them know."

Jesmine nodded. "I will father."

"We got off topic. You said you want to help them. They have their reasons for wanting to kill Dra'kesh. Countless people have their reasons for wanting the dragons gone. But none of that matters. What matters is what you want and why."

Jesmine closed her eyes, taking a deep breath. "I would like nothing more than to get vengeance on Sa'bara for what he's done, but that's not going to help me. It's not going to bring you or anyone else back. What I can do is try to stop it from happening again. To stop Dra'kesh's cruelty. Perhaps once they are free, they and the north can work together to liberate these lands from Sa'bara. I don't know. But what I do know," she said, opening her eyes and stared at him, "Is that I can show the world that the death of Eisandra was not some fluke, but that it is possible to beat these dragons again, and that if we work together, we can free ourselves from their control, and be able to decide how to live our lives without the fear of angering some uncaring and unforgiving dragon. Because no one should have to see their family melted before them because they didn't have enough money to pay some arbitrary fee, or have to talk to their dead father..." She trailed off, looking away.

"It's okay to be sad," he said, looking over the library, the light from the magic torches flickering. "Wait here, I'll get what you need," he said, less so walking, but walk-floating down the steps, which creaked under a non-existent weight, disappearing out of view.

Jesmine let out a sigh, collapsing once again. Slowly she

looked over to her father's body and swallowed a lump in her throat. "Even in death you help me. Thank you," she muttered.

"What father wouldn't give themselves to their children?" he responded as a leather-bound bag with metal latches over the flap floats over to her.

Jesmine reached for it as the weight of the bag sparked a curiosity. She pulled it into her lap, her father standing before her again. "My book wasn't this heavy."

"I know. This is something your mother wanted to give you when you were ready."

She looked down to the bag, a thin layer of dust breaking, undoing the latches, reaching in and feeling the cool outline of a book. She pulled it out, the torch lights reflecting the magically melded together rubies, diamonds, sapphires, emeralds and black garnets that formed a dragon's eye on the silver latch with no discernable keyhole that would unlock the strap that had mithril running along the edges. The intricate arcane designs were inlaid with mithril metal ran across the front and back portions. The spine was over two inches in thickness and had a draconic-shaped arcane symbol made to look like a red and mithril colored dragon breathing fire.

Jesmine ran her trembling fingers over the book, looking at the side of the pages, golden leaf siding with mithril painted arcane markings weaved along the sides, connecting the arcane symbols from the front, back, into a giant solid glyph. "This looks like mother's book, but hers was lost when she fought Eisandra."

"It's not her original, but it is the one she wanted you to have. She made it just for you."

Jesmine looked up and asked, "Do you know the command word to open it?"

"She wouldn't tell me. But since Jesmine was the word she used to open her book; it might not be too hard for you to guess."

She thought for a moment, running her fingers over the book's lock. She focused as the runes on her body gave off a faint glow, saying in elven-arcana, "Mother." A moment passed, and nothing happened.

"A nice try, but perhaps a little too focused?"

Jesmine nodded and closed her eyes and tried again. "Mother and Father," nothing happened.

"I thought that would have been it, perhaps something more inclusive but secretive? You know how she loved her secrets."

She thought for a moment, eyes lighting up. "I think I might know." She closed her eyes, focusing once more. Her tattoos glowed softly as she spoke in ancient-draconic-arcane, the command word equivalent of "Family."

The runes on the book lit up with a red radiance, the dragon on the spine appearing to breathe fire as the lock separated into two. The book opened, the pages seeming impossibly thin but were as sturdy and durable as thick vellum. Her eyes glowed, reading through the pages with a near impossible quickness, able to get the basics of what spell was on what page with just a glance. She closed her eyes, the book snapping shut and the latch merging back into one piece once again.

"I knew you could do it," he said cheerfully.

She kept her head down. "Thank you." She stood up and looked to her father, "Does this mean that your reason for staying is fulfilled and you'll pass on?"

"I was but—"

"Father!"

"If you are going to fight Dra'kesh and liberate our home, I will want to hear all about it. Which means you will need to live to tell me about it."

"You… mother was tough but you…"

"I don't want my precious songbird to throw her life away. I want you to live more than anything else."

Jesmine put the book back into the bag, closing her eyes. "I will. And I will return so you can rest knowing that you didn't die in vain."

"My death was tragic, but never in vain. Now go, all but Histra has left some time ago."

Jesmine raised her head, "What?"

"I could sense them leave my area. Why, I do not know, I've been here with you all this time."

Jesmine's eyes went wide. "I got to go."

"Be safe."

"I will," she responded, rushing to the staircase, taking one step before stopping. "And Father?"

"Yes?" he asked, standing by the staircase that led to the

library.

"Love you."

"Love you too," he replied before she ran up the stairs. She quickly cast a light orb as darkness enveloped her. Her footsteps pounded on the steps, rushing up, the door creaking opening as she approached.

Histra cracked her eyes open as the sudden movement caught her attention. She pushed herself up to her feet just as Jesmine reached the top. "Took you long enough. Did you find your book?"

"Yes. Where is everyone else?"

"They went to Ariana. They followed us here."

"Histra, hurry get on my back," Jesmine urged, crouching down for her to get on.

She sighed. "I am not a backpack," she remarked, climbing on.

"I can run faster than you, and we need to get to them," she explained, rushing out. Histra tightly held onto her, folding her wings. Jesmine sprinted in the direction of Ariana's home, and, turning to get an unobstructed view, seeing smoke rising into the sky. "Let's hope we're not too late."

When Dran knocked Kra'mek into Ariana's home, the orc landed on his back with a heavy thud, the door slamming behind them. The orc grunted, swinging his hammer at Dran, who narrowly dodged.

Kra'mek leapt to his feet, the wood creaking under his weight, glaring at Dran, "You're dead," he said in orcish, then speaking the command word, the hammer bursting into flames.

He remarked, falling back into the dining room, "Not good."

The orc roared, charging in after him, the dwarf throwing chairs at him, which he batted away, shattering them and lighting the pieces of dried wood on fire.

"I did not think that one through," he remarked, using the dining table to block the orc from charging right at him. Kra'mek simply smashed the table, which collapsed in upon itself, bursting into flames as he barged through.

While they played cat and mouse, the fire steadily spread faster and faster through the home. Dran desperately looked for something, anything he could use against Kra'mek, who was nipping at his heels.

Ariana smelled the burning of wood, her attention instantly

turning to her home, letting out a howl. Her body tensed, struggling against the net, ignoring the pain that shot through her, hooks tearing at her hide. A puff of purple haze enveloped her head. She held her breath, the gas forcing its way through her nostrils, and into her lungs. The weight of slumber pressing upon her, struggling growing ever weaker till sleep overtook her once more.

Zed continued his spell, Garran remarking. "Damn werewolves," he looked to Shana. "Cover me!"

She drew her bow, aiming in the direction where Alderin and Gnemi were last seen, Garran charging after them.

Alderin and Gnemi rushed around the elven home, the human with an arrow notched in his bow and Gnemi's crossbow cocked and loaded. "Keep moving, we'll try to isolate and take them out one at a time," Alderin said.

Moments later, Orla appeared in front of them. Her gaze intensified, yelling, "Found them!"

Alderin and Gnemi fired as Orla threw two daggers. The attacks whistled through the air. Gnemi's bolt hit her upper leg. Alderin's arrow piercing her chest armor. Her first dagger pierced into Alderin's gut. The second dagger whizzed right past his head.

Orla unsheathed two medium length swords, charging in. Alderin barely had time to register the pain as he dodged her attack. Gnemi just managed to roll out of the way. Crossbow slipping from his fingers.

Alderin raised his bow, deflecting the attack. Her blade sliced halfway through the bow before it snapped in twine. The top of the shaft flung back, smacking the human in the face as he hit her with the other half of the bow, scratching her cheek.

Gnemi charged in, feeling the soft ache of his earlier injury, Orla barely managing to block. She jumped back keeping the two in front of her, weapons at the ready. Alderin winced, feeling the sharp stabbing pain in his gut. Each step jostled the blade, blood staining his under armor. He pressed on with his attack.

Blades clanged, dirt kicked up, Orla falling back. Gnemi tried to get around her til she leapt back to the other side of an alley, gritting her teeth, pain shooting through her leg.

"Not falling for that," Alderin remarked, tensing in pain, resisting the urge to tend to his wound. They panted heavily in this surreal pause in the fighting.

Orla muttered in orcish. "Damn," before a sudden smile crept across her face. Garran rushed into the fight; axe held high.

Alderin turned to face the attack, Orla rushing in.

"Look out!" Gnemi cried out charging in, striking her in the leg.

Orla grunted, attacking him, their blades clashing. Gnemi's sword was knocked away, the orc awkwardly bending down to strike at him.

Alderin and Garran met head on, sword to axe. Garran's heavy strikes pushed him back while the human gripped with both hands just to stand up to the force of Garran's single-handed blows. He yelled in orcish. "You will pay for what you've done!"

Sweat poured down Alderin's brow, breath heavy, trying to keep the massive orc at bay.

Gnemi fell back, using the dead trees and bushes to his advantage, able to wiggle through the small openings. Orla rushed in after him, slowed by the dead brush.

Alderin's pain grew; the force of Garran's strikes reverberating through his blade, making it difficult to maintain his grip. With relentless rage, the orc struck over and over, with a metallic clang.

Gnemi faired a little better, dodging and deflecting Orla's attacks, guiding each one away from him rather than stopping them outright. The orc yelled in frustration, forced to bend down low to strike at him, exacerbating the pain in her leg.

As their fight raged on, the fires raged throughout Ariana's home. Shana watched with ever growing concern, keeping a look out for her companions.

Alderin panted heavily, the dagger slipping out, only the tip covered in blood. Garran struck with a heavy blow. He stumbled back, barely able to deflect it as he stared down the orc. A sharp piercing pain was felt through his leg. He yelled, leg giving out under him, falling to a knee. Garran swooped in, punching him in the face, the blow knocking him to the ground with a heavy thud, dried dirt kicking up.

"Alderin!" Gnemi yelled. Purple smoke appeared around him.

Orla broke off her attack, jumping back. "Zed! I had him!" she yelled, looking at him chanting in arcana, tusks glowing a soft purple.

Gnemi coughed, stumbling back into the dead brush, hanging limply from it, his blade clattering to the ground.

Zed stopped his chant, clearing his throat. "We don't have time to fight them. Kra'mek is in the burning building," he replied.

Garran pressed Alderin to the ground with his foot, who cried out in pain. "Good work Zed," he looked at Orla, "Grab the gnome, the more hostages we have the better," he remarked, keeping his foot pressed down on Alderin, ripping the sword from his grasp. "I am going to enjoy making you pay for all the trouble you've given me."

The human gasped for air under the orc's weight. Dirt clung to his sweaty face as Garran grabbed him by the back of his armor, dragging him to the front of Ariana's home. Fire licked at the windows, which cracked and shattered under the growing heat.

Dran and Kra'mek continued their combative dance, the heat curling more of his beard. Parts of the building began to crumble as Kra'mek yelled, "You will die for killing Karrun!" he charged him, barely dodging. The heat of the hammer caught some of his beard on fire, flames eating through it as he wiped the heavy amounts of blood that ran down the side of his face.

Dran stood steadfast, the orc swinging the hammer down. He threw the blood into Kra'mek's eyes causing the orc to fall back, the red liquid stinging and blinding him as he yelled wildly, swinging the flaming hammer. The dwarf dodged the attacks enough to grab his opponent and flung him over the shoulder. The orc flew three feet away back into the dining hall, landing a short distance from the burning elven corpse.

Kra'mek yelled out in pain while Dran took the moment to pat out the fire on his beard. He rushed into the living room, the fires blocking his only escape.

Kra'mek coughed as thick black smoke from the burning corpse wafted over him. He pushed back to his feet, rubbing the blood from his eyes. As his vision cleared, he yelled, "You have nowhere to run now," coughing heavily. His lungs burned as he charged Dran, but he only made it three steps before he stumbled and fell with a heavy thud. The burning in his lungs grew hotter as he forced himself back onto his feet, the searing pain growing throughout his body. He managed only a short distance, unable to breathe before he collapsed to the ground, dead.

Dran distanced himself, desperately looking for a way to escape. He coughed heavily; smoke filled the room. He took a step towards the kitchen hearing a voice yell into his ear, which sent a cold shiver down his spine, *"Wrong way! It's poisonous. Only death there."*

Parts of the ceiling crumbled as he fell to the ground, desperate to get any air. With no way out and the fires closing in he thought, *"I'm sorry sis, I won't be coming back."*

Meanwhile, Garran threw Alderin across the ground, his body rolling and smacking into an elven corpse, the arrow shaft snapping. He let out a groan of pain, Gnemi's body tossed like a rag doll beside Ariana. "Try putting out the fire Zed," Garran commanded.

"I'll try," he replied, facing the burning home, beginning to cast a spell.

Garran cracked his neck, holstering his axe and walking over to Alderin, who panted heavily. "Orla get ready to rush in once the fires die down. We don't have much time to save Kra'mek."

"Got it," she responded.

Garran kicked Alderin in the side, the human rolling and yelling in pain, body slamming into a nearby building. "After what we offered, you stole from me, and killed my friends. I'm not only going to kill you, I am going to make you suffer for all the pain you've caused me," he grunted, crouching down. "You won't die today… not tomorrow, not a month from now, but you will, and when you do, you will be begging for me to end your pitiful existence," he stated.

"Garran?" Orla asked with a slight tremble in her voice.

He grunted. "What is it?"

"Turn around!" she urged.

"Hmm?" he said, turning to see the fire being pulled away from the building. It swirled and flowed like a river of inferno up into the air, sucking up every flame, until not even the building itself was smoking. Higher and higher the flames swirled. His eyes widened. "Zed?"

He shook his head, watching with growing concern, taking a step back. The flames took the shape of a giant dragon, letting out a burning roar before flying down and striking at Garran.

He ran but, was unable to dodge the full brunt of the attack.

Deep gashes in his side were instantly cauterized as he yelled in pain. Shana fired several shots at the burning creature, which flew right through, catching on fire, and were quickly absorbed into the dragon.

Zed ended his spell cast, muttering while taking several steps back. "She's created a living fire dragon..." The dragon landing amongst them, its tail swiping at the orc, the fires burning him as he screamed in pain. It unleashed a fire breath at Shana, who hid behind the chimney, flames rushing past her, the intense heat lighting her hair ablaze. She tried to put it out, but the fire leapt from her hair and was absorbed by the fiery draconic being. "Retreat! Garran, we need to retreat!"

Garran groaned, pulling himself back to his feet, watching the dragon's fire tail knock Orla several feet away, parts of her clothes catching on fire, which were quickly absorbed back into the blazing beast. "Orla!" he yelled, reaching out to her as she groaned in pain.

Zed rushed over to him. "We need to run. We can't fight her like this."

Garran looked to him. "Find her!"

"She'll kill us before we do!" he shouted, the dragon turning its attention to the pair. Its head rose up, jaws opening wide, teeth burning. It unleashed another fiery breath just as the orcs leapt out of the way to avoid the attack, the heat of the inferno curling their hair.

Garran grunted from the pain of the burning wounds at his side. He looked back to the partially burned-out building behind the fire dragon, the flames distorting the air around them. "Kra'mek!" he screamed.

Zed grabbed him by the shoulder, pulling him back. "We have to go... NOW!"

He tensed, hearing no response. The fire dragon lashed out at him, claws striking at his arm, cutting three deep gashes that cauterized themselves the moment they were made. He howled in pain, falling back. He gave one last look at the fire dragon and back at the building. A pit formed in his stomach, yelling, "Retreat!"

Shana slid down the roof, leaping to the ground as they ran. The fire dragon gave chase through and out of the town, forcing them to the outskirts and back into the forest.

Jesmine took a deep breath, lifting the infernal creature into the air and with one last word, it disappeared into the sky. From her spot on top of the hill she looked down at the carnage that transpired. She closed her spellbook, looking over to Histra, who was still on her back. "I hope I wasn't too late," she said with a heavy pant.

"We'll see when we get there, and don't make a habit of me holding onto your back when you cast spells," she said.

"Histra..." Jesmine trailed off, running down the hill. "I'll do what I can," she remarked.

Alderin pushed himself back onto his feet, looking to Ariana's burned-out home, limping his way to it. The scent of burnt wood lingered heavily on the air. He tried to push open the blackened burnt door, but it collapsed upon itself, revealing Dran lying motionless in the center of the room. "Dran!" he yelled, stumbling over the door fragments.

"Dran, are you okay?" he asked, pushing him over, his beard and most of his hair completely burned away with severe burns over his face. "Dran!" he yelled, shaking his body. "Say something!"

"Ow..." he muttered, cracking his eye open.

Alderin let out a relieved chuckle, wincing in pain. "You're alive."

"Barely," he groaned, looking over to the dead and burned orc body. "Do me a favor and grab me my hammer, but don't breathe the air over there. It's poisonous..."

"We can worry about the hammer later," he said, dragging him out of the building just as Jesmine reached them.

"You're alive. Thank the Gods."

Dran coughed. "Scarcely," he remarked, Histra letting go of Jesmine, walking over to him, who chuckled when she approached "For once your ice aura feels great," he remarked with a cough.

She let out a sigh. "You had to get yourself burned. I'm not a miracle worker. Something like this will take time..." she groaned, looking over him, running her claws along his face. "It could have been worse," she grunted, "Much worse."

"I thought I was going to die but then all the fire disappeared," he remarked.

"That was me; I took control of the flames to make it appear like a living flame spell. It was the best I could do on short notice."

Alderin winced in pain, placing his hand on his side. "It certainly saved our lives. Thank you," he replied.

"You aren't out of the woods yet, you could bleed to death," remarked Histra.

Jesmine sighed, "Histra…"

She gave one last look over Dran. "You have no immediate concerns," she looked to Alderin, "You on the other hand, get the damn armor off," she remarked.

He nodded, wincing, removing his leather armor. "Jesmine, does this mean that you got your spellbook?"

She nodded, walking over to Ariana and Gnemi. "Yes," she said, checking on Gnemi before gingerly working to remove the net from Ariana. "Once we are all able to move, we should go."

"You don't have to tell me twice," remarked Dran, staring up into the sky. "I've had my fair share of ghosts and orcs for a lifetime."

"Now aren't you glad you didn't leave me in that cage? You'd all be dead if it wasn't for me," Histra said, digging her claws into Alderin's leg, working to pull out the arrow before marking around his wound, casting her spell.

"Histra, could you at least be a little more modest?" Jesmine asked, wincing as one of the net's hooks pricked her.

She didn't respond, slowly healing Alderin's wound as he chuckled softly, "This once, and only this once… I'll give it to her."

"Aye, me too," he groaned. Histra slowly and partially healed Alderin's wounds before working to ease Dran's burns.

Ariana sat up suddenly as consciousness came back to her sometime later, head almost hitting Jesmine in the face as the net was fully removed from her. "Ariana, relax. Everything is okay," Jesmine said, placing a hand on her shoulder.

Her ears perked, her nostrils flaring, looking around, her attention focused on her home. Her tail stopped wagging, ears folding back.

"Sorry about your home Ariana. The orc with the flaming hammer made a total mess of the place," Dran groaned, looking over to her, some of the burns on his face and body partially healed.

Ariana stood up but collapsed almost immediately after, as dizziness overcame her. "Careful, you were under that orc's sleeping spell. It's not something to get over. Honestly, I am surprised you are already awake," said Jesmine.

Ariana let out a huff, "I'm slightly resistant to magic. Another benefit of being a Lycan," she remarked, eyes suddenly going wide, looking around. "My bags! Where are my bags!?"

"Right over there," said Jesmine, pointing to them a few feet behind her.

Ariana let out a sigh of relief. "Thank the Gods," she said, dragging them over to her.

"After the fire…" she trailed off.

"I'll want to look over what's left."

"That's a bad idea," remarked Dran, leaning against the war hammer.

Ariana stared at him. "Why?"

"The smoke deeper in the home is poisonous. The orc was killed within seconds after breathing it in. I was lucky to be far enough away to be spared."

"I see…"

"I know it can't be easy, but let me do something to cheer you up," Jesmine said, pulling out her spellbook, everyone's eyes lighting up when they saw it.

"That's your spellbook?!" exclaimed Alderin, torn between keeping his eyes peeled and noticing the glimmer from the book.

"I've seen intricate spellbooks, but this tops our arcane master back home by a landslide," remarked Dran.

"It's a parting gift from my mother," she explained with a weak smile, flipping through the pages, and after several minutes of searching she stopped on a passage. "Ah, this one should do it."

"Should?" asked Ariana, ears perking.

"Nothing is certain till it is done. Hold out your cuffs and keep them still. This will take a while," she responded, beginning her incantation. The runes on her body and within the pages of the spellbook began to glow, hands running across the mithril cuffs, their own arcane markings glowing in kind.

Histra eyed Jesmine's book… her wings twitched, feeling a rush. Her claws tensed, eventually looking away. "Wake me when it's over," she remarked, curling up where she laid. A half an hour later the cuffs shifted, and a line formed, splitting the manacles, which clattered to the ground with a ringing clank.

Ariana let out a deep sigh of relief, rubbing her wrists and ankles. "It feels so good to get them off," she remarked, giving a big lipped grin, "Thank you Jesmine. I won't forget this for as long as I live."

"You are most welcome," she replied, standing up before a light-headed feeling overcame her, forcing her to sit back down. "That took more out of me than I thought."

"Take a moment, but it's best we get as far as we can from those cuffs as possible. Now that we have a chance to lose those orcs," Alderin said.

"I'll be fine… I just need a few minutes."

"Take the time you need after that we leave."

"Aye, the moment we lose them, the better off we'll be."

"But that leaves one nagging problem left for us," Histra said, sitting up, everyone turning to her. "How do we get across the river now that Rivera is cut off? After all, the dragons are looking for us."

After a moment of silence Jesmine spoke up, "Sabra. We'll head to Sabra."

Chapter 20 Fateful Decisions

Garran and his battered party returned to the scene of the battle in the waning hours of the day. A deathly silence surrounded them, their horses bucking and neighing uneasily. Bandages covered their cuts and burns, their bodies aching as they kept a vigilant watch. He dismounted from his horse with a heavy grunt, Shana slipping off her steed and rushing over to him.

"You're injures haven't healed. You might reopen the wounds," she warned.

Garran grunted, "I'm fine," shrugging her off, storming into Ariana's burnt-out shell of a home. Only seconds later his screams of anger and frustration were heard. Shana rushed in to see him standing over the dead partially burned body of his friend. His fists shook in rage, punching a nearby blackened burnt wall, breaking right through it. His hand dripped with blood as burnt splinters were driven into it.

"Garran," Shana said, approaching him.

"They won't get away with this. They will pay dearly for it!" he grunted, picking up the body of his friend with his good arm, carrying him out over his shoulder.

"We can't keep pushing on like this. We are too few," she warned, Garran saying nothing, walking past her.

Zed and Orla gritted their teeth seeing Garran placing the body on the back of his horse. "We will hold a quick ceremony and press on," he muttered.

"That will be difficult," Zed replied.

"We can track them with your magic. They shouldn't have gotten far. If we get the jump on them, we'll win," he remarked.

"I can't," he responded, shaking his head.

He stared daggers at him. "What?"

Zed lifted up the cuffs and collar, "They removed them. I can no longer track them."

"Then Shana can track her."

"Garran. We've been beaten."

"No!" He yelled as the horses neighed uneasily. "We haven't. We've only been unlucky. Look how easily they fell against our strength. They don't stand a chance," he grunted, mounting up.

The others look at each other then back to him, Shana speaking up. "This is madness. The reward from Sa'bara is not worth it."

"I don't give a damn about Sa'bara and what he wants. We are far past that. If I could I'd strangle him with my bare hands for the trouble, he's given us."

"You don't mean that," said Shana.

"Garran, take a moment to think about what you are saying," cautioned Orla.

Zed approached him. "I agree. Take a moment and calm down. Think about it. What if one of Sa'bara's informants are here? They could take your one moment of frustration out of context."

"I don't care. Curse them! Curse the dragons! They deserve to die for what they've done! We are a strong people; we don't deserve to be treated like mongrels, rewarded for being obedient little pets. We've done everything he has wanted. What he desires. And what is our reward for all our efforts? Nothing but death! We are skillful warriors. We are strong, brave, deserving of greatness, but look where we are. A dead town in the middle of nowhere!" he exclaimed.

"Garran, I know this isn't what we'd hoped for, but you can't give up and throw everything away like that," Shana said.

He grunted, "We've already lost everything. Bringing that werewolf back won't bring back the dead but killing those soft skins would brighten up my day," he remarked, riding off.

Shana sighed, looking over the others. "Once he calms down, I'll talk to him."

Orla remarked, "We know how he feels. But even we must admit when we've been bested."

"We weren't bested, they were merely lucky, and that's what's eating at him the most," Shana replied, mounting her horse.

Zed climbed back onto his. "This is a turn of events I wished that had never come to pass," he replied, heading off to the edge of the forest, where they spent the waning moments of sunlight building a bonfire. Kra'mek's body laid to rest on a pile of dead wood.

Garran held a torch in his hands as he gave one final remark. "You didn't deserve this death, but you died with honor, may your ashes find their way to Garthund, and he judges you worthy," he said, putting the torch to the wood which quickly caught fire. The thick dark clouds billowed out as the flames consumed the body. He walked away but only took a few steps before he began to cough hard, falling to one knee.

"Garran!" yelled Shana, rushing to him.

He coughed. "I'm fine. It's simply a little hard to breathe," he replied, Zed's eyes going wide.

"Everyone away from the fire! The wood contains Sa'bara's poison!" Zed warned.

Quickly they dragged Garran away.

The orc coughed heavily, struggling to breathe. "I won't let this stop me," he groaned, pushing himself back to his feet.

"Garran, you mustn't push yourself. We'll take a moment to recover," said Shana as they setup camp.

He laid in his own tent, coughing and hacking. Shana watched over him as the night dragged on. She tensed, the weight heavy on her eyes, heavier on her chest.

"Get some rest. I'll be here," he coughed.

Shana's shoulders dropped, "If you insist."

"I need you at your best," he replied with a weak smirk.

"I'll see you in the morning," she stated, leaving the hut, finding Zed standing at the entrance. "What do you think?"

"I'm not sure. The fact he didn't die quickly means he only got a small dose. We'll have to wait and see," he explained.

Shana sighed in relief. "There is still hope then."

"I'll look after him. He'll hate it, but he will need it tonight."

Shana patted him on the shoulder. "You're a good friend."

"Get some rest."

Orla spoke up, sitting on a tree stump, looking over to the town in the distance. "I'll keep watch."

Shana nodded, entering her personal tent while Zed entered Garran's.

He closed the entrance behind him. A small lantern hanging from the top of the tent provided a soft glow. "I don't need you to look after me. I'm not a child," Garran stated before unleashing a coughing fit.

"I know. I came to talk," replied Zed, sitting beside him. "Give up on chasing them."

"What?!" he snapped, trying to sit up but collapsed back down. "No. Once I recover, we will find them, kill them, and I will feel the satisfaction that *he* won't get one werewolf for his collection."

Zed took a deep breath and looked to him. "As your friend, I beg you. Don't go down this route. We've been through so much together. I'd hate for you to throw away everything over this."

"Beg? We don't beg," he groaned. "No. I am not throwing away anything. I've already lost everything. There is nothing left but to take this to the very end. To make them suffer, to punish them. To punish everyone who played a part in this misery. I'll find those random humans that helped them and kill them and everyone they care about. I'll take that werewolf's head and put it on a pike and laugh at Sa'bara who failed to get something he so badly wanted. I will make that human Alderin suffer the most. I won't stop till our friends are avenged," he said, coughing harder.

"There is no way I can talk you out of this?"

"When was the last time you ever talked me out of something that I had my mind set on?" he asked with a smirk.

"Never," he replied with a long sigh. He looked over to the hut's entrance then back at him.

"Tell me, my friend, that you're with me. We've been through so much over the years. We can't let this stop us."

"I'm with you to the end."

Garran grinned, his tusks and teeth showing through as Zed began to chant, his tusks glowing a soft green. "What are you doing?" he asked, after a while, looking at him curiously. Zed moved his hands over his body. "Careful, you said yourself that your healing magic is limited," he remarked. Zed's hands moved to his mouth. A burst of pain burned through his throat and lungs as a flow of air rushed into them. His eyes went wide, Zed's hand clamping down onto his mouth, holding his nose in the process. He gripped Zed's arm, trying in vain to fight against him.

"I'm sorry, my friend. I've tried so hard. Tried to urge you to take more sensible routes, to cut your losses and simply inform Sa'bara about what you know. But, in the end, it was my failure to help," he said, staring him in the eyes.

Garran squirmed and struggled. The pain burned through him, body growing weaker and weaker, poison coursing through his veins and lungs. Zed muttered in draconic-arcana, a small symbol glowing blue green unseen under his shirt. His massive orcish form shrunk down, thick orcish fingers reducing to green scaled claws.

Garran was already too weak to fight Zed's scaled down form. His yellow reptilian eyes focused on him, revealing himself to be a small kobold. His horns were engraved in less elegant runic markings and inlaid silver compared to Histra's. His orcish clothes were oversized and baggy on his smaller form.

Zed took a deep breath, Garran's eyes for the first time shook with fear. "As my friend you deserved to see me in my true form. For so long I wanted to show you, but I was forbidden. Know this is the hardest execution I've ever done, but his will must be followed. I did all I could to give myself a reason to ignore what you've said," he trailed off and looked back to the hut's entrance. "Don't worry. They will be spared. We will return and inform him of what we know. They will be rewarded for their attempts to serve him. And your betrayal won't be noted. You will have simply died by accident," he explained, muttering in draconic once again. His body shifted back to its orcish form. "Goodbye, my friend. I won't forget you," he said as Garran's eyes grew dim, the last of his life draining away.

Zed took a deep breath and sighed. "I will do what I can to avenge your death," he said, sitting there in quiet contemplation, keeping his head held low with one hand held to his chest.

Over the next few days, the party found the trail told to them by Amir, leading their way out of Du'ralia Forest. They remained mindful that the orcs and the avolarieans might still be on their trail, but without them magic-tracking Ariana, they rested a little easier with each passing day.

The plains south of the forest were dotted with small human settlements surrounded by farmland. Smaller forests and some rolling hills completed the vista. In the late afternoon they crested the top of a hill to see the moderately sized town of Sabra nestled up against the great Sa'bara River.

Wattle and Daub houses made the vast majority of homes. Farmers tilled the fields as fishermen stood on long wooden docks that reached out and bridged to a small island about thirty yards from the town. They threw their nets over the side of the dock, letting them gather fish as the waters rushed by.

"Do you think they have a way to get us across the river? I don't see any bridges that span to the other side," remarked Alderin.

"There is only one way we'll find out. I don't think Amir would lie to us," said Jesmine.

"Here's hoping," he replied as they headed into town. Ariana already had shifted back to her anthropomorphic form. People watched their approach with curiosity, but upon seeing Histra it quickly shifted to suspicion.

People up ahead ran deeper into the town. "This is going to be interesting," Histra remarked.

Dran's burns which had mostly healed, still left some scarring along the right side of face and hand. He rubbed his slowly growing facial hair as he approached her. "Just don't say anything to piss people off. You know, what you normally do."

She glared at him. "I know how to handle myself," she remarked.

"We know you can, Histra. Just… um," stated Jesmine.

"Just what?"

"Relax."

Histra sighed. "I'll see what I can do," she replied, reaching the outskirts of the town. Four lightly armed militia men approached.

"Hello!" one of them yelled.

Alderin responded as they slowly approached. "Greetings."

"What brings you to our town?" he asked, looking over the group with special attention to Histra with a glare. Her wings twitched in response.

"We've come to see Amir."

"Amir?" the guard responded, looking to the other guards, then back to him.

"Yes, he helped us earlier in our travels. Do you know where he is?"

"We'll take you to him," he responded, motioning for them to follow. They moved through the town's dirt streets as people watched and talked amongst themselves. They were taken to the far side of town, seeing the tallest building nearby, a stone church with a dragon statue placed at the very top of the roof, but they stopped a little down the road to a small simple single-story home. The guard knocked on the door. "Amir, you have visitors from out of town. They say they know you."

A few moments passed, the door opening. Amir stepped out; his eyes widened with surprise. "You're here."

Jesmine dismounted from her horse. "Yes."

"You all look terrible. Please come inside my humble home," he said, looking to the guards. "It's alright. These are the ones I mentioned."

"There really was a kobold then," the guard responded, looking over to Histra.

She glared. "Yes. *Shocking*, a kobold who can take care of herself," she remarked, storming into Amir's home.

"The mayor has been informed of their arrival, Amir," the guard said, leaning in close. "You know why."

He nodded.

"I hope we aren't causing too much trouble?" said Jesmine.

Amir smiled. "No. None at all. We rarely get visitors to our sleepy town. And though I've mentioned what happened when we came back, there has been some skepticism. I will admit, I wasn't expecting to see you again," he responded with a chuckle.

"Your faith in us is *astounding*," said Histra sarcastically.

"Amir, why is there a kobold here?" inquired a female voice from within the home.

"She's the healer I told you about, love," he replied, turning to the guards. "They're fine. They won't cause any trouble."

"We'll keep two guards nearby, just in case you need any help."

"I won't need it, but thank you," he replied, ushering everyone inside. Amir's home was a simple place, with wooden furnishings, a fireplace in the next room with a pot of stew that was slowly stirred by a middle-aged woman with soft bronzed skin, her long black hair tied into a single ponytail. Her brown eyes looked on those entering the home with concern, most of her attention focused on the kobold.

Histra walked into the dining and kitchen area. "Yes?"

The woman looked away. "Nothing."

"What I thought," she huffed.

"Histra, what did we just talk about?" asked Jesmine, walking up to her.

"I've done nothing wrong. I'm not a fan of someone's judging eyes," she growled, shooting the woman a look.

"And if you keep making comments like that with your vinegar laced words, you will give them reason to keep their judgements of you justified," The elf replied, Histra staring back for a moment before turning away.

She looked over to Amir, who closed the door behind him. "Amir?"

"Everyone, this is my lovely wife, Rina. Rina, these are the people that I ran into at the castle."

"The ones you said were going to Ami'ralia?"

"They're the ones, and from the looks of it, they ran into some trouble."

"Aye, a little from the orcs, but we managed to stop them. It's been over a week since we last saw them," replied Dran.

"I'm glad to see you all made it out of there in one piece," he said. He turned to Jesmine. "How was visiting your hometown?"

Rina looked at her husband curiously. "Hometown?"

Jesmine lowered her hood. "It was an experience that I will never forget," she replied.

"By the Gods, it's an elf!" Rina responded, stumbling back, her eyes transfixed on Jesmine's ears.

"I see you left *that* part out of your story," remarked Histra.

"Some facts did not need to be shared," Amir replied.

"Good. I prefer to limit attention drawn to us, and me."

"We thank you for your hospitality, and we hope not to take up too much of your time, but we are in need of your aid," said Jesmine.

"You need to cross the river?" asked Amir.

She nodded. "Yes."

"We lost the orcs, but we prefer to keep them off of our trail," Alderin explained.

"I understand," he said, turning to his wife. "Rina, I hate to burden you, but can you keep our guests' company while I go to see the mayor?"

"I will do what I can," she said, turning to the party. "We don't have much, but you are free to rest. You must be tired from your travel."

"I believe it's been the longest trip of my life," Gnemi said, climbing into a nearby chair. "Thank you for your kindness."

"We do what we can for others," she replied.

"If you'll excuse me, I will talk to the mayor and see if I can organize your way across the river," said Amir.

"Thank you. It means a lot to us," said Jesmine.

"I am doing what Toval would have wanted," he explained, grabbing his walking stick before leaving.

Dran walked over to Rina. "Thank you, miss, for your hospitality, and we apologize for the inconvenience."

She went back to the pot and stirred the food within. "No trouble at all. It's more surprising to have so many guests in our humble home."

"More like surprising to see a kobold in your home," Histra chimed in from the corner of the room.

"Histra!" Jesmine exclaimed.

"What? It's true, and I am doing what I can to not be a bother. I'm over here in the corner," she said, wings twitching.

"It is surprising to see a kobold walking around with others, but if Amir trusts you, so do I."

"That means so *much* to me," she replied sarcastically.

Jesmine sighed. "Sorry. Histra is a bit difficult at times."

"At times?" remarked Dran.

"Who has been healing your burned face over the last several days?" Histra said, giving him a cold glare.

"I only spoke the truth, and I thank you for the effort."

"Be glad your burns were within what I could do. If you break a bone or get stabbed, don't come crying to me for aid."

"I don't intend to have either happen to me."

"You didn't intend to get burned either, but guess what? It happened."

Jesmine walked over to Rina. "Sorry, we have an interesting group."

Rina nodded. "How do you put up with her?" she asked, looking over to Histra.

"Once you get past her outer shell you find out she's rather nice."

"Granted, her outer shell is a bit thick, and that's not counting the ice." Alderin said, the kobold shooting him a glare as he smirked.

She slowly nodded. "If you say so."

"Do you happen to have a place where I could sit and work privately?"

"The next room over should be okay, I hope. It was our

children's room until they moved out a few years ago."

"Thank you," said Jesmine, leaving the room.

"Where are you going?" asked Alderin.

"I'm going to continue to work on my project."

"Ah, putting those tools you went to pick up from your home to good use, I see."

"I wouldn't have had us go back for them otherwise," she replied, heading into the other room, cracking open the shutters, light pouring in before sitting down on a straw bed. She pulled out her spellbook, flipping through the pages until she found the one she was looking for. The elf ran a finger down the paper, reading diagrams with dozens of notes written all around them before pulling out a small set of engraving tools and the claw. After checking the book again, Jesmine took the appendage in one hand and a small, delicate metal engraving tool in the other. "I wish I had a bench and a clamp. That would make this so much easier," she muttered to herself.

She took a deep breath, reading from the book, tattoo markings glowing a soft white-blue color. The glow traveled down her hand to the tool, subtle runic markings glowing in kind along the side. Slowly she carved into the claw as the markings she has already made glowed the same color.

Back in the other room, Rina spoke. "My husband has told me that orcs were after you and that they, along with some avolarieans, attacked you."

Dran nodded. "Aye. It wasn't something we wanted to happen. At the time we didn't even know we were being followed."

"The avolarieans were a new threat. We never had any direct dealings with them before. If it wasn't for your husband and the others, I don't think we would have made it," said Alderin.

Gnemi chimed in with a heavy heart. "I think about those who didn't. They didn't know us, but they risked and gave their lives. It's something I will never forget no matter how long I live."

"I will let their families know. They will appreciate the kind words," said Rina, checking the food again. "I apologize there isn't much. I wasn't expecting company."

Dran raised his hand. "Your family has done enough. We have enough rations to last us."

Ariana, who was silent up to this time, spoke. "We also are

skillful enough to hunt any food we need," she said, idly rubbing her wrists. "We appreciate the thought."

"What are you again? My husband mentioned it, but I've never heard of anything like you except werewolves."

Ariana's ears twitched, turning in her direction. "Lycan."

"What?" she asked with curious concern.

"They are called Lycan, but I'm a wolfkin. We've been mistaken for them in the past. A curse of looking like a wolf. People tend make assumptions about what we are," she responded.

"I'm sorry to hear that and forgive me."

"It's alright. I'm very used to it."

"And you all came all this way just to get Jesmine to her home?"

"Yes. Having closure is important," Ariana said, looking off to the side.

"I can understand. Amir and I had several family members simply disappear during the elven extermination."

"We heard about that. You have our condolences."

"Though it's been thirty years, I can still..." she trailed off. "Sorry. Not the best topic to speak of with guests. Hopefully Amir can convince the mayor to let you cross the river."

Histra suddenly spoke up. "I've been wondering about that. The river is fraught with dangers, and Sa'bara isn't too keen to have many boats on it. I also didn't see a single one on your docks. How would we cross the river even if we get your mayor's stamp of approval?"

Rina looked to her. "It's not my place to say, but it doesn't conflict with any of his laws, if that is what you are wondering."

She slumped and leaned against the wall. "If you say so. Wake me if something happens. I'm going to try to get some rest."

"Sorry, Histra is distrustful by nature. She probably doesn't mean anything bad by it," Gnemi explained.

Rina nodded and looked over to the kobold. "If you say so."

By the time Amir returned the sun had nearly set over the horizon. Rina rushed over to him. "What did he say?"

"It was certainly not the easiest conversation of my life, but I got permission. There is only one catch."

"What is it?" Alderin asked.

"You have to go tonight. He wasn't too fond of the idea of a kobold walking around the village. It makes a lot of people uncomfortable."

Histra cracked open her eyes, stretching and yawning. "Imagine that," she said with a sarcastic sigh.

"How long till we have to go?" asked Alderin, waving off her comment.

"The three mages assigned to it are already preparing. You have about half an hour."

"That soon?" asked Dran.

"It was the best I could do. He also didn't like the idea of a kobold using our method, but the one she healed helped convince him otherwise."

"I guess he knows how to show appreciation eventually," Histra remarked.

Dran groaned. "Enough, Histra."

"You don't care. In a few weeks we'll part ways, and hopefully not have to bother each other ever again," she said, stranding up, stretching.

"I'll miss you, Histra," Gnemi said.

"I'm sure you will," she replied.

"I will…" the gnome said, smiling back.

"We'll be sure to be ready, and thank you again," said Alderin, making his way to Jesmine, who was intensely focused on her task. Alderin approached, clearing his throat and softly spoke. "Jesmine? We'll be leaving soon."

She pulled the tool away from the claw, the glow quickly fading. "Alright," she replied, closing and putting away her spellbook.

"If you don't mind me asking, what are you working on?"

"A parting gift for Histra," she replied. "Don't let her know. I want it to be a surprise."

"How much of a surprise can it be? She's seen you working on it for a while now."

"Yeah, but she doesn't know it's for her, does she?" she asked with a smile.

Alderin smirked. "True. Just be ready soon."

"I will," she replied, packing everything up. After they gave Rina one last thank you for her hospitality, they left, guiding their horses by the reins as Amir led them toward the docks. The few people out at this late hour gave them a wide berth.

"This is the friendliest town we've been to so far, which is not a very high bar to exceed," remarked Histra, catching the eyes of a few people on her.

"Histra," said Jesmine.

"I am not going to pretend I don't see it. I am fully aware why, and if you think this is bad, imagine if I went back with you."

Amir spoke up. "It's been decades since most of us have seen a kobold, but the last time they did, it was not a pleasant experience."

"And is that my fault? If a human went on a killing spree, would that mean you are all afraid of each other? No, no excuse," she retorted as they reached the docks.

"She talked about wanting to give Gnemi a real history lesson, but maybe someone should give Histra an equal lesson about the word 'empathy'..." Dran thought.

The smooth surface of the river was misleading to the speed and strength of its flow as water crashed up along the logs in the river, giving the docks a sway that made one feel uneasy.

Gnemi reached up to hold onto the wooden railings that provided a small sense of comfort as they walked to the tiny island up ahead. Three clothed figures, their faces covered with scarves, awaited them. Each held a staff with gold inlaid into the runic markings, which glowed a very bright dark blue. In their other hands were their leather-bound spellbooks, the runic markings on the pages glowing just as bright. Their focus was out across the river.

"Excellent timing. We arrived just as they are about to finish," commented Amir as they reached the island.

"Jesmine, do you know what spell they are casting?" Dran asked.

"It's hard to read a spell from the middle of the incantation, and I am not familiar with the human method of spell casting," she responded.

"If you want to mount up, now would be the time," Amir said.

"Mount up?" Alderin asked.

"You're going walk across and please hurry. Maintaining a spell of this caliber is difficult, even with three working together. But don't go too fast, otherwise they may not be able to keep up,"

Amir cautioned.

"Not keep up?" he asked.

"I know what he means," said Jesmine, climbing onto her horse. "Thank you for the advice," she added, everyone else following suit with Dran and Gnemi getting on Dariel.

"Come," said Ariana, crouching down, backpack filled with books on her back, motioning for Histra with her free hand.

Histra sighed, her wings slumping slightly. "I hate being carried around like this."

"With how you like to carry on, I am surprised you don't," said Alderin.

"I don't like the look of being in need to be carried," She explained, climbing onto Ariana's back, sitting on it, resting her legs over her shoulders.

"You don't need it, but it will be faster," said Jesmine.

The three mages ahead of them spoke in loud human-arcana. The smooth water surface of the river grew still from the base of the island where the glyphs and mages were and went outward with incredible speed. The section of smoothed river glowed with a faint blue hue which was only visible due to the waning sunlight.

"Go, and good luck getting home," said Amir, waving them off.

"We won't forget this," said Dran as they walked onto the water. The horses uneasily took the first steps, their hooves pressing down on the smooth semi-solid unfrozen water. Ariana felt the wetness of the river on her feet but instead of slipping through, she found the surface solid but cushioned like a stuffed feathered pillow. A soft blue glowing hue formed around the point of contact, which slowly faded over the next ten seconds as they walked.

Gnemi watched with amazement in his eyes. "This is a bridge of water!" he exclaimed. "And this goes all the way across?" he asked, looking back to the mages, who don't respond, keeping focus on their chanting and body movements with their staffs.

Jesmine answered. "Yes and no. The spell spans the river, but it's not bridging the entire river."

"What do you mean?"

She thought for a moment. "The easiest way to put it is that the entire path here is not solid. As we move across the water, the mages adjust where the solid water is for us to walk on, while what's behind us returns to normal. In other words, only a small section of the entire bridge is active at any one time."

"Ah, so if someone else decided to get on would it activate for them or is it just where we are?" he asks while they are walking.

"That depends on the spell and the caster. If the caster was with us, it would bet the latter, but seeing as they are staying where they are, it's the former."

"I'm impressed that a small town like that has skillful enough casters to maintain such a spell over such a long distance," remarked Dran.

"It feels weird to walk on it. It's cool and wet, yet solid, but not like ice," commented Ariana.

"Solid water that isn't frozen always felt weird to me," said Histra.

"When I talked to survivors of Sa'bara's extermination, some mentioned that they crossed the Great Sa'bara River by walking across it," said Jesmine, looking ahead, mindful to keep her horse within the soft glowing blue lines.

"So, it wasn't just hearing Amir's stories of what happened, or his offer to help, that convinced you that we should come here?"

"It was too much of a coincidence to ignore. My only concern was if they still had people to perform it."

Histra unfurled her wings slightly, replying. "Given the fact they hid their faces from me, they prefer it not to be known that they still possess the power."

"Ariana?" asked Alderin, riding beside her.

She looked up to him curiously, her ears perked. "Yes?"

"Now that you have your cuffs and collar off, what is it that you intend to do?"

Her ears went flat, looking away and out to the two moons in the sky. "When we began this, I was thinking of heading back to my hunting grounds with the books and supplies from my family, furthering my research, perhaps staying near my hometown and hunting there, but," she turned her attention back to him, "I might want to help get rid of that pesky problem of yours," she said with a toothy grin. "And perhaps I can find a remedy for Histra's mental problem."

"I have a memory issue. I'm not crazy," Histra retorted.

"I think curing Histra of her mental problems is a wonderful idea," Alderin said with a chuckle.

"Sorry, I meant *memory* problem," Ariana said, with a hint of sarcasm.

"Speaking of which," said Alderin, looking behind him to Jesmine, seeing that the mages working the spell were now well out of earshot. "Have you made a decision?"

"Sure, ask her in the middle of a raging river with no place to go," Histra said sarcastically.

"Histra, just don't. You were doing so well. but lately you have been...what's the word?"

"A 'bitch'," said Dran.

"That would be it, unfortunately," said Jesmine, Ariana giving the dwarf a look.

"What?"

"Nothing," remarked Ariana.

Histra sighed. "You are free to make whatever decision you want Jesmine, and I won't stop you. I won't stop any of you. I don't care about the other dragons. The only one I cared about is dead, and nothing will bring her back."

"Thankfully," remarked Dran.

"What was that?" she asked, glaring at him.

"You heard me, and you know very well you are in a minority when it comes to attitudes on the dragons."

She huffed. "I do, but I am not ashamed of it. I am proud of who I served. I will do a lot to survive, but I will not forsake my beliefs. None of you knew her like I did."

"How can you be sure your memories are not tainted nostalgia or something else? Or simply wrong?" asked Dran.

Her wings twitched, raising a claw before lowering it. "You're right."

"Furthermore you...did you say I was right?" asked Dran in shock.

"I did. Are you that surprised? What I do remember is limited. Was I in a place of great respect and power? I believe so, but as of right now, I know what I know to the best of my ability. Speak of what you will of the others, but don't speak ill of the one I served, and we can continue being friends, alright?"

Dran stared at her in surprise for a moment.

"What is it?"

"Nothing, nothing. Sorry, we got off topic, Jesmine, you were saying?" he asked.

"I thought about it. And the answer is yes. I'll help you," she said as there was a cheer from Dran, Alderin, and Gnemi.

"Thank the Gods. I honestly wouldn't know what to do if you didn't help. Everything was riding on you coming with," Alderin said.

"Aye. We'll head back to my home at Tundaholm right away."

"After we drop Histra off at the Four-Corner City," Jesmine said.

"Right, right. We mustn't forget that now."

Histra relaxed slightly. "Good, I was hoping not. After all I did to get you as far as we did, holding up your end of the bargain would be much appreciated," she replied as they continued down the water bridge.

Night now completely overtook the day and the faint glow of the path before them stood out more against the dark surface of the river. About two thirds of the way across it, a huge blue hue several yards ahead of them went off along the path of the bridge, the light of the bridge flickering for a moment, the horses neighing, sliding half a foot into the bridge. They wildly whined and nickered as they were almost thrown off the horses. "Easy girl," said Jesmine, trying to calm the horse.

Ariana tripped and stumbled forward, her feet and lower legs completely soaked in water, landing with a soft bounce on her shoulder, protecting the bag in front of her from impact. "Are you okay, Histra?" she asked.

"Yeah," she said, holding tightly onto the other bag's straps. "What happened?" she asked, the others working to get the horses back onto their hooves.

"I don't know," replied Gnemi.

"There was the light up ahead and then we found ourselves almost sinking into the river," remarked Dran.

"Something activated another section of bridge, putting a strain on the mages," said Jesmine, working to get back onto her horse. "It is most likely something that lives in the river."

"We should hurry it up then," said Dran, helping Gnemi get back onto the horse. The group picked up the pace. "I see something coming this way," he said, pointing down the river, subtle black humps in the water in a long, curved line moving over to them.

"I don't see anything," said Alderin.

"I see them, keep going," said Histra as they tried to urge the horses to move faster, but they were reluctant to do so. The creature broke the surface of the water, snapping at the bridge and the light that just faded away.

The being's slick scaled body splashed through the water across the bridge's path, a huge section glowing. The bridge flickered; the horses and Ariana sunk two feet into the water. Alderin found himself thrown from his horse, landing on a section of the water bridge that had yet to solidify, splashing into the river. The strong current pulled him under as he reached out to grip the hardening water of the bridge.

His hand slid against the slick surface, fingers digging into it, providing some hold against the water's current. He barely managed to poke his head out, gasping for air just as he slipped off. Water washed over his face, unable to call out for help. Ariana grabbed his hand with her own and with the other holding Cetas' reins, she pulled him back onto the bridge. The water that dripped from his body merged with it. He gasped for air, barely managing to say. "Thank you."

"Thank me later," she remarked. Only small sections of its body broke the water's surface, revealing its return approach while they were still stuck pulling the horses back onto the bridge.

"No time!" yelled Dran, eyes locked on the approaching being. A bright set of lights appeared off to the side of the bridge. The creature, just mere moments from another attack, turned and struck out at the bright glowing spheres.

Its head, with massive harp-curved jaws, snapped shut around them before splashing into the river, spraying water onto the group. Jesmine focused, creating more glowing spheres farther away, moving them in erratic patterns, causing the monster to swim after them.

Wasting no time, they pulled the horses back onto their hooves, riding as fast as they could across the remainder of the bridge. Alderin helped Jesmine's horse stay on track while she kept the spheres glowing bright, moving the creature farther and farther away until it gave up on them entirely.

When they finished crossing the bridge, light from a set of hidden glyphs set in stones near the river and those that connected the opposite banks faded out completely. Jesmine took a deep breath and relaxed, ending her spell in kind.

"That was amazing. How did you know that would work on whatever that was?" asked Gnemi now that the danger had passed.

"I didn't, but it was better than not doing anything," she explained.

"In other words, we got lucky," said Histra.

"We've been lucky a lot on this, wouldn't you agree?" asked Jesmine.

"I suppose," she shrugged.

"Now that we've crossed the river at the expense of seeing my life flash before my eyes twice, let's find a place to set up camp and get some rest," said Alderin.

"Best idea I've heard all night," said Dran as they headed off away from the river.

The next few weeks moving to the border were surprisingly uneventful. There was the occasional town, mostly filled with orcs, but there was no sign of any pursuers. Eventually came the day Histra had been waiting for all this time.

They stood on the edge of a large dirt road that led south. An occasional orc wagon rode by. She looked down the road, wings unfurling, holding a small bag filled with enough food to last her. The kobold looked over her shoulder to the others. "I understand that this is the farthest you'll take me," she remarked.

"I've been there once, I prefer not to go there again," said Jesmine.

She looked away. "I understand."

"It's only a day's travel at most," said Dran, approaching her.

"For you on horseback, perhaps two for me, but that won't be an issue. I can handle myself."

"We know you can," said Alderin as Gnemi walked beside her. "Histra?"

She looked over to him. "Yes?"

"It was nice knowing you," he said with a smile and held out his hand.

She looked down at it, then back at him. "What's that?"

"Something we gnomes do when seeing someone off."

"I don't recall seeing this before," she remarked, turning to him. "But…I'll give you this one," she said, then held out her claw like him.

"You're missing part of it," said Gnemi as he reached and shook her hand. "Good luck, Histra. I hope you find what you are looking for."

She looked down at the handshake with curiosity. "Thanks. And don't press us kobolds too much. You are far too forward with your questions."

"I'll try to remember that."

"If I happen to discover a cure for you, Histra, I'll be sure to send you a note. Don't expect me to go to that city, though," Ariana said.

"If any of you happen to be there, I'll be sure to make it pleasant," she responded, looking down the road. Dran looked over to Alderin, who gave a subtle nod. He reached for the poisoned water sac as Jesmine approached, hesitating as she walked past him.

"Before you go, Histra, there is something I want to give you," she said with a smile, crouching beside her.

"Give me something?" she asked, giving her a curious look.

She dug into her pouch and pulled out a necklace, leather straps weaved around a fully engraved claw that held it in place. She held it out to her. "I want you to have this."

Histra looked at it, then to her, holding out her claw. "It's the thing you've been working on," she remarked. Jesmine placed it into her claw. "It's cold…" she said, feeling a shiver run down her spine. "Wait, no…"

"It's a white dragon claw…specifically her claw, if what I was told is true."

Her claws tensed around it. "You had a piece of one of her claws?" she asked, gritting her teeth, giving Jesmine a piercing glare. Her look softened, "And you are giving it to me?"

"More importantly, if you use the word 'friend' in dragon tongue, it should…well give it a try and you'll see."

She looked down to the claw, her small talons running across it, looking back at Jesmine, who had a big smile on her face, failing to hide the sadness in her words. She closed her eyes, slipping the necklace around her while keeping the claw in her hand. She focused on it, saying in draconic, "Friend."

The runes on the claw began glowing a soft white blue, Histra feeling warmth. The heat of the sun on her white scales and the warm air all around her. She opened her eyes in surprise, looking over herself, then back at Jesmine.

"How do you feel?" she asked.

"Fine, just…" she looked down at the claw which faintly glowed. "It's suppressing my aura…"

"If you are going to deal with other kobolds, it might be easier for you not to freeze them."

"Well, white kobolds are normally known for our tolerance for cold, but I suppose these southern ones might not know much about that. They are all probably cozy with their jobs, all safe from any real problems in the world," she remarked.

"Do you like?" she asked.

"No, I do not like it," she replied as Jesmine's shoulders slumped.

"I know it was a risk giving you something of her like that…" she said as Histra raised her claw.

"Let me finish. I don't like it… I love it," she looked off to the side. "You had no reason to do this. None whatsoever."

"Yes, I know, but I didn't need a reason to want to do something nice for you."

She looked down and ran her claws along it. "I don't know what to say but…thank you."

"Well, that puts what I was going to give you to shame," said Dran as Histra's wings twitched.

"Hmm?"

Dran held out the water skin. "Since it will take a day or two for you to get there, perhaps a little extra water won't hurt."

"It wouldn't hurt…" she looked away for a moment.

"Here you go," said Dran, offering it.

"If I was going to go," she added.

Everyone looked at Histra with surprise. "What?" Alderin asked.

She looked over her shoulder to him. "Do you humans also have trouble hearing? I said I am not going to go."

"Up until now you only talked about wanting to go."

"Yes, but I have been thinking. Though Eisandra was in control of the place, and had white kobolds in charge, does that mean I am going to get any special treatment? No. And spending a decade in a cage as a slave freak sideshow has given me a rather strong distaste for the trade," she explained, turning to the group.

"What are going to do, then?" Jesmine asked.

"Well," she ran her claws along Eisandra's. "Seeing you gave me your only ancient dragon claw; I have to help you get a new one. It is only fair," she remarked.

"What?" asked Dran in surprise.

"Do dwarves have trouble hearing now, too?" she sighed. "I've said time and time again, I don't give a damn about the others, and if there is one thing I have learned from being with you all, is you need me to keep you all from dying. And since you are the only friends, I can legitimately recall having, that are still alive, I prefer to keep you all that way," she stated with a smile.

"This is going to be hard to explain back home," Dran said.

"Not my problem," she said, walking back to Ariana. "Hope you don't mind me staying. I know how much you were looking forward to not having me on your back anymore."

"Since your ice aura is not going to be an issue, you could ride with me," Jesmine said.

"I still don't like horses," she remarked.

"You'll have time to get to know them," she replied.

"Humph."

"If you are probably staying, and if Ariana helps you recover your memory, will you perhaps tell me more about kobold society and Eisandra?" Gnemi asked.

She looked to him. "Sure, why not? If you have a hand in getting me cured," she replied.

"I'll do what I can!"

"I'm sure you will," she said.

Alderin looked to Dran curiously, putting away the water skin. "We better get going then. Tundaholm is still a bit of a trek from here. Too bad you couldn't tell us sooner. We could have saved some time," he remarked.

"Aye, that would have been nice," Dran said.

"It was an important decision that I had to think very long and hard on," said Histra as Jesmine helped put her on her horse, which neighed uncomfortably. "See, horses don't like me."

"She'll get used to you," said Jesmine as she and the others mounted up. They turned toward the Sa'bara-Dra'kesh border, where the next step in their journey was set to begin.

ABOUT THE AUTHOR

A professional author for several years. Working hard to make
their dreams come true, and not letting life stop him from
achieving those goals. Proof of concept that hard work, dedication
and the help of those close to you, one can achieve anything.

www.ingramcontent.com/pod-product-compliance
Lightning Source LLC
Chambersburg PA
CBHW072015020726
47501CB00006B/1819